W9-BFG-941

*T*his story is set in New Bedford, Massachusetts, once the whaling capital of the world, where in the 18th Century a group of secret Jews emigrated from Portugal. Here in this bustling whaling village, many Jews became merchants, providing sea captains with necessary provisions such as oilskins, waterproof boots, and canvas bags.

Emanuel Aguilar knew more about whaling
than most nine-year-old boys.

His father Aaron owned a shop on the wharf,
where the town's whalers purchased their supplies.
Here one could find waterproof boots, compasses,
and barrels to store oil. The shop also sold
provisions such as molasses, potatoes, flour, and
salted meat.

Each year, as many as 500 ships set sail from the bustling port of New Bedford in search of whales, whose oil was used to make candles and to light the lamps in the days before electricity.

Emanuel loved talking with the whalers. Nobody could spin a story better than Captain Henshaw, and Emanuel never tired of listening to his seafaring adventures.

"Papa, when will I be old enough to go to sea?" he asked his father each time the tall, swaggering captain finished telling about one of his encounters with the mighty whale.

"The life of a whaler is lonely and dangerous,
Emanuel," his father cautioned. "Sometimes men go out
and never come back. Better you should grow up to be
a merchant like me."

But Emanuel didn't want to sell barrels, salted meat, and waterproof boots. He wanted to be like the mighty captain and not like his timid father.

It seemed like Papa was always afraid. The Aguilars were among the Jewish families who had left Portugal, where they had to keep their Judaism a secret. Here in New Bedford they carried their fear with them.

Every year at Hanukkah, for example, Emanuel pleaded with his father to put a whale oil menorah in the window to celebrate the Festival of Lights. But Papa always refused.

"Back in the land of my birth, it was against the law for Jews to practice their religion. Any Jew caught doing so was punished."

"This isn't Portugal, Papa. This is America! No one will put us in jail for being who we are," said Emanuel.

Emanuel couldn't understand his father's fears. He didn't understand why his family could only light Shabbat candles with the shades drawn. He didn't understand why he couldn't tell his Christian friends he was Jewish. And he didn't understand why he couldn't put a menorah in the window during the Festival of Lights.

On the first night of Hanukkah, Emanuel pleaded
with his father once again to light the menorah.
"This is the holiday to celebrate our religious freedom!"
   "Not tonight, Emanuel," said Papa, sighing.
"Perhaps tomorrow."
   On the second night, Emanuel asked again.
   "Not tonight, Emanuel," said Papa wearily. "Perhaps tomorrow."

By the seventh night, Emanuel realized that neither his father, nor their Jewish neighbors, had any intention of lighting their Hanukkah lamps.

Emanuel wanted to be more like the whalers who came into the shop—brave and strong and unafraid. Tomorrow, Captain Henshaw was venturing into the cold Atlantic to hunt whales. Emanuel decided to join him. That evening before packing his bags, he wrote his father a letter:

Dear Papa,

By the time you read this note I will be on Captain Henshaw's ship. I am not sure how long I will be gone. I need to know what it's like to be free. I hope someday you can be free, too.

Love, Emanuel

The next morning when Captain Henshaw set sail, Emanuel was hiding in a barrel in the belly of the ship. "Goodbye, father," he whispered as he sailed farther and farther from the familiar shores of New Bedford.

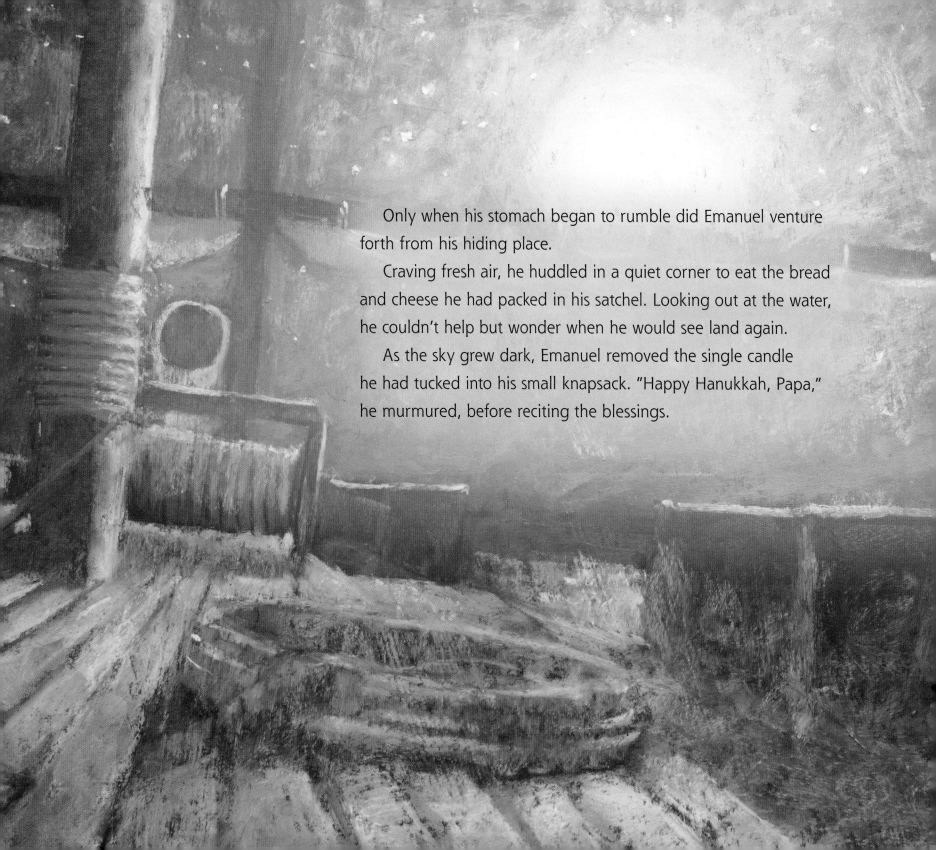

Only when his stomach began to rumble did Emanuel venture forth from his hiding place.

Craving fresh air, he huddled in a quiet corner to eat the bread and cheese he had packed in his satchel. Looking out at the water, he couldn't help but wonder when he would see land again.

As the sky grew dark, Emanuel removed the single candle he had tucked into his small knapsack. "Happy Hanukkah, Papa," he murmured, before reciting the blessings.

Suddenly the wind began to pick up, and ominous clouds rolled in. Before long, the sea began to toss the ship about.

"All hands on deck. A storm is brewing!" shouted Captain Henshaw.

Emanuel watched in horror as a giant bolt of lightning cracked the mast in two.

"We've lost the mast on the main sail," the Captain cried. "We'd best head back to New Bedford before it's too late."

The wind was blowing so hard that Emanuel
had to grab onto a rope in order to stay aboard.
"So this is what fear feels like," he thought. As he
watched the crew work tirelessly to secure the
ship, he saw a man approach. It was Jeremiah
Scott, a young blacksmith from town.

"Master Emanuel, is that you?" Jeremiah asked. "What are you doing here?"

"I snuck on board last night, and…"

"Never mind about that now. There's work to be done!
Just hold on tight while we get the ship back to port,"
Jeremiah ordered.

For hours, Captain Henshaw and his crew battled the 35-foot waves. Emanuel remembered what Papa said about whaling being lonely and dangerous. He had never felt more afraid in his entire life.

When the storm finally let up, everything became dark and still.

"Is it over, Mr. Scott? Are we almost home?" quavered Emanuel.

"Not yet. The ship has lost its bearings. The captain thinks the lighthouse was struck by lightning, and there are no stars to guide us."

Without a guiding light, the ship would surely get dashed against the rocks, Emanuel realized. Even Jeremiah Scott looked frightened.

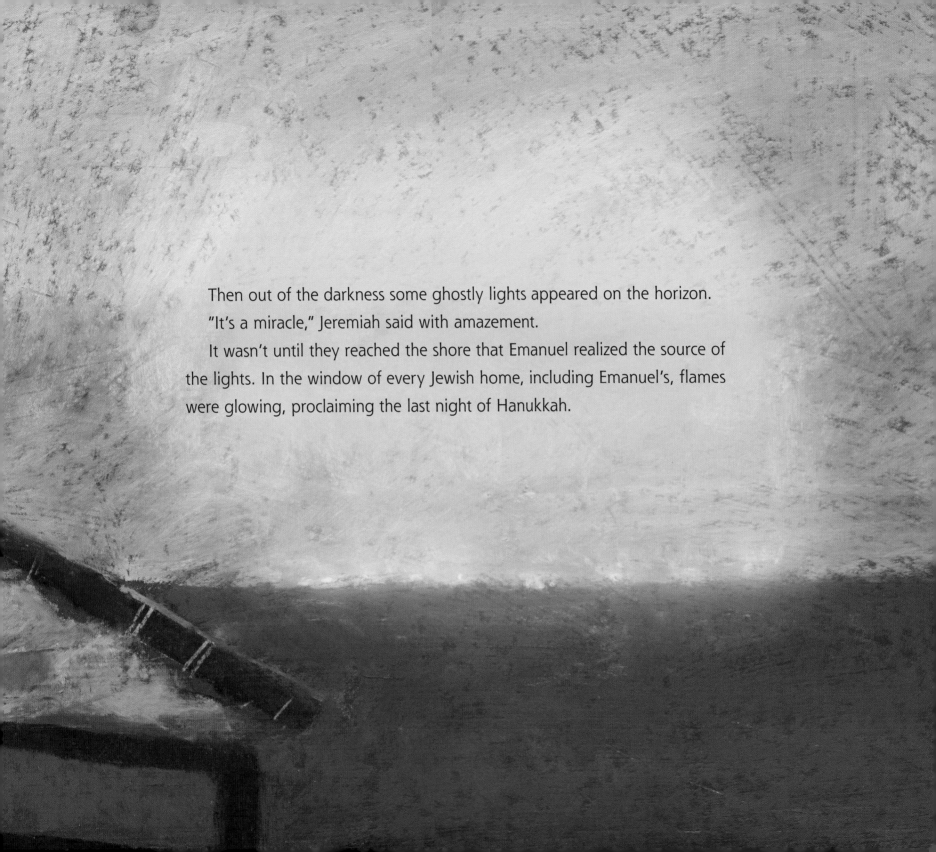

Then out of the darkness some ghostly lights appeared on the horizon.

"It's a miracle," Jeremiah said with amazement.

It wasn't until they reached the shore that Emanuel realized the source of the lights. In the window of every Jewish home, including Emanuel's, flames were glowing, proclaiming the last night of Hanukkah.

When Emanuel finally stepped off the ship, Papa was waiting. They embraced for a long time without speaking.

Finally, Emanuel said, "Papa, the oil lamps. We could see them from the ship! What happened?"

"After I read your letter I was so ashamed," Papa admitted. "I called our Jewish friends and neighbors together and convinced them to light the menorahs. You were right, Emanuel. It is not good to be ruled by fear."

"The flames helped us find our way home!" Emanuel exclaimed. "Thank you for showing us the way."

Papa smiled. "No, Emanuel. Thank you for showing me the way."

And together they returned home to celebrate the
last night of Hanukkah.

About Hanukkah

Hanukkah is an eight-day Festival of Lights that celebrates the victory of the Maccabees over the mighty armies of Syrian King Antiochus. According to legend, when the Maccabees came to restore the Holy Temple in Jerusalem, they found one jug of pure oil, enough to keep the menorah lit for just one day. But a miracle happened, and the oil burned for eight days. On each night of the holiday, we add an additional candle to the menorah, exchange gifts, play the game of dreidel, and eat fried latkes and *sufganiyot* (jelly donuts) to remember this victory for religious freedom.

About the Author

HEIDI SMITH HYDE is a graduate of Brandeis University and Harvard Graduate School of Education. A former religious school teacher, she is the Director of Education of Temple Sinai in Brookline, Massachusetts. She lives in Chestnut Hill with her husband and sons. Her books include *Feivel's Flying Horses*, a National Jewish Book Award Finalist, and *Mendel's Accordion*, a Sydney Taylor Notable Children's Book and winner of the Sugarman Award for Best Jewish Children's Book.

About the Illustrator

JAMEL AKIB was born in Leigh-on-Sea, Essex, England, to mixed English and Malaysian parentage. He moved to Sabah, North Borneo, at the age of five and later returned to England to pursue his education. He has a B.A. honors degree in illustration and is an award-winning artist. Married with two children, he lives in West Sussex, England. Jamel works in chalk pastels.

W9-AVZ-870

Primary Sources for Western Civilization

From Early Mesopotamia to the Reformation

Gary Forsythe

Texas Tech University

Kendall Hunt
publishing company

Cover photograph taken from The Rosetta Stone by E.A.W. Budge, published by Kegan Paul, Trench, Trubner & CO. (1904).

The famous Rosetta Stone, discovered by Napoleon's soldiers in the Nile Delta in 1799, now in the British Museum. It contains a text written in Greek, hieroglyphic Egyptian, and demotic Egyptian. The text led to the modern decipherment of the ancient Egyptian language and writing system.

Kendall Hunt
publishing company

www.kendallhunt.com
Send all inquiries to:
4050 Westmark Drive
Dubuque, IA 52004-1840

Copyright © 2011 by Gary Forsythe

ISBN 978-0-7575-9425-0

Kendall Hunt Publishing Company has the exclusive rights to reproduce this work,
to prepare derivative works from this work, to publicly distribute this work,
to publicly perform this work and to publicly display this work.

All rights reserved. No part of this publication may be reproduced,
stored in a retrieval system, or transmitted, in any form or by any
means, electronic, mechanical, photocopying, recording, or otherwise,
without the prior written permission of the copyright owner.

Printed in the United States of America
10 9 8 7 6 5 4 3 2

Contents

IV THE MIDDLE AGES   175

Introduction

V RENAISSANCE & REFORMATION 275

Introduction

THE ANCIENT NEAR EAST

Introduction

The two major river valleys of the Tigris and Euphrates and of the Nile were the homes of the two earliest civilizations of Mesopotamia and Egypt. They laid down the basic patterns of organized human existence in western Asia and the eastern Mediterranean for the next few thousands of years: people living in towns or cities, well-organized public religion, the use of writing systems for recording various kinds of information and human knowledge, and well-defined political institutions and law codes. During the third and second millennia B.C., there arose in this region of the world several distinct civilizations: the Sumerians, the Babylonians, the Assyrians, the Hurrians, the Hittites, the Minoans, and the Mycenaeans. Then during the first half of the first millennium B.C., three great empires dominated the history of this area: the Assyrian, the Neo-Babylonian, and the Persian Empires. Although most of these civilizations and empires are barely known to many people today, this complex of ancient Near Eastern cultures produced one of the most influential religious systems of world history: Judaism. Studying Mesopotamia, Egypt, and these other civilizations is rewarding and interesting in its own right, but it is especially important in helping us understand many of the ideas, beliefs, and practices that we encounter in The Old Testament. The readings in this part of the book provide you with an interesting sampling of the literature and thought of the Mesopotamians and Egyptians, which should allow you to appreciate more fully from the historical perspective how the ancient Hebrews developed their own distinctive religious culture out of this larger ancient Near Eastern environment. ✢

Reading I

The Sumerian King List

The following Mesopotamian text, composed c.2000 B.C., is a list of Sumerian rulers, stretching back into the distant past, and most of whom are mythical; but the text exhibits three basic features of Mesopotamian thought: (1) that the institution of kingship was of divine origin; (2) that in early times leadership within Mesopotamia was exercised at different times by different city-states; and (3) that as shown by the decreasing lengths of the kings' reigns, the Mesopotamians generally regarded human history as moving along a downward slope of gradual decline, unlike our modern assumption of scientific advancement, technological progress, and sustained economic growth.

Note: Parentheses are used by modern editors and translators to supply linguistic elements or words not actually present in the ancient text but required by the sense, whereas brackets are use to enclose modern restorations to damaged portions of the text.

(Taken from pp.265-266 of Ancient Near Eastern Texts Relating to the Old Testament, edited by James B. Pritchard, Third Edition, Princeton University Press 1969)

When kingship was lowered from heaven, kingship was (first) in Eridu. (In) Eridu, A-lulim (became) king and ruled 28,800 years. Alalgar ruled 36,000 years. Two kings (thus) ruled it for 64,800 years.

I drop (the topic) Eridu (because) its kingship was brought to Bad-tibira. (In) Bad-tibira, En-men-lu-Anna ruled 43,200 years; En-men-gal-Anna ruled 28,800 years; the god Dumu-zi, a shepherd, ruled 36,000 years. Three kings (thus) ruled it for 108,000 years. I drop (the topic) Bad-tibira (because) its kingship was brought to Larak. (In) Larak, En-sipa-zi-Anna ruled 28,800 years. One king (thus) ruled it for 28,800 years.

I drop (the topic) Larak (because) its kingship was brought to Sippar. (In) Sippar, En-men-dur-Anna became king and ruled 21,000 years. One king (thus) ruled it for 21,000 years.

I drop (the topic) Sippar (because) its kingship was brought to Shuruppak. (In) Shuruppak, Ubar-Tutu became king and ruled 18,600 years. One king (thus) ruled it for 18,600 years.

These are five cities, eight kings ruled them for 241,000 years. (Then) the Flood swept over (the earth).

After the Flood had swept over (the earth) (and) when kingship was lowered (again) from heaven, kingship was (first) in Kish. In Kish, Ga[...]ur became king and ruled 1,200 years--(original) destroyed! legible (only) to heavenly Nidaba (the goddess of writing)--ruled 960 years. [Pala-kinatim ruled 900 years; Nan- gish-lishma ruled ... years]; Bah[i]na ruled...years; BU.AN.[..]. [um] ruled [8]40 ye[ars]; Kalibum ruled 960 years; Qalumum ruled 840 years; Zuqaqip ruled 900 years; Atab ruled 600 years; [Mashda, son] of Atab ruled 840 years; Arwi'um, son of Mashda, ruled 720 years; Etana, a shepherd, he who ascended to heaven (and) who consolidated all countries, became king and ruled 1,560 (var.: 1,500) years; Balih, son of Etana, ruled 400 (var.: 410) years; En-me-nunna ruled 660 years; Melam-Kishi, son of En-me-nunna ruled 900 years; Bar-sal-nunna, son of En-me-nunna, ruled 1,200 years; Samug, son of Bar-sal-nunna, ruled 140 years; Tizkar, son of Samug, ruled 305 years; Ilku' ruled 900 years; Ilta-sadum ruled 1,200 years; En-men-barage-si, he who carried away as spoil the "weapon" of Elam, became king and ruled 900 years; Aka, son of En-men- barage-si, ruled 629 years. Twenty-three kings (thus) ruled it for 24,510 years, 3 months, and 3 1/2 days. Kish was defeated in battle (lit.: was smitten with weapons), its kingship was removed to Eanna (sacred precinct of Uruk).

In Eanna, Mes-kiag-gasher, the son of the (sun) god Utu, became high priest as well as king, and ruled 324 years. Mes-kiag-gasher went (daily) into the (Western) Sea and came forth (again) toward the (Sunrise) Mountains; En-me-kar, son of Mes-kiag-gasher, he who built Uruk, became king and ruled 420 years; the god Lugalbanda, a shepherd, ruled 1,200 years; the god Dumu-zi, a su.pes-fisherman'--his (native) city was Ku'a(ra),--ruled 100 years; the divine Gilgamesh, his father was a lillu, a high priest of Kullab, ruled 126 years; Ur-Nungal (var.: Ur-lugal), son of Gilgamesh, ruled 30 years; Utul-kalamma, son of Ur-nun-gal (var.: Ur-lugal), ruled 15 years; Laba[h...]ir ruled 9 years; En-nun-dara-Anna ruled 8 years; MES(?).HE, a smith, ruled 36 years; Melam-Anna ruled 6 years; Lugal-ki-tun(?) ruled 36 years. Twelve kings (thus) ruled it for 2,310 years.

Uruk was defeated in battle, its kingship was removed to Ur.

In Ur, Mes-Anne-pada became king, ruled 80 years; Mes-kiag-Nanna became king, ruled 36 years; [Elulu ruled 25 years; Balulu ruled 36 years. Four kings (thus) ruled it for 177 years. Ur was defeated in battle].

THE LEGEND OF SARGON

Sargon was one of the earliest great conquerors in history. He succeeded in uniting the separate city-states of early Mesopotamia into a single kingdom, and he founded a dynasty of rulers that lasted for more than a century, after which his united kingdom fell apart, and the Mesopotamians reverted to their separate city-states once again. Sargon soon became a great figure of legend and his greatness as a conqueror and ruler was embodied in a mythical story of his unusual birth, rescue from death while still a helpless infant, and his survival to realize his divinely ordained destiny as a great conqueror and ruler. Variations of this story were later associated with other great figures of the ancient world, who were the founders of nations or empires, such as Cyrus the Great of Persia, Moses in the Hebrew tradition, different heroes of ancient Greece, and Romulus and Remus, the twin founders of ancient Rome.

Note: Parentheses are used by modern editors and translators to supply linguistic elements or words not actually present in the ancient text but required by the sense, whereas brackets are use to enclose modern restorations to damaged portions of the text.

(Taken from p.119 of Ancient Near Eastern Texts Relating to the Old Testament, edited by James B. Pritchard, Third Edition, Princeton University Press 1969)

Sargon, the mighty king, king of Agade, am I. My mother was a high priestess, my father I knew not. The brother(s) of my father loved the hills. My city is Azupiranu, which is situated on the banks of the Euphrates. My mother, the high priestess, conceived me, in secret she bore me. She set me in a basket of rushes, with bitumen she sealed my lid. She cast me into the river which rose not (over) me. The river bore me up and carried me to Akki, the drawer of water. Akki, the drawer of water lifted me out as he dipped his e[w]er. Akki, the drawer of water, [took me] as his son (and) reared me. Akki, the drawer of water, appointed me as his gardener. While I was a gardener, Ishtar granted me (her) love, And for four and [...] years I exercised kingship. The black-headed [people] I ruled, I gov[erned]; Mighty [moun]tains with chip-axes of bronze I conquered, The upper ranges I scaled, The lower ranges I [trav]ersed, The sea [lan]ds three times I circled. Dilmun my [hand] cap[tured], [To] the great Der I [went up], I [...], [K]azallu I destroyed and [... ...]. Whatever king may come up after me, [...], Let him r[ule, let him govern] the black-headed [peo]ple; [Let him conquer] mighty [mountains] with chip-axe[s of bronze], [Let] him scale the upper ranges, [Let him traverse the lower ranges], Let him circle the sea [lan]ds three times! [Dilmun let his hand capture], Let him go up [to] the great Der and [...]! [...] from my city, Aga[de...] [...]...[...]. (the Remainder is broken away.)

READING 3

THE EPIC OF GILGAMESH

Gilgamesh, a legendary king of Uruk during the Sumerian period, emerged early on as a heroic figure among the Mesopotamians. Many stories were told about him and his supposed great deeds. By the time of the Old Babylonian Kingdom (c.1900-1600 B.C.) these stories had been fashioned into a continuous tale that is now generally termed *The Epic of Gilgamesh*. According to this long narrative poem, Gilgamesh is so full of strength and energy that he wears out his subjects, who then pray to the gods for relief. They in turn instruct one of the goddesses to fashion out of clay a mighty man named Enkidu, whom they send to Uruk to put Gilgamesh in his place. But after the two fight one another to a standstill, they become friends and then go off to perform great exploits, first killing the monstrous guardian of the great cedar forest (named Huwawa) and then slaying the bull of heaven that has been ravaging the land, because Ishtar, goddess of female beauty and sexuality, had offered herself to Gilgamesh, only to be scorned. After Enkidu offers another insult to Ishtar, the gods decree that Enkidu must die. After Enkidu falls sick and dies, the poem describes Gilgamesh's last major exploit, a quest for immortality, so that he would not succumb to death like his friend Enkidu. An important part of this quest involves Gilgamesh sailing off to a mysterious island in the sea, a place called Dilmun, where there live the only two mortals of Mesopotamian myth who were ever granted immortality by the gods. These two people are a married couple: Utnapishtim and his wife, who had survived the great flood that had once destroyed all life on earth. During Gilgamesh's visit on this island Utnapishtim tells him the story of this great flood, whose basic outline was later adopted and adapted by the authors of *Genesis* in *The Old Testament*. The two versions of this story, Mesopotamian vs. Hebrew, reveal important differences between the ways in which these peoples viewed the divine.

(Adapted from pp. 72-99 of Ancient Neare Eastern Texts Relating to the Old Testament, edited by James B. Pritchard, third edition, Princeton University Press, 1969)

PASSAGE **1** Enkidu's Dream

While on his sick bed, Enkidu has a dream in which he sees what awaits him in the Mesopotamian underworld after his death. It is a place of dreariness and gloom, where even the high and mighty rulers of the earth are humbled and forced to be the servants of the nether gods. Upon awakening from the dream, Enkidu tells Gilgamesh what he has seen; and the vision, along with Enkidu's death, shakes Gilgamesh to the core.

"My friend, I saw a dream last night: The heavens shouted, the earth responded;...
While I was standing between them There was a young man whose face was dark, Like
unto Zu was his face... like the talons of an eagle were his claws. he overpowered me. he
leaps. he submerged me. (text missing)... he transformed me, So that my arms were ... like
those of a bird. Looking at me, he leads me to the House of Darkness, The abode of Irkalla,
To the house which none leave who have entered it, On the road from which there is no
way back, To the house wherein the dwellers are bereft of light, Where dust is their fare
and clay their food. They are clothed like birds, with wings for garments, And see no light,
residing in darkness.'" In the House of Dust, which I entered, I looked at rulers, their crowns
put away; I saw princes, those born to the crown, Who had ruled the land from the days of
yore. These doubles... of Anu [god of heaven] and Enlil [god of storms] were serving meat
roasts; They were serving bake meats and pouring Cool water from the waterskins."

PASSAGE 2 The Advice of Siduri

While trying to find a source of immortality to avoid death, Gilgamesh encounters the
goddess Siduri (termed ale-wife) , who urges Gilgamesh to give up his quest. She advises
him to take joy in the simple pleasures of life, because the gods have reserved immortality
for themselves.

Gilgamesh said to Siduri: "He who with me underwent all hardships, Enkidu,
whom I loved dearly, Who with me underwent all hardships, Has now gone to the fate
of mankind! Day and night I have wept over him. I would not give him up for burial in
case... my friend should rise at my lamentation, seven days and seven nights, Until a
worm fell out of his nose. Since his passing I have not found life, I have roamed like a
hunter in the midst of the steppe. O ale-wife, now that I have seen thy face, Let me not
see the death which I ever dread."

The ale-wife said to him, to Gilgamesh: "Gilgamesh, whither rovest thou? The life
thou pursuest thou shalt not find. When the gods created mankind, Death for mankind
they set aside, Life in their own hands retaining. Thou, Gilgamesh, let full be thy belly,
Make thou merry. by day and by night. Of each day make thou a feast of rejoicing, Day
and night dance thou, and play. Let thy garments be sparkling fresh, Thy head be washed;
bathe thou in water. Pay heed to the little one that holds on to thy hand, Let thy spouse
delight in thy bosom! For this is the task of mankind!"

PASSAGE 3 The Mesopotamian Flood Story

After sailing to the distant island of Dilmun, Gilgamesh finally meets Utnapishtim, who
tells the story of the great flood: how and why the gods decided to destroy mankind, how
the god Ea warned Utnapishtim and urged him to build a huge boat to survive the flood,
and how Enlil bestowed immortality upon Utnapishtim and his wife.

Gilgamesh said to him, to Utnapishtim the Faraway: "I look at you now, Utnapishtim,
and your appearance is no different from mine; there is nothing strange in your features.
I thought I should find you like a hero prepared for battle, but you lie here taking your ease
on your back. Tell me how joinedst thou the Assembly of the gods, In thy quest of life."

Utnapishtim said to him, to Gilgamesh: "I will reveal to thee, Gilgamesh, a hidden
matter And a secret of the gods will I tell thee: Shurippak, a city which thou knowest, And
which on Euphrates' banks is situated, That city was ancient, as were the gods within it,
When their heart led the great gods to produce the flood. In those days the world teemed,
the people multiplied, the world bellowed like a wild bull, and the great god was aroused
by the clamor. Enlil heard the clamor, and he said to the gods in council, 'The uproar of
mankind is intolerable, and sleep is no longer possible by reason of the babel.' So the gods
in their hearts were moved to let loose the deluge. There were Anu, their father, Valiant

Enlil, their counselor, Ninurta, their assistant, Ennuge, their irrigator. Ninigiku-Ea was also present with them

Their words Ea [god of wisdom] repeats to the reed-hut: 'Reed-hut, reed-hut! Wall, wall! Reed-hut, hearken! Wall, reflect! Man of Shuruppak, son of Ubar-Tutu, Tear down this house, build a ship! Give up possessions, seek thou life. Forswear worldly goods and keep the soul alive! Aboard the ship take thou the seed of all living things. The ship that thou shalt build, Her dimensions shall be to measure. Equal shall be her width and her length. Like the Apsu thou shalt ceil her.'

I understood, and I said to Ea, my lord: 'Behold, my lord, what thou hast thus ordered, I will be honored to carry out. But what shall I answer the city, the people and elders?' Ea opened his mouth to speak, Saying to me, his servant: 'Thou shalt then thus speak unto them: I have learned that Enlil is hostile to me, So that I cannot reside in your city, Nor set my foot in Enlil's territory. To the Deep I will therefore go down, To dwell with my lord Ea. But upon you he will shower down abundance, The choicest birds, the rarest fishes. The land shall have its fill of harvest riches. He who at dusk orders the husk-greens, Will shower down upon you a rain of wheat.'

With the first glow of dawn, The land was gathered about me. (too fragmentary for translation) The little ones carried bitumen, While the grown ones brought all else that was needful. On the fifth day I laid her framework. One whole acre ... was her floor space, Ten dozen cubits the height of each of her walls, Ten dozen cubits each edge of the square deck. I laid out the contours and joined her together. I provided her with six decks, Dividing her thus into seven parts. Her floor plan I divided into nine parts. I hammered water-plugs into her. I saw to the punting-poles and laid in supplies. Six sar' measures... of bitumen I poured into the furnace, Three sar of asphalt I also poured inside. Three sar of oil the basket-bearers carried, Aside from the one sar of oil which the calking.. con- sumed, And the two sar of oil which the boatman stowed away. Bullocks I slaughtered for the people, And I killed sheep every day. Must, red wine, oil, and white wine... I gave the workmen to drink, as though river water, That they might feast as on New Year's Day....

the ship was completed. The launching was very difficult, So that they had to shift the floor plankS above and below, Until two-thirds of the structure had gone into the water. Whatever I had I loaded upon her: Whatever I had of silver I loaded upon her; Whatever I had of gold I loaded upon her; Whatever I had of all the living beings I loaded upon her. All my family and kin I made go aboard the ship. The beasts of the field, the wild creatures of the field, All the craftsmen I made go aboard.

Shamash [the sun god] had set for me a stated time: 'When he who orders unease at night, Will shower down a rain of blight, Board thou the ship and batten up the entrance!' That stated time had arrived: >He who orders unease at night, showers down a rain of blight. I watched the appearance of the weather. The weather was awesome to behold. I boarded the ship and battened up the entrance. To batten down ... the whole ship, to Puzur-Amurri, the boatman, I handed over the structure together with its contents.

With the first glow of dawn, A black cloud rose up from the horizon. Inside it Adad thunders, While Shullat and Hanish... go in front, Moving as heralds over hill and plain. Erragal... tears out the posts; Forth comes Ninurta and causes the dikes to follow. The Anunnaki lift up the torches, Setting the land ablaze with their glare. Consternation''' over Adad reaches to the heavens, Who turned to blackness all that had been light. The wide land was shattered like a pot! For one day the south-storm blew, Gathering speed as it blew, submerging the mountains, Overtaking the people like a battle. No one can see his fellow, Nor can the people be recognized from heaven.

The gods were frightened by the deluge, And, shrinking back, they ascended to the heaven of Anu. The gods cowered like dogs Crouched against the outer wall. Ishtar cried out like a woman in travail, The sweet-voiced mistress of the gods moans aloud: 'The olden days are alas turned to clay, Because I bespoke evil in the Assembly of the gods. How could I bespeak evil in the Assembly of the gods, Ordering battle for the destruction of my people, When it is I myself who give birth to my people. Like the spawn of the fishes they fill the sea!' The Aminnaki gods weep with her, The gods, all humbled, sit and weep, Their lips drawn tight, one and all.

Six days and six nights Blows the flood wind, as the south-storm sweeps the land. When the seventh day arrived, The flood -carrying south-storm subsided in the battle, Which it had fought like an army. The sea grew quiet, the tempest was still, the flood ceased. I looked at the weather: stillness had set in, And all of mankind had returned to clay. The landscape was as level as a flat roof. I opened a hatch, and light fell upon my face. Bowing low, I sat and wept, Tears running down on my face. I looked about for coast lines in the expanse of the sea: In each of fourteen... regions There emerged a region-mountain. On Mount Nisir... the ship came to a halt. Mount Nisir held the ship fast, Allowing no motion. One day, a second day, Mount Nisir held the ship fast, Allowing no motion. For a hird day, a fourth day, Mount Nisir held the ship fast, Allowing no motion. For a fifth, and a sixth day, Mount Nisir held the ship fast, Allowing no motion. When the seventh day arrived, I sent forth and set free a dove. The dove went forth, but came back; Since no resting-place for it was visible, she turned around. Then I sent forth and set free a swallow. The swallow went forth, but came back; Since no resting-place for it was visible, she turned around. Then I sent forth and set free a raven. The raven went forth and, seeing that the waters had diminished, He eats, circles, caws, and turns not around. Then I let out all to the four winds And offered a sacrifice. I poured out a libation on the top of the mountain. Seven and seven cult-vessels I set up, Upon their pot-stands I heaped cane, cedar wood, and myrtle.

The gods smelled the savor, The gods smelled the sweet savor, The gods crowded like flies about the sacrificer. When at length the great goddess [Ishtar] arrived, She lifted up the great jewels which Anu had fashioned to her liking: 'Ye gods here, as surely as this lapis is Upon my neck, I shall not forget, I shall be mindful of these days, forgetting them never. Let the gods come to the offering; But let not Enlil come to the offering, For he, unreasoning, brought on the deluge And my people consigned to destruction.' When at length Enlil arrived And saw the ship, Enlil was wroth, He was filled with wrath over the heavenly gods: 'Has some living soul escaped? No man was to survive the destruction!' Ninurta opened his mouth to speak, Saying to valiant Enlil: 'Who, other than Ea, can devise plans? It is Ea alone who knows every matter.' Ea opened his mouth to speak, Saying to valiant Enlil: 'Thou wisest of gods, thou hero, How couldst thou, unreasoning, bring on the deluge? On the sinner impose his sin, On the transgressor impose his transgression! Yet, be lenient, lest he be cut off, Be patient, lest he be dislodged! Instead of thy bringing on the deluge, Would that a lion had risen up to diminish mankind! Instead of thy bringing on the deluge, Would that a wolf had risen up to diminish mankind! Instead of thy bringing on the deluge, Would that a famine had risen up to lay low mankind! Instead of thy bringing on the deluge, Would that pestilence had risen up to smite down mankind! It was not I who disclosed the secret of the great gods. I let AtrahasiS see a dream, And he perceived the secret of the gods. Now then take counsel in regard to him!' Thereupon Enlil went aboard the ship. Holding me by the hand, he took me aboard. He took my wife aboard and made her kneel by my side. Standing between us, he touched our foreheads to bless us: 'Hitherto Utnapishtim has been but human. Henceforth Utnapishtim and his wife shall be like unto us gods. Utnapishtim shall reside far away, at the mouth of the rivers!' Thus they took me and made me reside far away, At the mouth of the rivers."

THE END OF THE POEM

Before Gilgamesh leaves the island of Dilmun, Utnapishtim tells Gilgamesh of a marvelous plant that grows at the bottom of the sea, called "man becomes young in old age." Thus, rather than giving Gilgamesh immortality, Utnapishtim provides him with a means of extending his life and becoming rejuvenated. Consequently, as Gilgamesh is sailing back across the sea, he plunges down to the bottom and retrieves the marvelous plant. After reaching land, Gilgamesh begins his journey back to uruk, but when he spots a cool spring of water, he pauses to bathe himself. After placing the marvelous plant on the ground, he lowers himself into the water; and while he is bathing, a snake smells the sweet fragrance of the plant, eats it, and immediately sheds its skin, emerging shiny and rejuvenated. Thus, it is the snake, not Gilgamesh, who succeeds in enjoying the benefit of the marvelous plant; and in a manner similar to what we encounter in *Genesis*, the snake is responsible for dooming mankind to mortality. The poem ends with Gilgamesh returning to uruk, saddened because his quest for immortality has failed, but he consoles himself with the knowledge that he has performed great deeds that will be remembered in times to come.

HAMMURABI'S LAW CODE

Among many other aspects of social and political organization, the early Mesopotamians developed the earliest coherent body of written law. Although we possess portions of law codes earlier than that of Hammurabi, they were written on clay tablets and have thus survived in a fragmentary condition. Hammurabi's law code, on the other hand, was inscribed upon a seven-foot tall pillar of stone, so that its provisions have remained largely undamaged up to the modern day.

Hammurabi was king of the Old Babylonian Kingdom (which flourished from c.1900 to C.1600 B.C.) and reigned during the pinnacle of its power and influence. His reign of forty-two years is generally thought by modern scholars to have occurred during the years 1792-1750 B.C. In the prologue to the law code Hammurabi portrays himself as having been placed in power by the principal gods of the Babylonians, and in a relief carving on the pillar Hammurabi is shown as receiving a ring and staff from the Mesopotamian god Shamash, the god of the sun and of justice. Thus, as was the case with many other ancient peoples, Hammurabi viewed his law code as of divine origin and having the sanction of the gods.

The following extracts from the law code offer us important insights into the behavior, beliefs, customs, and social and economic conditions of the Old Babylonian Kingdom.

(Taken from the translation of L. W. King with revisions by Gary Forsythe)

ADMINISTRATION OF JUSTICE

1. If any one ensnare another, putting a death spell upon him, but he can not prove it, then he that ensnared him shall be put to death.

2. If any one bring an accusation against a man, and the accused go to the river and leap into the river, if he sink in the river his accuser shall take possession of his house. But if the river prove that the accused is not guilty, and he escape unhurt, then he who had brought the accusation shall be put to death, while he who leaped into the river shall take possession of the house that had belonged to his accuser.

3. If any one bring an accusation of any crime before the elders, and does not prove what he has charged, he shall, if it be a capital offense charged, be put to death.

4. If he satisfy the elders to impose a fine of grain or money, he shall receive the fine that the action produces.

5. If a judge try a case, reach a decision, and present his judgment in writing; if later error shall appear in his decision, and it be through his own fault, then he shall pay twelve times the fine set by him in the case, and he shall be publicly removed from the judge's bench, and never again shall he sit there to render judgement.

6. If any one steal the property of a temple or of the court, he shall be put to death, and also the one who receives the stolen thing from him shall be put to death.

8. If any one steal cattle or sheep, or an ass, or a pig or a goat, if it belong to a god or to the court, the thief shall pay thirtyfold therefor; if they belonged to a commoner of the king he shall pay tenfold; if the thief has nothing with which to pay he shall be put to death.

10. If the purchaser does not bring the merchant and the witnesses before whom he bought the article, but its owner bring witnesses who identify it, then the buyer is the thief and shall be put to death, and the owner receives the lost article.

11. If the owner do not bring witnesses to identify the lost article, he is an evil-doer, he has traduced, and shall be put to death.

12. If the witnesses be not at hand, then shall the judge set a limit, at the expiration of six months. If his witnesses have not appeared within the six months, he is an evil-doer, and shall bear the fine of the pending case.

DAMAGE TO CROPS

53. If any one be too lazy to keep his dam in proper condition, and does not so keep it; if then the dam break and all the fields be flooded, then shall he in whose dam the break occurred be sold for money, and the money shall replace the grain which he has caused to be ruined.

54. If he be not able to replace the grain, then he and his possessions shall be divided among the farmers whose grain he has flooded.

55. If any one open his ditches to water his crop, but is careless, and the water flood the field of his neighbor, then he shall pay his neighbor grain for his loss.

56. If a man let in the water, and the water overflow the plantation of his neighbor, he shall pay ten gur of grain for every ten gan of land.

DEBT SERVITUDE

117. If any one fail to meet a claim for debt, and sell himself, his wife, his son, and daughter for money or give them away to forced labor: they shall work for three years in the house of the man who bought them, or the proprietor, and in the fourth year they shall be set free.

118. If he give a male or female slave away for forced labor, and the merchant sublease them, or sell them for money, no objection can be raised.

119. If any one fail to meet a claim for debt, and he sell the maid servant who has borne him children, for money, the money which the merchant has paid shall be repaid to him by the owner of the slave and she shall be freed.

MARRIAGE, DIVORCE, AND ADULTERY

127. If any one "point the finger" (slander) at a sister of a god or the wife of any one, and can not prove it, this man shall be taken before the judges and his brow shall be marked. (by cutting the skin, or perhaps hair.)

128. If a man take a woman to wife, but have no intercourse with her, this woman is no wife to him.

129. If a man's wife be surprised (*in flagrante delicto*) with another man, both shall be tied and thrown into the water, but the husband may pardon his wife and the king his slaves.

130. If a man violate the wife (betrothed or child-wife) of another man, who has never known a man, and still lives in her father's house, and sleep with her and be surprised, this man shall be put to death, but the wife is blameless.

131. If a man bring a charge against one's wife, but she is not surprised with another man, she must take an oath and then may return to her house.

132. If the "finger is pointed" at a man's wife about another man, but she is not caught sleeping with the other man, she shall jump into the river for her husband.

133. If a man is taken prisoner in war, and there is a sustenance in his house, but his wife leave house and court, and go to another house: because this wife did not keep her court, and went to another house, she shall be judicially condemned and thrown into the water.

134. If any one be captured in war and there is not sustenance in his house, if then his wife go to another house this woman shall be held blameless.

135. If a man be taken prisoner in war and there be no sustenance in his house and his wife go to another house and bear children; and if later her husband return and come to his home: then this wife shall return to her husband, but the children follow their father.

136. If any one leave his house, run away, and then his wife go to another house, if then he return, and wishes to take his wife back: because he fled from his home and ran away, the wife of this runaway shall not return to her husband.

137. If a man wish to separate from a woman who has borne him children, or from his wife who has borne him children: then he shall give that wife her dowry, and a part of the usufruct of field, garden, and property, so that she can rear her children. When she has brought up her children, a portion of all that is given to the children, equal as that of one son, shall be given to her. She may then marry the man of her heart.

138. If a man wishes to separate from his wife who has borne him no children, he shall give her the amount of her purchase money and the dowry which she brought from her father's house, and let her go.

139. If there was no purchase price he shall give her one mina of gold as a gift of release.

140. If he be a commoner, he shall give her one-third of a mina of gold.

141. If a man's wife, who lives in his house, wishes to leave it, plunges into debt, tries to ruin her house, neglects her husband, and is judicially convicted: if her husband offer her release, she may go on her way, and he gives her nothing as a gift of release. If her husband does not wish to release her, and if he take another wife, she shall remain as servant in her husband's house.

142. If a woman quarrel with her husband, and say: "You are not congenial to me," the reasons for her prejudice must be presented. If she is guiltless, and there is no fault on her part, but he leaves and neglects her, then no guilt attaches to this woman, she shall take her dowry and go back to her father's house.

143. If she is not innocent, but leaves her husband, and ruins her house, neglecting her husband, this woman shall be cast into the water.

144. If a man take a wife and this woman give her husband a maid-servant, and she bear him children, but this man wishes to take another wife, this shall not be permitted to him; he shall not take a second wife.

145. If a man take a wife, and she bear him no children, and he intend to take another wife: if he take this second wife, and bring her into the house, this second wife shall not be allowed equality with his wife.

146. If a man take a wife and she give this man a maid-servant as wife and she bear him children, and then this maid assume equality with the wife: because she has borne him children her master shall not sell her for money, but he may keep her as a slave, reckoning her among the maid-servants.

147. If she have not borne him children, then her mistress may sell her for money.

148. If a man take a wife, and she be seized by disease, if he then desire to take a second wife he shall not put away his wife, who has been attacked by disease, but he shall keep her in the house which he has built and support her so long as she lives.

149. If this woman does not wish to remain in her husband's house, then he shall compensate her for the dowry that she brought with her from her father's house, and she may go.

150. If a man give his wife a field, garden, and house and a deed therefor, if then after the death of her husband the sons raise no claim, then the mother may bequeath all to one of her sons whom she prefers, and need leave nothing to his brothers.

151. If a woman who lived in a man's house made an agreement with her husband, that no creditor can arrest her, and has given a document therefor: if that man, before he married that woman, had a debt, the creditor can not hold the woman for it. But if the woman, before she entered the man's house, had contracted a debt, her creditor can not arrest her husband therefor.

152. If after the woman had entered the man's house, both contracted a debt, both must pay the merchant.

153. If the wife of one man on account of another man has their mates (her husband and the other man's wife) murdered, both of them shall be impaled.

154. If a man be guilty of incest with his daughter, he shall be driven from the place (exiled).

155. If a man betroth a girl to his son, and his son have intercourse with her, but he (the father) afterward defile her, and be surprised, then he shall be bound and cast into the water (drowned).

156. If a man betroth a girl to his son, but his son has not known her, and if then he defile her, he shall pay her half a gold mina, and compensate her for all that she brought out of her father's house. She may marry the man of her heart.

157. If any one be guilty of incest with his mother after his father, both shall be burned.

158. If any one be surprised after his father with his chief wife, who has borne children, he shall be driven out of his father's house.

DISOWNING AND ACKNOWLEDGING CHILDREN

168. If a man wish to put his son out of his house, and declare before the judge: "I want to put my son out," then the judge shall examine into his reasons. If the son be guilty of no great fault, for which he can be rightfully put out, the father shall not put him out.

169. If he be guilty of a grave fault, which should rightfully deprive him of the filial relationship, the father shall forgive him the first time; but if he be guilty of a grave fault a second time the father may deprive his son of all filial relation.

170. If his wife bear sons to a man, or his maid-servant have borne sons, and the father while still living says to the children whom his maid-servant has borne: "My sons," and he count them with the sons of his wife; if then the father die, then the sons of the wife and of the maid-servant shall divide the paternal property in common. The son of the wife is to partition and choose.

171. If, however, the father while still living did not say to the sons of the maid-servant: "My sons," and then the father dies, then the sons of the maid-servant shall not share with the sons of the wife, but the freedom of the maid and her sons shall be granted. The sons of the wife shall have no right to enslave the sons of the maid; the wife shall take her dowry (from her father), and the gift that her husband gave her and deeded to her (separate from dowry, or the purchase-money paid her father), and live in the home of her husband: so long as she lives she shall use it, it shall not be sold for money. Whatever she leaves shall belong to her children.

185. If a man adopt a child and to his name as son, and rear him, this grown son can not be demanded back again.

186. If a man adopt a son, and if after he has taken him he injure his foster father and mother, then this adopted son shall return to his father's house.

188. If an artizan has undertaken to rear a child and teaches him his craft, he can not be demanded back.

189. If he has not taught him his craft, this adopted son may return to his father's house.

190. If a man does not maintain a child that he has adopted as a son and reared with his other children, then his adopted son may return to his father's house.

192. If a son of a paramour or a prostitute say to his adoptive father or mother: "You are not my father, or my mother," his tongue shall be cut off.

195. If a son strike his father, his hands shall be hewn off.

PERSONAL INJURY

196. If a man put out the eye of another man, his eye shall be put out.

197. If he break another man's bone, his bone shall be broken.

198. If he put out the eye of a commoner, or break the bone of a commoner, he shall pay one gold mina.

199. If he put out the eye of a man's slave, or break the bone of a man's slave, he shall pay one-half of its value.

200. If a man knock out the teeth of his equal, his teeth shall be knocked out.

201. If he knock out the teeth of a commoner, he shall pay one-third of a gold mina.

202. If any one strike the body of a man higher in rank than he, he shall receive sixty blows with an ox-whip in public.

203. If a free-born man strike the body of another free-born man or equal rank, he shall pay one gold mina.

204. If a commoner strike the body of another commoner, he shall pay ten shekels in money.

205. If the slave of a commoner strike the body of a commoner, his ear shall be cut off.

206. If during a quarrel one man strike another and wound him, then he shall swear, "I did not injure him wittingly," and pay the physicians.

207. If the man die of his wound, he shall swear similarly, and if he (the deceased) was a free-born man, he shall pay half a mina in money.

208. If he was a commoner, he shall pay one-third of a mina.

209. If a man strike a free-born woman so that she lose her unborn child, he shall pay ten shekels for her loss.

210. If the woman die, his daughter shall be put to death.

211. If a woman of the common class lose her child by a blow, he shall pay five shekels in money.

212. If this woman die, he shall pay half a mina.

213. If he strike the maid-servant of a man, and she lose her child, he shall pay two shekels in money.

214. If this maid-servant die, he shall pay one-third of a mina.

215. If a physician make a large incision with an operating knife and cure it, or if he open a tumor (over the eye) with an operating knife, and saves the eye, he shall receive ten shekels in money.

216. If the patient be a commoner, he receives five shekels.

217. If he be the slave of some one, his owner shall give the physician two shekels.

218. If a physician make a large incision with the operating knife, and kill him, or open a tumor with the operating knife, and cut out the eye, his hands shall be cut off.

219. If a physician make a large incision in the slave of a commoner, and kill him, he shall replace the slave with another slave.

220. If he had opened a tumor with the operating knife, and put out his eye, he shall pay half his value.

221. If a physician heal the broken bone or diseased soft part of a man, the patient shall pay the physician five shekels in money.

222. If he were a commoner, he shall pay three shekels.

223. If he were a slave his owner shall pay the physician two shekels.

DAMAGE TO PROPERTY

224. If a veterinary surgeon perform a serious operation on an ass or an ox, and cure it, the owner shall pay the surgeon one-sixth of a shekel as a fee.

225. If he perform a serious operation on an ass or ox, and kill it, he shall pay the owner one-fourth of its value.

226. If a barber, without the knowledge of his master, cut the sign of a slave on a slave not to be sold, the hands of this barber shall be cut off.

227. If any one deceive a barber, and have him mark a slave not for sale with the sign of a slave, he shall be put to death, and buried in his house. The barber shall swear: "I did not mark him wittingly," and shall be guiltless.

228. If a builder build a house for some one and complete it, he shall give him a fee of two shekels in money for each sar of surface.

229. If a builder build a house for some one, and does not construct it properly, and the house which he built fall in and kill its owner, then that builder shall be put to death.

230. If it kill the son of the owner the son of that builder shall be put to death.

231. If it kill a slave of the owner, then he shall pay slave for slave to the owner of the house.

232. If it ruin goods, he shall make compensation for all that has been ruined, and inasmuch as he did not construct properly this house which he built and it fell, he shall re-erect the house from his own means.

233. If a builder build a house for some one, even though he has not yet completed it; if then the walls seem toppling, the builder must make the walls solid from his own means.

234. If a shipbuilder build a boat of sixty gur for a man, he shall pay him a fee of two shekels in money.

235. If a shipbuilder build a boat for some one, and do not make it tight, if during that same year that boat is sent away and suffers injury, the shipbuilder shall take the boat apart and put it together tight at his own expense. The tight boat he shall give to the boat owner.

236. If a man rent his boat to a sailor, and the sailor is careless, and the boat is wrecked or goes aground, the sailor shall give the owner of the boat another boat as compensation.

237. If a man hire a sailor and his boat, and provide it with grain, clothing, oil and dates, and other things of the kind needed for fitting it: if the sailor is careless, the boat is wrecked, and its contents ruined, then the sailor shall compensate for the boat which was wrecked and all in it that he ruined.

238. If a sailor wreck any one's ship, but saves it, he shall pay the half of its value in money.

239. If a man hire a sailor, he shall pay him six gur of grain per year.

244. If any one hire an ox or an ass, and a lion kill it in the field, the loss is upon its owner.

245. If any one hire oxen, and kill them by bad treatment or blows, he shall compensate the owner, oxen for oxen.

246. If a man hire an ox, and he break its leg or cut the ligament of its neck, he shall compensate the owner with ox for ox.

247. If any one hire an ox, and put out its eye, he shall pay the owner one-half of its value.

248. If any one hire an ox, and break off a horn, or cut off its tail, or hurt its muzzle, he shall pay one-fourth of its value in money.

249. If any one hire an ox, and God strike it that it die, the man who hired it shall swear by God and be considered guiltless.

250. If while an ox is passing on the street (market) some one push it, and kill it, the owner can set up no claim in the suit (against the hirer).

251. If an ox be a goring ox, and it shown that he is a gorer, and he do not bind his horns, or fasten the ox up, and the ox gore a free-born man and kill him, the owner shall pay one-half a mina in money.

252. If he kill a man's slave, he shall pay one-third of a mina.

265. If a herdsman, to whose care cattle or sheep have been entrusted, be guilty of fraud and make false returns of the natural increase, or sell them for money, then shall he be convicted and pay the owner ten times the loss.

266. If the animal be killed in the stable by God (an accident), or if a lion kill it, the herdsman shall declare his innocence before God, and the owner bears the accident in the stable.

267. If the herdsman overlook something, and an accident happen in the stable, then the herdsman is at fault for the accident which he has caused in the stable, and he must compensate the owner for the cattle or sheep.

READING 5

EGYPTIAN BOOK OF THE DEAD

The famous pyramids of ancient Egypt were the everlasting tombs of the kings, whom the Egyptians regarded as incarnate gods on earth during their lifetime and as merging into the god Osiris after their death to become rulers over the dead. All Egyptians, however, aspired to a happy existence after their death, and they devoted what resources they had to this quest. In the course of time Egyptian priests developed a complex body of rituals and spells that were designed to ensure the deceased of a happy life in the West, the Egyptian name for the realm of the dead. Many of these rituals and spells were written on scrolls and buried with the dead as a guarantee for their safe passage into the West. These texts that were buried with the dead today generally go by the collective name of "The Egyptian Book of the Dead." The following is a small excerpt from this vast body of complex literature. This passage shows how the deceased had to undergo an ordeal of having his life judged by Osiris, the god of the dead. The deceased needed to convince his divine judges that he had lived a reasonably just life. If he did not, his heart, thought to be the core of a person's life and mind, was fed to a demon, who devoured it and thus annihilated the person forever. If the person received a favorable judgment on his life, he was allowed to enter the Field of Reeds, where he enjoyed an eternal existence similar to what he had experienced during his lifetime. In addition, the long series of denials contained in this text give us an interesting glimpse into ancient Egyptian views of conventional morality.

(Adapted from pp.34-36 of Ancient Near Eastern Texts Relating to the Old Testament, edited by James B. Pritchard, Third Edition, Princeton University Press 1969)

What is said on reaching the Broad-Hall of the Two Justices, absolving X [the deceased] of every sin which he has committed, and seeing the faces of the gods:

Hail to thee, O great god, lord of the Two justices! I have come to thee, my lord, I have been brought that I might see thy beauty. I know thee; I know thy name and the names of the forty-two gods who are with thee in the Broad-Hall of the Two Justices, who live on them who preserve evil and who drink their blood on that day of reckoning up character in the presence of Wennofer. Behold, "Sati-mertifi, Lord of justice," is thy name. I have come to thee; I have brought thee justice; I have expelled deceit for thee.

I have not committed evil against men. I have not mistreated cattle. I have not committed sin in the place of truth. I have not known that which is not. I have not seen evil.... My name has not reached the Master of the Barque. I have not blasphemed a god. I have not done violence to a poor man. I have not done that which the gods abominate. I have not defamed a slave to his superior. I have not made anyone sick. I have not made anyone weep. I have not killed. I have given no order to a killer. I have not caused anyone suffering. I have not cut down on the food-income in the temples. I have not damaged the bread of the gods. I have not taken the loaves of the blessed dead. I have not had sexual relations with a boy. I have not defiled myself. I have neither increased or diminished the grain-measure. I have not diminished the aroura. I have not falsified a half-aroura of land. I have not added to the weight of the balance. I have not weakened the plummet of the scales. I have not taken milk from the mouths of children. I have not driven cattle away from their pasturage. I have not snared the birds of the gods. I have not caught fish in their marshes. I have not held up the water in its season. I have not built a dam against running water. I have not quenched a fire at its proper time. I have not neglected the appointed times and their meat-offerings. I have not driven away the cattle of the god's property. I have not stopped a god on his procession. I am pure!...

WORDS TO BE SPOKEN BY X [the deceased]: Hail to you, ye gods who are in this Broad-Hall of the Two Justices! I know you; I know your names. I shall not fall for dread of you. Ye have not reported guilt of mine up to this god in whose retinue ye are; no deed of mine has come from you. Ye have spoken truth about me in the presence of the All-Lord, because I acted justly in Egypt. I have not been abusive to a god. No deed of mine has come from a king who is in his day. Hail to you who are in the Broad-Hall of the Two Justices, who have no deceit in your bodies, who live on truth and who eat of truth in the presence of Horus, who is in his sun disc. May ye rescue me from Babi, who lives on the entrails of elders on that day of the great reckoning. Behold me. I have come to you without sin, without guilt, without evil, without a witness against me, without one against whom I have taken action. I live on truth, and I eat of truth. I have done that which men said and that with which gods are content. I have satisfied a god with that which he desires. I have given bread to the hungry, water to the thirsty, clothing to the naked, and a ferry-boat to him who was marooned. I have provided divine offerings for the gods and mortuary offerings for the dead. So rescue me, you; protect me, you. Ye will not make report against me in the presence of the great god. I am one pure of mouth and pure of hands, one to whom "Welcome, welcome, in peace!" is said by those who see him, because I have heard those great words which the ass discussed with the cat in the house of the hippopotamus, when the witness was His-Face-Behind-Him and he gave out a cry. I have seen the splitting of the ished-tree in Rostau. I am one who has a concern for the gods, who knows the nature of their bodies. I have come here to testify to justice and to bring the scales to their proper position in the cemetery. O thou who art high upon his standard, Lord of the Atef-Crown, whose name has been made "Lord of Breath," mayest thou rescue me from thy messengers who give forth uncleanliness and create destruction, who have no covering up of their faces, because I have effected justice for the Lord of justice, being pure-my front is pure, my rear is clean, my middle is in the flowing water of justice; there is no part of me free of justice.... ... I will not announce thee," says the doorkeeper of the Broad-Hall of the Two Justices, "unless thou tellest my name." "Understander of Hearts, Searcher of Bodies is thy name." "Then to whom should I announce thee?" "To the god who is in his hour of service." "Thou shouldst tell it to the interpreter of the Two Lands." "Well, who is the interpreter of the Two Lands?" "It is Thoth." "Come," says Thoth, "why hast thou come?" "I have come here to be announced ... .. What is thy condition?" "I am pure of sin. I have protected myself from the strife of those who are in their days. I am not among them." "Then to whom shall I announce thee? I shall announce thee to him whose ceiling is of fire, whose walls are living serpents, and whose pavement is water. Who is he?" "He is Osiris." "Then go thou. Behold, thou art announced....

AS FOR HIM ON WHOSE BEHALF THIS BOOK IS MADE, HE SHALL BE PROSPEROUS AND HIS CHILDREN SHALL BE PROSPEROUS, WITHOUT GREED, BECAUSE HE SHALL BE A TRUSTED MAN OF the king AND HIS COURTIERS. LOAVES, JARS, BREAD, AND JOINTS OF MEAT SHALL BE GIVEN TO HIM FROM THE ALTAR OF the great god. HE CANNOT BE HELD BACK AT ANY DOOR OF THE WEST, BUT HE SHALL BE USHERED IN WITH the Kings of Upper and Lower Egypt, and he shall be in the retinue of Osiris. Right and true a million times!

Reading 6

An Egyptian Tale of Magic

Egypt was famous throughout the rest of the ancient world (as well as today) as the source of the most powerful magic. The following story not only represents Egypt's tradition of magic, but it is also a good example of popular Egyptian story telling. It was recorded on a papyrus during the Second Intermediate Period, but its historical setting is the Old Kingdom. The tale is portrayed as having been told to King Khufu, the pharaoh of Egypt's largest pyramid, concerning his father King Snefru. Furthermore, it is noteworthy that the magician in this story is not only a chief priest (i.e., one who possesses a wealth of expert religious knowledge), but one who is termed "the scribe of the book," that is, a man highly skilled in writing hieroglyphics: for in the realm of magic, writing is viewed as an important source of magical power. It is also noteworthy that this tale involves the use of magical power to part the waters of a lake, thereby resembling the story of how God parted the sea for the Hebrews fleeing from the land of Egypt. See *Exodus* 7.9-13 for a contest involving God's magic overcoming that of the Egyptian pharaoh's best magicians.

(Taken from The Literature of the Ancient Egyptians: Poems, Narratives, and Manuals of Instruction from the Third and Second Millennia B.C., by Adolf Erman, translated by A. M. Blackman, published by Methuen and Co. [London, 1927] pp.38-40)

Then Prince Daufre stood up to speak and said: I relate to thy majesty a wonder that came to pass in the time of thy father Snefru, one of the deeds of the cheif *kerheb* [learned priest], Zazamonkh. One day King Snefru was sad. So, he assembled the officers of the palace in order to seek for him a diversion, but he found none. Then said he, "Go, bring me the chief *kerheb*, the scribe of the book, Zazamonkh." And he was brought unto him straightway, and his majesty said unto him, "I had assembled the officers of the palace together in order to seek for me a diversion, but I could find none." And Zazamonkh said unto him, "If thy majesty would but betake thee to the Lake of the Great House [i.e., the palace], man thee a boat with all fair damsels from the inner apartments of thy palace. Then will the heart of thy majesty be diverted when thou shalt see how they row to and fro. Then, as thou viewest the pleasant nesting places of thy lake and viewest its fields and its pleasant banks, thine heart will be diverted thereby." His majesty said unto him, "I will do this. Get thee back to thine house, but I will go boating. Have brought to me twenty paddles of ebony inwrought with gold, the handles thereof being of sekeb wood inwrought with fine gold. Have brought to me twenty women of those with the fairest limbs and with beautious breasts and braided tresses, such as have not yet given birth. And moreover, have brought to me twenty nets, and give these nets to these women instead of their clothes."

And it was done according to all that his majesty commanded. And they rowed to and fro, and the heart of his majesty was glad when he beheld how they rowed. Then a leader became entangled with her braided tresses, and a fish pendant of new malachite fell into the water; and she became silent [i.e., stopped singing in time] and ceased rowing. And her side [of the boat] became silent and ceased rowing. Then said his majesty, "Is it that you will not row then?" And they said, "Our leader is silent and roweth not." And his majesty said unto her, "Wherefor rowest thou not?" And she said, "It is the fish pendant of new malachite that hath fallen into the water."

He had another brought to her and said, "I give thee this instead." And she said, "I want my pot downt to its bottom" [= I want my very own thing]. Then said his majesty, "Go, bring me the chief *kerheb* Zazamonkh." And he was brought straightway. And his majesty said, "Zazamonkh, my brother, I have done as thou saidest, and the heart of my majesty was diverted when I beheld how they rowed. But a fish pendant of new malachite, belonging to a leader, fell into the water; and she was silent and rowed not; and so she spoiled her side. And I said unto her, 'Wherefor rowest thou not?' And she said unto me, 'It is a fish pendant of new malachite that hath fallen into the water.' And I said unto her, 'Row, and lo, I will replace it.' And she said unto me, 'I want my pot down to its bottom.'"

Then the cheif *kerheb* Zazamonkh said his say of magic. Then he placed one side of the water of the lake upon the other and found the fish pendant lying on a potsherd. And he brought it and gave it to its mistress. Now, as to the water, it was twelve cubits deep [eighteen feet] in the middle, and it reached twenty-four cubitsd after it was turned back. Then he said his say of magic, and he brought the waters of the lake back to their place. And his majesty spent the whole day in merriment with the entire palace, and he rewarded the cheif *kerheb* Zazamonkh with all good things.

Lo, it is a wonder that came to ass in the time of thy father Snefru, one of the deeds of the cheif *kerheb*, the scribe of the book, Zazamonkh.

ASSYRIAN ANNALS OF KING ASHURNASIRPAL

The kings of the Assyrian Empire have left behind detailed accounts of their military conquests, testifying to the brutality and predatory nature of their reigns. The first great Assyrian conquering king was Ashurnasirpal, who ruled from 883 to 859 B.C.; and the following are extracts taken from a very long inscription that he erected to record his exploits for posterity.

(Taken from Babylonian and Assyrian Literature, tr. Rev. J. M. Rodwell, P. F. Collier and Son, New York 1901)

In my first campaign when the Sun-god guider of the lands threw over me his beneficent protection on the throne of my dominion I firmly seated myself; a sceptre the dread of man into my hands I took; my chariots (and) armies I collected; rugged paths, difficult mountains, which for the passage of chariots and armies was not suited I passed, and to the land of Nairi I went: Libie, their capital city, the cities Zurra and Abuqu Arura Arubie, situated within the limits of the land of Aruni and Etini, fortified cities, I took, their fighting-men in numbers I slew; their spoil, their wealth, their cattle I spoiled; their soldiers were discouraged; they took possession of a difficult mountain, a mountain exceedingly difficult; after them I did not proceed, for it was a mountain ascending up like lofty points of iron, and the beautiful birds of heaven had not reached up into it: like nests of the young birds in the midst of the mountain their defence they placed, into which none of the Kings my fathers had ever penetrated: in three days successfully on one large mountain, his courage vanquished opposition: along the feet of that mountain I crept and hid: their nests, their tents, I broke up; 200 of their warriors with weapons I destroyed; their spoil in abundance like the young of sheep I carried off; their corpses like rubbish on the mountains I heaped up; their relics in tangled hollows of the mountains I consumed; their cities I overthrew, I demolished, in fire I burned.

From the land of Nummi to the land of Kirruri I came down; the tribute of Kirruri of the territory of Zimizi, Zimira, Ulmanya, Adavas, Kargai, Harmasai, horses, (fish (?). oxen, horned sheep in numbers, copper, as their tribute I received: an officer to guard boundaries over them I placed. While in the land of Kirruri they detained me, the fear of Ashur my Lord overwhelmed the lands of Gilzanai and Khubuskai; horses, silver gold, tin, copper, kams of copper as their tribute they brought to me. From the land of Kirruri I withdrew; to a territory close by the town Khulun in Gilhi Bitani I passed: the cities of Khatu, Khalaru, Nistun, Irbidi, Mitkie, Arzanie, Zila, Khalue, cities of Gilhi situated in the environs of Uzie and Arue and Arardi powerful lands, I occupied: their soldiers in numbers I slew; their spoil, their riches I carried off; their soldiers were discouraged; the summits projecting over against the city of Nistun which were menacing like the storms of heaven, I captured; into which no one among the Princes my sires had ever penetrated; my soldiers like birds (of prey) rushed upon them; 260 of their warriors by the sword I smote down; their heads cut off in heaps I arranged; the rest of them like birds in a nest, in the rocks of the mountains nestled; their spoil, their riches from the midst of the mountains I brought down; cities which were in the midst of vast forests situated I overthrew, destroyed, burned in fire; the rebellious soldiers fled from before my arms; they came down; my yoke they received; impost tribute and a Viceroy I set over them. Bubu son of Bubua son of the Prefect of Nistun in the city of Arbela I flayed; his skin I stretched in contempt upon the wall. At that time an image of my person I made; a history of my supremacy upon it I wrote, and (on) a mountain of the land of Ikin(?) in the city of Ashurnasirpal at the foot I erected (it).

In my own eponym [yearly office] in the month of — and the 24th day (probably B.C. 882). in honor of Ashur and Ishtar the great gods my Lords, I quitted the city of Nineveh: to cities situated below Nipur and Pazate powerful countries I proceeded; Atkun, Nithu, Pilazi and 20 other cities in their environs I captured; many of their soldiers I slew; their spoil, their riches I carried off; the cities I burned with fire; the rebel soldiers fled from before my arms, submitted, and took my yoke; I left them in possession of their land.

From the cities below Nipur and Pazate I withdrew; the Tigris I passed; to the land of Commagene I approached; the tribute of Commagene and of the Moschi in kams of copper, sheep and goats I received; while in Commagene I was stationed, they brought me intelligence that the city Suri in Bit-Khalupe had revolted. The people of Hamath had slain their governor Ahiyababa the son of Lamamana they brought from Bit-Adini and made him their King. By help of Ashur and Yav the great gods who aggrandize my royalty, chariots, (and) an army, I collected: the banks of the Chaboras I occupied; in my passage tribute in abundance from Salman-haman-ilin of the city of Sadikannai and of Il-yav of the city of Sunai, silver, gold, tin, kam of copper, vestments of wool, vestments of linen I received.

To Suri which is in Bit-Halupe I drew near; the fear of the approach of Ashur my Lord overwhelmed them; the great men and the multitudes of the city, for the saving of their lives, coming up after me, submitted to my yoke; some slain, some living, some tongue-less I made: Ahiyababa son of Lamamana whom from Bit-Adini they had fetched, I captured; in the valor of my heart and the steadfastness of my soldiers I besieged the city; the soldiers, rebels all, were taken prisoners; the nobles to the principal palace of his land I caused to send; his silver, his gold, his treasure, his riches, copper (?)tin, kams, tabhani, hariati of copper, choice copper in abundance, alabaster and iron-stone of large size the treasures of his harem, his daughters and the wives of the rebels with their treasures, and the gods with their treasures, precious stones of the land of ... , his swift chariot, his horses, the harness, his chariot-yoke, trappings for horses, coverings for men, vestments of wool, vestments of linen, handsome altars of cedar, handsome ... , bowls of cedar-wood beautiful black coverings, beautiful purple coverings, carpets, his oxen, his sheep, his abundant spoil, which like the stars of heaven could not be reckoned, I carried off; Aziel as my lieutenant over them I placed; a trophy along the length of the great gate I erected: the rebellious nobles who had revolted against me and whose skins I had stripped off, I made into a trophy: some in the middle of the pile I left to decay; some on the top of the pile on stakes I impaled; some by the side of the pile I placed in order on stakes; many within view of my land I flayed; their skins on the walls I arranged; of the officers of the King's officer, rebels, the limbs I cut off; I brought Ahiyababa to Nineveh; I flayed, him and fastened his skin to the wall....

In honor of Ashur, the Sun-god and Yav, the gods in whom I trust, my chariots and army I collected at the head of the river Zupnat, the place of an image which Tiglath-Pileser and Tiglath-Adar, Kings of Assyria my fathers had raised; an image of My Majesty I constructed and put up with theirs. In those days I renewed the tribute of the land of Izala, oxen, sheep, goats: to the land of Kasyari I proceeded, and to Kinabu the fortified city of the province of Hulai. I drew near; with the impetuosity of my formidable attack I besieged and took the town; 600 of their fighting men with (my) arms I destroyed; 3,000 of their captives I consigned to the flames; as hostages I left not one of them alive; Hulai the governor of their town I captured by (my) hand alive; their corpses into piles I built; their boys and maidens I dishonored; Hulai the governor of their city I flayed: his skin on the walls of Damdamusa I placed in contempt; the city I overthrew demolished, burned with fire; the city of Mariru within their territory I took; 50 warrior fighting men by (my) weapons I destroyed; 200 of their captives in the flame I burned....

To Tila I drew near; a strong city with three forts facing each other: the soldiers to their strong forts and numerous army trusted and would not submit; my yoke they would not accept; (then,) with onset and attack I besieged the city; their fighting men with my weapons I destroyed; of their spoil, their riches, oxen and sheep, I made plunder; much booty I burned with fire; many soldiers I captured alive; of some I chopped off the hands and feet; of others the noses and ears I cut off; of many soldiers I destroyed the eyes; one pile of bodies while yet alive, and one of heads I reared up on the heights within their town; their heads in the midst I hoisted; their boys and their maidens I dishonored, the city I overthrew, razed and burned with fire....

From Bit-Adini I withdrew; the Euphrates, in a difficult part of it, I crossed in ships of hardened skins: I approached the land of Carchemish: the tribute of Sangara King of Syria, twenty talents of silver, sahri gold, bracelets of gold, scabbards of gold, 100 talents of copper, 250 talents of annui kami, hariate, nirmakate kibil of copper, the extensive furniture of his palace, of incomprehensible perfection different kinds of woods, ka and sara, 200 female slaves, vestments of wool, and linen; beautiful black coverings, beautiful purple coverings, precious stones, horns of buffaloes, white chariots, images of gold, their coverings, the treasures of his Royalty, I received of him; the chariots and warlike engines of the General of Carchemish I laid up in my magazines; the Kings of all those lands who had come out against me received my yoke; their hostages I received; they did homage in my presence.

To the land of Lebanon I proceeded. From Carchemish I withdrew and marched to the territory of Munzigani and Harmurga: the land of Ahanu I reduced; to Gaza the town of Lubarna of the Khatti I advanced; gold and vestments of linen I received: crossing the river Abrie I halted and then leaving that river approached the town of Kanulua a royal city belonging to Lubarna of the Khatti: from before my mighty arms and my formidable onset he fled in fear, and for the saving of his life submitted to my yoke; twenty talents of silver, one talent of gold, 100 talents in tin, 100 talents in annui, 1,000 oxen, 10,000 sheep, 1,000 vestments of wool, linen, nimati and ki woods coverings, ahusate thrones, kui wood, wood for seats, their coverings, sarai, zueri-wood, horns of kui in abundance, the numerous utensils of his palace, whose beauty could not be comprehended: ... pagatu(?) from the wealth of great Lords as his tribute I imposed upon him; the chariots and warlike engines of the land of the Khatti I laid up in my magazines; their hostages I took.

In those days (I received) the tribute of Guzi of the land of Yahanai, silver, gold, tin, ... oxen, sheep, vestments of wool and linen I received: from Kanalua the capital of Lubarna I withdrew....

In those days I occupied the environs of Lebanon; to the great sea of Phoenicia I went up: up to the great sea my arms I carried: to the gods I sacrificed; I took tribute of the Princes of the environs of the sea-coast, of the lands of Tyre, Sidon, Gebal, Maacah Maizai Kaizai, of Phoenicia and Arvad on the sea-coast - silver, gold, tin, copper, kam of copper, vestments of wool and linen, pagutu great and small, strong timber, wood of ki teeth of dolphins, the produce of the sea, I received as their tribute: my yoke they accepted; the mountains of Amanus I ascended; wood for bridges, pines, box, cypress, li-wood, I cut down; I offered sacrifices for my gods; a trophy of victory I made, and in a central place I erected it.

READING 8

THE OLD TESTAMENT

(Taken from the King James Version)

A. THE GARDEN OF EDEN

✢ Genesis

CHAPTER 3: **1** Now the serpent was more subtil than any beast of the field which the LORD God had made. And he said unto the woman, "Yea, hath God said, Ye shall not eat of every tree of the garden?" **2** And the woman said unto the serpent, "We may eat of the fruit of the trees of the garden: **3** But of the fruit of the tree which is in the midst of the garden, God hath said, 'Ye shall not eat of it, neither shall ye touch it, lest ye die.'" **4** And the serpent said unto the woman, "Ye shall not surely die: **5** For God doth know that in the day ye eat thereof, then your eyes shall be opened, and ye shall be as gods, knowing good and evil." **6** And when the woman saw that the tree was good for food, and that it was pleasant to the eyes, and a tree to be desired to make one wise, she took of the fruit thereof, and did eat, and gave also unto her husband with her; and he did eat. **7** And the eyes of them both were opened, and they knew that they were naked; and they sewed fig leaves together, and made themselves aprons. **8** And they heard the voice of the LORD God walking in the garden in the cool of the day: and Adam and his wife hid themselves from the presence of the LORD God amongst the trees of the garden. **9** And the LORD God called unto Adam, and said unto him, "Where art thou?" **10** And he said, "I heard thy voice in the garden, and I was afraid, because I was naked; and I hid myself." **11** And he said, "Who told thee that thou wast naked? Hast thou eaten of the tree, whereof I commanded thee that thou shouldest not eat?" **12** And the man said, "The woman whom thou gavest to be with me, she gave me of the tree, and I did eat." **13** And the LORD God said unto the woman, "What is this that thou hast done?" And the woman said, "The serpent beguiled me, and I did eat." **14** And the LORD God said unto the serpent, "Because thou hast done this, thou art cursed above all cattle, and above every beast of the field; upon thy belly shalt thou go, and dust shalt thou eat all the days of thy life: **15** And I will put enmity between thee and the woman, and between thy seed and her seed; it shall bruise thy head, and thou shalt bruise his heel." **16** Unto the woman he said, "I will greatly multiply thy sorrow and thy conception; in sorrow thou shalt bring forth children; and thy desire shall be to thy husband, and he shall rule over thee." **17** And unto Adam he said, "Because thou hast hearkened unto the voice of thy wife, and hast eaten of the tree, of which I commanded thee, saying, Thou shalt not eat of it: cursed is the ground for thy sake; in sorrow shalt thou eat of it all the days of thy life; **18** Thorns also and thistles shall it bring forth to thee; and thou shalt eat the herb of the field; **19** In the sweat of thy face shalt thou eat bread, till thou return unto the ground; for out of it wast thou taken: for dust thou art, and unto dust shalt thou return." **20** And Adam called his wife's name Eve; because she was the mother of all living. **21** Unto Adam also and to his wife did the LORD God make coats of skins, and clothed them. **22** And the LORD God said, "Behold, the man is become as one of us, to know good and evil: and now, lest he put forth his hand, and take also of the tree of life, and eat, and live for ever:" **23** Therefore the LORD God sent him forth from the garden of Eden, to till the ground from whence he was taken. **24** So he drove out the man; and he placed at the east of the garden of Eden Cherubims, and a flaming sword which turned every way, to keep the way of the tree of life.

B. THE BIBLICAL FLOOD STORY

✢ Genesis

CHAPTER 5: 1. This is the book of the generations of Adam. In the day that God created man, in the likeness of God made he him; **2.** Male and female created he them; and blessed them, and called their name Adam, in the day when they were created. **3.** And Adam lived an hundred and thirty years, and begat a son in his own likeness, and after his image; and called his name Seth: **4.** And the days of Adam after he had begotten Seth were eight hundred years: and he begat sons and daughters: **5.** And all the days that Adam lived were nine hundred and thirty years: and he died. **6.** And Seth lived an hundred and five years, and begat Enos: **7.** And Seth lived after he begat Enos eight hundred and seven years, and begat sons and daughters: **8.** And all the days of Seth were nine hundred and twelve years: and he died. **9.** And Enos lived ninety years, and begat Cainan: **10.** And Enos lived after he begat Cainan eight hundred and fifteen years, and begat sons and daughters: **11.** And all the days of Enos were nine hundred and five years: and he died. **12.** And Cainan lived seventy years and begat Mahalaleel: **13.** And Cainan lived after he begat Mahalaleel eight hundred and forty years, and begat sons and daughters: **14.** And all the days of Cainan were nine hundred and ten years: and he died. **15.** And Mahalaleel lived sixty and five years, and begat Jared: **16.** And Mahalaleel lived after he begat Jared eight hundred and thirty years, and begat sons and daughters: **17.** And all the days of Mahalaleel were eight hundred ninety and five years: and he died. **18.** And Jared lived an hundred sixty and two years, and he begat Enoch: **19.** And Jared lived after he begat Enoch eight hundred years, and begat sons and daughters: **20.** And all the days of Jared were nine hundred sixty and two years: and he died. **21.** And Enoch lived sixty and five years, and begat Methuselah: **22.** And Enoch walked with God after he begat Methuselah three hundred years, and begat sons and daughters: **23.** And all the days of Enoch were three hundred sixty and five years: **24.** And Enoch walked with God: and he was not; for God took him. **25.** And Methuselah lived an hundred eighty and seven years, and begat Lamech. **26.** And Methuselah lived after he begat Lamech seven hundred eighty and two years, and begat sons and daughters: **27.** And all the days of Methuselah were nine hundred sixty and nine years: and he died. **28.** And Lamech lived an hundred eighty and two years, and begat a son: **29.** And he called his name Noah, saying, "This same shall comfort us concerning our work and toil of our hands, because of the ground which the LORD hath cursed." **30.** And Lamech lived after he begat Noah five hundred ninety and five years, and begat sons and daughters: **31.** And all the days of Lamech were seven hundred seventy and seven years: and he died. **32.** And Noah was five hundred years old: and Noah begat Shem, Ham, and Japheth.

CHAPTER 6: **1.** And it came to pass, when men began to multiply on the face of the earth, and daughters were born unto them, **2.** That the sons of God saw the daughters of men that they were fair; and they took them wives of all which they chose. **3.** And the LORD said, "My spirit shall not always strive with man, for that he also is flesh: yet his days shall be an hundred and twenty years." **4.** There were giants in the earth in those days; and also after that, when the sons of God came in unto the daughters of men, and they bare children to them, the same became mighty men which were of old, men of renown. **5.** And God saw that the wickedness of man was great in the earth, and that every imagination of the thoughts of his heart was only evil continually. **6.** And it repented the LORD that he had made man on the earth, and it grieved him at his heart. **7.** And the LORD said, "I will destroy man whom I have created from the face of the earth; both man, and beast, and the creeping thing, and the fowls of the air; for it repenteth me that I have made them." **8.** But Noah found grace in the eyes of the LORD. **9.** These are the generations of Noah: Noah was a just man and perfect in his generations, and Noah walked with God. **10.** And Noah begat three sons, Shem, Ham, and Japheth. **11.** The earth also was corrupt before God, and the earth was filled with violence. **12.** And God looked upon the earth, and, behold, it was corrupt; for all flesh had corrupted his way upon the earth. **13.** And God said unto Noah, "The end of all flesh is come before me; for the earth is filled with violence through them; and, behold, I will destroy them with the earth. **14.** Make thee an ark of gopher wood; rooms shalt thou make in the ark, and shalt pitch it within and without with pitch. **15.** And this is the fashion which thou shalt make it of: The length of the ark shall be three hundred cubits, the breadth of it fifty cubits, and the height of it thirty cubits. **16.** A window shalt thou make to the ark, and in a cubit shalt thou finish it above; and the door of the ark shalt thou set in the side thereof; with lower, second, and third stories shalt thou make it. **17.** And, behold, I, even I, do bring a flood of waters upon the earth, to destroy all flesh, wherein is the breath of life, from under heaven; and every thing that is in the earth shall die. **18.** But with thee will I establish my covenant; and thou shalt come into the ark, thou, and thy sons, and thy wife, and thy sons' wives with thee. **19.** And of every living thing of all flesh, two of every sort shalt thou bring into the ark, to keep them alive with thee; they shall be male and female. **20.** Of fowls after their kind, and of cattle after their kind, of every creeping thing of the earth after his kind, two of every sort shall come unto thee, to keep them alive. **21.** And take thou unto thee of all food that is eaten, and thou shalt gather it to thee; and it shall be for food for thee, and for them." **22.** Thus did Noah; according to all that God commanded him, so did he.

CHAPTER 7: **1.** And the LORD said unto Noah, "Come thou and all thy house into the ark; for thee have I seen righteous before me in this generation. **2.** Of every clean beast thou shalt take to thee by sevens, the male and his female: and of beasts that are not clean by two, the male and his female. **3.** Of fowls also of the air by sevens, the male and the female; to keep seed alive upon the face of all the earth. **4.** For yet seven days, and I will cause it to rain upon the earth forty days and forty nights; and every living substance that I have made will I destroy from off the face of the earth." **5.** And Noah did according unto all that the LORD commanded him. **6.** And Noah was six hundred years old when the flood of waters was upon the earth. **7.** And Noah went in, and his sons, and his wife, and his sons' wives with him, into the ark, because of the waters of the flood. **8.** Of clean beasts, and of beasts that are not clean, and of fowls, and of every thing that creepeth upon the earth, **9.** There went in two and two unto Noah into the ark, the male and the female, as God had commanded Noah. **10.** And it came to pass after seven days, that the waters of the flood were upon the earth. **11.** In the six hundredth year of Noah's life, in the second month, the seventeenth day of the month, the same day were all the fountains of the great deep broken up, and the windows of heaven were opened. **12.** And the rain was upon the earth forty days and forty nights. **13.** In the selfsame day entered Noah, and Shem, and Ham, and Japheth, the sons of Noah, and Noah's wife, and the three wives of his sons with them, into the ark; **14.** They, and every beast after his kind, and all the cattle after their kind, and every creeping thing that creepeth upon the earth after his kind, and every fowl after his kind, every bird of every sort. **15.** And they went in unto Noah into the ark, two and two of all flesh, wherein is the breath of life. **16.** And they that went in, went in male and female of all flesh, as God had commanded him: and the LORD shut him in. **17.** And the flood was forty days upon the earth; and the waters increased, and bare up the ark, and it was lift up above the earth. **18.** And the waters prevailed, and were increased greatly upon the earth; and the ark went upon the face of the waters. **19.** And the waters prevailed exceedingly upon the earth; and all the high hills, that were under the whole heaven, were covered. **20.** Fifteen cubits upward did the waters prevail; and the mountains were covered. **21.** And all flesh died that moved upon the earth, both of fowl, and of cattle, and of beast, and of every creeping thing that creepeth upon the earth, and every man: **22.** All in whose nostrils was the breath of life, of all that was in the dry land, died. **23.** And every living substance was destroyed which was upon the face of the ground, both man, and cattle, and the creeping things, and the fowl of the heaven; and they were destroyed from the earth: and Noah only remained alive, and they that were with him in the ark. **24.** And the waters prevailed upon the earth an hundred and fifty days.

CHAPTER 8: 1. And God remembered Noah, and every living thing, and all the cattle that was with him in the ark: and God made a wind to pass over the earth, and the waters asswaged; **2.** The fountains also of the deep and the windows of heaven were stopped, and the rain from heaven was restrained; **3.** And the waters returned from off the earth continually: and after the end of the hundred and fifty days the waters were abated. **4.** And the ark rested in the seventh month, on the seventeenth day of the month, upon the mountains of Ararat. **5.** And the waters decreased continually until the tenth month: in the tenth month, on the first day of the month, were the tops of the mountains seen. **6.** And it came to pass at the end of forty days, that Noah opened the window of the ark which he had made: **7.** And he sent forth a raven, which went forth to and fro, until the waters were dried up from off the earth. **8.** Also he sent forth a dove from him, to see if the waters were abated from off the face of the ground; **9.** But the dove found no rest for the sole of her foot, and she returned unto him into the ark, for the waters were on the face of the whole earth: then he put forth his hand, and took her, and pulled her in unto him into the ark. **10.** And he stayed yet other seven days; and again he sent forth the dove out of the ark; **11.** And the dove came in to him in the evening; and, lo, in her mouth was an olive leaf pluckt off: so Noah knew that the waters were abated from off the earth. **12.** And he stayed yet other seven days; and sent forth the dove; which returned not again unto him any more. **13.** And it came to pass in the six hundredth and first year, in the first month, the first day of the month, the waters were dried up from off the earth: and Noah removed the covering of the ark, and looked, and, behold, the face of the ground was dry. **14.** And in the second month, on the seven and twentieth day of the month, was the earth dried. **15.** And God spake unto Noah, saying, **16.** "Go forth of the ark, thou, and thy wife, and thy sons, and thy sons' wives with thee. **17.** Bring forth with thee every living thing that is with thee, of all flesh, both of fowl, and of cattle, and of every creeping thing that creepeth upon the earth; that they may breed abundantly in the earth, and be fruitful, and multiply upon the earth." **18.** And Noah went forth, and his sons, and his wife, and his sons' wives with him: **19.** Every beast, every creeping thing, and every fowl, and whatsoever creepeth upon the earth, after their kinds, went forth out of the ark.   20. And Noah builded an altar unto the LORD; and took of every clean beast, and of every clean fowl, and offered burnt offerings on the altar.   21. And the LORD smelled a sweet savour; and the LORD said in his heart, "I will not again curse the ground any more for man's sake; for the imagination of man's heart is evil from his youth; neither will I again smite any more every thing living, as I have done.   22. While the earth remaineth, seedtime and harvest, and cold and heat, and summer and winter, and day and night shall not cease."

CHAPTER 9: **1.** And God blessed Noah and his sons, and said unto them, "Be fruitful, and multiply, and replenish the earth.   **2.** And the fear of you and the dread of you shall be upon every beast of the earth, and upon every fowl of the air, upon all that moveth upon the earth, and upon all the fishes of the sea; into your hand are they delivered.   **3.** Every moving thing that liveth shall be meat for you; even as the green herb have I given you all things.   **4.** But flesh with the life thereof, which is the blood thereof, shall ye not eat.   **5.** And surely your blood of your lives will I require; at the hand of every beast will I require it, and at the hand of man; at the hand of every man's brother will I require the life of man.   **6.** Whoso sheddeth man's blood, by man shall his blood be shed: for in the image of God made he man.   **7.** And you, be ye fruitful, and multiply; bring forth abundantly in the earth, and multiply therein."   **8.** And God spake unto Noah, and to his sons with him, saying,   **9.** "And I, behold, I establish my covenant with you, and with your seed after you;   **10.** And with every living creature that is with you, of the fowl, of the cattle, and of every beast of the earth with you; from all that go out of the ark, to every beast of the earth.   **11.** And I will establish my covenant with you, neither shall all flesh be cut off any more by the waters of a flood; neither shall there any more be a flood to destroy the earth."   **12.** And God said, "This is the token of the covenant which I make between me and you and every living creature that is with you, for perpetual generations: **13.** I do set my bow in the cloud, and it shall be for a token of a covenant between me and the earth.   **14.** And it shall come to pass, when I bring a cloud over the earth, that the bow shall be seen in the cloud: **15.** And I will remember my covenant, which is between me and you and every living creature of all flesh; and the waters shall no more become a flood to destroy all flesh.   **16.** And the bow shall be in the cloud; and I will look upon it, that I may remember the everlasting covenant between God and every living creature of all flesh that is upon the earth."   **17.** And God said unto Noah, "This is the token of the covenant, which I have established between me and all flesh that is upon the earth."

C. ABRAHAM'S SACRIFICE OF ISAAC

✤ Genesis

CHAPTER 22: **1** And it came to pass after these things, that God did tempt Abraham, and said unto him, "Abraham:" and he said, "Behold, here I am." **2** And he said, "Take now thy son, thine only son Isaac, whom thou lovest, and get thee into the land of Moriah; and offer him there for a burnt offering upon one of the mountains which I will tell thee of." **3** And Abraham rose up early in the morning, and saddled his ass, and took two of his young men with him, and Isaac his son, and clave the wood for the burnt offering, and rose up, and went unto the place of which God had told him. **4** Then on the third day Abraham lifted up his eyes, and saw the place afar off. **5** And Abraham said unto his young men, "Abide ye here with the ass; and I and the lad will go yonder and worship, and come again to you." **6** And Abraham took the wood of the burnt offering, and laid it upon Isaac his son; and he took the fire in his hand, and a knife; and they went both of them together. **7** And Isaac spake unto Abraham his father, and said, "My father:" and he said, "Here am I, my son." And he said, "Behold the fire and the wood: but where is the lamb for a burnt offering?"   **8** And Abraham said, "My son, God will provide himself a lamb for a burnt offering:" so they went both of them together.   **9** And they came to the place which God had told him of; and Abraham built an altar there, and laid the wood in order, and bound Isaac his son, and laid him on the altar upon the wood.   **10** And Abraham stretched forth his hand, and took the knife to slay his son.   **11** And the angel of the LORD called unto him out of heaven, and said, "Abraham, Abraham:" and he said, "Here am I."   **12** And he said, "Lay not thine hand upon the lad, neither do thou any thing unto him: for now I know that thou fearest God, seeing thou hast not withheld thy son, thine only son from me."   **13** And Abraham lifted up his eyes, and looked, and behold behind him a ram caught in a thicket by his horns: and Abraham went and took the ram, and offered him up for a burnt offering in the stead of his son.   **14** And Abraham called the name of that place Jehovahjireh: as it is said to this day, In the mount of the LORD it shall be seen.   **15** And the angel of the LORD called unto Abraham out of heaven the second time,   **16** And said, "By myself have I sworn, saith the LORD, for because thou hast done this thing, and hast not withheld thy son, thine only son: **17** That in blessing I will bless thee, and in multiplying I will multiply thy seed as the stars of the heaven, and as the sand which is upon the sea shore; and thy seed shall possess the gate of his enemies;   **18** And in thy seed shall all the nations of the earth be blessed; because thou hast obeyed my voice."

D. THE EXPOSURE OF MOSES

✣ Exodus

CHAPTER 1:   **7** And the children of Israel were fruitful, and increased abundantly, and multiplied, and waxed exceeding mighty; and the land was filled with them.   **8** Now there arose up a new king over Egypt, which knew not Joseph.   **9** And he said unto his people, "Behold, the people of the children of Israel are more and mightier than we: **10** Come on, let us deal wisely with them; lest they multiply, and it come to pass, that, when there falleth out any war, they join also unto our enemies, and fight against us, and so get them up out of the land."   **11** Therefore they did set over them taskmasters to afflict them with their burdens. And they built for Pharaoh treasure cities, Pithom and Raamses.   **12** But the more they afflicted them, the more they multiplied and grew. And they were grieved because of the children of Israel.   **13** And the Egyptians made the children of Israel to serve with rigour: **14** And they made their lives bitter with hard bondage, in morter, and in brick, and in all manner of service in the field: all their service, wherein they made them serve, was with rigour.   **15** And the king of Egypt spake to the Hebrew midwives, of which the name of the one was Shiphrah, and the name of the other Puah: **16** And he said, "When ye do the office of a midwife to the Hebrew women, and see them upon the stools; if it be a son, then ye shall kill him: but if it be a daughter, then she shall live."   **17** But the midwives feared God, and did not as the king of Egypt commanded them, but saved the men children alive.   **18** And the king of Egypt called for the midwives, and said unto them, "Why have ye done this thing, and have saved the men children alive?"   **19** And the midwives said unto Pharaoh, "Because the Hebrew women are not as the Egyptian women; for they are lively, and are delivered ere the midwives come in unto them."   **20** Therefore God dealt well with the midwives: and the people multiplied, and waxed very mighty.   **21** And it came to pass, because the midwives feared God, that he made them houses.   **22** And Pharaoh charged all his people, saying, "Every son that is born ye shall cast into the river, and every daughter ye shall save alive."
  CHAPTER 2:   **1** And there went a man of the house of Levi, and took to wife a daughter of Levi.   **2** And the woman conceived, and bare a son: and when she saw him

that he was a goodly child, she hid him three months.   **3** And when she could not longer hide him, she took for him an ark of bulrushes, and daubed it with slime and with pitch, and put the child therein; and she laid it in the flags by the river's brink.   **4** And his sister stood afar off, to wit what would be done to him.   **5** And the daughter of Pharaoh came down to wash herself at the river; and her maidens walked along by the river's side; and when she saw the ark among the flags, she sent her maid to fetch it.   **6** And when she had opened it, she saw the child: and, behold, the babe wept. And she had compassion on him, and said, "This is one of the Hebrews' children."   **7** Then said his sister to Pharaoh's daughter, "Shall I go and call to thee a nurse of the Hebrew women, that she may nurse the child for thee?"   **8** And Pharaoh's daughter said to her, "Go." And the maid went and called the child's mother.   **9** And Pharaoh's daughter said unto her, "Take this child away, and nurse it for me, and I will give thee thy wages." And the women took the child, and nursed it.   **10** And the child grew, and she brought him unto Pharaoh's daughter, and he became her son. And she called his name Moses: and she said, "Because I drew him out of the water."

E. THE MIRACLE OF THE BURNING BUSH

✣ Exodus

CHAPTER 3: **1** Now Moses kept the flock of Jethro his father in law, the priest of Midian: and he led the flock to the backside of the desert, and came to the mountain of God, even to Horeb.   **2** And the angel of the LORD appeared unto him in a flame of fire out of the midst of a bush: and he looked, and, behold, the bush burned with fire, and the bush was not consumed.   **3** And Moses said, "I will now turn aside, and see this great sight, why the bush is not burnt."   **4** And when the LORD saw that he turned aside to see, God called unto him out of the midst of the bush, and said, "Moses, Moses." And he said, "Here am I."   **5** And he said, "Draw not nigh hither: put off thy shoes from off thy feet, for the place whereon thou standest is holy ground."   **6** Moreover he said, "I am the God of thy father, the God of Abraham, the God of Isaac, and the God of Jacob." And Moses hid his face; for he was afraid to look upon God.   **7** And the LORD said, "I have surely seen the affliction of my people which are in Egypt, and have heard their cry by reason of their taskmasters; for I know their sorrows;   **8** And I am come down to deliver them out of the hand of the Egyptians, and to bring them up out of that land unto a good land and a large, unto a land flowing with milk and honey; unto the place of the Canaanites, and the Hittites, and the Amorites, and the Perizzites, and the Hivites, and the Jebusites.   **9** Now therefore, behold, the cry of the children of Israel is come unto me: and I have also seen the oppression wherewith the Egyptians oppress them.   **10** Come now therefore, and I will send thee unto Pharaoh, that thou mayest bring forth my people the children of Israel out of Egypt...."

F. THE TEN COMMANDMENTS

✣ Exodus

CHAPTER 19:   **16** And it came to pass on the third day in the morning, that there were thunders and lightnings, and a thick cloud upon the mount, and the voice of the trumpet exceeding loud; so that all the people that was in the camp trembled.   **17** And Moses brought forth the people out of the camp to meet with God; and they stood at the nether part of the mount.   **18** And mount Sinai was altogether on a smoke, because the LORD descended upon it in fire: and the smoke thereof ascended as the smoke of a furnace, and the whole mount quaked greatly. **19** And when the voice of the trumpet sounded long, and waxed louder and louder, Moses spake, and God answered him by a voice. **20** And the LORD came down upon mount Sinai, on the top of the mount: and the LORD called Moses up to the top of the mount; and Moses went up. **21** And the LORD said unto Moses, "Go down, charge the people, lest they break through unto the LORD to gaze, and many of them perish. **22** And let the priests also, which come near to the LORD, sanctify themselves, lest the LORD break forth upon them." **23** And Moses said unto the LORD, "The people cannot come up to mount Sinai: for thou chargedst us, saying, 'Set bounds about the mount, and sanctify it.'" **24** And the LORD said unto him, "Away, get thee down, and thou shalt come up, thou, and Aaron with thee: but let not the priests and the people break through to come up unto the LORD, lest he break forth upon them." **25** So Moses went down unto the people, and spake unto them.

CHAPTER 20: **1** And God spake all these words, saying, **2** "I am the LORD thy God, which have brought thee out of the land of Egypt, out of the house of bondage. **3** Thou shalt have no other gods before me. **4** Thou shalt not make unto thee any graven image, or any likeness of any thing that is in heaven above, or that is in the earth beneath, or that is in the water under the earth. **5** Thou shalt not bow down thyself to them, nor serve them: for I the LORD thy God am a jealous God, visiting the iniquity of the fathers upon the children unto the third and fourth generation of them that hate me; **6** And shewing mercy unto thousands of them that love me, and keep my commandments. **7** Thou shalt not take the name of the LORD thy God in vain; for the LORD will not hold him guiltless that taketh his name in vain. **8** Remember the sabbath day, to keep it holy. **9** Six days shalt thou labour, and do all thy work: **10** But the seventh day is the sabbath of the LORD thy God: in it thou shalt not do any work, thou, nor thy son, nor thy daughter, thy manservant, nor thy maidservant, nor thy cattle, nor thy stranger that is within thy gates: **11** For in six days the LORD made heaven and earth, the sea, and all that in them is, and rested the seventh day: wherefore the LORD blessed the sabbath day, and hallowed it. **12** Honour thy father and thy mother: that thy days may be long upon the land which the LORD thy God giveth thee. **13** Thou shalt not kill. **14** Thou shalt not commit adultery. **15** Thou shalt not steal. **16** Thou shalt not bear false witness against thy neighbour. **17** Thou shalt not covet thy neighbour's house, thou shalt not covet thy neighbour's wife, nor his manservant, nor his maidservant, nor his ox, nor his ass, nor any thing that is thy neighbour's." **18** And all the people saw the thunderings, and the lightnings, and the noise of the trumpet, and the mountain smoking: and when the people saw it, they removed, and stood afar off. **19** And they said unto Moses, "Speak thou with us, and we will hear: but let not God speak with us, lest we die." **20** And Moses said unto the people, "Fear not: for God is come to prove you, and that his fear may be before your faces, that ye sin not." **21** And the people stood afar off, and Moses drew near unto the thick darkness where God was. **22** And the LORD said unto Moses, "Thus thou shalt say unto the children of Israel, 'Ye have seen that I have talked with you from heaven. **23** Ye shall not make with me gods of silver, neither shall ye make unto you gods of gold. **24** An altar of earth thou shalt make unto me, and shalt sacrifice thereon thy burnt offerings, and thy peace offerings, thy sheep, and thine oxen: in all places where I record my name I will come unto thee, and I will bless thee. **25** And if thou wilt make me an altar of stone, thou shalt not build it of hewn stone: for if thou lift up thy tool upon it, thou hast polluted it. **26** Neither shalt thou go up by steps unto mine altar, that thy nakedness be not discovered thereon.'"

CHAPTER 21: **1** "Now these are the judgments which thou shalt set before them. **2** If thou buy an Hebrew servant, six years he shall serve: and in the seventh he shall go out free for nothing. **3** If he came in by himself, he shall go out by himself: if he were married, then his wife shall go out with him. **4** If his master have given him a wife, and she have born him sons or daughters; the wife and her children shall be her master's, and he shall go out by himself.   **5** And if the servant shall plainly say, I love my master, my wife, and my children; I will not go out free: **6** Then his master shall bring him unto the judges; he shall also bring him to the door, or unto the door post; and his master shall bore his ear through with an aul; and he shall serve him for ever.   **7** And if a man sell his daughter to be a maidservant, she shall not go out as the menservants do.   **8** If she please not her master, who hath betrothed her to himself, then shall he let her be redeemed: to sell her unto a strange nation he shall have no power, seeing he hath dealt deceitfully with her.   **9** And if he have betrothed her unto his son, he shall deal with her after the manner of daughters.   **10** If he take him another wife; her food, her raiment, and her duty of marriage, shall he not diminish.   **11** And if he do not these three unto her, then shall she go out free without money.   **12** He that smiteth a man, so that he die, shall be surely put to death.   **13** And if a man lie not in wait, but God deliver him into his hand; then I will appoint thee a place whither he shall flee.   **14** But if a man come presumptuously upon his neighbour, to slay him with guile; thou shalt take him from mine altar, that he may die.   **15** And he that smiteth his father, or his mother, shall be surely put to death.   **16** And he that stealeth a man, and selleth him, or if he be found in his hand, he shall surely be put to death.   **17** And he that curseth his father, or his mother, shall surely be put to death.   **18** And if men strive together, and one smite another with a stone, or with his fist, and he die not, but keepeth his bed: **19** If he rise again, and walk abroad upon his staff, then shall he that smote him be quit: only he shall pay for the loss of his time, and shall cause him to be thoroughly healed.   **20** And if a man smite his servant, or his maid, with a rod, and he die under his hand; he shall be surely punished.   **21** Notwithstanding, if he continue a day or two, he shall not be punished: for he is his money.

22 If men strive, and hurt a woman with child, so that her fruit depart from her, and yet no mischief follow: he shall be surely punished, according as the woman's husband will lay upon him; and he shall pay as the judges determine.   **23** And if any mischief follow, then thou shalt give life for life,   **24** Eye for eye, tooth for tooth, hand for hand, foot for foot,   **25** Burning for burning, wound for wound, stripe for stripe.   **26** And if a man smite the eye of his servant, or the eye of his maid, that it perish; he shall let him go free for his eye's sake.   **27** And if he smite out his manservant's tooth, or his maidservant's tooth; he shall let him go free for his tooth's sake.   **28** If an ox gore a man or a woman, that they die: then the ox shall be surely stoned, and his flesh shall not be eaten; but the owner of the ox shall be quit.   **29** But if the ox were wont to push with his horn in time past, and it hath been testified to his owner, and he hath not kept him in, but that he hath killed a man or a woman; the ox shall be stoned, and his owner also shall be put to death...."

G. THE BOOK OF JOB

This book of *The Old Testament* explores the perennial question of how evil can exist in a world controlled by an all-powerful and benevolent god, and why the good and innocent among us often suffer. This book, written during the period of the Persian Empire, reveals the influence of Zoroastrian cosmic dualism by juxtaposing God to Satan, who is the source of all of Job's afflictions. After Job enjoys a life of piety and prosperity, God permits Satan to test Job's religious faith by depriving him of all his children, possessions, and health until Job, as Satan has predicted, cries out in agony and questions God's justice. The book culminates in a confrontation between Job and God, in which the latter, speaking through the medium of a whirlwind, explains to Job that His will and knowledge are beyond all human comprehension and are not to be questioned. After Job submits himself to God's will, the book ends with Job being restored to his former state of prosperity.

CHAPTER 1:   **1** There was a man in the land of Uz, whose name was Job; and that man was perfect and upright, and one that feared God, and eschewed evil.   **2** And there were born unto him seven sons and three daughters.   **3** His substance also was seven thousand sheep, and three thousand camels, and five hundred yoke of oxen, and five hundred she asses, and a very great household; so that this man was the greatest of all the men of the east.   **4** And his sons went and feasted in their houses, every one his day; and sent and called for their three sisters to eat and to drink with them.   **5** And it was so, when the days of their feasting were gone about, that Job sent and sanctified them, and rose up early in the morning, and offered burnt offerings according to the number of them all: for Job said, "It may be that my sons have sinned, and cursed God in their hearts." Thus did Job continually.   **6** Now there was a day when the sons of God came to present themselves before the LORD, and Satan came also among them.   **7** And the LORD said unto Satan, "Whence comest thou?" Then Satan answered the LORD, and said, "From going to and fro in the earth, and from walking up and down in it."   **8** And the LORD said unto Satan, "Hast thou considered my servant Job, that there is none like him in the earth, a perfect and an upright man, one that feareth God, and escheweth evil?"   **9** Then Satan answered the LORD, and said, "Doth Job fear God for nought?   **10** Hast not thou made an hedge about him, and about his house, and about all that he hath on every side? thou hast blessed the work of his hands, and his substance is increased in the land.   **11** But put forth thine hand now, and touch all that he hath, and he will curse thee to thy face."   **12** And the LORD said unto Satan, "Behold, all that he hath is in thy power; only upon himself put not forth thine hand." So Satan went forth from the presence of the LORD.

CHAPTER 38:   **1** Then the LORD answered Job out of the whirlwind, and said,   **2** Who is this that darkeneth counsel by words without knowledge?   **3** Gird up now thy loins like a man; for I will demand of thee, and answer thou me.   **4** Where wast thou when I laid the foundations of the earth? declare, if thou hast understanding.   **5** Who hath laid the measures thereof, if thou knowest? or who hath stretched the line upon it?   **6** Whereupon are the foundations thereof fastened? or who laid the corner stone thereof;   **7** When the morning stars sang together, and all the sons of God shouted for joy?   **8** Or who shut up the sea with doors, when it brake forth, as if it had issued out of the womb?   **9** When I made the cloud the garment thereof, and thick darkness a swaddlingband for it,   **10** And brake up for it my decreed place, and set bars and doors,   **11** And said, Hitherto shalt thou come, but no further: and here shall thy proud waves be stayed?   **12** Hast thou commanded the morning since thy days; and caused the dayspring to know his place;   **13** That it might take hold of the ends of the earth, that the wicked might be shaken out of it?   **14** It is turned as clay to the seal; and they stand as a garment.   **15** And from the wicked their light is withholden, and the high arm shall be broken.   **16** Hast thou entered into the springs of the sea? or hast thou walked in the search of the depth?   **17** Have the gates of death been opened unto thee? or hast thou seen the doors of the shadow of death?   **18** Hast thou perceived the breadth of the earth? declare if thou knowest it all.   **19** Where is the way where light dwelleth? and as for darkness, where is the place thereof,   **20** That thou shouldest take it to the bound thereof, and that thou shouldest know the paths to the house thereof?   **21** Knowest thou it, because thou wast then born? or because the number of thy days is great?   **22** Hast thou entered into the treasures of the snow? or hast thou seen the treasures of the hail,   **23** Which I have reserved against the time of trouble, against the day of battle and war?   **24** By what way is the light parted, which scattereth the east wind upon the earth?   **25** Who hath divided a watercourse for the overflowing of waters, or a way for the lightning of thunder;   **26** To cause it to rain on the earth, where no man is; on the wilderness, wherein there is no man;   **27** To satisfy the desolate and waste ground; and to cause the bud of the tender herb to spring forth?   **28** Hath the rain a father? or who hath begotten the drops of dew?   **29** Out of whose womb came the ice? and the hoary frost of heaven, who hath gendered it?   **30** The waters are hid as with a stone, and the face of the deep is frozen.   **31** Canst thou bind the sweet influences of Pleiades, or loose the bands of Orion?   **32** Canst thou bring forth Mazzaroth in his season? or canst thou guide Arcturus with his sons?   **33** Knowest thou the ordinances of heaven? canst thou set the dominion thereof in the earth?   **34** Canst thou lift up thy voice to the clouds, that abundance of waters may cover thee?   **35** Canst thou send lightnings, that they may go and say unto thee, Here we are?   **36** Who hath put wisdom in the inward parts? or who hath given understanding to the heart?   **37** Who can number the clouds in wisdom? or who can stay the bottles of heaven,   **38** When the dust groweth into hardness, and the clods cleave fast together?   **39** Wilt thou hunt the prey for the lion? or fill the appetite of the young lions,   **40** When they couch in their dens, and abide in the covert to lie in wait?   **41** Who provideth for the raven his food? when his young ones cry unto God, they wander for lack of meat...."

Ancient Greece

Introduction

Although the peoples of the ancient Near East had made major strides in developing well-organized societies and in taking the first steps in pioneering basic technological and scientific discoveries, such as metallurgy and mathematics, their overall approach to the great mysteries of nature and the universe was based in myth: formulating imaginative stories that were designed to account for the causes of things. The ancient Greeks, although creators of their own highly colorful mythology, were the first people in the Western tradition who developed a modern-looking culture that was founded upon a rational approach to all aspects of human existence, nature, and the universe. Their alphabet of only 24 letters was so simple that it allowed a substantial portion of their population to be literate, and their distinctive form of political organization, the *polis*, or city-state, bestowed a considerable degree of freedom upon its citizens. As a result, the Greeks developed a culture in which many of its members succeeded in using their freedom and human reason to explore all facets of their surroundings. They therefore developed a very rich literature, which included poetry of all sorts, historical writing, drama, and philosophy. Many of these works stand at the beginning of the Western literary tradition and are still today regarded as great classics. Accordingly, while the Western tradition has been heavily influenced by the religious thought and literature of Judaism from the ancient Near East, it is also greatly indebted to the ancient Greeks as pioneers of rational inquiry and of political freedom. ✣

HOMER'S ILIAD

Homer's *Iliad*, a long epic poem later divided by Greek scholars into 24 books, narrates only a very small portion of the tale of the Trojan War, one of the most important Greek myths. The poem confines its attention to events of the ninth year of the ten-year war, beginning with the quarrel between Agamemnon (commander in chief of the Greek army) and Achilles (the greatest Greek warrior), resulting in terrible consequences for both the Greeks and Trojans. According to this Greek myth, the Trojan War began when Paris, one of the many sons of King Priam of Troy, came to Sparta in Greece, where he seduced Helen, the wife of King Memelaus of Sparta. After Paris took Helen back to Troy, the various small kingdoms of Greece were then mobilized by Memelaus' brother, King Agamemnon of Mycenae, the most important kingdom in early Greece. The Greek force sailed to Troy and began to carry on a war against the Trojans and their numerous allies. After ten years of fighting the Greeks succeeded in capturing Troy only through the stratagem of the wooden horse. After constructing a huge wooden horse and leaving it on the beach with their bravest warriors hiding inside it, the Greeks pretended to embark upon their ships to sail back to Greece. When the Trojans dragged the horse inside their fortified city to offer it to the gods, the Greek warriors emerged during the night, opened up the city gates to their fellow Greeks, and the city of Troy was sacked and destroyed.

The plot of the poem, however, concerns itself with events that occurred only during the ninth year of the war. In a fit of anger Agamemnon, the acknowledged commander-in-chief among the Greeks, dishonors the greatest Greek warrior Achilles, who in response withdraws himself and his Myrmidons from the fighting. When the Trojans rally and press the Greeks hard about their ships on the shore, Achilles grudgingly allows his best friend Patroclus to lead the Myrmidons back into battle in order to drive back the Trojans. But in the course of the fighting, Hector, the bravest of the Trojans and one of King Priam's sons, kills Patroclus. This so infuriates Achilles that he again enters the war and slaughters numerous Trojans. He even succeeds in encountering Hector and kills him to avenge fully Patroclus' death. Achilles is so full of grief for his dead friend and with anger against Hector that he mistreats Hector's dead body and refuses to give it back to the Trojans to receive a proper burial until Achilles is visited in the Greek camp by King Priam himself, who begs the slayer of his dear son to return his body. The following excerpt is taken from *The Iliad*'s 24th book and ends the poem. Thus, this magnificent epic poem, which concerns itself with great questions of life and death, friendship and hatred, striving after individual excellence and the defense of one's loved ones and fellow citizens, ends with the Trojans' awareness of their own impending doom and with Achilles' own inner knowledge that he also will not survive the war to return home to his own aged father.

(Taken from the translation of Samuel Butler)

At this, Iris [messenger of the gods], fleet as the wind, sped forth to deliver her message. She went to Priam's house, and found weeping and lamentation therein. His sons were seated round their father in the outer courtyard, and their raiment was wet with tears: the old man sat in the midst of them with his mantle wrapped close about his body, and his head and neck all covered with the filth which he had clutched as he lay grovelling in the mire. His daughters and his sons' wives went wailing about the house, as they thought of the many and brave men who lay dead, slain by the Argives. The messenger of Zeus stood by Priam and spoke softly to him, but fear fell upon him as she did so. "Take heart," she said, "Priam offspring of Dardanus, take heart and fear not. I bring no evil tidings, but am minded well towards you. I come as a messenger from Zeus, who though he be not near, takes thought for you and pities you. The lord of Olympus bids you go and ransom noble Hector, and take with you such gifts as shall give satisfaction to Achilles. You are to go alone, with no Trojan, save only some honoured servant who may drive your mules and waggon, and bring back to the city the body of him whom noble Achilles has slain. You are to have no thought, nor fear of death, for Zeus will send the slayer of Argus to escort you. When he has brought you within Achilles' tent, Achilles will not kill you nor let another do so, for he will take heed to his ways and sin not, and he will entreat a suppliant with all honourable courtesy."

Iris went her way when she had thus spoken, and Priam told his sons to get a mule waggon ready, and to make the body of the waggon fast upon the top of its bed. Then he went down into his fragrant store room, high vaulted, and made of cedar wood, where his many treasures were kept, and he called Hecuba his wife. "Wife," said he, "a messenger has come to me from Olympus, and has told me to go to the ships of the Achaeans to ransom my dear son, taking with me such gifts as shall give satisfaction to Achilles. What think you of this matter? for my own part I am greatly moved to pass through the of the Achaeans and go to their ships."

His wife cried aloud as she heard him, and said, "Alas, what has become of that judgement for which you have been ever famous both among strangers and your own people? How can you venture alone to the ships of the Achaeans, and look into the face of him who has slain so many of your brave sons? You must have a heart of iron, for if the cruel savage sees you and lays hold on you, he will know neither respect nor pity. Let us then weep Hector from afar here in our own house, for when I gave him birth the threads of overruling fate were spun for him that dogs should eat his flesh far from his parents, in the house of that terrible man on whose liver I would fain fasten and devour it. Thus would I avenge my son, who showed no cowardice when Achilles slew him, and thought neither of Right nor of avoiding battle as he stood in defence of Trojan men and Trojan women."

Then Priam said, "I would go, do not therefore stay me nor be as a bird of ill omen in my house, for you will not move me. Had it been some mortal man who had sent me some prophet or priest who divines from sacrifice I should have deemed him false and have given him no heed; but now I have heard the goddess and seen her face to face, therefore I will go and her saying shall not be in vain. If it be my fate to die at the ships of the Achaeans even so would I have it; let Achilles slay me, if I may but first have taken my son in my arms and mourned him to my heart's comforting." So saying he lifted the lids of his chests, and took out twelve goodly vestments. He took also twelve cloaks of single fold, twelve rugs, twelve fair mantles, and an equal number of shirts. He weighed out ten talents of gold, and brought moreover two burnished tripods, four cauldrons, and a very beautiful cup which the Thracians had given him when he had gone to them on an embassy; it was very precious, but he grudged not even this, so eager was he to ransom the body of his son....

They brought out a strong mule waggon, newly made, and set the body of the waggon fast on its bed. They took the mule yoke from the peg on which it hung, a yoke of boxwood with a knob on the top of it and rings for the reins to go through. Then they brought a yoke band eleven cubits long, to bind the yoke to the pole; they bound it on at the far end of the pole, and put the ring over the upright pin making it fast with three turns of the band on either side the knob, and bending the thong of the yoke beneath it. This done, they brought from the store chamber the rich ransom that was to purchase the body of Hector, and they set it all orderly on the waggon; then they yoked the strong harness mules which the Mysians had on a time given as a goodly present to Priam; but for Priam himself they yoked horses which the old king had bred, and kept for own use. Thus heedfully did Priam and his servant see to the yoking of their cars at the palace.

Then Hecuba came to them all sorrowful, with a golden goblet of wine in her right hand, that they might make a drink offering before they set out. She stood in front of the horses and said, "Take this, make a drink offering to father Zeus, and since you are minded to go to the ships in spite of me, pray that you may come safely back from the hands of your enemies...."

He washed his hands and took the cup from his wife; then he made the drink offering and prayed, standing in the middle of the courtyard and turning his eyes to heaven. "Father Zeus," he said, "that rulest from Ida, most glorious and most great, grant that I may be received kindly and compassionately in the tents of Achilles; and send your swift messenger upon my right hand, the bird of omen which is strongest and most dear to you of all birds, that I may see it with my own eyes and trust it as I go forth to the ships of the Danaans." So did he pray, and Zeus the lord of counsel heard his prayer. Forthwith he sent an eagle, the most unerring portent of all birds that fly, the dusky hunter that men also call the Black Eagle. His wings were spread abroad on either side as wide as the well made and well bolted door of a rich man's chamber. He came to them flying over the city upon their right hands, and when they saw him they were glad and their hearts took comfort within them.

The old man made haste to mount his chariot, and drove out through the inner gateway and under the echoing gatehouse of the outer court. Before him went the mules drawing the four wheeled waggon, and driven by wise Idaeus; behind these were the horses, which the old man lashed with his whip and drove swiftly through the city, while his friends followed after, wailing and lamenting for him as though he were on his road to death.

As soon as they had come down from the city and had reached the plain, his sons and sons in law who had followed him went back to Ilius. But Priam and Idaeus as they showed out upon the plain did not escape the ken of all seeing Zeus, who looked down upon the old man and pitied him; then he spoke to his son Hermes and said, "Hermes, for it is you who are the most disposed to escort men on their way, and to hear those whom you will hear, go, and so conduct Priam to the ships of the Achaeans that no other of the Danaans shall see him nor take note of him until he reach the son of Peleus." Thus he spoke and Hermes, guide and guardian, slayer of Argus, did as he was told. Forthwith he bound on his glittering golden sandals with which he could fly like the wind over land and sea; he took the wand with which he seals men's eyes in sleep, or wakes them just as he pleases, and flew holding it in his hand till he came to Troy and to the Hellespont. To look at, he was like a young man of noble birth in the hey day of his youth and beauty with the down just coming upon his face.

Now when Priam and Idaeus had driven past the great tomb of Ilius, they stayed their mules and horses that they might drink in the river, for the shades of night were falling, when, therefore, Idaeus saw Hermes standing near them he said to Priam, "Take heed, descendant of Dardanus; here is matter which demands consideration. I see a man who I think will presently fall upon us; let us fly with our horses, or at least embrace his knees and implore him to take compassion upon us?" When he heard this the old man's heart failed him, and he was in great fear; he stayed where he was as one dazed, and the hair stood on end over his whole body; but the bringer of good luck came up to him and took him by the hand, saying, "Whither, father, are you thus driving your mules and horses in the dead of night when other men are asleep? Are you not afraid of the fierce Achaeans who are hard by you, so cruel and relentless? Should some one of them see you bearing so much treasure through the darkness of the flying night, what would not your state then be? You are no longer young, and he who is with you is too old to protect you from those who would attack you. For myself, I will do you no harm, and I will defend you from any one else, for you remind me of my own father...."

The bringer of good luck then sprang on to the chariot, and seizing the whip and reins he breathed fresh spirit into the mules and horses. When they reached the trench and the wall that was before the ships, those who were on guard had just been getting their suppers, and the slayer of Argus threw them all into a deep sleep. Then he drew back the bolts to open the gates, and took Priam inside with the treasure he had upon his waggon. Ere long they came to the lofty dwelling of the son of Peleus for which the Myrmidons had cut pine and which they had built for their king; when they had built it they thatched it with coarse tussock grass which they had mown out on the plain, and all round it they made a large courtyard, which was fenced with stakes set close together. The gate was barred with a single bolt of pine which it took three men to force into its place, and three to draw back so as to open the gate, but Achilles could draw it by himself.

Hermes opened the gate for the old man, and brought in the treasure that he was taking with him for the son of Peleus. Then he sprang from the chariot on to the ground and said, "Sir, it is I, immortal Hermes, that am come with you, for my father sent me to escort you. I will now leave you, and will not enter into the presence of Achilles, for it might anger him that a god should befriend mortal men thus openly. Go you within, and embrace the knees of the son of Peleus: beseech him by his father, his lovely mother, and his son; thus you may move him." With these words Hermes went back to high Olympus.

Priam sprang from his chariot to the ground, leaving Idaeus where he was, in charge of the mules and horses. The old man went straight into the house where Achilles, loved of the gods, was sitting. There he found him with his men seated at a distance from him: only two, the hero Automedon, and Alcimus of the race of Ares, were busy in attendance about his person, for he had but just done eating and drinking, and the table was still there. King Priam entered without their seeing him, and going right up to Achilles he clasped his knees and kissed the dread murderous hands that had slain so many of his sons.

As when some cruel spite has befallen a man that he should have killed some one in his own country, and must fly to a great man's protection in a land of strangers, and all marvel who see him, even so did Achilles marvel as he beheld Priam. The others looked one to another and marvelled also, but Priam besought Achilles saying, "Think of your father, O Achilles like unto the gods, who is such even as I am, on the sad threshold of old age. It may be that those who dwell near him harass him, and there is none to keep war and ruin from him. Yet when he hears of you being still alive, he is glad, and his days are full of hope that he shall see his dear son come home to him from Troy; but I, wretched man that I am, had the bravest in all Troy for my sons, and there is not one of them left. I had fifty sons when the Achaeans came here; nineteen of them were from a single womb, and the others were borne to me by the women of my household. The greater part of them has fierce Ares [the war god] laid low, and Hector, him who was alone left, him who was the guardian of the city and ourselves, him have you lately slain; therefore I am now come to the ships of the Achaeans to ransom his body from you with a great ransom. Fear, O Achilles, the wrath of heaven; think on your own father and have compassion upon me, who am the more pitiable, for I have steeled myself as no man yet has ever steeled himself before me, and have raised to my lips the hand of him who slew my son."

Thus spoke Priam, and the heart of Achilles yearned as he bethought him of his father. He took the old man's hand and moved him gently away. The two wept bitterly Priam, as he lay at Achilles' feet, weeping for Hector, and Achilles now for his father and now for Patroclous, till the house was filled with their lamentation. But when Achilles was now sated with grief and had unburthened the bitterness of his sorrow, he left his seat and raised the old man by the hand, in pity for his white hair and beard; then he said, "Unhappy man, you have indeed been greatly daring; how could you venture to come alone to the ships of the Achaeans, and enter the presence of him who has slain so many of your brave sons? You must have a heart of iron: sit now upon this seat, and for all our grief we will hide our sorrows in our hearts, for weeping will not avail us. The immortals know no care, yet the lot they spin for man is full of sorrow; on the floor of Zeus' palace there stand two urns, the one filled with evil gifts, and the other with good ones. He for whom Zeus the lord of thunder mixes the gifts he sends, will meet now with good and now with evil fortune; but he to whom Zeus sends none but evil gifts will be pointed at by the finger of scorn, the hand of famine will pursue him to the ends of the world, and he will go up and down the face of the earth, respected neither by gods nor men. Even so did it befall Peleus; the gods endowed him with all good things from his birth upwards, for he reigned over the Myrmidons excelling all men in prosperity and wealth, and mortal though he was they gave him a goddess for his bride. But even on him too did heaven send misfortune, for there is no race of royal children born to him in his house, save one son who is doomed to die all untimely; nor may I take care of him now that he is growing old, for I must stay here at Troy to be the bane of you and your children. And you too, O Priam, I have heard that you were aforetime happy. They say that in wealth and plenitude of offspring you surpassed all that is in Lesbos, the realm of Makar to the northward, Phrygia that is more inland, and those that dwell upon the great Hellespont; but from the day when the dwellers in heaven sent this evil upon you, war and slaughter have been about your city continually. Bear up against it, and let there be some intervals in your sorrow. Mourn as you may for your brave son, you will take nothing by it. You cannot raise him from the dead, ere you do so yet another sorrow shall befall you."

Then the son of Peleus sprang like a lion through the door of his house, not alone, but with him went his two squires Automedon and Alcimus who were closer to him than any others of his comrades now that Patroclus was no more. These unyoked the horses and mules, and bade Priam's herald and attendant be seated within the house. They lifted the ransom for Hector's body from the waggon. but they left two mantles and a goodly shirt, that Achilles might wrap the body in them when he gave it to be taken home. Then he called to his servants and ordered them to wash the body and anoint it, but he first took it to a place where Priam should not see it, lest if he did so, he should break out in the bitterness of his grief, and enrage Achilles, who might then kill him and sin against the word of Zeus.

When the servants had washed the body and anointed it, and had wrapped it in a fair shirt and mantle, Achilles himself lifted it on to a bier, and he and his men then laid it on the waggon. He cried aloud as he did so and called on the name of his dear comrade, "Be not angry with me, Patroclus," he said, "if you hear even in the house of Hades that I have given Hector to his father for a ransom. It has been no unworthy one, and I will share it equitably with you." Achilles then went back into the tent and took his place on the richly inlaid seat from which he had risen, by the wall that was at right angles to the one against which Priam was sitting. "Sir," he said, "your son is now laid upon his bier and is ransomed according to desire; you shall look upon him when you take him away at daybreak; ... and now tell me and tell me true, for how many days would you celebrate the funeral rites of noble Hector? Tell me, that I may hold aloof from war and restrain the host." And Priam answered, "Since, then, you suffer me to bury my noble son with all due rites, do thus, Achilles, and I shall be grateful. You know how we are pent up within our city; it is far for us to fetch wood from the mountain, and the people live in fear. Nine days, therefore, will we mourn Hector in my house; on the tenth day we will bury him and there shall be a public feast in his honour; on the eleventh we will build a mound over his ashes, and on the twelfth, if there be need, we will fight." And Achilles answered, "All, King Priam, shall be as you have said. I will stay our fighting for as long a time as you have named." As he spoke he laid his hand on the old man's right wrist, in token that he should have no fear.

Thus then did Priam and his attendant sleep there in the forecourt, full of thought, while Achilles lay in an inner room of the house, with fair Briseis by his side. And now both gods and mortals were fast asleep through the livelong night, but upon Hermes alone, the bringer of good luck, sleep could take no hold for he was thinking all the time how to get King Priam away from the ships without his being seen by the strong force of sentinels. He hovered therefore over Priam's head and said, "Sir, now that Achilles has spared your life, you seem to have no fear about sleeping in the thick of your foes. You have paid a great ransom, and have received the body of your son; were you still alive and a prisoner the sons whom you have left at home would have to give three times as much to free you; and so it would be if Agamemnon and the other Achaeans were to know of your being here."

When he heard this the old man was afraid and roused his servant. Hermes then yoked their horses and mules, and drove them quickly through the host so that no man perceived them. When they came to the ford of eddying Xanthus, begotten of immortal Zeus, Hermes went back to high Olympus, and dawn in robe of saffron began to break over all the land. Priam and Idaeus then drove on toward the city lamenting and making moan, and the mules drew the body of Hector. No one neither man nor woman saw them, till Cassandra, fair as golden Aphrodite standing on Pergamus, caught sight of her dear father in his chariot, and his servant that was the city's herald with him. Then she saw him that was lying upon the bier, drawn by the mules, and with a loud cry she went about the city saying, "Come hither Trojans, men and women, and look on Hector; if ever you rejoiced to see him coming from battle when he was alive, look now on him that was the glory of our city and all our people." At this there was not man nor woman left in the city, so great a sorrow had possessed them. Hard by the gates they met Priam as he was bringing in the body. Hector's wife and his mother were the first to mourn him: they flew towards the waggon and laid their hands upon his head, while the crowd stood weeping round them. They would have stayed before the gates, weeping and lamenting the livelong day to the going down of the sun, had not Priam spoken to them from the chariot and said, "Make way for the mules to pass you. Afterwards when I have taken the body home you shall have your fill of weeping." On this the people stood asunder, and made a way for the waggon.

When they had borne the body within the house they laid it upon a bed and seated minstrels round it to lead the dirge, whereon the women joined in the sad music of their lament. Foremost among them all Andromache [Hector's wife] led their wailing as she clasped the head of mighty Hector in her embrace. "Husband," she cried, "you have died young, and leave me in your house a widow; he of whom we are the ill starred parents is still a mere child, and I fear he may not reach manhood. Ere he can do so our city will be razed and overthrown, for you who watched over it are no more you who were its saviour, the guardian of our wives and children. Our women will be carried away captives to the ships, and I among them; while you, my child, who will be with me will be put to some unseemly tasks, working for a cruel master. Or, may be, some Achaean will hurl you (O miserable death) from our walls, to avenge some brother, son, or father whom Hector slew; many of them have indeed bitten the dust at his hands, for your father's hand in battle was no light one. Therefore do the people mourn him. You have left, O Hector, sorrow unutterable to your parents, and my own grief is greatest of all, for you did not stretch forth your arms and embrace me as you lay dying, nor say to me any words that might have lived with me in my tears night and day for evermore." Bitterly did she weep the while, and the women joined in her lament....

Then King Priam spoke to them saying, "Bring wood, O Trojans, to the city, and fear no cunning ambush of the Argives, for Achilles when he dismissed me from the ships gave me his word that they should not attack us until the morning of the twelfth day." Forthwith they yoked their oxen and mules and gathered together before the city. Nine days long did they bring in great heaps wood, and on the morning of the tenth day with many tears they took trave Hector forth, laid his dead body upon the summit of the pile, and set the fire thereto. Then when the child of morning rosy fingered dawn appeared on the eleventh day, the people again assembled, round the pyre of mighty Hector. When they were got together, they first quenched the fire with wine wherever it was burning, and then his brothers and comrades with many a bitter tear gathered his white bones, wrapped them in soft robes of purple, and laid them in a golden urn, which they placed in a grave and covered over with large stones set close together. Then they built a barrow hurriedly over it keeping guard on every side lest the Achaeans should attack them before they had finished. When they had heaped up the barrow they went back again into the city, and being well assembled they held high feast in the house of Priam their king. Thus, then, did they celebrate the funeral of Hector tamer of horses.

ARISTOTLE ON POLITICS

Aristotle (384-322 B.C.) was one of the greatest philosophers ever to have lived. He came from the small town of Stageira in northern Greece, and his father served King Philip of Macedon (father of Alexander the Great) as his physician. After attending Plato's Academy in Athens, where he emerged as the star pupil, he returned to the northern Aegean to be the teacher of the young Alexander the Great. Aristotle eventually settled in Athens and founded his own philosophical school called the Lyceum; but from his habit of walking about while lecturing (*peripatein*) Aristotle's brand of philosophical inquiry was henceforth often termed the peripatetic school.

During his life Aristotle succeeded in writing very many treatises on numerous subjects: poetics, ethics, metaphysics, physics, and especially biology. He possessed the extraordinary ability to examine any major aspect of the world around him, to resolve it into its constituent parts, to employ his rigorous logic in making connections between them, and to arrive at general conclusions that brought clarity out of a seemingly random pile of empirical data. In fact, Aristotle's conclusions on matters of natural science were so insightful and convincing that they were regarded as valid and authoritative in western Europe during the Middle Ages and Renaissance until they began to be undermined by the discoveries of early modern science during the seventeenth century.

The Politics is an excellent example of Aristotle's ability to view the complex and chaotic history of the numerous Greek city-states and from all the empirical data to deduce general conclusions about the nature, effectiveness, and weaknesses of differently consti- tuted states. The work represents a summation of the political experience of the ancient Greeks and has exercised a major impact upon political thought in the Western tradition.

(Taken from the translation of Benjamin Jowett with revisions by Gary Forsythe)

FROM FAMILY TO THE POLIS

✢ Book I

1. EVERY STATE is a community of some kind, and every community is established with a view to some good; for mankind always act in order to obtain that which they think good. But, if all communities aim at some good, the state or political community, which is the highest of all, and which embraces all the rest, aims at good in a greater degree than any other, and at the highest good.

Some people think that the qualifications of a statesman, king, householder, and master are the same, and that they differ, not in kind, but only in the number of their subjects. For example, the ruler over a few is called a master; over more, the manager of a household; over a still larger number, a statesman or king, as if there were no difference between a great household and a small state. The distinction which is made between the king and the statesman is as follows: When the government is personal, the ruler is a king; when, according to the rules of the political science, the citizens rule and are ruled in turn, then he is called a statesman.

But all this is a mistake; for governments differ in kind, as will be evident to any one who considers the matter according to the method which has hitherto guided us. As in other departments of science, so in politics, the compound should always be resolved into the simple elements or least parts of the whole. We must therefore look at the elements of which the state is composed, in order that we may see in what the different kinds of rule differ from one another, and whether any scientific result can be attained about each one of them.

2. He who thus considers things in their first growth and origin, whether a state or anything else, will obtain the clearest view of them. In the first place there must be a union of those who cannot exist without each other; namely, of male and female, that the race may continue (and this is a union which is formed, not of deliberate purpose, but because, in common with other animals and with plants, mankind have a natural desire to leave behind them an image of themselves), and of natural ruler and subject, that both may be preserved. For that which can foresee by the exercise of mind is by nature intended to be lord and master, and that which can with its body give effect to such foresight is a subject, and by nature a slave; hence master and slave have the same interest....

Out of these two relationships between man and woman, master and slave, the first thing to arise is the family, and Hesiod is right when he says, "First house and wife and an ox for the plough," for the ox is the poor manÆs slave. The family is the association established by nature for the supply of menÆs everyday wants, and the members of it are called by Charondas æcompanions of the cupboard,Æ and by Epimenides the Cretan, æcompanions of the manger.Æ But when several families are united, and the association aims at something more than the supply of daily needs, the first society to be formed is the village. And the most natural form of the village appears to be that of a colony from the family, composed of the children and grandchildren, who are said to be suckled æwith the same milk.Æ And this is the reason why Greek states were originally governed by kings....

When several villages are united in a single complete community, large enough to be nearly or quite selfûsufficing, the state comes into existence, originating in the bare needs of life, and continuing in existence for the sake of a good life. And therefore, if the earlier forms of society are natural, so is the state, for it is the end of them, and the nature of a thing is its end. For what each thing is when fully developed, we call its nature, whether we are speaking of a man, a horse, or a family. Besides, the final cause and end of a thing is the best, and to be selfûsufficing is the end and the best. Hence it is evident that the state is a creation of nature, and that man is by nature a political animal....

THE THREE FORMS OF GOVERNMENT

✢ Book III

7. Having determined these points, we have next to consider how many forms of government there are, and what they are; and in the first place what are the true forms, for when they are determined the perversions of them will at once be apparent. The words constitution and government have the same meaning, and the government, which is the supreme authority in states, must be in the hands of one, or of a few, or of the many. The true forms

of government, therefore, are those in which the one, or the few, or the many, govern with a view to the common interest; but governments which rule with a view to the private interest, whether of the one or of the few, or of the many, are perversions. For the members of a state, if they are truly citizens, ought to participate in its advantages.

Of forms of government in which one rules, we call that which regards the common interests, monarchy or kingship; that in which more than one, but not many, rule, aristocracy; and it is so called, either because the rulers are the best men (*aristoi*), or because they have at heart the best interests of the state and of the citizens. But when the citizens at large administer the state for the common interest, the government is called by the generic name a polity. And there is a reason for this use of language. One man or a few may excel in virtue; but as the number increases it becomes more difficult for them to attain perfection in every kind of virtue, though they may in military virtue, for this is found in the masses. Hence in a polity the fighting men have the supreme power, and those who possess arms are the citizens (*politai*).

Of the above mentioned forms, the perversions are as follows: of monarchy, tyranny; of aristocracy, oligarchy; of polity, democracy. For tyranny is a kind of monarchy which has in view the interest of the monarch only; oligarchy has in view the interest of the wealthy; democracy, of the needy: none of them the common good of all.

POLITICAL SOUNDNESS OF THE MIDDLE CLASS

✣ Book IV

11. We have now to inquire what is the best constitution for most states, and the best life for most men, neither assuming a standard of virtue which is above ordinary persons, nor an education which is exceptionally favored by nature and circumstances, nor yet an ideal state which is an aspiration only, but having regard to the life in which the majority are able to share, and to the form of government which states in general can attain....

Now in all states there are three elements: one class is very rich, another very poor, and a third in the middle. It is admitted that moderation and the middle are best, and therefore it will clearly be best to possess the gifts of fortune in moderation; for in that condition of life men are most ready to follow rational principle. But he who greatly excels in beauty, strength, birth, or wealth, or on the other hand who is very poor, or very weak, or very much disgraced, finds it difficult to follow rational principle. Of these two the one sort grow into violent and great criminals, the others into rogues and petty rascals. And two sorts of offenses correspond to them, the one committed from violence, the other from roguery.

Again, the middle class is least likely to shrink from rule, or to be over ambitious for it; both of which are injuries to the state. Again, those who have too much of the goods of fortune, strength, wealth, friends, and the like, are neither willing nor able to submit to authority. The evil begins at home; for when they are boys, by reason of the luxury in which they are brought up, they never learn, even at school, the habit of obedience. On the other hand, the very poor, who are in the opposite extreme, are too degraded. So that the one class cannot obey, and can only rule despotically; the other knows not how to command and must be ruled like slaves. Thus arises a city, not of freemen, but of masters and slaves, the one despising, the other envying; and nothing can be more fatal to friendship and good fellowship in states than this: for good fellowship springs from friendship; when men are at enmity with one another, they would rather not even share the same path. But a city ought to be composed, as far as possible, of equals and similars; and these are generally the middle classes. Wherefore the city which is composed of middle class citizens is necessarily best constituted in respect of the elements of which we say the fabric of the state naturally consists. And this is the class of citizens which is most secure in a state, for they do not, like the poor, covet their neighborsÆ goods; nor do others covet theirs, as the poor covet the goods of the rich; and as they neither plot against others, nor are themselves plotted against, they pass through life safely.

Wisely then did Phocylides pray, "Many things are best in the mean; I desire to be of a middle condition in my city." Thus it is manifest that the best political community is formed by citizens of the middle class, and that those states are likely to be well administered in which the middle class is large, and stronger if possible than both the other classes, or at any rate than either singly; for the addition of the middle class turns the scale, and prevents either of the extremes from being dominant. Great then is the good fortune of a state in which the citizens have a moderate and sufficient property; for where some possess much, and the others nothing, there may arise an extreme democracy, or a pure oligarchy; or a tyranny may grow out of either extreme either out of the most rampant democracy, or out of an oligarchy; but it is not so likely to arise out of the middle constitutions and those akin to them.... The mean condition of states is clearly best, for no other is free from faction; and where the middle class is large, there are least likely to be factions and dissensions. For a similar reason large states are less liable to faction than small ones, because in them the middle class is large; whereas in small states it is easy to divide all the citizens into two classes who are either rich or poor, and to leave nothing in the middle. And democracies are safer and more permanent than oligarchies, because they have a middle class which is more numerous and has a greater share in the government; for when there is no middle class, and the poor greatly exceed in number, troubles arise, and the state soon comes to an end.

Reading 11

Herodotus, Father of History

The first great work of historical writing in the Western tradition was an account of the wars fought between the Greeks and Persians written by Herodotus, who is often justifiably termed "the father of history." When completed, this lengthy narrative was copied onto nine ancient papyrus scrolls, which we now call Books. It described the long complex and often hostile relationship between the numerous self-governing Greek city-states and the great imperial power of Persia ruled by a single all-powerful king. The first six books of this historical account traces the rise of the Persian Empire under the rule of its first three kings (Cyrus, his son Cambyses, and Darius), their conquests, and the affairs of the various Greek city-states as they were affected by the Persians. The last three books form the culmination of the entire work by narrating the great Persian invasion of mainland Greece during the years 480-479 B.C. led by King Xerxes, who wished to follow in the footsteps of the three earlier Persian kings by being a great conqueror. Despite the vast numerical superiority of the Persian army and navy, the Greek city-states temporarily put aside their mutual quarrels and united under the joint leadership of Sparta and Athens to defeat this invasion.

Herodotus was born in 484 B.C. just a few years before this great invasion, but his birthplace was not in mainland Greece, but in the city-state of Halicarnassus located in the southwestern edge of Anatolia. As part of the Asian continent, Anatolia belonged to the Persian Empire; and since the western coast of this region had long been inhabited by Greeks who had colonized the area from the Greek mainland, the Greek people as a whole were divided into two groups: those who enjoyed freedom in their own self-governing city-states, and those who owed allegiance to Persia. Thus, the principal theme of Herodotus' historical account is the contrast between the Greek love of political freedom and self-determination and the despotic power that the Persian king exercised over his subjects, whom the Greeks regarded as little better than slaves.

(Taken from the translation of George Rawlinson)

PREFACE TO THE HISTORY

THESE are the researches of Herodotus of Halicarnassus, which he publishes, in the hope of thereby preserving from decay the remembrance of what men have done, and of preventing the great and wonderful actions of the Greeks and the Barbarians from losing their due meed of glory; and withal to put on record what were their grounds of feuds.

A. DEBATE OF THE PERSIAN NOBLES

✠ Book III

Cyrus the Great (king 559-530 B.C.) had founded the Persian Empire by bringing much of western Asia under Persian control by military conquest. He was succeeded on the royal throne by his son Cambyses (king 530-522 B.C.). But when the latter died under mysterious circumstances while leading the Persian conquest of Egypt, the throne in the Persian homeland was seized by a royal pretender. A group of seven Persian nobles formed a conspiracy that overthrew this pretender and resulted in Darius emerging as the new king. In his description of these events Herodotus portrays these Persian noble conspirators as conducting a debate as to which form of government is best (monarchy / tyranny, aristocracy / oligarchy, or democracy / mob rule). This is the earliest account that we possess of a Greek writer discussing the relative merits of what soon became for the Greeks the three basic forms of government: rule by one person, rule by the few, or rule by the many. Many modern scholars have questioned whether following Cambyses' death, Persians nobles ever held a debate along these lines that typify Greek (not Persian) political thought. Whether they did or not, the passage neatly encapsulates how the ancient Greeks assessed the strengths and weaknesses of these three forms of government.

80 And now when five days were gone, and the hubbub had settled down, the conspirators met together to consult about the situation of affairs. At this meeting speeches were made, to which many of the Greeks give no credence, but they were made nevertheless. Otanes recommended that the management of public affairs should be entrusted to the whole nation. "To me," he said, "it seems advisable, that we should no longer have a single man to rule over us- the rule of one is neither good nor pleasant. Ye cannot have forgotten to what lengths Cambyses went in his haughty tyranny, and the haughtiness of the Magi ye have yourselves experienced. How indeed is it possible that monarchy should be a well-adjusted thing, when it allows a man to do as he likes without being answerable? Such licence is enough to stir strange and unwonted thoughts in the heart of the worthiest of men. Give a person this power, and straightway his manifold good things puff him up with pride, while envy is so natural to human kind that it cannot but arise in him. But pride and envy together include all wickedness- both of them leading on to deeds of savage violence. True it is that kings, possessing as they do all that heart can desire, ought to be void of envy; but the contrary is seen in their conduct towards the citizens. They are jealous of the most virtuous among their subjects, and wish their death; while they take delight in the meanest and basest, being ever ready to listen to the tales of slanderers. A king, besides, is beyond all other men inconsistent with himself. Pay him court in moderation, and he is angry because you do not show him more profound respect- show him profound respect, and he is offended again, because (as he says) you fawn on him. But the worst of all is, that he sets aside the laws of the land, puts men to death without trial, and subjects women to violence. The rule of the many, on the other hand, has, in the first place, the fairest of names, to wit, isonomy; and further it is free from all those outrages which a king is wont to commit. There, places are given by lot, the magistrate is answerable for what he does, and measures rest with the commonalty. I vote, therefore, that we do away with monarchy, and raise the people to power. For the people are all in all."

81 Such were the sentiments of Otanes. Megabyzus spoke next, and advised the setting up of an oligarchy:- "In all that Otanes has said to persuade you to put down monarchy," he observed, "I fully concur; but his recommendation that we should call the people to power seems to me not the best advice. For there is nothing so void of understanding, nothing so full of wantonness, as the unwieldy rabble. It were folly not to be borne, for men, while seeking to escape the wantonness of a tyrant, to give themselves up

to the wantonness of a rude unbridled mob. The tyrant, in all his doings, at least knows what is he about, but a mob is altogether devoid of knowledge; for how should there be any knowledge in a rabble, untaught, and with no natural sense of what is right and fit? It rushes wildly into state affairs with all the fury of a stream swollen in the winter, and confuses everything. Let the enemies of the Persians be ruled by democracies; but let us choose out from the citizens a certain number of the worthiest, and put the government into their hands. For thus both we ourselves shall be among the governors, and power being entrusted to the best men, it is likely that the best counsels will prevail in the state."

82 This was the advice which Megabyzus gave, and after him Darius came forward, and spoke as follows:- "All that Megabyzus said against democracy was well said, I think; but about oligarchy he did not speak advisedly; for take these three forms of government- democracy, oligarchy, and monarchy- and let them each be at their best, I maintain that monarchy far surpasses the other two. What government can possibly be better than that of the very best man in the whole state? The counsels of such a man are like himself, and so he governs the mass of the people to their heart's content; while at the same time his measures against evil-doers are kept more secret than in other states. Contrariwise, in oligarchies, where men vie with each other in the service of the commonwealth, fierce enmities are apt to arise between man and man, each wishing to be leader, and to carry his own measures; whence violent quarrels come, which lead to open strife, often ending in bloodshed. Then monarchy is sure to follow; and this too shows how far that rule surpasses all others. Again, in a democracy, it is impossible but that there will be malpractices: these malpractices, however, do not lead to enmities, but to close friendships, which are formed among those engaged in them, who must hold well together to carry on their villainies. And so things go on until a man stands forth as champion of the commonalty, and puts down the evil-doers. Straightway the author of so great a service is admired by all, and from being admired soon comes to be appointed king; so that here too it is plain that monarchy is the best government. Lastly, to sum up all in a word, whence, I ask, was it that we got the freedom which we enjoy?- did democracy give it us, or oligarchy, or a monarch? As a single man recovered our freedom for us, my sentence is that we keep to the rule of one. Even apart from this, we ought not to change the laws of our forefathers when they work fairly; for to do so is not well."

83 Such were the three opinions brought forward at this meeting; the four other Persians voted in favour of the last. Otanes, who wished to give his countrymen a democracy, when he found the decision against him, arose a second time, and spoke thus before the assembly:- "Brother conspirators, it is plain that the king who is to be chosen will be one of ourselves, whether we make the choice by casting lots for the prize, or by letting the people decide which of us they will have to rule over them, in or any other way. Now, as I have neither a mind to rule nor to be ruled, I shall not enter the lists with you in this matter. I withdraw, however, on one condition- none of you shall claim to exercise rule over me or my seed for ever." The six agreed to these terms, and Otanes withdraw and stood aloof from the contest. And still to this day the family of Otanes continues to be the only free family in Persia; those who belong to it submit to the rule of the king only so far as they themselves choose; they are bound, however, to observe the laws of the land like the other Persians.

B. THE VALUE OF POLITICAL FREEDOM

✦ Book V

Around 510 B.C. the Athenians overthrew a tyrant, who together with the previous rule of his father had controlled Athens over the preceding 36 years. The Athenians now organized their political affairs under a democratic form of government; and they soon scored a major military success over their hostile neighbors. In keeping with his principal theme of political freedom vs. slavery, Herodotus attributed Athens' victory at this time and Athenian greatness in general to their enjoyment of political freedom.

77 So when the Spartan army had broken up from its quarters thus ingloriously, the Athenians, wishing to revenge themselves, marched first against the Chalcideans. The Boeotians, however, advancing to the aid of the latter as far as the Euripus, the Athenians thought it best to attack them first. A battle was fought accordingly; and the Athenians gained a very complete victory, killing a vast number of the enemy, and taking seven hundred of them alive. After this, on the very same day, they crossed into Euboea, and engaged the Chalcideans with the like success; whereupon they left four thousand settlers upon the lands of the Hippobotae,- which is the name the Chalcideans give to their rich men. All the Chalcidean prisoners whom they took were put in irons, and kept for a long time in close confinement, as likewise were the Boeotians, until the ransom asked for them was paid; and this the Athenians fixed at two minae the man. The chains wherewith they were fettered the Athenians suspended in their citadel; where they were still to be seen in my day, hanging against the wall scorched by the Median flames, opposite the chapel which faces the west. The Athenians made an offering of the tenth part of the ransom-money: and expended it on the brazen chariot drawn by four steeds, which stands on the left hand immediately that one enters the gateway of the citadel. The inscription runs as follows: When Chalcis and Boeotia dared her might, Athens subdued their pride in valorous fight; Gave bonds for insults; and, the ransom paid, From the full tenths these steeds for Pallas made.

78 Thus did the Athenians increase in strength. And it is plain enough, not from this instance only, but from many everywhere, that freedom is an excellent thing since even the Athenians, who, while they continued under the rule of tyrants, were not a whit more valiant than any of their neighbours, no sooner shook off the yoke than they became decidedly the first of all. These things show that, while undergoing oppression, they let themselves be beaten, since then they worked for a master; but so soon as they got their freedom, each man was eager to do the best he could for himself. So fared it now with the Athenians.

C. DESPOTISM OF THE PERSIAN KING

✚ Book VII

While narrating how Xerxes mobilized his vast army for his invasion of Greece, and how he proceeded on his march, Herodotus tells the following story that is intended to show how the Persian system of royal rule rendered all the inhabitants of the empire, no matter their wealth and status, vulnerable to the caprice of an absolute monarch.

27 Now there lived in this city a certain Pythius, the son of Atys, a Lydian. This man entertained Xerxes and his whole army in a most magnificent fashion, offering at the same time to give him a sum of money for the war. Xerxes, upon the mention of money, turned to the Persians who stood by, and asked of them, "Who is this Pythius, and what wealth has he, that he should venture on such an offer as this?" They answered him, "This is the man, O king! who gave thy father Darius the golden plane-tree, and likewise the golden vine; and he is still the wealthiest man we know of in all the world, excepting thee."

28 Xerxes marvelled at these last words; and now, addressing Pythius with his own lips, he asked him what the amount of his wealth really was. Pythius answered as follows: "O king! I will not hide this matter from thee, nor make pretence that I do not know how rich I am; but as I know perfectly, I will declare all fully before thee. For when thy journey was noised abroad, and I heard thou wert coming down to the Grecian coast, straightway, as I wished to give thee a sum of money for the war, I made count of my stores, and found them to be two thousand talents of silver, and of gold four millions of Daric staters, wanting seven thousand. All this I willingly make over to thee as a gift; and when it is gone, my slaves and my estates in land will be wealth enough for my wants."

29 This speech charmed Xerxes, and he replied, "Dear Lydian, since I left Persia there is no man but thou who has either desired to entertain my army, or come forward of his own free will to offer me a sum of money for the war. Thou hast done both the one and the other, feasting my troops magnificently, and now making offer of a right noble sum. In return, this is what I will bestow on thee. Thou shalt be my sworn friend from this day; and the seven thousand staters which are wanting to make up thy four millions I will supply, so that the full tale may be no longer lacking, and that thou mayest owe the completion of the round sum to me. Continue to enjoy all that thou hast acquired hitherto; and be sure to remain ever such as thou now art. If thou dost, thou wilt not repent of it so long as thy life endures."...

38 The army had begun its march, when Pythius the Lydian, affrighted at the heavenly portent, and emboldened by his gifts, came to Xerxes and said- "Grant me, O my lord! a favour which is to thee a light matter, but to me of vast account." Then Xerxes' who looked for nothing less than such a prayer as Pythius in fact preferred, engaged to grant him whatever he wished, and commanded him to tell his wish freely. So Pythius, full of boldness, went on to say: "O my lord! thy servant has five sons; and it chances that all are called upon to join thee in this march against Greece. I beseech thee, have compassion upon my years; and let one of my sons, the eldest, remain behind, to be my prop and stay, and the guardian of my wealth. Take with thee the other four; and when thou hast done all that is in thy heart, mayest thou come back in safety."

39 But Xerxes was greatly angered, and replied to him: "Thou wretch! darest thou speak to me of thy son, when I am myself on the march against Greece, with sons, and brothers, and kinsfolk, and friends? Thou, who art my bond-slave, and art in duty bound to follow me with all thy household, not excepting thy wife! Know that man's spirit dwelleth in his ears, and when it hears good things, straightway it fills all his body with delight; but no sooner does it hear the contrary than it heaves and swells with passion. As when thou didst good deeds and madest good offers to me, thou wert not able to boast of having out-done the king in bountifulness, so now when thou art changed and grown impudent, thou shalt not receive all thy deserts, but less. For thyself and four of thy five sons, the entertain-ment which I had of thee shall gain protection; but as for him to whom thou clingest above the rest, the forfeit of his life shall be thy punishment." Having thus spoken, forthwith he commanded those to whom such tasks were assigned to seek out the eldest of the sons of Pythius, and having cut his body asunder, to place the two halves. One on the right, the other on the left, of the great road, so that the army might march out between them.

D. THE BATTLE OF THERMOPYLAE

✤ Book VII

The first major military engagement between the Greeks and Persians led by Xerxes occurred at a narrow pass in northern Greece called Thermopylae (the Hot Gates), where the much smaller forces of the Greeks had at least a reasonable chance to hold back the far larger army of the Persians, but the Persians eventually discovered an alternative route that enabled them to surround and annihilate the Greek defenders.

201 King Xerxes pitched his camp in the region of Malis called Trachinia, while on their side the Greeks occupied the narrows. These narrows the Greeks in general call Thermopylae (the Hot Gates); but the natives, and those who dwell in the neighbourhood, call them Pylae (the Gates). Here then the two armies took their stand; the one master of

all the region lying north of Trachis, the other of the country extending southward of that place to the verge of the continent.

202 The Greeks who at this spot awaited the coming of Xerxes were the following:- From Sparta, three hundred men-at-arms; from Arcadia, a thousand Tegeans and Mantineans, five hundred of each people; a hundred and twenty Orchomenians, from the Arcadian Orchomenus; and a thousand from other cities: from Corinth, four hundred men; from Phlius, two hundred; and from Mycenae eighty. Such was the number from the Peloponnese. There were also present, from Boeotia, seven hundred Thespians and four hundred Thebans.

203 Besides these troops, the Locrians of Opus and the Phocians had obeyed the call of their countrymen, and sent, the former all the force they had, the latter a thousand men. For envoys had gone from the Greeks at Thermopylae among the Locrians and Phocians, to call on them for assistance, and to say- "They were themselves but the vanguard of the host, sent to precede the main body, which might every day be expected to follow them. The sea was in good keeping, watched by the Athenians, the Eginetans, and the rest of the fleet. There was no cause why they should fear; for after all the invader was not a god but a man; and there never had been, and never would be, a man who was not liable to misfortunes from the very day of his birth, and those misfortunes greater in proportion to his own greatness. The assailant therefore, being only a mortal, must needs fall from his glory." Thus urged, the Locrians and the Phocians had come with their troops to Trachis.

204 The various nations had each captains of their own under whom they served; but the one to whom all especially looked up, and who had the command of the entire force, was the Spartan, Leonidas.... Leonidas had come to be king of Sparta quite unexpectedly.

205 Having two elder brothers, Cleomenes and Dorieus, he had no thought of ever mounting the throne. However, when Cleomenes died without male offspring, as Dorieus was likewise deceased, having perished in Sicily, the crown fell to Leonidas, who was older than Cleombrotus, the youngest of the sons of Anaxandridas, and, moreover, was married to the daughter of Cleomenes. He had now come to Thermopylae, accompanied by the three hundred men which the law assigned him, whom he had himself chosen from among the citizens, and who were all of them fathers with sons living....

206 The force with Leonidas was sent forward by the Spartans in advance of their main body, that the sight of them might encourage the allies to fight, and hinder them from going over to the Medes, as it was likely they might have done had they seen that Sparta was backward. They intended presently, when they had celebrated the Carneian festival, which was what now kept them at home, to leave a garrison in Sparta, and hasten in full force to join the army. The rest of the allies also intended to act similarly; for it happened that the Olympic festival fell exactly at this same period. None of them looked to see the contest at Thermopylae decided so speedily; wherefore they were content to send forward a mere advanced guard. Such accordingly were the intentions of the allies.

207 The Greek forces at Thermopylae, when the Persian army drew near to the entrance of the pass, were seized with fear; and a council was held to consider about a retreat. It was the wish of the Peloponnesians generally that the army should fall back upon the Peloponnese, and there guard the Isthmus. But Leonidas, who saw with what indignation the Phocians and Locrians heard of this plan, gave his voice for remaining where they were, while they sent envoys to the several cities to ask for help, since they were too few to make a stand against an army like that of the Medes.

208 While this debate was going on, Xerxes sent a mounted spy to observe the Greeks, and note how many they were, and see what they were doing. He had heard, before he came out of Thessaly, that a few men were assembled at this place, and that at their head were certain Spartans, under Leonidas, a descendant of Herakles. The horseman rode up to the camp, and looked about him, but did not see the whole army; for such as were on the further side of the wall (which had been rebuilt and was now carefully guarded) it was not possible for him to behold; but he observed those on the outside, who were encamped in front of the rampart. It chanced that at this time the Spartans held the outer guard, and were seen by the spy, some of them engaged in gymnastic exercises, others combing their long hair. At this the spy greatly marvelled, but he counted their number, and when he had taken accurate note of everything, he rode back quietly; for no one pursued after him, nor paid any heed to his visit. So he returned, and told Xerxes all that he had seen.

209 Upon this, Xerxes, who had no means of surmising the truth- namely, that the Spartans were preparing to do or die manfully- but thought it laughable that they should be engaged in such employments, sent and called to his presence Demaratus the son of Ariston [a former Spartan king, now living in exile as an advisor to Xerxes], who still remained with the army. When he appeared, Xerxes told him all that he had heard, and questioned him concerning the news, since he was anxious to understand the meaning of such behaviour on the part of the Spartans. Then Demaratus said "I spake to thee, O king! concerning these men long since, when we had but just begun our march upon Greece; thou, however, didst only laugh at my words, when I told thee of all this, which I saw would come to pass. Earnestly do I struggle at all times to speak truth to thee, sire; and now listen to it once more. These men have come to dispute the pass with us; and it is for this that they are now making ready. 'Tis their custom, when they are about to hazard their lives, to adorn their heads with care. Be assured, however, that if thou canst subdue the men who are here and the Spartans who remain in Sparta, there is no other nation in all the world which will venture to lift a hand in their defence. Thou hast now to deal with the first kingdom and town in Greece, and with the bravest men." Then Xerxes, to whom what Demaratus said seemed altogether to surpass belief, asked further "how it was possible for so small an army to contend with his?" "O king!" Demaratus answered, "let me be treated as a liar, if matters fall not out as I say."

210 But Xerxes was not persuaded any the more. Four whole days he suffered to go by, expecting that the Greeks would run away. When, however, he found on the fifth that they were not gone, thinking that their firm stand was mere impudence and recklessness, he grew wroth, and sent against them the Medes and Cissians, with orders to take them alive and bring them into his presence. Then the Medes rushed forward and charged the Greeks, but fell in vast numbers: others however took the places of the slain, and would not be beaten off, though they suffered terrible losses. In this way it became clear to all, and especially to the king, that though he had plenty of combatants, he had but very few warriors. The struggle, however, continued during the whole day.

211 Then the Medes, having met so rough a reception, withdrew from the fight; and their place was taken by the band of Persians under Hydarnes, whom the king called his "Immortals": they, it was thought, would soon finish the business. But when they joined battle with the Greeks, 'twas with no better success than the Median detachment- things went much as before- the two armies fighting in a narrow space, and the barbarians using shorter spears than the Greeks, and having no advantage from their numbers. The Spartans fought in a way worthy of note, and showed themselves far more skilful in fight than their adversaries, often turning their backs, and making as though they were all flying away, on which the barbarians would rush after them with much noise and shouting, when the Spartans at their approach would wheel round and face their pursuers, in this way destroying vast numbers of the enemy. Some Spartans likewise fell in these encounters, but only a very few. At last the Persians, finding that all their efforts to gain the pass availed nothing, and that, whether they attacked by divisions or in any other way, it was to no purpose, withdrew to their own quarters.

212 During these assaults, it is said that Xerxes, who was watching the battle, thrice leaped from the throne on which he sat, in terror for his army. Next day the combat was renewed, but with no better success on the part of the barbarians. The Greeks were so few that the barbarians hoped to find them disabled, by reason of their wounds, from offering any further resistance; and so they once more attacked them. But the Greeks were drawn up in detachments according to their cities, and bore the brunt of the battle in turns- all except the Phocians, who had been stationed on the mountain to guard the pathway. So, when the Persians found no difference between that day and the preceding, they again retired to their quarters.

213 Now, as the king was in great strait, and knew not how he should deal with the emergency, Ephialtes, the son of Eurydemus, a man of Malis, came to him and was admitted to a conference. Stirred by the hope of receiving a rich reward at the king's hands, he had come to tell him of the pathway which led across the mountain to Thermopylae; by which disclosure he brought destruction on the band of Greeks who had there withstood the barbarians. This Ephialtes afterwards, from fear of the Spartans, fled into Thessaly; and during his exile, in an assembly of the Amphictyons held at Pylae, a price was set upon his head by the Pylagorae. When some time had gone by, he returned from exile, and went to Anticyra, where he was slain by Athenades, a native of Trachis....

215 Great was the joy of Xerxes on this occasion; and as he approved highly of the enterprise which Ephialtes undertook to accomplish, he forthwith sent upon the errand Hydarnes, and the Persians under him. The troops left the camp about the time of the lighting of the lamps. The pathway along which they went was first discovered by the Malians of these parts, who soon afterwards led the Thessalians by it to attack the Phocians, at the time when the Phocians fortified the pass with a wall, and so put themselves under covert from danger. And ever since, the path has always been put to an ill use by the Malians....

217 The Persians took this path, and, crossing the Asopus, continued their march through the whole of the night, having the mountains of Oeta on their right hand, and on their left those of Trachis. At dawn of day they found themselves close to the summit. Now the hill was guarded, as I have already said, by a thousand Phocian men-at-arms, who were placed there to defend the pathway, and at the same time to secure their own country. They had been given the guard of the mountain path, while the other Greeks defended the pass below, because they had volunteered for the service, and had pledged themselves to Leonidas to maintain the post.

218 The ascent of the Persians became known to the Phocians in the following manner:- During all the time that they were making their way up, the Greeks remained unconscious of it, inasmuch as the whole mountain was covered with groves of oak; but it happened that the air was very still, and the leaves which the Persians stirred with their feet made, as it was likely they would, a loud rustling, whereupon the Phocians jumped up and flew to seize their arms. In a moment the barbarians came in sight, and, perceiving men arming themselves, were greatly amazed; for they had fallen in with an enemy when they expected no opposition. Hydarnes, alarmed at the sight, and fearing lest the Phocians might be Spartans, inquired of Ephialtes to what nation these troops belonged. Ephialtes told him the exact truth, whereupon he arrayed his Persians for battle. The Phocians, galled by the showers of arrows to which they were exposed, and imagining themselves the special object of the Persian attack, fled hastily to the crest of the mountain, and there made ready to meet death; but while their mistake continued, the Persians, with Ephialtes and Hydarnes, not thinking it worth their while to delay on account of Phocians, passed on and descended the mountain with all possible speed.

219 The Greeks at Thermopylae received the first warning of the destruction which the dawn would bring on them from the seer Megistias, who read their fate in the victims as he was sacrificing. After this deserters came in, and brought the news that the Persians were marching round by the hills: it was still night when these men arrived. Last of all, the scouts came running down from the heights, and brought in the same accounts, when the day was just beginning to break. Then the Greeks held a council to consider what they should do, and here opinions were divided: some were strong against quitting their post, while others contended to the contrary. So when the council had broken up, part of the troops departed and went their ways homeward to their several states; part however resolved to remain, and to stand by Leonidas to the last.

220 It is said that Leonidas himself sent away the troops who departed, because he tendered their safety, but thought it unseemly that either he or his Spartans should quit the post which they had been especially sent to guard. For my own part, I incline to think that Leonidas gave the order, because he perceived the allies to be out of heart and unwilling to encounter the danger to which his own mind was made up. He therefore commanded them to retreat, but said that he himself could not draw back with honour; knowing that, if he stayed, glory awaited him, and that Sparta in that case would not lose her prosperity....

222 So the allies, when Leonidas ordered them to retire, obeyed him and forthwith departed....

223 At sunrise Xerxes made libations, after which he waited until the time when the marketplace is wont to fill, and then began his advance. Ephialtes had instructed him thus, as the descent of the mountain is much quicker, and the distance much shorter, than the way round the hills, and the ascent. So the barbarians under Xerxes began to draw nigh; and the Greeks under Leonidas, as they now went forth determined to die, advanced much further than on previous days, until they reached the more open portion of the pass. Hitherto they had held their station within the wall, and from this had gone forth to fight at the point where the pass was the narrowest. Now they joined battle beyond the defile, and carried slaughter among the barbarians, who fell in heaps. Behind them the captains of the squadrons, armed with whips, urged their men forward with continual blows. Many were thrust into the sea, and there perished; a still greater number were trampled to death by their own soldiers; no one heeded the dying. For the Greeks, reckless of their own safety and desperate, since they knew that, as the mountain had been crossed, their destruction was nigh at hand, exerted themselves with the most furious valour against the barbarians.

224 By this time the spears of the greater number were all shivered, and with their swords they hewed down the ranks of the Persians; and here, as they strove, Leonidas fell fighting bravely, together with many other famous Spartans, whose names I have taken care to learn on account of their great worthiness, as indeed I have those of all the three hundred. There fell too at the same time very many famous Persians: among them, two sons of Darius, Abrocomes and Hyperanthes, his children by Phratagune, the daughter of Artanes. Artanes was brother of King Darius, being a son of Hystaspes, the son of Arsames; and when he gave his daughter to the king, he made him heir likewise of all his substance; for she was his only child.

225 Thus two brothers of Xerxes here fought and fell. And now there arose a fierce struggle between the Persians and the Spartans over the body of Leonidas, in which the Greeks four times drove back the enemy, and at last by their great bravery succeeded in bearing off the body. This combat was scarcely ended when the Persians with Ephialtes approached; and the Greeks, informed that they drew nigh, made a change in the manner of their fighting. Drawing back into the narrowest part of the pass, and retreating even behind the cross wall, they posted themselves upon a hillock, where they stood all drawn up together in one close body, except only the Thebans. The hillock whereof I speak is at the entrance of the straits, where the stone lion stands which was set up in honour of Leonidas. Here they defended themselves to the last, such as still had swords using them,

and the others resisting with their hands and teeth; till the barbarians, who in part had pulled down the wall and attacked them in front, in part had gone round and now encircled them upon every side, overwhelmed and buried the remnant which was left beneath showers of missile weapons....

E. THE BATTLE OF SALAMIS

✣ Book VIII

Although the Greek cause had suffered a major setback at Thermopylae, the heroic stand of those who had died there galvanized the Greeks to defend their homeland. The Greek navy now took up a position in a confined area formed by the small island of Salamis and Attica, the land of the Athenian state. Like Thermopylae, this confined space favored the smaller Greek navy and offered the larger Persian fleet no real advantage, but luckily for the Greeks, Persian overconfidence prompted them to attack the Greeks near Salamis. The result was a smashing victory for the Greeks. Salamis therefore proved decisive in destroying the persians' best chance to subdue Greece. Then in the following year (479 B.C.), as described in Book IX of Herodotus, the Persian invasion ended catastrophically when Mardonius was defeated and killed in a major land battle at plataea, just north of Athens. The failure of Xerxes' invasion of Greece marked the halt of Persian expansion and paved the way for the confidence that characterized Greek culture during its classical period.

68 Mardonius [Xerxes' cousin and son-in-law] accordingly went round the entire assemblage, beginning with the Sidonian monarch, and asked this question; to which all gave the same answer, advising to engage the Greeks, except only Artemisia, who spake as follows: "Say to the king, Mardonius, that these are my words to him: I was not the least brave of those who fought at Euboea, nor were my achievements there among the meanest; it is my right, therefore, O my lord, to tell thee plainly what I think to be most for thy advantage now. This then is my advice. Spare thy ships, and do not risk a battle; for these people are as much superior to thy people in seamanship, as men to women. What so great need is there for thee to incur hazard at sea? Art thou not master of Athens, for which thou didst undertake thy expedition? Is not Greece subject to thee? Not a soul now resists thy advance. They who once resisted, were handled even as they deserved. Now learn how I expect that affairs will go with thy adversaries. If thou art not over-hasty to engage with them by sea, but wilt keep thy fleet near the land, then whether thou abidest as thou art, or marchest forward towards the Peloponnese, thou wilt easily accomplish all for which thou art come hither. The Greeks cannot hold out against thee very long; thou wilt soon part them asunder, and scatter them to their several homes. In the island where they lie, I hear they have no food in store; nor is it likely, if thy land force begins its march towards the Peloponnese, that they will remain quietly where they are- at least such as come from that region. Of a surety they will not greatly trouble themselves to give battle on behalf of the Athenians. On the other hand, if thou art hasty to fight, I tremble lest the defeat of thy sea force bring harm likewise to thy land army. This, too, thou shouldst remember, O king; good masters are apt to have bad servants, and bad masters good ones. Now, as thou art the best of men, thy servants must needs be a sorry set. These Egyptians, Cyprians, Cilicians, and Pamphylians, who are counted in the number of thy subject-allies, of how little service are they to thee!"

69 As Artemisia spake, they who wished her well were greatly troubled concerning her words, thinking that she would suffer some hurt at the king's hands, because she exhorted him not to risk a battle; they, on the other hand, who disliked and envied her, favoured as she was by the king above all the rest of the allies, rejoiced at her declaration, expecting that her life would be the forfeit. But Xerxes, when the words of the

several speakers were reported to him, was pleased beyond all others with the reply of Artemisia; and whereas, even before this, he had always esteemed her much, he now praised her more than ever. Nevertheless, he gave orders that the advice of the greater number should be followed; for he thought that at Euboea the fleet had not done its best, because he himself was not there to see- whereas this time he resolved that he would be an eye-witness of the combat.

70 Orders were now given to stand out to sea; and the ships proceeded towards Salamis, and took up the stations to which they were directed, without let or hindrance from the enemy. The day, however, was too far spent for them to begin the battle, since night already approached: so they prepared to engage upon the morrow....

84 The [Greek] fleet had scarce left the land when they were attacked by the barbarians. At once most of the Greeks began to back water, and were about touching the shore, when Ameinias of Palline, one of the Athenian captains, darted forth in front of the line, and charged a ship of the enemy. The two vessels became entangled, and could not separate, whereupon the rest of the fleet came up to help Ameinias, and engaged with the Persians. Such is the account which the Athenians give of the way in which the battle began; but the Eginetans maintain that the vessel which had been to Egina for the Aeacidae, was the one that brought on the fight. It is also reported, that a phantom in the form of a woman appeared to the Greeks, and, in a voice that was heard from end to end of the fleet, cheered them on to the fight; first, however, rebuking them, and saying- "Strange men, how long are ye going to back water?"

85 Against the Athenians, who held the western extremity of the line towards Eleusis, were placed the Phoenicians; against the Spartans, whose station was eastward towards the Piraeus, the Ionians. Of these last a few only followed the advice of Themistocles, to fight backwardly; the greater number did far otherwise. I could mention here the names of many trierarchs who took vessels from the Greeks, but I shall pass over all excepting Theomestor, the son of Androdamas, and Phylacus, the son of Histiaeus, both Samians. I show this preference to them, inasmuch as for this service Theomestor was made tyrant of Samos by the Persians, which Phylacus was enrolled among the king's benefactors, and presented with a large estate in land. In the Persian tongue the king's benefactors are called Orosangs.

86 Far the greater number of the Persian ships engaged in this battle were disabled, either by the Athenians or by the Eginetans. For as the Greeks fought in order and kept their line, while the barbarians were in confusion and had no plan in anything that they did, the issue of the battle could scarce be other than it was. Yet the Persians fought far more bravely here than at Euboea, and indeed surpassed themselves; each did his utmost through fear of Xerxes, for each thought that the king's eye was upon himself.

87 What part the several nations, whether Greek or barbarian, took in the combat, I am not able to say for certain; Artemisia, however, I know, distinguished herself in such a way as raised her even higher than she stood before in the esteem of the king. For after confusion had spread throughout the whole of the king's fleet, and her ship was closely pursued by an Athenian trireme, she, having no way to fly, since in front of her were a number of friendly vessels, and she was nearest of all the Persians to the enemy, resolved on a measure which in fact proved her safety. Pressed by the Athenian pursuer, she bore straight against one of the ships of her own party, a Calyndian, which had Damasithymus, the Calyndian king, himself on board. I cannot say whether she had had any quarrel with the man while the fleet was at the Hellespont, or no- neither can I decide whether she of set purpose attacked his vessel, or whether it merely chanced that the Calyndian ship came in her way- but certain it is that she bore down upon his vessel and sank it, and that thereby she had the good fortune to procure herself a double advantage. For the commander of the Athenian trireme, when he saw her bear down on one of the enemy's fleet, thought immediately that her vessel was a Greek, or else had deserted from the Persians, and was now fighting on the Greek side; he therefore gave up the chase, and turned away to attack others.

88 Thus in the first place she saved her life by the action, and was enabled to get clear off from the battle; while further, it fell out that in the very act of doing the king an injury she raised herself to a greater height than ever in his esteem. For as Xerxes beheld the fight, he remarked (it is said) the destruction of the vessel, whereupon the bystanders observed to him- "Seest thou, master, how well Artemisia fights, and how she has just sunk a ship of the enemy?" Then Xerxes asked if it were really Artemisia's doing; and they answered, "Certainly; for they knew her ensign": while all made sure that the sunken vessel belonged to the opposite side. Everything, it is said, conspired to prosper the queen- it was especially fortunate for her that not one of those on board the Calyndian ship survived to become her accuser. Xerxes, they say, in reply to the remarks made to him, observed- "My men have behaved like women, my women like men!"

89 There fell in this combat Ariabignes, one of the chief commanders of the fleet, who was son of Darius and brother of Xerxes; and with him perished a vast number of men of high repute, Persians, Medes, and allies. Of the Greeks there died only a few; for, as they were able to swim, all those that were not slain outright by the enemy escaped from the sinking vessels and swam across to Salamis. But on the side of the barbarians more perished by drowning than in any other way, since they did not know how to swim. The great destruction took place when the ships which had been first engaged began to fly; for they who were stationed in the rear, anxious to display their valour before the eyes of the king, made every effort to force their way to the front, and thus became entangled with such of their own vessels as were retreating.

90 In this confusion the following event occurred: certain Phoenicians belonging to the ships which had thus perished made their appearance before the king, and laid the blame of their loss on the Ionians, declaring that they were traitors, and had wilfully destroyed the vessels. But the upshot of this complaint was that the Ionian captains escaped the death which threatened them, while their Phoenician accusers received death as their reward. For it happened that, exactly as they spoke, a Samothracian vessel bore down on an Athenian and sank it, but was attacked and crippled immediately by one of the Eginetan squadron. Now the Samothracians were expert with the javelin, and aimed their weapons so well, that they cleared the deck of the vessel which had disabled their own, after which they sprang on board, and took it. This saved the Ionians. Xerxes, when he saw the exploit, turned fiercely on the Phoenicians- (he was ready, in his extreme vexation, to find fault with any one)- and ordered their heads to be cut off, to prevent them, he said, from casting the blame of their own misconduct upon braver men. During the whole time of the battle Xerxes sat at the base of the hill called Aegaleos, over against Salamis; and whenever he saw any of his own captains perform any worthy exploit he inquired concerning him; and the man's name was taken down by his scribes, together with the names of his father and his city. Ariaramnes too, a Persian, who was a friend of the Ionians, and present at the time whereof I speak, had a share in bringing about the punishment of the Phoenicians.

91 When the rout of the barbarians began, and they sought to make their escape to Phalerum, the Eginetans, awaiting them in the channel, performed exploits worthy to be recorded. Through the whole of the confused struggle the Athenians employed themselves in destroying such ships as either made resistance or fled to shore, while the Eginetans dealt with those which endeavoured to escape down the strait; so that the Persian vessels were no sooner clear of the Athenians than forthwith they fell into the hands of the Eginetan squadron....

96 As soon as the sea-fight was ended, the Greeks drew together to Salamis all the wrecks that were to be found in that quarter, and prepared themselves for another

engagement, supposing that the king would renew the fight with the vessels which still remained to him. Many of the wrecks had been carried away by a westerly wind to the coast of Attica, where they were thrown upon the strip of shore called Colias....

97 Xerxes, when he saw the extent of his loss, began to be afraid lest the Greeks might be counselled by the Ionians, or without their advice might determine to sail straight to the Hellespont and break down the bridges there; in which case he would be blocked up in Europe, and run great risk of perishing. He therefore made up his mind to fly; but, as he wished to hide his purpose alike from the Greeks and from his own people, he set to work to carry a mound across the channel to Salamis, and at the same time began fastening a number of Phoenician merchant ships together, to serve at once for a bridge and a wall. He likewise made many warlike preparations, as if he were about to engage the Greeks once more at sea. Now, when these things were seen, all grew fully persuaded that the king was bent on remaining, and intended to push the war in good earnest. Mardonius, however, was in no respect deceived; for long acquaintance enabled him to read all the king's thoughts. Meanwhile, Xerxes, though engaged in this way, sent off a messenger to carry intelligence of his misfortune to Persia....

113 King Xerxes and his army waited but a few days after the sea-fight, and then withdrew into Boeotia by the road which they had followed on their advance. It was the wish of Mardonius to escort the king a part of the way; and as the time of year was no longer suitable for carrying on war, he thought it best to winter in Thessaly, and wait for the spring before he attempted the Peloponnese. After the army was come into Thessaly, Mardonius made choice of the troops that were to stay with him....

115 Xerxes, after this, left Mardonius in Thessaly, and marched away himself, at his best speed, toward the Hellespont. In five-and-forty days he reached the place of passage, where he arrived with scarce a fraction, so to speak, of his former army. All along their line of march, in every country where they chanced to be, his soldiers seized and devoured whatever corn they could find belonging to the inhabitants; while, if no corn was to be found, they gathered the grass that grew in the fields, and stripped the trees, whether cultivated or wild, alike of their bark and of their leaves, and so fed themselves. They left nothing anywhere, so hard were they pressed by hunger. Plague too and dysentery attacked the troops while still upon their march, and greatly thinned their ranks. Many died; others fell sick and were left behind in the different cities that lay upon the route, the inhabitants being strictly charged by Xerxes to tend and feed them. Of these some remained in Thessaly, others in Siris of Paeonia, others again in Macedon. Here Xerxes, on his march into Greece, had left the sacred car and steeds of Zeus; which upon his return he was unable to recover; for the Paeonians had disposed of them to the Thracians, and, when Xerxes demanded them back, they said that the Thracian tribes who dwelt about the sources of the Strymon had stolen the mares as they pastured.

Reading 12

Thucydides, The Scientific Historian

Following the stunning Greek defeat of Xerxes' invasion of Greece, Sparta continued to be the strongest military power in mainland Greece by leading an alliance of other Greek city-states known as the Peloponnesian League, but they soon found their rival in Athens, which now emerged as the strongest naval power. Once Xerxes was defeated, the Greek city-states of Anatolia, long discontented as Persian subjects, rose up in rebellion; and in order to maintain their independence from Persia, they formed an alliance headed by Athens, initially centered on the island of Delos and hence termed the Delian League by modern scholars. The purpose of the alliance was for the various states to furnish men, money, and ships for naval campaigns against Persia for their common defense. After about fifteen years of fighting, the Persians finally gave up trying to reconquer the Greek states that had rebelled from them. But when some members of the Delian League attempted to slack off and withdraw from the alliance, they found that the Athenians, now possessing superior naval power, used their might to force their reluctant allies to continue to provide them with annual payments. Thus, what had begun as a voluntary alliance system soon became an Athenian empire, in which the Athenians exercised naval supremacy in the Aegean. As the result of receiving a substantial annual tribute from their numerous Greek subjects, by 450 B.C. Athens had become the richest state in Greece and was using the tribute to maintain its large navy and to beautify Athens itself with public buildings and temples, such as the Parthenon. This power and prosperity attracted many of the leading intellects to Athens and made it the cultural center of the Greek world.

Athens' naval supremacy also had the effect of dividing much of the Greek world into two groups: those who were allied to Sparta, and those who were subject to Athens. Eventually minor conflicts between parties of these two groups sparked off a tremendous war that involved all parties in a desperate struggle for victory. This war, which lasted for 27 years (431-404 B.C.) and did much to destroy the prosperity of Classical Greece, is known as the Peloponnesian War. We owe our knowledge of this war to Thucydides, an Athenian, who lived during this conflict and wrote an extremely detailed historical account of this war. He is generally recognized as the greatest historian of ancient Greece and one of the greatest historians of all time. Besides chronicling the events of this particular war in detail, Thucydides succeeded in portraying these human actions in universal terms, showing how intelligence, chance, boldness, miscalculations, lack of resolve, etc. affected the outcome of events, and how the pressures of war eroded public morality of all parties involved.

(Taken from the translation of Richard Crawley with revisions by Gary Forsythe)

A. THUCYDIDES' METHODS OF RESEARCH AND WRITING HISTORY

✥ Book I

22 With reference to the speeches in this history, some were delivered before the war began, others while it was going on; some I heard myself, others I got from various quarters; it was in all cases difficult to carry them word for word in one's memory, so my habit has been to make the speakers say what was in my opinion demanded of them by the various occasions, of course adhering as closely as possible to the general sense of what they really said. And with reference to the narrative of events, far from permitting myself to derive it from the first source that came to hand, I did not even trust my own impressions, but it rests partly on what I saw myself, partly on what others saw for me, the accuracy of the report being always tried by the most severe and detailed tests possible. My conclusions have cost me some labor from the want of coincidence between accounts of the same occurrences by different eye-witnesses, arising sometimes from imperfect memory, sometimes from undue partiality for one side or the other. The absence of romance in my history will, I fear, detract somewhat from its interest; but if it be judged useful by those inquirers who desire an exact knowledge of the past as an aid to the interpretation of the future, which in the course of human things must resemble if it does not reflect it, I shall be content. In fine, I have written my work, not as an essay which is to win the applause of the moment, but as a possession for all time....

B. SPARTA DECLARES WAR ON ATHENS

✥ Book I

After some of Sparta's Peloponnesian allies complained to Sparta of Athenian aggression, the Spartans held an assembly of their adult male citizens to hear both their allies' complaints and the Athenians' reply. Then they debated what should be done. After listening to speeches made by one of their two kings (Archidamus) and one of their five annually elected ephors (Sthenelaidas), the Spartan assembly decided that the Athenians were guilty of breaking their treaty with Sparta, and Sparta was now ready to wage war upon Athens.

79 Such were the words of the Athenians. After the Spartans had heard the complaints of the allies against the Athenians, and the observations of the latter, they made all withdraw, and consulted by themselves on the question before them. The opinions of the majority all led to the same conclusion; the Athenians were open aggressors, and war must be declared at once. But Archidamus, the Spartan king, came forward, who had the reputation of being at once a wise and a moderate man, and made the following speech:

80 "I have not lived so long, Spartans, without having had the experience of many wars, and I see those among you of the same age as myself, who will not fall into the common misfortune of longing for war from inexperience or from a belief in its advantage and its safety. This, the war on which you are now debating, would be one of the greatest magnitude, on a sober consideration of the matter. In a struggle with Peloponnesians and neighbors our strength is of the same character, and it is possible to move swiftly on the different points. But a struggle with a people who live in a distant land, who have also an extraordinary familiarity with the sea, and who are in the highest state of preparation in every other department; with wealth private and public, with ships, and horses, and hoplites, and a population such as no one other Greek place can equal, and lastly a number of tributary allies- what can justify us in rashly beginning such a struggle? wherein is our trust that we should rush on it unprepared? Is it in our ships? There we are inferior; while if we are to practise and become a match for them, time must intervene.

81 Is it in our money? There we have a far greater deficiency. We neither have it in our treasury, nor are we ready to contribute it from our private funds. Confidence might possibly be felt in our superiority in hoplites and population, which will enable us to invade and devastate their lands. But the Athenians have plenty of other land in their empire, and can import what they want by sea. Again, if we are to attempt an insurrection of their allies, these will have to be supported with a fleet, most of them being islanders. What then is to be our war? For unless we can either beat them at sea, or deprive them of the revenues which feed their navy, we shall meet with little but disaster. Meanwhile our honor will be pledged to keeping on, particularly if it be the opinion that we began the quarrel. For let us never be elated by the fatal hope of the war being quickly ended by the devastation of their lands. I fear rather that we may leave it as a legacy to our children; so improbable is it that the Athenian spirit will be the slave of their land, or Athenian experience be cowed by war.

82 "Not that I would bid you be so unfeeling as to suffer them to injure your allies, and to refrain from unmasking their intrigues; but I do bid you not to take up arms at once, but to send and remonstrate with them in a tone not too suggestive of war, nor again too suggestive of submission, and to employ the interval in perfecting our own preparations. The means will be, first, the acquisition of allies, Greek or barbarian it matters not, so long as they are an accession to our strength naval or pecuniary- I say Greek or barbarian, because the odium of such an accession to all who like us are the objects of the designs of the Athenians is taken away by the law of self-preservation- and secondly the development of our home resources. If they listen to our embassy, so much the better; but if not, after the lapse of two or three years our position will have become materially strengthened, and we can then attack them if we think proper. Perhaps by that time the sight of our preparations, backed by language equally significant, will have disposed them to submission, while their land is still untouched, and while their counsels may be directed to the retention of advantages as yet undestroyed. For the only light in which you can view their land is that of a hostage in your hands, a hostage the more valuable the better it is cultivated. This you ought to spare as long as possible, and not make them desperate, and so increase the difficulty of dealing with them. For if while still unprepared, hurried away by the complaints of our allies, we are induced to lay it waste, have a care that we do not bring deep disgrace and deep perplexity upon Peloponnese. Complaints, whether of communities or individuals, it is possible to adjust; but war undertaken by a coalition for sectional interests, whose progress there is no means of foreseeing, does not easily admit of creditable settlement.

83 "And none need think it cowardice for a number of confederates to pause before they attack a single city. The Athenians have allies as numerous as our own, and allies that pay tribute, and war is a matter not so much of arms as of money, which makes arms of use. And this is more than ever true in a struggle between a continental and a maritime power. First, then, let us provide money, and not allow ourselves to be carried away by the talk of our allies before we have done so: as we shall have the largest share of responsibility for the consequences be they good or bad, we have also a right to a tranquil inquiry respecting them.

84 "And the slowness and procrastination, the parts of our character that are most assailed by their criticism, need not make you blush. If we undertake the war without preparation, we should by hastening its commencement only delay its conclusion: further, a free and a famous city has through all time been ours. The quality which they condemn

is really nothing but a wise moderation; thanks to its possession, we alone do not become insolent in success and give way less than others in misfortune; we are not carried away by the pleasure of hearing ourselves cheered on to risks which our judgment condemns; nor, if annoyed, are we any the more convinced by attempts to exasperate us by accusation. We are both warlike and wise, and it is our sense of order that makes us so. We are warlike, because self-control contains honor as a chief constituent, and honor bravery. And we are wise, because we are educated with too little learning to despise the laws, and with too severe a self-control to disobey them, and are brought up not to be too knowing in useless matters- such as the knowledge which can give a specious criticism of an enemy's plans in theory, but fails to assail them with equal success in practice- but are taught to consider that the schemes of our enemies are not dissimilar to our own, and that the freaks of chance are not determinable by calculation. In practice we always base our preparations against an enemy on the assumption that his plans are good; indeed, it is right to rest our hopes not on a belief in his blunders, but on the soundness of our provisions. Nor ought we to believe that there is much difference between man and man, but to think that the superiority lies with him who is reared in the severest school.

85 These practices, then, which our ancestors have delivered to us, and by whose maintenance we have always profited, must not be given up. And we must not be hurried into deciding in a day's brief space a question which concerns many lives and fortunes and many cities, and in which honor is deeply involved- but we must decide calmly. This our strength peculiarly enables us to do. As for the Athenians, send to them on the matter of Potidaea, send on the matter of the alleged wrongs of the allies, particularly as they are prepared with legal satisfaction; and to proceed against one who offers arbitration as against a wrongdoer, law forbids. Meanwhile do not omit preparation for war. This decision will be the best for yourselves, the most terrible to your opponents." Such were the words of Archidamus. Last came forward Sthenelaidas, one of the ephors for that year, and spoke to the Spartans as follows:

86 "The long speech of the Athenians I do not pretend to understand. They said a good deal in praise of themselves, but nowhere denied that they are injuring our allies and Peloponnese. And yet if they behaved well against the Persians then, but ill towards us now, they deserve double punishment for having ceased to be good and for having become bad. We meanwhile are the same then and now, and shall not, if we are wise, disregard the wrongs of our allies, or put off till to-morrow the duty of assisting those who must suffer to-day. Others have much money and ships and horses, but we have good allies whom we must not give up to the Athenians, nor by lawsuits and words decide the matter, as it is anything but in word that we are harmed, but render instant and powerful help. And let us not be told that it is fitting for us to deliberate under injustice; long deliberation is rather fitting for those who have injustice in contemplation. Vote therefore, Spartans, for war, as the honor of Sparta demands, and neither allow the further aggrandizement of Athens, nor betray our allies to ruin, but with the gods let us advance against the aggressors."

87 With these words he, as ephor, himself put the question to the assembly of the Spartans. He said that he could not determine which was the loudest acclamation (their mode of decision is by acclamation not by voting); the fact being that he wished to make them declare their opinion openly and thus to increase their ardor for war. Accordingly he said: "All Spartans who are of opinion that the treaty has been broken, and that Athens is guilty, leave your seats and go there," pointing out a certain place; "all who are of the opposite opinion, there." They accordingly stood up and divided; and those who held that the treaty had been broken were in a decided majority. Summoning the allies, they told them that their opinion was that Athens had been guilty of injustice, but that they wished to convoke all the allies and put it to the vote; in order that they might make war, if they decided to do so, on a common resolution....

C. ATHENS DECIDES THE FATE OF MYTILENE

✢ Book III

In the fourth year of the war (428 B.C.) one of Athens' major subjects, the city-state of Mytilene in the island of Lesbos, attempted to revolt and join the side of Sparta. Athens, however, learned of these plans before the revolt was fully in operation; and as a result, swift and decisive Athenian intervention prevented the revolt from succeeding. The Athenians were then faced with how and to what extent the people of Mytilene should be punished. After debating this matter in the citizen assembly, they initially decided by a slim majority vote to kill all adult males and to enslave all women and children of Mytilene so as to terrorize all their other subjects to keep them from contemplating similar actions. But given the extreme harshness of their decision, the matter was reopened for a second debate, and a less harsh decision was taken toward Mytilene. In the following passage Thucydides shows how the Athenians wrestled with these difficult issues in an open public debate.

35 Arrived at Mytilene, Paches [the Athenian general] reduced Pyrrha and Eresus; and finding the Spartan, Salaethus, in hiding in the town, sent him off to Athens, together with the Mytilenians that he had placed in Tenedos, and any other persons that he thought concerned in the revolt. He also sent back the greater part of his forces, remaining with the rest to settle Mytilene and the rest of Lesbos as he thought best.

36 Upon the arrival of the prisoners with Salaethus, the Athenians at once put the latter to death, although he offered, among other things, to procure the withdrawal of the Peloponnesians from Plataea, which was still under siege; and after deliberating as to what they should do with the former, in the fury of the moment determined to put to death not only the prisoners at Athens, but the whole adult male population of Mytilene, and to make slaves of the women and children. It was remarked that Mytilene had revolted without being, like the rest, subjected to the empire; and what above all swelled the wrath of the Athenians was the fact of the Peloponnesian fleet having ventured over to Ionia to her support, a fact which was held to argue a long meditated rebellion. They accordingly sent a trireme to communicate the decree to Paches, commanding him to lose no time in dispatching the Mytilenians. The morrow brought repentance with it and reflection on the horrid cruelty of a decree, which condemned a whole city to the fate merited only by the guilty. This was no sooner perceived by the Mytilenian ambassadors at Athens and their Athenian supporters, than they moved the authorities to put the question again to the vote; which they the more easily consented to do, as they themselves plainly saw that most of the citizens wished some one to give them an opportunity for reconsidering the matter. An assembly was therefore at once called, and after much expression of opinion upon both sides, Cleon, son of Cleaenetus, the same who had carried the former motion of putting the Mytilenians to death, the most violent man at Athens, and at that time by far the most powerful with the commons, came forward again and spoke as follows:

37 "I have often before now been convinced that a democracy is incapable of empire, and never more so than by your present change of mind in the matter of Mytilene. Fears or plots being unknown to you in your daily relations with each other, you feel just the same with regard to your allies, and never reflect that the mistakes into which you may be led by listening to their appeals, or by giving way to your own compassion, are full of danger to yourselves, and bring you no thanks for your weakness from your allies; entirely forgetting that your empire is a despotism and your subjects disaffected conspirators, whose obedience is ensured not by your suicidal concessions, but by the superiority given you by your own strength and not their loyalty. The most alarming feature in the case is the constant change of measures with which we appear to be threatened, and our seeming ignorance of the fact

that bad laws which are never changed are better for a city than good ones that have no authority; that unlearned loyalty is more serviceable than quick-witted insubordination; and that ordinary men usually manage public affairs better than their more gifted fellows. The latter are always wanting to appear wiser than the laws, and to overrule every proposition brought forward, thinking that they cannot show their wit in more important matters, and by such behavior too often ruin their country; while those who mistrust their own cleverness are content to be less learned than the laws, and less able to pick holes in the speech of a good speaker; and being fair judges rather than rival athletes, generally conduct affairs successfully. These we ought to imitate, instead of being led on by cleverness and intellectual rivalry to advise your people against our real opinions.

38 "For myself, I adhere to my former opinion, and wonder at those who have proposed to reopen the case of the Mytilenians, and who are thus causing a delay which is all in favor of the guilty, by making the sufferer proceed against the offender with the edge of his anger blunted; although where vengeance follows most closely upon the wrong, it best equals it and most amply requites it. I wonder also who will be the man who will maintain the contrary, and will pretend to show that the crimes of the Mytilenians are of service to us, and our misfortunes injurious to the allies. Such a man must plainly either have such confidence in his rhetoric as to adventure to prove that what has been once for all decided is still undetermined, or be bribed to try to delude us by elaborate sophisms. In such contests the state gives the rewards to others, and takes the dangers for herself. The persons to blame are you who are so foolish as to institute these contests; who go to see an oration as you would to see a sight, take your facts on hearsay, judge of the practicability of a project by the wit of its advocates, and trust for the truth as to past events not to the fact which you saw more than to the clever strictures which you heard; the easy victims of new-fangled arguments, unwilling to follow received conclusions; slaves to every new paradox, despisers of the commonplace; the first wish of every man being that he could speak himself, the next to rival those who can speak by seeming to be quite up with their ideas by applauding every hit almost before it is made, and by being as quick in catching an argument as you are slow in foreseeing its consequences; asking, if I may so say, for something different from the conditions under which we live, and yet comprehending inadequately those very conditions; very slaves to the pleasure of the ear, and more like the audience of a rhetorician than the council of a city.

39 "In order to keep you from this, I proceed to show that no one state has ever injured you as much as Mytilene. I can make allowance for those who revolt because they cannot bear our empire, or who have been forced to do so by the enemy. But for those who possessed an island with fortifications; who could fear our enemies only by sea, and there had their own force of triremes to protect them; who were independent and held in the highest honor by you- to act as these have done, this is not revolt- revolt implies oppression; it is deliberate and wanton aggression; an attempt to ruin us by siding with our bitterest enemies; a worse offence than a war undertaken on their own account in the acquisition of power. The fate of those of their neighbors who had already rebelled and had been subdued was no lesson to them; their own prosperity could not dissuade them from affronting danger; but blindly confident in the future, and full of hopes beyond their power though not beyond their ambition, they declared war and made their decision to prefer might to right, their attack being determined not by provocation but by the moment which seemed propitious. The truth is that great good fortune coming suddenly and unexpectedly tends to make a people insolent; in most cases it is safer for mankind to have success in reason than out of reason; and it is easier for them, one may say, to stave off adversity than to preserve prosperity. Our mistake has been to distinguish the Mytilenians as we have done: had they been long ago treated like the rest, they never would have so far forgotten themselves, human nature being as surely made arrogant by consideration as it is awed by firmness.

Let them now therefore be punished as their crime requires, and do not, while you condemn the aristocracy, absolve the people. This is certain, that all attacked you without distinction, although they might have come over to us and been now again in possession of their city. But no, they thought it safer to throw in their lot with the aristocracy and so joined their rebellion! Consider therefore: if you subject to the same punishment the ally who is forced to rebel by the enemy, and him who does so by his own free choice, which of them, think you, is there that will not rebel upon the slightest pretext; when the reward of success is freedom, and the penalty of failure nothing so very terrible? We meanwhile shall have to risk our money and our lives against one state after another; and if successful, shall receive a ruined town from which we can no longer draw the revenue upon which our strength depends; while if unsuccessful, we shall have an enemy the more upon our hands, and shall spend the time that might be employed in combating our existing foes in warring with our own allies.

40 "No hope, therefore, that rhetoric may instil or money purchase, of the mercy due to human infirmity must be held out to the Mytilenians. Their offence was not involuntary, but of malice and deliberate; and mercy is only for unwilling offenders. I therefore, now as before, persist against your reversing your first decision, or giving way to the three failings most fatal to empire- pity, sentiment, and indulgence. Compassion is due to those who can reciprocate the feeling, not to those who will never pity us in return, but are our natural and necessary foes: the orators who charm us with sentiment may find other less important arenas for their talents, in the place of one where the city pays a heavy penalty for a momentary pleasure, themselves receiving fine acknowledgments for their fine phrases; while indulgence should be shown towards those who will be our friends in future, instead of towards men who will remain just what they were, and as much our enemies as before. To sum up shortly, I say that if you follow my advice you will do what is just towards the Mytilenians, and at the same time expedient; while by a different decision you will not oblige them so much as pass sentence upon yourselves. For if they were right in rebelling, you must be wrong in ruling. However, if, right or wrong, you determine to rule, you must carry out your principle and punish the Mytilenians as your interest requires; or else you must give up your empire and cultivate honesty without danger. Make up your minds, therefore, to give them like for like; and do not let the victims who escaped the plot be more insensible than the conspirators who hatched it; but reflect what they would have done if victorious over you, especially they were the aggressors. It is they who wrong their neighbor without a cause, that pursue their victim to the death, on account of the danger which they foresee in letting their enemy survive; since the object of a wanton wrong is more dangerous, if he escape, than an enemy who has not this to complain of. Do not, therefore, be traitors to yourselves, but recall as nearly as possible the moment of suffering and the supreme importance which you then attached to their reduction; and now pay them back in their turn, without yielding to present weakness or forgetting the peril that once hung over you. Punish them as they deserve, and teach your other allies by a striking example that the penalty of rebellion is death. Let them once understand this and you will not have so often to neglect your enemies while you are fighting with your own confederates."

41 Such were the words of Cleon. After him Diodotus, son of Eucrates, who had also in the previous assembly spoken most strongly against putting the Mytilenians to death, came forward and spoke as follows:

42 "I do not blame the persons who have reopened the case of the Mytilenians, nor do I approve the protests which we have heard against important questions being frequently debated. I think the two things most opposed to good counsel are haste and passion; haste usually goes hand in hand with folly, passion with coarseness and narrowness of mind. As for the argument that speech ought not to be the exponent of action, the man who uses it must be either senseless or interested: senseless if he believes it possible to treat of the uncertain future through any other medium; interested if, wishing to carry a disgraceful measure and doubting his ability to speak well in a bad cause, he thinks to frighten opponents and hearers by well-aimed calumny. What is still more intolerable is to accuse a speaker of making a display in order to be paid for it. If ignorance only were imputed, an unsuccessful speaker might retire with a reputation for honesty, if not for wisdom; while the charge of dishonesty makes him suspected, if successful, and thought, if defeated, not only a fool but a rogue. The city is no gainer by such a system, since fear deprives it of its advisers; although in truth, if our speakers are to make such assertions, it would be better for the country if they could not speak at all, as we should then make fewer blunders. The good citizen ought to triumph not by frightening his opponents but by beating them fairly in argument; and a wise city, without over-distinguishing its best advisers, will nevertheless not deprive them of their due, and, far from punishing an unlucky counsellor, will not even regard him as disgraced. In this way successful orators would be least tempted to sacrifice their convictions to popularity, in the hope of still higher honors, and unsuccessful speakers to resort to the same popular arts in order to win over the multitude.

43 "This is not our way; and, besides, the moment that a man is suspected of giving advice, however good, from corrupt motives, we feel such a grudge against him for the gain which after all we are not certain he will receive, that we deprive the city of its certain benefit. Plain good advice has thus come to be no less suspected than bad; and the advocate of the most monstrous measures is not more obliged to use deceit to gain the people, than the best counsellor is to lie in order to be believed. The city and the city only, owing to these refinements, can never be served openly and without disguise; he who does serve it openly being always suspected of serving himself in some secret way in return. Still, considering the magnitude of the interests involved, and the position of affairs, we orators must make it our business to look a little farther than you who judge offhand; especially as we, your advisers, are responsible, while you, our audience, are not so. For if those who gave the advice, and those who took it, suffered equally, you would judge more calmly; as it is, you visit the disasters into which the whim of the moment may have led you upon the single person of your adviser, not upon yourselves, his numerous companions in error.

44 "However, I have not come forward either to oppose or to accuse in the matter of Mytilene; indeed, the question before us as sensible men is not their guilt, but our interests. Though I prove them ever so guilty, I shall not, therefore, advise their death, unless it be expedient; nor though they should have claims to indulgence, shall I recommend it, unless it be clearly for the good of the country. I consider that we are deliberating for the future more than for the present; and where Cleon is so positive as to the useful deterrent effects that will follow from making rebellion capital, I, who consider the interests of the future quite as much as he, as positively maintain the contrary. And I require you not to reject my useful considerations for his specious ones: his speech may have the attraction of seeming the more just in your present temper against Mytilene; but we are not in a court of justice, but in a political assembly; and the question is not justice, but how to make the Mytilenians useful to Athens.

45 "Now of course communities have enacted the penalty of death for many offences far lighter than this: still hope leads men to venture, and no one ever yet put himself in peril without the inward conviction that he would succeed in his design. Again, was there ever city rebelling that did not believe that it possessed either in itself or in its alliances resources adequate to the enterprise? All, states and individuals, are alike prone to err, and there is no law that will prevent them; or why should men have exhausted the list of punishments in search of enactments to protect them from evildoers? It is probable that in early times the penalties for the greatest offences were less severe, and that, as these were disregarded, the penalty of death has been by degrees in most cases arrived at, which is itself disregarded in like manner. Either then some means of terror more terrible than this must be discovered, or it must be owned that this restraint is useless; and that as long as poverty gives men the courage of necessity, or plenty fills them with the ambition which belongs to insolence and pride, and the other conditions of life remain each under the thraldom of some fatal and master passion, so long will the impulse never be wanting to drive men into danger. Hope also and cupidity, the one leading and the other following, the one conceiving the attempt, the other suggesting the facility of succeeding, cause the widest ruin, and, although invisible agents, are far stronger than the dangers that are seen. Fortune, too, powerfully helps the delusion and, by the unexpected aid that she sometimes lends, tempts men to venture with inferior means; and this is especially the case with communities, because the stakes played for are the highest, freedom or empire, and, when all are acting together, each man irrationally magnifies his own capacity. In fine, it is impossible to prevent, and only great simplicity can hope to prevent, human nature doing what it has once set its mind upon, by force of law or by any other deterrent force whatsoever.

46 "We must not, therefore, commit ourselves to a false policy through a belief in the efficacy of the punishment of death, or exclude rebels from the hope of repentance and an early atonement of their error. Consider a moment. At present, if a city that has already revolted perceive that it cannot succeed, it will come to terms while it is still able to refund expenses, and pay tribute afterwards. In the other case, what city, think you, would not prepare better than is now done, and hold out to the last against its besiegers, if it is all one whether it surrender late or soon? And how can it be otherwise than hurtful to us to be put to the expense of a siege, because surrender is out of the question; and if we take the city, to receive a ruined town from which we can no longer draw the revenue which forms our real strength against the enemy? We must not, therefore, sit as strict judges of the offenders to our own prejudice, but rather see how by moderate chastisements we may be enabled to benefit in future by the revenue-producing powers of our dependencies; and we must make up our minds to look for our protection not to legal terrors but to careful administration. At present we do exactly the opposite. When a free community, held in subjection by force, rises, as is only natural, and asserts its independence, it is no sooner reduced than we fancy ourselves obliged to punish it severely; although the right course with freemen is not to chastise them rigorously when they do rise, but rigorously to watch them before they rise, and to prevent their ever entertaining the idea, and, the insurrection suppressed, to make as few responsible for it as possible.

47 "Only consider what a blunder you would commit in doing as Cleon recommends. As things are at present, in all the cities the people is your friend, and either does not revolt with the oligarchy, or, if forced to do so, becomes at once the enemy of the insurgents; so that in the war with the hostile city you have the masses on your side. But if you butcher the people of Mytilene, who had nothing to do with the revolt, and who, as soon as they got arms, of their own motion surrendered the town, first you will commit the crime of killing your benefactors; and next you will play directly into the hands of the higher classes, who when they induce their cities to rise, will immediately have the people on their side, through your having announced in advance the same punishment for those who are guilty and for those who are not. On the contrary, even if they were guilty, you ought to seem not to notice it, in order to avoid alienating the only class still friendly to us. In short, I consider it far more useful for the preservation of our empire voluntarily to put up with injustice, than to put to death, however justly, those whom it is our interest to keep alive. As for Cleon's idea that in punishment the claims of justice and expediency can both be satisfied, facts do not confirm the possibility of such a combination.

48 "Confess, therefore, that this is the wisest course, and without conceding too much either to pity or to indulgence, by neither of which motives do I any more than Cleon wish you to be influenced, upon the plain merits of the case before you, be persuaded by me to try calmly those of the Mytilenians whom Paches sent off as guilty, and to leave the rest undisturbed. This is at once best for the future, and most terrible to your enemies at the present moment; inasmuch as good policy against an adversary is superior to the blind attacks of brute force."

49 Such were the words of Diodotus. The two opinions thus expressed were the ones that most directly contradicted each other; and the Athenians, notwithstanding their change of feeling, now proceeded to a division, in which the show of hands was almost equal, although the motion of Diodotus carried the day. Another trireme was at once sent off in haste, for fear that the first might reach Lesbos in the interval, and the city be found destroyed; the first ship having about a day and a night's start. Wine and barley-cakes were provided for the vessel by the Mytilenian ambassadors, and great promises made if they arrived in time; which caused the men to use such diligence upon the voyage that they took their meals of barley-cakes kneaded with oil and wine as they rowed, and only slept by turns while the others were at the oar. Luckily they met with no contrary wind, and the first ship making no haste upon so horrid an errand, while the second pressed on in the manner described, the first arrived so little before them, that Paches had only just had time to read the decree, and to prepare to execute the sentence, when the second put into port and prevented the massacre. The danger of Mytilene had indeed been great.

50 The other party whom Paches had sent off as the prime movers in the rebellion, were upon Cleon's motion put to death by the Athenians, the number being rather more than a thousand. The Athenians also demolished the walls of the Mytilenians, and took possession of their ships. Afterwards tribute was not imposed upon the Lesbians; but all their land, except that of the Methymnians, was divided into three thousand allotments, three hundred of which were reserved as sacred for the gods, and the rest assigned by lot to Athenian shareholders, who were sent out to the island. With these the Lesbians agreed to pay a rent of two minae a year for each allotment, and cultivated the land themselves. The Athenians also took possession of the towns on the continent belonging to the Mytilenians, which thus became for the future subject to Athens. Such were the events that took place at Lesbos....

D. THE MELIAN DIALOGUE

✥ Book V

The corrosive effects of the war upon morality and decency are best illustrated by how the Athenians treated the population of the small island of melos in 416 B.C. Until then the islanders had been neutral parties, but the Athenians now decided that their neutral status represented an embarrassment to Athenian naval power. Thucydides' account of the dialogue between the Athenians and the Melians, as well as the annihilation of the latter by the former, is one of the most chilling illustrations of the doctrine of "might makes right" in the realm of warfare.

84 THE next summer Alcibiades sailed with twenty ships to Argos and seized the suspected persons still left of the Spartan faction to the number of three hundred, whom the Athenians forthwith lodged in the neighboring islands of their empire. The Athenians also made an expedition against the isle of Melos with thirty ships of their own, six Chian, and two Lesbian vessels, sixteen hundred hoplites, three hundred archers, and twenty mounted archers from Athens, and about fifteen hundred hoplites from the allies and the islanders. The Melians are a colony of Sparta that would not submit to the Athenians like the other islanders, and at first remained neutral and took no part in the struggle, but afterwards upon the Athenians using violence and plundering their territory, assumed an attitude of open hostility. Cleomedes, son of Lycomedes, and Tisias, son of Tisimachus, the generals, encamping in their territory with the above armament, before doing any harm to their land, sent envoys to negotiate. These the Melians did not bring before the people, but bade them state the object of their mission to the magistrates and the few; upon which the Athenian envoys spoke as follows:

85 Athenians: "Since the negotiations are not to go on before the people, in order that we may not be able to speak straight on without interruption, and deceive the ears of the multitude by seductive arguments which would pass without refutation (for we know that this is the meaning of our being brought before the few), what if you who sit there were to pursue a method more cautious still? Make no set speech yourselves, but take us up at whatever you do not like, and settle that before going any farther. And first tell us if this proposition of ours suits you."

86 The Melian commissioners answered: "To the fairness of quietly instructing each other as you propose there is nothing to object; but your military preparations are too far advanced to agree with what you say, as we see you are come to be judges in your own cause, and that all we can reasonably expect from this negotiation is war, if we prove to have right on our side and refuse to submit, and in the contrary case, slavery."

87 Athenians: "If you have met to reason about presentiments of the future, or for anything else than to consult for the safety of your state upon the facts that you see before you, we will give over; otherwise we will go on."

88 Melians: "It is natural and excusable for men in our position to turn more ways than one both in thought and utterance. However, the question in this conference is, as you say, the safety of our country; and the discussion, if you please, can proceed in the way which you propose."

89 Athenians: "For ourselves, we shall not trouble you with specious pretences- either of how we have a right to our empire because we overthrew the Persians, or are now attacking you because of wrong that you have done us- and make a long speech which would not be believed; and in return we hope that you, instead of thinking to influence us by saying that you did not join the Spartans, although their colonists, or that you have done us no wrong, will aim at what is feasible, holding in view the real sentiments of us both; since you know as well as we do that right, as the world goes, is only in question between equals in power, while the strong do what they can and the weak suffer what they must."

90 Melians: "As we think, at any rate, it is expedient- we speak as we are obliged, since you enjoin us to let right alone and talk only of interest- that you should not destroy what is our common protection, the privilege of being allowed in danger to invoke what is fair and right, and even to profit by arguments not strictly valid if they can be got to pass current. And you are as much interested in this as any, as your fall would be a signal for the heaviest vengeance and an example for the world to meditate upon."

91 Athenians: "The end of our empire, if end it should, does not frighten us: a rival empire like Sparta, even if Sparta was our real antagonist, is not so terrible to the van-quished as subjects who by themselves attack and overpower their rulers. This, however, is a risk that we are content to take. We will now proceed to show you that we are come here in the interest of our empire, and that we shall say what we are now going to say, for the preservation of your country; as we would fain exercise that empire over you without trouble, and see you preserved for the good of us both."

92 Melians: "And how, pray, could it turn out as good for us to serve as for you to rule?"

93 Athenians: "Because you would have the advantage of submitting before suffering the worst, and we should gain by not destroying you."

94 Melians: "So that you would not consent to our being neutral, friends instead of enemies, but allies of neither side."

95 Athenians: "No; for your hostility cannot so much hurt us as your friendship will be an argument to our subjects of our weakness, and your enmity of our power."

96 Melians: "Is that your subjects' idea of equity, to put those who have nothing to do with you in the same category with peoples that are most of them your own colonists, and some conquered rebels?"

97 Athenians: "As far as right goes, they think one has as much of it as the other, and that if any maintain their independence it is because they are strong, and that if we do not molest them it is because we are afraid; so that besides extending our empire we should gain in security by your subjection; the fact that you are islanders and weaker than others rendering it all the more important that you should not succeed in baffling the masters of the sea."

98 Melians: "But do you consider that there is no security in the policy which we indicate? For here again if you debar us from talking about justice and invite us to obey your interest, we also must explain ours, and try to persuade you, if the two happen to coincide. How can you avoid making enemies of all existing neutrals who shall look at case from it that one day or another you will attack them? And what is this but to make greater the enemies that you have already, and to force others to become so who would otherwise have never thought of it?"

99 Athenians: "Why, the fact is that continentals generally give us but little alarm; the liberty which they enjoy will long prevent their taking precautions against us; it is rather islanders like yourselves, outside our empire, and subjects smarting under the yoke, who would be the most likely to take a rash step and lead themselves and us into obvious danger."

100 Melians: "Well then, if you risk so much to retain your empire, and your subjects to get rid of it, it were surely great baseness and cowardice in us who are still free not to try everything that can be tried, before submitting to your yoke."

101 Athenians: "Not if you are well advised, the contest not being an equal one, with honor as the prize and shame as the penalty, but a question of self-preservation and of not resisting those who are far stronger than you are."

102 Melians: "But we know that the fortune of war is sometimes more impartial than the disproportion of numbers might lead one to suppose; to submit is to give ourselves over to despair, while action still preserves for us a hope that we may stand erect."

103 Athenians: "Hope, danger's comforter, may be indulged in by those who have abundant resources, if not without loss at all events without ruin; but its nature is to be extravagant, and those who go so far as to put their all upon the venture see it in its true colors only when they are ruined; but so long as the discovery would enable them to guard against it, it is never found wanting. Let not this be the case with you, who are weak and hang on a single turn of the scale; nor be like the vulgar, who, abandoning such security as human means may still afford, when visible hopes fail them in extremity, turn to invisible, to prophecies and oracles, and other such inventions that delude men with hopes to their destruction."

104 Melians: "You may be sure that we are as well aware as you of the difficulty of contending against your power and fortune, unless the terms be equal. But we trust that the gods may grant us fortune as good as yours, since we are just men fighting against unjust, and that what we want in power will be made up by the alliance of the Spartans, who are bound, if only for very shame, to come to the aid of their kindred. Our confidence, therefore, after all is not so utterly irrational."

105 Athenians: "When you speak of the favor of the gods, we may as fairly hope for that as yourselves; neither our pretensions nor our conduct being in any way contrary to what men believe of the gods, or practise among themselves. Of the gods we believe, and of men we know, that by a necessary law of their nature they rule wherever they can. And it is not as if we were the first to make this law, or to act upon it when made: we found it existing before us, and shall leave it to exist for ever after us; all we do is to make use of it, knowing that you and everybody else, having the same power as we have, would do the same as we do. Thus, as far as the gods are concerned, we have no fear and no reason to fear that we shall be at a disadvantage. But when we come to your notion about the Spartans, which leads you to believe that shame will make them help you, here we bless your simplicity but do not envy your folly. The Spartans, when their own interests or their country's laws are in question, are the worthiest men alive; of their conduct towards others much might be said, but no clearer idea of it could be given than by shortly saying that of all the men we know they are most conspicuous in considering what is agreeable honorable, and what is expedient just. Such a way of thinking does not promise much for the safety which you now unreasonably count upon."

106 Melians: "But it is for this very reason that we now trust to their respect for expediency to prevent them from betraying the Melians, their colonists, and thereby losing the confidence of their friends in Greece and helping their enemies."

107 Athenians: "Then you do not adopt the view that expediency goes with security, while justice and honor cannot be followed without danger; and danger the Spartans generally court as little as possible."

108 Melians: "But we believe that they would be more likely to face even danger for our sake, and with more confidence than for others, as our nearness to Peloponnese makes it easier for them to act, and our common blood ensures our fidelity."

109 Athenians: "Yes, but what an intending ally trusts to is not the goodwill of those who ask his aid, but a decided superiority of power for action; and the Spartans look to this even more than others. At least, such is their distrust of their home resources that it is only with numerous allies that they attack a neighbor; now is it likely that while we are masters of the sea, they will cross over to an island?"

110 Melians: "But they would have others to send. The Cretan Sea is a wide one, and it is more difficult for those who command it to intercept others, than for those who wish to elude them to do so safely. And should the Spartans miscarry in this, they would fall upon your land, and upon those left of your allies whom Brasidas [a successful Spartan general] did not reach; and instead of places which are not yours, you will have to fight for your own country and your own confederacy."

111 Athenians: "Some diversion of the kind you speak of you may one day experience, only to learn, as others have done, that the Athenians never once yet withdrew from a siege for fear of any. But we are struck by the fact that, after saying you would consult for the safety of your country, in all this discussion you have mentioned nothing which men might trust in and think to be saved by. Your strongest arguments depend upon hope and the future, and your actual resources are too scanty, as compared with those arrayed against you, for you to come out victorious. You will therefore show great blindness of judgment, unless, after allowing us to retire, you can find some counsel more prudent than this. You will surely not be caught by that idea of disgrace, which in dangers that are disgraceful, and at the same time too plain to be mistaken, proves so fatal to mankind; since in too many cases the very men that have their eyes perfectly open to what they are rushing into, let the thing called disgrace, by the mere influence of a seductive name, lead them on to a point at which they become so enslaved by the phrase as in fact to fall wilfully into hopeless disaster, and incur disgrace more disgraceful as the companion of error, than when it comes as the result of misfortune. This, if you are well advised, you will guard against; and you will not think it dishonorable to submit to the greatest city in Greece, when it makes you the moderate offer of becoming its tributary ally, without ceasing to enjoy the country that belongs to you; nor when you have the choice given you between war and security, will you be so blinded as to choose the worse. And it is certain that those who do not yield to their equals, who keep terms with their superiors, and are moderate towards their inferiors, on the whole succeed best. Think over the matter, therefore, after our withdrawal, and reflect once and again that it is for your country that you are consulting, that you have not more than one, and that upon this one deliberation depends its prosperity or ruin."

112 The Athenians now withdrew from the conference; and the Melians, left to themselves, came to a decision corresponding with what they had maintained in the discussion, and answered: "Our resolution, Athenians, is the same as it was at first. We will not in a moment deprive of freedom a city that has been inhabited these seven hundred years; but we put our trust in the fortune by which the gods have preserved it until now, and in the help of men, that is, of the Spartans; and so we will try to save ourselves. Meanwhile we invite you to allow us to be friends to you and foes to neither party, and to retire from our country after making such a treaty as shall seem fit to us both."

113 Such was the answer of the Melians. The Athenians now departing from the conference said: "Well, you alone, as it seems to us, judging from these resolutions, regard what is future as more certain than what is before your eyes, and what is out of sight, in your eagerness, as already coming to pass; and as you have staked most on, and trusted most in, the Spartans, your fortune, and your hopes, so will you be most completely deceived."

114 The Athenian envoys now returned to the army; and the Melians showing no signs of yielding, the generals at once betook themselves to hostilities, and drew a line of circumvallation around the Melians, dividing the work among the different states. Subsequently the Athenians returned with most of their army, leaving behind them a certain number of their own citizens and of the allies to keep guard by land and sea. The force thus left stayed on and besieged the place.

115 About the same time the Argives invaded the territory of Phlius and lost eighty men cut off in an ambush by the Phliasians and Argive exiles. Meanwhile the Athenians at Pylos took so much plunder from the Spartans that the latter, although they still refrained from breaking off the treaty and going to war with Athens, yet proclaimed that any of their people that chose might plunder the Athenians. The Corinthians also commenced hostilities with the Athenians for private quarrels of their own; but the rest of the Peloponnesians stayed quiet. Meanwhile the Melians attacked by night and took the part of the Athenian lines over against the market, and killed some of the men, and brought in grain and all else that they could find useful to them, and so returned and kept quiet, while the Athenians took measures to keep better guard in future.

116 Summer was now over. The next winter the Spartans intended to invade the Argive territory, but arriving at the frontier found the sacrifices for crossing unfavorable, and went back again. This intention of theirs gave the Argives suspicions of certain of their fellow citizens, some of whom they arrested; others, however, escaped them. About the same time the Melians again took another part of the Athenian lines which were but feebly garrisoned. Reinforcements afterwards arriving from Athens in consequence, under the command of Philocrates, son of Demeas, the siege was now pressed vigorously; and some treachery taking place inside, the Melians surrendered at discretion to the Athenians, who put to death all the grown men whom they took, and sold the women and children for slaves, and subsequently sent out five hundred colonists and inhabited the place themselves.

Plato on the Death of Socrates

Among other things, the ancient Greeks created philosophy, which is itself a Greek word, meaning "love of wisdom." During the sixth century B.C. the earliest Greek philosophers explored many aspects of the natural world around them and were thus more akin to modern scientists than what we today regard as philosophers. But during the second half of the fifth century B.C. Greek philosophers began to concentrate most of their speculations upon the nature of us human beings and how we can best organize our affairs and communities to maximize justice and happiness. Central to this new focus was Socrates, an Athenian born in 469 B.C.

Unfortunately, Socrates did not bother setting down any of his thoughts in writing, but his most famous pupil, Plato (427-347 B.C.) made his beloved teacher the central figure in virtually all his philosophical works, cast in dialogue form in which various characters (including Socrates, of course) engage in lengthy conversations and investigations into important philosophical concepts: what is friendship, what is piety, what are love and beauty, what is the best way in which to organize a state, how do we learn, what is justice, do we have an immortal soul, and what happens to it after we die, etc.

In 399 B.C., when Socrates was seventy years old, he was prosecuted by three fellow Athenians for holding inappropriate views concerning the nature of the gods and for corrupting the young men of Athens by teaching them these things. The trial came before a jury of 501 Athenians. Each party to the case was allowed to speak for a specified period of time, after which the members of the jury immediately voted for condemnation or acquittal by dropping black or white pebbles in a jar. The jury voted 280 for Socrates' condemnation vs. 220 for his acquittal. Then a second phase of the trial was quickly transacted, in which the penalty was assessed and imposed. Socrates was not only found guilty of the charges brought against him, but he was condemned to death. Whereupon he was arrested and confined to prison until he was executed by being required to drink a poisonous draft of hemlock.

The following three writings of Plato give us a vivid portrayal of the trial, imprisonment, and execution of Socrates. The first writing, *The Apology* (meaning "The Reply"), is Plato's rendering of what Socrates said before the Athenian jury in response to his accusers. The second work, *The Crito*, is a typically Platonic philosophical work in that it is a discussion of a very important moral or philosophical concept: are we ever justified in doing wrong, even when we are ourselves the victims of injustice? This latter question is much more than an abstract discussion, because Socrates' dear friend Crito is trying to convince Socrates that he should allow his friends to arrange his escape from prison, because Socrates' condemnation to death was unjust. The third writing, called *The Phaedo*, is a very long dialogue set in prison just before Socrates drinks the fatal hemlock, and it is appropriately concerned with the question of whether we have an immortal soul, and what happens to it when we die, a matter with which Socrates must have been much concerned at the time leading up to his death. The only portion of this dialogue reproduced here is the description of Socrates' death.

(Taken from the translation of Benjamin Jowett with revisions by Gary Forsythe)

A. THE APOLOGY

1 How you, O Athenians, have been affected by my accusers, I cannot tell; but I know that they almost made me forget who I was—so persuasively did they speak; and yet they have hardly uttered a word of truth. But of the many falsehoods told by them, there was one which quite amazed me;—I mean when they said that you should be upon your guard and not allow yourselves to be deceived by the force of my eloquence. To say this, when they were certain to be detected as soon as I opened my lips and proved myself to be anything but a great speaker, did indeed appear to me most shameless—unless by the force of eloquence they mean the force of truth; for is such is their meaning, I admit that I am eloquent. But in how different a way from theirs! Well, as I was saying, they have scarcely spoken the truth at all; but from me you shall hear the whole truth: not, however, delivered after their manner in a set oration duly ornamented with words and phrases. No, by heaven! but I shall use the words and arguments which occur to me at the moment; for I am confident in the justice of my cause (Or, I am certain that I am right in taking this course.): at my time of life I ought not to be appearing before you, O men of Athens, in the character of a juvenile orator—let no one expect it of me. And I must beg of you to grant me a favour:—If I defend myself in my accustomed manner, and you hear me using the words which I have been in the habit of using in the agora, at the tables of the money-changers, or anywhere else, I would ask you not to be surprised, and not to interrupt me on this account. For I am more than seventy years of age, and appearing now for the first time in a court of law, I am quite a stranger to the language of the place; and therefore I would have you regard me as if I were really a stranger, whom you would excuse if he spoke in his native tongue, and after the fashion of his country:—Am I making an unfair request of you? Never mind the manner, which may or may not be good; but think only of the truth of my words, and give heed to that: let the speaker speak truly and the judge decide justly.

2 And first, I have to reply to the older charges and to my first accusers, and then I will go on to the later ones. For of old I have had many accusers, who have accused me falsely to you during many years; and I am more afraid of them than of Anytus and his associates, who are dangerous, too, in their own way. But far more dangerous are the others, who began when you were children, and took possession of your minds with their falsehoods, telling of one Socrates, a wise man, who speculated about the heaven above, and searched into the earth beneath, and made the worse appear the better cause. The disseminators of this tale are the accusers whom I dread; for their hearers are apt to fancy that such enquirers do not believe in the existence of the gods. And they are many, and their charges against me are of ancient date, and they were made by them in the days when you were more impressible than you are now—in childhood, or it may have been in youth—and the cause when heard went by default, for there was none to answer. And hardest of all, I do not know and cannot tell the names of my accusers; unless in the chance

case of a Comic poet. All who from envy and malice have persuaded you—some of them having first convinced themselves—all this class of men are most difficult to deal with; for I cannot have them up here, and cross-examine them, and therefore I must simply fight with shadows in my own defence, and argue when there is no one who answers. I will ask you then to assume with me, as I was saying, that my opponents are of two kinds; one recent, the other ancient: and I hope that you will see the propriety of my answering the latter first, for these accusations you heard long before the others, and much oftener. Well, then, I must make my defence, and endeavour to clear away in a short time, a slander which has lasted a long time. May I succeed, if to succeed be for my good and yours, or likely to avail me in my cause! The task is not an easy one; I quite understand the nature of it. And so leaving the event with God, in obedience to the law I will now make my defence.

3 I will begin at the beginning, and ask what is the accusation which has given rise to the slander of me, and in fact has encouraged Meletus to proof this charge against me. Well, what do the slanderers say? They shall be my prosecutors, and I will sum up their words in an affidavit: 'Socrates is an evil-doer, and a curious person, who searches into things under the earth and in heaven, and he makes the worse appear the better cause; and he teaches the aforesaid doctrines to others.' Such is the nature of the accusation: it is just what you have yourselves seen in the comedy of Aristophanes (Aristoph., Clouds.), who has introduced a man whom he calls Socrates, going about and saying that he walks in air, and talking a deal of nonsense concerning matters of which I do not pretend to know either much or little—not that I mean to speak disparagingly of any one who is a student of natural philosophy. I should be very sorry if Meletus could bring so grave a charge against me. But the simple truth is, O Athenians, that I have nothing to do with physical speculations. Very many of those here present are witnesses to the truth of this, and to them I appeal. Speak then, you who have heard me, and tell your neighbours whether any of you have ever known me hold forth in few words or in many upon such matters...You hear their answer. And from what they say of this part of the charge you will be able to judge of the truth of the rest.

4 As little foundation is there for the report that I am a teacher, and take money; this accusation has no more truth in it than the other. Although, if a man were really able to instruct mankind, to receive money for giving instruction would, in my opinion, be an honour to him. There is Gorgias of Leontium, and Prodicus of Ceos, and Hippias of Elis, who go the round of the cities, and are able to persuade the young men to leave their own citizens by whom they might be taught for nothing, and come to them whom they not only pay, but are thankful if they may be allowed to pay them. There is at this time a Parian philosopher residing in Athens, of whom I have heard; and I came to hear of him in this way:—I came across a man who has spent a world of money on the Sophists, Callias, the son of Hipponicus, and knowing that he had sons, I asked him: 'Callias,' I said, 'if your two sons were foals or calves, there would be no difficulty in finding some one to put over them; we should hire a trainer of horses, or a farmer probably, who would improve and perfect them in their own proper virtue and excellence; but as they are human beings, whom are you thinking of placing over them? Is there any one who understands human and political virtue? You must have thought about the matter, for you have sons; is there any one?' 'There is,' he said. 'Who is he?' said I; 'and of what country? and what does he charge?' 'Evenus the Parian,' he replied; 'he is the man, and his charge is five minae.' Happy is Evenus, I said to myself, if he really has this wisdom, and teaches at such a moderate charge. Had I the same, I should have been very proud and conceited; but the truth is that I have no knowledge of the kind.

5 I dare say, Athenians, that some one among you will reply, 'Yes, Socrates, but what is the origin of these accusations which are brought against you; there must have been something strange which you have been doing? All these rumours and this talk about you

would never have arisen if you had been like other men: tell us, then, what is the cause of them, for we should be sorry to judge hastily of you.' Now I regard this as a fair challenge, and I will endeavour to explain to you the reason why I am called wise and have such an evil fame. Please to attend then. And although some of you may think that I am joking, I declare that I will tell you the entire truth. Men of Athens, this reputation of mine has come of a certain sort of wisdom which I possess. If you ask me what kind of wisdom, I reply, wisdom such as may perhaps be attained by man, for to that extent I am inclined to believe that I am wise; whereas the persons of whom I was speaking have a superhuman wisdom which I may fail to describe, because I have it not myself; and he who says that I have, speaks falsely, and is taking away my character. And here, O men of Athens, I must beg you not to interrupt me, even if I seem to say something extravagant. For the word which I will speak is not mine. I will refer you to a witness who is worthy of credit; that witness shall be the God of Delphi—he will tell you about my wisdom, if I have any, and of what sort it is. You must have known Chaerephon; he was early a friend of mine, and also a friend of yours, for he shared in the recent exile of the people, and returned with you. Well, Chaerephon, as you know, was very impetuous in all his doings, and he went to Delphi and boldly asked the oracle to tell him whether—as I was saying, I must beg you not to interrupt—he asked the oracle to tell him whether anyone was wiser than I was, and the Pythian prophetess answered, that there was no man wiser. Chaerephon is dead himself; but his brother, who is in court, will confirm the truth of what I am saying.

6 Why do I mention this? Because I am going to explain to you why I have such an evil name. When I heard the answer, I said to myself, What can the god mean? and what is the interpretation of his riddle? for I know that I have no wisdom, small or great. What then can he mean when he says that I am the wisest of men? And yet he is a god, and cannot lie; that would be against his nature. After long consideration, I thought of a method of trying the question. I reflected that if I could only find a man wiser than myself, then I might go to the god with a refutation in my hand. I should say to him, 'Here is a man who is wiser than I am; but you said that I was the wisest.' Accordingly I went to one who had the reputation of wisdom, and observed him—his name I need not mention; he was a politician whom I selected for examination—and the result was as follows: When I began to talk with him, I could not help thinking that he was not really wise, although he was thought wise by many, and still wiser by himself; and thereupon I tried to explain to him that he thought himself wise, but was not really wise; and the consequence was that he hated me, and his enmity was shared by several who were present and heard me. So I left him, saying to myself, as I went away: Well, although I do not suppose that either of us knows anything really beautiful and good, I am better off than he is,— for he knows nothing, and thinks that he knows; I neither know nor think that I know. In this latter particular, then, I seem to have slightly the advantage of him. Then I went to another who had still higher pretensions to wisdom, and my conclusion was exactly the same. Whereupon I made another enemy of him, and of many others besides him.

7 Then I went to one man after another, being not unconscious of the enmity which I provoked, and I lamented and feared this: but necessity was laid upon me,—the word of God, I thought, ought to be considered first. And I said to myself, Go I must to all who appear to know, and find out the meaning of the oracle. And I swear to you, Athenians, by the dog I swear! —for I must tell you the truth—the result of my mission was just this: I found that the men most in repute were all but the most foolish; and that others less esteemed were really wiser and better. I will tell you the tale of my wanderings and of the 'Herculean' labours, as I may call them, which I endured only to find at last the oracle irrefutable. After the politicians, I went to the poets; tragic, dithyrambic, and all sorts. And there, I said to myself, you will be instantly detected; now you will find out that you are more ignorant than they are. Accordingly, I took them some of the most elaborate

passages in their own writings, and asked what was the meaning of them—thinking that they would teach me something. Will you believe me? I am almost ashamed to confess the truth, but I must say that there is hardly a person present who would not have talked better about their poetry than they did themselves. Then I knew that not by wisdom do poets write poetry, but by a sort of genius and inspiration; they are like diviners or sooth-sayers who also say many fine things, but do not understand the meaning of them. The poets appeared to me to be much in the same case; and I further observed that upon the strength of their poetry they believed themselves to be the wisest of men in other things in which they were not wise. So I departed, conceiving myself to be superior to them for the same reason that I was superior to the politicians.

8 At last I went to the artisans. I was conscious that I knew nothing at all, as I may say, and I was sure that they knew many fine things; and here I was not mistaken, for they did know many things of which I was ignorant, and in this they certainly were wiser than I was. But I observed that even the good artisans fell into the same error as the poets;—because they were good workmen they thought that they also knew all sorts of high matters, and this defect in them overshadowed their wisdom; and therefore I asked myself on behalf of the oracle, whether I would like to be as I was, neither having their knowledge nor their ignorance, or like them in both; and I made answer to myself and to the oracle that I was better off as I was.

9 This inquisition has led to my having many enemies of the worst and most dangerous kind, and has given occasion also to many calumnies. And I am called wise, for my hearers always imagine that I myself possess the wisdom which I find wanting in others: but the truth is, O men of Athens, that God only is wise; and by his answer he intends to show that the wisdom of men is worth little or nothing; he is not speaking of Socrates, he is only using my name by way of illustration, as if he said, He, O men, is the wisest, who, like Socrates, knows that his wisdom is in truth worth nothing. And so I go about the world, obedient to the god, and search and make enquiry into the wisdom of any one, whether citizen or stranger, who appears to be wise; and if he is not wise, then in vindication of the oracle I show him that he is not wise; and my occupation quite absorbs me, and I have no time to give either to any public matter of interest or to any concern of my own, but I am in utter poverty by reason of my devotion to the god.

10 There is another thing:—young men of the richer classes, who have not much to do, come about me of their own accord; they like to hear the pretenders examined, and they often imitate me, and proceed to examine others; there are plenty of persons, as they quickly discover, who think that they know something, but really know little or nothing; and then those who are examined by them instead of being angry with themselves are angry with me: This confounded Socrates, they say; this villainous misleader of youth!—and then if somebody asks them, Why, what evil does he practise or teach? they do not know, and cannot tell; but in order that they may not appear to be at a loss, they repeat the ready-made charges which are used against all philosophers about teaching things up in the clouds and under the earth, and having no gods, and making the worse appear the better cause; for they do not like to confess that their pretence of knowledge has been detected— which is the truth; and as they are numerous and ambitious and energetic, and are drawn up in battle array and have persuasive tongues, they have filled your ears with their loud and inveterate calumnies. And this is the reason why my three accusers, Meletus and Anytus and Lycon, have set upon me; Meletus, who has a quarrel with me on behalf of the poets; Anytus, on behalf of the craftsmen and politicians; Lycon, on behalf of the rhetoricians: and as I said at the beginning, I cannot expect to get rid of such a mass of calumny all in a moment. And this, O men of Athens, is the truth and the whole truth; I have concealed nothing, I have dissembled nothing. And yet, I know that my plainness of speech makes them hate me, and what is their hatred but a proof that I am speaking the truth?—Hence has arisen the prejudice against me; and this is the reason of it, as you will find out either in this or in any future enquiry....

17 Strange, indeed, would be my conduct, O men of Athens, if I who, when I was ordered by the generals whom you chose to command me at Potidaea and Amphipolis and Delium, remained where they placed me, like any other man, facing death—if now, when, as I conceive and imagine, God orders me to fulfil the philosopher's mission of searching into myself and other men, I were to desert my post through fear of death, or any other fear; that would indeed be strange, and I might justly be arraigned in court for denying the existence of the gods, if I disobeyed the oracle because I was afraid of death, fancying that I was wise when I was not wise. For the fear of death is indeed the pretence of wisdom, and not real wisdom, being a pretence of knowing the unknown; and no one knows whether death, which men in their fear apprehend to be the greatest evil, may not be the greatest good. Is not this ignorance of a disgraceful sort, the ignorance which is the conceit that a man knows what he does not know? And in this respect only I believe myself to differ from men in general, and may perhaps claim to be wiser than they are:—that whereas I know but little of the world below, I do not suppose that I know: but I do know that injustice and disobedience to a better, whether God or man, is evil and dishonourable, and I will never fear or avoid a possible good rather than a certain evil. And therefore if you let me go now, and are not convinced by Anytus, who said that since I had been prosecuted I must be put to death; (or if not that I ought never to have been prosecuted at all); and that if I escape now, your sons will all be utterly ruined by listening to my words—if you say to me, Socrates, this time we will not mind Anytus, and you shall be let off, but upon one condition, that you are not to enquire and speculate in this way any more, and that if you are caught doing so again you shall die;—if this was the condition on which you let me go, I should reply: Men of Athens, I honour and love you; but I shall obey God rather than you, and while I have life and strength I shall never cease from the practice and teaching of philosophy, exhorting any one whom I meet and saying to him after my manner: You, my friend,—a citizen of the great and mighty and wise city of Athens,—are you not ashamed of heaping up the greatest amount of money and honour and reputation, and caring so little about wisdom and truth and the greatest improvement of the soul, which you never regard or heed at all? And if the person with whom I am arguing, says: Yes, but I do care; then I do not leave him or let him go at once; but I proceed to interrogate and examine and cross-examine him, and if I think that he has no virtue in him, but only says that he has, I reproach him with undervaluing the greater, and overvaluing the less. And I shall repeat the same words to every one whom I meet, young and old, citizen and alien, but especially to the citizens, inasmuch as they are my brethren. For know that this is the command of God; and I believe that no greater good has ever happened in the state than my service to the God. For I do nothing but go about persuading you all, old and young alike, not to take thought for your persons or your properties, but first and chiefly to care about the greatest improvement of the soul. I tell you that virtue is not given by money, but that from virtue comes money and every other good of man, public as well as private. This is my teaching, and if this is the doctrine which corrupts the youth, I am a mischievous person. But if any one says that this is not my teaching, he is speaking an untruth. Wherefore, O men of Athens, I say to you, do as Anytus bids or not as Anytus bids, and either acquit me or not; but whichever you do, understand that I shall never alter my ways, not even if I have to die many times.

18 Men of Athens, do not interrupt, but hear me; there was an understanding between us that you should hear me to the end: I have something more to say, at which you may be inclined to cry out; but I believe that to hear me will be good for you, and therefore I beg that you will not cry out. I would have you know, that if you kill such an one as I am, you will injure yourselves more than you will injure me. Nothing will injure me, not Meletus nor yet Anytus—they cannot, for a bad man is not permitted to injure a better than himself. I do not deny that Anytus may, perhaps, kill him, or drive him into exile, or deprive him of civil rights; and he may imagine, and others may imagine, that he is inflicting a great injury upon him: but there I do not agree. For the evil of doing as he is doing—the evil of unjustly taking away the life of another—is greater far. And now, Athenians, I am not going to argue for my own sake, as you may think, but for yours, that you may not sin against the God by condemning me, who am his gift to you. For if you kill me you will not easily find a successor to me, who, if I may use such a ludicrous figure of speech, am a sort of gadfly, given to the state by God; and the state is a great and noble steed who is tardy in his motions owing to his very size, and requires to be stirred into life. I am that gadfly which God has attached to the state, and all day long and in all places am always fastening upon you, arousing and persuading and reproaching you. You will not easily find another like me, and therefore I would advise you to spare me. I dare say that you may feel out of temper (like a person who is suddenly awakened from sleep), and you think that you might easily strike me dead as Anytus advises, and then you would sleep on for the remainder of your lives, unless God in his care of you sent you another gadfly. When I say that I am given to you by God, the proof of my mission is this:—if I had been like other men, I should not have neglected all my own concerns or patiently seen the neglect of them during all these years, and have been doing yours, coming to you individually like a father or elder brother, exhorting you to regard virtue; such conduct, I say, would be unlike human nature. If I had gained anything, or if my exhortations had been paid, there would have been some sense in my doing so; but now, as you will perceive, not even the impudence of my accusers dares to say that I have ever exacted or sought pay of any one; of that they have no witness. And I have a sufficient witness to the truth of what I say—my poverty.

19 Some one may wonder why I go about in private giving advice and busying myself with the concerns of others, but do not venture to come forward in public and advise the state. I will tell you why. You have heard me speak at sundry times and in divers places of an oracle or sign which comes to me, and is the divinity which Meletus ridicules in the indictment. This sign, which is a kind of voice, first began to come to me when I was a child; it always forbids but never commands me to do anything which I am going to do. This is what deters me from being a politician. And rightly, as I think. For I am certain, O men of Athens, that if I had engaged in politics, I should have perished long ago, and done no good either to you or to myself. And do not be offended at my telling you the truth: for the truth is, that no man who goes to war with you or any other multitude, honestly striving against the many lawless and unrighteous deeds which are done in a state, will save his life; he who will fight for the right, if he would live even for a brief space, must have a private station and not a public one.

20 I can give you convincing evidence of what I say, not words only, but what you value far more—actions. Let me relate to you a passage of my own life which will prove to you that I should never have yielded to injustice from any fear of death, and that 'as I should have refused to yield' I must have died at once. I will tell you a tale of the courts, not very interesting perhaps, but nevertheless true. The only office of state which I ever held, O men of Athens, was a member of the boule: the tribe Antiochis, which is my tribe, had the presidency at the trial of the generals who had not taken up the bodies of the slain after the battle of Arginusae; and you proposed to try them in a body, contrary to law, as you all thought afterwards; but at the time I was the only one of the Prytanes who was opposed to the illegality, and I gave my vote against you; and when the orators threatened to impeach and arrest me, and you called and shouted, I made up my mind that I would run the risk, having law and justice with me, rather than take part in your injustice because I feared imprisonment and death. This happened in the days of the democracy. But when the oligarchy of the Thirty was in power, they sent for me and four others into the rotunda, and bade us bring Leon the Salaminian from Salamis, as they wanted to put him to death. This was a specimen of the sort of commands which they were always giving with the view of implicating as many as possible in their crimes; and then I showed, not in word only but in deed, that, if I may be allowed to use such an expression, I cared not a straw for death, and that my great and only care was lest I should do an unrighteous or unholy thing. For the strong arm of that oppressive power did not frighten me into doing wrong; and when we came out of the rotunda the other four went to Salamis and fetched Leon, but I went quietly home. For which I might have lost my life, had not the power of the Thirty shortly afterwards come to an end. And many will witness to my words.

21 Now do you really imagine that I could have survived all these years, if I had led a public life, supposing that like a good man I had always maintained the right and had made justice, as I ought, the first thing? No indeed, men of Athens, neither I nor any other man. But I have been always the same in all my actions, public as well as private, and never have I yielded any base compliance to those who are slanderously termed my disciples, or to any other. Not that I have any regular disciples. But if any one likes to come and hear me while I am pursuing my mission, whether he be young or old, he is not excluded. Nor do I converse only with those who pay; but any one, whether he be rich or poor, may ask and answer me and listen to my words; and whether he turns out to be a bad man or a good one, neither result can be justly imputed to me; for I never taught or professed to teach him anything. And if any one says that he has ever learned or heard anything from me in private which all the world has not heard, let me tell you that he is lying.

22 But I shall be asked, Why do people delight in continually conversing with you? I have told you already, Athenians, the whole truth about this matter: they like to hear the cross-examination of the pretenders to wisdom; there is amusement in it. Now this duty of cross-examining other men has been imposed upon me by God; and has been signified to me by oracles, visions, and in every way in which the will of divine power was ever intimated to any one. This is true, O Athenians, or, if not true, would be soon refuted. If I am or have been corrupting the youth, those of them who are now grown up and have become sensible that I gave them bad advice in the days of their youth should come forward as accusers, and take their revenge; or if they do not like to come themselves, some of their relatives, fathers, brothers, or other kinsmen, should say what evil their families have suffered at my hands. Now is their time. Many of them I see in the court. There is Crito, who is of the same age and of the same deme with myself, and there is Critobulus his son, whom I also see. Then again there is Lysanias of Sphettus, who is the father of Aeschines—he is present; and also there is Antiphon of Cephisus, who is the father of Epigenes; and there are the brothers of several who have associated with me. There is Nicostratus the son of Theosdotides, and the brother of Theodotus (now Theodotus himself is dead, and therefore he, at any rate, will not seek to stop him); and there is Paralus the son of Demodocus, who had a brother Theages; and Adeimantus the son of Ariston, whose brother Plato is present; and Aeantodorus, who is the brother of Apollodorus, whom I also see. I might mention a great many others, some of whom Meletus should have produced as witnesses in the course of his speech; and let him still produce them, if he has forgotten—I will make way for him. And let him say, if he has any testimony of the sort which he can produce. Nay, Athenians, the very opposite is the truth. For all these are ready to witness on behalf of the corrupter, of the injurer of their kindred, as Meletus and Anytus call me; not the corrupted youth only—there might have been a motive for that—but their uncorrupted elder relatives. Why should they too support me with their testimony? Why, indeed, except for the sake of truth and justice, and because they know that I am speaking the truth, and that Meletus is a liar....

(Following the jury's decision to condemn Socrates to death, he furhter replies)

29 Not much time will be gained, O Athenians, in return for the evil name which you will get from the detractors of the city, who will say that you killed Socrates, a wise man; for they will call me wise, even although I am not wise, when they want to reproach you. If you had waited a little while, your desire would have been fulfilled in the course of nature. For I am far advanced in years, as you may perceive, and not far from death. I am speaking now not to all of you, but only to those who have condemned me to death. And I have another thing to say to them: you think that I was convicted because I had no words of the sort which would have procured my acquittal—I mean, if I had thought fit to leave nothing undone or unsaid. Not so; the deficiency which led to my conviction was not of words— certainly not. But I had not the boldness or impudence or inclination to address you as you would have liked me to do, weeping and wailing and lamenting, and saying and doing many things which you have been accustomed to hear from others, and which, as I maintain, are unworthy of me. I thought at the time that I ought not to do anything common or mean when in danger: nor do I now repent of the style of my defence; I would rather die having spoken after my manner, than speak in your manner and live. For neither in war nor yet at law ought I or any man to use every way of escaping death. Often in battle there can be no doubt that if a man will throw away his arms, and fall on his knees before his pursuers, he may escape death; and in other dangers there are other ways of escaping death, if a man is willing to say and do anything. The difficulty, my friends, is not to avoid death, but to avoid unrighteousness; for that runs faster than death. I am old and move slowly, and the slower runner has overtaken me, and my accusers are keen and quick, and the faster runner, who is unrighteousness, has overtaken them. And now I depart hence condemned by you to suffer the penalty of death,—they too go their ways condemned by the truth to suffer the penalty of villainy and wrong; and I must abide by my award—let them abide by theirs. I suppose that these things may be regarded as fated,—and I think that they are well.

30 And now, O men who have condemned me, I would fain prophesy to you; for I am about to die, and in the hour of death men are gifted with prophetic power. And I prophesy to you who are my murderers, that immediately after my departure punishment far heavier than you have inflicted on me will surely await you. Me you have killed because you wanted to escape the accuser, and not to give an account of your lives. But that will not be as you suppose: far otherwise. For I say that there will be more accusers of you than there are now; accusers whom hitherto I have restrained: and as they are younger they will be more inconsiderate with you, and you will be more offended at them. If you think that by killing men you can prevent some one from censuring your evil lives, you are mistaken; that is not a way of escape which is either possible or honourable; the easiest and the noblest way is not to be disabling others, but to be improving yourselves. This is the prophecy which I utter before my departure to the judges who have condemned me.

31 Friends, who would have acquitted me, I would like also to talk with you about the thing which has come to pass, while the magistrates are busy, and before I go to the place at which I must die. Stay then a little, for we may as well talk with one another while there is time. You are my friends, and I should like to show you the meaning of this event which has happened to me. O my judges—for you I may truly call judges—I should like to tell you of a wonderful circumstance. Hitherto the divine faculty of which the internal oracle is the source has constantly been in the habit of opposing me even about trifles, if I was going to make a slip or error in any matter; and now as you see there has come upon me that which may be thought, and is generally believed to be, the last and worst evil. But the oracle made no sign of opposition, either when I was leaving my house in the morning, or when I was on my way to the court, or while I was speaking, at anything which I was going to say; and yet I have often been stopped in the middle of a speech, but now in nothing I either said or did touching the matter in hand has the oracle opposed me. What do I take to be the explanation of this silence? I will tell you. It is an intimation that what has happened to me is a good, and that those of us who think that death is an evil are in error. For the customary sign would surely have opposed me had I been going to evil and not to good.

32 Let us reflect in another way, and we shall see that there is great reason to hope that death is a good; for one of two things—either death is a state of nothingness and utter unconsciousness, or, as men say, there is a change and migration of the soul from this world to another. Now if you suppose that there is no consciousness, but a sleep like the sleep of him who is undisturbed even by dreams, death will be an unspeakable gain. For if a person were to select the night in which his sleep was undisturbed even by dreams, and were to compare with this the other days and nights of his life, and then were to tell us how many days and nights he had passed in the course of his life better and more pleasantly than this one, I think that any man, I will not say a private man, but even the great king will not find many such days or nights, when compared with the others. Now if death be of such a nature, I say that to die is gain; for eternity is then only a single night. But if death is the journey to another place, and there, as men say, all the dead abide, what good, O my friends and judges, can be greater than this? If indeed when the pilgrim arrives in the world below, he is delivered from the professors of justice in this world, and finds the true judges who are said to give judgment there, Minos and Rhadamanthus and Aeacus and Triptolemus, and other sons of God who were righteous in their own life, that pilgrimage will be worth making. What would not a man give if he might converse with Orpheus and Musaeus and Hesiod and Homer? Nay, if this be true, let me die again and again. I myself, too, shall have a wonderful interest in there meeting and conversing with Palamedes, and Ajax the son of Telamon, and any other ancient hero who has suffered death through an unjust judgment; and there will be no small pleasure, as I think, in comparing my own sufferings with theirs. Above all, I shall then be able to continue my search into true and false knowledge; as in this world, so also in the next; and I shall find out who is wise, and who pretends to be wise, and is not. What would not a man give, O judges, to be able to examine the leader of the great Trojan expedition; or Odysseus or Sisyphus, or numberless others, men and women too! What infinite delight would there be in conversing with them and asking them questions! In another world they do not put a man to death for asking questions: assuredly not. For besides being happier than we are, they will be immortal, if what is said is true.

33 Wherefore, O judges, be of good cheer about death, and know of a certainty, that no evil can happen to a good man, either in life or after death. He and his are not neglected by the gods; nor has my own approaching end happened by mere chance. But I see clearly that the time had arrived when it was better for me to die and be released from trouble; wherefore the oracle gave no sign. For which reason, also, I am not angry with my condemners, or with my accusers; they have done me no harm, although they did not mean to do me any good; and for this I may gently blame them. Still I have a favour to ask of them. When my sons are grown up, I would ask you, O my friends, to punish them; and I would have you trouble them, as I have troubled you, if they seem to care about riches, or anything, more than about virtue; or if they pretend to be something when they are really nothing,—then reprove them, as I have reproved you, for not caring about that for which they ought to care, and thinking that they are something when they are really nothing. And if you do this, both I and my sons will have received justice at your hands. The hour of departure has arrived, and we go our ways—I to die, and you to live. Which is better God only knows.

B. THE CRİTO

Chap. 1

    Socrates: WHY have you come at this hour, Crito? it must be quite early.

    Crito: Yes, certainly.

    Soc: What is the exact time?

    Cr: The dawn is breaking.

    Soc: I wonder the keeper of the prison would let you in.

    Cr: He knows me because I often come, Socrates; moreover. I have done him a kindness.

    Soc: And are you only just come?

    Cr: No, I came some time ago.

    Soc: Then why did you sit and say nothing, instead of awakening me at once?

    Cr: Why, indeed, Socrates, I myself would rather not have all this sleeplessness and sorrow. But I have been wondering at your peaceful slumbers, and that was the reason why I did not awaken you, because I wanted you to be out of pain. I have always thought you happy in the calmness of your temperament; but never did I see the like of the easy, cheerful way in which you bear this calamity.

    Soc: Why, Crito, when a man has reached my age he ought not to be repining at the prospect of death.

    Cr: And yet other old men find themselves in similar misfortunes, and age does not prevent them from repining.

    Soc: That may be. But you have not told me why you come at this early hour.

    Cr: I come to bring you a message which is sad and painful; not, as I believe, to yourself but to all of us who are your friends, and saddest of all to me.

    Soc: What! I suppose that the ship has come from Delos, on the arrival of which I am to die?

    Cr: No, the ship has not actually arrived, but she will probably be here to-day, as persons who have come from Sunium tell me that they have left her there; and therefore to-morrow, Socrates, will be the last day of your life.

Chap. 2

    Soc: Very well, Crito; if such is the will of the gods, I am willing; but my belief is that there will be a delay of a day.

    Cr: Why do you say this?

    Soc: I will tell you. I am to die on the day after the arrival of the ship?

    Cr: Yes; that is what the authorities say.

    Soc: But I do not think that the ship will be here until to-morrow; this I gather from a vision which I had last night, or rather only just now, when you fortunately allowed me to sleep.

    Cr: And what was the nature of the vision?

    Soc: There came to me the likeness of a woman, fair and comely, clothed in white raiment, who called to me and said: "O Socrates- The third day hence, to Phthia shalt thou go," [a quotation from Homer's *Iliad*].

    Cr: What a singular dream, Socrates!

    Soc: There can be no doubt about the meaning Crito, I think.

Chap. 3

    Cr: Yes: the meaning is only too clear. But, O! my beloved Socrates, let me entreat you once more to take my advice and escape. For if you die I shall not only lose a friend who can never be replaced, but there is another evil: people who do not know you and me will believe that I might have saved you if I had been willing to give money, but that I did not care. Now, can there be a worse disgrace than this- that I should be thought to value money more than the life of a friend? For the many will not be persuaded that I wanted you to escape, and that you refused.

Soc: But why, my dear Crito, should we care about the opinion of the many? Good men, and they are the only persons who are worth considering, will think of these things truly as they happened.

Cr: But do you see. Socrates, that the opinion of the many must be regarded, as is evident in your own case, because they can do the very greatest evil to anyone who has lost their good opinion?

Soc: I only wish, Crito, that they could; for then they could also do the greatest good, and that would be well. But the truth is, that they can do neither good nor evil: they cannot make a man wise or make him foolish; and whatever they do is the result of chance.

Chap. 4

Cr: Well, I will not dispute about that; but please to tell me, Socrates, whether you are not acting out of regard to me and your other friends: are you not afraid that if you escape hence we may get into trouble with the informers for having stolen you away, and lose either the whole or a great part of our property; or that even a worse evil may happen to us? Now, if this is your fear, be at ease; for in order to save you, we ought surely to run this or even a greater risk; be persuaded, then, and do as I say.

Soc: Yes, Crito, that is one fear which you mention, but by no means the only one.

Cr: Fear not. There are persons who at no great cost are willing to save you and bring you out of prison; and as for the informers, you may observe that they are far from being exorbitant in their demands; a little money will satisfy them. My means, which, as I am sure, are ample, are at your service, and if you have a scruple about spending all mine, here are strangers who will give you the use of theirs; and one of them, Simmias the Theban, has brought a sum of money for this very purpose; and Cebes and many others are willing to spend their money too. I say, therefore, do not on that account hesitate about making your escape, and do not say, as you did in the court, that you will have a difficulty in knowing what to do with yourself if you escape. For men will love you in other places to which you may go, and not in Athens only; there are friends of mine in Thessaly, if you like to go to them, who will value and protect you, and no Thessalian will give you any trouble.

Chap. 5

Nor can I think that you are justified, Socrates, in betraying your own life when you might be saved; this is playing into the hands of your enemies and destroyers; and moreover , I should say that you were betraying your children; for you might bring them up and educate them; instead of which you go away and leave them, and they will have to take their chance; and if they do not meet with the usual fate of orphans, there will be small thanks to you. No man should bring children into the world who is unwilling to persevere to the end in their nurture and education. But you are choosing the easier part, as I think, not the better and manlier, which would rather have become one who professes virtue in all his actions, like yourself. And, indeed, I am ashamed not only of you, but of us who are your friends, when I reflect that this entire business of yours will be attributed to our want of courage. The trial need never have come on, or might have been brought to another issue; and the end of all, which is the crowning absurdity, will seem to have been permitted by us, through cowardice and baseness, who might have saved you, as you might have saved yourself, if we had been good for anything (for there was no difficulty in escaping); and we did not see how disgraceful, Socrates, and also miserable all this will be to us as well as to you. Make your mind up then, or rather have your mind already made up, for the time of deliberation is over, and there is only one thing to be done, which must be done, if at all, this very night, and which any delay will render all but impossible; I beseech you therefore, Socrates, to be persuaded by me, and to do as I say.

Chap. 6

Soc: Dear Crito, your zeal is invaluable, if a right one; but if wrong, the greater the zeal the greater the evil; and therefore we ought to consider whether these things shall be done or not. For I am and always have been one of those natures who must be guided by reason, whatever the reason may be which upon reflection appears to me to be the best; and now that this fortune has come upon me, I cannot put away the reasons which I have before given: the principles which I have hitherto honored and revered I still honor, and unless we can find other and better principles on the instant, I am certain not to agree with you; no, not even if the power of the multitude could inflict many more imprisonments, confiscations, deaths, frightening us like children with hobgoblin terrors. But what will be the fairest way of considering the question? Shall I return to your old argument about the opinions of men, some of which are to be regarded, and others, as we were saying, are not to be regarded? Now were we right in maintaining this before I was condemned? And has the argument which was once good now proved to be talk for the sake of talking; in fact an amusement only, and altogether vanity? That is what I want to consider with your help, Crito: whether, under my present circumstances, the argument appears to be in any way different or not; and is to be allowed by me or disallowed. That argument, which, as I believe, is maintained by many who assume to be authorities, was to the effect, as I was saying, that the opinions of some men are to be regarded, and of other men not to be regarded. Now you, Crito, are a disinterested person who are not going to die to-morrow- at least, there is no human probability of this, and you are therefore not liable to be deceived by the circumstances in which you are placed. Tell me, then, whether I am right in saying that some opinions, and the opinions of some men only, are to be valued, and other opinions, and the opinions of other men, are not to be valued. I ask you whether I was right in maintaining this?

Cr: Certainly.

Soc: The good are to be regarded, and not the bad?

Cr: Yes.

Soc: And the opinions of the wise are good, and the opinions of the unwise are evil?

Cr: Certainly.

Chap. 7

Soc: And what was said about another matter? Was the disciple in gymnastics supposed to attend to the praise and blame and opinion of every man, or of one man only- his physician or trainer, whoever that was?

Cr: Of one man only.

Soc: And he ought to fear the censure and welcome the praise of that one only, and not of the many?

Cr: That is clear.

Soc: And he ought to live and train, and eat and drink in the way which seems good to his single master who has understanding, rather than according to the opinion of all other men put together?

Cr: True.

Soc: And if he disobeys and disregards the opinion and approval of the one, and regards the opinion of the many who have no understanding, will he not suffer evil?

Cr: Certainly he will.

Soc: And what will the evil be, whither tending and what affcting, in the disobedient person?

Cr: Clearly, affecting the body; that is what is destroyed by the evil.

Soc: Very good; and is not this true, Crito, of other things which we need not separately enumerate? In the matter of just and unjust, fair and foul, good and evil, which are the subjects of our present consultation, ought we to follow the opinion of the many and to fear them; or the opinion of the one man who has understanding, and whom we ought to fear and reverence more than all the rest of the world: and whom deserting we shall destroy and injure that principle in us which may be assumed to be improved by justice and deteriorated by injustice; is there not such a principle?

Cr: Certainly there is, Socrates.

Chap. 8

Soc: Take a parallel instance; if, acting under the advice of men who have no understanding, we destroy that which is improvable by health and deteriorated by disease- when that has been destroyed, I say, would life be worth having? And that is- the body?

Cr: Yes.

Soc: Could we live, having an evil and corrupted body?

Cr: Certainly not.

Soc: And will life be worth having, if that higher part of man be depraved, which is improved by justice and deteriorated by injustice? Do we suppose that principle, whatever it may be in man, which has to do with justice and injustice, to be inferior to the body?

Cr: Certainly not.

Soc: More honored, then?

Cr: Far more honored.

Soc: Then, my friend, we must not regard what the many say of us: but what he, the one man who has understanding of just and unjust, will say, and what the truth will say. And therefore you begin in error when you suggest that we should regard the opinion of the many about just and unjust, good and evil, honorable and dishonorable. Well, someone will say, "But the many can kill us."

Cr: Yes, Socrates; that will clearly be the answer.

Soc: That is true; but still I find with surprise that the old argument is, as I conceive, unshaken as ever. And I should like to know Whether I may say the same of another proposition- that not life, but a good life, is to be chiefly valued?

Cr: Yes, that also remains.

Soc: And a good life is equivalent to a just and honorable one- that holds also?

Cr: Yes, that holds.

Chap. 9

Soc: From these premises I proceed to argue the question whether I ought or ought not to try to escape without the consent of the Athenians: and if I am clearly right in escaping, then I will make the attempt; but if not, I will abstain. The other considerations which you mention, of money and loss of character, and the duty of educating children, are, I fear, only the doctrines of the multitude, who would be as ready to call people to life, if they were able, as they are to put them to death- and with as little reason. But now, since the argument has thus far prevailed, the only question which remains to be considered is, whether we shall do rightly either in escaping or in suffering others to aid in our escape and paying them in money and thanks, or whether we shan not do rightly; and if the latter, then death or any other calamity which may ensue on my remaining here must not be allowed to enter into the calculation.

Cr: I think that you are right, Socrates; how then shall we proceed?

Soc: Let us consider the matter together, and do you either refute me if you can, and I will be convinced; or else cease, my dear friend, from repeating to me that I ought to escape against the wishes of the Athenians: for I am extremely desirous to be persuaded by you, but not against my own better judgment. And now please to consider my first position, and do your best to answer me.

Cr: I will do my best.

Chap. 10

Soc: Are we to say that we are never intentionally to do wrong, or that in one way we ought and in another way we ought not to do wrong, or is doing wrong always evil and dishonorable, as I was just now saying, and as has been already acknowledged by us? Are all our former admissions which were made within a few days to be thrown away? And have we, at our age, been earnestly discoursing with one another all our life long only to discover that we are no better than children? Or are we to rest assured, in spite of the opinion of the many, and in spite of consequences whether better or worse, of the truth of what was then said, that injustice is always an evil and dishonor to him who acts unjustly? Shall we affirm that?

Cr: Yes.

Soc: Then we must do no wrong?

Cr: Certainly not.

Soc: Nor when injured injure in return, as the many imagine; for we must injure no one at all?

Cr: Clearly not.

Soc: Again, Crito, may we do evil?

Cr: Surely not, Socrates.

Soc: And what of doing evil in return for evil, which is the morality of the many-is that just or not?

Cr: Not just.

Soc: For doing evil to another is the same as injuring him?

Cr: Very true.

Soc: Then we ought not to retaliate or render evil for evil to anyone, whatever evil we may have suffered from him. But I would have you consider, Crito, whether you really mean what you are saying. For this opinion has never been held, and never will be held, by any considerable number of persons; and those who are agreed and those who are not agreed upon this point have no common ground, and can only despise one another, when they see how widely they differ. Tell me, then, whether you agree with and assent to my first principle, that neither injury nor retaliation nor warding off evil by evil is ever right. And shall that be the premise of our agreement? Or do you decline and dissent from this? For this has been of old and is still my opinion; but, if you are of another opinion, let me hear what you have to say. If, however, you remain of the same mind as formerly, I will proceed to the next step.

Cr: You may proceed, for I have not changed my mind.

Soc: Then I will proceed to the next step, which may be put in the form of a question: Ought a man to do what he admits to be right, or ought he to betray the right?

Cr: He ought to do what he thinks right.

Chap. 11

Soc: But if this is true, what is the application? In leaving the prison against the will of the Athenians, do I wrong any? or rather do I not wrong those whom I ought least to wrong? Do I not desert the principles which were acknowledged by us to be just? What do you say?

Cr: I cannot tell, Socrates, for I do not know.

Soc: Then consider the matter in this way: Imagine that I am about to play truant (you may call the proceeding by any name which you like), and the laws and the government come and interrogate me: "Tell us, Socrates," they say; "what are you about? are you going by an act of yours to overturn us- the laws and the whole State, as far as in you lies? Do you imagine that a State can subsist and not be overthrown, in which the decisions of law have no power, but are set aside and overthrown by individuals?" What will be our answer, Crito, to these and the like words? Anyone, and especially a clever rhetorician, will have a good deal to urge about the evil of setting aside the law which requires a sentence to be carried out; and we might reply, "Yes; but the State has injured us and given an unjust sentence." Suppose I say that?

Cr: Very good, Socrates.

Chap. 12

Soc: "And was that our agreement with you?" the law would say, "or were you to abide by the sentence of the State?" And if I were to express astonishment at their saying this, the law would probably add: "Answer, Socrates, instead of opening your eyes: you are in the habit of asking and answering questions. Tell us what complaint you have to make against us which justifies you in attempting to destroy us and the State? In the first place did we not bring you into existence? Your father married your mother by our aid and begat you. Say whether you have any objection to urge against those of us who regulate marriage?" None, I should reply. "Or against those of us who regulate the system of nurture and education of children in which you were trained? Were not the laws, who have the charge of this, right in commanding your father to train you in music and gymnastic?" Right, I should reply. "Well, then, since you were brought into the world and nurtured and educated by us, can you deny in the first place that you are our child and slave, as your fathers were before you? And if this is true you are not on equal terms with us; nor can you think that you have a right to do to us what we are doing to you. Would you have any right to strike or revile or do any other evil to a father or to your master, if you had one, when you have been struck or reviled by him, or received some other evil at his hands?- you would not say this? And because we think right to destroy you, do you think that you have any right to destroy us in return, and your country as far as in you lies? And will you, O professor of true virtue, say that you are justified in this? Has a philosopher like you failed to discover that our country is more to be valued and higher and holier far than mother or father or any ancestor, and more to be regarded in the eyes of the gods and of men of understanding? also to be soothed, and gently and reverently entreated when angry, even more than a father, and if not persuaded, obeyed? And when we are punished by her, whether with imprisonment or stripes, the punishment is to be endured in silence; and if she leads us to wounds or death in battle, thither we follow as is right; neither may anyone yield or retreat or leave his rank, but whether in battle or in a court of law, or in any other place, he must do what his city and his country order him; or he must change their view of what is just: and if he may do no violence to his father or mother, much less may he do violence to his country." What answer shall we make to this, Crito? Do the laws speak truly, or do they not?

Cr: I think that they do.

Chap. 13

Soc: Then the laws will say: "Consider, Socrates, if this is true, that in your present attempt you are going to do us wrong. For, after having brought you into the world, and nurtured and educated you, and given you and every other citizen a share in every good that we had to give, we further proclaim and give the right to every Athenian, that if he does not like us when he has come of age and has seen the ways of the city, and made our acquaintance, he may go where he pleases and take his goods with him; and none of us laws will forbid him or interfere with him. Any of you who does not like us and the city, and who wants to go to a colony or to any other city, may go where he likes, and take his goods with him. But he who has experience of the manner in which we order justice and administer the State, and still remains, has entered into an implied contract that he will do as we command him. And he who disobeys us is, as we maintain, thrice wrong: first, because in disobeying us he is disobeying his parents; secondly, because we are the authors of his education; thirdly, because he has made an agreement with us that he will duly obey our commands; and he neither obeys them nor convinces us that our commands are wrong; and we do not rudely impose them, but give him the alternative of obeying or convincing us; that is what we offer and he does neither.

Chap. 14

These are the sort of accusations to which, as we were saying, you, Socrates, will be exposed if you accomplish your intentions; you, above all other Athenians." Suppose I ask, why is this? they will justly retort upon me that I above all other men have acknowledged the agreement. "There is clear proof," they will say, "Socrates, that we and the city were not displeasing to you. Of all Athenians you have been the most constant resident in the city, which, as you never leave, you may be supposed to love. For you never went out of the city either to see the games, except once when you went to the Isthmus, or to any other place unless when you were on military service; nor did you travel as other men do. Nor had you any curiosity to know other States or their laws: your affections did not go beyond us and our State; we were your especial favorites, and you acquiesced in our government of you; and this is the State in which you begat your children, which is a proof of your satisfaction. Moreover, you might, if you had liked, have fixed the penalty at banishment in the course of the trial-the State which refuses to let you go now would have let you go then. But you pretended that you preferred death to exile, and that you were not grieved at death. And now you have forgotten these fine sentiments, and pay no respect to us, the laws, of whom you are the destroyer; and are doing what only a miserable slave would do, running away and turning your back upon the compacts and agreements which you made as a citizen. And first of all answer this very question: Are we right in saying that you agreed to be governed according to us in deed, and not in word only? Is that true or not?" How shall we answer that, Crito? Must we not agree?

Cr: There is no help, Socrates.

Soc: Then will they not say: "You, Socrates, are breaking the covenants and agreements which you made with us at your leisure, not in any haste or under any compulsion or deception, but having had seventy years to think of them, during which time you were at liberty to leave the city, if we were not to your mind, or if our covenants appeared to you to be unfair. You had your choice, and might have gone either to Sparta or Crete, which you often praise for their good government, or to some other Greek or foreign State. Whereas you, above all other Athenians, seemed to be so fond of the State, or, in other words, of us her laws (for who would like a State that has no laws?), that you never stirred out of her: the halt, the blind, the maimed, were not more stationary in her than you were. And now you run away and forsake your agreements. Not so, Socrates, if you will take our advice; do not make yourself ridiculous by escaping out of the city.

Chap. 15

For just consider, if you transgress and err in this sort of way, what good will you do, either to yourself or to your friends? That your friends will be driven into exile and deprived of citizenship, or will lose their property, is tolerably certain; and you yourself, if you fly to one of the neighboring cities, as, for example, Thebes or Megara, both of which are well-governed cities, will come to them as an enemy, Socrates, and their government will be against you, and all patriotic citizens will cast an evil eye upon you as a subverter of the laws, and you will confirm in the minds of the judges the justice of their own condemnation of you. For he who is a corrupter of the laws is more than likely to be corrupter of the young and foolish portion of mankind. Will you then flee from well-ordered cities and virtuous men? and is existence worth having on these terms? Or will you go to them without shame, and talk to them, Socrates? And what will you say to them? What you say here about virtue and justice and institutions and laws being the best things among men? Would that be decent of you? Surely not. But if you go away from well-governed States to Crito's friends in Thessaly, where there is great disorder and license, they will be charmed to have the tale of your escape from prison, set off with ludicrous particulars of the manner in which you were wrapped in a goatskin or some other disguise, and metamorphosed as the fashion of runaways is- that is very likely; but will there be no one to remind you that in your old age you violated the most sacred laws from a miserable desire of a little more life? Perhaps not, if you keep them in a good temper; but if they are out of temper you will hear many degrading things; you will live, but how?- as the flatterer of all men, and the servant of all men; and doing what?- eating and drinking in Thessaly, having gone abroad in order that you may get a dinner. And where will be your fine sentiments about justice and virtue then? Say that you wish to live for the sake of your children, that you may bring them up and educate them- will you take them into Thessaly and deprive them of Athenian citizenship? Is that the benefit which you would confer upon them? Or are you under the impression that they will be better cared for and educated here if you are still alive, although absent from them; for that your friends will take care of them? Do you fancy that if you are an inhabitant of Thessaly they will take care of them, and if you are an inhabitant of the other world they will not take care of them? Nay; but if they who call themselves friends are truly friends, they surely will.

Chap. 16

Listen, then, Socrates, to us who have brought you up. Think not of life and children first, and of justice afterwards, but of justice first, that you may be justified before the princes of the world below. For neither will you nor any that belong to you be happier or holier or juster in this life, or happier in another, if you do as Crito bids. Now you depart in innocence, a sufferer and not a doer of evil; a victim, not of the laws, but of men. But if you go forth, returning evil for evil, and injury for injury, breaking the covenants and agreements which you have made with us, and wronging those whom you ought least to wrong, that is to say, yourself, your friends, your country, and us, we shall be angry with you while you live, and our brethren, the laws in the world below, will receive you as an enemy; for they will know that you have done your best to destroy us. Listen, then, to us and not to Crito."

Chap. 17

This is the voice which I seem to hear murmuring in my ears, like the sound of the flute in the ears of the mystic; that voice, I say, is humming in my ears, and prevents me from hearing any other. And I know that anything more which you will say will be in vain. Yet speak, if you have anything to say.

Cr: I have nothing to say, Socrates.

Soc: Then let me follow the intimations of the will of God.

C. THE PHAEDO

Chap. 1

Echecrates: Were you yourself, Phaedo, in the prison with Socrates on the day when he drank the poison?

Phaedo: Yes, Echecrates, I was.

Ech: I wish that you would tell me about his death. What did he say in his last hours? We were informed that he died by taking poison, but no one knew anything more; for no Phliasian ever goes to Athens now, and a long time has elapsed since any Athenian found his way to Phlius, and therefore we had no clear account.

Phaed: Did you not hear of the proceedings at the trial?

Ech: Yes; someone told us about the trial, and we could not understand why, having been condemned, he was put to death, as appeared, not at the time, but long afterwards. What was the reason of this?

Phaed: An accident, Echecrates. The reason was that the stern of the ship which the Athenians send to Delos happened to have been crowned on the day before he was tried.

Ech: What is this ship?

Phaed: This is the ship in which, as the Athenians say, Theseus went to Crete when he took with him the fourteen youths, and was the saviour of them and of himself. And they were said to have vowed to Apollo at the time, that if they were saved they would make an annual pilgrimage to Delos. Now this custom still continues, and the whole period of the voyage to and from Delos, beginning when the priest of Apollo crowns the stern of the ship, is a holy season, during which the city is not allowed to be polluted by public executions; and often, when the vessel is detained by adverse winds, there may be a very considerable delay. As I was saying, the ship was crowned on the day before the trial, and this was the reason why Socrates lay in prison and was not put to death until long after he was condemned.

Chap. 2

Ech: What was the manner of his death, Phaedo? What was said or done? And which of his friends had he with him? Or were they not allowed by the authorities to be present? And did he die alone?

Phaed. No; there were several of his friends with him.

Ech. If you have nothing to do, I wish that you would tell me what passed, as exactly as you can.

Phaed. I have nothing to do, and will try to gratify your wish. For to me, too, there is no greater pleasure than to have Socrates brought to my recollection, whether I speak myself or hear another speak of him.

Ech. You will have listeners who are of the same mind with you, and I hope that you will be as exact as you can.

Phaed. I remember the strange feeling which came over me at being with him. For I could hardly believe that I was present at the death of a friend, and therefore I did not pity him, Echecrates; his mien and his language were so noble and fearless in the hour of death that to me he appeared blessed. I thought that in going to the other world he could not be without a divine call, and that he would be happy, if any man ever was, when he arrived there, and therefore I did not pity him as might seem natural at such a time. But neither could I feel the pleasure which I usually felt in philosophical discourse (for philosophy was the theme of which we spoke). I was pleased, and I was also pained, because I knew that he was soon to die, and this strange mixture of feeling was shared by us all; we were laughing and weeping by turns....

Chap. 3

Phaed: I will begin at the beginning, and endeavor to repeat the entire conversation. You must understand that we had been previously in the habit of assembling early in the morning at the court in which the trial was held, and which is not far from the prison. There we remained talking with one another until the opening of the prison doors (for they were not opened very early), and then went in and generally passed the day with Socrates. On the last morning the meeting was earlier than usual; this was owing to our having heard on the previous evening that the sacred ship had arrived from Delos, and therefore we agreed to meet very early at the accustomed place....

Chap. 63

Socrates: "... As for Me already, as the tragic poet would say, the voice of fate calls. Soon I must drink the poison; and I think that I had better repair to the bath first, in order that the women may not have the trouble of washing my body after I am dead."

Chap. 64

When he had done speaking, Crito said: "And have you any commands for us, Socrates-anything to say about your children, or any other matter in which we can serve you?" "Nothing particular," he said: "only, as I have always told you, I would have you look to yourselves; that is a service which you may always be doing to me and mine as well as to yourselves. And you need not make professions; for if you take no thought for yourselves, and walk not according to the precepts which I have given you, not now for the first time, the warmth of your professions will be of no avail." "We will do our best," said Crito. "But in what way would you have us bury you?" "In any way that you like; only you must get hold of me, and take care that I do not walk away from you." Then he turned to us, and added with a smile: "I cannot make Crito believe that I am the same Socrates who have been talking and conducting the argument; he fancies that I am the other Socrates whom he will soon see, a dead body-and he asks, How shall he bury me? And though I have spoken many words in the endeavor to show that when I have drunk the poison I shall leave you and go to the joys of the blessed-these words of mine, with which I comforted you and myself, have had, I perceive, no effect upon Crito. And therefore I want you to be surety for me now, as he was surety for me at the trial: but let the promise be of another sort; for he was my surety to the judges that I would remain, but you must be my surety to him that I shall not remain, but go away and depart; and then he will suffer less at my death, and not be grieved when he sees my body being burned or buried. I would not have him sorrow at my hard lot, or say at the burial, 'Thus we lay out Socrates,' or, 'Thus we follow him to the grave or bury him;' for false words are not only evil in themselves, but they infect the soul with evil. Be of good cheer, then, my dear Crito, and say that you are burying my body only, and do with that as is usual, and as you think best."

Chap. 65

When he had spoken these words, he arose and went into the bath chamber with Crito, who bade us wait; and we waited, talking and thinking of the subject of discourse, and also of the greatness of our sorrow; he was like a father of whom we were being bereaved, and we were about to pass the rest of our lives as orphans. When he had taken the bath his children were brought to him-(he had two young sons and an elder one); and the women of his family also came, and he talked to them and gave them a few directions in the presence of Crito; and he then dismissed them and returned to us. Now the hour of sunset was near, for a good deal of time had passed while he was within. When he came out, he sat down with us again after his bath, but not much was said. Soon the jailer, who was the servant of the Eleven [officials in charge of the prison[, entered and stood by him, saying: "To you, Socrates, whom I know to be the noblest and gentlest and best of all who ever came to this place, I will not impute the angry feelings of other men, who rage and swear at me when, in obedience to the authorities, I bid them drink the poison-indeed, I am sure that you will not be angry with me; for others, as you are aware, and not I, are the guilty cause. And so fare you well, and try to bear lightly what must needs be; you know my errand." Then bursting into tears he turned away and went out. Socrates looked at him and said: "I return your good wishes, and will do as you bid." Then, turning to us, he said, "How charming the man is: since I have been in prison he has always been coming to see me, and at times he would talk to me, and was as good as could be to me, and now see how generously he sorrows for me. But we must do as he says, Crito; let the cup be brought, if the poison is prepared: if not, let the attendant prepare some." "Yet," said Crito, "the sun is still upon the hilltops, and many a one has taken the draught late, and after the announcement has been made to him, he has eaten and drunk, and indulged in sensual delights; do not hasten then, there is still time." Socrates said: "Yes, Crito, and they of whom you speak are right in doing thus, for they think that they will gain by the delay; but I am right in not doing thus, for I do not think that I should gain anything by drinking the poison a little later; I should be sparing and saving a life which is already gone: I could only laugh at myself for this. Please then to do as I say, and not to refuse me."

Chap. 66

Crito, when he heard this, made a sign to the servant, and the servant went in, and remained for some time, and then returned with the jailer carrying a cup of poison. Socrates said: "You, my good friend, who are experienced in these matters, shall give me directions how I am to proceed." The man answered: "You have only to walk about until your legs are heavy, and then to lie down, and the poison will act." At the same time he handed the cup to Socrates, who in the easiest and gentlest manner, without the least fear or change of color or feature, looking at the man with all his eyes, Echecrates, as his manner was, took the cup and said: "What do you say about making a libation out of this cup to any god? May I, or not?" The man answered: "We only prepare, Socrates, just so much as we deem enough." "I understand," he said: "yet I may and must pray to the gods to prosper my journey from this to that other world-may this, then, which is my prayer, be granted to me." Then holding the cup to his lips, quite readily and cheerfully he drank off the poison. And hitherto most of us had been able to control our sorrow; but now when we saw him drinking, and saw too that he had finished the draught, we could no longer forbear, and in spite of myself my own tears were flowing fast; so that I covered my face and wept over myself, for certainly I was not weeping over him, but at the thought of my own calamity in having lost such a companion. Nor was I the first, for Crito, when he found himself unable to restrain his tears, had got up and moved away, and I followed; and at that moment. Apollodorus, who had been weeping all the time, broke out in a loud cry which made cowards of us all. Socrates alone retained his calmness: "What is this strange outcry?" he said. "I sent away the women mainly in order that they might not offend in this way, for I have heard that a man should die in peace. Be quiet, then, and have patience." When we heard that, we were ashamed, and refrained our tears; and he walked about until, as he said, his legs began to fail, and then he lay on his back, according to the directions, and the man who gave him the poison now and then looked at his feet and legs; and after a while he pressed his foot hard and asked him if he could feel; and he said, "no;" and then his leg, and so upwards and upwards, and showed us that he was cold and stiff. And he felt them himself, and said: "When the poison reaches the heart, that will be the end." He was beginning to grow cold about the groin, when he uncovered his face, for he had covered himself up, and said (they were his last words)-he said: "Crito, I owe a cock to Asclepius; will you remember to pay the debt?" "The debt shall be paid," said Crito; "is there anything else?" There was no answer to this question; but in a minute or two a movement was heard, and the attendants uncovered him; his eyes were set, and Crito closed his eyes and mouth.

Chap. 67

Such was the end, Echecrates, of our friend, whom I may truly call the wisest, and justest, and best of all the men whom I have ever known.

Reading 14

The Maccabean Revolt

The Hellenistic world, resulting from the conquest of the Persian Empire by Alexander the Great, broke down the political and cultural barriers between Greece and the ancient Near East. The blending together of these two different cultural traditions (termed syncretism by modern scholars) proceeded relatively peacefully. One major exception to this general rule was the clash between Jewish monotheism and Greek polytheism. The Jewish response to Hellenistic culture was varied and complex. Many Jews left their homeland and migrated to other cities in search of job opportunities. By the end of the second century B.C., for example, Jews comprised a substantial minority in the large cosmopolitan cities of Alexandria in Egypt and Antioch in Syria, where many Jews adopted Hellenistic culture in varying degrees. Although Judah itself remained more isolated from the surrounding Hellenistic culture, it was not unaffected by it.

The following passage is taken from *I Maccabees*, a sacred book of the Jews, included in the Catholic *Bible* among *The Apocrypha*, but excluded from the Protestant version of *The Bible*. This text describes how King Antiochus IV Epiphanes, ruler of the Seleucid Empire, in 167 B.C. attempted to impose polytheism upon the Jews of Judah and also tried to stamp out the traditional practices of the Jews: their sacred literature, circumcision, their dietary rules, and especially their monotheism. The gymnasium mentioned in 1.14 epitomized Greek culture: young men exercising naked, which would have inadvertently exposed their own lack of circumcision. This imposition of Hellenistic culture upon the people of Judah provoked a violent uprising from the Jews, who engaged in a guerilla war against Jewish Hellenizers and the agents of the Seleucid king, finally ending in the defeat of the latter and the vindication of Jewish religious freedom, henceforth commemorated by the annual celebration of Hanukkah.

(Taken from the King James Version)

CHAPTER 1. **1** And it happened, after that Alexander son of Philip, the Macedonian, who came out of the land of Chettiim [Greece], had smitten Darius king of the Persians and Medes, that he reigned in his stead, the first over Greece, **2** And made many wars, and won many strong holds, and slew the kings of the earth, **3** And went through to the ends of the earth, and took spoils of many nations, insomuch that the earth was quiet before him; whereupon he was exalted and his heart was lifted up. **4** And he gathered a mighty strong host and ruled over countries, and nations, and kings, who became tributaries unto him. **5** And after these things he fell sick, and perceived that he should die.

6 Wherefore he called his servants, such as were honourable, and had been brought up with him from his youth, and parted his kingdom among them, while he was yet alive.   **7** So Alexander reigned twelves years, and then died.   **8** And his servants bare rule every one in his place.   **9** And after his death they all put crowns upon themselves; so did their sons after them many years: and evils were multiplied in the earth.   **10** And there came out of them a wicked root Antiochus surnamed Epiphanes, son of Antiochus the king, who had been an hostage at Rome, and he reigned in the hundred and thirty and seventh year of the kingdom of the Greeks [175 B.C.].   **11** In those days went there out of Israel wicked men, who persuaded many, saying, Let us go and make a covenant with the heathen that are round about us: for since we departed from them we have had much sorrow.   **12** So this device pleased them well.   **13** Then certain of the people were so forward herein, that they went to the king, who gave them licence to do after the ordinances of the heathen: **14** Whereupon they built a place of exercise [a Greek gymnasium] at Jerusalem according to the customs of the heathen: **15** And made themselves uncircumcised, and forsook the holy covenant, and joined themselves to the heathen, and were sold to do mischief.   **16** Now when the kingdom was established before Antiochus, he thought to reign over Egypt that he might have the dominion of two realms.   **17** Wherefore he entered into Egypt with a great multitude, with chariots, and elephants, and horsemen, and a great navy,   **18** And made war against Ptolemee king of Egypt: but Ptolemee was afraid of him, and fled; and many were wounded to death.   **19** Thus they got the strong cities in the land of Egypt and he took the spoils thereof.   **20** And after that Antiochus had smitten Egypt, he returned again in the hundred forty and third year [169 B.C.], and went up against Israel and Jerusalem with a great multitude,   **21** And entered proudly into the sanctuary, and took away the golden altar, and the candlestick of light, and all the vessels thereof,   **22** And the table of the shewbread, and the pouring vessels, and the vials. and the censers of gold, and the veil, and the crown, and the golden ornaments that were before the temple, all which he pulled off.   **23** He took also the silver and the gold, and the precious vessels: also he took the hidden treasures which he found.   **24** And when he had taken all away, he went into his own land, having made a great massacre, and spoken very proudly.   **25** Therefore there was a great mourning in Israel, in every place where they were;   **26** So that the princes and elders mourned, the virgins and young men were made feeble, and the beauty of women was changed.   **27** Every bridegroom took up lamentation, and she that sat in the marriage chamber was in heaviness,   **28** The land also was moved for the inhabitants thereof, and all the house of Jacob was covered with confusion.   **29** And after two years fully expired [167 B.C.] the king sent his chief collector of tribute unto the cities of Juda, who came unto Jerusalem with a great multitude,   **30** And spake peaceable words unto them, but all was deceit: for when they had given him credence, he fell suddenly upon the city, and smote it very sore, and destroyed much people of Israel.   **31** And when he had taken the spoils of the city, he set it on fire, and pulled down the houses and walls thereof on every side.   **32** But the women and children took they captive, and possessed the cattle.   **33** Then builded they the city of David with a great and strong wall, and with mighty towers, and made it a strong hold for them.   **34** And they put therein a sinful nation, wicked men, and fortified themselves therein.   **35** They stored it also with armour and victuals, and when they had gathered together the spoils of Jerusalem, they laid them up there, and so they became a sore snare: **36** For it was a place to lie in wait against the sanctuary, and an evil adversary to Israel.   **37** Thus they shed innocent blood on every side of the sanctuary, and defiled it: **38** Insomuch that the inhabitants of Jerusalem fled because of them: whereupon the city was made an habitation of strangers, and became strange to those that were born in her; and her own children left her.   **39** Her sanctuary was laid waste like a wilderness, her feasts were turned into mourning, her sabbaths into reproach her honour into contempt.   **40** As had been her glory, so was her dishonour increased, and her excellency was turned into mourning.   **41** Moreover king Antiochus wrote to his whole kingdom, that all should be one people,   **42** And every one should leave his laws: so all the heathen agreed according to the commandment of the king.   **43** Yea, many also of the Israelites consented to his religion, and sacrificed unto idols, and profaned the sabbath.   **44** For the king had sent letters by messengers unto Jerusalem and the cities of Juda that they should follow the strange laws of the land,   **45** And forbid burnt offerings, and sacrifice, and drink offerings, in the temple; and that they should profane the sabbaths and festival days: **46** And pollute the sanctuary and holy people: **47** Set up altars, and groves, and chapels of idols, and sacrifice swine's flesh, and unclean beasts: **48** That they should also leave their children uncircumcised, and make their souls abominable with all manner of uncleanness and profanation: **49** To the end they might forget the law, and change all the ordinances.   **50** And whosoever would not do according to the commandment of the king, he said, he should die.   **51** In the selfsame manner wrote he to his whole kingdom, and appointed overseers over all the people, commanding the cities of Juda to sacrifice, city by city.   **52** Then many of the people were gathered unto them, to wit every one that forsook the law; and so they committed evils in the land;   **53** And drove the Israelites into secret places, even wheresoever they could flee for succour.   **54** Now the fifteenth day of the month Casleu, in the hundred forty and fifth year [167 B.C.], they set up the abomination of desolation upon the altar, and builded idol altars throughout the cities of Juda on every side;   **55** And burnt incense at the doors of their houses, and in the streets.   **56** And when they had rent in pieces the books of the law which they found, they burnt them with fire.   **57** And whosoever was found with any the book of the testament, or if any committed to the law, the king's commandment was, that they should put him to death.   **58** Thus did they by their authority unto the Israelites every month, to as many as were found in the cities.   **59** Now the five and twentieth day of the month they did sacrifice upon the idol altar, which was upon the altar of God.   **60** At which time according to the commandment they put to death certain women, that had caused their children to be circumcised.   **61** And they hanged the infants about their necks, and rifled their houses, and slew them that had circumcised them.   **62** Howbeit many in Israel were fully resolved and confirmed in themselves not to eat any unclean thing.   **63** Wherefore the rather to die, that they might not be defiled with meats, and that they might not profane the holy covenant: so then they died.   **64** And there was very great wrath upon Israel.

CHAPTER 2.   **1** In those days arose Mattathias the son of John, the son of Simeon, a priest of the sons of Joarib, from Jerusalem, and dwelt in Modin.   **2** And he had five sons, Joannan, called Caddis: **3** Simon; called Thassi: **4** Judas, who was called Maccabeus: **5** Eleazar, called Avaran: and Jonathan, whose surname was Apphus.   **6** And when he saw the blasphemies that were committed in Juda and Jerusale,   **7** He said, Woe is me! wherefore was I born to see this misery of my people, and of the holy city, and to dwell there, when it was delivered into the hand of the enemy, and the sanctuary into the hand of strangers?   **8** Her temple is become as a man without glory.   **9** Her glorious vessels are carried away into captivity, her infants are slain in the streets, her young men with the sword of the enemy.   **10** What nation hath not had a part in her kingdom and gotten of her spoils?   **11** All her ornaments are taken away; of a free woman she is become a bondslave.   **12** And, behold, our sanctuary, even our beauty and our glory, is laid waste, and the Gentiles have profaned it.   **13** To what end therefore shall we live any longer?   **14** Then Mattathias and his sons rent their clothes, and put on sackcloth, and mourned very sore.   **15** In the mean while the king's officers, such as compelled the people to revolt, came into the city Modin, to make them sacrifice.   **16** And when many of Israel came unto them, Mattathias also and his sons came together.   **17** Then answered the king's officers, and said to Mattathias on this wise, "Thou art a ruler, and an honourable and great man in this city, and strengthened with sons and brethren: **18** Now therefore come thou first, and fulfil the king's commandment, like as all the heathen have done, yea, and the men of Juda also, and such as remain at Jerusalem: so shalt thou and thy house be in the number of the king's friends, and thou and thy children shall be honoured with silver and gold, and many rewards."   **19** Then Mattathias answered and spake with a loud voice, "Though all the nations that are under the king's dominion obey him, and fall away every one from the religion of their fathers, and give consent to his commandments: **20** Yet will I and my sons and my brethren walk in the covenant of our fathers.   **21** God forbid that we should forsake the law and the ordinances.   **22** We will not hearken to the king's words, to go from our religion, either on the right hand, or the left."   **23** Now when he had left speaking these words, there came one of the Jews in the sight of all to sacrifice on the altar which was at Modin, according to the king's commandment.   **24** Which thing when Mattathias saw, he was inflamed with zeal, and his reins trembled, neither could he forbear to shew his anger according to judgment: wherefore he ran, and slew him upon the altar.   **25** Also the king's commissioner, who compelled men to sacrifice, he killed at that time, and the altar he pulled down.   **26** Thus dealt he zealously for the law of God like as Phinees did unto Zambri the son of Salom.   **27** And Mattathias cried throughout the city with a loud voice, saying, "Whosoever is zealous of the law, and maintaineth the covenant, let him follow me."   **28** So he and his sons fled into the mountains, and left all that ever they had in the city.   **29** Then many that sought after justice and judgment went down into the wilderness, to dwell there: **30** Both they, and their children, and their wives; and their cattle; because afflictions increased sore upon them.   **31** Now when it was told the king's servants, and the host that was at Jerusalem, in the city of David, that certain men, who had broken the king's commandment, were gone down into the secret places in the wilderness,   **32** They pursued after them a great number, and having overtaken them, they camped against them, and made war against them on the sabbath day.   **33** And they said unto them, "Let that which ye have done hitherto suffice; come forth, and do according to the commandment of the king, and ye shall live."   **34** But they said, "We will not come forth, neither will we do the king's commandment, to profane the sabbath day."   **35** So then they gave them the battle with all speed.   **36** Howbeit they answered them not, neither cast they a stone at them, nor stopped the places where they lay hid;   **37** But said, "Let us die all in our innocency: heaven and earth will testify for us, that ye put us to death wrongfully."   **38** So they rose up against them in battle on the sabbath, and they slew them, with their wives and children and their cattle, to the number of a thousand people.   **39** Now when Mattathias and his friends understood hereof, they mourned for them right sore.   **40** And one of them said to another, "If we all do as our brethren have done, and fight not for our lives and laws against the heathen, they will now quickly root us out of the earth."   **41** At that time therefore they decreed, saying, "Whosoever shall come to make battle with us on the sabbath day, we will fight against him; neither will we die all, as our brethren that were murdered im the secret places."   **42** Then came there unto him a company of Assideans who were mighty men of Israel, even all such as were voluntarily devoted unto the law.   **43** Also all they that fled for persecution joined themselves unto them, and were a stay unto them.   **44** So they joined their forces, and smote sinful men in their anger, and wicked men in their wrath: but the rest fled to the heathen for succour.   **45** Then Mattathias and his friends went round about, and pulled down the altars: **46** And what children soever they found within the coast of Israel uncircumcised, those they circumcised valiantly.   **47** They pursued also after the proud men, and the work prospered in their hand.   **48** So they recovered the law out of the hand of the Gentiles, and out of the hand of kings, neither suffered they the sinner to triumph. **49** Now when the time drew near that Mattathias should die, he said unto his sons, "Now hath pride and rebuke gotten strength, and the time of destruction, and the wrath of indignation: **50** Now therefore, my sons, be ye zealous for the law, and give your lives for the covenant of your fathers…. **66** As for Judas Maccabeus, he hath been mighty and strong, even from his youth up: let him be your captain, and fight the battle of the people. **67** Take also unto you all those that observe the law, and avenge ye the wrong of your people. **68** Recompense fully the heathen, and take heed to the commandments of the law." **69** So he blessed them, and was gathered to his fathers. **70** And he died in the hundred forty and sixth year [166 B.C.], and his sons buried him in the sepulchres of his fathers at Modin, and all Israel made great lamentation for him.

CHAPTER 3. **1** Then his son Judas, called Maccabeus, rose up in his stead. **2** And all his brethren helped him, and so did all they that held with his father, and they fought with cheerfulness the battle of Israel. **3** So he gat his people great honour, and put on a breastplate as a giant, and girt his warlike harness about him, and he made battles, protecting the host with his sword. **4** In his acts he was like a lion, and like a lion's whelp roaring for his prey. **5** For He pursued the wicked, and sought them out, and burnt up those that vexed his people. **6** Wherefore the wicked shrunk for fear of him, and all the workers of iniquity were troubled, because salvation prospered in his hand. **7** He grieved also many kings, and made Jacob glad with his acts, and his memorial is blessed for ever. **8** Moreover he went through the cities of Juda, destroying the ungodly out of them, and turning away wrath from Israel: **9** So that he was renowned unto the utmost part of the earth, and he received unto him such as were ready to perish. **10** Then Apollonius gathered the Gentiles together, and a great host out of Samaria, to fight against Israel. **11** Which thing when Judas perceived, he went forth to meet him, and so he smote him, and slew him: many also fell down slain, but the rest fled. **12** Wherefore Judas took their spoils, and Apollonius' sword also, and therewith he fought all his life long. **13** Now when Seron, a prince of the army of Syria, heard say that Judas had gathered unto him a multitude and company of the faithful to go out with him to war; **14** He said, "I will get me a name and honour in the kingdom; for I will go fight with Judas and them that are with him, who despise the king's commandment." **15** So he made him ready to go up, and there went with him a mighty host of the ungodly to help him, and to be avenged of the children of Israel. **16** And when he came near to the going up of Bethhoron, Judas went forth to meet him with a small company: **17** Who, when they saw the host coming to meet them, said unto Judas, "How shall we be able, being so few, to fight against so great a multitude and so strong, seeing we are ready to faint with fasting all this day?" **18** Unto whom Judas answered, "It is no hard matter for many to be shut up in the hands of a few; and with the God of heaven it is all one, to deliver with a great multitude, or a small company: **19** For the victory of battle standeth not in the multitude of an host; but strength cometh from heaven. **20** They come against us in much pride and iniquity to destroy us, and our wives and children, and to spoil us: **21** But we fight for our lives and our laws. **22** Wherefore the Lord himself will overthrow them before our face: and as for you, be ye not afraid of them." **23** Now as soon as he had left off speaking, he leapt suddenly upon them, and so Seron and his host was overthrown before him. **24** And they pursued them from the going down of Bethhoron unto the plain, where were slain about eight hundred men of them; and the residue fled into the land of the Philistines. **25** Then began the fear of Judas and his brethren, and an exceeding great dread, to fall upon the nations round about them: **26** Insomuch as his fame came unto the king, and all nations talked of the battles of Judas. **27** Now when king Antiochus heard these things, he was full of indignation: wherefore he sent and gathered together all the forces of his realm, even a very strong army.   **28** He opened also his treasure, and gave his soldiers pay for a year, commanding them to be ready whensoever he should need them.   **29** Nevertheless, when he saw that the money of his treasures failed and that the tributes in the country were small, because of the dissension and plague, which he had brought upon the land in taking away the laws which had been of old time;   **30** He feared that he should not be able to bear the charges any longer, nor to have such gifts to give so liberally as he did before: for he had abounded above the kings that were before him.   **31** Wherefore, being greatly perplexed in his mind, he determined to go into Persia, there to take the tributes of the countries, and to gather much money.   **32** So he left Lysias, a nobleman, and one of the blood royal, to oversee the affairs of the king from the river Euphrates unto the borders of Egypt: **33** And to bring up his son Antiochus, until he came again.   **34** Moreover he delivered unto him the half of his forces, and the elephants, and gave him charge of all things that he would have done, as also concerning them that dwelt in Juda and Jerusalem: **35** To wit, that he should send an army against them, to destroy and root out the strength of Israel, and the remnant of Jerusalem, and to take away their memorial from that place;   **36** And that he should place strangers in all their quarters, and divide their land by lot.   **37** So the king took the half of the forces that remained, and departed from Antioch, his royal city, the hundred forty and seventh year [165 B.C.]; and having passed the river Euphrates, he went through the high countries.   **38** Then Lysias chose Ptolemee the son of Dorymenes, Nicanor, and Gorgias, mighty men of the king's friends: **39** And with them he sent forty thousand footmen, and seven thousand horsemen, to go into the land of Juda, and to destroy it, as the king commanded.   **40** So they went forth with all their power, and came and pitched by Emmaus in the plain country.   **41** And the merchants of the country, hearing the fame of them, took silver and gold very much, with servants, and came into the camp to buy the children of Israel for slaves: a power also of Syria and of the land of the Philistines joined themselves unto them.   **42** Now when Judas and his brethren saw that miseries were multiplied, and that the forces did encamp themselves in their borders: for they knew how the king had given commandment to destroy the people, and utterly abolish them;   **43** They said one to another, "Let us restore the decayed fortune of our people, and let us fight for our people and the sanctuary."   **44** Then was the congregation gathered together, that they might be ready for battle, and that they might pray, and ask mercy and compassion.   **45** Now Jerusalem lay void as a wilderness, there was none of her children that went in or out: the sanctuary also was trodden down, and aliens kept the strong hold; the heathen had their habitation in that place; and joy was taken from Jacob, and the pipe with the harp ceased.   **46** Wherefore the Israelites assembled themselves together, and came to Maspha, over against Jerusalem; for in Maspha was the place where they prayed aforetime in Israel.   **47** Then they fasted that day, and put on sackcloth, and cast ashes upon their heads, and rent their clothes,   **48** And laid open the book of the law, wherein the heathen had sought to paint the likeness of their images.   **49** They brought also the priests' garments, and the firstfruits, and the tithes: and the Nazarites they stirred up, who had accomplished their days.   **50** Then cried they with a loud voice toward heaven, saying, "What shall we do with these, and whither shall we carry them away?   **51** For thy sanctuary is trodden down and profaned, and thy priests are in heaviness, and brought low.   **52** And lo, the heathen are assembled together against us to destroy us: what things they imagine against us, thou knowest.   **53** How shall we be able to stand against them, except thou, O God, be our help?"   **54** Then sounded they with trumpets, and cried with a loud voice.   **55** And after this Judas ordained captains over the people, even captains over thousands, and over hundreds, and over fifties, and over tens.   **56** But as for such as were building houses, or had betrothed wives, or were planting vineyards, or were fearful, those he commanded that they should return, every man to his own house, according to the law.   **57** So the camp removed, and pitched upon the south side of Emmaus.   **58** And Judas said, "arm yourselves, and be valiant men, and see that ye be in readiness against the morning, that ye may fight with these nations, that are assembled together against us to destroy us and our sanctuary: **59** For it is better for us to die in battle, than to behold the calamities of our people and our sanctuary.   **60** Nevertheless, as the will of God is in heaven, so let him do."

CHAPTER 4.   **1** Then took Gorgias five thousand footmen, and a thousand of the best horsemen, and removed out of the camp by night;   **2** To the end he might rush in upon the camp of the Jews, and smite them suddenly. And the men of the fortress were his guides.   **3** Now when Judas heard thereof he himself removed, and the valiant men with him, that he might smite the king's army which was at Emmaus,   **4** While as yet the forces were dispersed from the camp.   **5** In the mean season came Gorgias by night into the camp of Judas: and when he found no man there, he sought them in the mountains: for said he, "These fellows flee from us."   **6** But as soon as it was day, Judas shewed himself in the plain with three thousand men, who nevertheless had neither armour nor swords to their minds.   **7** And they saw the camp of the heathen, that it was strong and well harnessed, and compassed round about with horsemen; and these were expert of war.   **8** Then said Judas to the men that were with him, "Fear ye not their multitude, neither be ye afraid of their assault...."   **12** Then the strangers lifted up their eyes, and saw them coming over against them.   **13** Wherefore they went out of the camp to battle; but they that were with Judas sounded their trumpets.   **14** So they joined battle, and the heathen being discomfited fled into the plain.   **15** Howbeit all the hindmost of them were slain with the sword: for they pursued them unto Gazera, and unto the plains of Idumea, and Azotus, and Jamnia, so that there were slain of them upon a three thousand men.   **16** This done, Judas returned again with his host from pursuing them,   **17** And said to the people, "Be not greedy of the spoil inasmuch as there is a battle before us,   **18** And Gorgias and his host are here by us in the mountain: but stand ye now against our enemies, and overcome them, and after this ye may boldly take the spoils."   **19** As Judas was yet speaking these words, there appeared a part of them looking out of the mountain: **20** Who when they perceived that the Jews had put their host to flight and were burning the tents; for the smoke that was seen declared what was done: **21** When therefore they perceived these things, they were sore afraid, and seeing also the host of Judas in the plain ready to fight,   **22** They fled every one into the land of strangers.   **23** Then Judas returned to spoil the tents, where they got much gold, and silver, and blue silk, and purple of the sea, and great riches.   **24** After this they went home, and sung a song of thanksgiving, and praised the Lord in heaven: because it is good, because his mercy endureth forever.   **25** Thus Israel had a great deliverance that day.   **26** Now all the strangers that had escaped came and told Lysias what had happened: **27** Who, when he heard thereof, was confounded and discouraged, because neither such things as he would were done unto Israel, nor such things as the king commanded him were come to pass.   **28** The next year [164 B.C.] therefore following Lysias gathered together threescore thousand choice men of foot, and five thousand horsemen, that he might subdue them.   **29** So they came into Idumea, and pitched their tents at Bethsura, and Judas met them with ten thousand men.   **30** And when he saw that mighty army, he prayed and said, "Blessed art thou, O Saviour of Israel, who didst quell the violence of the mighty man by the hand of thy servant David, and gavest the host of strangers into the hands of Jonathan the son of Saul, and his armourbearer;   **31** Shut up this army in the hand of thy people Israel, and let them be confounded in their power and horsemen: **32** Make them to be of no courage, and cause the boldness of their strength to fall away, and let them quake at their destruction: **33** Cast them down with the sword of them that love thee, and let all those that know thy name praise thee with thanksgiving."   **34** So they joined battle; and there were slain of the host of Lysias about five thousand men, even before them were they slain.   **35** Now when Lysias saw his army put to flight, and the manliness of Judas' soldiers, and how they were ready either to live or die valiantly, he went into Antiochia, and gathered together a company of strangers, and having made his army greater than it was, he purposed to come again into Judea.   **36** Then said Judas and his brethren, "Behold, our enemies are discomfited: let us go up to cleanse and dedicate the sanctuary."   **37** Upon this all the host assembled themselves together, and went up into mount Sion.   **38** And when they saw the sanctuary desolate, and the altar profaned, and the gates burned up, and shrubs growing in the courts as in a forest, or in one of the mountains, yea, and the priests' chambers pulled down;   **39** They rent their clothes, and made great lamentation, and cast ashes upon their heads,   **40** And fell down flat to the ground upon their faces, and blew an alarm with the trumpets, and cried toward heaven.   **41** Then Judas appointed certain men to fight against those that were in the fortress, until he had cleansed the sanctuary.   **42** So he chose priests of blameless conversation, such as had pleasure in the law: **43** Who cleansed the sanctuary, and bare out the defiled stones into an unclean place.   **44** And when as they consulted what to do with the altar of burnt offerings, which was profaned;   **45** They thought it best to pull it down, lest it should be a reproach to them, because the heathen had defiled it: wherefore they pulled it down,   **46** And laid up the stones in the mountain of the temple in a convenient place, until there should come a prophet to shew what should be done with them.   **47** Then they took whole stones according to the law, and built a new altar according to the former;   **48** And made up the sanctuary, and the things that were within the temple, and hallowed the courts.   **49** They made also new holy vessels, and into the temple they brought the candlestick, and the altar of burnt offerings, and of incense, and the table.   **50** And upon the altar they burned incense, and the lamps that were upon the candlestick they lighted, that they might give light in the temple.   **51** Furthermore they set the loaves upon the table, and spread out the veils, and finished all the works which they had begun to make.   **52** Now on the five and twentieth day of the ninth month, which is called the month Casleu, in the hundred forty and eighth year [164 B.C.], they rose up betimes in the morning,   **53** And offered sacrifice according to the law upon the new altar of burnt offerings, which they had made.   **54** Look, at what time and what day the heathen had profaned it, even in that was it dedicated with songs, and citherns, and harps, and cymbals.   **55** Then all the people fell upon their faces, worshipping and praising the God of heaven, who had given them good success.   **56** And so they kept the dedication of the altar eight days and offered burnt offerings with gladness, and sacrificed the sacrifice of deliverance and praise.   **57** They decked also the forefront of the temple with crowns of gold, and with shields; and the gates and the chambers they renewed, and hanged doors upon them.   **58** Thus was there very great gladness among the people, for that the reproach of the heathen was put away.   **59** Moreover Judas and his brethren with the whole congregation of Israel ordained, that the days of the dedication of the altar should be kept in their season from year to year by the space of eight days, from the five and twentieth day of the month Casleu, with mirth and gladness.   **60** At that time also they builded up the mount Sion with high walls and strong towers round about, lest the Gentiles should come and tread it down as they had done before.   **61** And they set there a garrison to keep it, and fortified Bethsura to preserve it; that the people might have a defence against Idumea.

Ancient Rome

Introduction

The ancient Greeks developed such a sophisticated form of culture that it eventually became the prestige culture of the entire Mediterranean area with other non-Greek peoples adopting and adapting their alphabetic writing system, architecture, sculpture, painting, mythology, and literature. On the other hand, the Greeks were so bound to their city-state form of organization that they never succeeded in uniting into a single Greek nation. The task of developing a workable unified Mediterranean society was left up to the Romans. Like other Mediterranean peoples, they were heavily influenced by Greek culture from their earliest days, and by adopting many of its features, the Romans developed their own cultural identity that was both similar to but different from that of the Greeks. In addition, the Romans exhibited an uncanny ability for political organization that enabled them to create a long-lasting imperial system. Like many peoples, the Romans proved themselves to be great conquerors; however, unlike many such peoples, they followed up their conquests with effective political organization and social integration that ultimately won the loyalty of Rome's subjects. The following readings display the cultural indebtedness of the Romans to the Greeks in the areas of historical writing, politics, oratory, and philosophy; they also illustrate how the Romans succeeded in providing the culturally diverse inhabitants of the Roman Empire with a commonly shared form of civilization. In addition, once Christianity developed out of Hellenistic Judaism, the unity and tranquility of the Roman Empire, despite the phenomenon of persecution, greatly facilitated the spread of this new religion. ✣

LIVY, HISTORIAN OF THE ROMAN REPUBLIC

Livy (59 B.C.-17 A.D.) was a contemporary of Rome's first emperor, Augustus,. His *History of Rome*, our single most important source of information for the history of the Roman Republic, narrated Roman affairs from the mythical foundation of the city (traditionally dated to 753 B.C.) down to the year 9 B.C. The following excerpts from this vast narrative are representative of the work as a whole and portray Rome and the Roman people at three different stages: at the very beginning of the community, during their emergence as the dominant power in Italy, and at the height of its greatest power when engaged in its second titanic struggle with Carthage.

(Taken from the translation of the Rev. Canon Roberts in the Everyman Library [1912])

A. ROME'S FOUNDATION STORY

✤ Book I

Livy begins his history with the story (already well established by his day) of Rome's mythical foundation by the twins Romulus and Remus, who were supposed to be descended from the great Trojan hero Aeneas, one of the few Trojan survivors of the mythical Greek capture and destruction of Troy. Thus, this foundation story forged a direct link between Rome's origins and one of the most important myths of the Greeks.

1 To begin with, it is generally admitted that after the capture of Troy [traditionally dated by the ancients to 1184 B.C.] , whilst the rest of the Trojans were massacred, against two of them, Aeneas and Antenor, -the Achaeans refused to exercise the rights of war, partly owing to old ties of hospitality, and partly because these men had always been in favor of making peace and surrendering Helen.... He [Aeneas] first visited Macedonia, then was carried down to Sicily in quest of a settlement; from Sicily he directed his course to the Laurentian territory [in central Italy]. Here, too, the name of Troy is found, and here the Trojans disembarked, and as their almost infinite wanderings had left them nothing but their arms and their ships, they began to plunder the neighborhood. The Aborigines, who occupied the country, with their king Latinus at their head, came hastily together

117

from the city and the country districts to repel the inroads of the strangers by force of arms…. A formal treaty was made between the leaders and mutual greetings exchanged between the armies. Latinus received Aeneas as a guest in his house, and there, in the presence of his tutelary deities, completed the political alliance by a domestic one, and gave his daughter in marriage to Aeneas. This incident confirmed the Trojans in the hope that they had reached the term of their wanderings and won a permanent home. They built a town, which Aeneas called Lavinium after his wife….

[We now pick up Livy's narrative after skipping over his brief account of about 400 years of mythical kings, descended from Trojan Aeneas, who ruled a town near the later site of Rome called Alba]

3 … He was succeeded by Proca, who had two sons, Numitor and Amulius. To Numitor, the elder, he bequeathed the ancient throne of the Silvian house. Violence, however, proved stronger than either the father's will or the respect due to the brother's seniority; for Amulius expelled his brother and seized the crown. Adding crime to crime, he murdered his brother's sons and made the daughter, Rea Silvia, a Vestal virgin; thus, under the presence of honoring her, depriving her of all hopes of issue.

4 But the Fates had, I believe, already decreed the origin of this great city and the foundation of the mightiest empire under heaven. The Vestal was forcibly violated and gave birth to twins. She named Mars as their father, either because she really believed it, or because the fault might appear less heinous if a deity were the cause of it. But neither gods nor men sheltered her or her babes from the king's cruelty; the priestess was thrown into prison, the boys were ordered to be thrown into the river. By a heaven-sent chance it happened that the Tiber was then overflowing its banks, and stretches of standing water prevented any approach to the main channel. Those who were carrying the children expected that this stagnant water would be sufficient to drown them, so under the impression that they were carrying out the king's orders they exposed the boys at the nearest point of the overflow, where the Ficus Ruminalis (said to have been formerly called Romularis) now stands. The locality was then a wild solitude. The tradition goes on to say that after the floating cradle in which the boys had been exposed had been left by the retreating water on dry land, a thirsty she-wolf from the surrounding hills, attracted by the crying of the children, came to them, gave them her teats to suck and was so gentle towards them that the king's flock-master found her licking the boys with her tongue. According to the story, his name was Faustulus. He took the children to his hut and gave them to his wife Larentia to bring up. Some writers think that Larentia, from her unchaste life, had got the nickname of "She-wolf" amongst the shepherds, and that this was the origin of the marvellous story.

As soon as the boys, thus born and thus brought up, grew to be young men they did not neglect their pastoral duties, but their special delight was roaming through the woods on hunting expeditions. As their strength and courage were thus developed, they used not only to lie in wait for fierce beasts of prey, but they even attacked brigands when loaded with plunder. They distributed what they took amongst the shepherds, with whom, surrounded by a continually increasing body of young men, they associated themselves in their serious undertakings and in their sports and pastimes.

5 It is said that the festival of the Lupercalia, which is still observed, was even in those days celebrated on the Palatine hill. This hill was originally called Pallantium from a city of the same name in Arcadia; the name was afterwards changed to Palatium. Evander, an Arcadian, had held that territory many ages before, and had introduced an annual festival from Arcadia in which young men ran about naked for sport and wantonness, in honor of the Lycaean Pan, whom the Romans afterwards called Inuus. The existence of this festival was widely recognised, and it was while the two brothers were engaged in it that the brigands, enraged at losing their plunder, ambushed them.

Romulus successfully defended himself, but Remus was taken prisoner and brought before Amulius, his captors impudently accusing him of their own crimes. The principal charge brought against them was that of invading Numitor's lands with a body of young men whom they had got together, and carrying off plunder as though in regular warfare. Remus accordingly was handed over to Numitor for punishment.

Faustulus had from the beginning suspected that it was royal offspring that he was bringing up, for he was aware that the boys had been exposed at the king's command and the time at which he had taken them away exactly corresponded with that of their exposure. He had, however, refused to divulge the matter prematurely, until either a fitting opportunity occurred or necessity demanded its disclosure. The necessity came first. Alarmed for the safety of Remus he revealed the state of the case to Romulus.

It so happened that Numitor also, who had Remus in his custody, on hearing that he and his brother were twins and comparing their ages and the character and bearing so unlike that of one in a servile condition, began to recall the memory of his grandchildren, and further inquiries brought him to the same conclusion as Faustulus; nothing was wanting to the recognition of Remus. So the king Amulius was being enmeshed on all sides by hostile purposes. Romulus shrunk from a direct attack with his body of shepherds, for he was no match for the king in open fight. They were instructed to approach the palace by different routes and meet there at a given time, whilst from Numitor's house Remus lent his assistance with a second band he had collected. The attack succeeded and the king was killed.

6 At the beginning of the fray, Numitor gave out that an enemy had entered the City and was attacking the palace, in order to draw off the Alban soldiery to the citadel, to defend it. When he saw the young men coming to congratulate him after the assassination, he at once called a council of his people and explained his brother's infamous conduct towards him, the story of his grandsons, their parentage and bringing up, and how he recognised them. Then he proceeded to inform them of the tyrant's death and his responsibility for it. The young men marched in order through the midst of the assembly and saluted their grandfather as king; their action was approved by the whole population, who with one voice ratified the title and sovereignty of the king.

After the government of Alba was thus transferred to Numitor, Romulus and Remus were seized with the desire of building a city in the locality where they had been exposed. There was the superfluous population of the Alban and Latin towns, to these were added the shepherds: it was natural to hope that with all these Alba would be small and Lavinium small in comparison with the city which was to be founded. These pleasant anticipations were disturbed by the ancestral curse -ambition-which led to a deplorable quarrel over what was at first a trivial matter. As they were twins and no claim to precedence could be based on seniority, they decided to consult the tutelary deities of the place by means of augury as to who was to give his name to the new city, and who was to rule it after it had been founded. Romulus accordingly selected the Palatine as his station for observation, Remus the Aventine.

7 Remus is said to have been the first to receive an omen: six vultures appeared to him. The augury had just been announced to Romulus when double the number appeared to him. Each was saluted as king by his own party. The one side based their claim on the priority of the appearance, the other on the number of the birds. Then followed an angry altercation; heated passions led to bloodshed; in the tumult Remus was killed. The more common report is that Remus contemptuously jumped over the newly raised walls and was forthwith killed by the enraged Romulus, who exclaimed, "So shall it be henceforth with every one who leaps over my walls." Romulus thus became sole ruler, and the city was called after him, its founder.

B. THE BATTLE OF SENTINUM (295 B.C.)

✤ Book X

By 295 B.C. the Romans were involved in the final stages of their conquest of peninsular Italy, but their growing power prompted four major peoples (the Etruscans, the Umbrians, the Samnites, and the Gauls) to unite to oppose Rome. Under the command of their two highly experienced consuls of the year (Quintus Fabius Maximus Rullianus and Publius Decius Mus) the Romans encountered and shattered this powerful coalition at Sentinum in Umbria. Rome's conquest of Italy was now merely a matter of time (finally completed in 264 B.C.), but the battle was also made famous by the consul Decius offering himself in sacrifice in a solemn ritual called *devotio*, which vowed both the Roman commander and the opposing enemy forces to the gods of the underworld for death and destruction.

27 After crossing the Apennines, the consuls descended into the district of Sentinum and fixed their camp about four miles' distance from the enemy. The four nations [Samnites, Gauls, Etruscans, and Umbrians] consulted together as to their plan of action, and it was decided that they should not all be mixed up in one camp nor go into battle at the same time. The Gauls were linked with the Samnites, the Umbrians with the Etruscans. They fixed upon the day of battle, the brunt of the fighting was to be reserved for the Gauls and Samnites, in the midst of the struggle the Etruscans and Umbrians were to attack the Roman camp. These arrangements were upset by three deserters, who came in the secrecy of night to Fabius and disclosed the enemy's plans. They were rewarded for their information and dismissed with instructions to find out and report whatever fresh decision was arrived at. The consuls sent written instructions to Fulvius and Postumius [two other commanders stationed elsewhere] to bring their armies up to Clusium and ravage the enemy's country on their march as far as they possibly could. The news of these ravages brought the Etruscans away from Sentinum to protect their own territory.

Now that they had got them out of the way, the consuls tried hard to bring on an engagement. For two days they sought to provoke the enemy to fight, but during those two days nothing took place worth mentioning; a few fell on both sides and enough exasperation was produced to make them desire a regular battle without, however, wishing to hazard everything on a decisive conflict. On the third day the whole force on both sides marched down into the plain.

Whilst the two armies were standing ready to engage, a hind driven by a wolf from the mountains ran down into the open space between the two lines with the wolf in pursuit. Here they each took a different direction, the hind ran to the Gauls, the wolf to the Romans. Way was made for the wolf between the ranks; the Gauls speared the hind. On this a soldier in the front rank exclaimed: "In that place where you see the creature sacred to Diana lying dead, flight and carnage will begin; here the wolf, whole and unhurt, a creature sacred to Mars, reminds us of our Founder and that we too are of the race of Mars." The Gauls were stationed on the right, the Samnites on the left. Q. Fabius posted the first and third legions on the right wing, facing the Samnites; to oppose the Gauls, Decius had the fifth and sixth legions, who formed the Roman left. The second and fourth legions were engaged in Samnium with L. Volumnius the proconsul. When the armies first met they were so evenly matched that had the Etruscans and Umbrians been present, whether taking part in the battle or attacking the camp, the Romans must have been defeated.

28 But although neither side was gaining any advantage and Fortune had not yet indicated in any way to whom she would grant the victory, the fighting on the right wing was very different from that on the left. The Romans under Fabius were acting more on the defensive and were protracting the contest as long as possible. Their commander knew that it was the habitual practice of both the Gauls and the Samnites to make a furious

attack to begin with, and if that were successfully resisted, it was enough; the courage of the Samnites gradually sank as the battle went on, whilst the Gauls, utterly unable to stand heat or exertion, found their physical strength melting away; in their first efforts they were more than men, in the end they were weaker than women. Knowing this, he kept the strength of his men unimpaired against the time when the enemy usually began to show signs of defeat. Decius, as a younger man, possessing more vigor of mind, showed more dash; he made use of all the strength he possessed in opening the attack, and as the infantry battle developed too slowly for him, he called on the cavalry. Putting himself at the head of a squadron of exceptionally gallant troopers, he appealed to them as the pick of his soldiers to follow him in charging the enemy, for a two-fold glory would be theirs if victory began on the left wing and, in that wing, with the cavalry. Twice they swept aside the Gaulish horse. Making a third charge, they were carried too far, and whilst they were now fighting desperately in the midst of the enemy's cavalry they were thrown into consternation by a new style of warfare. Armed men mounted on chariots and baggage wagons came on with a thunderous noise of horses and wheels, and the horses of the Roman cavalry, unaccustomed to that kind of uproar, became uncontrollable through fright; the cavalry after their victorious charges, were now scattered in frantic terror; horses and men alike were overthrown in their blind flight. Even the standards of the legionaries were thrown into confusion, and many of the front rank men were crushed by the weight of the horses and vehicles dashing through the lines. When the Gauls saw their enemy thus demoralised they did not give them a moment's breathing space in which to recover themselves, but followed up at once with a fierce attack. Decius shouted to his men and asked them whither they were fleeing, what hope they had in flight; he tried to stop those who were retreating and recall the scattered units. Finding himself unable, do what he would, to check the demoralisation, he invoked the name of his father, P. Decius, and cried: "Why do I any longer delay the destined fate of my family? This is the privilege granted to our house that we should be an expiatory sacrifice to avert dangers from the State. Now will I offer the legions of the enemy together with myself as a sacrifice to Tellus and the Dii Manes." When he had uttered these words he ordered the priest, M. Livius, whom he had kept by his side all through the battle, to recite the prescribed form in which he was to devote "himself and the legions of the enemy on behalf of the army of the Roman people, the Quirites." He was accordingly devoted in the same words and wearing the same garb as his father, P. Decius, at the battle of Veseris in the Latin war [340 B.C.]. After the usual prayers had been recited he uttered the following awful curse: "I carry before me terror and rout and carnage and blood and the wrath of all the gods, those above and those below. I will infect the standards, the armor, the weapons of the enemy with dire and manifold death, the place of my destruction shall also witness that of the Gauls and Samnites." After uttering this imprecation on himself and on the enemy he spurred his horse against that part of the Gaulish line where they were most densely massed and leaping into it was slain by their missiles.

29 From this moment the battle could hardly have appeared to any man to be dependent on human strength alone. After losing their leader, a thing which generally demoralises an army, the Romans arrested their flight and recommenced the struggle. The Gauls, especially those who were crowded round the consul's body, were discharging their missiles aimlessly and harmlessly as though bereft of their senses; some seemed paralysed, incapable of either fight or flight. But, in the other army, the priest Livius, to whom Decius had transferred his attendants and whom he had commissioned to act as propraetor, announced in loud tones that the consul's death had freed the Romans from all danger and given them the victory, the Gauls and Samnites were made over to Tellus the Mother and the Dii Manes, Decius was summoning and dragging down to himself the army which he had devoted together with himself, there was terror everywhere among the enemy, and the Furies were lashing them into madness. Whilst the battle was thus being restored, L. Cornelius Scipio and C. Marcius were ordered by Fabius to bring up the reserves from the rear to the support of his colleagues. There they learnt the fate of P. Decius, and it was a powerful encouragement to them to dare everything for the republic. The Gauls were standing in close order covered by their shields, and a hand-to-hand fight seemed no easy matter, but the staff officers gave orders for the javelins which were lying on the ground between the two armies to be gathered up and hurled at the enemy's shield wall. Although most of them stuck in their shields and only a few penetrated their bodies, the closely massed ranks went down, most of them falling without having received a wound, just as though they had been struck by lightning. Such was the change that Fortune had brought about in the Roman left wing. On the right Fabius, as I have stated, was protracting the contest. When he found that neither the battle-shout of the enemy, nor their onset, nor the discharge of their missiles were as strong as they had been at the beginning, he ordered the officers in command of the cavalry to take their squadrons round to the side of the Samnite army, ready at a given signal to deliver as fierce a flank attack as possible. The infantry were at the same time to press steadily forwards and dislodge the enemy. When he saw that they were offering no resistance, and were evidently worn out, he massed all his support which he had kept in reserve for the supreme moment, and gave the signal for a general charge of infantry and cavalry. The Samnites could not face the onslaught and fled precipitately past the Gauls to their camp, leaving their allies to fight as best they could. The Gauls were still standing in close order behind their shield wall. Fabius, on hearing of his colleague's death, ordered a squadron of Campanian horse, about 500 strong, to go out of action and ride round to take the Gauls in the rear. The principes of the third legion were ordered to follow, and, wherever they saw the enemy's line disordered by the cavalry, to press home the attack and cut them down. He vowed a temple and the spoils of the enemy to Jupiter Victor, and then proceeded to the Samnite camp to which the whole crowd of panic-struck fugitives was being driven. As they could not all get through the gates, those outside tried to resist the Roman attack and a battle began close under the rampart. It was here that Gellius Egnatius, the captain-general of the Samnites, fell. Finally the Samnites were driven within their lines and the camp was taken after a brief struggle. At the same time the Gauls were attacked in the rear and overpowered; 25,000 of the enemy were killed in that day's fighting and 8000 made prisoners. The victory was by no means a bloodless one, for P. Decius lost 7000 killed and Fabius 1700. After sending out a search party to find his colleague's body, Fabius had the spoils of the enemy collected into a heap and burnt as a sacrifice to Jupiter Victor. The consul's body could not be found that day as it was buried under a heap of Gauls; it was discovered the next day and brought back to camp amidst the tears of the soldiers. Fabius laid aside all other business in order to pay the last rites to his dead colleague; the obsequies were conducted with every mark of honor and the funeral oration sounded the well-deserved praises of the deceased consul.

C. THE REPUBLICAN CONSTITUTION IN ACTION (211 B.C.)

✤ Book XXVI

The following excerpt comes from the middle of Livy's narrative of the Second Punic or Hannibalic War (218-201 B.C.) and well illustrates the standard workings of the Roman governmental system at this time. The passage begins with the newly elected consuls convening the senate, which proceeds to decide various important issues concerning the allocation of military forces for the different theaters of this war. The passage then describes the trial of Cn. Fulvius for military incompetence exhibited during the previous year. Fulvius was prosecuted before the assembly of Roman citizens (acting as a jury) by the plebeian tribune C. Sempronius Blaesus (serving in the capacity of a public prosecutor).

1 The new consuls, Cn, Fulvius Centimalus and P. Sulpicius Galba, entered upon office on the 15th of March, and at once convened a meeting of the senate in the Capitol to discuss questions of State, the conduct of the war and the distribution of the provinces and the armies. The retiring consuls- Q. Fulvius and Appius Claudius- retained their commands and were instructed to prosecute the siege of Capua unremittingly until they had effected its capture. The recovery of this city was the main concern of the Romans now. What determined them was not only the bitter resentment which its defection had evoked, a feeling which was never more justified in the case of any city, but also the certainty they felt that, as in its revolt it had drawn many communities with it, owing to its greatness and strength, so its recapture would create amongst these communities a feeling of respect for the power whose sovereignty they had formerly acknowledged. The praetors of the past year, M. Junius in Etruria and P. Sempronius in Gaul, had their commands extended and were each to retain the two legions they had. M. Marcellus was to act as proconsul and finish the war in Sicily with the army which he had. If he needed reinforcements he was to take them from the troops which P. Cornelius was commanding in Sicily, but none were to be selected from those who had been forbidden by the senate to take a furlough or return home before the end of the war. The province of Sicily was assigned to C. Sulpicius, and he was to take over the two legions which were with P. Cornelius; any reinforcements he needed were to be supplied from the army of Cn. Fulvius which had been so disgracefully routed and cut up the previous year in Apulia. The soldiers who had so disgraced themselves were placed under the same conditions with regard to length of service as the survivors of Cannae. As an additional brand of ignominy the men of both these armies were forbidden to winter in towns or to construct winter quarters for themselves within ten miles of any town. The two legions which Q. Mucius had commanded in Sardinia were given to L. Cornelius, and any additional force he might require was to be raised by the consuls. T. Otacilius and M. Valerius were ordered to cruise off the coasts of Sicily and Greece respectively with the fleets and soldiers they had previously commanded. The former had a hundred ships with two legions on board; the latter, fifty ships and one legion. The total strength of the Roman armies engaged on land and sea this year amounted to twenty-five legions.

2 At the beginning of the year a despatch from L. Marcius was laid before the senate. The senators fully appreciated the successful way in which he had conducted his operations, but a good many of them were indignant at the honorific title he had assumed. The superscription of the letter was "The propraetor to the senate," though the imperium had not been conferred upon him by an order of the people nor with the sanction of the senate. An evil precedent had been set, they said, when a commander was chosen by his army, and the solemn procedure at elections, after the auspices were duly taken, was transferred to camps and provinces far away from the magistrates and the laws, and left to the caprice of the soldiers. Some thought the senate ought to take the matter up, but it was thought better to adjourn the consideration of it until the horsemen who had brought the despatch had left the City. With regard to the food and clothing of the army, they ordered a reply to be sent to the effect that both these matters would be attended to by the senate. They refused, however, to allow the despatch to be addressed "To the propraetor L. Marcius," lest it should appear that the question which was to be discussed had been prejudged. After the messengers had been dismissed the consuls gave this question priority over everything else, and it was unanimously agreed that the tribunes should consult the plebs as soon as possible as to whom they wished to have sent to Spain with the imperium as commander-in-chief to take over the army which Cn. Scipio had commanded. The tribunes undertook to do so, and due notice of the question was given to the Assembly. But the citizens were preoccupied with a controversy of a very different nature. C. Sempronius Blaesus had fixed a day for bringing Cn. Fulvius to trial for losing his army in Apulia, and made a very bitter attack upon him beforehand in the Assembly. "Many commanders," he said, "have through rashness and inexperience led their armies into most dangerous positions, but Cn. Fulvius is the only one who has demoralised his army by every form of vice before betraying them. They may with perfect truth be said to have been destroyed before they saw the enemy; they owed their defeat to their own commander, not to Hannibal. "Now no man, when he is going to vote, takes sufficient trouble to find out what sort of a man it is to whom he is entrusting the supreme command of the army. Think of the difference between Tiberius Sempronius and Cn. Fulvius. Tiberius Sempronius had an army of slaves given to him, but in a short time, thanks to the discipline he maintained and the wise use he made of his authority, there was not a man amongst them who when he was in the field of battle gave a thought to his birth or his condition. Those men were a protection to our allies and a terror to our enemies. They snatched, as though from the very jaws of Hannibal, cities like Cumae and Beneventum and restored them to Rome. Cn. Fulvius, on the other hand, had an army of Roman citizens, born of respectable parents, brought up as free men, and he infected them with the vices of slaves, and made them such that they were insolent and riotous amongst our allies, weaklings and cowards in face of the enemy; they could not stand even the war-cry of the Carthaginians, let alone their charge. Good heavens! no wonder the soldiers gave ground, when their commander was the first to run away; the wonder is that any stood their ground and fell, and that all did not accompany Cn. Fulvius in his panic and flight. C. Flaminius, L. Paulus, L. Postumius, and the two Scipios, Cnaeus and Publius, all chose to fall in battle rather than desert their armies, when they were hemmed in by the foe. Cn. Fulvius came back to Rome as the all-but solitary herald of the annihilation of his army. After the army had fled from the field of Cannae it was deported to Sicily, not to return till the enemy had evacuated Italy, and a similar decree was recently passed in the case of Fulvius' legions. But, shame to relate, the commander himself remained unpunished after his flight from a battle brought on by his own headstrong folly; he is free to pass the rest of his life where he passed it in youth-in stews and brothels-whilst his soldiers, whose only fault is that they copied their commander, are practically sent into exile and have to undergo a service of disgrace. So unequal are the liberties enjoyed in Rome by the rich and the poor, the men of rank and the men of the people."

3 In his defence Fulvius threw all the blame upon his men. They clamored, he said, for battle, and he led them out, not at the moment, for it was late in the day, but on the following morning. Though they were drawn up on favorable ground, at an early hour they found either the terror of the enemy's name or the strength of his attack too much for them. When they were all flying in disorder he was swept away by the rush as Varro was at Cannae and as many other commanders have been at different times. What help would he have given to the republic by staying there alone? unless indeed his death would have warded off other national disasters. His failure was not due to lack of supplies, or to incautiously taking up a position on unfavorable ground; he had not been ambushed through insufficient reconnoitring; he had been beaten in a fair fight on an open field. Men's tempers, on whichever side they were, were beyond his control, a man's natural disposition made him either brave or cowardly. The speeches of the prosecutor and the defendant occupied two days, on the third day the witnesses were produced. Besides all the other serious charges brought against him, a great many men stated on oath that the panic and flight began with the praetor, and that when the soldiers found that they were left to themselves, and thought that their commander had good ground for fear,

they too turned their backs and fled. The prosecutor had in the first instance asked for a fine, but the evidence which had been given roused the anger of the people to such an extent that they insisted upon a capital charge being laid. This led to a fresh contest. As the prosecutor during the first two days had limited the penalty to a fine and only on the third day made the charge a capital one, the defendant appealed to the other tribunes, but they refused to interfere with their colleague. It was open to him by ancient custom to proceed either by statute law or by customary precedent, whichever he preferred, until he had obtained judgment, whether the penalty were a capital or a pecuniary one. On this Sempronius announced that he should prosecute C. Fulvius on the charge of treason and requested the City praetor to convene the Assembly for the purpose on the appointed day. Then the accused tried another way of escape. His brother Quintus was in high favor with the people at the time, owing to his former successes and the general conviction that he would soon take Capua, and the defendant hoped that he might be present at his trial. Quintus wrote to the senate for their permission, appealing to their compassion and begging to be allowed to defend his brother's life, but they told him in reply that it would militate against the interests of the State for him to leave Capua. Just before the day of trial Cn. Fulvius went into exile at Tarquinii. The plebs affirmed by resolution his legal status as exile and all the consequences it involved.

Reading 16

Polybius on the Roman Constitution

F following Rome's decisive defeat of Macedonia in 168 B.C., the Romans used their victory by rounding up 2000 prominent Greeks from various city-states and brought them to Rome to serve as hostages to guarantee the future good behavior of Greece. Among these hostages was Polybius. His father had been a prominent public figure, and Polybius himself (being in his early thirties when taken to Rome) was just beginning to follow in his father's footsteps. Shortly after arriving in Rome, Polybius became closely associated with several leading Romans; and as the result of his firsthand experience of the Roman political and military system, he soon decided to write a detailed historical account of Rome's rise to Mediterranean dominance in order to explain this remarkable phenomenon to his fellow Greeks, many of whom at the time knew rather little about the Romans. In the sixth book of his narrative Polybius paused to engage in a lengthy digression in which he provided his readers with a general description of the Roman constitution of his day.

(Taken from the translation of W. R. Paton in the Loeb Classical Library Series)

2. I am aware that some will wonder why I have deferred until the present occasion my account of the Roman constitution, thus being obliged to interrupt the due course of my narrative. Now, that I have always regarded this account as one of the essential parts of my whole design, I have, I am sure, made evident in numerous passages and chiefly in the prefatory remarks dealing with the fundamental principles of this history, where I said that the best and most valuable result I aim at is that readers of my work may gain a knowledge how it was and by virtue of what peculiar political institutions that in less than fifty-three years [220-167 B.C.] nearly the whole world was overcome and fell under the single dominion of Rome, a thing the like of which had never happened before.... What chiefly attracts and chiefly benefits students of history is just this: the study of causes and the consequent power of choosing what is best in each case. Now the chief cause of success or the reverse in all matters is the form of a state's constitution ; for springing from this, as from a fountain-head, all designs and plans of action not only originate, but reach their consummation.

   3. ... Most of those whose object it has been to instruct us methodically concerning such matters, distinguish three kinds of constitutions, which they call kingship, " aristocracy, and democracy. Now we should, I think, be quite justified in asking them to

enlighten us as to whether they represent these three to be the sole varieties or rather to be the best; for in either case my opinion is that they are wrong. For it is evident that we must regard as the best constitution a combination of all these three varieties, since we have had proof of this not only theoretically but by actual experience, Lycurgus having been the first to draw up a constitution(that of Sparta(on this principle. Nor on the other hand can we admit that these are the only three varieties ; for we have witnessed monarchical and tyrannical governments, which while they differ very widely from kingship, yet bear a certain resemblance to it, this being the reason why monarchs in general falsely assume and use, as far as I they can, the regal title. There have also been several oligarchical constitutions which seem to bear some likeness to aristocratic ones, though the divergence is, generally, as wide as possible. The same holds good about democracies.

4. The truth of what I say is evident from the following considerations. It is by no means every monarchy which we can call straight off a kingship, but only that which is voluntarily accepted by the subjects and where they are governed rather by an appeal to their reason than by fear and force. Nor again can we style every oligarchy an aristocracy, but only that where the government is in the hands of a selected body of the justest and wisest men. Similarly that is no true democracy in which the whole crowd of citizens is free to do whatever they wish or purpose, but when, in a community where it is traditional and customary to reverence the gods, to honour our parents, to respect our elders, and to obey the laws, the will of the greater number prevails, this is to be called a democracy. We should therefore assert that there are six kinds of governments, the three above mentioned which are in everyone's mouth and the three which are naturally allied to them, I mean monarchy, oligarchy, and mob-rule. Now the first of these to come into being is monarchy, its growth being natural and unaided ; and next arises kingship derived from monarchy by the aid of art and by the correction of defects. Monarchy first changes into its vicious allied form, tyranny ; and next, the abolishment of both gives birth to aristocracy. Aristocracy by its very nature degenerates into oligarchy ; and when the commons inflamed by anger take vengeance on this government for its unjust rule, democracy comes into being ; and in due course the licence and lawlessness of this form of government produces mob-rule to complete the series. The truth of what I have just said will be quite clear to anyone who pays due attention to such beginnings, origins, and changes as are in each case natural. For he alone who has seen how each form naturally arises and develops, will be able to see when, how, and where the growth, perfection, change, and end of each are likely to occur again. And it is to the Roman constitution above all that this method, I think, may be successfully applied, since from the outset its formation and growth have been due to natural causes....

11. ... I am quite aware that to those who have been born and bred under the Roman Republic my account of it will seem somewhat imperfect owing to the omission of certain details. For as they have complete knowledge of it and practical acquaintance with all its parts, having been familiar with these customs and institutions from childhood, they will not be struck by the extent of the information give but will demand in addition all I have omitted : they will not think that the author has purposely omitted small peculiarities, but that owing to ignorance he has been silent regarding the origins of many things and some points of capital importance. Had I mentioned them, they would not have been impressed by my doing so, regarding them as small and trivial points.... .The three kinds of government that I spoke of above all shared in the control of the Roman state. And such fairness and propriety in all respects was shown in the use of these three elements for drawing the constitution and in its subsequent administration that it was impossible even for a native to pronounce with certainty whether the whole system was aristocratic,

democratic, or monarchical. This was indeed only natural. For if one fixed one's eyes on the power of the consuls, the constitution seemed completely monarchical and royal; if on that of the senate it seemed again to be aristocratic; and when one looked at the power of the masses, it seemed clearly to be a democracy. The parts of the state falling under the control of each element were and with a few modifications still are as follows.

12. The consuls, previous to leading out their legions, exercise authority in Rome over all public affairs, since all the other magistrates except the tribunes are under them and bound to obey them, and it is they who introduce embassies to the senate. Besides this it is they who consult the senate on matters of urgency, they who carry out in detail the provisions of its decrees. Again as concerns all affairs of state administered by the people it is their duty to take these under their charge, to summon assemblies, to introduce measures, and to preside over the execution of the popular decrees. As for preparation for war and the general conduct of operations in the field, here their power is almost uncontrolled; for they are empowered to make what demands they choose on the allies, to appoint military tribunes, to levy soldiers and select those who are fittest for service. They also have the right of inflicting, when on active service, punishment on anyone under their command ; and they are authorized to spend any sum they decide upon from the public funds, being accompanied by a quaestor who faithfully executes their instructions. So that if one looks at this part of the administration alone, one may reasonably pronounce the constitution to be a pure monarchy or kingship....

13. To pass to the senate. In the first place it has the control of the treasury, all revenue and expenditure being regulated by it. For with the exception of payments made to the consuls, the quaestors are not allowed to disburse for any particular object without a decree of the senate. And even the item of expenditure which is far heavier and more important than any other(the outlay every five years by the censors on public works, whether constructions or repairs(is under the control of the senate, which makes a grant to the censors for the purpose. Similarly crimes committed in Italy which require a public investigation, such as treason, conspiracy, poisoning, and assassination, are under the jurisdiction of the senate. Also if any private person or community in Italy is in need of arbitration or indeed claims damages or requires succour or protection, the senate attends to all such matters. It also occupies itself with the dispatch of all embassies sent to countries outside of Italy for the purpose either of settling differences, or of offering friendly advice, or indeed of imposing demands, or of receiving submission, or of declaring war ; and in like manner with respect to embassies arriving in Rome it decides what reception and what answer should be given to them. All these matters are in the hands of the senate, nor have the people anything whatever to do with them. So that again to one residing in Rome during the absence of the consuls the constitution appears to be entirely aristocratic; and this is the conviction of many Greek states and many of the kings, as the senate manages all business connected with them.

14. After this we are naturally inclined to ask what part in the constitution is left for the people, considering that the senate controls all the particular matters I mentioned, and, what is most important, manages all matters of revenue and expenditure, and considering that the consuls again have uncontrolled authority as regards armaments and operations in the field. But nevertheless there is a part and a very important part left for the people. For it is the people which alone has the right to confer honours and inflict punishment, the only bonds by which kingdoms and states and in a word human society in general are held together. For where the distinction between these is overlooked or is observed but ill applied, no affairs can be properly administered. How indeed is this possible when good and evil men are held in equal estimation ? It is by the people, then, in many cases that offences punishable by a fine are tried when the accused have held the highest office ; and they are the only court which may try on capital charges. As regards the latter they have a practice which is praiseworthy and should be mentioned. Their usage allows those on trial for their lives when found guilty liberty to depart openly, thus inflicting voluntary exile on themselves, if even only one of the tribes that pronounce the verdict has not yet voted. Such exiles enjoy safety in the territories of Naples, Praeneste, Tibur, and other allied communities. Again it is the people who bestow office on the deserving, the noblest reward of virtue in a state ; the people have the power of approving or rejecting laws, and what is most important of all, they deliberate on the question of war and peace. Furthermore, in the case of alliances, terms of peace, and treaties, it is the people who ratify all these or the reverse. Thus here again one might plausibly say that the people's share in the government is the greatest, and that the constitution is a democratic one.

15. Having stated how political power is distributed among the different parts of the state, I will now explain how each of the three parts is enabled, if they wish, to counteract or co-operate with the others. The consul, when he leaves with his army invested with the powers I mentioned, appears indeed to have absolute authority in all matters necessary for carrying out his purpose; but in fact he requires the support of the people and the senate, and is not able to bring his operations to a conclusion without them. For it is obvious that the legions require constant supplies, and without the consent of the senate, neither grain, clothing, nor pay can be provided; so that the commander's plans come to nothing, if the senate chooses to be deliberately negligent and obstructive. It also depends on the senate whether or not a general can carry out completely his conceptions and designs, since it has the right of either superseding him when his year's term of office has expired or of retaining him in command. Again it is in its power to celebrate with pomp and to magnify the successes of a general or on the other hand to obscure and belittle them. For the processions they call triumphs, in which the generals bring the actual spectacle of their achievements before the eyes of their fellow-citizens, cannot be properly organized and sometimes even cannot be held at all, unless the senate consents and provides the requisite funds. As for the people it is most indispensable for the consuls to conciliate them, however far away from home they may be ; for, as I said, it is the people which ratifies or annuls terms of peace and treaties, and what is most important, on laying down office the consuls are obliged to account for their actions to the people. So that in no respect is it safe for the consuls to neglect keeping in favour with both the senate and the people.

16. The senate again, which possesses such great power, is obliged in the first place to pay attention to the commons in public affairs and respect the wishes of the people, and it cannot carry out inquiries into the most grave and important offences against the state, punishable with death, and their correction, unless the senate's decree is confirmed by the people. The same is the case in matters which directly affect the senate itself. For if anyone introduces a law meant to deprive the senate of some of its traditional authority, or to abolish the precedence and other distinctions of the senators or even to curtail them of their private fortunes, it is the people alone which has the power of passing or rejecting any such measure. And what is most important is that if a single one of the tribunes interposes, the senate is unable to decide finally about any matter, and cannot even meet and hold sittings ; and here it is to be observed that the tribunes are always obliged to act as the people decree and to pay every attention to their wishes. Therefore, for all these reasons the senate is afraid of the masses and must pay due attention to the popular will.

17. Similarly, again, the people must be submissive to the senate and respect its members both in public and in private. Through the whole of Italy a vast number of contracts, which it would not be easy to enumerate, are given out by the censors for the construction and repair of public buildings, and besides this there are many things which are farmed, such

as navigable rivers, harbours, gardens, mines, lands, in fact everything that forms part of the Roman dominion. Now all these matters are undertaken by the people, and one may almost say that everyone is interested in these contracts and the work they involve. For certain people are the actual purchasers from the censors of the contracts, others are the partners of these first, others stand surety for them, others pledge their own fortunes to the state for this purpose. Now in all these matters the senate is supreme. It can grant extension of time ; it can relieve the contractor if any accident occurs ; and if the work proves to be absolutely impossible to carry out it can liberate him from his contract. There are in fact many ways in which the senate can either benefit or injure those who manage public property, as all these matters are referred to it. What is even more important is that the judges in most civil trials, whether public or private, are appointed from its members, where the action involves large interests. So that all citizens being at the mercy of the senate, and looking forward with alarm to the uncertainty of litigation, are very shy of obstructing or resisting its decisions. Similarly, everyone is reluctant to oppose the projects of the consuls as all are generally and individually under their authority when in the field.

18. Such being the power that each part has of hampering the others or co-operating with them, their union is adequate to all emergencies, so that it is impossible to find a better political system than this. For whenever the menace of some common danger from abroad compels them to act in concord and support each other, so great does the strength of the state become, that nothing which is requisite can be neglected, as all are zealously competing in devising means of meeting the need of the hour, nor can any decision arrived at fail to be executed promptly, as all are co-operating both in public and in private to the accomplishment of the task they have set themselves; and consequently this peculiar form of constitution possesses an irresistible power of attaining every object upon which it is resolved. When again they are freed from external menace, and reap the harvest of good fortune and affluence which is the result of their success, and in the enjoyment of this prosperity are corrupted by flattery and idleness and wax insolent and overbearing, as indeed happens often enough, it is then especially that we see the state providing itself a remedy for the evil from which it suffers. For when one part having grown out of proportion to the others aims at supremacy and tends to become too predominant, it is evident that, as for the reasons above given none of the three is absolute, but the purpose of the one can be counterworked and thwarted by the others, none of them will excessively outgrow the others or treat them with contempt. All in fact remains in statu quo, on the one hand, because any aggressive impulse is sure to be checked and from the outset each estate stands in dread of being interfered with by the others....

51. The constitution of Carthage seems to me to have been originally well contrived as regards its most distinctive points. For there were kings, and the house of Elders was an aristocratical force, and the people were supreme in matters proper to them, the entire frame of the state much resembling that of Rome and Sparta. But at the time when they entered on the Hannibalic War, the Carthaginian constitution had degenerated, and that of Rome was better. For as every body or state or action has its natural periods first of growth, then of prime, and finally of decay, and as everything in them is at its best when they are in their prime, it was for this reason that the difference between the two states manifested itself at this time. For by as much as the power and prosperity of Carthage had been earlier than that of Rome, by so much had Carthage already begun to decline; while Rome was exactly at her prime, as far at least as her system of government was concerned. Consequently, the multitude at Carthage had already acquired the chief voice in deliberations ; while at Rome the senate still retained this ; and hence, as in one ease the masses deliberated and in the other the most eminent men, the Roman decisions on public affairs were superior, so that although they met with complete disaster, they were finally by the wisdom of their counsels victorious over the Carthaginians in the war.

52. But to pass to differences of detail, such as, to begin with, the conduct of war, the Carthaginians naturally are superior at sea both in efficiency and equipment, because seamanship has long been their national craft, and they busy themselves with the sea more than any other people ; but as regards military service on land the Romans are much more efficient. They indeed devote their whole energies to this matter, whereas the Carthaginians entirely neglect their infantry, though they do pay some slight attention to their cavalry. The reason of this is that the troops they employ are foreign and mercenary, whereas those of the Romans are natives of the soil and citizens. So that in this respect also we must pronounce the political system of Rome to be superior to that of Carthage, the Carthaginians continuing to depend for the maintenance of their freedom on the courage of a mercenary force but the Romans on their own valour and on the aid of their allies. Consequently, even if they happen to be worsted at the outset, the Romans redeem defeat by final success, while it is the contrary with the Carthaginians. For the Romans, fighting as they are for their country and their children, never can abate their fury but continue to throw their whole hearts into the struggle until they get the better of their enemies. It follows that though the Romans are, as I said, much less skilled in naval matters, they are on the whole successful at sea owing to the gallantry of their men ; for although skill in seamanship is of no small importance in naval battles, it is chiefly the courage of the marines that turns the scale in favour of victory. Now not only do Italians in general naturally excel Phoenicians and Africans in bodily strength and personal courage, but by their institutions also they do much to foster a spirit of bravery in the young men. A single instance will suffice to indicate the pains taken by the state to turn out men who will be ready to endure everything in order to gain a reputation in their country for valour.

53. Whenever any illustrious man dies, he is carried at his funeral into the forum to the so-called rostra, sometimes conspicuous in an upright posture and more rarely reclined. Here with all the people standing round, a grown-up son, if he has left one who happens to be present, or if not some other relative mounts the rostra and discourses on the virtues and successful achievements of the dead. As a consequence the multitude and not only those who had a part in these achievements, but those also who had none, when the facts are recalled to their minds and brought before their eyes, are moved to such sympathy that the loss seems to be not confined to the mourners, but a public one affecting the whole people. Next after the interment and the performance of the usual ceremonies, they place the image of the departed in the most conspicuous position in the house, enclosed in a wooden shrine. This image is a mask reproducing with remarkable fidelity both the features and complexion of the deceased. On the occasion of public sacrifices they display these images, and decorate them with much care, and when any distinguished member of the family dies they take them to the funeral, putting them on men who seem to them to bear the closest resemblance to the original in stature and carriage. These representatives wear togas, with a purple border if the deceased was a consul or praetor, whole purple if he was a censor, and embroidered with gold if he had celebrated a triumph or achieved anything similar. They all ride in chariots preceded by the fasces, axes, and other insignia by which the different magistrates are wont to be accompanied according to the respective dignity of the offices of state held by each during his life ; and when they arrive at the rostra they all seat themselves in a row on ivory chairs. There could not easily be a more ennobling spectacle for a young man who aspires to fame and virtue. For who would not be inspired by the sight of the images of men renowned for their excellence, all together and as if alive and breathing ? What spectacle could be more glorious than this?

54. Besides, he who makes the oration over the man about to be buried, when he has finished speaking of him recounts the successes and exploits of the rest whose images are present, beginning from the most ancient. By this means, by this constant renewal of

the good report of brave men, the celebrity of those who performed noble deeds is rendered immortal, while at the same time the fame of those who did good service to their country becomes known to the people and a heritage for future generations. But the most important result is that young men are thus inspired to endure every suffering for the public welfare in the hope of winning the glory that attends on brave men. What I say is confirmed by the facts. For many Romans have voluntarily engaged in single combat in order to decide a battle, not a few have faced certain death, some in war to save the lives of the rest, and others in peace to save the republic. Some even when in office have put their own sons to death contrary to every law or custom, setting a higher value on the interest of their country than on the ties of nature that bound them to their nearest and dearest. Many such stories about many men are related in Roman history, but one told of a certain person will suffice for the present as an example and as a confirmation of what I say.

55. It is narrated that when Horatius Cocles was engaged in combat with two of the enemy at the far end of the bridge over the Tiber that lies in the front of the town, he saw large reinforcements coming up to help the enemy, and fearing lest they should force the passage and get into the town, he turned round and called to those behind him to retire and cut the bridge with all speed. His order was obeyed, and while they were cutting the bridge, he stood to his ground receiving many wounds, and arrested the attack of the enemy who were less astonished at his physical strength than at his endurance and courage. The bridge once cut, the enemy were prevented from attacking; and Cocles, plunging into the river in full armour as he was, deliberately sacrificed his life," regarding the safety of his country and the glory which in future would attach to his name as of more importance than his present existence and the years of life which remained to him. Such, if I am not wrong, is the eager emulation of achieving noble deeds engendered in the Roman youth by their institutions.

56. Again, the laws and customs relating to the acquisition of wealth are better in Rome than at Carthage. At Carthage nothing which results in profit is regarded as disgraceful; at Rome nothing is considered more so than to accept bribes and seek gain from improper channels.' For no less strong than their approval of money-making by respectable means is their condemnation of unscrupulous gain from forbidden sources. A proof of this is that at Carthage candidates for office practise open bribery, whereas at Rome death is the penalty for it. Therefore as the rewards offered to merit are the opposite in the two cases, it is natural that the steps taken to gain them should also be dissimilar. But the quality in which the Roman commonwealth is most distinctly superior is in my opinion the nature of their religious convictions. I believe that it is the very thing which among other peoples is an object of reproach, I mean superstition, which maintains the cohesion of the Roman State. These matters are clothed in such pomp and introduced to such an extent into their public and private life that nothing could exceed it, a fact which will surprise many. My own opinion at least is that they have adopted this course for the sake of the common people. It is a course which perhaps would not have been necessary had it been possible to form a state composed of wise men, but as every multitude is fickle, full of lawless desires, unreasoned passion, and violent anger, the multitude must be held in by invisible terrors and suchlike pageantry. For this reason I think, not that the ancients acted rashly and at haphazard in introducing among the people notions concerning the gods and beliefs in the terrors of the underworld, but that the moderns are most rash and foolish in banishing such beliefs. The consequence is that among the Greeks, apart from other things, members of the government, if they are entrusted with no more than a talent [of silver, weighing about sixty pounds], though they have ten copyists and as many seals and twice as many witnesses, cannot keep their faith ; whereas among the Romans those who as magistrates and legates are dealing with large sums of money maintain correct conduct just because they have pledged their faith by oath. Whereas elsewhere it is a rare thing to find a man who keeps his hands off public money, and whose record is clean in this respect, among the Romans one rarely comes across a man who has been detected in such conduct....

57. That all existing things are subject to decay and change is a truth that scarcely needs proof; for the course of nature is sufficient to force this conviction on us. There being two agencies by which every kind of state is liable to decay, the one external and the other a growth of the state itself, we can lay down no fixed rule about the former, but the latter is a regular process. I have already stated what kind of state is the first to come into being, and what the next, and how the one is transformed into the other ; so that those who are capable of connecting the opening propositions of this inquiry with its conclusion will now be able to foretell the future unaided. And what will happen is, I think, evident. When a state has weathered many great perils and subsequently attains to supremacy and uncontested sovereignty, it is evident that under the influence of long established prosperity, life will become more extravagant and the citizens more fierce in their rivalry regarding office and other objects than they ought to be. As these defects go on increasing, the beginning of the change for the worse will be due to love of office and the disgrace entailed by obscurity, as well as to extravagance and purse-proud display; and for this change the populace will be responsible when on the one hand they think they have a grievance against certain people who have shown themselves grasping, and when, on the other hand, they are puffed up by the flattery of others who aspire to office. For now, stirred to fury and swayed by passion in all their counsels, they will no longer consent to obey or even to be the equals of the ruling caste, but will demand the lion's share for themselves. When this happens, the state will change its name to the finest sounding of all, freedom and democracy, but will change its nature to the worst thing of all, mob-rule. Having dealt with the origin and growth of the Roman Republic, and with its prime and its present condition, and also with the differences for better or worse between it and others, I may now close this discourse more or less so.

58. But, drawing now upon the period immediately subsequent to the date at which I abandoned my narrative to enter on this digression, I will make brief and summary mention of one occurrence ; so that, as if exhibiting a single specimen of a good artist's work, I may make manifest not by words only but by actual fact the perfection and strength of principle of the Republic such as it then was. Hannibal, when, after his victory over the Romans at Cannae, the eight thousand who garrisoned the camp fell into his hands, after making them all prisoners, allowed them to send a deputation to those at home on the subject of their ransom and release. Upon their naming ten of their most distinguished members, he sent them off after making them swear that they would return to him. One of those nominated just as he was going out of the camp said he had forgotten something and went back, and after recovering the thing he had left behind again took his departure, thinking that by his return he had kept his faith and absolved himself of his oath. Upon their arrival in Rome they begged and entreated the senate not to grudge the prisoners their release, but to allow each of them to pay three minae and return to his people ; for Hannibal, they said, had made this concession. The men deserved to be released, for they had neither been guilty of cowardice in the battle nor had they done anything unworthy of Rome ; but having been left behind to guard the camp, they had, when all the rest had perished in the battle, been forced to yield to circumstances and surrender to the enemy. But the Romans, though they had met with severe reverses in the war, and had now, roughly speaking, lost all their allies and were in momentary expectation of Rome itself being placed in peril, after listening to this plea, neither disregarded their dignity under the pressure of calamity, nor neglected to take into consideration every proper step ; but seeing that Hannibal's object in acting thus was both to obtain funds and to deprive

the troops opposed to him of their high spirit, by showing that, even if defeatedi they might hope for safety, they were so far from acceding to this request, that they did not allow their pity for their kinsmen, or the consideration of the service the men would render them, to prevail, but defeated Hannibal's calculations and the hopes he had based on them by refusing to ransom the men, and at the same time imposed by law on their own troops the duty of either conquering or dying on the field, as there was no hope of safety for them if defeated. Therefore after coming to this decision they dismissed the nine delegates who returned of their own free will, as bound by their oath, while as for the man who had thought to free himself from the oath by a ruse they put him in irons and returned him to the enemy ; so that Hannibal's joy at his victory in the battle was not so great as his dejection, when he saw with amazement how steadfast and high-spirited were the Romans in their deliberations.

Reading 17

Cicero and the Late Republic

In less than a century after Polybius had described the Roman constitution and Roman public morals in such glowing terms, Roman society and politics had undergone serious decline, which ultimately resulted in the destruction of the Republic and its replacement by the Principate of the emperors, a form of hereditary monarchy. Our single best source of information for the years 65-43 B.C. are the voluminous writings of Cicero, Rome's greatest orator and trial lawyer. Besides possessing many of his public and courtroom speeches and essays on politics and philosophy, we are fortunate to have 955 letters exchanged between himself and numerous friends. The following four passages are taken from this enormous body of written material and offer an exciting, though dismal, view of the corruption that had become widespread in Roman society during the final decades of the Republic.

A. A CORRUPT TRIAL

✤ Letter to Atticus I. 16

Cicero's most deadly political enemy was Publius Clodius Pulcher, a member of an old patrician family, but who built up a large political following among the urban poor of Rome. He was therefore opposed by the more conservative leaders of the Roman senate; and when Clodius became implicated in a scandal involving the desecration of religious rites, his political enemies seized upon the issue and eventually brought him to trial on the matter, but as Cicero described in a letter to his friend Atticus, Clodius succeeded in getting off by widespread use of bribery.

(Taken from the translation of E. R. Winstedt in the Loeb Classical Library Series)

If you want to know the cause of the acquittal, it was the empty pockets and disreputable quality of the jury; and that it happened at all was due to the plan of Hortensius. He was afraid that Fufius would veto the bill that was proposed in accordance with the senate's decree. He did not see that it was better for Clodius to be left in disgrace and eating humble pie than for the trial to be held before an unreliable jury; but he was led by his hatred to bring the case to trial quickly, since he said that Clodius' throat could be cut even by a sword made of lead. As to the trial itself, if you want to know, it was quite incredible how it went.... You've never seen a bigger bunch of crooks seated in a gambling-den: tarnished senators, threadbare equites, and tribunes, not moneyers so much as money makers. Yet, there were a few men of quality whom Clodius could not put to flight at the scrutiny of jurors.... In the court, as each question was referred to the court during the preliminaries, their opinions were unanimous and as strict as could be. The accused was granted nothing, the prosecutor was given more than he asked for. Well, Hortensius began to gloat about his foresight. There wasn't a soul who thought Clodius still on trial and not condemned one thousand times already. When I was called as a witness (I think that you must have heard the story), the supporters of Clodius shouted, the jury rose and stood around me, baring their throats, and indicating to Clodius that they would die for me;... and so, when I was thus being defended by the jury as if I were the saviour of my country, the defendant was shattered by their voices, and all his counsel collapsed. More-over, on the next day a crowd gathered at my house every bit as large as the one which escorted me home at the end of my consulship. Our splendid high court clamored that they would not come unless the court was guarded. The question was referred to the court. There was only one vote against a guard. The question was raised in the senate. A decree was made, very impressive, very complimentary; the jury was praised, the mag-istrates were told to act. Nobody thought that Clodius would offer any defense. "But tell me now, Muses, (as Homer says) how first the fire was lit." You know that Calvus, one of the young sparks, the singer of my praises,... inside two days, using one slave (and he a one-time gladiator), fixed the whole thing. He got people to come and see him. He made promises. He stood as surety. He made gifts. On top of all that—ye gods, it's scandalous— some of the jury even got, as the final titbit of their reward, nights with certain women and introductions to some of the young nobles. So, there was a complete flight of the men of standing. The Forum was full of slaves, and yet 25 of the jury were still brave enough to prefer even to risk their lives in the face of instant danger than to bring the whole state to ruin. There were 31 more anxious to be paid than to have a worthwhile reputation. Catulus saw one of them: "What did you want to ask us for a guard to protect you for? Were you frightened that your profits would be snatched?" There you are, as briefly as I can, what the trial was like, and why Clodius got off.

B. VIOLENCE AT A TRIAL

✣ Letter to his Brother Quintus II. 3.2

In order to oppose the violence organized by Clodius' followers in Rome, Titus Annius Milo organized similar gangs of toughs who clashed from time to time with those of Clodius. These violent political activities plagued the streets of Rome for about five years (57-52 B.C.) until Clodius was finally killed, and Milo was forced to go into exile. The fol-lowing excerpt from a letter of Cicero, written to his brother, who happened to be away from Rome on state business, describes a scene at a trial held in early 56 B.C.

⤳   *(Taken from the translation of W. Glynn Williams in the Loeb Classical Library)*

Milo appeared in court on February 6th. Pompey made a speech. At least he tried to. When he got up, you see, Clodius' gangs began to shout. They kept it up all through his speech, not just shouting, but curses and swearing too. Pompey refused to be stopped. He's got courage. He said all that he had to say, sometimes even getting a bit of silence.... Anyway, as he finished, Clodius got up. He was greeted with such a roar from our chaps (for we'd decided to return the compliment) that he completely lost control of himself and couldn't speak. Pompey's speech ended about an hour after noon. The din went on for two hours, swearing and the filthiest ditties about Clodius and his sister being bandied about. Pale with fury, he began to shout to his supporters, "Who's starving the people to death?" "Pompey," the gangs replied. "Who wants to go to Alexandria?" he asked. "Pompey," they replied. "Whom do you want to go?" "Crassus" came the answer. He was there too, not wishing Milo any good either. About an hour later, it seemed as if someone had given Clodius' men an order to start spitting at us. Our men's tempers rose. They began to jostle us to make us give ground. Our men charged, the gangs took to their heels, Clodius was thrown off the speaker's platform, I took to my heels too, in case anything happened in the crowd. Pompey went home. I didn't go to the senate either, to avoid having to hold my tongue on such an important question, or to tread on the toes of the men of standing in a defense of Pompey. Bibulus, Curio, Favonius, and young Servilius were all criticizing him.

C. THE EVE OF CIVIL WARLETTERS TO HIS FRIENDS VIII. 14.2-3

As the threat of civil war between Caesar and Pompey loomed on the horizon during the year 50 B.C., Cicero was absent from Rome in order to serve as governor of the Roman province of Cilicia (southeastern Anatolia). Thus, in order to stay in touch with the most recent political news, Cicero asked a younger associate, Marcus Caelius Rufus, to keep him informed by letter. In the following passage Caelius sums up with political astuteness the situation as it stood in August of 50 B.C.

(Taken from the translation of W. Glynn Williams in the Loeb Classical Library)

With regard to the general political situation, I have repeatedly told you in my letters that I foresee no peace that can last a year; and the nearer the struggle-and there is bound to be a struggle-approaches, the more clearly do we see the danger of it. The point at issue, on which those who are at the head of affairs are going to fight, is this: Gnaeus Pompey is determined not to allow Gaius Caesar to be elected consul unless he has handed over his army and his provinces. Caesar, on the other hand, is convinced that there is no safety for him if he once quits his army. He proposes, however, this compromise: that both should deliver up their armies. So it is that their vaunted mutual attachment and detestable alliance is not merely degenerating into private bickering but is breaking out into war.... Amid all this discord I see that Pompey will have on his side the senate and the body of jurors; all who live a life of fear, or but little hope, will join Caesar: for his army is altogether above comparison. Only may we have time enough to consider the resources of each and choose our side!

D. DEATH OF CLODIUS

The following passage is from an ancient commentary on Cicero's speech delivered on behalf of Milo when charged with Clodius' murder in 52 B.C. This passage explains the background to the trial and offers a striking picture of the political violence of the late republic.

(Taken from the translation of N. H. Watts in the Loeb Classical Library)

Cicero gave this speech on 7 April in the third consulship of Pompey (52 B.C.). During the trial Pompey stationed troops in the Forum and the temples surrounding it.... Titus Annius

Milo, Publius Plautius Hypsaeus, and Quintus Metellus Scipio were rival candidates for the consulship. Largesse was openly distributed; and in addition, they surrounded themselves with squads of armed men. A fierce feud existed between Milo and Clodius, since Milo was a firm friend of Cicero and had given strenuous support as plebeian tribune to Cicero's recall from exile (57 B.C.). After Cicero's return Publius Clodius remained just as hostile towards Cicero, and so he backed Hypsaeus and Scipio against Milo. Milo and Clodius frequently fought out their feud in Rome with their own gangs. They were both equally ruthless, but Milo acted for the better men. Now, while Milo was standing for the consulship, Clodius was campaigning in the same year for the praetorship; and he reckoned that his tenure would be undermined if Milo achieved the position of consul. The consular elections were considerably delayed, and it became impossible to complete them because of the reckless hostilities of the candidates. Hence, by January there were still no consuls or praetors in office, and election-day was all the time being postponed as before. Milo in fact wanted the elections to be completed as soon as might be: he felt confident of the support of the good men (since he was opposing Clodius) and of the people, since he had been generous in his largesse and had paid for sumptuous theatrical performances and gladiatorial shows (at a cost of three personal fortunes, according to Cicero). The other candidates preferred delay.... Now, on 20 January ... Milo set out for Lanuvium, his home town, of which he was then dictator, to install a priest on the next day. At about 3 p.m. just beyond Bovillae he was confronted by Clodius, who was on his way back from Aricia, where he had been addressing the town officials. The spot was quite near the shrine of Bona Dea. Clodius was on horseback with about 30 slaves armed with swords and unencumbered, the usual practice when on the move in those days. In addition, he had three friends with him: one an equestrian called Gaius Causinius Schola, and two who were well-known plebeians, Publius Pomponius and Gaius Clodius. Milo was travelling in a carriage with his wife Fausta, daughter of the dictator Lucius Sulla, and a relative called Marcus Fufius. Behind them was a long column of slaves, including some gladiators such as the famous Eudamus and Birria. They were at the far end of the line, moving fairly slowly; and they started a brawl with Clodius' slaves. As Clodius glanced back menacingly at this uproar, Birria hurled a lance, which pierced his shoulder. With the fight under way, more of Milo's entourage ran up, while the wounded Clodius was carried to a near-by inn in Bovillae. Milo heard that he had been injured, and he decided that it would be dangerous to leave Clodius alive, while his death would be a relief, even if there were penalties to be paid. Thus, he ordered that he should be turned out of the inn.... The skulking Clodius was therefore hauled out and finished off with many wounds. His body was left in the road, since Clodius' slaves were either dead or lying low with grave injuries. It was picked up by a senator, Sextus Teidius, who happened to be returning to Rome from the country. He had the body taken to Rome in his litter, and he retraced his steps the way he had come. The corpse reached Rome before about 7 p.m. and was surrounded in the hall of Clodius' house by a great crowd of slaves and rabble, weeping copiously; and the feeling aroused by the affair was intensified by his wife Fulvia, who displayed his wounds with unrestrained grief. At dawn the next day a still bigger crowd of the same sort gathered, and several well-known men were seen there.... Here assembled Titus Munatius Plancus the brother of the orator Lucius Plancus, and Quintus Pompeius Rufus grandson of the dictator Sulla through his daughter. Both men were plebeian tribunes. At their suggestion the ignorant mob carried the body to the Forum, naked and battered as it was, in the same attitude as it had had on its couch, so that the wounds were clearly visible. Then they placed it on the speaker's platform. Plancus and Pompeius, being supporters of Milo's rivals, held a public meeting there and inflamed people against Milo. Then the clerk Sextus Cloelius persuaded the people to take the body into the senate-house and cremate it, using benches, tables, other furniture, and notebooks belonging to the clerks. This set fire to the senate-house itself, and the blaze spread to the Basilica Porcia next door. Furthermore, the Clodius crowd attacked the homes of Milo (who was away),... but they were driven back with arrows.... The destruction of the senate-house caused a good deal more feeling among the public than the death of Clodius.... Consular elections still could not be conducted owing to the disorderliness of the candidates and the activities of gangs. Then a senatorial decree was enacted as a first step, requiring that ... Pompey should levy troops throughout Italy. He very quickly organized a force.

TACITUS, HISTORIAN OF IMPERIAL ROME

Tacitus (born ca. 60 and died ca. 125 A.D.) was the greatest historian of imperial Rome. Little is known about his life, but he seems to have come from a family of northern Italy or of southern Gaul [France] and enjoyed a rather distinguished senatorial career. His historical account of the Principate is extremely detailed and gives us our best view into the workings of the Roman imperial government and of the constant intrigues and scandals that surrounded the imperial court and involved members of the Roman upper class, especially the senatorial aristocracy. The following two excerpts are taken from Tacitus' work entitled *The Annals*, which treated the period from the death of Augustus in 14 A.D. to the death of Nero in 68 A.D. They specifically concern the reign of Nero (r. 54-68 A.D.), who was Rome's first teenage emperor and exhibited interests all too typical of his youth. He eventually showed himself to be unfit to exercise imperial power, was faced with a major rebellion in the provinces, and committed suicide before his enemies could seize and arrest him.

(Taken from the translation of Albert J. Church and William J. Brodribb)

A. NERO THE GANG BANGER

✤ Book XIII

25 In the consulship of Quintus Volusius and Publius Scipio [56 A.D.], there was peace abroad, but a disgusting licentiousness at home on the part of Nero, who in a slave's disguise, so as to be unrecognized, would wander through the streets of Rome, to brothels and taverns, with comrades, who seized on goods exposed for sale and inflicted wounds on any whom they encountered, some of these last knowing him so little that he even received blows himself, and showed the marks of them in his face. When it was notorious that the emperor was the assailant, and the insults on men and women of distinction were multiplied, other persons too on the strength of a licence once granted under Nero's name, ventured with impunity on the same practices, and had gangs of their own, till night presented the scenes of a captured city.

Julius Montanus, a senator, but one who had not yet held any office, happened to encounter the prince in the darkness, and because he fiercely repulsed his attack and then on recognizing him begged for mercy, as though this was a reproach, forced to destroy himself. Nero was for the future more timid, and surrounded himself with soldiers and a number of gladiators, who, when a fray began on a small scale and seemed a private affair, were to let it alone, but, if the injured persons resisted stoutly, they rushed in with their swords.

B. ΠERO THE ΜATRICIDE

In the fifth year of his reign (59 A.D.) Nero shed himself of his mother Agrippina and her unwanted interference into matters of state by cold-bloodedly carrying out her murder and then passing it off as a justified execution of a dangerous conspiratress. This act of calculated murder can perhaps be regarded as constituting Nero's loss of his political virginity. Getting off scott free from having perpetrated such a heinous crime seems to have convinced him that he could enjoy his absolute power just as he pleased.

✣ Book XIV

1 In the year of the consulship of Caius Vipstanus and Caius Fonteius, Nero deferred no more a long meditated crime. Length of power had matured his daring, and his passion for Poppaea daily grew more ardent. As the woman had no hope of marriage for herself or of Octavia's divorce while Agrippina lived, she would reproach the emperor with incessant vituperation and sometimes call him in jest a mere ward who was under the rule of others, and was so far from having empire that he had not even his liberty. 'Why,' she asked, 'was her marriage put off? Was it, forsooth, her beauty and her ancestors, with their triumphal honors, that failed to please, or her being a mother, and her sincere heart? No; the fear was that as a wife at least she would divulge the wrongs of the Senate, and the wrath of the people at the arrogance and rapacity of his mother. If the only daughter in law Agrippina could bear was one who wished evil to her son, let her be restored to her union with Otho. She would go anywhere in the world, where she might hear of the insults heaped on the emperor, rather than witness them, and be also involved in his perils.' These and the like complaints, rendered impressive by tears and by the cunning of an adulteress, no one checked, as all longed to see the mother's power broken, while not a person believed that the son's hatred would steel his heart to her murder.

 2 Cluvius relates that Agrippina in her eagerness to retain her influence went so far that more than once at midday, when Nero, even at that hour, was flushed with wine and feasting, she presented herself attractively attired to her half intoxicated son and offered him her person, and that when kinsfolk observed wanton kisses and caresses, portending infamy, it was Seneca who sought a female's aid against a woman's fascinations, and hurried in Acte, the freed girl, who alarmed at her own peril and at Nero's disgrace, told him that the incest was notorious, as his mother boasted of it, and that the soldiers would never endure the rule of an impious sovereign. Fabius Rusticus tells us that it was not Agrippina, but Nero, who lusted for the crime, and that it was frustrated by the adroitness of that same freed girl. Cluvius's account, however, is also that of all other authors, and popular belief inclines to it, whether it was that Agrippina really conceived such a monstrous wickedness in her heart, or perhaps because the thought of a strange passion seemed comparatively credible in a woman, who in her girlish years had allowed herself to be seduced by Lepidus in the hope of winning power, had stooped with a like ambition to the lust of Pallas, and had trained herself for every infamy by her marriage with her uncle [the Emperor Claudius, r. 41-54 A.D.].

 3 Nero accordingly avoided secret interviews with her, and when she withdrew to her gardens or to her estates at Tusculum and Antium, he praised her for courting repose. At last, convinced that she would be too formidable, wherever she might dwell, he resolved to destroy her, merely deliberating whether it was to be accomplished by poison, or by the sword, or by any other violent means. Poison at first seemed best, but, were it to be administered at the imperial table, the result could not be referred to chance after the recent circumstances of the death of Britannicus. Again, to tamper with the servants of a woman who, from her familiarity with crime, was on her guard against treachery, appeared to be extremely difficult, and then, too, she had fortified her constitution by the use of antidotes. How again the dagger and its work were to be kept secret, no one could suggest, and it was feared too that whoever might be chosen to execute such a crime would spurn the order. An ingenious suggestion was offered by Anicetus, a freedman, commander of the fleet at Misenum, who had been tutor to Nero in boyhood and had a hatred of Agrippina which she reciprocated. He explained that a vessel could be constructed, from which a part might by a contrivance be detached, when out at sea, so as to plunge her unawares into the water. 'Nothing,' he said, 'allowed of accidents so much as the sea, and should she be overtaken by shipwreck, who would be so unfair as to impute to crime an offence committed by the winds and waves? The emperor would add the honor of a temple and of shrines to the deceased lady, with every other display of filial affection.'

4 Nero liked the device, favored as it also was by the particular time, for he was celebrating Minerva's five days' festival at Baiae. Thither he enticed his mother by repeated assurances that children ought to bear with the irritability of parents and to soothe their tempers, wishing thus to spread a rumor of reconciliation and to secure Agrippina's acceptance through the feminine credulity, which easily believes what joy. As she approached, he went to the shore to meet her (she was coming from Antium), welcomed her with outstretched hand and embrace, and conducted her to Bauli. This was the name of a country house, washed by a bay of the sea, between the promontory of Misenum and the lake of Baiae. Here was a vessel distinguished from others by its equipment, seemingly meant, among other things, to do honor to his mother; for she had been accustomed to sail in a trireme, with a crew of marines. And now she was invited to a banquet, that night might serve to conceal the crime. It was well known that somebody had been found to betray it, that Agrippina had heard of the plot, and in doubt whether she was to believe it, was conveyed to Baiae in her litter. There some soothing words allayed her fear; she was graciously received, and seated at table above the emperor. Nero prolonged the banquet with various conversation, passing from a youth's playful familiarity to an air of constraint, which seemed to indicate serious thought, and then, after protracted festivity, escorted her on her departure, clinging with kisses to her eyes and bosom, either to crown his hypocrisy or because the last sight of a mother on the even of destruction caused a lingering even in that brutal heart.

5 A night of brilliant starlight with the calm of a tranquil sea was granted by heaven, seemingly, to convict the crime. The vessel had not gone far, Agrippina having with her two of her intimate attendants, one of whom, Crepereius Gallus, stood near the helm, while Acerronia, reclining at Agrippina's feet as she reposed herself, spoke joyfully of her son's repentance and of the recovery of the mother's influence, when at a given signal the ceiling of the place, which was loaded with a quantity of lead, fell in, and Crepereius was crushed and instantly killed. Agrippina and Acerronia were protected by the projecting sides of the couch, which happened to be too strong to yield under the weight. But this was not followed by the breaking up of the vessel; for all were bewildered, and those too, who were in the plot, were hindered by the unconscious majority. The crew then thought it best to throw the vessel on one side and so sink it, but they could not themselves promptly unite to face the emergency, and others, by counteracting the attempt, gave an opportunity of a gentler fall into the sea. Acerronia, however, thoughtlessly exclaiming that she was Agrippina, and imploring help for the emperor's mother, was despatched with poles and oars, and such naval implements as chance offered. Agrippina was silent and was thus the less recognized; still, she received a wound in her shoulder. She swam, then met with some small boats which conveyed her to the Lucrine lake, and so entered her house.

6 There she reflected how for this very purpose she had been invited by a lying letter and treated with conspicuous honor, how also it was near the shore, not from being driven by winds or dashed on rocks, that the vessel had in its upper part collapsed, like a mechanism anything but nautical. She pondered too the death of Acerronia; she looked at her own wound, and saw that her only safeguard against treachery was to ignore it. Then she sent her freedman Agerinus to tell her son how by heaven's favor and his good fortune she had escaped a terrible disaster; that she begged him, alarmed, as he might be, by his mother's peril, to put off the duty of a visit, as for the present she needed repose. Meanwhile, pretending that she felt secure, she applied remedies to her wound, and fomentations to her person. She then ordered search to be made for the will of Acerronia, and her property to be sealed, in this alone throwing off disguise.

7 Nero, meantime, as he waited for tidings of the consummation of the deed, received information that she had escaped with the injury of a slight wound, after having so far encountered the peril that there could be no question as to its author. Then, paralysed with terror and protesting that she would show herself the next moment eager for vengeance, either arming the slaves or stirring up the soldiery, or hastening to the Senate and the people, to charge him with the wreck, with her wound, and with the destruction of her friends, he asked what resource he had against all this, unless something could be at once devised by Burrus and Seneca. He had instantly summoned both of them, and possibly they were already in the secret. There was a long silence on their part; they feared they might remonstrate in vain, or believed the crisis to be such that Nero must perish, unless Agrippina were at once crushed. Thereupon Seneca was so far the more prompt as to glance back on Burrus, as if to ask him whether the bloody deed must be required of the soldiers. Burrus replied 'that the praetorians were attached to the whole family of the Caesars, and remembering Germanicus would not dare a savage deed on his offspring. It was for Anicetus to accomplish his promise.' Anicetus, without a pause, claimed for himself the consummation of the crime. At those words, Nero declared that that day gave him empire, and that a freedman was the author of this mighty boon. 'Go,' he said, 'with all speed and take with you the men readiest to execute your orders.' He himself, when he had heard of the arrival of Agrippina's messenger, Agerinus, contrived a theatrical mode of accusation, and, while the man was repeating his message, threw down a sword at his feet, then ordered him to be put in irons, as a detected criminal, so that he might invent a story how his mother had plotted the emperor's destruction and in the shame of discovered guilt had by her own choice sought death.

8 Meantime, Agrippina's peril being universally known and taken to be an accidental occurrence, everybody, the moment he heard of it, hurried down to the beach. Some climbed projecting piers; some the nearest vessels; others, as far as their stature allowed, went into the sea; some, again, stood with outstretched arms, while the whole shore rung with wailings, with prayers and cries, as different questions were asked and uncertain answers given. A vast multitude streamed to the spot with torches, and as soon as all knew that she was safe, they at once prepared to wish her joy, till the sight of an armed and threatening force scared them away. Anicetus then surrounded the house with a guard, and having burst open the gates, dragged off the slaves who met him, till he came to the door of her chamber, where a few still stood, after the rest had fled in terror at the attack. A small lamp was in the room, and one slave girl with Agrippina, who grew more and more anxious, as no messenger came from her son, not even Agerinus, while the appearance of the shore was changed, a solitude one moment, then sudden bustle and tokens of the worst catastrophe. As the girl rose to depart, she exclaimed, 'Do you too forsake me?' and looking round saw Anicetus, who had

with him the captain of the trireme, Herculeius, and Obaritus, a centurion of marines. 'If,' said she, 'you have come to see me, take back word that I have recovered, but if you are here to do a crime, I believe nothing about my son; he has not ordered his mother's murder.' The assassins closed in round her couch, and the captain of the trireme first struck her head violently with a club. Then, as the centurion bared his sword for the fatal deed, presenting her person, she exclaimed, 'Smite my womb,' and with many wounds she was slain.

9 So far our accounts agree. That Nero gazed on his mother after her death and praised her beauty, some have related, while others deny it. Her body was burnt that same night on a dining couch, with a mean funeral; nor, as long as Nero was in power, was the earth raised into a mound, or even decently closed. Subsequently, she received from the solicitude of her domestics, a humble sepulchre on the road to Misenum, near the country house of Caesar the Dictator, which from a great height commands a view of the bay beneath. As soon as the funeral pile was lighted, one of her freedmen, surnamed Mnester, ran himself through with a sword, either from love of his mistress or from the fear of destruction. Many years before Agrippina had anticipated this end for herself and had spurned the thought. For when she consulted the astrologers about Nero, they replied that he would be emperor and kill his mother. 'Let him kill her,' she said, 'provided he is emperor.'

10 But the emperor, when the crime was at last accomplished, realised its portentous guilt. The rest of the night, now silent and stupified, now and still oftener starting up in terror, bereft of reason, he awaited the dawn as if it would bring with it his doom. He was first encouraged to hope by the flattery addressed to him, at the prompting of Burrus, by the centurions and tribunes, who again and again pressed his hand and congratulated him on his having escaped an unforeseen danger and his mother's daring crime. Then his friends went to the temples, and, an example having once been set, the neighboring towns of Campania testified their joy with sacrifices and deputations. He himself, with an opposite phase of hypocrisy, seemed sad, and almost angry at his own deliverance, and shed tears over his mother's death. But as the aspects of places change not, as do the looks of men, and as he had ever before his eyes the dreadful sight of that sea with its shores (some too believed that the notes of a funereal trumpet were heard from the surrounding heights, and wailings from the mother's grave), he retired to Naples and sent a letter to the Senate, the drift of which was that Agerinus, one of Agrippina's confidential freedmen, had been detected with the dagger of an assassin, and that in the consciousness of having planned the crime she had paid its penalty.

11 He even revived the charges of a period long past, how she had aimed at a share of empire, and at inducing the praetorian cohorts to swear obedience to a woman, to the disgrace of the Senate and people; how, when she was disappointed, in her fury with the soldiers, the Senate, and the populace, she opposed the usual donative and largess, and organised perilous prosecutions against distinguished citizens. What efforts had it cost him to hinder her from bursting into the Senate house and giving answers to foreign nations! He glanced too with indirect censure at the days of Claudius, and ascribed all the abominations of that reign to his mother, thus seeking to show that it was the State's good fortune which had destroyed her. For he actually told the story of the shipwreck; but who could be so stupid as to believe that it was accidental, or that a shipwrecked woman had sent one man with a weapon to break through an emperor's guards and fleets? So now it was not Nero, whose brutality was far beyond any remonstrance, but Seneca who was in ill repute, for having written a confession in such a style.

12 Still there was a marvellous rivalry among the nobles in decreeing thanksgivings at all the shrines, and the celebration with annual games of Minerva's festival, as the day on which the plot had been discovered; also, that a golden image of Minerva with a statue of the emperor by its side should be set up in the Senate house, and that Agrippina's birthday should be classed among the inauspicious days. Thrasea Paetus, who had been used to pass over previous flatteries in silence or with brief assent, then walked out of the Senate, thereby imperilling himself, without communicating to the other senators any impulse towards freedom. There occurred too a thick succession of portents, which meant nothing. A woman gave birth to a snake, and another was killed by a thunderbolt in her husband's embrace. Then the sun was suddenly darkened and the fourteen districts of the city were struck by lightning. All this happened quite without any providential design; so much so, that for many subsequent years Nero prolonged his reign and his crimes. Still, to deepen the popular hatred towards his mother, and prove that since her removal, his clemency had increased, he restored to their ancestral homes two distinguished ladies, Junia and Calpurnia, with two ex praetors, Valerius Capito and Licinius Gabolus, whom Agrippina had formerly banished. He also allowed the ashes of Lollia Paulina to be brought back and a tomb to be built over them. Iturius and Calvisius, whom he had himself temporarily exiled, he now released from their penalty. Silana indeed had died a natural death at Tarentum, whither she had returned from her distant exile, when the power of Agrippina, to whose enmity she owed her fall, began to totter, or her wrath was at last appeased.

13 While Nero was lingering in the towns of Campania, doubting how he should enter Rome, whether he would find the Senate submissive and the populace enthusiastic, all the vilest courtiers, and of these never had a court a more abundant crop, argued against his hesitation by assuring him that Agrippina's name was hated and that her death had heightened his popularity. 'He might go without a fear,' they said, 'and experience in his person men's veneration for him.' They insisted at the same time on preceding him. They found greater enthusiasm than they had promised, the tribes coming forth to meet him, the Senate in holiday attire, troops of their children and wives arranged according to sex and age, tiers of seats raised for the spectacle, where he was to pass, as a triumph is witnessed. Thus elated and exulting over his people's slavery, he proceeded to the Capitol, performed the thanksgiving, and then plunged into all the excesses, which, though ill restrained, some sort of respect for his mother had for a while delayed.

14 He had long had a fancy for driving a four horse chariot, and a no less degrading taste for singing to the harp, in a theatrical fashion, when he was at dinner. This he would remind people was a royal custom, and had been the practice of ancient chiefs; it was celebrated too in the praises of poets and was meant to show honor to the gods. Songs indeed, he said, were sacred to Apollo, and it was in the dress of a singer that that great and prophetic deity was seen in Roman temples as well as in Greek cities. He could no longer be restrained, when Seneca and Burrus thought it best to concede one point that he might not persist in both. A space was enclosed in the Vatican valley where he might manage his horses, without the spectacle being public. Soon he actually invited all the people of Rome, who extolled him in their praises, like a mob which craves for amusements and rejoices when a prince draws them the same way. However, the public exposure of his shame acted on him as an incentive instead of sickening him, as men expected. Imagining that he mitigated the scandal by disgracing many others, he brought on the stage descendants of noble families, who sold themselves because they were paupers. As they have ended their days, I think it due to their ancestors not to hand down their names. And indeed the infamy is his who gave them wealth to reward their degradation rather than to deter them from degrading themselves. He prevailed too on some well known Roman knights, by immense presents, to offer their services in the amphitheatre; only pay from one who is able to command, carries with it the force of compulsion.

15 Still, not yet wishing to disgrace himself on a public stage, he instituted some games under the title of 'juvenile sports,' for which people of every class gave in their names. Neither rank nor age nor previous high promotion hindered any one from practising the art of a Greek or Latin actor and even stooping to gestures and songs unfit for a man. Noble ladies too actually played disgusting parts, and in the grove, with which Augustus had surrounded the lake for the naval fight, there were erected places for meeting and refreshment, and every incentive to excess was offered for sale. Money too was distributed, which the respectable had to spend under sheer compulsion and which the profligate gloried in squandering. Hence a rank growth of abominations and of all infamy. Never did a more filthy rabble add a worse licentiousness to our long corrupted morals. Even, with virtuous training, purity is not easily upheld; far less amid rivalries in vice could modesty or propriety or any trace of good manners be preserved. Last of all, the emperor himself came on the stage, tuning his lute with elaborate care and trying his voice with his attendants. There were also present, to complete the show, a guard of soldiers with centurions and tribunes, and Burrus, who grieved and yet applauded. Then it was that Roman knights were first enrolled under the title of Augustani [an organized group of the emperor's fans], men in their prime and remarkable for their strength, some, from a natural frivolity, others from the hope of promotion. Day and night they kept up a thunder of applause, and applied to the emperor's person and voice the epithets of deities. Thus they lived in fame and honor, as if on the strength of their merits.

Reading 19

The Meditations of Marcus Aurelius

As a result of the principle of hereditary monarchy that formed the basis of the Roman Principate, the Roman Empire experienced ups and downs in accordance with the character and judgment of the various emperors. In sharp contrast to the immature and corrupt Nero, as revealed in the previous reading, stands Marcus Aurelius (emperor 161-180). As a youth he developed a keen interest in philosophy and endeavored throughout his life to live up to its high moral standards; and the public record of his life indicates that he succeeded rather well in doing so. The following passages come from a short philosophical work that Marcus Aurelius wrote in Greek, and whose title is usually translated into English as Meditations. Running throughout the entire work are three themes that had long been integral to Greek philosophy:

1. That human beings have a dual nature, body and soul, with the latter serving as the ruler of the former; and that as rational animals, humans are designed by nature to use reason to govern their actions and behavior.

2. That all things in life and in the universe are subject to constant change; and that all human beings enjoy a physical existence that is quite insignificant with respect to eternity and the totality of the universe.

3. That we are all duty-bound to love our fellow man and to treat one another with decency and to correct one another's faults through gentle reasoning.

Despite his position as the all-mighty ruler of the Roman Empire, Marcus Aurelius held the second and third of these three principles before himself as constant reminders that in the long scheme of things he was no more important than other people, and that he must rule his subjects with humanity.

(Taken from the translation of George Long in the Harvard Classics [1909-1914] Vol. II. Part 3)

Book I

FROM my grandfather Verus [I learned] good morals and the government of my temper. From the reputation and remembrance of my father, modesty and a manly character. From my mother, piety and beneficence, and abstinence, not only from evil deeds, but even from evil thoughts; and further simplicity in my way of living, far removed from the habits of the rich. From my great-grandfather, not to have frequented public schools, and to have had good teachers at home, and to know that on such things a man should spend liberally. From my governor, to be neither of the green nor of the blue party at the games in the Circus, nor a partizan either of the Parmularius or the Scutarius at the gladiators' fights; from him too I learned endurance of labour, and to want little, and to work with my own hands, and not to meddle with other people's affairs, and not to be ready to listen to slander. From Diognetus, not to busy myself about trifling things, and not to give credit to what was said by miracle-workers and jugglers about incantations and the driving away of demons and such things; and not to breed quails [for fighting], nor to give myself up passionately to such things; and to endure freedom of speech; and to have become intimate with philosophy; and to have been a hearer, first of Bacchius, then of Tandasis and Marcianus; and to have written dialogues in my youth; and to have desired a plank bed and skin, and whatever else of the kind belongs to the Grecian discipline.

From Rusticus I received the impression that my character required improvement and discipline; and from him I learned not to be led astray to sophistic emulation, nor to writing on speculative matters, nor to delivering little hortatory orations, nor to showing myself off as a man who practises much discipline, or does benevolent acts in order to make a display; and to abstain from rhetoric, and poetry, and fine writing; and not to walk about in the house in my outdoor dress, nor to do other things of the kind; and to write my letters with simplicity, like the letter which Rusticus wrote from Sinuessa to my mother; and with respect to those who have offended me by words, or done me wrong, to be easily disposed to be pacified and reconciled, as soon as they have shown a readiness to be reconciled, and to read carefully, and not to be satisfied with a superficial understanding of a book; nor hastily to give my assent to those who talk overmuch; and I am indebted to him for being acquainted with the discourses of Epictetus, which he communicated to me out of his own collection.

From Apollonius I learned freedom of will and undeviating steadiness of purpose; and to look to nothing else, not even for a moment, except to reason; and to be always the same in sharp pains, on the occasion of the loss of a child, and in long illness; and to see clearly in a living example that the same man can be both most resolute and yielding, and not peevish in giving his instruction; and to have had before my eyes a man who clearly considered his experience and his skill in expounding philosophical principles as the smallest of his merits; and from him I learned how to receive from friends what are esteemed favours, without being either humbled by them or letting them pass unnoticed. From Sextus, a benevolent disposition, and the example of a family governed in a fatherly manner, and the idea of living conformably to nature; and gravity without affectation, and to look carefully after the interests of friends, and to tolerate ignorant persons, and those who form opinions without consideration: he had the power of readily accommodating himself to all, so that intercourse with him was more agreeable than any flattery; and at the same time he was most highly venerated by those who associated with him; and he had the faculty both of discovering and ordering, in an intelligent and methodical way, the principles necessary for life; and he never showed anger or any other passion, but was entirely free from passion, and also most affectionate; and he could express approbation without noisy display, and he possessed much knowledge without ostentation. From Alexander, the grammarian, to refrain from fault-finding, and not in a reproachful way to chide those who uttered any barbarous or solecistic or strange-sounding expression; but dexterously to introduce the very expression which ought to have been used, and in the way of answer or giving confirmation, or joining in an inquiry about the thing itself, not about the word, or by some other fit suggestion. From Fronto I learned to observe what envy and duplicity and hypocrisy are in a tyrant, and that generally those among us who are called Patricians are rather deficient in paternal affection.

From Alexander the Platonic, not frequently nor without necessity to say to any one, or to write in a letter, that I have no leisure; nor continually to excuse the neglect of duties required by our relation to those with whom we live, by alleging urgent occupations. From Catulus, not to be indifferent when a friend finds fault, even if he should find fault without reason, but to try to restore him to his usual disposition; and to be ready to speak well of teachers, as it is reported of Domitius and Athenodotus; and to love my children truly.

✦ Book IV

Consider, for example, the times of Vespasian [Roman emperor 69-79]. Thou wilt see all these things, people marrying, bringing up children, sick, dying, warring, feasting, trafficking, cultivating the ground, flattering, obstinately arrogant, suspecting, plotting, wishing for some to die, grumbling about the present, loving, heaping up treasure, desiring consulship, kingly power. Well, then, that life of these people no longer exists at all. Again, remove to the times of Trajan [Roman emperor 98-117]. Again, all is the same. Their life, too, is gone. In like manner view also the other epochs of time and of whole nations, and see how many after great efforts soon fell and were resolved into the elements. But chiefly thou shouldst think of those whom thou hast thyself known distracting themselves about idle things, neglecting to do what was in accordance with their proper constitution, and to hold firmly to this and to be content with it. And herein it is necessary to remember that the attention given to everything has its proper value and proportion. For thus thou wilt not be dissatisfied, if thou appliest thyself to smaller matters no further than is fit....

It is no evil for things to undergo change, and no good for things to subsist in consequence of change. Time is like a river made up of the events which happen, and a violent stream; for as soon as a thing has been seen, it is carried away, and another comes in its place, and this will be carried away too. Everything which happens is as familiar and well known as the rose in spring and the fruit in summer; for such is disease, and death, and calumny, and treachery, and whatever else delights fools or vexes them. In the series of things those which follow are always aptly fitted to those which have gone before; for this series is not like a mere enumeration of disjointed things, which has only a necessary sequence, but it is a rational connection: and as all existing things are arranged together harmoniously, so the things which come into existence exhibit no mere succession, but a certain wonderful relationship....

If any god told thee that thou shalt die to-morrow, or certainly on the day after to-morrow, thou wouldst not care much whether it was on the third day or on the morrow, unless thou wast in the highest degree mean-spirited-for how small is the difference?-so think it no great thing to die after as many years as thou canst name rather than to-morrow. Think continually how many physicians are dead after often contracting their eyebrows over the sick; and how many astrologers after predicting with great pretensions the deaths of others; and how many philosophers after endless discourses on death or immortality; how many heroes after killing thousands; and how many tyrants who have used their power over men's lives with terrible insolence as if they were immortal; and how many cities are entirely dead, so to speak, Helice and Pompeii and Herculaneum, and others innumerable. Add to the reckoning all whom thou hast known, one after another. One man after burying another has been laid out dead, and another buries him; and all this in a short time. To conclude, always observe how ephemeral and worthless human things are, and what was yesterday a little mucus, to-morrow will be a mummy or ashes. Pass then through this little space of time conformably to nature, and end thy journey in content, just as an olive falls off when it is ripe, blessing nature who produced it, and thanking the tree on which it grew. Be like the promontory against which the waves continually break, but it stands firm and tames the fury of the water around it.

✚ Book VI

Take care that thou art not made into a Caesar, that thou art not dyed with this dye; for such things happen. Keep thyself then simple, good, pure, serious, free from affectation, a friend of justice, a worshiper of the gods, kind, affectionate, strenuous in all proper acts. Strive to continue to be such as philosophy wished to make thee. Reverence the gods, and help men. Short is life. There is only one fruit of this terrene life, a pious disposition and social acts.

Do everything as a disciple of Antoninus [Marcus Aurelius' adoptive father and Roman emperor 138-161]. Remember his constancy in every act which was conformable to reason, and his evenness in all things, and his piety, and the serenity of his countenance, and his sweetness, and his disregard of empty fame, and his efforts to understand things; and how he would never let anything pass without having first most carefully examined it and clearly understood it; and how he bore with those who blamed him unjustly without blaming them in return; how he did nothing in a hurry; and how he listened not to calumnies, and how exact an examiner of manners and actions he was; and not given to reproach people, nor timid, nor suspicious, nor a sophist; and with how little he was satisfied, such as lodging, bed, dress, food, servants; and how laborious and patient; and how he was able on account of his sparing diet to hold out to the evening, not even requiring to relieve himself by any evacuations except at the usual hour; and his firmness and uniformity in his friendships; and how he tolerated freedom of speech in those who opposed his opinions; and the pleasure that he had when any man showed him anything better; and how religious he was without superstition. Imitate all this that thou mayest have as good a conscience, when thy last hour comes, as he had.

Reading 20

Life in the Roman Empire

Although formally written literary works of all sorts, transmitted to us through a complex manuscript tradition, form the overwhelming bulk of our information about the ancient Greek and Roman world, we also possess a vast quantity of informally written, non-literary material, preserved in the form of inscriptions on stone or bronze or writings on papyrus or other similar material, which provide us with glimpses into all aspects of daily ancient life often ignored by our formally written literary sources. The following material is an infinitesimal fraction of our surviving non-literary evidence and is designed to illustrate the nature and variety of this material and to show how it sheds important light upon the living conditions of the Roman Empire.

A. Invitation to a Birthday Party

The following text, written on a very thin piece of wood (which served as a kind of note paper), was found at the ancient site of a Roman military settlement in northern England near Hadrian's Wall. The text, dating to about 100 A.D., is a letter written by the wife of a Roman officer and sent to the woman's sister who was living with her husband at another nearby Roman military settlement.

(Taken from THE VINDOLANDA WRITING-TABLETS (TABULAE VINDOLANDENSES II), by ALAN K. BOWMAN AND J. DAVID THOMAS [British Museum Press 1990] p.257)

Claudia Severa sends greetings to her Lepidina: On 11 September, sister, for the day of the celebration of my birthday, I give you a warm invitation to make sure that you come to us, to make the day more enjoyable for me by your arrival, if you are present (?). Give my greetings to your Cerialis. My Aelius and my little son send him their greetings. I shall expect you, sister. Farewell, sister, my dearest soul, as I hope to prosper, and hail.

B. A Private Endowment for Children

The following text comes from a funerary monument from the town of Terracina, located on the western coast of central Italy. It records an excerpt from the will of a wealthy woman concerning the establishment of a fund to assist the rearing of 100 boys and 100 girls in the community by providing them with a monthly allowance until they came of age. The money set aside for this purpose was to be invested by the local municipal government, and only its interest was to be spent to support the children. As each child came of age, he or she was to be replaced by another boy or girl, so that the total number of children thus supported always remained at 200.

(Taken from Roman Civilization, Source Book II, The Empire, by Naphtali Lewis and Meyer Reinhold [Columbia University Press 1955] p.352)

Caelia Macrina daughter of Gaius left 300,000 sesterces in her will for the construction of this monument, and ... thousand sesterces for its decoration and upkeep. She also left 1,000,000 sesterces to the town of Terracina in memory of her son Macer, so that out of the income from this money child-assistance subsidies might be paid to one hundred boys and one hundred girls—to each citizen boy 5 denarii each month, to each citizen girl 3 denarii each month, the boys up to sixteen years, the girls up to fourteen years—in such a way that the payments should always be received by groups of a hundred boys and a hundred girls.

C. FROM THE WALLS OF POMPEII

The following brief texts were either painted or scratched on the walls of buildings in Pompeii and were preserved when the town was buried by the eruption of Mount Vesuvius in 79 A.D.

(Taken from Roman Civilization, Source Book II, The Empire, by Naphtali Lewis and Meyer Reinhold [Columbia University Press 1955] pp.359-61)

Twenty pairs of gladiators of Decimus Lucretius Satrius Valens, and ten pairs of gladiators of Decimus Lucretius Valens, his son, will fight at Pompeii on April 8, 9, 10, 11, 12. There will be a full card of wild beast combats, and awnings (for the spectators). Aemilius Celer (painted this sign), all alone in the moonlight.

A copper pot is missing from this shop. 65 sesterces reward if anybody brings it back, 20 sesterces if he reveals the thief so we can get our property back.

Take your lewd looks and flirting eyes off another man's wife, and show some decency on your face!

Anybody in love, come here. I want to break Venus' ribs with a club and cripple the goddess' loins. If she can pierce my tender breast, why can't I break her head with a club?

[A prostitute's sign] I am yours for 2 asses cash.

D. FUNERARY INSCRIPTIONS

The following epitaphs are simply a very small sample taken from tens of thousands of funerary inscriptions that have been discovered at numerous ancient sites of the Roman empire. They offer interesting glimpses into the lives and attitudes of many ordinary Romans.

(Taken from Roman Civilization, Source Book II, The Empire, by Naphtali Lewis and Meyer Reinhold [Columbia University Press 1955] pp.283-6)

Here lies Amymone, wife of Marcus, most good and most beautiful, wool spinner, dutiful, modest, careful, chaste, stay-at-home.

To the spirits of the departed. Gaius Calpenius Hermes built this for himself and his family and for his freedmen and freedwomen and their descendants, and for Antistia Coetonis, his wife. This place of burial shall not pass to an heir belonging to another family. He built a chamber on the right of the entrance; he placed sarcophagi on the pavement outside; and opposite (the entrance) and to the left, in two walls, made niches with funerary urns and sarcophagi.

To the spirits of the departed. Gaius Tullius Hesper built this tomb for himself, where his bones are to be placed. If anyone does violence to them or removes them hence, I wish for him that he may live a long time in bodily pain, and that when he dies the gods below may not receive him.

Marcus Vocusius Crescens, freedman of Marcus, built this in his lifetime for himself and Vocusia Veneria, his very good wife, and Petronius Vocusianus, his son, soldier of the Third Praetorian Cohort, aged 18 years, 3 months, 18 days. If anyone tries to sell, buy, or break open this repository, then he shall pay a penalty of 20,000 sesterces to the municipality of Aquileia, and the informer shall receive one fourth.

Gaius Julius Mygdonius, a Parthian by origin, born a freeman, captured when a youth and sold into slavery in Roman territory. When I became a citizen with fate's kind help, I got together a nest egg against the day when I reached fifty. Ever since youth I sought to attain my old age; now receive me gladly, O stone; with you I shall be freed from care.

You see me a corpse, passers-by. My civilian name was Apollonis, my native town Apamea, but now in the soil of Nicomedia the thread of destiny spun by the Fates holds me fast to the ground.

Eight times he won in athletic games, but in the ninth boxing match he met his fated end. Play, laugh, passer-by, knowing that you too must die. His wife Alexandria erected this memorial out of his money as a remembrance. If anyone dares to disturb this monument, he shall pay a fine Of 2,500 denarii to the fisc.

I lived dear to my family, I gave up my life yet a maiden. Here I lie dead and I am ashes, and these ashes are earth. But if the earth is a goddess, I am a goddess, I am not dead. I beg you, stranger, do not desecrate my bones. Mus, lived thirteen years.

To the spirits of the departed. To Cerellia Fortunata, dearest wife, with whom he lived forty years without the slightest cause for complaint, Marcus Antonius Encolpus built this.... Do not pass by this epitaph, wayfarer, but stop, listen, and learn, then go. There is no boat in Hades, no ferryman Charon, no caretaker Aeacus, no Cerberus dog. All we dead below have become bones and ashes, nothing more. I have spoken you true go now, wayfarer, lest even though dead I seem to you garrulous.

Pompeius Catussa, Sequanian, plasterer, to his wife incomparable and most kind to him, who lived with me 5 years, 6 months, 18 days without any kind of fault, erected this in his lifetime for himself and his wife, and consecrated it while under construction.

All you who read this, go bathe in the baths of Apollo, as I used to do with my wife-I wish I still could.

To the spirits of the departed. In this tomb lies a lifeless body, whose spirit was received among the gods, for thus he deserved, Lucius Statius Onesimus, merchant of the Appian Way for many years, a man most trustworthy above all men, whose reputation is recorded forever, who lived sixty-eight years, more or less, without blemish. Statia Crescentina, his wife, built this for her well-deserving husband most worthy and deserving, with whom she lived in good accord without dissensions.

To the spirits of the departed. You wanted to precede me, most sainted wife, and you have left me behind in tears. If there is anything good in the regions below—as for me, I lead a worthless life without you—be happy there too, sweetest Thalassia, nurse of a Roman senator and married to me for forty years. Paprius Vitalis, of the painters' craft, her husband, built this for his incomparable wife, himself, and their family.

To the departed spirit of Mevia Sophe. Gaius Maenius Cimber to his most sainted wife and protectress, my heart's desire, who lived with me 18 years, 3 months, 13 days, which I lived with her without cause for complaint. But now I complain to her spirit and demand her back of Dis, or else, ye gods, give me back to my wife, who lived with me so harmoniously to her dying day. Mevia Sophe, bring it to pass, if the spirits of the departed have any influence, that I need not suffer such a criminal separation any longer.

Stranger, so may the earth rest lightly upon you after death as you do no damage here; or if anyone does damage, may the gods above not approve of him and the gods below not receive him, and may the earth rest heavily upon him.

Tomb of a sainted cherished soul, sacred to the spirits of the departed. Furia Spes, freedwoman, to Sempronius Firmus, husband most dear to me. As boy and girl we were bound by mutual love at first sight. I lived with him but a very short time, and during the time we should have lived together we were separated by an evil hand. I beg of you, most holy spirit of the departed, take good care of my dear one, and please be most kind to him in the hours of the night, so that I may see him and he may wish me too to persuade fate to let me come and be with him tenderly and speedily.

To the spirits of the departed. Titus Flavius Martialis lies here. What I ate and drank is with me here; what I left behind is gone forever.

Sacred to the spirits of the departed. To Aurelia Vercella, my wife most sweet, who lived seventeen years, more or less. I was not, I was, I am not, I have no more desires. Anthimus, her husband.

Reading 21

The Story of Trimalchio

The following passage is taken from Petronius' *Satyricon*, a novel written about 60 A.D. during the reign of Nero. The scene is a lavish banquet in the mansion of a filthy rich freedman, a freed slave, named Trimalchio, who ostentatiously flaunts his wealth before his dinner guests at every opportunity. Here he tells in brief his life story, from rags to riches, so to speak. Although fictional and obviously exaggerated for comic effect, this portrait of a self-made man, beginning in slavery and ending in extraordinary wealth, does in fact represent the way in which many slaves in Roman society obtained their freedom and became successful businessmen and respected citizens of the Roman Empire.

(Translated by Gary Forsythe)

75 I ask you, friends, to make yourselves at home: for I too was once like you, but I have arrived at this station by my own ability. A little brain work makes the man; all the rest is garbage. I buy well; I sell well. One person will tell you one thing, and another person another. I am bursting with good fortune.... But as I had started to say, my diligence has brought me to this fortune. When I came from Asia, I was as big as this here lamp stand. Every day I used to measure myself at its top; and in order to have a bearded chin more quickly, I smeared my lips from the oil of the lamp. Nevertheless, for fourteen years I was my master's favorite; And where's the dishonor in doing what one's master tells him? All the same, I managed to get into my mistress' good graces, too (you know what I mean: I hold my tongue, as I am not one to boast).

76 But as the gods would have it, I became the master in the house and took on my master's very own brain. Why say more? He made me joint heir with the emperor, and I received a senator's fortune. Yet, no one ever has enough. I wanted to go into business. To make a long story short, I built five ships, loaded them with wine (worth gold at the time), and sent them to Rome. You would have thought that I had ordered it: all the ships were wrecked. That's what happened. No lie. On one day Neptune [god of the sea] swallowed thirty million sesterces. Do you think that I gave up? No, by Hercules, this loss was just a taste for me, as if nothing had happened. I made other ships, bigger, better, and luckier ones, so that no one could say that I wasn't a bold fellow. You know, a great ship holds great boldness. Again I loaded them with wine, bacon, beans, perfume, and slaves. At this point Fortunata [Trimalchio's wife] did a loyal thing. She sold all her jewelry and clothes and put one hundred gold coins in my hand. This was the leaven of my fortune. What the gods will happens quickly. From one voyage I raked in ten million sesterces. I immediately bought up all the estates that had been my former master's. I built a house; I bought up

slaves and teams of draft animals. Whatever I touched grew like a honeycomb. But after I began to have more than all my native town has, I let well enough alone, took myself out of the business, and started loaning money to freedmen [for conducting business].

While I was reluctant to carry on my business, an astrologer, who happened to come to our town, urged me to do so. He is a little Greek guy, named Serapa, a counselor of the gods. He has even told me things that I had forgotten. He has laid out for me everything from needle and thread. He knows my insides. The only thing that he has not told me is what I had for dinner yesterday. You would have thought that he had always lived with me....

77 ... "You have made your wife a lady from those [low] circumstances. You are not fortunate in your friends. No one ever returns an equal favor to you. You own large landed estates. You are nurturing a viper under your wing." And why should I not tell you that there still remains to my life thirty years, four months, and two days. In addition, I will soon receive an inheritance. All this my fate tells me.

But if it should happen that I join my estates to Apulia [over into the next state], I will have lived long enough. Meanwhile, while Mercury [god of money-making] watches out for me, I have built this house. As you know, it was a cottage. Now it's a shrine. It has four dining rooms, twenty bedrooms, two marble porticos, an upstairs dining room, a bedroom in which I myself sleep, a boudoir of this viper [Trimalchio's wife], and an excellent butler's pantry;... and there are many other things that I'll soon show you. Believe me. Have a penny; you're worth a penny. Have something, and you'll be treated like something. So, your friend here [pointing to himself], who was a frog, is now a king.

THE NEW TESTAMENT

The four Gospels (*Matthew*, *Mark*, *Luke*, and *John*) provide us with our most important information concerning the life and acts of Jesus. The first four passages presented here illustrate different aspects of Jesus' teachings and interaction with rival Jewish sects during his day (primarily the Sadducees and Pharisees). On the other hand, *The Acts of the Apostles* give us a good picture of how Christianity developed during the first generation following the crucifixion. The last two passages, taken from this latter book of *The New Testament*, show how Christianity slowly divorced itself from Judaism and largely became a religious movement involving the non-Jewish population of the Roman Empire.

❧ *(Taken from the King James Version)*

A. THE GREATEST COMMANDMENT

✢ The Gospel According to Mark

CHAPTER 12: ... **13** And they send unto him certain of the Pharisees and of the Herodians, to catch him in his words. **14** And when they were come, they say unto him, Master, we know that thou art true, and carest for no man: for thou regardest not the person of men, but teachest the way of God in truth: Is it lawful to give tribute to Caesar, or not? **15** Shall we give, or shall we not give? But he, knowing their hypocrisy, said unto them, Why tempt ye me? bring me a penny, that I may see it. **16** And they brought it. And he saith unto them, Whose is this image and superscription? And they said unto him, Caesar's. **17** And Jesus answering said unto them, Render to Caesar the things that are Caesar's, and to God the things that are God's. And they marvelled at him. **18** Then come unto him the Sadducees, which say there is no resurrection; and they asked him, saying, **19** Master, Moses wrote unto us, If a man's brother die, and leave his wife behind him, and leave no children, that his brother should take his wife, and raise up seed unto his brother. **20** Now there were seven brethren: and the first took a wife, and dying left no seed. **21** And the second took her, and died, neither left he any seed: and the third likewise. **22** And the seven had her, and left no seed: last of all the woman died also. **23** In the resurrection therefore, when they shall rise, whose wife shall she be of them? for the seven had her to wife. **24** And Jesus answering said unto them, Do ye not therefore err, because ye know not the scriptures, neither the power of God? **25** For when they shall rise from the dead, they neither marry, nor are given in marriage; but are as the angels which are in heaven.   **26** And as touching the dead, that they rise: have ye not read in the book of Moses, how in the bush God spake unto him, saying, I am the God of Abraham, and the God of Isaac, and the God of Jacob?   **27** He is not the God of the dead, but the God of the living: ye therefore do greatly err.   **28** And one of the scribes came, and having heard them reasoning together, and perceiving that he had answered them well, asked him, Which is the first commandment of all?   **29** And Jesus answered him, The first of all the commandments is, Hear, O Israel; The Lord our God is one Lord: **30** And thou shalt love the Lord thy God with all thy heart, and with all thy soul, and with all thy mind, and with all thy strength: this is the first commandment.   **31** And the second is like, namely this, Thou shalt love thy neighbour as thyself. There is none other commandment greater than these. **32** And the scribe said unto him, Well, Master, thou hast said the truth: for there is one God; and there is none other but he: **33** And to love him with all the heart, and with all the understanding, and with all the soul, and with all the strength, and to love his neighbour as himself, is more than all whole burnt offerings and sacrifices.   **34** And when Jesus saw that he answered discreetly, he said unto him, Thou art not far from the kingdom of God. And no man after that durst ask him any question.

B. THE SPIRIT VS. THE LETTER OF THE LAW

✤ The Gospel According to Matthew

CHAPTER 12.   1 At that time Jesus went on the sabbath day through the corn; and his disciples were an hungred, and began to pluck the ears of corn and to eat.   **2** But when the Pharisees saw it, they said unto him, Behold, thy disciples do that which is not lawful to do upon the sabbath day.   **3** But he said unto them, Have ye not read what David did, when he was an hungred, and they that were with him;   **4** How he entered into the house of God, and did eat the shewbread, which was not lawful for him to eat, neither for them which were with him, but only for the priests?   **5** Or have ye not read in the law, how that on the sabbath days the priests in the temple profane the sabbath, and are blameless?   **6** But I say unto you, That in this place is one greater than the temple.   **7** But if ye had known what this meaneth, I will have mercy, and not sacrifice, ye would not have condemned the guiltless.   **8** For the Son of man is Lord even of the sabbath day.   **9** And when he was departed thence, he went into their synagogue: **10** And, behold, there was a man which had his hand withered. And they asked him, saying, Is it lawful to heal on the sabbath days? that they might accuse him.   **11** And he said unto them, What man shall there be among you, that shall have one sheep, and if it fall into a pit on the sabbath day, will he not lay hold on it, and lift it out?   **12** How much then is a man better than a sheep? Wherefore it is lawful to do well on the sabbath days.   **13** Then saith he to the man, Stretch forth thine hand. And he stretched it forth; and it was restored whole, like as the other.

C. THE END OF DAYS

✤ The Gospel According to Matthew

CHAPTER 24.   1 And Jesus went out, and departed from the temple: and his disciples came to him for to shew him the buildings of the temple.   **2** And Jesus said unto them, See ye not all these things? verily I say unto you, There shall not be left here one stone upon another, that shall not be thrown down.   **3** And as he sat upon the mount of Olives, the disciples came unto him privately, saying, Tell us, when shall these things be? and what shall be the sign of thy coming, and of the end of the world?   **4** And Jesus answered and said unto them, Take heed that no man deceive you.   **5** For many shall come in my name, saying, I am Christ; and shall deceive many.   **6** And ye shall hear of wars and rumours of wars: see that ye be not troubled: for all these things must come to pass, but the end is not yet.   **7** For nation shall rise against nation, and kingdom against kingdom: and there shall be famines, and pestilences, and earthquakes, in divers places.   **8** All these are the beginning of sorrows.   **9** Then shall they deliver you up to be afflicted, and shall kill you: and ye shall be hated of all nations for my name's sake.   **10** And then shall many be offended, and shall betray one another, and shall hate one another.   **11** And many false prophets shall rise, and shall deceive many.   **12** And because iniquity shall abound, the love of many shall wax cold.   **13** But he that shall endure unto the end, the same shall be saved.   **14** And this gospel of the kingdom shall be preached in all the world for a witness unto all nations; and then shall the end come.   **15** When ye therefore shall see the abomination of desolation, spoken of by Daniel the prophet, stand in the holy place, (whoso readeth, let him understand:)   **16** Then let them which be in Judaea flee into the mountains: **17** Let him which is on the housetop not come down to take any thing out of his house: **18** Neither let him which is in the field return back to take his clothes.   **19** And woe unto them that are with child, and to them that give suck in those days!   **20** But pray ye that your flight be not in the winter, neither on the sabbath day: **21** For then shall be great tribulation, such as was not since the beginning of the world to this time, no, nor ever shall be.   **22** And except those days should be shortened, there should no flesh be saved: but for the elect's sake those days shall be shortened.   **23** Then if any man shall say unto you, Lo, here is Christ, or there; believe it not.   **24** For there shall arise false Christs, and false prophets, and shall shew great signs and wonders; insomuch that, if it were possible, they shall deceive the very elect.   **25** Behold, I have told you before.   **26** Wherefore if they shall say unto you, Behold, he is in the desert; go not forth: behold, he is in the secret chambers; believe it not.   **27** For as the lightning cometh out of the east, and shineth even unto the west; so shall also the coming of the Son of man be.   **28** For wheresoever the carcase is, there will the eagles be gathered together.   **29** Immediately after the tribulation of those days shall the sun be darkened, and the moon shall not give her light, and the stars shall fall from heaven, and the powers of the heavens shall be shaken: **30** And then shall appear the sign of the Son of man in heaven: and then shall all the tribes of the earth mourn, and they shall see the Son of man coming in the clouds of heaven with power and great glory.   **31** And he shall send his angels with a great sound of a trumpet, and they shall gather together his elect from the four winds, from one end of heaven to the other. **32** Now learn a parable of the fig tree; When his branch is yet tender, and putteth forth leaves, ye know that summer is nigh: **33** So likewise ye, when ye shall see all these things, know that it is near, even at the doors.   **34** Verily I say unto you, This generation shall not pass, till all these things be fulfilled.   **35** Heaven and earth shall pass away, but my words shall not pass away.   **36** But of that day and hour knoweth no man, no, not the angels of heaven, but my Father only.   **37** But as the days of Noe were, so shall also the coming of the Son of man be.   **38** For as in the days that were before the flood they were eating and drinking, marrying and giving in marriage, until the day that Noe entered into the ark,   **39** And knew not until the flood came, and took them all away; so shall also the coming of the Son of man be.   **40** Then shall two be in the field; the one shall be taken, and the other left.   **41** Two women shall be grinding at the mill; the one shall be taken, and the other left.   **42** Watch therefore: for ye know not what hour your Lord doth come.   **43** But know this, that if the goodman of the house had known in what watch the thief would come, he would have watched, and would not have suffered his house to be broken up.   **44** Therefore be ye also ready: for in such an hour as ye think not the Son of man cometh.   **45** Who then is a faithful and wise servant, whom his lord hath made ruler over his household, to give them meat in due season?   **46** Blessed is that servant, whom his lord when he cometh shall find so doing.   **47** Verily I say unto you, That he shall make him ruler over all his goods.   **48** But and if that evil servant shall say in his heart, My lord delayeth his coming;   **49** And shall begin to smite his fellowservants, and to eat and drink with the drunken;   **50** The lord of that servant shall come in a day when he looketh not for him, and in an hour that he is not aware of,   **51** And shall cut him asunder, and appoint him his portion with the hypocrites: there shall be weeping and gnashing of teeth.

D. THE DISTURBANCE IN THE TEMPLE OF JERUSALEM

✤ The Gospel According to Matthew

CHAPTER 21.   **1** And when they drew nigh unto Jerusalem, and were come to Bethphage, unto the mount of Olives, then sent Jesus two disciples,   **2** Saying unto them, Go into the village over against you, and straightway ye shall find an ass tied, and a colt with her: loose them, and bring them unto me.   **3** And if any man say ought unto you, ye shall say, The Lord hath need of them; and straightway he will send them.   **4** All this was done, that it might be fulfilled which was spoken by the prophet, saying,   **5** Tell ye the daughter of Sion, Behold, thy King cometh unto thee, meek, and sitting upon an ass, and a colt the foal of an ass.   **6** And the disciples went, and did as Jesus commanded them,   **7** And brought the ass, and the colt, and put on them their clothes, and they set him thereon.   **8** And a very great multitude spread their garments in the way; others cut down branches from the trees, and strawed them in the way.   **9** And the multitudes that went before, and that followed, cried, saying, Hosanna to the son of David: Blessed is he that cometh in the name of the Lord; Hosanna in the highest.   **10** And when he was come into Jerusalem, all the city was moved, saying, Who is this?   **11** And the multitude said, This is Jesus the prophet of Nazareth of Galilee.   **12** And Jesus went into the temple of God, and cast out all them that sold and bought in the temple, and overthrew the tables of the moneychangers, and the seats of them that sold doves,   **13** And said unto them, It is written, My house shall be called the house of prayer; but ye have made it a den of thieves.   **14** And the blind and the lame came to him in the temple; and he healed them.   **15** And when the chief priests and scribes saw the wonderful things that he did, and the children crying in the temple, and saying, Hosanna to the son of David; they were sore displeased,   **16** And said unto him, Hearest thou what these say? And Jesus saith unto them, Yea; have ye never read, Out of the mouth of babes and sucklings thou hast perfected praise?   **17** And he left them, and went out of the city into Bethany; and he lodged there....   **23** And when he was come into the temple, the chief priests and the elders of the people came unto him as he was teaching, and said, By what authority doest thou these things? and who gave thee this authority?   **24** And Jesus answered and said unto them, I also will ask you one thing, which if ye tell me, I in like wise will tell you by what authority I do these things.   **25** The baptism of John, whence was it? from heaven, or of men? And they reasoned with themselves, saying, If we shall say, From heaven; he will say unto us, Why did ye not then believe him?   **26** But if we shall say, Of men; we fear the people; for all hold John as a prophet.   **27** And they answered Jesus, and said, We cannot tell. And he said unto them, Neither tell I you by what authority I do these things.   **28** But what think ye? A certain man had two sons; and he came to the first, and said, Son, go work to day in my vineyard.   **29** He answered and said, I will not: but afterward he repented, and went.   **30** And he came to the second, and said likewise. And he answered and said, I go, sir: and went not.   **31** Whether of them twain did the will of his father? They say unto him, The first. Jesus saith unto them, Verily I say unto you, That the publicans and the harlots go into the kingdom of God before you. 32 For John came unto you in the way of righteousness, and ye believed him not: but the publicans and the harlots believed him: and ye, when ye had seen it, repented not afterward, that ye might believe him.   33 Hear another parable: There was a certain householder, which planted a vineyard, and hedged it round about, and digged a winepress in it, and built a tower, and let it out to husbandmen, and went into a far country: 34 And when the time of the fruit drew near, he sent his servants to the husbandmen, that they might receive the fruits of it.   35 And the husbandmen took his servants, and beat one, and killed another, and stoned another.   36 Again, he sent other servants more than the first: and they did unto them likewise.   37 But last of all he sent unto them his son, saying, They will reverence my son.   38 But when the husbandmen saw the son, they said among themselves, This is the heir; come, let us kill him, and let us seize on his inheritance.   39 And they caught him, and cast him out of the vineyard, and slew him.   40 When the lord therefore of the vineyard cometh, what will he do unto those husbandmen?   41 They say unto him, He will miserably destroy those wicked men, and will let out his vineyard unto other husbandmen, which shall render him the fruits in their seasons.   42 Jesus saith unto them, Did ye never read in the scriptures, The stone which the builders rejected, the same is become the head of the corner: this is the Lord's doing, and it is marvellous in our eyes?   43 Therefore say I unto you, The kingdom of God shall be taken from you, and given to a nation bringing forth the fruits thereof.   44 And whosoever shall fall on this stone shall be broken: but on whomsoever it shall fall, it will grind him to powder.   45 And when the chief priests and Pharisees had heard his parables, they perceived that he spake of them.   46 But when they sought to lay hands on him, they feared the multitude, because they took him for a prophet.

CHAPTER 18.   1 After these things Paul departed from Athens, and came to Corinth;   2 And found a certain Jew named Aquila, born in Pontus, lately come from Italy, with his wife Priscilla; (because that Claudius had commanded all Jews to depart from Rome:) and came unto them.   3 And because he was of the same craft, he abode with them, and wrought: for by their occupation they were tentmakers.   4 And he reasoned in the synagogue every sabbath, and persuaded the Jews and the Greeks.   5 And when Silas and Timotheus were come from Macedonia, Paul was pressed in the spirit, and testified to the Jews that Jesus was Christ.   6 And when they opposed themselves, and blasphemed, he shook his raiment, and said unto them, Your blood be upon your own heads; I am clean; from henceforth I will go unto the Gentiles.   7 And he departed thence, and entered into a certain man's house, named Justus, one that worshipped God, whose house joined hard to the synagogue.   8 And Crispus, the chief ruler of the synagogue, believed on the Lord with all his house; and many of the Corinthians hearing believed, and were baptized.   9 Then spake the Lord to Paul in the night by a vision, Be not afraid, but speak, and hold not thy peace: 10 For I am with thee, and no man shall set on thee to hurt thee: for I have much people in this city.   11 And he continued there a year and six months, teaching the word of God among them.   12 And when Gallio was the deputy of Achaia, the Jews made insurrection with one accord against Paul, and brought him to the judgment seat,   13 Saying, This fellow persuadeth men to worship God contrary to the law.   14 And when Paul was now about to open his mouth, Gallio said unto the Jews, If it were a matter of wrong or wicked lewdness, O ye Jews, reason would that I should bear with you: 15 But if it be a question of words and names, and of your law, look ye to it; for I will be no judge of such matters.   16 And he drave them from the judgment seat.   17 Then all the Greeks took Sosthenes, the chief ruler of the synagogue, and beat him before the judgment seat. And Gallio cared for none of those things.   18 And Paul after this tarried there yet a good while, and then took his leave of the brethren, and sailed thence into Syria, and with him Priscilla and Aquila; having shorn his head in

Cenchrea: for he had a vow. **19** And he came to Ephesus, and left them there: but he himself entered into the synagogue, and reasoned with the Jews. **20** When they desired him to tarry longer time with them, he consented not; **21** But bade them farewell, saying, I must by all means keep this feast that cometh in Jerusalem: but I will return again unto you, if God will. And he sailed from Ephesus. **22** And when he had landed at Caesarea, and gone up, and saluted the church, he went down to Antioch. **23** And after he had spent some time there, he departed, and went over all the country of Galatia and Phrygia in order, strengthening all the disciples.

E. CHRISTIANITY TRANSCENDS JUDAISM

✣ The Acts of the Apostles

CHAPTER 11. **1** There was a certain man in Caesarea called Cornelius, a centurion of the band called the Italian band, **2** A devout man, and one that feared God with all his house, which gave much alms to the people, and prayed to God alway. **3** He saw in a vision evidently about the ninth hour of the day an angel of God coming in to him, and saying unto him, Cornelius. **4** And when he looked on him, he was afraid, and said, What is it, Lord? And he said unto him, Thy prayers and thine alms are come up for a memorial before God. **5** And now send men to Joppa, and call for one Simon, whose surname is Peter: **6** He lodgeth with one Simon a tanner, whose house is by the sea side: he shall tell thee what thou oughtest to do. **7** And when the angel which spake unto Cornelius was departed, he called two of his household servants, and a devout soldier of them that waited on him continually; **8** And when he had declared all these things unto them, he sent them to Joppa. **9** On the morrow, as they went on their journey, and drew nigh unto the city, Peter went up upon the housetop to pray about the sixth hour: **10** And he became very hungry, and would have eaten: but while they made ready, he fell into a trance, **11** And saw heaven opened, and a certain vessel descending upon him, as it had been a great sheet knit at the four corners, and let down to the earth: **12** Wherein were all manner of fourfooted beasts of the earth, and wild beasts, and creeping things, and fowls of the air. **13** And there came a voice to him, Rise, Peter; kill, and eat. **14** But Peter said, Not so, Lord; for I have never eaten any thing that is common or unclean. **15** And the voice spake unto him again the second time, What God hath cleansed, that call not thou common. **16** This was done thrice: and the vessel was received up again into heaven. **17** Now while Peter doubted in himself what this vision which he had seen should mean, behold, the men which were sent from Cornelius had made enquiry for Simon's house, and stood before the gate, **18** And called, and asked whether Simon, which was surnamed Peter, were lodged there. **19** While Peter thought on the vision, the Spirit said unto him, Behold, three men seek thee. **20** Arise therefore, and get thee down, and go with them, doubting nothing: for I have sent them. **21** Then Peter went down to the men which were sent unto him from Cornelius; and said, Behold, I am he whom ye seek: what is the cause wherefore ye are come? **22** And they said, Cornelius the centurion, a just man, and one that feareth God, and of good report among all the nation of the Jews, was warned from God by an holy angel to send for thee into his house, and to hear words of thee. **23** Then called he them in, and lodged them. And on the morrow Peter went away with them, and certain brethren from Joppa accompanied him. **24** And the morrow after they entered into Caesarea. And Cornelius waited for them, and he had called together his kinsmen and near friends. **25** And as Peter was coming in, Cornelius met him, and fell down at his feet, and worshipped him. **26** But Peter took him up, saying, Stand up; I myself also am a man. **27** And as he talked with him, he went in, and found many that were come together. **28** And he said unto them,

Ye know how that it is an unlawful thing for a man that is a Jew to keep company, or come unto one of another nation; but God hath shewed me that I should not call any man common or unclean.   29 Therefore came I unto you without gainsaying, as soon as I was sent for: I ask therefore for what intent ye have sent for me?   30 And Cornelius said, Four days ago I was fasting until this hour; and at the ninth hour I prayed in my house, and, behold, a man stood before me in bright clothing,   31 And said, Cornelius, thy prayer is heard, and thine alms are had in remembrance in the sight of God. 32 Send therefore to Joppa, and call hither Simon, whose surname is Peter; he is lodged in the house of one Simon a tanner by the sea side: who, when he cometh, shall speak unto thee.   33 Immediately therefore I sent to thee; and thou hast well done that thou art come. Now therefore are we all here present before God, to hear all things that are commanded thee of God.   34 Then Peter opened his mouth, and said, Of a truth I perceive that God is no respecter of persons: 35 But in every nation he that feareth him, and worketh righteousness, is accepted with him.   36 The word which God sent unto the children of Israel, preaching peace by Jesus Christ: (he is Lord of all:)   37 That word, I say, ye know, which was published throughout all Judaea, and began from Galilee, after the baptism which John preached;   38 How God anointed Jesus of Nazareth with the Holy Ghost and with power: who went about doing good, and healing all that were oppressed of the devil; for God was with him.   39 And we are witnesses of all things which he did both in the land of the Jews, and in Jerusalem; whom they slew and hanged on a tree: 40 Him God raised up the third day, and shewed him openly;   41 Not to all the people, but unto witnesses chosen before God, even to us, who did eat and drink with him after he rose from the dead.   42 And he commanded us to preach unto the people, and to testify that it is he which was ordained of God to be the Judge of quick and dead.   43 To him give all the prophets witness, that through his name whosoever believeth in him shall receive remission of sins.   44 While Peter yet spake these words, the Holy Ghost fell on all them which heard the word.   45 And they of the circumcision which believed were astonished, as many as came with Peter, because that on the Gentiles also was poured out the gift of the Holy Ghost.   46 For they heard them speak with tongues, and magnify God. Then answered Peter,   47 Can any man forbid water, that these should not be baptized, which have received the Holy Ghost as well as we?   48 And he commanded them to be baptized in the name of the Lord. Then prayed they him to tarry certain days.

F. THE CHRISTIANS ABANDON CIRCUMCISION

✢ The Acts of the Apostles

CHAPTER 15.   1 And certain men which came down from Judaea taught the brethren, and said, Except ye be circumcised after the manner of Moses, ye cannot be saved.   **2** When therefore Paul and Barnabas had no small dissension and disputation with them, they determined that Paul and Barnabas, and certain other of them, should go up to Jerusalem unto the apostles and elders about this question.   **3** And being brought on their way by the church, they passed through Phenice and Samaria, declaring the conversion of the Gentiles: and they caused great joy unto all the brethren.   **4** And when they were come to Jerusalem, they were received of the church, and of the apostles and elders, and they declared all things that God had done with them.   **5** But there rose up certain of the sect of the Pharisees which believed, saying, That it was needful to circumcise them, and to command them to keep the law of Moses.   **6** And the apostles and elders came together for to consider of this matter.   **7** And when there had been much disputing, Peter rose up, and said unto them, Men and brethren, ye know how that a good while ago God made choice among us, that the Gentiles by my mouth should hear the word of the gospel, and believe.   8 And God, which knoweth the hearts, bare them witness, giving them the Holy Ghost, even as he did unto us;   9 And put no difference between us and them, purifying their hearts by faith.   10 Now therefore why tempt ye God, to put a yoke upon the neck of the disciples, which neither our fathers nor we were able to bear?   11 But we believe that through the grace of the LORD Jesus Christ we shall be saved, even as they.   12 Then all the multitude kept silence, and gave audience to Barnabas and Paul, declaring what miracles and wonders God had wrought among the Gentiles by them.   13 And after they had held their peace, James answered, saying, Men and brethren, hearken unto me: 14 Simeon hath declared how God at the first did visit the Gentiles, to take out of them a people for his name.   15 And to this agree the words of the prophets; as it is written,   16 After this I will return, and will build again the tabernacle of David, which is fallen down; and I will build again the ruins thereof, and I will set it up: 17 That the residue of men might seek after the Lord, and all the Gentiles, upon whom my name is called, saith the Lord, who doeth all these things.   18 Known unto God are all his works from the beginning of the world.   19 Wherefore my sentence is, that we trouble not them, which from among the Gentiles are turned to God: 20 But that we write unto them, that they abstain from pollutions of idols, and from fornication, and from things strangled, and from blood.   21 For Moses of old time hath in every city them that preach him, being read in the synagogues every sabbath day.   22 Then pleased it the apostles and elders with the whole church, to send chosen men of their own company to Antioch with Paul and Barnabas; namely, Judas surnamed Barsabas and Silas, chief men among the brethren: 23 And they wrote letters by them after this manner; The apostles and elders and brethren send greeting unto the brethren which are of the Gentiles in Antioch and Syria and Cilicia.   24 Forasmuch as we have heard, that certain which went out from us have troubled you with words, subverting your souls, saying, Ye must be circumcised, and keep the law: to whom we gave no such commandment: 25 It seemed good unto us, being assembled with one accord, to send chosen men unto you with our beloved Barnabas and Paul,   26 Men that have hazarded their lives for the name of our Lord Jesus Christ.   27 We have sent therefore Judas and Silas, who shall also tell you the same things by mouth.   28 For it seemed good to the Holy Ghost, and to us, to lay upon you no greater burden than these necessary things;   29 That ye abstain from meats offered to idols, and from blood, and from things strangled, and from fornication: from which if ye keep yourselves, ye shall do well. Fare ye well.   30 So when they were dismissed, they came to Antioch: and when they had gathered the multitude together, they delivered the epistle: 31 Which when they had read, they rejoiced for the consolation. 32 And Judas and Silas, being prophets also themselves, exhorted the brethren with many words, and confirmed them.

CHRISTIANITY IN THE ROMAN EMPIRE

Judaism and Christianity were the only two strictly monotheistic religions of the ancient Mediterranean world. Christianity, of course, derived its monotheism from Judaism. There was relatively little, if any, conflict among the various polytheistic religions, because they usually simply equated one set of gods with another, but no such easy equation and avoidance of conflict was possible with strict monotheism. Nevertheless, since Judaism had existed for several centuries before the establishment of the Roman Empire, the Romans granted the Jews within their empire various rights and privileges that exempted them from having to participate in polytheistic ceremonies celebrated in the cities of the Roman Empire. The Roman government, however, did not extend such toleration to Christianity, because not long after it came into existence, it divorced itself from Judaism and became a new-fangled religion of the Roman Empire that did not tolerate polytheism. Thus, within a relatively short period of time the Roman government outlawed Christianity, partly because Christians refused to acknowledge the gods of the Roman state. As the result of their basic incompatibility with one another, Christians soon found themselves being persecuted by the Roman government until, following Constantine's conversion to Christianity, the latter religion was no longer outlawed. The following four passages illustrate the phenomenon of persecution and martyrdom that characterized the early history of Christianity in Roman society.

A. THE NERONIAN PERSECUTION

✣ Tacitus, *Annals* XV. 44

During the summer of **64** A.D. a fire accidentally broke out in the city of Rome and caused tremendous damage. Despite its accidental cause, rumors soon circulated that the Emperor Nero had deliberately set the fire. In order to divert popular suspicion from himself, Nero tried to attach the blame for the fire on the community of Christians in the city. Tacitus describes this event in the following words, which represent our earliest account in a non-Christian source of interaction between the Roman state and the Christians.

(Taken from the translation of Albert J. Church and William J. Brodribb)

But all human efforts, the lavish gifts of the emperor, and the propitiations of the gods did not banish the sinister belief that the conflagration was the result of an order.

Consequently, to get rid of it, Nero fastened the guilt and inflicted the most exquisite tortures on a class hated for their abominations, called Christians by the populace. Christus, from whom it had its origin, suffered the extreme penalty during the reign of Tiberius at the hands of one of our procurators, Pontius Pilatus; and a most mischievous superstition, thus checked for the moment, again broke out not only in Judea, the source of the evil, but even in Rome, where hideous and shameful things from every part of the world find their centre and become popular. Accordingly, an arrest was first made of all who pleaded guilty; then, upon their information an immense multitude was convicted, not so much of the crime of firing the city, as of hatred against mankind. Mockery of every sort was added to their deaths. Covered with the skins of beasts, they were torn by dogs and perished, or they were nailed to crosses or were doomed to the flames and burnt to serve as a nightly illumination, when daylight had expired. Nero offered his gardens for the spectacle and was exhibiting a show in the circus, while he mingled with the people in the dress of a charioteer or stood aloft on a car. Hence, even for criminals who deserved extreme and exemplary punishment, there arose a feeling of compassion; for it was not, as it seemed, for the public good, but to glut one man's cruelty, that they were being destroyed.

B. LETTERS OF PLINY AND TRAJAN

✣ Book X. 96-7

While serving as provincial governor of Bithynia and Pontus (northwestern Asia Minor) in 111-112 A.D., Pliny wrote numerous letters to the Emperor Trajan to seek his advice on various legal and governmental questions. The following exchange of letters sheds important light on the early relationship between Christians and the Roman government.

(Taken from the translation of William Melmoth and revised by W. M. L. Hutchinson in the Loeb Classical Library)

Pliny to the Emperor Trajan: It is my rule, Sir, which I inviolably observe, to refer myself to you in all my doubts; for who is more capable of guiding my uncertainty or informing my ignorance? Having never been present at any trials of the Christians, I am unacquainted with the method and limits to be observed either in examining or punishing them. Whether any difference is to be made on account of age, or no distinction allowed between the youngest and the adult; whether repentance admits to a pardon, or if a man has been once a Christian it avails him nothing to recant; whether the mere profession of Christianity, albeit without crimes, or only the crimes associated there-with are punishable - in all these points I am greatly doubtful. In the meanwhile, the method that I have observed towards those who have been denounced to me as Christians is this. I interrogated them whether they were Christians; if they confessed it I repeated the question twice again, adding the threat of capital punishment; if they still persevered, I ordered them to be executed. For whatever the nature of their creed might be, I could at least feel no doubt that contumacy and inflexible obstinacy deserved chastisement. There were others also possessed with the same infatuation, but being citizens of Rome, I directed them to be carried thither. These accusations spread (as is usually the case) from the feet of the matter being investigated, and several forms of the mischief came to light. A placard was put up without any signature, accusing a large number of persons by name. Those who denied that they were or had ever been Christians, who repeated after me an invocation to the gods and offered adoration with wine and frankincense to your image, which I had ordered to be brought for that purpose, together with those of the gods, and who finally cursed Christ—none of which acts, it is said, those who are really Christians can be forced into performing—these I thought it proper to discharge. Others who were aimed by that informer at first confessed themselves Christians, and then denied it; true, they had been of that persuasion but they had quitted it, some, three years, others many years, and a few as much as twenty-five years ago. They all worshipped your statue and the images of the gods and cursed Christ. They affirmed, however, the whole of their guilt, or their error, was that they were in the habit of meeting on a certain fixed day before it was light, when they sang in alternate verses a hymn to Christ, as to a god, and bound themselves by a solemn oath, not to do any wicked deeds, but never to commit any fraud, theft or adultery, never to falsify their word, nor deny a trust when they should be called upon to deliver it up; after which it was their custom to separate and then reassemble to partake of food—but food of an ordinary and innocent kind. Even this practice, however, they had abandoned after the publication of my edict, by which, according to your orders, I had forbidden political associations. I judged it so much the more necessary to extract the real truth with the assistance of torture from two female slaves, who were styled deaconesses: but I could discover nothing more than depraved and excessive superstition. I therefore adjourned the proceedings and betook myself at once to your counsel. For the matter seemed to me well worth referring to you, especially considering the numbers endangered. Persons of all ranks and ages and of both sexes are and will be involved in the prosecution. For this contagious superstition is not confined to the cities only, but has spread through the villages and rural districts; it seems possible, however, to check and cure it. IT is certain at least that the temples, which had been almost deserted, begin now to be frequented; and the sacred festivals, after a long intermission, are again revived; while there is the general demand for sacrificial animals, which for some time past have met with but few purchasers. From hence it is easy to imagine what multitudes may be reclaimed from this error, if a door be left open to repentance.

TRAJAN TO PLINY: The method that you have pursued, my dear Pliny, in sifting the cases of those denounced to you as Christians is extremely proper. It is not possible to lay down any general rule which can be applied as the fixed standard in all cases of this nature. No search should be made for these people; when they are denounced and found guilty, they must be punished; with the restriction, however, that when the party denies himself to be a Christian and shall give proof that he is not (that is, by adoring our Gods), he shall be pardoned on the ground of repentance, even though he may have formerly incurred suspicion. Informations without the accuser's name subscribed must not be admitted in evidence against anyone, as it is introducing a very dangerous precedent and by no means is agreeable to the spirit of the age.

C. LEGAL INTERROGATION OF CHRISTIANS

The following passage comes from a Christian account of the martyrdom of six Christians in North Africa in 180 A.D. The passage reproduces the transcript of the legal proceedings that occurred before the Roman provincial governor.

(Taken from Roman Civilization, Source Book II, The Empire, ed. by Naphtali Lewis and Meyer Reinhold [Columbia University Press 1955] pp.593-5)

In the consulship of Praesens (for the second time) and Claudianus, on July 17, Speratus, Nartzalus, Cittinus, Donata, Sccunda, and Vestia were put on trial in the governor's council chamber at Carthage. The proconsul Saturninus said, "You can secure the indulgence of our lord the emperor if you return to your senses." Speratus said, "We have never done any wrong; we have lent ourselves to no injustice; we have never spoken ill of anyone; but when we have been ill-treated, we have given thanks, because we honor our emperor." The proconsul Saturninus said, "We also are religious, and our religion is simple; and we swear by the genius of our lord the emperor and pray for his welfare, as you too ought to do." Speratus said, "If you grant me your undivided attention, I will tell you the mystery of simplicity." Saturninus said, "I shall not grant you a hearing, if you begin to speak evil about our sacred rites; but swear rather by the genius of our lord the emperor." Speratus said, "The empire of this world I do not recognize, but rather I serve that God whom no man has seen nor can see with human eyes. I have not committed theft; if I buy anything, I pay the tax, because I recognize my Lord, the King of kings and Emperor of all peoples." The proconsul Saturninus said to the others, "Cease to be of this persuasion." Speratus said, "It is an evil persuasion to commit murder, or to bear false witness." The proconsul Saturninus said, "Do not participate in this madness." Cittinus said, "We have none other to fear except only our Lord God who is in heaven." Donata said, "Honor to Caesar as to Caesar, but fear to God." Vestia said, "I am a Christian." Secunda said, "What I am, that I wish to be." The proconsul Saturninus said to Speratus, "Do you persist in being a Christian?" Speratus said, "I am a Christian;" and they all concurred with him. The proconsul Saturninus said, "Do you desire some time to reconsider?" Speratus said, "In a matter so just there is no reconsidering." The proconsul Saturninus said, "What are the things in your box?" Speratus said, "The Books and the letters of Paul, a just man." The proconsul Saturninus said, "Take a postponement of thirty days and reconsider." Speratus said again, "I am a Christian;" and they all concurred with him. The proconsul Saturninus read out the decree from the tablet: "Since Speratus, Nartzalus, Cittinus, Donata, Vestia, Secunda, and the rest who have confessed that they live according to the rite of the Christians have obstinately persevered when an opportunity was offered them to return to the practice of the Romans, it is my decision that they be punished with the sword." Speratus said, "We give thanks to God." Narttalus said, "Today we are martyrs in heaven; thanks to God!" The proconsul Saturninus ordered the herald to proclaim: "I have ordered the execution of Speratus, Nartzalus, Cittinus, Veturius, Felix, Aquilinus, Lactantius, Januaria, Generosa, Vestia, Donata, and Secunda." They all said, "Thanks be to God!" And so they were crowned with martyrdom all together: and they reign with the Father, the Son, and the Holy Ghost forever and ever. Amen.

D. THE CONVERSION OF CONSTANTINE

✦ Lactantius, *On the Deaths of the Persecutors* 44

During the year 312 A.D. the two imperial contenders, Constantine and Maxentius, fought a civil war for control of the western half of the Roman Empire. The fighting culminated in the battle of the Mulvian Bridge spanning the Tiber River just a few miles north of Rome. Before this engagement Constantine was prompted in a dream to seek the divine assistance of the god of the Christians. The following account was written by a contemporary Christian named Lactantius. His treatise, entitled *On the Deaths of the Persecutors*, was designed to show how those who had persecuted Christians in recent years had all met with a bad end.

(Taken from Vol. VII of Ante-Nicene Fathers, tr. by Alexander Roberts and James Donaldson)

And now a civil war broke out between Constantine and Maxentius. Although Maxentius kept himself within Rome, because the soothsayers had foretold that if he went out of it, he should perish, yet he conducted the military operations by able generals. In forces he exceeded his adversary; for he had not only his fatherÆs army, which deserted from Severus, but also his own, which he had lately drawn together out of Mauritania and Italy. They fought, and the troops of Maxentius prevailed. At length Constantine, with steady courage and a mind prepared for every event, led his whole forces to the neighbourhood of Rome, and encamped them opposite to the Milvian bridge. The anniversary of the reign of Maxentius approached, that is, the sixth day before the kalends of November [October 27]. and the fifth year of his reign was drawing to an end.

Constantine was directed in a dream to cause the heavenly sign to be delineated on the shields of his soldiers, and so to proceed to battle. He did as he had been commanded, and he marked on their shields the letter X [the Greek letter chi] with a perpendicular line drawn through it and turned round thus at the top [i.e., P = the Greek letter rho], being the cipher of Christ. Armed with this sign, his troops stood to arms. The enemies advanced, but without their emperor, and they crossed the bridge. The armies met, and fought with the utmost exertions of valour, and firmly maintained their ground. In the meantime a sedition arose at Rome, and Maxentius was reviled as one who had abandoned all concern for the safety of the commonweal; and suddenly, while he conducted the chariot races on the anniversary of his reign, the people cried with one voice, ôConstantine cannot be overcome!ö Dismayed at this, Maxentius burst from the assembly, and having called some senators together, ordered the Sibylline books [traditional books of Roman prophecies] to be searched. In them it was found that:ù

ôOn the same day the enemy of the Romans should perish.ö

Led by this response to the hopes of victory, he went to the field. The bridge in his rear was broken down. At sight of that the battle grew hotter. The hand of the Lord prevailed, and the forces of Maxentius were routed. He fled towards the broken bridge; but the multitude pressing on him, he was driven headlong into the Tiber.

This destructive war being ended, Constantine was acknowledged as emperor, with great rejoicings, by the senate and people of Rome.

IV

The Middle Ages

Introduction

The Germanic invasions of the Roman Empire and the rise of Islam destroyed the Mediterranean unity that had been the Roman Empire. In its place arose three distinct cultural regions: the Byzantine Empire of the eastern Mediterranean; the Islamic Empire comprising, in part, the southern areas of the Mediterranean; and the various Germanic kingdoms of Western Europe. The first of these was a continuation of the eastern Greek half of the Roman Empire, which carried on the high cultural traditions of both the ancient Greeks and Romans, combined with Christianity, until the Ottoman Turks captured Constantinople in 1453. The third of these cultural regions gradually developed into Medieval Europe. The formation of the latter culture was a slow process and resulted from the gradual synthesis of three rather different traditions: the culture of the Roman Empire, the simple warlike society of the Germanic invaders, and Christianity. During the Middle Ages a Christian worldview, centered upon God and eternity, replaced the secular civic culture of the Roman Empire. The complex urban culture of the latter largely disappeared and was replaced by a simple society and economy based on large landed plantations called manors (hence the term *manorialism*), and the complex political system of the Roman Empire gave way to a rather simple form of monarchy, an outgrowth of the kingship of the Germanic tribes. It was not until the period of the High or Late Middle Ages (1050–1350) that Medieval Europe began to advance politically, economically, and intellectually with the rise of centralized monarchies in England and France, the revival of town life with a newly emerging middle class and incipient capitalism, and the rise of Medieval universities. ✛

Reading 24

Gregory of Tours, History of the Franks

G regory of Tours (538-594) was not only a Christian bishop of Tours, but the author of *The History of the Franks*, our single most important source of information about Gaul during the later fifth and sixth centuries. His account reveals the odd mixture of Christianity and the cut-throat nature of early Germanic society. Gregory's Christian perspective in writing history is clearly evident throughout the whole work, which records numerous miracles to demonstrate the validity of the one true religion. In fact, the first book of this work is a brief summary of events from God's creation of the world and Adam and Eve in the Garden of Eden, major events recorded in The Old and New Testaments, and the first four centuries of our era. Gregory's narrative focuses upon the careers and actions of leading Christian bishops of this region of Western Europe, the wars fought among the various Germanic kings, and the power struggles and treacherous behavior within the royal families. His account of King Clovis' reign (481-511) perhaps best epitomizes all these characteristics that defined the culture of Western Europe during the early Medieval period.

(Taken from the translation of Ernest Brehaut)

A. PREFACE

With liberal culture on the wane, or rather perishing in the Gallic cities there were many deeds being done both good and evil: the heathen were raging fiercely; kings were growing more cruel; the church. attacked by heretics, was defended by Catholics; while the Christian faith was in general devoutly cherished, among some it was growing cold; the churches also were enriched by the faithful or plundered by traitors-and no grammarian skilled in the dialectic art could be found to describe these matters either in prose or verse; and many were lamenting and saying: "Woe to our day, since the pursuit of letters has perished from among us and no one can be found among the people who can set forth the deeds of the present on the written page." Hearing continually these complaints and others like them I [have undertaken] to commemorate the past, order that it may come to the knowledge of the future; and although my speech is rude, I have been unable to be silent as to the struggles between the wicked and the upright; and I have been especially (encouraged because, to my surprise, it has often been said by men of our day, that few understand the learned words of the rhetorician but many the rude language of the common people. I have decided also that for the reckoning of the years the first book shall begin with the very beginning of the world, and I have given its chapters below.

B. REIGN OF KING CLOVIS

✣ Book II

27. After these events Childeric died and Clovis his son reigned in his stead. In the fifth year of his reign Siagrius, king of the Romans, son of Egidius, had his seat in the city of Soissons which Egidius, who has been mentioned before, once held. And Clovis came against him with Ragnachar, his kinsman, because he used to possess the kingdom, and demanded that they make ready a battlefield. And Siagrius did not delay nor was he afraid to resist. And so they fought against each other and Siagrius, seeing his army crushed, turned his back and fled swiftly to king Alaric at Toulouse. And Clovis sent to Alaric to send him back, otherwise he was to know that Clovis would make war on him for his refusal. And Alaric was afraid that he would incur the anger of the Franks on account of Siagrius, seeing it is the fashion of the Goths to be terrified, and he surrendered him in chains to Clovis' envoys. And Clovis took him and gave orders to put him under guard, and when he had got his kingdom he directed that he be executed secretly..

At that time many churches were despoiled by Clovis' army, since he was as yet involved in heathen error. Now the army had taken from a certain church a vase of wonderful size and beauty, along with the remainder of the utensils for the service of the church. And the bishop of the church sent messengers to the king asking that the vase at least be returned, if he could not get back any more of the sacred dishes. On hearing this the king said to the messenger: "Follow us as far as Soissons, because all that has been taken is to be divided there and when the lot assigns me that dish I will do what the father asks." Then when he came to Soissons and all the booty was set in their midst, the king said: "I ask of you, brave warriors, not to refuse to grant me in addition to my share, yonder dish," that is, he was speaking of the vase just mentioned. In answer to the speech of the king those of more sense replied: "Glorious king, all that we see is yours, and we ourselves are subject to your rule. Now do what seems well(pleasing to you; for no one is able to resist your power." When they said this a foolish, envious and excitable fellow lifted his battle(ax and struck the vase, and cried in a loud voice: "You shall get nothing here except what the lot fairly bestows on you." At this all were stupefied, but the king endured the insult with the gentle(ness of patience, and taking the vase he handed it over to the messenger of the church, nursing the wound deep in his heart. And at the end of the year he ordered the whole army to come with their equipment of armor, to show the brightness of their arms on the field of March. And when he was reviewing them all carefully, he came to the man who struck the vase, and said to him "No one has brought armor so carelessly kept as you; for neither your spear nor sword nor ax is in serviceable condition." And seizing his ax he cast it to the earth, and when the other had bent over somewhat to pick it up, the king raised his hands and drove his own ax into the man's head. "This," said he, "'is what you did at Soissons to the vase." Upon the death of this man, he ordered the rest to depart, raising great dread of himself by this action. He made many wars and gained many victories. In the tenth year of his reign he made war on the Thuringi and brought them under his dominion.

28. Now the king of the Burgundians was Gundevech, of the family of king Athanaric the persecutor, whom we have mentioned before. He had four sons: Gundobad, Godegisel, Chilperic and Godomar. Gundobad killed his brother Chilperic with the sword, and sank his wife in water with a stone tied to her neck. His two daughters he condemned to exile;

the older of these, who became a nun, was called Chrona, and the younger Clotilda. And as Clovis often sent embassies to Burgundy, the maiden Clotilda was found by his envoys. And when they saw that she was of good bearing and wise, and learned that she was of the family of the king, they reported this to King Clovis, and he sent an embassy to Gundobad without delay asking her in marriage. And Gundobad was afraid to refuse, and surrendered her to the men, and they took the girl and brought her swiftly to the king. The king was very glad when he saw her, and married her, having already by a concubine a son named Theodoric.

29. He had a first-born son by queen Clotilda, and as his wife wished to consecrate him in baptism, she tried unceasingly to persuade her husband, saying: "The gods you worship are nothing, and they will be unable to help themselves or any one else. For they are graven out of stone or wood or some metal. And the names you have given them are names of men and not of gods, as Saturn, who is declared to have fled in fear of being banished from his kingdom by his son; as Jove himself, the foul perpetrator of all shameful crimes, committing incest with men, mocking at his kinswomen, not able to refrain from intercourse with his own sister as she herself says: Jovisque et soror et conjunx. What could Mars or Mercury do? They are endowed rather with the magic arts than with the power of the divine name. But he ought rather to be worshipped who created by his word heaven and earth, the sea and all that in them is out of a state of nothingness, who made the sun shine, and adorned the heavens with stars, who filled the waters with creeping things, the earth with living things and the air with creatures that fly, at whose nod the earth is decked with grow-ing crops, the trees with fruit, the vines with grapes, by whose hand mankind was created, by whose generosity all that creation serves and helps man whom he created as his own."

But though the queen said this the spirit of the king was by no means moved to belief, and he said: "It was at the command of our gods that all things were created and came forth, and it is plain that your God has no power and, what is more, he is proven not to belong to the family of the gods." Meantime the faithful queen made her son ready for baptism; she gave command to adorn the church with hangings and curtains, in order that he who could not moved by persuasion might be urged to belief by this mystery. The boy, whom they named Ingomer, died after being baptized, still wearing the white garments in which he became regenerate. At this the king was violently angry, and reproached the queen harshly, saying: "If the boy had been dedicated in the name of my gods he would certainly have lived; but as it is, since he was baptized in the name of your God, he could not live at all." To this the queen said: "I give thanks to the omnipotent God, creator of all, who has judged me not wholly unworthy, that he should deign to take to his kingdom one born from my womb. My soul is not stricken with grief for his sake, because I know that, summoned from this world as he was in his baptismal garments, he will be fed by the vision of God." After this she bore another son, whom she named Chlodomer at baptism; and when he fell sick, the king said: "It is impossible that anything else should happen to him than happened to his brother, namely, that being baptized in the name of your Christ, should die at once." But through the prayers of his mother, and the Lord's command, he became well.

30. The queen did not cease to urge him to recognize the true God and cease worshipping idols. But he could not be influenced in any way to this belief, until at last a war arose with the Alamanni, in which he was driven by necessity to confess what before he had of his free will denied. It came about that as the two armies were fighting fiercely, there was much slaughter, and Clovis's army began to be in danger of destruction. He saw it and raised his eyes to heaven, and with remorse in his heart he burst into tears and cried: "Jesus Christ, whom Clotilda asserts to be the son of the living God, who art said to give aid to those in distress, and to bestow victory on those who hope in thee, I beseech the glory of thy aid, with the vow that if thou wilt grant me victory over these enemies, and I shall know that power which she says that people dedicated in thy name have had

from thee, I will believe in thee and be baptized in thy name. For I have invoked my own gods but, as I find, they have withdrawn from aiding me; and therefore I believe that they possess no power, since they do not help those who obey them. I now call upon thee, I desire to believe thee only let me be rescued from my adversaries." And when he said thus, the Alamanni turned their backs, and began to disperse in flight. And when they saw that their king was killed, they submitted to the dominion of Clovis, saying: "Let not the people perish further, we pray; we are yours now." And he stopped the fighting, and after encouraging his men, retired in peace and told the queen how he had had merit to win the victory by calling on the name of Christ. This happened in the fifteenth year of his reign.

31. Then the queen asked saint Remigius, bishop of Rheims, to summon Clovis secretly, urging him to introduce the king to the word of salvation. And the bishop sent for him secretly and began to urge him to believe in the true God, maker of heaven and earth, and to cease worshipping idols, which could help neither themselves nor any one else. But the king said: "I gladly hear you, most holy father; but there remains one thing: the people who follow me cannot endure to abandon their gods; but I shall go and speak to them according to your words." He met with his followers, but before he could speak the power of God anticipated him, and all the people cried out together: "O pious king, we reject our mortal gods, and we are ready to follow the immortal God whom Remigius preaches." This was reported to the bishop, who was greatly rejoiced, and bade them get ready the baptismal font. The squares were shaded with tapestried canopies, the churches adorned with white curtains, the baptistery set in order, the aroma of incense spread, candles of fragrant odor burned brightly, and the whole shrine of the baptistery was filled with a divine fragrance: and the Lord gave such grace to those who stood by that they thought they were placed amid the odors of paradise. And the king was the first to ask to be baptized by the bishop. Another Constantine advanced to the baptismal font, to terminate the disease of ancient leprosy and wash away with fresh water the foul spots that had long been borne. And when he entered to be baptized, the saint of God began with ready speech: "Gently bend your neck, Sigamber; worship what you burned; burn what you worshipped." The holy bishop Remigius was a man of excellent wisdom and especially trained in rhetorical studies, and of such surpassing holiness that he equalled the miracles of Silvester [the pope who allegedly baptized Emperor Constantine]. For there is extant a book of his life which tells that he raised a dead man. And so the king confessed all-powerful God in the Trinity, and was baptized in the name of the Father, Son and holy Spirit, and was anointed with the holy ointment with the sign of the cross of Christ. And of his army more than 3000 were baptized. His sister also, Albofled, was baptized, who not long after passed to the Lord. And when the king was in mourning for her, the holy Remigius sent a letter of consolation which began in this way: "The reason of your mourning pains me, and pains me greatly, that Albofled your sister, of good memory, has passed ; away. But I can give you this comfort, that her departure from the world was such that she ought to be envied rather than e mourned." Another sister also was converted, Lanthechild by name, who had fallen into the heresy of the Arians, and she confessed that the Son and the holy Spirit were equal to the Father, and was anointed....

38. Clovis received an appointment to the consulship from the emperor Anastasius [of Constantinople], and in the church of the blessed Martin he clad himself in the purple tunic and chlamys, and placed a diadem on his head. Then he mounted his horse, and in the most generous manner he gave gold and silver as he passed along the way which is between the gate of the entrance [of the church of St. Martin] and the church of the city, scattering it among the people who were there with his own hand, and from that day he was called consul or Augustus. Leaving Tours he went to Paris and there he established the seat of his kingdom. There also Theodoric came to him....

When King Clovis was dwelling at Paris, he sent secretly to the son of Sigibert saying: "Behold your father has become an . old man and limps in his weak foot. If he should die," said he, 'Of due right his kingdom would be yours together with our friendship." Led on by greed the son plotted to kill his father. And when his father went out from the city of Cologne and crossed the Rhine and was intending to journey through the wood Buchaw, as he slept at midday in his tent, his son sent assassins in against him, and killed him there, in the idea that he would get his kingdom. But by God's judgment he walked into the pit that he had cruelly dug for his father. He sent messengers to king Clovis to tell about his father's death, and to say: "My father is dead, and I have his treasures in my possession, and also his kingdom. Send men to me, and I shall gladly transmit to you from his treasures whatever pleases you." And Clovis replied: "I thank you for your good will, and I ask that you show the treasures to my men who come, and after that you shall possess all yourself." When they came, he showed his father's treasures. And when they were looking at the different things he said: "It was in this little chest that my father used to put his gold coins." "Thrust in your hand," said they, "to the bottom, and uncover the whole." When he did so, and was much bent over, one of them lifted his hand and dashed his battle (ax against his head, and so in a shameful manner he incurred the death which he had brought on his father. Clovis heard that Sigibert and his son had been slain, and came to the place and summoned all the people, saying: "Hear what has happened. When I," said he, "was sailing down the river Scheldt Cloderic, son of my kinsman, was in pursuit of his own father asserting that I wished him killed. And when his father was fleeing through the forest of Buchaw, he set highwaymen upon him, and gave him over to death, and slew him. And when he was opening the treasures, he was slain himself by some one or other. Now I know nothing at all of these matters. For I cannot shed the blood of my own kinsmen, which it is a crime to do. But since this has happened, I give you my advice, if it seems acceptable; turn to me, that you may be under my protection." They listened to this, and giving applause with both shields and voices, they raised him on a shield, and made him king over them. He received Sigibert's kingdom with his treasures, and placed the people, too, under his rule. For God was laying his enemies low every day under his hsand, and was increasing his kingdom, because he walked with an upright heart before him, and did what was pleasing in his eyes.

41. After this he turned to Chararic. When he had fought with Siagrius this Chararic had been summoned to help Clovis, but stood at a distance, aiding neither side, but awaiting the outcome, in order to form a league of friendship with him to whom victory came. For this reason Clovis was angry, and went out against him. He entrapped and captured him and his son also, and kept them in prison, and gave them the tonsure; he gave orders to ordain Chararic priest and his son deacon. And when Chararic complained of his degradation and wept, it is said that his son remarked: "It was on green wood," said he, "that these twigs were cut, and they are not altogether withered. They will shoot out quickly, and be able to grow; may he perish as swiftly who has done this." This utterance was reported to the ears of Clovis, namely, that they were threatening to let their hair grow, and kill him. And he ordered them both to be put to death. When they were dead, he took their kingdom with the treasures and people.

42. Ragnachar was then king at Cambrai, a man so unrestrained in his wantonness that he scarcely had mercy for his own near relatives. He had a counselor Farro, who defiled himself with a like vileness. And it was said that when food, or a gift, or anything whatever was brought to the king, he was wont to say that: it was enough for him and his Farro. And at this thing the Franks were in a great rage. And so it happened that Clovis gave golden armlets and belts, but all only made to resemble gold-for it was bronze gilded so as to deceive-these he gave to Ragnachar's leudes to be invited to attack him. Moreover, when Clovis had set his army in motion against him, and Ragnachar was

continually sending spies to get information, on the return of his messengers, he used to ask how strong the force was. And they would answer: is a great sufficiency for you and your Farro." Clovis came and made war on him, and he saw that his army was beaten and prepared to slip away in flight, but was seized by his army, and with his hands tied behind his back, he was taken with Ricchar his brother before Clovis. And Clovis said to him: "Why have you humiliated our family in permitting yourself to be bound? It would have been better for you to die." And raising his ax he dashed it against his head, and he turned to his brother and said: "If you had aided your brother, he would not have been bound" And in the same way he smote him with his ax and killed him. After their death their betrayers perceived that the gold which they had received from the king was false. When they told the king of this, it is said that he answered: "Rightly," said he, "does he receive this kind of gold, who of his own will brings his own master to death;" it ought to suffice them that they were alive and were not put to death, to mourn amid torments the wicked betrayal of their masters. When they heard this, they prayed for mercy, saying it was enough for them if they were allowed to live The kings named above were kinsmen of Clovis, and their brother Rignomer by name, was slain by Clovis' order at the city of Mans. When they were dead Clovis received all their kingdom and treasures And having killed many other kings and his nearest relatives, of whom he was jealous lest they take the kingdom from him, he extended his rule over all the Gauls. However, he gathered his people together at one time, it is said, and spoke of the kinsmen whom he had himself destroyed. "Woe to me, who have remained as a stranger among foreigners, and have none of my kinsmen to give me aid if adversity comes." But he said this not because of grief at their death but by way of a ruse, if perchance he should be able to find some one still to kill.

43. After all this he died at Paris, and was buried in the church of the holy apostles, which he himself had built together with his queen Clotilda. He passed away in the fifth year after the battle; of VouillΘ, and all the days of his reign were thirty years, and his age was forty-five. From the death of St. Martin to the death of king Clovis, which happened in the eleventh year of the episcopate of Licinius, bishop of Tours, one hundred and twelve years are reckoned. Queen Clotilda came to Tours after the death of her husband and served there in the church of St. Martin, and dwelt in the place with the greatest chastity and kindness all the days of her life, rarely visiting Paris.

C. A FALSE PROPHET

✛ Book X

25. Now in the Gauls the disease I have mentioned attacked the province of Marseilles, and a great famine oppressed Angers, Nantes, and Mans. These are the beginning of sorrows according to what the Lord says in the Gospel: "There shall be pestilence and famines and earthquakes in different places and false Christs and false prophets shall arise and give signs and prodigies in the heavens so as to put the elect astray" as is true at the present time. For a certain man of Bourges, as he himself told later, went into the deep woods to cut logs which he needed for a certain work and a swarm of flies surrounded him, as a result of which he was considered crazy for two years; whence it may be believed that they were a wickedness sent by the devil. Then he passed through the neighboring cities and went to the province of Arles and there wore skins and prayed like one of the devout, and to make a fool of him the enemy gave him the power of divination.

After this he rose from his place and left the province mentioned in order to become more expert in wickedness, and entered the territory of GΘvaudan, conducting himself as a great man and not afraid to say that he was Christ. He took with him a woman who passed as his sister to whom he gave the name of Mary. A multitude of people flocked to him bringing the sick, whom he touched and restored to health. They who came to him brought him also gold and silver and garments. These he distributed among the poor to deceive them the more easily, and throwing himself on the ground and praying with the woman I have mentioned and rising, he would give orders to the bystanders to worship him in turn. He foretold the future and announced that disease would come to some, to others losses and to others health. But all this he did by some arts and trickeries of the devil. A great multitude of people was led astray by him, not only the common ilk but bishops of the church. More than three thousand people followed him.

Meantime he began to spoil and plunder those whom he met on the road; the booty, however, he gave to those who had nothing. He threatened with death bishops and citizens, because they disdained to worship him. He entered La Velay and went to the place called Puy and halted with all his host at the churches near there, marshalling his line of battle to make war on Aurilius who was then bishop, and sending messengers forward, naked men who danced and played and announced his coming. The bishop was amazed at this and sent strong men to ask what his doings meant. One of these, the leader, bent down as if to embrace his knees and check his passage and [the impostor] ordered him to be seized and spoiled. But the other at once drew his sword and cut him into bits and that Christ who ought rather to be named anti(Christ fell dead; and all who were with him dispersed. Mary was tortured and revealed all his impostures and deceits. But the men whom he had excited to a belief in him by the trickery of the devil never returned to their sound senses, but they always said that this man was Christ in a sense and that Mary had a share in his divine nature. Moreover, through all the Gauls many appeared who attracted poor women to themselves by trickery and influenced them to rave and declare their leaders holy, and they made a great show before the people. I have seen some of them and have rebuked the most and endeavored to recall them from error.

THE EPIC OF BEOWULF

The *Epic of Beowulf* is the earliest major literary work in the history of the English language. It was written in Anglo-Saxon or Old English probably during the early 700's. The poem consists of two distinct episodes, both involving Beowulf as the central character. In the first episode Beowulf is a young Germanic warrior, summoned across the sea with his band of loyal followers to rid the feasting hall of King Hrothgar of the nightly visitations of a monster named Grendel, which dwells at the bottom of a nearby lake. The second half of the poem, which forms the text below, is set fifty years later when Beowulf is an aged king of the Geats, a Germanic people situated somewhere in Scandanavia. In this episode Beowulf is called out to protect his people from the devastation caused by a raging dragon. Although Beowulf succeeds in slaying the monster, he is mortally wounded in the combat and dies; and the poem ends with Beowulf's heroic funeral. This work therefore represents the warrior ethos and world-view of early Anglo-Saxon society, and it exhibits the nature of the Germanic war band and the personal prowess required of its leader.

(Taken from the translation of Chauncey Brewster Tinker)

THEREAFTER in later days by reason of the crash of battle it fell thus; after Hygelac was laid low, and Heardred had been slain by war swords piercing beneath the shield, at the time when the War-Scylfings, fierce battle-wolves, fell upon him among his victorious people and overwhelmed the nephew of Hereric in war, after that, the broad kingdom came into the hand of Beowulf. He ruled it well for fifty winters, -and the king, aged guardian of the land, was old,-until a certain dragon began to hold sway on dark nights and work his will, one who on a high mound kept watch over a treasure-hoard in a steep and rocky cave. Beneath it lay a path, unknown to men. But a certain slave entered there and eagerly took from the heathen hoard; he seized with his hand a cup, bright with gold. Nor did he give it back, albeit he had beguiled the keeper of the hoard with thievish craft. The king, best of heroes, learned of that deed, and he was filled with wrath.

NOWISE of his own freewill and purpose did slave seek out the dragons hoard, and bring sore harm upon himself, but in dire need, this thrall of one among the children of men had fled from wrathful blows, a homeless Wretch, haunted by sin, and he had entered there. But soon it had come to pass that awful terror seized upon the invader ;.... just as the terror got hold of him he saw the precious cup.

Many olden treasures were lying in that cave of earth where a certain man in days of yore had hidden away the dear possessions, taking thought for the great bequest of his noble kin. Death had snatched away those men in times gone by, and, at the last, the one who tarried longest there of all that mighty line was mourning for his friends; yet he would fain live that he might enjoy for a little time those olden treasures.

There was a new mound ready on the plain, near to the cliff hard by the ocean-waves, made fast by cunning craft. Thither the keeper of rings bore that heavy store of beaten gold, the princely treasures; and he spoke a few words : ANow do thou hold, oh-Earth-since heroes could not hold-this princely treasure, for, lo ! in thee at first the good men found it. Every man of my people who hath yielded up this life, dread slaughter, death in war, hath swept away;-they had known the pleasures of the hall! None have I to wield the sword, none to burnish the plated beaker, the precious drinking-cup;-the warrior-heroes are departed otherwhere. The hard helmet, decked with gold, must be bereft of its adornments; they sleep who once did brighten it, they who prepared the masks of war. Likewise the coat of mail which, amid the crash of shields, was proof against the bite of swords in battle, moulders with the hero; the byrnie may no longer make far journeys with the war-leader, together with heroes. There is no joy of harp, no mirth of the gleewood, no good hawk swinging through the hall, no swift horse beating with his hoof the castle-yard. Baleful death hath sent forth many mortals on their way. @Thus, alone and heavy-hearted, he sorrowfully lamented for them all, mournfully weeping by day and night until the surge of death touched at his heart.

Then the beauteous hoard, standing all open, had been found by the old twilight foe, the naked venomous dragon, he who, wrapped in flames, haunteth the mounds, and flies by night begirt with fire; of him the dwellers in the land are sore afraid. It is his wont to find out some hoard in the earth, where, old in winters, he shall guard the heathen gold,-but naught the better will he fare for that!

Thus for three hundred winters the scourge of the people had held the vast treasure-cave within the earth, until a certain man angered him in his heart, and bore away a plated beaker to his lord, and prayed his master for a covenant of peace. Thus the hoard was plundered, and a part of the treasure taken away. But his boon was granted to that wretched man. His lord beheld for the first time that handiwork of ancient men.

Soon as the dragon woke, strife was begun; fierce at heart he sniffed along the rock, and found out the tracks of his foe, for with secret craft he had gone on too far, hard by the dragons head. So the man not doomed to die easily escapeth woe and banishment, even he whom the grace of the Lord upholdeth. The keeper of the hoard sought eagerly along the ground, he wished to find the man who had wrought him this mischief in his sleep. Wroth and hot-hearted, he circled oft around the mound without;-but there was none upon the waste. Yet he rejoiced in the thought of battle, in warfare to come. At times he would turn back to the mound, and seek his precious cup. Soon he discovered that some one of menfolk had found out the gold, his splendid treasure.

Impatiently the keeper of the hoard waited till even was come; the guardian of the mound was mad with wrath; the foe wished to repay them with fire and burning for the loss of his dear cup. And the day departed, even as the dragon wished. No longer, then, would he abide at his den, but went forth flaming, all girdled with fire. Fearful was the beginning for the men of that land, even as the end was bitter, which straight thereafter fell upon their gracious lord.

THEN the monster began to spew forth coals of fire and burn the bright dwellings; the scourging flame leaped forth, terrifying the people; the loathed flier of the air meant to leave naught in that place alive. The warfare of the dragon, the vengeance of the deadly foe, near and far was manifest, how the destroyer hated and humbled the Geatish folk. Ere break of day he shot back to his hoard again, to his dark and secret hall. He had encompassed the men of that land with flame, with fire and burning, trusting for defence in his mound, his wall, and his might in warfare;-his trust betrayed him!

And forthwith the terror was made known unto Beowulf, how for a truth his own home, best of halls, the gift-seat of the Geats, had melted away in waves of fire. The good man suffered pain at heart, most grievous sorrow; the wise hero thought that, sinning against the ancient laws, he had provoked to anger the Almighty, the Lord eternal; his breast within him surged with dark thoughts, as was not his wont.

The fire-dragon with his burning coals had utterly destroyed the fortress, stronghold of the people, the water-washed fastness. Therefore the war-king, chief of the Weders, devised revenge upon him. Then the defence of warriors, lord of heroes, bade them make him a wondrous battle-shield, all of iron; for he knew full well that a shield of linden wood from the forest could avail him naught against the flame. But the valiant prince was doomed to meet the end of his fleeting days, of this worldly life, and the dragon too, though he had long held the hoarded treasure.

But the ring-prince scorned to seek out the wide-flying pest with a host of men, a great army; he had no fear of the combat for himself, nor did he esteem at all the dragon's war-might, his strength and prowess; forasmuch as aforetime, though in narrow straits, he had come safe through many a contest, many a battle-crash, after the time that he, crowned with victory, cleansed Hrothgar's hall, and closed in fight with Grendel's kin of loathed race.

Nor was that the least of contests in which Hygelac, son of Hrethel, was slain in the storm of battle, when the king of the Geats, kind lord of the people, smitten by the sword, died a bloody death in Friesland. Thence Beowulf came off by his own strength, swimming the waves; upon his arm he had thirty suits of armor, when all alone he went down to the sea. The Hetwaras, who had borne out their shields against him, had no cause to boast of their warfare, for few escaped from that war-wolf unto their home. So the son of Ecgtheow, wretched and alone, swam over the expanse of the waters back to his own people. There Hygd offered him the kingdom and the treasure, wealth and royal throne, for she put no trust in her child, that he would be able to hold the native seats against foreign tribes, now that Hygelac was dead. Yet none the sooner could the bereaved people persuade the prince on any conditions to become Heardred's lord and take the kingdom; nevertheless he upheld Heardred among the people with friendly counsel, with favor, and with honor, until he grew older and ruled the Weder-Geats.

But banished men, the sons of Ohthere, came to his land from overseas; they had rebelled against the lord of the Scylfings, the great prince, best of the sea-kings that dealt out treasure in the Swedish land. Thus Heardred's death was brought about; Hygelac's son, destitute, there received the allotted death-wound by blows of the sword. And, after the fall of Heardred, the son of Ongentheow returned unto his home, and suffered Beowulf to have the royal throne, and rule over the Geats,-he was a good king!

IN later days Beowulf bethought him of retribution for the prince's fall; he befriended the wretched Eadgils. Sailing over the broad sea, he supported the son of Ohthere with his army, with his warriors and weapons. Thereafter Eadgils avenged himself for his drear and bitter exile, and took the life of the king.

Thus the son of Ecgtheow had come safe through his every conflict, every perilous fight and brave adventure, even unto that great day in which he was to give battle to the dragon. Then the lord of the Geats, being filled with wrath, went forth with twelve companions to look upon the serpent. He had learned how the feud arose, the deadly hatred toward his men, for he had received the goodly treasurecup from the hand of him who found it. He was the thirteenth in the band, even the man who had caused the beginning of the feud, a captive sad at heart. Him they compelled in downcast mood to guide them to the spot. Unwillingly he went to where he knew that earth-hall stood, a cavern under ground, hard by the struggling waves and the surge of the waters; within, it was full of jewels and filigrees. The awful guardian, a ready fighter, had long watched o'er his golden treasures under the earth. No easy task was it for any man to purchase entrance there.

Then the king, strong in battle, the bounteous lord of the Geats, sat him down upon the headland, while he bade farewell to his hearth-companions. His spirit was full of sorrow, wavering, and ready to depart; Wyrd [fate] was upon him, she who was to come unto that aged man, to seek out the treasure of his soul and put asunder the life from the body; no long time was it now that the prince's soul was to be enwrapped in flesh. Beowulf, son of Ecgtheow, spoke : "In my youth I passed through many a battle-onset, many an hour of strife; I remember all. I was seven winters old when the treasure-prince, dear lord of the people, received me from the hand of my father; King Hrethel had me and held me as his own; he gave me of his treasure and his food, remembering our kinship. Never, while a thane in his hall, was I a whit less dear to him than any of his sons, Herebeald, ,Ixthcyn, or Hygelac my lord. For the eldest born a kinsman's deed did strew the bed of death, as was not meet, for Haethcyn laid him low, him his dear lord, with a bolt from his bow of horn; he missed the mark, and shot his kinsman down,-with the bloody dart brother did brother slay. It was a deed sinfully committed, not to be atoned, sickening to the heart, yet however it were, the prince must needs depart from life unavenged.

"In like manner it is a piteous thing for an aged man to live to see his young son swinging upon the gallows; he utters his lament, his song of woe, while his son hangeth there for the raven's delight, and he, old and full of years, can do naught to help him. Ever at morn he will be minded of his son's departure, nor will he care to await another heir within his home, since this one, through the pangs of death, hath received for his deeds. Worn with sorrow, he seeth in his son's dwelling, all bereft of revelry, a deserted wine-hall, where the winds linger;-riders and heroes are sleeping in the grave; there is no sound of harp, no joy within the courts, as formerly there was."

"THEN he goes to his bed, chanting in his loneliness a song of lamentation for the departed one; fields and dwelling-place, all seemed too empty for him. Even so suffered the defence of the Weders, while his heart within him surged with sorrow in memory of Herebeald. In nowise could he avenge the feud upon the murderer; none the sooner with hostile deeds could he wreak his hatred on the warrior, though he was not dear to him. Then, because of the sorrow which that wound cost him, he gave ober the joys of men; he chose the light of God. He left to his sons, as a rich man is wont, his land and chief cities, when he departed from life.

Then, after the death of Hrethel, there was feud and strife, contest and fierce hostility between the Geats and the Swedes over the wide water; and the sons of Ongentheow grew bold and eager for warfare; they would not keep the peace beyond the seas, but made many terrible inroads around Hreosnabeorh. For that my kinsmen took revenge, for the feud and the treachery, as was well known, although one bought it with his life,-a heavy price; Haethcyn, lord of the Geats, fell in that war. But I heard men say that in the morning, when Ongentheow met with Eofor, brother avenged brother upon the murderer, with the edge of the sword; the helmet was split asunder,-Ongentheow, the aged Scylfing, fell, pale in death; the hand that smote remembered feuds enough, it did not withhold the death-blow.

"Then in my warfare it was granted me to pay Hygelac with my flashing sword for the treasures he had given me. He bestowed upon me land, a dwelling-place and the joys of a home. He did not need to seek out a worse warrior among the Gifths or the Spear-Danes or in the Swedish realm, and hire him for pay. Ever was I wont to be before him in his host, alone in the van. And even so all my life long will I wage warfare, while lasts this sword which has often served me early and late, ever since in my valor I slew Daeghrefn with my hand, him who was champion of the Hugas. By no means was he suffered to carry spoils, fair breast-adornments, unto the Frisian king, for the standard-keeper fell in battle, a prince in his might; he was not slain with the sword,-the grapple of war crushed his body and the beating of his heart. But now the edge of the sword, hand and hard blade, must do battle for the treasure."

Beowulf spoke; for the last time he uttered boastful words: "In the days of my youth I ventured on many battles; and even now will I, the aged guardian of my people, go into the fight and do memorable deeds, if the great destroyer come forth to me out of his cavern." Then for the last time he greeted each of the men, bold helmet-wearers, his own dear companions. "I would not bear a sword or any weapon against the Serpent, if I knew how else I could maintain my boast against the monster, as I did of old against Grendel. But I look for hot battle-fire there, for the venomous blast of his nostrils; therefore I have upon me shield and byrnie. I will not flee one foot's breadth from the keeper of that mound, but it shall be with us twain at the wall as Wyrd, lord of every man, allotteth. I am eager in spirit, so that I forbear boasting against the winged warrior. But do ye men tarry upon the mound with your armor upon you, clad in your byrnies, to see which of us twain after the strife shall survive the deadly woundings. It is no exploit for you, nor for the might of any man, save mine alone to measure strength with the monster and do heroic deeds. I will boldly win the gold, or else battle, yea an evil death, shall take away your lord."

Then the mighty warrior rose up with his shield, stern under his helmet; he bore his battle-mail beneath the stony cliffs; he trusted in his single strength. That is no coward's way! And he beheld hard by the wall,-he of noble worth, who had passed through many wars and clashing battles when armed hosts close in fight,-where stood an arch of stone and a stream breaking out thence from the mound; the surge of the stream was hot with battle-fire. The hero could not abide near the hoard anywhere unburned, because of the dragon's flame.

Then the lord of the Geats, for he was wroth, sent forth a word from his breast. The stout-hearted warrior stormed; his voice battle-clear, entered in and rang under the hoary rock. The keeper of the hoard knew the speech of men, and his hatred was stirred. There was no more time to seek for peace. First came forth out of the rock the breath of the evil beast, the hot reek of battle. The earth resounded. The hero beneath the mound lord of the Geats, swung up his shield against the awful foe, and the heart of the coiled monster grew eager to go out to the strife. Already the good warrior-king had drawn his sword, that olden heirloom, undulled of edge. Each of those destroyers was struck with terror by the other. Stout-hearted stood that prince of friends against his tall shield, while the dragon coiled himself quickly together; Beowulf awaited him in his armor.

Then the flaming dragon, curving like a bow, advanced upon him, hastening to his fate. A shorter time did the shield protect well the life and body of the mighty king than his hopes had looked for, if haply he were to get victory in the combat at that time, early in the day; but Wyrd did not thus appoint for him. The lord of the Geats lifted his hand and smote the hideous-gleaming foe with his mighty sword, in such wise that the brown blade weakened as it fell upon the bone, and bit less deeply than its lord had need of, when sore beset. Then, at the sword-stroke, the keeper of the mound was furious in spirit. He cast forth devouring fire. Far and wide shot the deadly flame. The lord of the Geats nowise boasted of victory, for his naked warsword, his excellent blade, weakened in the fight, as was not meet. It was no easy course for the mighty son of Ecgtheow to forsake his earth for ever; yet he was doomed against is will to take up his abode in a dwelling otherwhere. So every man must quit these fleeting days.

It was not long ere the fighters closed again. The keeper of the hoard plucked up his courage; his breast heaved anew with his venomous breathing. He who erewhile ruled the people was hard put to it, being encompassed by fire. In nowise did his own companions, sons of heroes, surround him in a band with warlike valor, but they took refuge in the wood to save their lives. There was but one among them whose heart surged with sorrows. Naught can ever put aside the bond of friendship in him who thinketh aright.

HE was called Wiglaf, son of Weohstan, a beloved warrior, lord of the Scylfings, kinsman of Aelfhere. He saw his lord suffering the heat under his helmet; and he remembered all the benefits which Beowulf had given him in time past, the rich dwelling-place of the Wagmundings, and every folk-right which his father possessed. And he could not forbear, but seized the shield, the yellow linden, with his hand, and drew forth his old sword. This was known among men as an heirloom of Eanmund, son of Ohthere, whom, when a friendless exile, Weohstan slew in fight with the edge of the sword; he bore to his kinsman the brown-hued helmet, the ringed byrnie, the old giant-sword that Onela had given him; they were his comrade's war-harness, his ready armor. He spoke not of the feud, though he had killed his brother's son. He held the spoils, the sword and byrnie, for many years until his son could do a hero's deeds, like his father before him. Then he gave to him, among the Geats, war-harness of all kinds without number, when, full of years, he passed forth out of life along his last way.

This was the first time that the young warrior was to engage in the storm of war with his high lord. But his heart melted not within him, nor did his kinsman's heirloom weaken in the fight. That the dragon learned after they had come together.

Wiglaf spoke many fitting words, saying to his companions,-for his soul was sad within him: "I remember the time when, as we drank the mead in the beer-hall, we promised our lord, him who gave us these rings, that we would repay him for the war-harness, for helmets and hard swords, if need like this befell him. Of his own will he chose us from his host for this adventure, urged us to do gloriously, and gave me these treasures, since he deemed us good spearmen, keen helm-bearers, albeit our lord, defender of his people, had thought to do this mighty work alone, for that he of all men hath performed most of famed exploits and daring deeds. Now the day is come when our lord needs the might of good warriors. Let us on to his help, whilst the heat is upon him, and the grim terror of the fire.

"God knows of me that I would much rather that the flame should enwrap my body with my king's. Methinks it unseemly that we should bear our shields back to our home, unless we can first strike down the foe and defend the life of the Weders' king. Full well I know that it is not according to his old deserts that he alone of all the Geatish force should endure the pain and sink in the fight. There shall be one sword and one helmet, one shield and one byrnie in common unto us."

Then he sped through the noisome smoke, bearing his war-helmet to the aid of his lord; he spoke a few words: "Beloved Beowulf, now do thou all things well, as thou of old sworest in the days of thy youth that thou wouldst not let thy glory fade while thou didst live. Now, O resolute hero, famed for thy deeds, thou must defend thy life with all thy might. Lo, I will help thee."

After these words, the dragon, awful monster, flashing with blazing flames, came on all wroth a second time to meet his hated foemen. Wiglaf's shield was burned away to the boss in the waves of fire; the byrnie could give no help to the young spear-warrior. But the youth went quickly under his kinsman's shield, since his own had been burned to ashes in the fire. Then again the war-king took thought for his glory; mightily he smote with his battle-sword so that it stood in the dragon's head, driven by force. Naegling was shivered in pieces; Beowulf's sword, old and graymarked, weakened in the fight;-it was not granted that the iron blade should help him in the strife. Too strong was the hand, as I have heard, which by its blow overtaxed all swords whatsoever; so that he fared none the better for it, when he bore into the fight a weapon wondrous hard.

Then the destroyer of people, the dread fire-dragon, for the third time was mindful of the feud. He rushed on the brave hero, when ground was yielded him. Hot and fierce, he seized upon Beowulf's whole neck with his sharp teeth. He was all bloodied over with his lifeblood; the gore welled forth in streams.

THEN I have heard men tell how, in the king's great need, Wiglaf, the hero, showed forth unceasing courage, skill and valor, as was natural to him; he heeded not the dragon's head (though the brave hero's hand was burned as he helped his kinsman), but the armed man smote the evil beast a little lower down, insomuch that the bright and plated sword drove into him, and the fire began to wane forthwith. Then the king recovered himself once more; he drew the short-sword, keen and sharp in battle, which he wore on his byrnie. The defence of the Weders cut the Serpent asunder in the middle. They struck down the foe; their might drove forth his life, and thus they twain, noble kinsmen, destroyed him. Even such should a man be, a thane good at need. That was the king's last hour of victory by his own great deeds, the last of his worldly work.

But the wound which the earth-dragon had given him began to burn and swell; presently he found that poison, deadly venom, was surging in his breast. Then the prince, still wise in mind, moved along so that he might seat him by the mound; he saw that work of giants, saw how the rocky arches standing firm on their pillars, upheld within the earthhall everlasting. Then the thane, surpassing good, taking water, with his hands bathed the great king, his own dear lord, all gory and wearied with battle, and loosened his helmet.

Beowulf spoke and uttered words, despite his wound, his piteous battle-hurt; full well he knew that his life of earthly joy was spent, that the appointed number of his days was run, and Death exceeding near : "Now would I give my war-harness unto my son, had I been granted any heir, born of my body, to come after me. Fifty winters have I ruled this people; yet there was never a king of all the neighbor tribes who durst attack me with the sword or oppress me with terror. In my home I awaited what the times held in store for me, kept well mine own, sought out no wily quarrels, swore not many a false oath. In all this I can rejoice, though death-sick with my wounds, inasmuch as the Ruler of men cannot reproach me with murder of kinsmen, when my life parteth from my body. Now do thou, dear Wiglaf, lightly go and view the hoard 'neath the gray rock, now the dragon lieth low, sleepeth sore wounded, bereft of his treasure. Do thou make haste that I may behold the olden treasures, that store of gold, and look upon those bright and curious gems; and thus, having seen the treasured wealth, I may the easier quit life and the kingdom which long I have ruled."

And I have heard how the song of Weohstan, after these words, quickly obeyed his wounded lord, sick from the battle; he bore his ringed mail-shirt, the woven battle-sark, 'neath the roof of the cave. And the brave thane, exultant victor, as he went by the seat, saw many precious jewels, much glistering gold lying upon the ground and wondrous treasures on the wall, and the den of the dragon, the old twilight-flier; bowls lay there, vessels of bygone men, with none to brighten them, their adornments fallen away. There was many a helmet old and rusty, many an armring cunningly twisted. Treasure of gold found in the earth can easily puff with pride the heart of any man, hide it who will. Likewise he saw a banner all of gold standing ere, high above the hoard, greatest of wonders, woven by skill of hand; from it there one a ray of light, so that he could see the cavern floor, and examine the fair jewels. Naught was to be seen of the dragon there, for the sword had undone him!

Thus I have heard how one man alone at his own free will plundered the hoard within the cave, the old work of the giants, how he laid in his bosom beakers and dishes; he took the banner, too, that brightest of beacons. The old lord's blade, with its iron edge, had sorely injured him who long had been the owner of these treasures, who at midnight had borne about the fiery terror, dreadfully surging, hot before the hoard, until he died the death.

The messenger was in haste, eager to return, enriched with spoils. The great-hearted man was spurred with longing to know whether he would find alive the lord of the Weders, grievously sick, in the place where he had left him. And bringing the treasures, he found the great prince, his lord, bleeding, at the point of death; he began to sprinkle him again with water until the word's point broke through the treasure of his heart, and Beowulf spoke, aged and sorrowful, as he gazed upon the gold: "I utter thanks unto the Ruler of all, King of Glory, the everlasting Lord, for these fair things, which here I look upon, inasmuch as ere my death-day I have been able to win them for my people. I have sold and paid mine aged life for the treasure-hoard. Fulfil ye now the needs of the people. Here can I be no more. Bid the brave warriors rear a splendid mound at the sea-cape after my body is burned. There on Whale's Nest shall it tower high as a memorial for my people, so that seafarers, they who drive from far their great ships over the misty floods, may in aftertime call it 'Beowulf's Mound.'"

The great-hearted king took from his neck the ring of gold; gave to his thane, the youthful warrior, his helmet gold-adorned, his ring and his byrnie, bade him enjoy them well.

"Thou art the latest left of all our kin, the Waegmundings. Wyrd hath swept away all thy kinsmen, heroes in their might, to the appointed doom. I must go after them."

That was the old king's last word from the thoughts of his heart, ere he yielded to the bale-fire, the hotly surging flames. His soul departed from out his bosom unto the reward of the righteous.

THUS it went full hard with the young man see his best-beloved friend lying lifeless on the ground, faring most wretchedly. His destroyer lay there too, the horrid earth-dragon, bereft of life, crushed in ruin. No longer could the coiled serpent rule over treasure-hoards, for the edge of the sword, the hard, battle-notched work of the hammer, had destroyed him, and he had fallen to the ground near his hoard-hall, stilled by the wounding. No more in play did he whirl through the air at midnight, and show himself forth, proud of his treasure, for he sank to earth by the mighty hand of the battle-chief.

Indeed, as I have heard, it hath prospered few men in the world, even though mighty, however daring in their every deed, to rush on against the breath of a venomous foe, or to disturb his treasure-hall, if they found the keeper waking, abiding in his mound. Beowulf paid with his death for his share in the splendid riches. Both of them had reached the end of this fleeting life.

It was not long thereafter that the cowards left the wood, those faint-hearted traitors, the ten of them together, even they who in their lord's great need had not dared to brandish the spear. But shamefully now they bore their shields, their war-armor, to where the old man lay. They looked upon Wiglaf. The wearied warrior was sitting by his lord's shoulder; he was trying to revive him with water, but it availed him naught. He could not stay the chieftain's life on earth, though dearly he wished it, nor change the will of God in aught. The judgment of the Lord was wont to rule the deeds of every man, even as still it doth.

And straightway the youth had a fierce and ready answer for those whose courage had failed them. Wiglaf, son of Weohstan, spoke, sad at heart, as he looked upon those hated men: "Lo! he who is minded to speak the truth may say that the liege lord, he who gave you these treasures, even the battle-armor in which ye are standing,-what time at the alebench the king gave oft unto his thanes, sitting in the hall, helms and byrnies, the choicest far or near which he could find,-that he utterly and wretchedly wasted that war-harness. Nowise did the king need to boast of his comrades in arms when strife overtook him; yet God, the Lord of victory, granted him unaided to avenge himself with the sword, when he had need of valor. Little protection could I give him in the fight; and yet I tried what was beyond my power,to help my kinsman. It was ever the worse for the deadly foe when I smote him with the sword, the fire less fiercely flamed from his head. Too few defenders thronged about their lord when the dread moment fell. Now, all sharing of treasure, all gifts of swords, all hope, all rights of home, shall cease from your kin. Every man of your house shall roam, bereft of tribal rights, as soon as the princes in far countries hear of your flight, your inglorious deed. Death is better for every man than a life of shame!"

THEN he bade announce the issue of the fight to the stronghold up over the sea-cliff, where the sad warrior-band had been sitting by their shields the morning long, looking either for the death or the return of their dear lord. Little did he keep silence of the new tidings, he who rode up the headland, but truthfully spoke before them all: "Now the chief of the Weder people, lord of the Geats, source of all our joy, is fast in the bed of death; he lieth low in slaughter because of the Dragon's deeds. Beside him lieth his deadly adversary, slain by the wounding of the knife; for with the sword he could nowise wound the monster. Wiglaf, the son of Weohstan, sitteth over Beowulf, the living hero by the dead; over his head with weary heart he keepeth watch for friend and foe.

"Now the people may look for a season of war as soon as the fall of the king is published abroad among the Franks and the Frisians. A fierce strife with the Hugas arose when Hygelac came with a fleet upon the Frisian land; there the Hetwaras vanquished him in battle; by their valor, with an overwhelming army, they forced the mailed warrior to sink in the fight; he fell amid his host. The prince gave no spoils to his warriors. Ne'er since then has the favor of the Merovingian been granted unto us.

Nor do I anywise look for peace or truth from the Swedes, for 'twas widely known that Ongentheow took the life of Haethcyn, son of Hrethel, near Ravenswood, what time the War-Scylfings in vainglory did first attack the Geats. Straightway the aged father of Ohthere, old and terrible, retaliated he slew Haethcyn, the-sea-king, the old man rescued his wife, though robbed of her gold, his spouse, the mother of Ohthere and Onela, and then he followed after his deadly foes, until they escaped with difficulty into Ravenswood, deprived of their lord. Then with a great army he beset the remnant left by the sword, weary with their wounds; oft during all that night did he threaten woe to the hapless band; said that on the morrow he would slay them with the edge of the sword, and hang some of them on the gallows for a delight to the birds.

"With daybreak comfort came to the heavy-hearted men, when they heard Hygelac's horn and the blast of his trumpet, as the good king came marching on in their track with his mighty men.

Far and wide was to be seen the bloody track of Swedes and Geats, the warriors' deadly strife,-how the peoples, each with each, stirred up the feud. Then the good chief Ongentheow, aged and downcast, retreated with his comrades to the stronghold, the warrior turned back towards the upland; he had learned of the proud chief's warfare, of Hygelac's might in the battle. He trusted not in resistance, trusted not that he could defy the seamen, the ocean-farers, and defend his treasure, his children and wife; the old man drew back thence under the earth-wall.

"Then chase was given to the Swedish folk and Hygelac's standard reared. Forth they went over that peace-plain, until the Hrethlings thronged up to the inclosure. There Ongentheow, the white-haired, was driven to bay with the edge of the sword, so that the mighty king was forced to submit to the sole will of Eofor. Wulf, son of Wonred, struck at him fiercely with his weapon so that at the blow the blood burst forth in streams from 'neath his hair. Yet the aged Scylfing was not daunted; but the king quickly repaid that deadly stroke with worse exchange, when he turned upon him. The swift son of Wonred could not return the blow to that aged man, for Ongentheow had first cleft through the helmet on his head, so that he was forced to bow; stained with blood, he fell to earth. But he was not yet doomed, for he raised himself up, though the wound had touched him nearly. Then, when his brother lay prostrate, Hygelac's brave thane let his broad blade, his old giant-sword, break through the wall of shields down into the-giant-fashioned helm, and the king, defence of the people, bowed him low,-he was mortally wounded.

"There were many who bound up the wounds of the brother; upraised him quickly when the place was cleared for them, so that they could be masters of the battle-field; meanwhile the one warrior stripped the other,-Eofor took from Ongentheow his iron byrnie, his hard and hilted sword, with his helmet, too.

They bore unto Hygelac the old man's war-harness. He received the spoils, and graciously promised them rewards among his people; and he performed it even so. The lord of the Geats, the son of Hrethel, when he had returned home, repaid Eofor and Wulf for their deadly fight with treasure exceeding great; he gave unto each of them a hundred thousand in 'land and twisted rings; nor needed any man on earth reproach him with those rewards, since they had won glory in the fight. And, moreover, as a pledge of his favor, he gave unto Eofor his only daughter in marriage, for an honor to his home.

"Such is the feud and the enmity, the deadly strife of nations, for which, as I ween, the Swedish people will attack us, soon as they learn that our lord is dead, he who upheld our treasure and our realm against the foe, wrought good for his people, and furthermore did great and glorious deeds.

"Now we had best hasten to go and look upon our king, and then bring our ring-bestower along his way to the pyre. No mean thing shall be burned with the hero, for the hoard of treasure, of untold riches, has been bitterly purchased; and now at the last, he has bought these jewels with his own life. Fire shall devour them, flames shall enwrap them. No warrior shall bear away any of the treasure for a memorial, no fair maiden shall wear upon her neck the jeweled adornment; but rather, bereft of her gold and sad at heart, she shall tread the land of the stranger often and often, now that the chieftain has quitted laughter, mirth and glee. Therefore many a spear, cold in the morning, must needs be clasped by the fingers, uplifted in the hand; the sound of the harp shall not waken the warrior, but the wan raven, eager o'er the doomed, shall chatter freely, telling the eagle how he sped at the feast, when with the wolf he plundered the slain."

Thus the bold hero told his hated tidings : he spoke not falsely as touching facts or words. All the band arose; sadly they went, with welling tears, beneath the Eagle's Cliff to look upon the marvel. And they found him who had given them treasure in days gone by, found him in his resting-place, lifeless on the sand. Gone was the hero's final day, for the warrior-king, lord of the Weders, had died a wondrous death.

But first they beheld there a stranger being, the loathsome beast lying over against him on the plain; the fiery dragon, awful monster, was all scorched with flames. He was fifty foot-measurements long where he lay. At times he had been wont to rejoice in the air at the night season; thereafter down returning unto his den. Now he was fast in the clutch of death; he had enjoyed the last of his caverns. By him stood bowls and flagons; dishes lay there, and precious swords, rusty and eaten through, as if they had remained in earth's bosom a thousand winters; for a spell had been wound about that vast heritage, that gold of bygone men, so that none could touch the ring-hall, save as God himself, the King of victory-He is man's Defence-should grant unto whom He would, even unto whatsoever man should seem good to Him, to open up the hoard.

THEN it was evident that their way did not prosper, who had unrighteously hidden the riches beneath the mound. The guardian had slain some few of the people and the feud was dreadfully avenged. It is ever a wonder when a strong hero reacheth the end of his destined days, then when he may no longer dwell among his kinsmen in the mead-hall. This was the lot of Beowulf when he went out unto the guardian of the mound and the deadly strife; himself he knew not what was to part him from the world. Thus the mighty princes, who put the treasure there, uttered a deep curse upon it to hold it till doomsday, saying that the men who plundered that place should be guilty of sins, imprisoned in idolfanes, fast bound in the bonds of hell, and visited with plagues. But Beowulf was not greedy for gold; he had rather looked for the ,grace of the Almighty.

Wiglaf, son of Weohstan, spoke : "Often, for the sake of one man, must many suffer, even as now it hath befallen us. We could not teach our dear lord, keeper of the realm, any counsel,-that he should not go out against the guardian of the gold, but let him lie where long he had been, let him dwell in his haunts till the end of the world. He held to his high fate. The hoard is dearly bought and opened to our view; too cruel was the fate that enticed the king thither. I went within and looked upon all the riches of that cave, since a way had been opened, though not in gentle wise, and a passage granted me in under the earth-wall. Hurriedly I seized with my hands a vast burden of treasure; I bore it out hither to my king. And he was yet alive, still conscious and wise of mind. Many things did the aged man speak in his sorrow; and he bade me greet you, prayed that ye would build upon the place of burning a high mound, great and glorious, in memory of the deeds of your lord, inasmuch as he was the worthiest warrior among men over the broad earth, while he could still enjoy the wealth of his cities.

"Let us now hasten to go and see the heap of treasures cunningly wrought, the wonder 'neath the wall; I will guide you that ye may behold and see, near at hand, abundance of rings and ample gold. When we come out thence, let the bier be forthwith made ready, and then let us bear our master, our beloved lord, to where he shall tarry long, safe in the keeping of the Almighty."

And the son of Weohstan, the hero bold in battle, bade that they give command to many warriors, owners of homes, rulers of men, to bring from far wood for the pyre to where the good king lay, saying: "Now shall fire consume, while the wan flame is waxing high, the chief among warriors, him who oft withstood the shower of darts, what time the storm of arrows urged by the string flew over the wall of shields, and the shaft fulfilled its duty, as, with its feather-fittings, it eagerly sped the barb."

Now the wise son of Weohstan summoned together seven of the king's best thanes from out the troop, and, himself the eighth, went with them 'neath the hostile roof; one of the warriors, who went at the head, bore in his hand a flaming torch. And when the men had seen some portion of the treasure in the cave, lying there unguarded, and wasting away, in nowise did they choose by lot who should despoil that hoard; and little did it grieve any man among them that the precious treasures were straightway borne out thence.

Moreover, they shoved the Dragon, that serpent, over the-sea-cliff, let the wave take him and the waters engulf the keeper of treasure.

There the twisted gold of every sort, past counting, was laden upon a wain; the prince, the hoary warrior, was borne away unto Whale's Nest.

THEN the Geatish people fashioned for him a mighty pile upon the ground, all hung with helms, and war-shields, and bright byrnies, even as he had entreated them; and in the midst of it the sorrowing men laid their great king, their beloved lord. Then the warriors began to kindle the greatest of funeral fires upon the mound. Uprose the wood-smoke, black above the flame; blazing fire roared (mingled with a sound of weeping when the tumult of the wind was stilled), until, hot within the breast, it had consumed the bony frame. Sad at heart, with care-laden soul, they mourned the fall of their lord. Likewise, the aged wife, with hair upbound, sorrowing in heart, sang a dirge of lamentation for Beowulf; oft said she dreaded sore that evil days would come upon her, and much bloodshed, fear of the warrior, and shame and bondage. Heaven swallowed up the smoke.

Then the Weder people made a mound upon the cliff,- it was high and broad, to be seen afar of seafaring men; and ten days they built it, the war-hero=s beacon. They made a wall round about the ashes of the fire, even as the wisest of men could most worthily devise it there. Within the mound they put the rings and the jewels, all the adornments which the brave-hearted men had taken from the hoard; they let the earth hold the treasure of heroes, put the gold in the ground, where it still remains, as useless unto men as it was of yore.

Then warriors, sons of princes, twelve in all, rode around about the mound; they would bewail their sorrow, mourn their king, utter the dirge, and speak of their hero; they praised his courage and greatly commended his mighty deeds. Thus it is fitting that a man should praise his lord in words and cherish him in heart when he must forth from the fleeting body. So the Geatish people, companions of his hearth, mourned the fall of their lord; said that he was a mighty king, the mildest and kindest of men, most gracious to his people, and most desirous of praise.

READING 26

THE ORIGINAL ASSASSINS OF ISLAM

Not long after Muhammad's death a deep division occurred among his followers, resulting in the formation of the two major subgroups of Islam: the Sunni and the Shia sects, which in turn over time became further subdivided into other groups. As the result of their minority status within Islam, the Shia sect often adopted a very militant (if not violent) stance toward Sunni Islam. The following passage is an interesting illustration of this phenomenon. It is taken from *The Travels of Marco Polo*. Born in Venice in 1254, he set out with his father and uncle in 1271 at the age of seventeen on a trading mission that took them across Asia to China. During their twenty years of travel they encountered many different peoples and cultures of Asia, made possible by the unifying rule of the Mongols. Years later, after returning home, Marco Polo had his adventures written down and published by a professional story teller of Pisa, Rusticello by name. The passage reproduced here is set forth in connection with Marco Polo's outward journey through Mesopotamia and Iran. The assassins described here were members of a radical Islamic sect, established in 1092 in the mountains of northern Iran south of the Caspian Sea, whence they gradually spread westward as far as Syria, where the crusaders encountered them. They took their name from the drug that they were given: hashish. They were thus known as the *ashishin* in Arabic. They were sent out by their leader to assassinate fellow Muslims of whom their leader disapproved.

(Taken from the translation of Yule and Cordier [1920] with revisions by Gary Forsythe)

Mulehet is a country in which the Old Man of the Mountain dwelt in former days; and the name means "Place of the Aram." The Old Man was called in their language ALOADIN. He had caused a certain valley between two mountains to be enclosed, and had turned it into a garden, the largest and most beautiful that ever was seen, filled with every variety of fruit. In it were erected pavilions and palaces the most elegant that can be imagined, all covered with gilding and exquisite painting. And there were fountains too, flowing freely with wine and milk and honey and water; and numbers of ladies and of the most beautiful damsels in the world, who could play on all manner of instruments, and sung most sweetly, and danced in a manner that it was charming to behold. For the Old Man desired to make his people believe that this was actually Paradise. So he had fashioned it after the description

197

that Muhammad gave of his Paradise, to wit, that it should be a beautiful garden running with conduits of wine and milk and honey and water, and full of lovely women for the delectation of all its inmates. And sure enough the Muslims of those parts believed that it was Paradise!

Now no man was allowed to enter the Garden save those whom he intended to be his *ASHISHIN* [assassins]. There was a Fortress at the entrance to the Garden, strong enough to resist all the world, and there was no other way to get in. He kept at his Court a number of the youths of the country, from 12 to 20 years of age, such as had a taste for soldiering, and to these he used to tell tales about Paradise, just as Muhammad had been wont to do, and they believed in him just as the Muslims believe in Muhammad. Then he would introduce them into his garden, some four, or six, or ten at a time, having first made them drink a certain potion [hashish] that cast them into a deep sleep, and then causing them to be lifted and carried in. So when they awoke, they found themselves in the Garden. When therefore they awoke, and found themselves in a place so charming, they deemed that it was Paradise in very truth. And the ladies and damsels dallied with them to their hearts' content, so that they had what young men would have; and with their own good will they never would have quitted the place.

Now this Prince whom we call the Old One kept his Court in grand and noble style, and made those simple hill-folks about him believe firmly that he was a great Prophet. And when he wanted one of his *Ashishin* to send on any mission, he would cause that potion whereof I spoke to be given to one of the youths in the garden, and then had him carried into his Palace. So when the young man awoke, he found himself in the Castle, and no longer in that Paradise; whereat he was not over well pleased. He was then conducted to the Old Man's presence, and bowed before him with great veneration as believing himself to be in the presence of a true Prophet. The Prince would then ask whence he came, and he would reply that he came from Paradise! and that it was exactly such as Muhammad had described it in the Law. This of course gave the others who stood by, and who had not been admitted, the greatest desire to enter therein. So when the Old Man would have any Prince slain, he would say to such a youth: "Go thou and slay So and So; and when thou returnest my Angels shall bear thee into Paradise. And shouldst thou die, nevertheless, even so will I send my Angels to carry thee back into Paradise." So he caused them to believe; and thus there was no order of his that they would not confront any peril to execute, for the great desire they had to get back into that Paradise of his. And in this manner the Old One got his people to murder any one whom he desired to get rid of. Thus, too, the great dread that he inspired all Princes withal, made them become his tributaries in order that he might abide at peace and amity with them.

Now it came to pass, in the year of Christ's Incarnation, 1252, that Ala6, Lord of the Tartars of the Levant, heard tell of these great crimes of the Old Man, and resolved to make an end of him. So he took and sent one of his Barons with a great Army to that Castle, and they besieged it for three years, but they could not take it, so strong was it. And indeed if they had had food within it never would have been taken. But after being besieged those three years they ran short of victual, and were taken. The Old Man was put to death with all his men; and the Castle with its Garden of Paradise was levelled with the ground. And since that time he has had no successor; and there was an end to all his villainies.

Einhard, The Life of Charlemagne

Einhard's biography of Charlemagne not only provides us with important information concerning the greatest Frankish king of the early and central Middle Ages, but it also represents the best single example of the relative success of Charlemagne's program to revive learning and scholarship throughout western Europe, whose culture had still not recovered from the devastating consequences of the Germanic invasions that had ended the Roman Empire in those regions. As often noted, Einhard used as his literary model the famous series of biographies of Roman emperors from Augustus to Domitian written by Suetonius during the early second century.

(Taken from the translation of Samuel Epes Turner)

PREFACE

SINCE I have taken upon myself to narrate the public and private life, and no small part of the deeds, of my lord and foster-father, the most lent and most justly renowned King Charles, I have condensed the matter into as brief a form as possible. I have been careful not to omit any facts that could come to my knowledge, but at the same time not to offend by a prolix style those minds that despise everything modern, if one can possibly avoid offending by a new work men who seem to despise also the masterpieces of antiquity, the works of most learned and luminous writers. Very many of them, I have no doubt, are men devoted to a life of literary leisure, who feel that the affairs of the present generation ought not to be passed by, and who do not consider everything done today as unworthy of mention and deserving to be given over to silence and oblivion , but are nevertheless seduced by lust of immortality to celebrate the glorious deeds of other times by some sort of composition rather than to deprive posterity of the mention of their own names by not writing at all.

Be this as it may, I see no reason why I should refrain from entering upon a task of this kind, since no man can write with more accuracy than I of events that took place about me, and of facts concerning which I had personal knowledge, ocular demonstration as the saying goes, and I have no means of ascertaining whether or not any one else has the subject in hand.

In any event, I would rather commit my story to writing, and hand it down to posterity in partnership with others, so to speak, than to suffer the most glorious life of this most excellent king, the greatest of all the princes of his day, and his illustrious deeds, hard for men of later times to imitate, to be wrapped in the darkness of oblivion.

But there are still other reasons, neither unwarrantable nor insufficient, in my opinion, that urge me to write on this subject, namely, the care that King Charles bestowed upon me in my childhood, and my constant friendship with himself and his children after I took up my abode at court. In this way he strongly endeared me to himself, and made me greatly his debtor as well in death as in life, so that were I unmindful of the benefits conferred upon me, to keep silence concerning the most glorious and illustrious deeds of a man who claims so much at my hands, and suffer his life to lack due eulogy and written memorial, as if he had never lived, I should deservedly appear ungrateful, and be so considered, albeit my powers are feeble, scanty, next to nothing indeed, and not at all adapted to write and set forth a life that would tax the eloquence of a Cicero. I submit the book. It contains the history of a very great and distinguished man; but there is nothing in it to wonder at besides his deeds, except the fact that I, who am a barbarian, and very little versed in the Roman language, seem to suppose myself capable of writing gracefully and respectably in Latin, and to carry my presumption so far as to disdain the sentiment that Cicero is said in the first book of the *Tusculan Disputations* to have expressed when speaking of the Latin authors. His words are: "It is an outrageous abuse both of time and literature for a man to commit his thoughts to writing without having the ability either to arrange them or elucidate them, or attract readers by some charm of style." This dictum of the famous orator might have deterred me from writing if I had not made up my mind that it was better to risk the opinions of the world, and put my little talents for composition to the test, than to slight the memory of so great a man for the sake of sparing myself.

1. The Merovingian Family

The Merovingian family, from which the Franks used to choose their kings, is commonly said to have lasted until the time of Childeric, who was deposed, shaved, and thrust into the cloister by command of the Roman Pontiff Stephen. But although, to all outward appearance, it ended with him, it had long since been devoid of vital strength, and conspicuous only from bearing the empty epithet Royal; the real power and authority in the kingdom lay in the hands of the chief officer of the court, the so-called Mayor of the Palace, and he was at the head of affairs. There was nothing left the King to do but to be content with his name of King, his flowing hair, and long beard, to sit on his throne and play the ruler, to give ear to the ambassadors that came from all quarters, and to dismiss them, as if on his own responsibility, in words that were, in fact, suggested to him, or even imposed upon him. He had nothing that he could call his own beyond this vain title of King and the precarious support allowed by the Mayor of the Palace in his discretion, except a single country seat, that brought him but a very small income. There was a dwelling house upon this, and a small number of servants attached to it, sufficient to perform the necessary offices. When he had to go abroad, he used to ride in a cart, drawn by a yoke of oxen driven, peasant-fashion, by a Ploughman; he rode in this way to the palace and to the general assembly of the people, that met once a year for the welfare of the kingdom, and he returned him in like manner. The Mayor of the Palace took charge of the government and of everything that had to be planned or executed at home or abroad.

2. Charlemagne's Ancestors

At the time of Childeric's deposition, Pepin, the father of King Charles, held this office of Mayor of the Palace, one might almost say, by hereditary right; for Pepin's father, Charles

[Martel, 715-741], had received it at the hands of his father, Pepin, and filled it with distinction. It was this Charles that crushed the tyrants who claimed to rule the whole Frank land as their own, and that utterly routed the Saracens, when they attempted the conquest of Gaul, in - -two great battles-one in Aquitania, near the town of Poitiers, and the other on the River Berre, near Narbonne-and compelled them to return to Spain. This honor was usually conferred by the people only upon men eminent from their illustrious birth and ample wealth. For some years, ostensibly under King the father of King Charles, Childeric, Pepin, shared the duties inherited from his father and grandfather most amicably with his brother, Carloman. The latter, then, for reasons unknown, renounced the heavy cares of an earthly crown and retired to Rome. Here he exchanged his worldly garb for a cowl, and built a monastery on Mt. Oreste, near the Church of St. Sylvester, where he enjoyed for several years the seclusion that he desired, in company with certain others who had the same object in view. But so many distinguished Franks made the pilgrimage to Rome to fulfill their vows, and insisted upon paying their respects to him, as their former lord, on the way, that the repose which he so much loved was broken by these frequent visits, and he was driven to change his abode. Accordingly when he found that his plans were frustrated by his many visitors, he abandoned the mountain, and withdrew to the Monastery of St. Benedict, on Monte Cassino, in the province of Samnium, and passed the rest there in the exercise of religion.

3. Charlemagne's Accession

Pepin, however, was raised by decree of the Roman pontiff, from the rank of Mayor of the Palace to that of King, and ruled alone over the Franks for fifteen years or more. He died of dropsy in Paris at the close of the Aquitanian War, which he had waged with William, Duke of Aquitania, for nine successive years, and left his two sons, Charles and Carloman, upon whim, by the grace of God, the succession devolved.

The Franks, in a general assembly of the people, made them both kings on condition that they should divide the whole kingdom equally between them, Charles to take and rule the part that had to belonged to their father, Pepin, and Carloman the part which their uncle, Carloman had governed. The conditions were accepted, and each entered into the possession of the share of the kingdom that fell to him by this arrangement; but peace was only maintained between them with the greatest difficulty, because many of Carloman's party kept trying to disturb their good understanding, and there were some even who plotted to involve them in a war with each other. The event, however, which showed the danger to have been rather imaginary than real, for at Carloman's death his widow [Gerberga] fled to Italy with her sons and her principal adherents, and without reason, despite her husband's brother put herself and her children under the protection of Desiderius, King of the Lombards. Carloman had succumbed to disease after ruling two years in common with his brother and at his death Charles was unanimously elected King of the Franks....

6. Lombard War

After bringing this war to an end and settling matters in Aquitania (his associate in authority had meantime departed this life), he was induced, by the prayers and entreaties of Hadrian [pope 772-795], Bishop of the city of Rome, to wage war on the Lombards. His father before him had undertaken this task at the request of Pope Stephen [752-757], but under great difficulties, for certain leading Franks, of whom he usually took counsel, had so vehemently opposed his design as to declare openly that they would leave the King and go home. Nevertheless, the war against the Lombard King Astolf had been taken up and very quickly concluded. Now, although

Charles seems to have had similar, or rather just the same grounds for declaring war that his father had, the war itself differed from the preceding one alike in its difficulties and its issue. Pepin, to be sure, after besieging King Astolf a few days in Pavia, had compelled him to give hostages, to restore to the Romans the cities and castles that he had taken, and to make oath that he would not attempt to seize them again: but Charles did not cease, after declaring war, until he had exhausted King Desiderius by a long siege, and forced him to surrender at discretion; driven his son Adalgis, the last hope of the Lombards, not only -from his kingdom, but from all Italy; restored to the Romans all that they had lost; subdued Hruodgaus, Duke of Friuli, who was plotting revolution; reduced all Italy to his power, and set his son Pepin as king over it. At this point I should describe Charles' difficult passage over the Alps into Italy, and the hardships that the Franks endured in climbing the trackless mountain ridges, the heaven-aspiring cliffs and ragged peaks, if it were not my purpose in this work to record the manner of his life rather than the incidents of the wars that he waged. Suffice it to say that this war ended with the subjection of Italy, the banishment of King Desiderius for life, the expulsion of his son Adalgis from Italy, and the restoration of the conquests of the Lombard kings to Hadrian, the head of the Roman Church.

7. Saxon War

At the conclusion of this struggle, the Saxon war, that seems to have been only laid aside for the time , was taken up again. No war ever undertaken by the Frank nation was carried on with such persistence and bitterness, or cost so much labor, because the Saxons, like almost all the tribes of Germany, were a fierce people, given to the worship of devils, and hostile to our religion, and did not consider it dishonorable to transgress and violate all law, human and divine. Then there were peculiar circumstances that tended to cause a breach of peace every day. Except in a few places, where large forests or mountain ridges intervened and made the bounds certain, the line between ourselves and the Saxons passed almost in its whole extent through an open country, so that there was no end to the murders thefts and arsons on both sides. In this way the Franks became so embittered that they at last resolved to make reprisals no longer, but to come to open war with the Saxons. Accordingly war was begun against them, and was waged for thirty-three successive years with great fury; more, however, to the disadvantage of the Saxons than of the Franks. It could doubtless have been brought to an end sooner, had it not been for the faithlessness of the Saxons. It is hard to say how often they were conquered, and, humbly submitting to the King, promised to do what was enjoined upon them, without hesitation the required hostages, gave and received the officers sent them from the King. They were sometimes so much weakened and reduced that they promised to renounce the worship of devils, and to adopt Christianity, but they were no less ready to violate these terms than prompt to accept them, so that it is impossible to tell which came easier to them to do; scarcely a year passed from the beginning of the war without such changes on their part. But the King did not suffer his high purpose and steadfastness - firm alike in good and evil fortune - to be wearied by any fickleness on their part, or to be turned from the task that he had undertaken, on the contrary, he never allowed their faithless behavior to go unpunished, but either took the field against them in person, or sent his counts with an army to wreak vengeance and exact righteous satisfaction. At last, after conquering and subduing all who had offered resistance, he took ten thousand of those that lived on the banks of the Elbe, and settled them, with their wives and children, in many different bodies here and there in Gaul and Germany. The war that had lasted so many years was at length ended by their acceding to the terms offered by the King; which were renunciation of their national religious customs and the worship of devils, acceptance of the sacraments of the Christian faith and religion, and union with the Franks to form one people....

13. War with the Huns

The war against the Avars, or Huns, followed, and, except the Saxon war, was the greatest that he waged; he took it up with more spirit than any of his other wars, and made far greater preparations for it. He conducted one campaign in person in Pannonia, of which the Huns then had possession. He entrusted all subsequent operations to his son, Pepin, and the governors of the provinces, to counts even, and lieutenants. Although they most vigorously prosecuted the war, it only came to a conclusion after a seven years' struggle. The utter depopulation of Pannonia, and the site of the Khan's palace, now a desert, where not a trace of human habitation is visible bear witness how many battles were fought in those years, and how much blood was shed. The entire body of the Hun nobility perished in this contest, and all its glory with it. All the money and treasure that had been years amassing was seized, and no war in which the Franks have ever engaged within the memory of man brought them such riches and such booty. Up to that time the Huns had passed for, a poor people, but so much gold and silver was found in the Khan's palace, and so much valuable spoil taken in battle, that one may well think that the Franks took justly from the Huns what the Huns had formerly taken unjustly from other nations. Only two of the chief men of the Franks fell in this war - Eric, Duke of Friuli, who was killed in Tarsatch, a town on the coast of Liburnia by the treachery of the inhabitants; and Gerold, Governor of Bavaria, who met his death in Pannonia, slain, with two men that were accompanying him, by an unknown hand while he was marshaling his forces for battle against the Huns, and riding up and down the line encouraging his men. This war was otherwise almost a bloodless one so far as the Franks were concerned, and ended most satisfactorily, although by reason of its magnitude it was long protracted....

15. Extent of Charlemagne's Conquests

Such are the wars, most skillfully planned and successfully fought, which this most powerful king waged during the forty-seven years of his reign. He so largely increased the Frank kingdom, which was already great and strong when he received it at his father's hands, that more than double its former territory was added to it. The authority of the Franks was formerly confined to that part of Gaul included between the Rhine and the Loire, the Ocean and the Balearic Sea; to that part of Germany which is inhabited by the so-called Eastern Franks, and is bounded by Saxony and the Danube, the Rhine and the Saale-this stream separates the Thuringians from the Sorabians; and to the country of the Alemanni and Bavarians. By the wars above mentioned he first made tributary Aquitania, Gascony, and the whole of the region of the Pyrenees as far as the River Ebro, which rises in the land of the Navarrese, flows through the most fertile districts of Spain, and empties into the Balearic Sea, beneath the walls of the city of Tortosa. He next reduced and made tributary all Italy from Aosta to Lower Calabria, where the boundary line runs between the Beneventans and the [Byzantine] Greeks, a territory more than a thousand miles" long; then Saxony, which constitutes no small part of Germany, and is reckoned to be twice as wide as the country inhabited by the Franks, while about equal to it in length; in addition, both Pannonias, Dacia beyond the Danube, and Istria, Liburnia, and Dalmatia, except the cities on the coast, which he left to the [Byzantine] Greek Emperor for friendship's sake, and because of the treaty that he had made with him. In fine, he vanquished and made tributary all the wild and barbarous tribes dwelling in Germany between the Rhine and the Vistula, the Ocean and the Danube, all of which speak very much the same language, but differ widely from one another in customs and dress. The chief among them are the Welatabians, the Sorabians, the Abodriti, and the Bohemians, and he had to make war upon these; but the rest, by far the larger number, submitted to him of their own accord....

22. Personal Appearance

Charles was large and strong, and of lofty stature, though not disproportionately tall (his height is well known to have been seven times the length of his foot); the upper part of his head was round, his eyes very large and animated, nose a little long, hair fair, and face laughing and merry. Thus his appearance was always stately and dignified, whether he was standing or sitting; although his neck was thick and somewhat short, and his belly rather prominent; but the symmetry of the rest of his body concealed these defects. His gait was firm, his whole carriage manly, and his voice clear, but not so strong as his size led one to expect. His health was excellent, except during the four years preceding his death, when he was subject to frequent fevers; at the last he even limped a little with one foot. Even in those years he consulted rather his own inclinations than the advice of physicians, who were almost hateful to him, because they wanted him to give up roasts, to which he was accustomed, and to eat boiled meat instead. In accordance with the national custom, he took frequent exercise on horseback and in the chase, accomplishments in which scarcely any people in the world can equal the Franks. He enjoyed the exhalations from natural warm springs, and often practised swimming, in which he was such an adept that none could surpass him; and hence it was that he built his palace at Aixla-Chapelle, and lived there constantly during his latter years until his death. He used not only to invite his sons to his bath, but his nobles and friends, and now and then a troop of his retinue or body guard, so that a hundred or more persons sometimes bathed with him....

25. Studies

Charles had the gift of ready and fluent speech, and could express whatever he had to say with the utmost clearness. He was not satisfied with command of his native language merely, but gave attention to the study of foreign ones, and in particular was such a master of Latin that he could speak it as well as his native tongue; but he could understand Greek better than he could speak it. He was so eloquent, indeed, that he might have passed for a teacher of eloquence. He most zealously cultivated the liberal arts, held those who taught them in great esteem, and conferred great honors upon them. He took lessons in grammar of the deacon Peter of Pisa, at that time an aged man. Another deacon, Albin of Britain, surnamed Alcuin, a man of Saxon extraction, who was the greatest scholar of the day, was his teacher in other branches of learning. The King spent much time and labour with him studying rhetoric, dialectics, and especially astronomy; he learned to reckon, and used to investigate the motions of the heavenly bodies most curiously, with an intelligent scrutiny. He also tried to write, and used to keep tablets and blanks in bed under his pillow, that at leisure hours he might accustom his hand to form the letters; however, as he did not begin his efforts in due season, but late in life, they met with ill success....

28. Charlemagne Crowned Emperor

When he made his last journey thither, he also had other ends in view. The Romans had inflicted many injuries upon the Pontiff Leo, tearing out his eyes and cutting out his tongue, so that he had been comp lied to call upon the King for help. Charles accordingly went to Rome, to set in order the affairs of the Church, which were in great confusion, and passed the whole winter there. It was then that he received the titles of Emperor and Augustus, to which he at first had such an aversion that he declared that he would not have set foot in the Church the day that they were conferred, although it was a great feast-day, if he could have foreseen the design of the Pope. He bore very patiently with the jealousy which the Roman emperors [of Constantinople] showed upon his assuming these titles, for they took this step very ill; and by dint of frequent embassies and letters, in which he addressed them as brothers, he made their haughtiness yield to his magnanimity, a quality in which he was unquestionably much their superior....

30. Coronation of Louis and Charlemagne's Death

Toward the close of his life, when he was broken by ill-health and old age, he summoned Louis, Kigi of Aquitania, his onlv surviving son by Hildegard, and gathered together all the chief men of the whole kingdom of the Franks in a solemn assembly. He appointed Louis, with their unanimous consent, to rule with himself over the whole kingdom and constituted him heir to the imperial name; then, placing the diadem upon his son's head, he bade him be proclaimed Emperor and is step was hailed by all present favor, for it really seemed as if God had prompted him to it for the kingdom's good; it increased the King's dignity, and struck no little terror into foreign nations. After sending his son son back to Aquitania, although weak from age he set out to hunt, as usual, near his palace at Aix-la-Chapelle, and passed the rest of the autumn in the chase, returning thither about the first of November. While wintering there, he was seized, in the month of January, with a high fever Jan 22 814], and took to his bed. As soon as he was taken sick, he prescribed for himself abstinence from food, as he always used to do in case of fever, thinking that the disease could be driven off , or at least mitigated, by fasting. Besides the fever, he suffered from a pain in the side, which the Greeks call pleurisy; but he still persisted in fasting, and in keeping up his strength only by draughts taken at very long intervals. He died January twenty-eighth, the seventh day from the time that he took to his bed, at nine o'clock in the morning, after partaking of the holy communion, in the seventy-second year of his age and the forty-seventh of his reign.

31. Burial

His body was washed and cared for in the usual manner, and was then carried to the church, and interred amid the greatest lamentations of all the people. There was some question at first where to lay him, because in his lifetime he had given no directions as to his burial; but at length all agreed that he could nowhere be more honorably entombed than in the very basilica that he had built in the town at his own expense, for love of God and our Lord Jesus Christ, and in honor of the Holy and Eternal Virgin, His Mother. He was buried there the same day that he died, and a gilded arch was erected above his tomb with his image and an inscription. The words of the inscription were as follows: "In this tomb lies the body of Charles, the Great and Orthodox Emperor, who gloriously extended the kingdom of the Franks, and reigned prosperously for forty-seven years. He died at the age of seventy, in the year of our Lord 814, the 7th Indiction, on the 28th day of January."

Reading 28

Capitulare de Villis

The following document was probably issued around the year 795 by Louis the Pious, one of the sons of Charlemagne, to establish regulations for the management of manors in Aquitaine (southwestern France). These provisions allow us to reconstruct a fairly detailed picture of what these manors must have contained, how they looked, and how they operated.

(Taken from pp.25-33 of Volume I of Introduction to Contemporary Civilization in the West: A Source Book, Columbia University Press 1946)

1. We wish that our estates which we have instituted to serve our needs discharge their services to us entirely and to no other men.

2. Our people shall be well taken care of and reduced to poverty by no one.

3. Our stewards shall not presume to put our people to their own service, either to force them to work, to cut wood, or to do any other task for them. And they shall accept no gifts from them, either horse, ox, cow, pig, sheep, little pig, lamb, or anything else excepting bottles of wine or other beverage, garden produce, fruits, chickens, and eggs.

4. If any of our people does injury to us either by stealing or by some other offense he shall make good the damage and for the remainder of the legal satisfaction he shall be punished by whipping, with the exception of homicide and arson cases which are punishable by fines. The stewards, for injuries of our people to other men, shall endeavor to secure justice according to the practices which they have, as is the law. Instead of paying fines our people, as we have said, shall be whipped. Freemen who live in our domains or estates shall make good the injuries they do according to their law and the fines which they have incurred shall be paid for our use either in cattle or in equivalent value.

5. When our stewards ought to see that our work is done, the sowing, plowing, harvesting, cutting of hay, or gathering of grapes, let each one at the proper season and in each and every place organize and oversee what is to be done that it may be done well. If a steward shall not be in his district or cannot be in some place let him choose a good substitute from our people or another in high repute to direct our affairs that they may be successfully accomplished. And he shall diligently see to it that a trustworthy man is delegated to take care of this work.

6.   We wish our stewards to give a tithe of all our products to the churches on our domains and that the tithe not be given to the churches of another except to those entitled to it by ancient usage. And our churches shall not have clerics other than our own, that is, of our people or our palace.

7.   Each steward shall perform his services fully, just as it has been prescribed, and if the necessity should arise that more must be done then he shall determine whether he should increase the service or the day-work.

8.   Our stewards shall take care of our vines in their district and cultivate them well. And they shall put the wine in good vessels and carefully see to it that none is lost. And other required wine which is not from our vines they shall buy for provisioning the royal estates. And when they have bought more than is needed for this provisioning they shall inform us so that we can let them know what is to be done with it. For they shall put the product of our vines to our use. The wine which those persons on our estates pay as rent shall be put in our cellars.

9.   We wish that each steward in his district have measures of the modius, sextarius, the situla of eight sextarii, and the corbus, the same as we have in our palace.

10.   Our mayors, foresters, stablemen, cellarers, deans, toll-collectors, and other officers shall do the regular and fixed labor and pay the due of pigs for their holdings and fulfill well their offices in return for the manual labor remitted them. And if any mayor holds a benefice he shall send his representative so that the manual labor and other services will be performed for him.

11.   No steward shall take lodging for his own need or for his dogs from our people or from those in the forests.

12.   No steward shall maintain at the expense of anyone else our hostages placed on our estates.

13.   The stewards shall take good care of the stallions and not allow them to remain in one pasture too long lest they damage it. And if there should be any unsound or too old or about to die they shall inform us in good time before the season for putting them with the mares.

14.   They shall take good care of our mares and separate them from the colts at the right time. And when the fillies increase in number they shall also be separated to form a new herd.

15.   Our stewards shall have our foals sent to the palace in the winter at the Feast of Saint Martin.

16.   We wish that our stewards fully perform in the manner established for them whatever we or the queen or our officers, the seneschal or the butler, in our name or that of the queen command. If anyone shall not do this through negligence he shall abstain from drink from the time that it is made known to him until he comes into our presence or that of the queen and seeks pardon from us. And if the steward is with the army, on guard duty, or on a mission or otherwise engaged and he commands his assistants to do something and they fail to do it, then they shall come afoot to the palace and abstain from food and drink until they have given their reasons for not doing it. Then they shall receive their sentence, a whipping or whatever we or the queen deem appropriate.

17.   Each steward shall have as many men taking care of the bees for our use as he has estates in his district.

18.   At our mills the stewards shall have hens and geese according to the nature of the mill or as many more as is possible.

19.   In our barns on the chief estates they shall have at least 100 chickens and 30 geese and on our lesser estates at least 50 chickens and 12 geese.

20.   Each steward shall have the produce [of the fowl] brought always in abundance to the manor every year and besides shall inspect it three or four or more times.

21.   Each steward shall have fish-ponds on our estates where they were before and if it is possible to enlarge them, he shall do so. Where there were none before and it is now possible to have them let them be constructed.

22.   Those who hold vines from us shall have no less than three or four circles of grapes for our use.

23.   On each of our estates the stewards shall have cow-barns, pigsties, sheepfolds, and stables for goats, as many as possible, and never be without them. And they shall further have for performing their services cows furnished by our serfs so that our barns and teams are not in the least diminished by the services of work on our demesne. And when they are charged with furnishing food they shall have lame but healthy oxen and cows, and horses that are not mangy, and other healthy animals. They shall not on that account strip, as we have said, the cow-barns or the plough-beasts.

24.   Each steward shall be responsible that whatever ought to be supplied for our table is all good and excellent and prepared carefully and cleanly. And each steward shall have grain for two meals for each day of the service that he is charged with supplying our table. Similarly the other provisions shall be good in all respects, the flour as well as the meat.

25.   The stewards shall make known on the first of September whether or not there is pasturage for the hogs.

26.   The mayors shall not have more land in their administration than they can get about and oversee in one day.

27.   Our houses shall constantly have fire and watch service that they may be safe. And when royal envoys or legates are coming to or leaving the palace, in no wise shall they exercise the right of bed and board in our manor houses except by our special order or that of the queen. But the count in his district or those persons who have been accustomed of old to caring for envoys and legates shall continue to do so as before. And pack-horses and other necessary things shall be provided in the customary fashion that they may come to the palace or depart in a fashion befitting them.

28.   We wish that every year in Lent on Palm Sunday, which is called Hosanna Sunday, our stewards carefully render according to our instructions the money arising from the products of our land after we know for the particular year what our income is.

29.   Each steward shall see to it that anyone of our people who have cases to plead shall not of necessity have to come to us so that he will not lose through negligence

days on which he ought to be working. And if one of our serfs has some rights to claim outside our lands, his master shall do all that he can to secure justice for him. In case the serf shall not be able to get justice his master shall not permit him to exhaust himself in his efforts but shall see to it that the matter is made known to us by himself or by his representative.

30.   Of those things that our stewards ought to provide for our needs, we wish them to put aside all the products due us from them, and what must be placed in the wagons for the army, taking it from the homes as well as from the herdsmen and that they know how much they have reserved for this purpose.

31.   They shall set aside each year what they ought to give as food and maintenance to the workers entitled to it and to the women working in the women's quarters and shall give it fully at the right time and make known to us what they have done with it and where they got it.

32.   Each steward shall see to it that he always has the very best seed by purchase or otherwise.

33.   After the above things have been set aside and after the sowing and other works have been done, all that remains of all the products shall be preserved until we give word to what extent they shall be sold or stored according to our order.

34.   At all times it is to be seen to with diligence that whatever is worked upon or made with the hands such as lard, smoked meat, salted meat, newly salted meat, wine, vinegar, mulberry wine, cooked wine, fermentations, mustard, cheese, butter, malt, beer, mead, honey, wax, and flour shall be prepared or made with the greatest cleanliness.

35.   We wish that fat be made of the fat sheep and pigs. Moreover the stewards shall have in each estate not less than two fattened oxen either there to be made into fat or to be sent to us.

36.   Our woods and forests shall be well taken care of and where there shall be a place for a clearing let it be cleared. Our stewards shall not allow the fields to become woods and where there ought to be woods they shall not allow anyone to cut too much or damage them. And they shall look carefully after our wild beasts in the forests and also take care of the goshawks and sparrowhawks reserved for our use. They shall collect diligently our tax for the use of our forests and if our stewards or our mayors or their men put their pigs for fattening in our forests they shall be the first to pay the tenth of them to give a good example so that thereafter the other men will pay the tenth in full.

37.   The stewards shall keep our fields and cultivated lands in good shape and care for the meadows at the right time.

38.   They shall always have sufficient fat geese and chickens for our use when they ought to provide it or send it to us.

39.   We wish that the stewards collect the chickens and eggs which the lesser officials and the holders of mansi pay each year and when they are not needed that they have them sold.

40.   Each steward shall always have on our estates for the sake of adornment unusual birds, peacocks, pheasants, ducks, pigeons, partridges, and turtle-doves.

41. The buildings on our estates and the fences which enclose them shall be well taken care of and the stables and kitchens, bake-houses and presses shall be carefully ordered so that the workers in our service can perform their duties fittingly and very cleanly.

42. Each manor shall have in the store-room counterpanes, bolsters, pillows, bedclothes, table and bench covers, vessels of brass, lead, iron, and wood, andirons, chains, pot-hooks, adzes, axes, augurs, knives, and all sorts of tools so that it will not be necessary to seek them elsewhere or to borrow them. And the stewards shall be responsible that the iron instruments sent to the army are in good condition and when they are returned that they are put back into the store-room.

43. For our women's work-shops the stewards shall provide the materials at the right time as it has been established, that is flax, wool, woad, vermilion dye, madder, wool-combs, teasels, soap, grease, vessels and the other lesser things which are necessary there.

44. Of the minor foods two-thirds shall be sent for our service each year, vegetables as well as fish, cheese, butter, honey, mustard, vinegar, millet, panic, dried and fresh herbs, radishes, and turnips; similarly wax, soap, and other lesser things. Whatever is left shall be made known to us in an inventory as we have said above. The stewards shall by no means neglect to do this as they have up to now because we wish to check by the two-thirds sent to us what that third is which remains.

45. Each steward shall have good workmen in his districtiron-workers, goldsmiths, silversmiths, leather-workers, turners, carpenters, shield-makers, fishermen, fowlers or falconers, soap-makers, brewers who know how to make beer, cider, perry or any other beverage fit to drink, bakers who can make bread for our needs, net-makers who are skilled in making nets for hunting as well as fishing or for taking birds, and other workmen whose listing would be a lengthy matter.

46. They shall take good care of our walled game preserves which the people call parks and always repair them in time and on no account delay so that it becomes necessary to rebuild them. They shall do the same for all the buildings.

47. Our hunters and falconers and other servitors who attend us zealously in the palace shall receive assistance on our estates in carrying out what we or the queen have ordered by our letters when we send them on any of our affairs, or when the seneschal or butler instructs them to do anything on our authority.

48. The wine-presses on our estates shall be well taken care of. The stewards shall see to it that no one presumes to press our grapes with his feet but that all is done cleanly and honestly.

49. The women's quarters, that is, their houses, heated rooms, and sittingrooms, shall be well ordered and have good fences around them and strong gates that our work may be done well.

50. Each steward shall see to it that there are as many horses in one stable as ought to be there and as many attendants as should be with them. And those stablemen who are free and hold benefices in that district shall live off their benefices. Similarly if they are men of the domain who hold mansi they shall live off them. Those who do not have such shall receive maintenance from the demesne.

51. Each steward shall see to it that in no manner wicked men conceal our seed under the ground or do otherwise with the result that our harvests are smaller. And likewise, concerning other misdeeds, they shall watch them so that they can do no harm.

52. We wish that our stewards render justice to our coloni [tenant farmers] and serfs and to the coloni living on our estates, to the different men fully and entirely such as they are due.

53. Each steward shall see to it that our men in their districts in no way become robbers or evil-doers.

54. Each steward shall see to it that our people work well at their tasks and do not go wandering off to markets.

55. We wish that whatever our stewards have sent, supplied, or set aside for our use they shall record in an inventory; whatever they have dispensed in another; and what is left they shall also make known to us in an inventory.

56. Each steward shall hold frequent audiences in his district, administer justice, and see to it that our peoples live uprightly.

57. If any of our serfs wishes to say anything to us about our affairs over and above his steward, the steward shall not obstruct the means of his coming to us. If the steward knows that his assistants wish to come to the palace to speak against him then he shall make known to the palace the arguments against them so that their denunciations in our ears may not engender disgust. Accordingly we wish to know whether they come from necessity or without sufficient cause.

58. When our pups are committed to the stewards to be raised, the steward shall feed them at his own expense or entrust them to his assistants, that is to the mayors and deans or to the cellarers, who shall feed them well at their own expense unless it happens that by our order or that of the queen they are to be fed on our estate at our expense. In that case the steward shall send a man for this work who will feed them well. And he shall set aside what is to be fed them so that it will not be necessary for him to go to the kennels every day.

59. Each steward when he should give service shall send every day three librae of wax and eight sextaria of soap; besides this he shall do his best to send six librae of wax wherever we shall be with our attendants on the Feast of Saint Andrew; he shall do likewise at Mid-Lent.

60. On no account shall mayors be selected from the powerful men but from those of middling estate who are trustworthy.

61. Each steward when he should give service shall have his malt brought to the palace and at the same time have the master brewers come who are to make good beer there.

62. That we may know what and how much of everything we have, each steward every year at Christmas shall report those of our revenues which they hold, everything differentiated clearly and orderly. That is, an accounting of the land cultivated with the oxen which our ploughmen drive and that which is cultivated by the holders of mansi who owe us labor-service; of the payments of pigs, the taxes, the income from judgments and fines and from the beasts taken in our forests without our permission and from the other compositions; an accounting of the mills, forests, fields, bridges, and ships; of the free men and the hundred-men who owe service

for parts of our domain; of the markets, vineyards and of those who pay us wine; of the hay, firewood, torches, planks and other lumber; of the income from the waste-land; of the vegetables, millet, panic, wool, flax, and hemp; of the fruit of the trees, of the big and little nuts, of the graftings of various trees, of the gardens, turnips, fishponds, hides, skins and horns; of the honey, wax, fat, tallow, and soap; of the mulberry wine, cooked wine, mead, and vinegar; of the beer, new and old wine, new and old grain, chickens and eggs, and geese; of the fishermen, smiths, shield-makers and leather-workers; of the troughs, boxes, and cases; of the turners and saddlers; of the forges and mines, that is iron, lead, and other mines; of those paying taxes; and of the colts and fillies.

63. Of all the above mentioned things nothing that we require shall seem hard to our stewards for we wish the stewards to require them from their assistants in the same fashion without any hardship. And all things which any man shall have in his house or on his estates our stewards ought also to have on our estates.

64. Our carts which accompany the army, that is, the war-carts, shall be well-constructed, and their coverings be good, with hides on top and so sown together that if the necessity of swimming waters should arise they can cross rivers without any water getting to the provisions inside and in this fashion our things may, as we said, get across without damage. And we wish that flour for our use be put in each cart, that is 12 modii, and that they put in those in which wine is sent 12 modii of our measure. In each cart let them have a shield, a lance, a quiver, and a bow.

65. The fish in our fish-ponds shall be sold and others put in their place so that they may always have fish in them. However, when we are not coming to our estates they shall be sold and our stewards shall dispose of them to our advantage.

66. The stewards shall report to us the number of male and female goats and their horns and skins; and they shall bring to us annually newly salted cuts of fat goats.

67. The stewards shall inform us about any vacant mansi or any newly acquired serfs if they have any in their district for whom they have no place.

68. We wish that each steward always have ready good barrels bound with iron which they can send to the army or to the palace and that the stewards do not make containers of leather.

69. The stewards at all times shall report to us how many wolves each one has taken and shall send the skins to us. And in the month of May they shall hunt down and destroy the whelps with poison, traps, pits, and dogs.

70. We wish that the stewards have all sorts of plants in the garden, namely, lilies, roses, fenugreek, costmary, sage, rue, southernwood, cucumbers, pumpkins, squash, kidney-beans, cumin, rosemary, caraway, chick-peas, squill, gladiolus, dragon-arum, anise, colosynth, heliotrope, spicknel, seseli, lettuce, fennel-flower, rocket, garden cress, burdock, penny-royal, horse-parsley, parsley, celery, lovage, juniper, dill, sweet-fennel, endive, dittany, mustard, savory, water-mint, garden mint, apple-mint, tansy, catnip, centaury, garden-poppy, beets, hazel-wort, marshmallows, tree-hibiscus, mallows, carrots, parsnip, garden-orach, amaranth, kohlrabi, cabbages, onions, chives, leeks, radishes, shallots, cibols, garlic, madder, teasel, garden beans, Moorish peas, coriander, chervil, capers, clary. And the gardener shall have house-leek growing on his house. As for trees, we wish that they have various kinds of apple, pear, and plum trees, sorb, medlar, chestnut,

peach trees of different kinds, quince, filbert, almond, mulberry, laurel, pine, fig, walnut, and cherry trees of various kinds. Names of apple trees: gozmaringa, geroldinga, crevedella, spirauca, sweet ones and sour ones, and all the kind that keep, as well as those which are eaten when picked and those that are forced. They shall have three or four kinds of pears which will keep, sweet ones, cooking, and late pears.

READING 29

FUNERAL OF A VIKING NOBLE

During the ninth and tenth centuries Vikings (also termed Norsemen) used their highly sea-worthy long ships to expand westward from Denmark and Norway to settle in northern France, throughout the British Isles, and to colonize Iceland, Greenland, and even one place on the coast of Newfoundland. The Vikings of Sweden traveled eastward across the Baltic Sea and used the river system of northeastern Europe to establish trading posts throughout the region now occupied by the Baltic States, Ukraine, and Russia. This Viking expansion did much to establish long-distance trade routes that were fundamental in the economic growth of Medieval Europe during the High Middle Ages.

The Viking funeral described below occurred in the year 922 in a settlement on the Volga River in what is now Russia. This account is taken from the memoir of an Arab official who personally witnessed these proceedings.

(Taken from the translation of H. M. Snyser, pp.97-101 of Franciplegius: Medieval and Linguistic Studies in Honor of Francis Peabody Meagoun Jr., edited by Jess B. Bessinger Jr. and Robert P. Creed, New York University Press 1965)

I had always been told that when a chieftain of theirs dies, many things took place, of which burning was the least. I was very interested to get information about this. One day I heard that one of their leading men had died. They laid him in a grave and closed it over him for ten days, till they had finished cutting and sewing clothes for him.

This is how things are done. For one of the poorer men among them they take a small boat and lay him in it and burn him; but when it is a question of a rich man, they gather his wealth and divide it into three parts: one third for his family, one third for making clothes for him, and one third to make the liquor that they drink on the day that his slave girl is killed and burned with her master. They are indeed much addicted to liquor: for they drink day and night. Often one has died with a beaker in his hand.

When a chieftain dies, his family say to his slave girls and men servants, "which of you will die with him?" Then, one of them says, "I will." When he has said this, he is forced to do it and is not free to retract. Even if he wanted to, it would not be allowed. It is mostly the slave girls who do this.

So, when the man of whom I am speaking died, they said to his slave girls, "which of you will die with him?" One of them said, "I will." Two slave girls were given the task of waiting on her and staying with her wherever she went; and often they would even wash her hands and feet. Then they began seeing to the man's things—cutting out his clothes and preparing everything that ought to be there, while the slave girl drank and sang joyfully everyday and seemed to be looking forward to a coming happiness.

215

When the day came when he and his slave girl were to be burned, I went to the river where his ship lay. It had been dragged ashore. Four props of birch wood and other wood had been set ready for it; and also, something that looked like a great stack of wood had been laid all around. The ship was then dragged up onto this and set in place on this wood pile. The men began walking to and fro, talking in a language that I did not understand. Meanwhile the dead man still lay in his grave; for they had not taken him out. Then they brought a bench, set it in the ship, and covered it with rugs and cushions of Byzantine silk. Then, an old woman, whom they call the Angel of Death, came and spread these rugs out over the bench. She was in charge of sewing the clothes and arranging the corpse; and it is also she who kills the girl. I saw that she was an old hag-like woman, thickset and grim looking.

When they came to his grave, they cleared the earth off of it and also took the woodwork away. They stripped him of the clothes in which he had died. I noticed that he had turned black because of the cold in that land. They had laid liquor, fruit, and a lute in the grave with him; and all these they now took out. Oddly enough, the corpse did not stink, and nothing about it had changed except the color of the flesh. Then they dressed him in underbreaches, breaches, boots, coat, and a caftan of silk brocade with gold buttons on it. They set on his head a silk brocade hood of sable fur, carried him into the tent that stood on the ship, and laid him on the rugs and propped him up with cushions. Then they brought liquor, fruit, and sweet smelling plants and laid them beside him. They also brought bread, meat, and leeks and threw them in front of him. Then they brought a dog, cut it in two, and threw it into the ship. Next, they brought all his weapons and laid them beside him. Then they took two horses and made them gallop about until they sweated. Whereupon they cut them to pieces with swords and threw their flesh into the ship. In the same way they brought two cows, and these too they cut to pieces and threw into the ship. Then they brought a cock and hen, killed them, and threw them in.

Meanwhile, the slave girl who had chosen to be killed was walking to and fro. She would go inside one or other of their tents, and the owner of the tent would made love with her saying "tell your master that I did this simply for love of him." When it came to the Friday afternoon, they took the slave girl to a thing like a door frame which they had made. she sat herself on the palms of the hands of some men and stretched up high enough to look over the door frame. She said something in her own language. At this, they sat her down. Then, they lifted her up again, and she did as she had done the first time. At this, they sat her down and lifted her up for the third time, and she did as she had done the first two times. Then they handed her a hen, and she cut its head off and threw it. They took the hen and threw it into the ship. I then questioned the interpreter about what she had done. He replied, "the first time that they lifted her up, she said `look, I see my father and mother'; the second time she said `look, I see all my dead kinsmen sitting there'; the third time she said `look, I see my master sitting in paradise. Paradise is fair and green, and there are men and young lads with him. He is calling me. Let me go to him'."

Then they went off with her towards the ship. She took off two arm rings that she was wearing and gave them to the old woman called the Angel of Death, the one who was going to kill her. Then she took off two ankle rings that she was wearing and gave them to two other women, daughters of the one known as the Angel of Death. Next, they led her on board the ship but did not let her go into the tent. Then came some men who had shields and sticks, and they handed her a beaker of liquor. She sang over it and drank it all. The interpreter told me, "now with this she is bidding farewell to all her friends." Next, another beaker was handed to her. She took it and made her singing long and drawn out, but the old woman hurried her to make her drink it all and go into the tent where her master was. I was watching her, and she looked quite dazed. She tried to go into the tent but stuck her head between it and the ship's side. Then the old woman took hold of her head and managed to get it inside the tent; and the old woman herself went inside with her.

The men began to beat their shields with sticks, so that no sound of her shreeking could be heard for fear that other girls should become frightened and not want to seek death with their masters. Then six men went into the tent, and they all made love with her. After this they laid her down beside her dead master. Two held her legs, and two her hands; and the woman called the Angel of Death wound a cord with knotted ends around her neck, passing the ends out on either side and handing them to two men to pull. Then she stepped forward with a broad bladed dagger and began to drive it in and pluck it out again between the girl's ribs while the two men throttled her with the cord; and so she died.

After this, whoever was the closest kinsman of the dead man came forward. He took a wooden stick and set light to it. Then he walked backwards with his back to the ship and his face to the people, holding the stick in one hand and with the other hand laid on his backside. He was naked. In this fashion the wood that they had put just under the ship was set on fire, Immediately after they had laid the slain slave girl beside her master. Then the people came forward with wood and timber. Each brought a stick with its tip on fire and threw it onto the wood lying under the ship. So, the flames took hold, first on the wood, then on the ship, then on the tent, and the man and woman and everything inside the ship. Thereupon a strong fierce wind sprang up, so that the flames grew stronger, and the ship blazed up even more.

A man of the Rus was standing beside me, and I heard him talking to the interpreter who was near him. I asked the latter what the man had said to him, and he answered "he said that you Arabs are stupid." I said "why so?" He answered, "why, because you take the people whom you most love and honor and throw them into the ground, and the earth and creeping creatures and growing things destroy them. We on the other hand burn them up in an instant, so that they go to paradise in that very hour." Then he gave a roar of laughter; and when I asked him about that, he replied, "for love of him his lord has sent this wind to carry him away at the right time." In fact, no great time passed before the ship, timber, slave girl, and her master had all turned into ashes and so into dust.

After this, on the spot where the ship had first stood when they dragged it up out of the river, they built something that looked like a round mound. In the middle of it they set up a big post of birch wood, on which they wrote this man's name and the name of the king of the Rus. Then they went on their way.

THE RULE OF SAINT BENEDICT

Monasticism was one of the most important and characteristic features of Medieval Christianity. Over the centuries there came into existence a large number of different monastic orders, but the earliest and perhaps the most influential was the Benedictine order, originating with the monastery at Monte Cassino established in 535 by Saint Benedict. In order to regulate the proper functioning of the monastery, a charter, known as The Rule of Saint Benedict, was composed; and it became a model followed by other monastic orders, as each did their best to formulate the ideal religious life of monks.

(Taken from pp.274-314 of Select Historical Documents of the Middle Ages, by Ernest F. Henderson, London 1903)

2. What the Abbot should be like.

An abbot who is worthy to preside over a monastery ought always to remember what he is called, and carry out with his deeds the name of a Superior. For he is believed to be Christ's representative, since he is called by His name, the apostle saying: " Ye have received the spirit of adoption of sons, whereby we call Abba, Father." And so the abbot should not grant that he may not teach, or decree, or order, any thing apart from the precept of the Lord; but his order or teaching should be sprinkled with the ferment of divine justice in the minds of his disciples. Let the abbot always be mindful that, at the tremendous judgment of God, both things will be weighed in the balance: his teaching and the obedience of his disciples. And let the abbot know that whatever the father of the family finds of less utility among the sheep is laid to the fault of the shepherd. Only in a case where the whole diligence of their pastor shall have been bestowed on an unruly and disobedient flock, and his whole care given to their morbid actions, shall that pastor, absolved in the judgment of the Lord, be free to say to the Lord with the prophet: " I have not hid Thy righteousness within my heart, I have declared Thy faithfulness and Thy salvation, but they despising have scorned me." And then at length let the punishment for the disobedient sheep under his care be death itself prevailing against them. Therefore, when any one receives the name of abbot, he ought to rule over his disciples with a double teaching; that is, let him show forth all good and holy things by deeds more than by words. So that to ready disciples he may propound the mandates of God in words; but, to the hard-hearted and the more simple-minded, he may show forth the divine precepts by his deeds. But as to all the things that he has taught to his disciples to be wrong, he shall show by his deeds that they are not to be done; lest, preaching to others, he himself shall be found worthy of blame....

3. About calling in the brethren to take council.

As often as anything especial is to be done in the monastery, the abbot shall call together the whole congregation, and shall himself explain the question at issue. And, having heard the advice of the brethren, he shall think it over by himself, and shall do what he considers most advantageous. And for this reason, moreover, we have said that all ought to be called to take counsel: because often it is to a younger person that God reveals what is best. The brethren, moreover, with all subjection of humility, ought so to give their advice, that they do not presume boldly to defend what seems good to them; but it should rather depend on the judgment of the abbot; so that whatever he decides to be the more salutary, they should all agree to it. But even as it behoves the disciples to obey the master, so it is fitting that he should providently and justly arrange all matters. In all things, indeed, let all follow the Rule as their guide; and let no one rashly deviate from it. Let no one in the monastery follow the inclination of his own heart; and let no one boldly presume to dispute with his abbot, within or without the monastery. But, if he should so presume, let him be subject to the discipline of the Rule. The abbot, on the other hand, shall do all things fearing the Lord and observing the Rule; knowing that he, without a doubt, shall have to render account to God as to a most impartial judge, for all his decisions. But if any lesser matters for the good of the monastery are to be decided upon, he shall employ the counsel of the elder members alone, since it is written: " Do all things with counsel, and after it is done thou wilt not repent."

5. Concerning obedience.

The first grade of humility is obedience without delay. This becomes those who, on account of the holy service which they have professed, or on account of the fear of hell or the glory of eternal life consider nothing dearer to them than Christ: so that, so soon as anything is commanded by their superior, they may not know how to suffer delay in doing it, even as if it were a divine command. Concerning whom the Lord said: " As soon as he heard of me he obeyed me." And again he said to the learned men: " He who heareth you heareth me." Therefore let all such, straightway leaving their own affairs and giving up their own will, with unoccupied hands and leaving incomplete what they were doing the foot of obedience being foremost, follow with their deeds the voice of him who orders. And, as it were, in the same moment, let the aforesaid command of the master and the perfected work of the disciple both together in the swiftness of the fear of God, be called into being by those who are possessed with a desire of advancing to eternal life....

6. Concerning silence.

Let us do as the prophet says: "I said, I will take heed to my ways that I sin not with my tongue, I have kept my mouth with a bridle: I was dumb with silence, I held my peace even from good; and my sorrow was stirred." Here the prophet shows that if one ought at times, for the sake of silence, to refrain from good sayings; how much more, as a punishment for sin, ought one U> cease from evil words And therefore, if anything is to be asked of the prior, let it be asked with all humility and subjection of reverence; lest one seem to speak more than is fitting. Scurrilities, however, or idle words and those exciting laughter, we condemn in all places with a lasting prohibition: nor do we permit a disciple to open his mouth for such sayings.

7. Concerning humility.

The sixth grade of humility is, that a monk be contented with all lowliness or extremity, and consider himself, with regard to everything which is enjoined on him, as a poor and unworthy workman; saying to himself with the prophet: " I was reduced to nothing and was ignorant; I was made as the cattle before thee, and I am always with thee." The seventh grade of humility is, not only that he, with his tongue, pronounce himself viler and more worthless than all; but that he also believe it in the innermost workings of his heart; humbling himself and saying with the. prophet, etc The eighth degree of humility is that a monk do nothing except what the common rule of the monastery, or the example of his elders, urges him to do. The ninth degree of humility is that a monk restrain his tongue from speaking; and, keeping silence, do not speak until he is spoken to. The tenth grade of humility is that he be not ready, and easily inclined, to laugh The eleventh grade of humility is that a monk, when he speaks, speak slowly and without laughter, humbly with gravity, using few and reasonable words; and that he be not loud of voice The twelfth grade of humility is that a monk, shall not only with his heart but also with his body, always show humility to all who see him: that is, when at work, in the oratory, in the monastery, in the garden, on the road, in the fields. And everywhere, sitting or walking or standing, let him always be with head inclined, his looks fixed upon the ground; remembering every hour that he is guilty of his sins. Let him think that he is already being presented before the tremendous judgment of God, saying always to himself in his heart what that publican of the gospel, fixing his eyes on the earth, said: " Lord I am not worthy, I a sinner, so much as to lift up mine eyes unto Heaven."

8. Concerning the divine offices at night.

In the winter time, that is from the Calends of November until Easter, according to what is reasonable, they must rise at the eighth hour of the night, so that they rest a little more than half the night, and rise when they have already digested. But let the time that remains after vigils be kept for meditation by those brothers who are in any way behind hand with the psalter or lessons. From Easter, moreover, until the aforesaid Calends of November, let the hour of keeping vigils be so arranged that, a short interval being observed in which the brethren may go out for the necessities of nature, the matins, which are always to take place with the dawning light, may straightway follow.

16. How Divine Service shall be held through the day.

As the prophet says: " Seven times in the day do I praise Thee." Which sacred number of seven will thus be fulfilled by us if, at matins, at the first, third, sixth, ninth hours, at vesper time and at "completorium" we perform the duties of our service; for it is of these hours of the day that he said: "Seven times in the day do I praise Thee." For, concerning nocturnal vigils, the same prophet says: "At midnight I arose to confess unto thee." Therefore, at these times, let us give thanks to our Creator concerning the judgments of his righteousness; that is, at matins, etc and at night we will rise and confess to him. [There then follows a long list of psalms] ....

22. How the monks shall sleep.

They shall sleep separately in separate beds. They shall receive positions for their beds, after the manner of their characters, according to the dispensation of their abbot. If it can be done, they shall all sleep in one place. If, however, their number do not permit it, they shall rest by tens or twenties, with elders who will concern themselves about them. A candle shall always be burning in that same cell until early in the morning. They shall sleep clothed, and girt with belts or with ropes; and they shall not have their knives at their sides while they sleep, lest perchance in a dream they should wound the sleepers. And let the monks be always on the alert; and, when the signal is given, rising without delay, let them hasten to mutually prepare themselves for the service of God with all gravity and modesty, however. The younger brothers shall not have beds by themselves, but interspersed among those of the elder ones. And when they rise for the service of God, they shall exhort each other mutually with moderation, on account of the excuses that those who are sleepy are inclined to make.

27. What care the abbot should exercise with regard to the excommunicated.

With all solicitude the abbot shall exercise care with regard to delinquent brothers: " They that be whole need not a physician, but they that are sick." And therefore he ought to use every means, as a wise physician, to send in as it were secret consolers that is, wise elder brothers who, as it were secretly, shall console the wavering brother and lead him to the atonement of humility. And they shall comfort him lest he be swallowed up by overmuch sorrow. On the contrary, as the same apostle says, charity shall be confirmed in him, and he shall be prayed for by all. For the abbot should greatly exert his solicitude, and take care with all sagacity and industry, lest he lose any of the sheep entrusted to him. For he should know that he has undertaken the care of weak souls, not the tyranny over sound ones. And he shall fear the threat of the prophet through whom the Lord says: "Ye did take that which ye saw to be strong, and that which was weak ye did cast out." And let him imitate the pious example of the good Shepherd, who, leaving the ninety and nine sheep upon the mountains, went out to seek the one sheep that had gone astray: and He had such compassion upon its infirmity, that He deigned to place it upon His sacred shoulders, and thus to carry it back to the flock.

28. Concerning those who, being often rebuked, do not amend.

If any brother, having frequently been rebuked for any fault, do not amend even after he has been excommunicated, a more severe rebuke shall fall upon him; that is, the punishment of the lash shall be inflicted upon him. But if he do not even then amend; or, if perchance which God forbid, swelled with pride he try even to defend his works: then the abbot shall act as a wise physician. If he have applied the fomentations, the ointments of exhortation, the medicaments of the Divine Scriptures; if he have proceeded to the last blasting of excommunication, or to blows with rods, and if he see that his efforts avail nothing: let him also what is greater call in the prayer of himself and all the brothers for him: that God who can do all things may work a cure upon an infirm brother. But if he be not healed even in this way, then at last the abbot may use the pruning knife, as the apostle says: "Remove evU from you," etc.: lest one diseased sheep contaminate the whole flock.

33. Whether the monks should have any thing of their own.

More than any thing else is this special vice to be cut off root and branch from the monastery, that one should presume to give or receive anything without the order of the abbot, or should have anything of his own. He should have absolutely not anything: neither a book, nor tablets, nor a pen nothing at all. For indeed it is not allowed to the monks to have their own bodies or wills in their own power. But all things necessary they must expect from the Father of the monastery; nor is it allowable to have anything which the abbot did not give or permit. All things shall be common to all, as it is written: "Let not any man presume or call anything his own." But if any one shall have been discovered delighting in this most evil vice: being warned once and again, if he do not amend, let him be subjected to punishment.

34. Whether all ought to receive necessaries equally.

As it is written: "It was divided among them singly, according as each had need": whereby we do not say far from it that there should be an excepting of persons, but a consideration for infirmities. Wherefore he who needs less, let him thank God and not be dismayed; but he who needs more, let him be humiliated on account of his infirmity, and not exalted on account of the mercy that is shown him. And thus all members will be in peace. Above all, let not the evil of murmuring appear, for any cause, through any word or sign whatever. But, if such a murmurer is discovered, he shall be subjected to stricter discipline.

38. Concerning the weekly reader.

At the tables of the brothers when they eat, the reading should not fail; nor may any one at random dare to take up the book and begin to read there; but he who is about to read for the whole week shall begin his duties on Sunday. And, entering upon his office after mass and communion, he shall ask all to pray for him, that God may avert from him the spirit of elation. And this verse shall be said in the oratory three times by all, he however beginning it: " O Lord open Thou my lips and my mouth shall show forth Thy praise." And thus, having received the benediction, he shall enter upon his duties as reader. And there shall be the greatest silence at table, so that the muttering or the voice of no one shall be heard there, except that of the reader alone. But whatever things are necessary to those eating and drinking, the brothers shall so furnish them to each other in turn, that no one shall need to ask for anything. But if, nevertheless, something is wanted, it shall rather be sought by the employment of some sign than by the voice. Nor shall any one presume there to ask questions concerning the reading or anything else; nor shall an opportunity be given: unless perhaps the prior wishes to say something, briefly, for the purpose of edifying. Moreover the brother who reads for the week shall receive bread and wine before he begins to read, on account of the holy communion, and lest, perchance, it might be injurious for him to sustain a fast. Afterwards, moreover, he shall eat with the weekly cooks and the servitors. The brothers, moreover, shall read or sing not in rotation; but the ones shall do so who will edify their hearers.

39. We believe, moreover, that, for the daily refection of the sixth as well as of the ninth hour, two cooked dishes, on account of the infirmities of the different ones, are enough for all tables: so that whoever, perchance, can not eat of one may partake of the other. Therefore let two cooked dishes suffice for all the brothers: and, if it is possible to obtain apples or growing vegetables, a third may be added. One full pound of bread shall suffice for a day, whether there be one refection, or a breakfast and a supper. But if they are going to have supper, the third part of that same pound shall be reserved by the cellarer, to be given back to those who are about to sup. But if, perchance, some greater labour shall have been performed, it shall be in the will and the power of the abbot, if it is expedient, to increase anything; surfeiting above all things being guarded against, so that indigestion may never seize a monk: for nothing is so contrary to every Christian as surfeiting, as our Lord says: " Take heed to yourselves, lest your hearts be overcharged with surfeiting." But to younger boys the same quantity shall not be served, but less than that to the older ones; moderation being observed in all things. But the eating of the flesh of quadrupeds shall be abstained from altogether by every one, excepting alone the weak and the sick.

48. Concerning the daily manual labour.

Idleness is the enemy of the soul. And therefore, at fixed times, the brothers ought to be occupied in manual labour; and again, at fixed times, in sacred reading. Therefore we believe that, according to this disposition, both seasons ought to be arranged; so that, from Easter until the Calends of October, going out early, from the first until the fourth hour they shall do what labour may be necessary. Moreover, from the fourth hour until about the sixth, they shall be free for reading. After the meal of the sixth hour, moreover, rising from table, they shall rest in their beds with all silence; or, perchance, he that wishes to read may so read to himself that he do not disturb another. And the nona [the second meal] shall be gone through with more moderately about the middle of the eighth hour; and again they shall work at what is to be done until Vespers. But, if the exigency or poverty of the place demands that they be occupied by themselves in picking fruits, they shall not be dismayed: for then they are truly monks if they live by the labours of their hands; as did also our fathers and the apostles. Let all things be done with moderation, however, on account of the faint-hearted. From the Calends of October, moreover, until the beginning of Lent they shall be free for reading until the second full hour. At the second hour the tertia [morning service] shall be held, and all shall labour at the task which is enjoined upon them until the ninth. The first signal, moreover, of the ninth hour having been given, they shall each one leave off his work; and be ready when the second signal strikes. Moreover, after the refection they shall be free for their readings or for psalms. But in the days of Lent, from dawn until the third full hour, they shall be free for their readings; and, until the tenth full hour, they shall do the labour that is enjoined on them. In which days of Lent they shall all receive separate books from the library; which they shall read entirely through in order. These books are to be given out on the first day of Lent. Above all there shall certainly be appointed one or two elders, who shall go round the monastery at the hours in which the brothers are engaged in reading, and see to it that no troublesome brother chance to be found who is open to idleness and trifling, and is not intent on his reading; being not only of no use to himself, but also stirring up others. If such a one may it not happen be found, he shall be admonished once and a second time. If he do not amend, he shall be subject under the Rule to such punishment that the others may have fear. Nor shall brother join brother at unsuitable hours. Moreover, on Sunday all shall engage in reading: excepting those who are deputed to various duties. But if anyone be so negligent and lazy that he will not or can not read, some task shall be imposed upon him which he can do; so that he be not idle. On feeble or delicate brothers such a labour or art is to be imposed, that they shall neither be idle, nor shall they be so oppressed by the violence of labour as to be driven to take flight. Their weakness is to be taken into consideration by the abbot.

58. Concerning the manner of receiving brothers.

When any new comer applies for conversion, an easy entrance shall not be granted him: but, as the apostle says, " Try the spirits if they be of God." Therefore, if he who comes perseveres in knocking, and is seen after four or five days to patiently endure the insults inflicted upon him, and the difficulty of ingress, and to persist in his demand: entrance shall be allowed him, and he shall remain for a few days in the cell of the guests. After this, moreover, he shall be in the cell of the novices, where he shall meditate and eat and sleep. And an elder shall be detailed off for him who shall be capable of saving souls, who shall altogether intently watch over him, and make it a care to see if he reverently seek God, if he be zealous in the service of God, in obedience, in suffering shame. And all the harshness and roughness of the means through which God is approached shall be told him in advance. If he promise perseverance in his steadfastness, after the lapse of two months this Rule shall be read to him in order, and it shall be said to him: Behold the law under which thou dost wish to serve; if thou canst observe it, enter; but if thou canst not, depart freely. If he have stood firm thus far, then he shall be led into the aforesaid cell of the novices; and again he shall be proven with all patience. And, after the lapse of six months, the Rule shall be read to him; that he may know upon what he is entering. And, if he stand firm thus far, after four months the same Rule shall again be re-read to him. And if, having deliberated with himself, he shall promise to keep everything, and to obey all the commands that are laid upon him: then he shall be received in the congregation; knowing that it is decreed, by the law of the Rule, that from that day he shall not be allowed to depart from the monastery, nor to shake free his neck from the yoke of the Rule, which, after such tardy deliberation, he was at liberty either to refuse or receive. He who is to be received, moreover, shall, in the oratory, in the presence of all, make promise concerning his steadfastness and the change in his manner of life and his obedience to God and to His saints; so that if, at any time, he act contrary, he shall know that he shall be condemned by Him whom he mocks. Concerning which promise he shall make a petition in the name of the saints whose relics are there, and of the abbot who is present. Which petition he shall write with his own hand. Or, if he really be not learned in letters, another, being asked by him, shall write it. And that novice shall make his sign; and with his own hand shall place it [the petition] above the altar. And when he has placed it there, the novice shall straightway commence this verse: " Receive me oh Lord according to thy promise and I shall live, and do not cast me down from my hope." Which verse the whole congregation shall repeat three times, adding: " Glory be to the Father." Then that brother novice shall prostrate himself at the feet of each one, that they may pray for him. And, already, from that day, he shall be considered as in the congregation. If he have any property, he shall either first present it to the poor, or, making a solemn donation, shall confer it on the monastery, keeping nothing at all for himself: as one, forsooth, who from that day, shall know that he shall not have power even over his own body. Straightway, therefore in the oratory, he shall take off his own garments in which he was clad, and shall put on the garments of the monastery. Moreover, those garments which he has taken off shall be placed in the vestiary to be preserved; so that if, at any time, the devil persuading him, he shall consent to go forth from the monastery may it not happen, then, taking off the garments of the monastery, he may be cast out. That petition of his, nevertheless, which the abbot took from above the altar, he shall not receive again; but it shall be preserved in the monastery.

66. Concerning the doorkeepers of the monastery.

At the door of the monastery shall be placed a wise old man who shall know how to receive a reply and to return one; whose ripeness of age will not permit him to trifle. Which doorkeeper ought to have a cell next to the door; so that those arriving may always find one present from whom they may receive a reply. And straightway, when any one has knocked, or a poor man has called out, he shall answer, " Thanks be to God! " or shall give the blessing; and with all the gentleness of the fear of God he shall hastily give a reply with the fervour of charity. And if this doorkeeper need assistance he may receive a younger brother.

A monastery, moreover, if it can be done, ought so to be arranged that everything necessary, that is, water, a mill, a garden, a bakery, may be made use of, and different arts be carried on, within the monastery; so that there shall be no need for the monks to wander about outside. For this is not at all good for their souls. We wish, moreover, that this Rule be read very often in the congregation; lest any of the brothers excuse himself on account of ignorance.

Reading 31

THE MEDIEVAL PAPACY

A. POPE GREGORY I ON CONVERTING THE ANGLES

The following is the text of a letter written in 596 by Pope Gregory to an abbot in France concerning the mission of Augustine, who had been sent out to England to convert the Angles and Saxons to Christianity. The pope's suggestions on the techniques to be used in winning pagans over to the new religion are interesting.

(Taken from Selected Epistles of Gregory the Great, tr. by J. Barmby, Library of Nicene and Post Nicene Fathers, Second Series, Volume XIII [1895] pp. 84-5)

Since the departure of our congregation which is with thee, we have been in a state of great suspense from having heard nothing of the success of your journey. But when all-mighty God shall have brought you to our most reverent brother Augustine, tell him that I have long been considering with myself about the case of the Angles: to wit, that the temples of idols in that nation should not be destroyed, but that the idols themselves that are in them should be. Let holy water be prepared and sprinkled in these temples, and altars constructed and relics deposited, since if these same temples are well built, it is needful that they should be transferred from the worship of idols to the service of the true god. Thus, when the people themselves see that these temples are not destroyed, they may put away error from their heart and, knowing and adoring the true god, may have recourse with more familiarity to the place to which they have been accustomed. In addition, since they are wont to kill many oxen in sacrifice to demons, they should also have some solemnity of this kind in a changed form, so that on the day of dedication or on the anniversaries of the holy martyrs, whose relics are deposited there, they may make for themselves tents of the branches of trees around these temples that have been changed into churches and celebrate the solemnity with religious feasts. Nor let them any longer sacrifice animals to the Devil, but slay animals to the praise of God for their own eating and return thanks to the giver of all for their fullness, so that while some joys are reserved for them outwardly, they may be able the more easily to incline their minds to inward joys. For it is undoubtedly impossible to cut away everything at once from hard hearts, since one who strives to ascend to the highest place must needs rise by steps or paces and not by leaps. Thus, to the people of Israel in Egypt the Lord did indeed make himself known, but still he reserved to them in His own worship the use of the sacrifices which they were accustomed to offer to the Devil, enjoining them to immolate animals in sacrifice to Himself to the end that, their hearts being changed, they should omit some things in the sacrifice and retain others, so that though the animals were the same as what they had been accustomed to offer, nevertheless, as they immolated them to God and not to idols, they should be no longer the same sacrifices. This then it is necessary for thy love to say to our afore-said brother that he, being now in that country, may consider well how he should arrange all things. God keep thee safe, most beloved son.

B. THE DONATION OF CONSTANTINE

The following text, known as The Donation of Constantine, was written during the time of Charlemagne and served for centuries to give the papacy a claim to exercise power in secular affairs in the countries of Western Europe. This document purports to be a grant made by the Emperor Constantine, the first Christian emperor (ruled 312-337), to Pope Silvester. During the fifteenth century, when Western learning and study of classical languages and texts had revived and become sophisticated, the great Renaissance scholar, Lorenzo Vala, succeeded in demonstrating by analysis of its language and content that this document was an early Medieval forgery, but before Vala's scholarly demonstration the text had served the papacy well.

(Taken from Select Historical Documents of the Middle Ages, by Ernest F. Henderson, London 1903 pp.325-9)

We decree that his holy Roman church shall be honoured with veneration; and that, more than our empire and earthly throne, the most sacred seat of St. Peter shall be gloriously exalted; we giving to it the imperial power, and dignity of glory, and vigour and honour. And we ordain and decree that he shall have the supremacy as well over the four chief seats Antioch, Alexandria, Constantinople and Jerusalem, as also over all the churches of God in the whole world....

To those same holy apostles, my masters, St. Peter and St. Paul; and, through them, also to St. Sylvester, our father, the chief pontiff and universal pope of the city of Rome, and to all the pontiffs his successors, who until the end of the world shall be about to sit in the seat of St. Peter: we con- cede and, by this present, do confer, our imperial Lateran palace, which is preferred to, and ranks above, all the palaces in the whole world; then a diadem, that is, the crown of our head, and at the same time the tiara; and, also, the shoulder band, that is, the collar that usually surrounds our impe- rial neck; and also the purple mantle, and crimson tunic, and all the imperial raiment; and the same rank as those presiding over the imperial cavalry; conferring also the imperial sceptres, and, at the same time, the spears and standards; also the banners and different imperial ornaments, and all the advantage of our high im- perial position, and the glory of our power....

We also decreed this, that this same venerable one our father Sylvester, the supreme pontiff, and all the pontiffs his successors, might use and bear upon their heads to the praise of God and for the honour of St. Peter the diadem; that is, the crown which we have granted him from our own head, of purest gold and precious gems. But he, the most holy pope, did not at all allow that crown of gold to be used over the clerical crown which he wears to the glory of St. Peter; but we placed upon his most holy head, with our own hands, a tiara of gleaming splendour representing the glorious resurrection of our Lord. And, holding the bridle of his horse, out of reverence for St. Peter we per- formed for him the duty of groom; decreeing that all the pontiffs his successors, and they alone, may use that tiara in processions.

In imitation of our own power, in order that for that cause the supreme pontificate may not deteriorate, but may rather be adorned with power and glory even more than is the dignity of an earthly rule: behold, we give over to the oft-mentioned most blessed pontiff, our father Sylvester the universal pope, as well our palace, as has been said, as also the city of Rome and all the provinces, districts and cities of Italy or of the western regions; and relinquishing them, by our inviolable gift, to the power and sway of himself or the pontiffs his successors do decree, by this our godlike charter and imperial constitu- tion, that it shall be (so) arranged; and do concede that they (the palaces, provinces, etc.) shall lawfully remain with the holy Roman church.

Wherefore we have perceived it to be fitting that our empire and the power of our kingdom should be trans- ferred and changed to the regions of the East; and that, in the province of Byzantium, in a most fitting place, a city should be built in our name; and that our empire should there be established. For, where the supremacy of priests and the head of the Christian religion has been established by a heavenly Ruler, it is not just that there an earthly ruler should have jurisdiction. We decree, moreover, that all these things which, through this our imperial charter and through other godlike commands, we have established and confirmed, shall remain uninjured and unshaken until the end of the world....

C. DICTATE OF THE POPE

The following list of 27 propositions was composed in 1075 and became part of the official register of Pope Gregory VII. This document is generally known as The Dictate of the Pope (*Dictatus Papae*). Its formulation constituted part of the reform movement in the Roman Catholic Church during the eleventh century and played an important role in the emergence of the papacy as a well organized and powerful institution throughout Western Europe for the next two centuries.

(Taken from Select Historical Documents of the Middle Ages, by Ernest F. Henderson, London 1903 pp.366-7)

1.   That the Roman church was founded by God alone

2.   That the Roman pontiff alone can with right be called universal.

3.   That he alone can depose or reinstate bishops.

4.   That, in a council, his legate, even if a lower grade, is above all bishops, and can pass sentence of deposition against them.

5.   That the pope may depose the absent.

6.   That, among other things, we ought not to remain in the same house with those excommunicated by him.

7.   That for him alone is it lawful, according to the needs of the time, to make new laws, to assemble together new congregations, to make an abbey of a canonry; and, on the other hand, to divide a rich bishopric and unite the poor ones.

8.   That he alone may use the imperial insignia.

9.   That of the pope alone all princes shall kiss the feet.

10.   That his name alone shall be spoken in the churches.

11.   That this is the only name in the world.

12.   That it may be permitted to him to depose emperors.

13.   That he may be permitted to transfer bishops if need be.

14.   That he has power to ordain a clerk of any church he may wish.

15.   That he who is ordained by him may preside over another church but may not hold a subordinate position, and that such an one may not receive a higher grade from any bishop.

16.   That no synod shall be called a general one without his order.

17.   That no chapter and no book shall be considered canonical without his authority.

18.   That a sentence passed by him may be retracted by no one; and that he himself, alone of all, may retract it.

19.   That he himself may be judged by no one.

20.   That no one shall dare to condemn one who appeals to the apostolic chair.

21.   That to the latter should be referred the more important cases of every church.

22.   That the Roman church has never erred; nor will it err to all eternity, the Scripture bearing witness.

23.   That the Roman pontiff, if he have been canonically ordained, is undoubtedly made a saint by the merits of St. Peter; St. Ennodius, bishop of Pavia, bearing witness, and many holy fathers agreeing with him, as is contained in the decrees of St. Symmachus the pope.

24.   That, by his command and consent, it may be lawful for subordinates to bring accusations.

25.   That he may depose and reinstate bishops without assembling a synod.

26.   That he who is not at peace with the Roman church shall not be considered catholic.

27.   That he may absolve subjects from their fealty to wicked men.

Reading 32

Magna Charta

Following a twelve-year war with France (1202-1214), which ended in English defeat and the loss of all its feudal holdings in northern and western France, the barons of King John of England broke out into rebellion and forced him to sign in 1215 one of the most important documents for the early constitutional history of England: *Magna Charta*. King John had ignored many traditional rights and privileges of Englishmen during the war with France in order to raise money for the waging of the war. The power struggle between the barons and the king resulted in the latter being forced to acknowledge the rights and privileges of the latter. *Magna Charta* therefore established the important constitutional precedent that kings of England were to rule their subjects according to traditional customs and laws, not in accordance with their arbitrary will. Although most of the following provisions pertain to feudal rights and obligations that eventually became outmoded, out of others grew important legal and constitutional principles. For example, s.14 asserted the right of Englishmen to have representatives summoned by the king into parliament whenever he needed to impose taxes or other obligations upon his subjects. Out of s.39 grew the important legal idea that no subject could be arrested, punished, or dispossessed by the king or his officials except by the law of the land or by a judgment of the person's peers; and s.61 affirmed the right of the king's subjects to petition him for redress of any of their grievances. All three of these ideas were eventually enshrined in the U.S. Constitution.

(Taken from Source Problems in English History, ed. A. B. White and W. Notestein, published by Harper and Brothers [New York 1915])

Note: Eleven of the more arcane provisions have been omitted from this version of the text.

1. In the first place we have granted to God, and by this our present charter confirmed for us and our heirs for ever that the English church shall be free, and shall have her rights entire, and her liberties inviolate; and we will that it be thus observed; which is apparent from this that the freedom of elections, which is reckoned most important and very essential to the English church, we, of our pure and unconstrained will, did grant, and did by our charter confirm and did obtain the ratification of the same from our lord, Pope Innocent III., before the quarrel arose between us and our barons: and this we will observe, and our will

is that it be observed in good faith by our heirs forever. We have also granted to all freemen of our kingdom, for us and our heirs forever, all the underwritten liberties, to be had and held by them and their heirs, of us and our heirs forever.

2. If any of our earls or barons, or others holding of us in chief by military service shall have died, and at the time of his death his heir shall be of full age and owe "relief," he shall have his inheritance on payment of the ancient relief, namely the heir or heirs of an earl, 100 pounds for a whole earl'sbarony; the heir or heirs of a baron, 100 pounds for a whole barony; the heiror heirs of a knight, 100 shillings at most for a whole knight's fee; and whoever owes less let him give less, according to the ancient custom of fiefs.

3. If, however, the heir of any of the aforesaid has been under age and inwardship, let him have his inheritance without relief and without fine when he comes of age.

4. The guardian of the land of an heir who is thus under age, shall take from the land of the heir nothing but reasonably produce, reasonable customs, andreasonable services, and that without destruction or waste of men or goods; and if we have committed the wardship of the lands of any such minor to the sheriff, or to any other who is responsible to us for its issues, and he has made destruction or waste of what he holds in wardship, we will take of him amends, and the land shall be committed to two lawful and discreet men of that fee, who shall be responsible for the issues to us or to him to whom we shall assign them; and if we have given or sold the wardship of any such land to anyone and he has therein made destruction or waste, he shall lose that wardship, and it shall be transferred to two lawful and discreet men of that fief, who shall be responsible to us in like manner as aforesaid.

5. The guardian, moreover, so long as he has the wardship of the land, shall keep up the houses, parks, fishponds, stanks, mills, and other things pertaining to the land, out of the issues of the same land; and he shall restore to the heir, when he has come to full age, all his land, stocked with ploughs and "waynage," according as the season of husbandry shall require, andthe issues of the land can reasonably bear.

6. Heirs shall be married without disparagement [loss of status], yet so that before the marriage takes place, the nearest in blood to that heir shall have notice.

7. A widow, after the death of her husband, shall forthwith and without difficulty have her marriage portion and inheritance; nor shall she give anything for her dower, or for her marriage portion, or for the inheritance which her husband and she held on the day of the death of that husband; and she may remain in the house of her husband for fourty days after his death, within which time her dower shall be assigned to her.

8. No widow shall be compelled to marry, so long as she prefers to live without a husband; provided always that she gives security not to marry without our consent, if she holds of us, or without the consent of the lord of whom she holds, if she holds of another.

9. Neither we nor our bailiffs shall seize any land or rent for any debt, so long as the chattels of the debtor are sufficient to repay the debt; nor shallthe sureties of the debtor be distrained so long as the principal debtor is able to satisfy the debt; and if the principal debtor shall fail to pay the debt, having nothing wherewith to pay it, then the sureties shall answer for the debt; and let them have the lands and rents of the debtor, if they desire them, until they are indemnified for the debt which they

have paid for him, unless the principal debtor can show proof that he is discharged thereof as against the said sureties.

10. If one who has borrowed from the Jews any sum, great or small, die before that loan can be repaid, the debt shall not bear interest while the heir is under age, of whomsoever he may hold; and if the debt fall into our hands, we will not take anything except the principal sum contained in the bond.

11. And if anyone die indebted to the Jews, his wife shall have her dower and pay nothing of that debt; and if any children of the deceased are left under age, necessaries shall be provided for them in keeping with the holding of the deceased; and out of the residue the debt shall be paid, reserving, however, service due to feudal lords; in like manner let it be done touching debts due to others than Jews.

12. No scutage [shield money] nor aid shall be imposed on our kingdom, unless by common counsel of our kingdom, except for ransoming our person, for making our eldest son a knight, and for once marrying our eldest daughter; and for these there shall not be levied more than a reasonable aid. In like manner it shall be done concerning aids from the city of London.

13. And the city of London shall have all its ancient liberties and free customs, as well by land as by water; furthermore, we decree and grant that all other cities, boroughs, towns, and ports shall have all their liberties and free customs.

14. And for obtaining the common counsel of the kingdom concerning the assessing of an aid (except in the three cases aforesaid) or of a scutage, we will cause to be summoned the archbishops, bishops, abbots, earls, and greater barons, severally by our letters; and we will moreover cause to be summoned generally, through our sheriffs and bailiffs, all others who hold of us in chief, for a fixed date, namely, after the expiry of at least forty days, and at a fixed place; and in all letters of such summons we will specify the reason of the summons. And when the summons has thus been made, the business shall proceed on the day appointed, according to the counsel of such as are present, although not all who were summoned have come.

15. We will not for the future grant to anyone license to take an aid from his own free tenants, except to ransom his body, to make his eldest son a knight, and once to marry his eldest daughter; and on each of these occasions there shall be levied only a reasonable aid.

17. Common pleas shall not follow our court, but shall be held in some fixed place.

18. Inquests of novel disseisin, of mort d'ancester, and of darrein presentment, shall not be held elsewhere than in their own county courts and that in manner following,—We, or, if we should be out of the realm, our chief justiciar, will send two justiciars through every county four times a year, who shall, along with four knights of the county chosen by the county, hold the said assize in the county court, on the day and in the place of meeting of that court.

19. And if any of the said assizes cannot be taken on the day of the county court, let there remain of the knights and freeholders, who were present at the county court on that day, as many as may be required for the efficient making of judgments, according as the business be more or less.

20. A freeman shall not be amerced [fined] for a slight offense, except in accordance with the degree of the offense; and for a grave offense he shall be amerced in

accordance with the gravity of the offense, yet saving always his "contenement;" and a merchant in the same way, saving his "merchandise;" and a villein shall be amerced in the same way, saving his "wainage"— if they have fallen into our mercy: and none of the aforesaid amercements shall be imposed except by the oath of honest men of the neighborhood.

21. Earls and barons shall not be amerced except through their peers, and only in accordance with the degree of the offense.

22. A clerk shall not be amerced in respect of his lay holding except after the manner of the others aforesaid; further, he shall not be amerced in accordance with the extent of his ecclesiastical benefice.

23. No village or individual shall be compelled to make bridges at river-banks, except those who from of old were legally bound to do so.

24. No sheriff, constable, coroners, or others of our bailiffs, shall hold pleas of our Crown.

26. If anyone holding of us a lay fief shall die, and our sheriff or bailiff shall exhibit our letters patent of summons for a debt which the deceased owed to us, it shall be lawful for our sheriff or bailiff to attach and catalogue chattels of the deceased, found upon the lay fief, to the value of that debt, at the sight of law-worthy men, provided always that nothing whatever be thence removed until the debt which is evident shall be fully paid to us; and the residue shall be left to the executors to fulfil the will of the deceased; and if there be nothing due from him to us, all the chattels shall go to the deceased, saving to his wife and children their reasonable shares.

27. If any freeman shall die intestate, his chattels shall be distributed by the hands of his nearest kinsfolk and friends, under supervision of the church, saving to everyone the debts which the deceased owed to him.

28. No constable or other bailiff of ours shall take corn or other provisions from anyone without immediately tendering money therefor, unless he can have postponement thereof by permission of the seller.

29. No constable shall compel any knight to give money in lieu of castle-guard, when he is willing to perform it in his own person, or (if he cannot do it from any reasonable cause) then by another responsible man. Further, if we have led or sent him upon military service, he shall be relieved from guard in proportion to the time during which he has been on service because of us.

30. No sheriff or bailiff of ours, or other person, shall take the horses or carts of any freeman for transport duty, against the will of the said freeman.

31. Neither we nor our bailiffs shall take, for our castles or for any other work of ours, wood which is not ours, against the will of the owner of that wood.

32. We will not retain beyond one year and one day, the lands of those who have been convicted of felony, and the lands shall thereafter be handed over to the lords of the fiefs.

33. All kiddles for the future shall be removed altogether from Thames and Medway, and throughout all England, except upon the seashore.

35. Let there be one measure of wine throughout our whole realm; and one measure of ale; and one measure of corn, to wit, "the London quarter;" and one width of cloth (whether dyed, or russet, or "halberget"), to wit, two ells within the selvages; of weights also let it be as of measures.

36. Nothing in future shall be given or taken for a writ of inquisition of life or limbs, but freely it shall be granted, and never denied.

38. No bailiff for the future shall, upon his own unsupported complaint, put anyone to his "law," without credible witnesses brought for this purpose.

39. No freeman shall be taken or imprisoned or disseised [disinherited] or exiled or in any way destroyed, nor will we go upon him nor send upon him, except by the lawful judgment of his peers or by the law of the land.

40. To no one will we sell, to no one will we refuse or delay, right or justice.

41. All merchants shall have safe and secure exit from England, and entry to England, with the right to tarry there and to move about as well by land as by water, for buying and selling by the ancient and right customs, quit from all evil tolls, except (in time of war) such merchants as are of the land at war with us. And if such are found in our land at the beginning of the war, they shall be detained, without injury to their bodies or goods, until information be received by us, or by our chief justiciar, how the merchants of our land found in the land at war with us are treated; and if our men are safe there, the others shall be safe in our land.

42. It shall be lawful in future for any one (excepting always those imprisoned or outlawed in accordance with the law of the kingdom, and natives of any country at war with us, and merchants, who shall be treated as is above provided) to leave our kingdom and to return, safe and secure by land and water, except for a short period in time of war, on grounds of public policy— reserving always the allegiance due to us.

45. We will appoint as justices, constables, sheriffs, or bailiffs only such as know the law of the realm and mean to observe it well.

46. All barons who have founded abbeys, concerning which they hold charters from the kings of England, or of which they have long-continued possession, shall have the wardship of them, when vacant, as they ought to have.

48. All evil customs connected with forests and warrens, foresters and warreners, sheriffs and their officers, river-banks and their wardens, shall immediately be inquired into in each county by twelve sworn knights of the same county chosen by the honest men of the same county, and shall, within forty days of the said inquest, be utterly abolished, so as never to be restored, provided always that we previously have intimation thereof, or our justiciar, if we should not be in England.

49. We will immediately restore all hostages and charters delivered to us by Englishmen, as sureties of the peace or of faithful service.

51. As soon as peace is restored, we will banish from the kingdom all foreign-born knights, cross-bowmen, serjeants, and mercenary soldiers, who have come with horses and arms to the kingdom's hurt.

52. If any one has been dispossessed or removed by us, without the legal judgment of his peers, from his lands, castles, franchises, or from his right, we will immediately

restore them to him; and if a dispute arise over this, then let it be decided by the five-and-twenty barons of whom mention is made below in the clause for securing the peace. Moreover, for all those possessions, from which anyone has, without the lawful judgment of his peers, been disseised or removed, by our father, King Henry, or by our brother, King Richard, and which we retain in our hand (or which are possessed by others, to whom we are bound to warrant them) we shall have respite until the usual term of crusaders; excepting those things about which a plea has been raised, or an inquest made by our order, before our taking of the cross; but as soon as we return from our expedition (or if perchance we desist from the expedition) we will immediately grant full justice therein.

54. No one shall be arrested or imprisoned upon the appeal of a woman, for the death of any other than her husband.

55. All fines made with us unjustly and against the law of the land, and all amercements imposed unjustly and against the law of the land, shall be entirely remitted, or else it shall be done concerning them according to the decision of the five-and-twenty barons of whom mention is made below in the clause for securing the peace, or according to the judgment of the majority of the same, along with the aforesaid Stephen, archbishop of Canterbury, if he can be present, and such others as he may wish to bring with him for this purpose, and if he cannot be present, the business shall nevertheless proceed without him, provided always that if anyone or more of the aforesaid five-and-twenty barons are in a similar suit, they shall be removed as far as concerns this particular judgment, others being substituted in their places after having been selected by the rest of the same five-and-twenty for this purpose only, and after having been sworn.

56. If we have disseised or removed Welshmen from lands or liberties, or other things, without the legal judgment of their peers in England or in Wales, they shall be immediately restored to them; and if a dispute arise over this, then let it be decided in the marches by the judgment of their peers; for tenements in England according to the law of England, for tenements in Wales according to the law of Wales, and for tenements in the marches according to the law of the marches. Welshmen shall do the same to us and ours.

57. Further, for all those possessions from which any Welshman has, withoutthe lawful judgment of his peers, been disseised or removed by King Henry our father or King Richard our brother, and which we retain in our hand (or which are possessed by others, to whom we are bound to warrant them) we shall have respite until the usual term of crusaders; excepting those things about which a plea has been raised or an inquest made by our order before we took the cross; but as soon as we return (or if perchance we desist from our expedition), we will immediately grant full justice in accordance with the laws of the Welsh and in relation to the foresaid regions.

60. Moreover, all these aforesaid customs and liberties, the observance of which we have granted in our kingdom as far as pertains to us toward our men, shall be observed by all of our kingdom, as well clergy as laymen, as far as pertains to them toward their men.

61. Since, moreover, for God and the amendment of our kingdom and for the better allaying of the quarrel that has arisen between us and our barons, we have granted all these concessions, desirous that they should enjoy them in complete and firm

endurance forever, we give and grant to them the underwritten security, namely, that the barons choose five-and-twenty barons of the kingdom, whomsoever they will, who shall be bound with all their might, to observe and hold, and cause to be observed, the peace and liberties we have granted and confirmed to them by this our present Charter, so that if we, or our justiciar, or our bailiffs or anyone of our officers, shall in anything be at fault toward anyone, or shall have broken any one of the articles of the peace or of this security, and the offense be notified to four barons of the foresaid five-and-twenty, the said four barons shall repair to us (or our justiciar, if we are out of the realm) and, laying the transgression before us, petition to have that transgression redressed without delay. And if we shall not have corrected the transgression (or, in the event of our being out of the realm, if our justiciar shall not have corrected it) within forty days, reckoning from the time it has been intimated to us (or to our justiciar, if we should be out of the realm), the four barons aforesaid shall refer that matter to the rest of the five-and-twenty barons, and those five-and-twenty barons shall, together with the community of the whole land, distrain and distress us in all possible ways, namely, by seizing our castles, lands, possessions, and in any other way they can, until redress has been obtained as they deem fit, saving harmless our own person, and the persons of our queen and children; and when redress has been obtained, they shall resume their old relations toward us. And let whoever in the country desires it, swear to obey the orders of the said five-and-twenty barons for the execution of all the aforesaid matters, and along with them, to molest us to the utmost of his power; and we publicly and freely grant leave to everyone who wishes to swear, and we shall never forbid anyone to swear. All those, moreover, in the land who of themselves and of their own accord are unwilling to swear to the twenty-five to help them in constraining and molesting us, we shall by our command compel the same to swear to the effect aforesaid. And if anyone of the five-and-twenty barons shall have died or departed from the land, or be incapacitated in any other manner which would prevent the foresaid provisions being carried out, those of the said twenty-five barons who are left shall choose another in his place according to their own judgment, and he shall be sworn in the same way as the others. Further, in all matters, the execution of which is intrusted to these twenty-five barons, if perchance these twenty-five are present, that which the majority of those present ordain or command shall be held as fixed and established, exactly as if the whole twenty-five had concurred in this; and the said twenty-five shall swear that they will faithfully observe all that is aforesaid, and cause it to be observed with all their might. And we shall procure nothing from any one, directly or indirectly, whereby any part of these concessions and liberties might be revoked or diminished; and if any such thing has been procured, let it be void and null, and we shall never use it personally or by another.

62. And all the ill-will, hatreds, and bitterness that have arisen between us and our men, clergy and lay, from the date of the quarrel, we have completely remitted and pardoned everyone. Moreover, all trespasses occasioned by the said quarrel, from Easter in the sixteenth year of our reign till the restoration of peace, we have fully remitted to all, both clergy and laymen, and completely forgiven, as far as pertains to us. And, on this head, we have caused to be made for them letters testimonial patent of the lord Stephen, archbishop of Canterbury, of the lord Henry, archbishop of Dublin, of the bishops aforesaid, and of Master Pandulf as touching this security and the concessions aforesaid.

63.   Wherefore it is our will, and we firmly enjoin, that the English Church be free, and that the men in our kingdom have and hold all the aforesaid liberties, rights, and concessions, well and peaceably, freely and quietly, fully and wholly, for themselves and their heirs, of us and our heirs, in all respects and in all places forever, as is aforesaid. An oath, moreover, has been taken, as well on our part as on the part of the barons, that all these conditions aforesaid shall be kept in good faith and without evil intent.

Given under our hand, the above-named and many others being witnesses— in the meadow which is called Runnymede, between Windsor and Staines, on the fifteenth day of June, in the seventeenth year of our reign.

READING 33

THE CRUSADES

A. THE SPEECH OF POPE URBAN II

✥ From Robert the Monk

I n November of 1095 Pope Urban II, while conducting papal business in the French town of Clermont, delivered a speech that marked the beginning of the Crusades, in which western Europeans, authorized by the pope, carried out a holy war to capture areas of the eastern Mediterranean in order to make them safe for pilgrims traveling to the Holy Land. The westward migration of the Seljuk Turks during the late eleventh century had disrupted both the Islamic and Byzantine Empires and had also prevented Christian pilgrims from traveling safely to Jerusalem.

⫍ *(Taken from The First Crusade: The Accounts of Eye-Witnesses and Participants, by August C. Krey, Princeton University Press 1921, pp.30-3)*

"Oh, race of Franks, race from across the mountains, race chosen and beloved by God-as shines forth in very many of your works-set apart from all nations by the situation of your country, as well as by your Catholic faith and the honor of the Holy Church! To you our discourse is addressed, and for you our exhortation is intended. We wish you to know what a grievous cause has led us to your country, what peril, threatening you and all the faithful, has brought us.

From the confines of Jerusalem and the city of Constantinople a horrible tale has gone forth and very frequently has been brought to our ears; namely, that a race from the kingdom of the Persians, an accursed race, a race utterly alienated from God, a generation, forsooth, which has neither directed its heart nor entrusted its spirit to God, has invaded the lands of those Christians and has depopulated them by the sword, pillage, and fire; it has led away a part of the captives into its own country, and a part it has destroyed by cruel tortures; it has either entirely destroyed the churches of God or appropriated them for the rites of its own religion. They destroy the altars, after having defiled them with their uncleanness. They circumcise the Christians, and the blood of the circumcision they either spread upon the altars or pour into the vases of the baptismal font. When they wish to torture people by a base death, they perforate their navels, and, dragging forth the end of the intestines, bind it to a stake; then with flogging they lead the victim around until his viscera have gushed forth, and he falls prostrate upon the ground. Others they bind to a post and pierce with arrows. Others they compel to extend their necks, and then, attacking them with naked swords, they attempt to cut through the neck with a single blow. What shall I say of the abominable rape of the women? To speak of it is worse than to be silent. The kingdom of the Greeks is now dismembered by them and deprived of territory so vast in extent that it can not be traversed in a march of two months. On whom, therefore, is the task of avenging these wrongs and of recovering this territory incumbent, if not upon you ? You, upon whom above other nations God has conferred remarkable glory in arms, great courage, bodily energy, and the strength to humble the hairy scalp of those who resist you.

Let the deeds of your ancestors move you and incite your minds to manly achievements; likewise, the glory and greatness of King Charles the Great, and his son Louis, and of your other kings, who have destroyed the kingdoms of the pagans, and have extended in these lands the territory of the Holy Church. Let the Holy Sepulchre of the Lord, our Saviour, which is possessed by unclean nations, especially move you, and likewise the holy places, which are now treated with ignominy and irreverently polluted with filthiness. Oh, most valiant soldiers and descendants of invincible ancestors, be not degenerate, but recall the valor of your forefathers!

However, if you are hindered by love of children, parents, and wives, remember what the Lord says in the Gospel, 'He that loveth father, or mother more than me, is not worthy of me.'17 'Everyone that hath forsaken houses, or brethren, or sisters, or father, or mother, or wife, or children, or lands for my name's sake shall receive an hundred-fold and shall inherit everlasting life.'18 Let none of your possessions detain you, no solicitude for your family affairs, since this land which you inhabit, shut in on all sides by the sea and surrounded by mountain peaks, is too narrow for your large population; nor does it abound in wealth; and it furnishes scarcely food enough for its cultivators. Hence it is that you murder and devour one another, that you wage war, and that frequently you perish by mutual wounds. Let therefore hatred depart from among you, let your quarrels end, let wars cease, and let all dissensions and controversies slumber. Enter upon the road to the Holy Sepulchre; wrest that land from the wicked race, and subject it to yourselves. That land which, as the Scripture says, 'floweth with milk and honey'19 was given by God into the possession of the children of Israel.

Jerusalem is the navel of the world; the land is fruitful above others, like another paradise of delights. This the Redeemer of the human race has made illustrious by His advent, has beautified by His presence, has consecrated by suffering, has redeemed by death, has glorified by burial. This royal city, therefore, situated at the center of the world, is now held captive by His enemies, and is in subjection to those who do not know God, to the worship of the heathen. Therefore, she seeks and desires to be liberated and does not cease to implore you to come to her aid. From you, especially, she asks succor, because, as we have already said, God has conferred upon you, above all nations, great glory in arms. Accordingly, undertake this journey for the remission of your sins, with the assurance of the imperishable glory of the kingdom of heaven."

When Pope Urban had said these and very many similar things in his urbane discourse, he so influenced to one purpose the desires of all who were present that they cried out, "God wills it! God wills it!" When the venerable Roman pontiff heard that, with eyes uplifted to heaven he gave thanks to God and, with his hand commanding silence, said: "Most beloved brethren, to-day is manifest in you what the Lord says in the Gospel, 'Where two or three are gathered together in My name there am I in the midst of them.' Unless the Lord God had been present in your minds, all of you would not have uttered the same cry. For, although the cry issued from numerous mouths, yet the origin of the cry was one. Therefore I say to you that God, who implanted this in your breasts, has drawn it forth from you. Let this then be your battle-cry in combat, because this word is given to you by

God. When an armed attack is made upon the enemy, let this one cry be raised by all the soldiers of God: 'God wills it! God wills it!'

"And we do not command or advise that the old, or the feeble, or those unfit for bearing arms, undertake this journey; nor ought women to set out at all without their husbands, or brothers, or legal guardians. For such are more of a hindrance than aid, more of a burden than an advantage. Let the rich aid the needy; and, according to their means, let them take with them experienced soldiers. The priests and clerks of any order are not to go without the consent of their bishops; for this journey would profit them nothing if they went without such permission. Also, it is not fitting that laymen should enter upon the pilgrimage without the blessing of their priests.

Whoever, therefore, shall determine upon this holy pilgrimage and shall make his vow to God to that effect and shall offer himself to Him as a living sacrifice, holy, acceptable unto God, shall wear the sign of the cross of the Lord on his forehead, or on his breast. When, having truly fulfilled his vow, he wishes to return, let him place the cross on his back between his shoulders. Such, indeed, by two-fold action will fulfil the precept of the Lord, as He commands in the Gospel, 'He that doth not take his cross and follow after me, is not worthy of me.'"

B. THE SLAUGHTER OF JEWS

✤ From Albert of Aachen

One unfortunate subsidiary result of crusading zeal was attacks upon Jews, who were harrassed, beaten, or even killed for being descendants of those who had been responsible for crucifying Jesus, and who had been too set in their ways to embrace the one true religion of Christianity. The following episode occurred during the summer of 1096 and was part of the so-called Peasant Crusade, the first of the three phases that formed the First Crusade of 1096-1102.

(Taken from The First Crusade: The Accounts of Eye-Witnesses and Participants, by August C. Krey, Princeton University Press 1921, pp.54-5)

At the beginning of summer in the same year in which Peter and Gottschalk, after collecting an army, had set out, there assembled in like fashion a large and innumerable host of Christians from diverse kingdoms and lands; namely, from the realms of France, England, Flanders, and Lorraine. ... I know not whether by a judgment of the Lord, or by some error of mind, they rose in a spirit of cruelty against the Jewish people scattered throughout these cities and slaughtered them without mercy, especially in the Kingdom of Lorraine, asserting it to be the beginning of their expedition and their duty against the enemies of the Christian faith. This slaughter of Jews was done first by citizens of Cologne. These suddenly fell upon a small band of Jews and severely wounded and killed many; they destroyed the houses and synagogues of the Jews and divided among themselves a very large amount of money. When the Jews saw this cruelty, about two hundred in the silence of the night began flight by boat to Neuss. The pilgrims and crusaders discovered them, and after taking away all their possessions, inflicted on them similar slaughter, leaving not even one alive.

Not long after this, they started upon their journey, as they had vowed, and arrived in a great multitude at the city of Mainz. There Count Emico, a nobleman, a very mighty man in this region, was awaiting, with a large band of Teutons, the arrival of the pilgrims who were coming thither from diverse lands by the King's highway.

The Jews of this city, knowing of the slaughter of their brethren, and that they themselves could not escape the hands of so many, fled in hope of safety to Bishop Rothard. They put an infinite treasure in his guard and trust, having much faith in his protection, because he was Bishop of the city. Then that excellent Bishop of the city cautiously set aside the incredible amount of money received from them. He placed the Jews in the very spacious hall of his own house, away from the sight of Count Emico and his followers, that they might remain safe and sound in a very secure and strong place.

But Emico and the rest of his band held a council and, after sunrise, attacked the Jews in the hall with arrows and lances. Breaking the bolts and doors, they killed the Jews, about seven hundred in number, who in vain resisted the force and attack of so many thousands. They killed the women, also, and with their swords pierced tender children of whatever age and sex. The Jews, seeing that their Christian enemies were attacking them and their children, and that they were sparing no age, likewise fell upon one another, brother, children, wives, and sisters, and thus they perished at each other's hands. Horrible to say, mothers cut the throats of nursing children with knives and stabbed others, preferring them to perish thus by their own hands rather than to be killed by the weapons of the uncircumcised.

From this cruel slaughter of the Jews a few escaped; and a few because of fear, rather than because of love of the Christian faith, were baptized. With very great spoils taken from these people, Count Emico, Clarebold, Thomas, and all that intolerable company of men and women then continued on their way to Jerusalem, directing their course towards the Kingdom of Hungary, where passage along the royal highway was usually not denied the pilgrims.

C. THE CAPTURE OF JERUSALEM (JULY 15, 1099)

✢ From the *Gesta Francorum*

The so-called peasant Crusade ended in disaster with most of its participants being killed by the Turks after the former had landed in Anatolia. The second phase of this First Crusade was much better organized by several prominent leaders of Western Europe. After traveling by land to Constantinople and uniting their forces with those of Emperor Alexius to capture Nicaea in western Anatolia, the Crusaders advanced successfully across Anatolia, descended into Syria, captured Edessa in Mesopotamia, took Antioch in northern Syria, and finally descended upon Jerusalem itself, whose capture made this crusading expedition the single most successful one during the entire two centuries of the Crusades. The following account displays both the Christian piety and savagry of the crusaders.

(Taken from The First Crusade: The Accounts of Eye-Witnesses and Participants, *by August C. Krey, Princeton University Press 1921, pp.256-7)*

At length, our leaders decided to beleaguer the city with siege machines, so that we might enter and worship the Saviour at the Holy Sepulchre. They constructed wooden towers and many other siege machines. Duke Godfrey made a wooden tower and other siege devices, and Count Raymond did the same, although it was necessary to bring wood from a considerable distance. However, when the Saracens saw our men engaged in this work, they greatly strengthened the fortifications of the city and increased the height of the turrets at night. On a certain Sabbath night, the leaders, after having decided which parts of the wall were weakest, dragged the tower and the machines to the eastern side of the city. Moreover, we set up the tower at earliest dawn and equipped and covered it on the first, second, and third days of the week. The Count of St. Gilles erected his tower on the plain to the south of the city.

While all this was going on, our water supply was so limited that no one could buy enough water for one denarius to satisfy or quench his thirst. Both day and night, on the fourth and fifth days of the week, we made a determined attack on the city from all sides. However, before we made this assault on the city, the bishops and priests persuaded all, by exhorting and preaching, to honor the Lord by marching around Jerusalem in a great procession, and to prepare for battle by prayer, fasting, and almsgiving. Early on the sixth day of the week we again attacked the city on all sides, but as the assault was unsuccessful, we were all astounded and fearful. However, when the hour approached on which our Lord Jesus Christ deigned to suffer on the Cross for us, our knights began to fight bravely in one of the towers-namely, the party with Duke Godfrey and his brother, Count Eustace. One of our knights, named Lethold, clambered up the wall of the city, and no sooner had he ascended than the defenders fled from the walls and through the city. Our men followed, killing and slaying even to the Temple of Solomon, where the slaughter was so great that our men waded in blood up to their ankles.

Count Raymond brought his army and his tower up near the wall from the south, but between the tower and the wall there was a very deep ditch. Then our men took counsel how they might fill it, and had it proclaimed by heralds that anyone who carried three stones to the ditch would receive one denarius. The work of filling it required three days and three nights, and when at length the ditch was filled, they moved the tower up to the wall, but the men defending this portion of the wall fought desperately with stones and fire. When the Count heard that the Franks were already in the city, he said to his men, "Why do you loiter? Lo, the Franks are even now within the city." The Emir who commanded the Tower of St. David surrendered to the Count and opened that gate at which the pilgrims had always been accustomed to pay tribute. But this time the pilgrims entered the city, pursuing and killing the Saracens up to the Temple of Solomon, where the enemy gathered in force. The battle raged throughout the day, so that the Temple was covered with their blood. When the pagans had been overcome, our men seized great numbers, both men and women, either killing them or keeping them captive, as they wished. On the roof of the Temple a great number of pagans of both sexes had assembled, and these were taken under the protection of Tancred and Gaston of Beert. Afterward, the army scattered throughout the city and took possession of the gold and silver, the horses and mules, and the houses filled with goods of all kinds.

Later, all of our people went to the Sepulchre of our Lord, rejoicing and weeping for joy, and they rendered up the offering that they owed. In the morning, some of our men cautiously ascended to the roof of the Temple and attacked the Saracens, both men and women, beheading them with naked swords; the remainder sought death by jumping down into the temple. When Tancred heard of this, he was filled with anger.

D. ARAB PERCEPTIONS OF THE FRANKS

✤ From the Syrian Arab Usama

The Crusades not only resulted in the clash between two different cultures on the battlefield, but also their clash of their respectives cultures in peaceful settings. The following anecdotes, taken from the writings of a Syrian Arab named Usama, who lived during the late twelfth century, illustrates the interaction between Christians and Muslims in the Levant during this period.

(Taken from Arab Historians of the Crusades, by Francesco Gabrieli, [University of California Press, 1969] pp.76-80)

The ruler of Munaitira wrote to my uncle asking him to send a doctor to treat some of his followers who were ill. My uncle sent a Christian called Thabit. After only ten days he returned and we said 'You cured them quickly!' This was his story: They took me to see a knight who had an abscess on his leg, and a woman with consumption. I applied a poultice to the leg, and the abscess opened and began to heal. I prescribed a cleansing and refreshing diet for the woman. Then there appeared a Frankish doctor, who said: 'This man has no idea how to cure these people!' He turned to the knight and said: 'Which would you prefer, to live with one leg or to die with two?' When the knight replied that he would prefer to live with one leg, he sent for a strong man and a sharp axe. They arrived, and I stood by to watch. The doctor supported the leg on a block of wood, and said to the man: 'Strike a mighty blow, and cut cleanly!' And there, before my eyes, the fellow struck the knight one blow, and then another, for the first had not finished the job. The marrow spurted out of the leg, and the patient died instantaneously. Then the doctor examined the woman and said; 'She has a devil in her head who is in love with her. Cut her hair off!' This was done, and she went back to eating her usual Frankish food, garlic and mustard, which made her illness worse. 'The devil has got into her brain,' pronounced the doctor. He took a razor and cut a cross on her head, and removed the brain so that the inside of the skull was laid bare. This he rubbed with salt; the woman died instantly. At this juncture I asked whether they had any further need of me, and as they had none I came away, having learnt things about medical methods that I never knew before....

The Franks are without any vestige of a sense of honour and jealousy. If one of them goes along the street with his wife and meets a friend, this man will take the woman's hand and lead her aside to talk, while the husband stands by waiting until she has finished her conversation. If she takes too long about it he leaves her with the other man and goes on his way. Here is an example of this from my personal experience: while I was in Nablus I stayed with a man called Mu'izz, whose house served as an inn for Muslim travellers. Its windows overlooked the street. On the other side of the read hvea a Frank who sold wine for the merchants; he would take a bottle of wine from one of them and publicize it, announcing that such-and-such a merchant had just opened a hogshead of it, and could be found at such-and-such a place by anyone wishing to buy some; '... and I will give him the first right to the wine in this bottle.'

Now this man returned home one day and found a man in bed with his wife. 'What are you doing here with my wife?' he demanded. 'I was tired,' replied the man, 'and so I came in to rest.' 'And how do you come to be in my bed?' 'I found the bed made up, and lay down to sleep.' 'And this woman slept with you, I suppose?' 'The bed,' he replied, 'is hers. How could I prevent her getting into her own bed?' 'I swear if you do it again I shall take you to court!' And this was his only reaction, the height of his outburst of jealousy!

I heard a similar case from a bath attendant called Salim from Ma'arra, who worked in one of my father's bath-houses. This is his tale: I earned my living in Ma'arra by opening a bathhouse. One day a Frankish knight came in. They do not follow our custom of wearing a cloth round their waist while they are at the baths, and this fellow put out his hand, snatched off my loin-cloth and threw it away. He saw at once that I had just recently shaved my pubic hair. 'Salim!' he exclaimed. I came toward him and he pointed to that part of me. 'Salim! It's magnificent! You shall certainly do the same for me!' And he lay down flat on his back. His hair there was as long as his beard. T shaved him, and when he had felt the place with his hand and found it agreeably smooth he said: 'Salim, you must certainly do the same for my Dama.' In their language Dama means lady, or wife. He sent his valet to fetch his wife, and when they arrived and the valet had brought her in, she lay down on her back, and he said to me: 'Do to her what you did to me.' So I shaved her pubic hair, while her husband stood by watching me. Then he thanked me and paid me for my services.

You will observe a strange contradiction in their character: they are without jealousy or a sense of honour, and yet at the same time they have the courage that as a rule springs only from the sense of honour and a readiness to take offence....

There are some Franks who have settled in our land and taken to living like Muslims. These are better than those who have just arrived from their homelands, but they are the exception, and cannot be taken as typical. I came across one of them once when I sent a friend on business to Antioch, which was governed by Todros ibn as-Safi, a friend of mine. One day he said to my friend: 'A Frankish friend has invited me to visit him; come with me so that you can see how they live.' 'I went with him,' said my friend, 'and we came to the house of one of the old knights who came with the first expedition. This man had retired from the army, and was living on the income of the property he owned in Antioch. He had a fine table brought out, spread with a splendid selection of appetizing food. He saw that I was not eating, and said: 'Don't worry, please; eat what you like, for I don't eat Frankish food. I have Egyptian cooks and eat only what they serve. No pig's flesh ever comes into my house!' So I ate, although cautiously, and then we left. Another day, as I was passing through the market, a Frankish woman advanced on me, addressing me in her barbaric language with words I found incomprehensible. A crowd of Franks gathered round us and I gave myself up for lost, when suddenly this knight appeared, saw me and came up. 'What do you want with this man?' 'This man,' she replied, 'killed my brother Urso.' This Urso was a knight from Apamea who was killed by a soldier from Hamät. The old man scolded the woman. 'This man is a merchant, a city man, not a fighter, and he lives nowhere near where your brother was killed.' Then he turned on the crowd, which melted away, and shook hands with me. Thus the fact that I ate at his table saved my life....

This is an example of Frankish barbarism, God damn them! When I was in Jerusalem I used to go to the Masjid al-Aqsa, beside which is a small oratory which the Franks have made into a church. Whenever I went into the mosque, which was in the hands of Templars who were friends of mine, they would put the little oratory at my disposal, so that I could say my prayers there. One day I had gone in, said the Allah akhbar and risen to begin my prayers, when a Frank threw himself on me from behind, lifted me up and turned me so that I was facing east. 'That is the way to pray!' he said. Some Templars at once intervened, seized the man and took him out of my way, while I resumed my prayer. But the moment they stopped watching him he seized me again and forced me to face east, repeating that this was the way to pray. Again the Templars intervened and took him away. They apologized to me and said: 'He is a foreigner who has just arrived today from his homeland in the north, and he has never seen anyone pray facing any other direction than east.' 'I have finished my prayers,' I said, and left, stupefied by the fanatic who had been so perturbed and upset to see someone praying facing the Kaba!

E. THE CHILDREN'S CRUSADE

In 1212 occurred the so-called Children's Crusade, in which large numbers of children from Germany and France abandoned their homes and families and marched southward toward the Mediterranean coast. The French children descended upon the port city of Marseille, where two unscrupulous sea captains embarked them upon seven ships; and the children either died by shipwreck or were brought to Alexandria in Egypt, where they were sold into slavery. Many of the children from Germany succeeded in crossing the Alps and made their way to Genoa, Rome, or Brundisium. They seem to have thought that when they reached the Mediterranean, God would part the waters for them, and they could walk to Jerusalem, where they would regain possession of the holy city through their piety.

✍   *(Taken from Epidemics of the Middle Ages, by J. F. C. Becker, London 1859, pp.355-8)*

Chronicle of Alderic, Monk of Liege: There happened in this year an expedition of young children miraculously, as it were, assembling from all parts; they came first from the parts of the city of Vendome of the Parish [in France], who when they were about thirty thousand, came to Marseilles as wishing to go over the sea against the Saracens. But ribald and bad men joined to them, so corrupted the whole army, that, some perishing in the sea, some being put up for sale, few of so great a multitude returned, but of those who escaped thence the Pope gave a commandment, that when they should be old enough, they should go over the sea, having been marked with the cross. And the betrayers of these children are said to have been Hugh Ferreus and William Porcus, merchants of Marseilles, who being owners of ships, ought, so they promised them, to carry them over the sea for God's sake, without payment, and filled seven large ships with them, and when they had come with two days' sailing to Saint Peter's Island to the Hermit's Rock, a tempest arose and two ships perished, and all the children of those ships were drowned, and, after a time (as is said) Pope Gregory IX. founded in the same island the Church of the New Innocents, and appointed twelve prebendaries, and there are in that church the bodies of the children, which the sea threw up there, and to this day they are shown to pilgrims uncorrupted. But the betrayers succeeded in taking the other five ships to Bugia and Alexandria, and there they sold all those children to the princes of the Saracens and to merchants, from whom the Caliph bought for himself 400 all clerks, because thus he would separate them from the others, among whom were eighty all priests, and he treated them more honourably than was his wont. It is that Caliph of whom I have spoken above who studied at Paris in the dress of a clerk, and learned fully all that is known among us, and he now lately has left off sacrificing camel's flesh. The princes of the Saracens being assembled at Baldach in the same year in which the children were sold, they slew in their presence eighteen of these children by different kinds of martyrdom, because they would by no means relinquish the Christian faith, but cherished it diligently in slavery: he who said this, and was one of the above-said clerks whom the Caliph bought for himself, has faithfully reported that he has never heard that one of the above-said children apostatised from the Christian faith. And the two aforesaid betrayers, Hugh Ferreus and William Porcus, afterwards went to Mirabel, prince of the Saracens of Sicily, and wished to arrange with him the betrayal of the Emperor Frederic, but the Emperor by the grace of God triumphed over them, and hanged Mirabel with his two sons and those two traitors on one gallows, and after eighteen years he who reported this added that Mashemuch of Alexandria still kept carefully seven hundred, not now children, but men of full age.

Caffari, a contemporary Genoese statesman: But in the month of August, on the Sabbath day, on the 25th, a certain Teutonic boy, named Nicolas, entered the city of Genoa for purposes of pilgrimage, and with him a great multitude of pilgrims carrying crosses and staves, in the judgment of a working man more than 7000, men and women, boys and girls. And on the Lord's day following they departed from the city; but many men, women, boys, and girls of that number remained at Genoa.

Historical Fragment of an Unknown Author: At that time there was made a foolish expedition, young and silly persons taking the mark of the cross without any discretion, rather for curiosity than for their salvation. Persons of both sexes, boys and girls, not under age only, but also grown up, married women with virgins, set out, going with empty purses not only through all Germany, but also through parts of Gaul and Burgundy; neither could they by any means be restrained by their parents and friends, but used all efforts to join that expedition, so that everywhere in the towns and in the country they left their tools and whatever they had in hand at the time, and joined the bands as they passed by. And as for such novelties we are often a folk of easy faith, many thought that this came to pass not through lightness of mind, but by a divine inspiration and a kind of piety. For which reason they also succoured them in their expenses, furnishing food and other necessary things.

But when the clergy and some others of sounder mind spoke against it, and judged that expedition vain and useless, the lads vehemently cavilled, saying, that the clerks were unbelievers, and that they opposed this thing for envy and covetousness, rather than for truth and righteousness. But forasmuch as no affair that is commenced without the balancing of reason and without vigour of counsel, attains to a good conclusion; after this foolish multitude arrived at the parts of Italy, they were separated and scattered through the cities and towns, and many were kept by the inhabitants of the land as servants and handmaids. Others are said to have reached the sea, who were taken prisoners by the sailors and mariners, and carried to other distant parts of the earth. But the rest coming to Rome, when they saw that they could go no further, not being sustained with any authority, at last became aware that their labour was frivolous and empty: and yet they were by no means absolved from the vow of the cross, except the boys under the age of discretion, and those who were oppressed with old age. Therefore, thus deceived and perplexed, they began to return; and they who formerly used to pass through the countries in parties and troops, and never without the song of encouragement, now returning, singly and in silence, barefooted and famished, were a scoffing to all men: also many virgins were ravished, and lost the flower of their chastity.

Chronicle of Bishop Sicard of Cremona: In the same year, 1212, under the guidance of boys seemingly of twelve years, who said that they had seen a vision, and who took the sign of the cross, in the parts of Cologne, an innumerable multitude of poor people of either sex, and of boys, made pilgrimage through Germany, marked with the cross; and they came into Italy, saying with one heart and one voice, that they would cross the seas dry-shod, and recover the Holy Land of Jerusalem by the power of God. But at the end it all as it were came to nought.

F. THE FALL OF ACRE

✣ From Ludolph von Suchern

During the late 1200's the Mamluk warriors of Egypt succeeded in defending Syria from the Mongols, who had sacked and destroyed Baghdad in 1258, thereby bringing the Abbasid dynasty to an end. These same Mamluks also slowly captured all the fortified towns and cities of the crusaders. The last of these to fall was Acre, which had long served as the chief seaport for the crusaders. With its capture in 1292 the crusaders were completely expelled from the Holy Land. Many withdrew to the eastern Mediterranean islands of Cyprus and Rhodes, which for several generations thereafter served as the eastern-most outposts of Western Europe against the advance of the Ottoman Turks, who ended the Byzantine Empire in 1453 by their capture of Constantinople.

✍ *(Taken from The Crusades: A Reader, by S. J. Allen and Emilie Amt, University of Toronto Press 2003, pp.359-62)*

After having told of the glories and beauties of Acre, I will now briefly tell you of its fall and ruin, and the cause of its loss, even as I heard the tale told by right truthful men, who well remembered it. While, then, the grand doings of which I have spoken were going on in

Acre, at the instigation of the devil there arose a violent and hateful quarrel in Lombardy between the Guelphs and the Ghibellines [that is, between two factions in Italian politics], which brought all evil upon the Christians. Those Lombards who dwelt at Acre took sides in this same quarrel, especially the Pisans and Genoese, both of whom had an exceedingly strong party in Acre. These men made treaties and truces with the Saracens, to the end that they might the better fight against one another within the city. When Pope Urban [IV] heard of this, he grieved for Christendom and for the Holy Land, and sent 12,000 mercenary troops across the sea to help the Holy Land and Christendom. When these men came across the sea to Acre, they did no good, but abode by day and by night in taverns and places of ill repute, took and plundered merchants and pilgrims in the public streets, broke the treaty [with the Muslims], and did much evil.

Melot Sapheraph, sultan of Babylon, an exceedingly wise man, most potent in arms and bold in action, when he heard of this, and knew of the hateful quarrels of the people of Acre, called together his counselors and held a parliament in Babylon, wherein he complained that the truces had frequently been broken and violated, to the prejudice of himself and his people. After a debate had been held upon this matter, he gathered together a mighty host, and reached the city of Acre without any resistance, because of their quarrels with one another, cutting down and wasting all the vineyards and fruit trees and all the gardens and orchards, which are most lovely thereabout When the master of the Templars, a very wise and brave knight, saw this, he feared that the fall of the city was at hand, because of the quarrels of the citizens. He took counsel with his brethren about how peace could be restored, and then went out to meet the sultan, who was his own very especial friend, to ask him whether they could by any means repair the broken truce. He obtained these terms from the sultan, to wit, that because of his love for the sultan and the honor in which the sultan held him, the broken truce might be restored by every man in Acre paying one Venetian penny. So the master of the Templars was glad, and, departing from the sultan, called together all the people and preached a sermon to them in the Church of St. Cross, setting forth how, by his prayers, he had prevailed upon the sultan to grant that the broken treaty might be restored by a payment of one Venetian penny by each man, that therewith everything might be settled and quieted. He advised them by all means to do so, declaring that the quarrels of the citizens might bring a worse evil upon the city than this-as indeed they did. But when the people heard this, they cried out with one voice that he was the betrayer of the city, and was guilty of death. The master, when he heard this, left the church, hardly escaped alive from the hands of the people, and took back their answer to the sultan.

When the sultan heard this, knowing that, owing to the quarrels of the people, none of them would make any resistance, he pitched his tents, set up sixty [siege] machines, dug many mines beneath the city walls, and for forty days and nights, without any respite, assailed the city with fire, stones, and arrows, so that [the air] seemed to be stiff with arrows. I have heard a very honorable knight say that a lance which he was about to hurl from a tower among the Saracens was all notched with arrows before it left his hand. There were at that time in the Sultans army 600,000 armed men, divided into three companies; so that 100,000 continually besieged the city, and when they were weary another 100,000 took their place .., [and] 200,000 stood before the gates of the city ready for battle, and the duty of the remaining 200,000 was to supply them with everything that they needed. The gates were never closed, nor was there an hour of the day without some hard fight being fought against the Saracens by the Templars or other brethren dwelling therein, But the numbers of the Saracens grew so fast that after 100,000 of them had been slain, 200,000 came back. Yet, even against all this host, they would not have lost the city had they but helped one another faithfully; but when they were fighting outside the city, one party would run away and leave the other to be slain, while within the city one party would not defend the castle or palace belonging to the other, but purposely let the other party's castles, palaces, and strong places be stormed and taken by the enemy, and each one knew and believed his own castle and place to be so strong that he cared not for any other's castle or strong place. During this confusion the masters and brethren of the [military] orders alone defended themselves, and fought unceasingly against the Saracens, until they were nearly all slain; indeed, the master and brethren of the house of the Teutonic Order, together with their followers and friends, all fell dead at one and the same time.

As this went on with many battles and thousands slain on either side, at last the fulfillment of their sins and the time of the fall of the city drew near, when the fortieth day of its siege was come, in the year of our Lord 1292, on the twelfth day of the month of May, the most noble and glorious city of Acre, the flower, chief and pride of all the cities of the East, was taken The [Frankish] people of the other cities, to wit, Jaffa, Tyre, Sidon and Ascalon, when they heard this, left all their property behind and fled to Cyprus. When first the Saracens took Acre, they got in through a breach in the wall near the king of Jerusalem's castle; and when they were among the people of the city within, one party still would not help the other, but each defended his own castle and palace, and the Saracens had a much longer siege, and fought at much less advantage when they were within the city than when they were outside: for it was wondrously fortified.

Nevertheless, more than 100,000 men escaped to Cyprus. I have heard from a most honorable lord, and from other truthful men who were present, that more than 500 most noble ladies and maidens, the daughters of kings and princes, came down to the seashore, when the city was about to fall, carrying with them all their jewels and ornaments of gold and precious stones, of priceless value, in their bosoms, and cried aloud, [asking] whether there were any sailor there who would take all their jewels, and take whichever of them he chose to wife, if only he would take them, even naked, to some safe land or island. A sailor received them all into his ship, took them across to Cyprus, with all their goods, for nothing, and went his way But who he was, whence he came, or -whither he went, no man knows to this day. Very many other noble ladies and damsels were drowned or slain. It would take long to tell what grief and anguish was there.

While the Saracens were within the city, but before they had taken it, fighting from castle to castle, from one palace and strong place to another, so many men perished on either side that they walked over their corpses as it were over a bridge. When all the inner city was lost, all who still remained alive fled into the exceedingly strong castle of the Templars, which was immediately besieged on all sides by the Saracens; yet the Christians bravely defended it for two months, and before it almost all the nobles and chiefs of the sultan's army fell dead: for when the city inside the walls was burned, yet the towers of the city, and the Templars' castle, which was in the city, remained, and with these the people of the city kept the Saracens within the city from getting out, as before they had hindered their coming in, until of all the Saracens who had entered the city not one remained alive, but all fell by fire or by the sword. When the Saracen nobles saw the others lying dead, and themselves unable to escape from the city, they fled for refuge into the mines which they had dug under the great tower, that they might make their way through the wall and so get out. But the Templars and others who were in the castle, seeing that they could not hurt the Saracens with stones and the like, because of the mines wherein they were, undermined the great tower of the castle, and flung it down upon the mines and the Saracens therein, and all perished alike.

When the other Saracens outside the city saw that they had thus, as it were, failed utterly, they treacherously made a truce with the Templars and Christians on the condition that they should yield up the castle, taking all their goods with them, and should destroy it, but should rebuild the city on certain terms, and dwell therein in peace as before. The Templars and Christians, believing this, gave up the castle and marched out of it, and came down from the city towers. When the Saracens had by this means got possession both of the castle and of the city towers, they slew all the Christians alike, and led away the captives to Babylon. Thus Acre has remained empty and deserted even to this day ... When the glorious city of Acre thus fell, all the eastern people sang of its fall in hymns of lamentation, such as they are wont to sing over the tombs of their dead, bewailing the beauty, the grandeur, and the glory of Acre even to this day.

CHARTER OF THE LIBERTIES OF LORRIS

One of the most important phenomena during the High Middle Ages (1050-1350) was the growth of towns and cities, resulting from population growth and increased demand for manufactured goods. These towns and cities fostered the development of free-market capitalism and the formation of a new middle class situated between the serfs and the landed nobility. Since towns proved to be far more profitable than Medieval manors, kings often issued charters permitting towns to form on their land, so that the kings could impose taxes and fees upon various activities and thereby accumulate greater wealth. The following charter exhibits many standard features of royal grants authorizing the creation of towns during this period. This document was issued by King Louis VII of France in 1155, to establish the town of Lorris, to define the King's share in the town's commerce, and to specify what duties and rights the town's inhabitants enjoyed. Item 18 was a standard provision of such charters and allowed persons (primarily serfs) to take up residence in Lorris and to become a free member of the community if within the space of one full year no one attempted to assert feudal claims upon him. Thus, these Medieval towns became important vehicles by which serfs could escape their manors and gain their freedom in order to have the chance to pursue new economic opportunities.

(Taken from pp.312-5 of Volume III of The History of Civilization from the Fall of the Roman Empire to the French Revolution, by F. Guizot, translated by William Hazlitt [London 1875])

1. Let whoever shall have a house in the parish of Lorris pay a quitrent of six deniers only for his house, and each acre of land which he shall have in this parish; and if he make such an acquisition, let that be the quitrent of his house.

2. Let no inhabitant of the parish of Lorris pay a duty of entry nor any tax for his food, and let him not pay any duty of measurement for the corn which his labor, or that of the animals which he may have shall procure him, and let him pay no duty for the wine which he shall get from his vines.

3. Let none of them go on a [military] expedition on foot or horseback, whence he cannot return home the same day if he desire to do so.

4. Let none of them pay toll to ttampes or Orleans, or to Milly, which is in GAtinais, or to Melun.

5. Let no one who has property in the parish of Lorris lose any of it for any misdeed whatsoever, unless the said misdeed be committed against us or any of our guests.

6. Let no one going to the fairs or markets of Lorris, or in returning, be stopped or inconvenienced unless he shall have committed some misdeed that same day; and let no one on a fair or market day at Lorris, seize the bail given by his security; unless the bail be given the same day.

7. Let forfeitures of sixty sous be reduced to five, that of five sous to twelve deniers, and the provost's fee in cases of plaint, to four deniers.

8. Let no man of Lorris be forced to go out of it to plead before the lord king.

9. Let no one, neither us nor any other, take any tax, offering, or exaction from the men of Lorris.

10. Let no one sell wine at Lorris with public notice, except the king, who shall sell his wine in his cellar with that notice.

11. We will have at Lorris, for our service and that of the queen, a credit of a full fortnight, in the articles of provisions; and if any inhabitant have received a gage from the lord king, he shall not be bound to keep it more than eight days, unless he please.

12. If any have had a quarrel with another, but without breaking a closed house, and if it be accommodated without plaint brought before the provost, no fine shall be due, on this account, to us or to our provost; and if there has been a plaint they can still come to an agreement when they shall have paid the fine. And if any one bear plaint against another, and there has been no fine awarded against either one to the other, they shall not, on that account, owe anything to us or our provost.

13. If any one owe an oath to another, let the latter have permission to remit it.

14. If any men of Lorris have rashly given their pledge of a duel, and if with the consent of the provost they accommodate it before the pledges have been given, let each pay two sous and a half; and if the pledges have been given, let each pay seven sous and a half; and if the duel has been between men having the right of fighting in the list, then let the hostages of the conquered pay one hundred and twelve sous.

15. Let no man of Lorris do forced work for us, unless it be twice a year to take our wine to Orleans, and nowhere else; and those only shall do this work who shall have horses and carts, and they shall be informed Of it beforehand; and they shall receive no lodging from us. The laborers also shall bring wood for our kitchen.

16. No one shall be detained in prison if he can furnish bail for his appearance in court.

17. Whoever desires to sell his property may do so; and having received the price, he may leave the town, free and unmolested, if he please so to do, unless he has committed any misdeed in the town.

18. Whoever shall have remained a year and a day in the parish of Lorris without any claim having pursued him thither, and without the right having been interdicted him, whether by us or our provost, he shall remain there free and tranquil.

19. No one shall plead against another unless it be to recover, and ensure the observance of, what is his due.

20. When the men of Lorris shall go to Orleans with merchandise, they shall pay, upon leaving the town, one denier for their cart, when they go not for the sake of the fair; and when they go for the sake of the fair and the market, they shall pay, upon leaving Orleans, four deniers for each cart, and on entering, two deniers.

21. At marriages in Lorris, the public crier shall have no fee, nor he who keeps watch.

22. No cultivator of the parish of Lorris, cultivating his land with the plow, shall give, in the time of harvest more than one hermine [six bushels] of rye to all the serjeants of Lorris.

23. If any knight or serjeant find, in our forests, horses or other animals belonging to the men of Lorris, he must not take them to any other than to the provost of Lorris; and if any animal of the parish of Lorris be put to flight by bulls, or assailed by flies, have entered our forest, or leaped our banks, the owner of the animal shall owe no fine to the provost, if he can swear that the animal has entered in spite of his keeper. But if the animal entered with the knowledge of his keeper, the owner shall pay twelve deniers, and as much for each animal, if there be more than one.

24. There shall be at Lorris no duty paid for using the oven.

25. There shall be at Lorris no watch rate.

26. All men of Lorris who shall take salt or wine to Orleans, shall pay only one denier for each cart.

27. No men of Lorris shall owe any fine to the provost of Ptampes, nor to the provost of Pithiviers nor to any in GAtinais.

28. None among them shall pay the entry dues in Ferri&es, nor in Chateau-Landon, nor in Puiseaux, nor in Nibelle.

29. Let the men of Lorris take the dead wood in the forest for their own use.

30. Whosoever, in the market of Lorris, shall have bought or sold anything, and shall have forgotten to pay the duty, may pay it within eight days without being troubled, if he can swear that he did not withhold the right wittingly.

31. No man of Lorris having a house or a vineyard, or a meadow, or a field, or any buildings in the domain of St. Benedict, shall be under the jurisdiction of the abbot of St. Benedict or his serjeant, unless it be with regard to the quit-rent in kind, to which he is bound; and, in that case, he shall not go out of Lorris to be judged.

32. If any of the men of Lorris be accused of anything, and the accuser cannot prove it by witness, he shall clear himself by a single oath from the assertion of his accuser.

33. No man of this parish shall pay any duty because of what he shall buy or sell for his use on the territory of the precincts, nor for what he shall buy on Wednesday at the market.

34. These customs are granted to the men of Lorris, and they are common to the men who inhabit Courpalais, Chanteloup, and the bailiwick of Harpard.

35. We order that whenever the provost shall be changed in the town, he shall swear faithfully to observe these customs; and the same shall be done by new serjeants when they shall be instituted.

Given at Orleans in the year of our Lord 1155.

Boccaccio on the Black Death

Giovanni Boccaccio (1313-1375), a native of Florence, was one of the leading literary figures in the early years of the Italian Renaissance. His most famous literary work, *The Decameron*, was a large collection of tales revealing the full range of human behavior during Boccaccio's day. The work was not written in Latin, the universal language of scholarship at that time, but in Italian. It therefore represents one of the earliest and finest examples of so-called vernacular literature that arose in Western Europe as the High Middle Ages came to an end and gave way to the Renaissance.

Although *The Decameron* is a work of fiction, Boccaccio places it in a historical setting: the first major outbreak of the bubonic plague (or black death) in Florence in the year 1348, which Boccaccio describes in horrific detail in his preface to the work. During the two or three years in which this epidemic devastated Western Europe (1348-1350) approximately one-third of the entire human population died. This sudden enormous loss of life halted the population growth that had characterized the High Middle Ages, thus forming a profound chronological boundary between the High Middle Ages and the Renaissance.

(Taken from the translation of M. Rigg, Boccaccio: The Decameron, London 1921, Vol. I pp. 5-11)

I say, then, that the years of the beatific incarnation of the Son of God had reached the tale of one thousand three hundred and forty eight, when in the illustrious city of Florence, the fairest of all the cities of Italy, there made its appearance that deadly pestilence, which, whether disseminated by the influence of the celestial bodies, or sent upon us mortals by God in His just wrath by way of retribution for our iniquities, had had its origin some years before in the East, whence, after destroying an innumerable multitude of living beings, it had propagated itself without respite from place to place, and so calamitously, had spread into the West.

In Florence, despite all that human wisdom and forethought could devise to avert it, as the cleansing of the city from many impurities by officials appointed for the purpose, the refusal of entrance to all sick folk, and the adoption of many precautions for the preservation of health; despite also humble supplications addressed to God, and often repeated both in public procession and otherwise by the devout; towards the beginning of the spring of the said year the doleful effects of the pestilence began to be horribly apparent by symptoms that shewed as if miraculous.

Not such were they as in the East, where an issue of blood from the nose was a manifest sign of inevitable death; but in men and women alike it first betrayed itself by the emergence of certain tumors in the groin or the armpits, some of which grew as large as a common apple, others as an egg, some more, some less, which the common folk called gavoccioli. From the two said parts of the body this deadly gavocciolo soon began to propagate and spread itself in all directions indifferently; after which the form of the malady began to change, black spots or livid making their appearance in many cases on the arm or the thigh or elsewhere, now few and large, then minute and numerous. And as the gavocciolo had been and still were an infallible token of approaching death, such also were these spots on whomsoever they shewed themselves. Which maladies seemed set entirely at naught both the art of the physician and the virtue of physic; indeed, whether it was that the disorder was of a nature to defy such treatment, or that the physicians were at fault - besides the qualified there was now a multitude both of men and of women who practiced without having received the slightest tincture of medical science - and, being in ignorance of its source, failed to apply the proper remedies; in either case, not merely were those that covered few, but almost all within three days from the appearance of the said symptoms, sooner or later, died, and in most cases without any fever or other attendant malady.

Moreover, the virulence of the pest was the greater by reason that the intercourse was apt to convey it from the sick to the whole, just as fire devours things dry or greasy when they are brought close to it, the evil went yet further, for not merely by speech or association with the sick was the malady communicated to the healthy with consequent peril of common death; but any that touched the clothes of the sick or aught else that had been touched, or used by these seemed thereby to contract the disease.

So marvelous sounds that which I have now to relate, that, had not many, and I among them, observed it with their own eyes, I had hardly dared to credit it, much less to set it down in writing, though I had had it from the lips of a credible witness.

I say, then, that such was the energy of the contagion of the said pestilence, that it was not merely propagated from man to mail, but, what is much more startling, it was frequently observed, that things which had belonged to one sick or dead of the disease, if touched by some other living creature, not of the human species, were the occasion, not merely of sickening, but of an almost instantaneous death. Whereof my own eyes (as I said a little before) had cognisance, one day among others, by the following experience. The rags of a poor man who had died of the disease being strewn about the open street, two hogs came thither, and after, as is their wont, no little trifling with their snouts, took the rags between their teeth and tossed them to and fro about their chaps; whereupon, almost immediately, they gave a few turns, and fell down dead, as if by poison, upon the rags which in an evil hour they had disturbed.

In which circumstances, not to speak of many others of a similar or even graver complexion, diverse apprehensions and imaginations were engendered in the minds of such as were left alive, inclining almost all of them to the same harsh resolution, to wit, to shun and abhor all contact with the sick and all that belonged to them, thinking thereby to make each his own health secure. Among whom there were those who thought that to live temperately and avoid all excess would count for much as a preservative against seizures of this kind. Wherefore they banded together, and dissociating themselves from all others, formed communities in houses where there were no sick, and lived a separate and secluded life, which they regulated with the utmost care, avoiding every kind of luxury, but eating and drinking moderately of the most delicate viands and the finest wines, holding converse with none but one another, lest tidings of sickness or death should reach them, and diverting their minds with music and such other delights as they could devise. Others, the bias of whose minds was in the opposite direction, maintained, that to drink freely, frequent places of public resort, and take their pleasure with song and revel, sparing to satisfy no appetite, and to laugh and mock at no event, was the sovereign remedy for so great an evil: and that which they affirmed they also put in practice, so far as they were able, resorting day and night, now to this tavern, now to that, drinking with an entire disregard of rule or measure, and by preference making the houses of others, as it were, their inns, if they but saw in them aught that was particularly to their taste or liking; which they, were readily able to do, because the owners, seeing death imminent, had become as reckless of their property as of their lives; so that most of the houses were open to all comers, and no distinction was observed between the stranger who presented himself and the rightful lord. Thus, adhering ever to their inhuman determination to shun the sick, as far as possible, they ordered their life. In this extremity of our city's suffering and tribulation the venerable authority of laws, human and divine, was abased and all but totally dissolved for lack of those who should have administered and enforced them, most of whom, like the rest of the citizens, were either dead or sick or so hard bested for servants that they were unable to execute any office; whereby every man was free to do what was right in his own eyes.

Not a few there were who belonged to neither of the two said parties, but kept a middle course between them, neither laying the same restraint upon their diet as the former, nor allowing themselves the same license in drinking and other dissipations as the latter, but living with a degree of freedom sufficient to satisfy their appetite and not as recluses. They therefore walked abroad, carrying in the hands flowers or fragrant herbs or diverse sorts of spices, which they frequently raised to their noses, deeming it an excellent thing thus to comfort the brain with such perfumes, because the air seemed to be everywhere laden and reeking with the stench emitted by the dead and the dying, and the odours of drugs.

Some again, the most sound, perhaps, in judgment, as they were also the most harsh in temper, of all, affirmed that there was no medicine for the disease superior or equal in efficacy to flight; following which prescription a multitude of men and women, negligent of all but themselves, deserted their city, their houses, their estates, their kinsfolk, their goods, and went into voluntary exile, or migrated to the country parts, as if God in visiting men with this pestilence in requital of their iniquities would not pursue them with His wrath wherever they might be, but intended the destruction of such alone as remained within the circuit of the walls of the city; or deeming perchance, that it was now time for all to flee from it, and that its last hour was come.

Of the adherents of these diverse opinions not all died, neither did all escape; but rather there were, of each sort and in every place many that sickened, and by those who retained their health were treated after the example which they themselves, while whole, had set, being everywhere left to languish in almost total neglect. Tedious were it to recount, how citizen avoided citizen, how among neighbors was scarce found any that shewed fellow-feeling for another, how kinsfolk held aloof, and never met, or but rarely; enough that this sore affliction entered so deep into the minds of men and women, that in the horror thereof brother was forsaken by brother nephew by uncle, brother by sister, and oftentimes husband by wife: nay, what is more, and scarcely to be believed, fathers and mothers were found to abandon their own children, untended, unvisited, to their fate, as if they had been strangers. Wherefore the sick of both sexes, whose number could not be estimated, were left without resource but in the charity of friends (and few such there were), or the interest of servants, who were hardly to be had at high rates and on unseemly terms, and being, moreover, one and all, men and women of gross understanding, and for the most part unused to such offices, concerned themselves no further than to supply the immediate and expressed wants of the sick, and to watch them die; in which service they themselves not seldom perished with their gains. In consequence of which dearth of servants and dereliction of the sick by neighbors, kinsfolk and friends, it came to pass-a thing, perhaps, never before heard of-that no woman, however dainty, fair or well-born she might be, shrank, when stricken with the disease, from the ministrations of a man, no matter whether he were young or no, or scrupled to expose to him every part of her body, with no more shame than if he had been a woman, submitting of necessity to that which her malady required; wherefrom, perchance, there resulted in after time some loss of modesty in such as recovered. Besides which many succumbed, who with proper attendance, would, perhaps, have escaped death; so that, what with the virulence of the plague and the lack of due attendance of the sick, the multitude of the deaths, that daily and nightly took place in the city, was such that those who heard the tale-not to say witnessed the fact-were struck dumb with amazement. Whereby, practices contrary to the former habits of the citizens could hardly fail to grow up among the survivors.

It had been, as to-day it still is, the custom for the women that were neighbors and of kin to the deceased to gather in his house with the women that were most closely connected with him, to wail with them in common, while on the other hand his male kinsfolk and neighbors, with not a few of the other citizens, and a due proportion of the clergy according to his quality, assembled without, in front of the house, to receive the corpse; and so the dead man was borne on the shoulders of his peers, with funeral pomp of taper and dirge, to the church selected by him before his death. Which rites, as the pestilence waxed in fury, were either in whole or in great part disused, and gave way to others of a novel order. For not only did no crowd of women surround the bed of the dying, but many passed from this life unregarded, and few indeed were they to whom were accorded the lamentations and bitter tears of sorrowing relations; nay, for the most part, their place was taken by the laugh, the jest, the festal gathering; observances which the women, domestic piety in large measure set aside, had adopted with very great advantage to their health. Few also there were whose bodies were attended to the church by more than ten or twelve of their neighbors, and those not the honorable and respected citizens; but a sort of corpse-carriers drawn from the baser ranks, who called themselves becchini and performed such offices for hire, would shoulder the bier, and with hurried steps carry it, not to the church of the dead man's choice, but to that which was nearest at hand, with four or six priests in front and a candle or two, or, perhaps, none; nor did the priests distress themselves with too long and solemn an office, but with the aid of the becchini hastily consigned the corpse to the first tomb which they found untenanted. The condition of the lower, and, perhaps, in great measure of the middle ranks, of the people shewed even worse and more deplorable; for, deluded by hope or constrained by poverty, they stayed in their quarters, in their houses where they sickened by thousands a day, and, being without service or help of any kind, were, so to speak, irredeemably devoted to the death which overtook them. Many died daily or nightly in the public streets; of many others, who died at home, the departure was hardly observed by their neighbors, until the stench of their putrefying bodies carried the tidings; and what with their corpses and the corpses of others who died on every hand, the whole place was a sepulchre.

It was the common practice of most of the neighbors, moved no less by fear of contamination by the putrefying bodies than by charity towards the deceased, to drag the corpses out of the houses with their own hands, aided, perhaps, by a porter, if a porter was to be had, and to lay them in front of the doors, where any one who made the round might have seen, especially in the morning, more of them than he could count; afterwards they would have biers brought up or in default, planks, whereon they laid them. Nor was it once twice only that one and the same bier carried two or three corpses at once; but quite a considerable number of such cases occurred, one bier sufficing for husband and wife, two or three brothers, father and son, and so forth. And times without number it happened, that as two priests, bearing the cross, were on their way to perform the last office for some one, three or four biers were brought up by the porters in rear of them, so that, whereas the priests supposed that they had but one corpse to bury, they discovered that there were six or eight, or sometimes more. Nor, for all their number, were their obsequies honored by either tears or lights or crowds of mourners rather, it was come to this, that a dead man was then of no more account than a dead goat would be to-day.

POETRY FROM MEDIEVAL UNIVERSITIES

Although young men arrived at the various Medieval universities prepared to study well defined disciplines and to earn their degrees, their book learning equipped them with literary talents that some used to express their non-academic experiences, thoughts, and feelings all too typical of the human condition. In addition, despite the fact that they lived in a thoroughly Christian environment, their poetry is full of allusions to Greek and Roman divinities and mythological figures in order to express the students' enjoyment of the pleasures of this world.

(Taken from Wine, Women, and Song: Mediaeval Latin Students' Songs, by John Addington Symonds [London 1884])

A. FLORA

Rudely blows the winter blast,
Withered leaves are falling fast,
Cold hath hushed the birds at last.
　While the heavens were warm and glowing,
　　Nature's offspring loved in May;
　But man's heart no debt is owing
　　To such change of month or day
　　As the dumb brute-beasts obey.
Oh, the joys of this possessing!
How unspeakable the blessing
　That my Flora yields to-day!

Labour long I did not rue,
Ere I won my wages due,
And the prize I played for drew.
　Flora with her brows of laughter,
　　Gazing on me, breathing bliss,

Draws my yearning spirit after,
 Sucks my soul forth in a kiss:
 Where's the pastime matched with this?
Oh, the joys of this possessing!
How unspeakable the blessing
 Of my Flora's loveliness!

Truly mine is no harsh doom,
While in this secluded room
Venus lights for me the gloom!
 Flora faultless as a blossom
  Bares her smooth limbs for mine eyes;
 Softly shines her virgin bosom,
  And the breasts that gently rise
  Like the hills of Paradise.
Oh, the joys of this possessing!
How unspeakable the blessing
 When my Flora is the prize!

From her tender breasts decline,
In a gradual curving line,
Flanks like swansdown white and fine.
 On her skin the touch discerneth
  Naught of rough; 'tis soft as snow:
 'Neath the waist her belly turneth
  Unto fulness, where below
  In Love's garden lilies blow.
Oh, the joys of this possessing!
How unspeakable the blessing!
 Sweetest sweets from Flora flow!

Ah! should Jove but find my fair,
He would fall in love, I swear,
And to his old tricks repair:
 In a cloud of gold descending
  As on Danae's brazen tower,
 Or the sturdy bull's back bending,
  Or would veil his godhood's power
  In a swan's form for one hour.
Oh, the joys of this possessing!
How unspeakable the blessing!
 How divine my Flora's flower!

B. THE CONFESSION OF GOLIAS

Boiling in my spirit's veins
 With fierce indignation,
From my bitterness of soul
 Springs self-revelation:
Framed am I of flimsy stuff,
 Fit for levitation,

Like a thin leaf which the wind
  Scatters from its station.

While it is the wise man's part
  With deliberation
On a rock to base his heart's
  Permanent foundation,
With a running river I
  Find my just equation,
Which beneath the self-same sky
  Hath no habitation.

Carried am I like a ship
  Left without a sailor,
Like a bird that through the air
  Flies where tempests hale her;
Chains and fetters hold me not,
  Naught avails a jailer;
Still I find my fellows out,
  Toper, gamester, railer.

To my mind all gravity
  Is a grave subjection;
Sweeter far than honey are
  Jokes and free affection.
All that Venus bids me do,
  Do I with erection,
For she ne'er in heart of man
  Dwelt with dull dejection.

Down the broad road do I run,
  As the way of youth is;
Snare myself in sin, and ne'er
  Think where faith and truth is;
Eager far for pleasure more
  Than soul's health, the sooth is,
For this flesh of mine I care,
  Seek not ruth where ruth is.

Prelate, most discreet of priests,
  Grant me absolution!
Dear's the death whereof I die,
  Sweet my dissolution;
For my heart is wounded by
  Beauty's soft suffusion;
All the girls I come not nigh,
  Mine are in illusion.

'Tis most arduous to make
  Nature's self surrender;

Seeing girls, to blush and be
  Purity's defender!
We young men our longings ne'er
  Shall to stern law render,
Or preserve our fancies from
  Bodies smooth and tender.

Who, when into fire he falls,
  Keeps himself from burning?
Who within Pavia's walls
  Fame of chaste is earning?
Venus with her finger calls
  Youths at every turning,
Snares them with her eyes, and thralls
  With her amorous yearning.

If you brought Hippolitus
  To Pavia Sunday,
He'd not be Hippolitus
  On the following Monday;
Venus there keeps holiday
  Every day as one day;
'Mid these towers in no tower dwells
  Venus Verecunda.

In the second place I own
  To the vice of gaming:
Cold indeed outside I seem,
  Yet my soul is flaming:
But when once the dice-box hath
  Stripped me to my shaming,
Make I songs and verses fit
  For the world's acclaiming.

In the third place, I will speak
  Of the tavern's pleasure;
For I never found nor find
  There the least displeasure;
Nor shall find it till I greet
  Angels without measure,
Singing requiems for the souls
  In eternal leisure.

In the public-house to die
  Is my resolution;
Let wine to my lips be nigh
  At life's dissolution:
That will make the angels cry,
  With glad elocution,
"Grant this toper, God on high,
  Grace and absolution!"

With the cup the soul lights up,
  Inspirations flicker;
Nectar lifts the soul on high
  With its heavenly ichor:
To my lips a sounder taste
  Hath the tavern's liquor
Than the wine a village clerk
  Waters for the vicar.

Nature gives to every man
  Some gift serviceable;
Write I never could nor can
  Hungry at the table;
Fasting, any stripling to
  Vanquish me is able;
Hunger, thirst, I liken to
  Death that ends the fable.

Nature gives to every man
  Gifts as she is willing;
I compose my verses when
  Good wine I am swilling,
Wine the best for jolly guest
  Jolly hosts are filling;
From such wine rare fancies fine
  Flow like dews distilling.

Such my verse is wont to be
  As the wine I swallow;
No ripe thoughts enliven me
  While my stomach's hollow;
Hungry wits on hungry lips
  Like a shadow follow,
But when once I'm in my cups,
  I can beat Apollo.

Never to my spirit yet
  Flew poetic vision
Until first my belly had
  Plentiful provision;
Let but Bacchus in the brain
  Take a strong position,
Then comes Phoebus flowing in
  With a fine precision.

There are poets, worthy men,
  Shrink from public places,
And in lurking-hole or den
  Hide their pallid faces;
There they study, sweat, and woo
  Pallas and the Graces,

But bring nothing forth to view
  Worth the girls' embraces.

Fasting, thirsting, toil the bards,
  Swift years flying o'er them;
Shun the strife of open life,
  Tumults of the forum;
They, to sing some deathless thing,
  Lest the world ignore them,
Die the death, expend their breath,
  Drowned in dull decorum.

Lo! my frailties I've betrayed,
  Shown you every token,
Told you what your servitors
  Have against me spoken;
But of those men each and all
  Leave their sins unspoken,
Though they play, enjoy to-day,
  Scorn their pledges broken.

Now within the audience-room
  Of this blessed prelate,
Sent to hunt out vice, and from
  Hearts of men expel it;
Let him rise, nor spare the bard,
  Cast at him a pellet;
He whose heart knows not crime's smart,
  Show my sin and tell it!

I have uttered openly
  All I knew that shamed me,
And have spued the poison forth
  That so long defamed me;
Of my old ways I repent,
  New life hath reclaimed me;
God beholds the heart—'twas man
  Viewed the face and blamed me.

Goodness now hath won my love,
  I am wroth with vices;
Made a new man in my mind,
  Lo, my soul arises!
Like a babe new milk I drink—
  Milk for me suffices,
Lest my heart should longer be
  Filled with vain devices.

Thou Elect of fair Cologne,
  Listen to my pleading!

Spurn not thou the penitent;
  See, his heart is bleeding!
Give me penance! what is due
  For my faults exceeding
I will bear with willing cheer,
  All thy precepts heeding.

Lo, the lion, king of beasts,
  Spares the meek and lowly;
Toward submissive creatures he
  Tames his anger wholly.
Do the like, ye powers of earth,
  Temporal and holy!
Bitterness is more than's right
  When 'tis bitter solely.

HELOISE AND ABELARD

The intellectual reawakening of Western Europe is perhaps best exemplified by the establishment of numerous universities during the High Middle Ages. One of the greatest thinkers of the early twelfth century was Peter Abelard (1079-1142), who taught philosophy at the cathedral of Notre Dame in Paris. The following passage is taken from Abelard's autobiographical work entitled *Story of My Misfortunes*. Besides telling the story of Abelard's career as a well-respected and famous teacher of Medieval philosophy, the work has as its central theme the powerful love affair between himself and a much younger female student named Heloise. On the one hand, the narrative illustrates the age-old theme of the power of passion that always has and always will bring members of the opposite sex together. On the other hand, the story illustrates how such powerful passions affected people's personal lives in the cultural context of Medieval society.

(Taken from Story of My Misfortunes, by Peter Abelard, translated by Henry Adams Bello, MacMillan [New York] 1922)

At the very outset of my work there [Paris], I set about completing the glosses on Ezekiel which I had begun at Laon. These proved so satisfactory to all who read them that they came to believe me no less adept in lecturing on theology than I had proved myself to be in the field of philosophy. Thus my school was notably increased in size by reason of my lectures on subjects of both these kinds, and the amount of financial profit as well as glory which it brought me cannot be concealed from you, for the matter was widely talked of. But prosperity always puffs up the foolish, and worldly comfort enervates the soul, rendering it an easy prey to carnal temptations. Thus I, who by this time had come to regard myself as the only philosopher remaining in the whole world, and had ceased to fear any further disturbance of my peace, began to loosen the rein on my desires, although hitherto I had always lived in the utmost continence. And the greater progress I made in my lecturing on philosophy or theology, the more I departed alike from the practice of the philosophers and the spirit of the divines in the uncleanness of my life. For it is well known, methinks, that philosophers, and still more those who have devoted their lives to arousing the love of sacred study, have been strong above all else in the beauty of chastity. Thus did it come to pass that while I was utterly absorbed in pride and sensuality, divine grace, the cure for both diseases, was forced upon me, even though I, forsooth, would fain have shunned it. First was I punished for my sensuality, and then for my pride. For my sensuality I lost those things whereby I practiced it; for my pride, engendered in me by my knowledge of letters ù and it is even as the Apostle said: "Knowledge puffeth itself up."

(I Corinthians viii, I) ù I knew the humiliation of seeing burned the very book in which I most gloried. And now it is my desire that you should know the stories of these two happenings, understanding them more truly from learning the very facts than from hearing what is spoken of them, and in the order in which they came about.

Because I had ever held in abhorrence the foulness of prostitutes, because I had diligently kept myself from all excesses and from association with the women of noble birth who attended the school, because I knew so little of the common talk of ordinary people, perverse and subtly flattering chance gave birth to an occasion for casting me lightly down from the heights of my own exaltation. Nay, in such case not even divine goodness could redeem one who, having been so proud, was brought to such shame, were it not for the blessed gift of grace.

Now there dwelt in that same city of Paris a certain young girl named Heloise, the niece of a canon who was called Fulbert. Her uncle's love for her was equalled only by his desire that she should have the best education which he could possibly procure for her. Of no mean beauty, she stood out above all by reason of her abundant knowledge of letters. Now this virtue is rare among women, and for that very reason it doubly graced the maiden, and made her the most worthy of renown in the entire kingdom.

It was this young girl whom I, after carefully considering all those qualities which are wont to attract lovers, determined to unite with myself in the bonds of love, and indeed the thing seemed to me very easy to be done. So distinguished was my name, and I possessed such advantages of youth and comeliness, that no matter what woman I might favour with my love, I dreaded rejection of none. Then, too, I believed that I could win the maiden's consent all the more easily by reason of her knowledge of letters and her zeal therefor; so, even if we were parted, we might yet be together in thought with the aid of written messages. Perchance, too, we might be able to write more boldly than we could speak, and thus at all times could we live in joyful intimacy. Thus, utterly aflame with my passion for this maiden, I sought to discover means whereby I might have daily and familiar speech with her, thereby the more easily to win her consent.

For this purpose I persuaded the girl's uncle, with the aid of some of his friends, to take me into his household ù for he dwelt hard by my school ù in return for the payment of a small sum. My pretext for this was that the care of my own household was a serious handicap to my studies, and likewise burdened me with an expense far greater than I could afford. Now, he was a man keen in avarice, and likewise he was most desirous for his niece that her study of letters should ever go forward, so, for these reasons, I easily won his consent to the fulfillment of my wish, for he was fairly agape for my money, and at the same time believed that his niece would vastly benefit by my teaching. More even than this, by his own earnest entreaties he fell in with my desires beyond anything I had dared to hope, opening the way for my love; for he entrusted her wholly to my guidance, begging me to give her instruction whensoever I might be free from the duties of my school, no matter whether by day or night, and to punish her sternly if ever I should find her negligent of her tasks. In all this the man's simplicity was nothing short of astounding to me; I should not have been more smitten with wonder if he had entrusted a tender lamb to the care of a ravenous wolf.

When he had thus given her into my charge, not alone to be taught but even to be disciplined, what had he done save to give free scope to my desires, and to offer me every opportunity, even if I had not sought it, to bend her to my will with threats and blows if I failed to do so with caresses? There were, however, two things which particularly served to allay any foul suspicion: his own love for his niece, and my former reputation for continence. Why should I say more? We were united first in the dwelling that sheltered our love, and then in the hearts that burned with it. Under the pretext of study we spent our hours in the happiness of love, and learning held out to us the secret opportunities that our passion craved. Our speech was more of love than of the books which lay open before us; our kisses far outnumbered our reasoned words. Our hands sought less the book than each other's bosoms; love drew our eyes together far more than the lesson drew them to the pages of our text. In order that there might be no suspicion, there were, indeed, sometimes blows, but love gave them, not anger; they were the marks, not of wrath, but of a tenderness surpassing the most fragrant balm in sweetness. What followed? No degree in love's progress was left untried by our passion, and if love itself could imagine any wonder as yet unknown, we discovered it. And our inexperience of such delights made us all the more ardent in our pursuit of them, so that our thirst for one another was still unquenched.

In measure as this passionate rapture absorbed me more and more, I devoted less time to philosophy and to the work of the school. Indeed it became loathsome to me to go to the school or to linger there; the labour, moreover, was very burdensome, since my nights were vigils of love and my days of study. My lecturing became utterly careless and lukewarm; I did nothing because of inspiration, but everything merely as a matter of habit. I had become nothing more than a reciter of my former discoveries, and though I still wrote poems, they dealt with love, not with the secrets of philosophy. Of these songs you yourself well know how some have become widely known and have been sung in many lands, chiefly, methinks, by those who delighted in the things of this world. As for the sorrow, the groans, the lamentations of my students when they perceived the preoccupation, nay, rather the chaos, of my mind, it is hard even to imagine them.

A thing so manifest could deceive only a few, no one, methinks, save him whose shame it chiefly bespoke, the girl's uncle, Fulbert. The truth was often enough hinted to him, and by many persons, but he could not believe it, partly, as I have said, by reason of his boundless love for his niece, and partly because of the well-known continence of my previous life. Indeed we do not easily suspect shame in those whom we most cherish, nor can there be the blot of foul suspicion on devoted love. Of this St. Jerome in his epistle to Sabinianus (Epist. 48) says: "We are wont to be the last to know the evils of our own households, and to be ignorant of the sins of our children and our wives, though our neighbours sing them aloud." But no matter how slow a matter may be in disclosing itself, it is sure to come forth at last, nor is it easy to hide from one what is known to all. So, after the lapse of several months, did it happen with us. Oh, how great was the uncle's grief when he learned the truth, and how bitter was the sorrow of the lovers when we were forced to part! With what shame was I overwhelmed, with what contrition smitten because of the blow which had fallen on her I loved, and what a tempest of misery burst over her by reason of my disgrace! Each grieved most, not for himself, but for the other. Each sought to allay, not his own sufferings, but those of the one he loved. The very sundering of our bodies served but to link our souls closer together; the plentitude of the love which was denied to us inflamed us more than ever. Once the first wildness of shame had passed, it left us more shameless than before, and as shame died within us the cause of it seemed to us ever more desirable. And so it chanced with us as, in the stories that the poets tell, it once happened with Mars and Venus when they were caught together.

It was not long after this that Heloise found that she was pregnant, and of this she wrote to me in the utmost exultation, at the same time asking me to consider what had best be done. Accordingly, on a night when her uncle was absent, we carried out the plan we had determined on, and I stole her secretly away from her uncle's house, sending her without delay to my own country. She remained there with my sister until she gave birth to a son, whom she named Astrolabe. Meanwhile her uncle, after his return, was almost mad with grief; only one who had then seen him could rightly guess the burning agony of his sorrow and the bitterness of his shame. What steps to take against me, or what snares to set for me, he did not know. If he should kill me or do me some bodily hurt, he feared greatly lest his dear-loved niece should be made to suffer for it among my kinsfolk. He had no power to seize me and imprison me somewhere against my will, though I make no doubt he would have done so quickly enough had he been able or dared, for I had taken measures to guard against any such attempt.

At length, however, in pity for his boundless grief, and bitterly blaming myself for the suffering which my love had brought upon him through the baseness of the deception I had practiced, I went to him to entreat his forgiveness, promising to make an amends that he himself might decree. I pointed out that what had happened could not seem incredible to any one who had ever felt the power of love, or who remembered how, from the very beginning of the human race, women had cast down even the noblest men to utter ruin. And in order to make amends even beyond his extremest hope, I offered to marry her whom I had seduced, provided only the thing could be kept secret, so that I might suffer no loss of reputation thereby. To this he gladly assented, pledging his own faith and that of his kindred, and sealing with kisses the pact which I had sought of him ù and all this that he might the more easily betray me.

Forthwith I repaired to my own country, and brought back thence my mistress, that I might make her my wife. She, however, most violently disapproved of this, and for two chief reasons: the danger thereof, and the disgrace which it would bring upon me. She swore that her uncle would never be appeased by such satisfaction as this, as, indeed, afterwards proved only too true. She asked how she could ever glory in me if she should make me thus inglorious, and should shame herself along with me. What penalties, she said, would the world rightly demand of her if she should rob it of so shining a light! What curses would follow such a loss to the Church, what tears among the philosophers would result from such a marriage! How unfitting, how lamentable it would be for me, whom nature had made for the whole world, to devote myself to one woman solely, and to subject myself to such humiliation! She vehemently rejected this marriage, which she felt would be in every way ignominious and burdensome to me. Besides dwelling thus on the disgrace to me, she reminded me of the hardships of married life, to the avoidance of which the Apostle exhorts us, saying: "Art thou loosed from a wife ? seek not a wife. But and if thou marry, thou hast not sinned; and if a virgin marry, she hath not sinned. Nevertheless such shall have trouble in the flesh: but I spare you" (I Corinthians vii, 27). And again: "But I would have you to be free from cares" (I Corinthians vii, 32). But if I would heed neither the counsel of the Apostle nor the exhortations of the saints regarding this heavy yoke of matrimony, she bade me at least consider the advice of the philosophers, and weigh carefully what had been written on this subject either by them or concerning their lives. Even the saints themselves have often and earnestly spoken on this subject for the purpose of warning us. Thus St. Jerome, in his first book against Jovinianus, makes Theophrastus set forth in great detail the intolerable annoyances and the endless disturbances of married life, demonstrating with the most convincing arguments that no wise man should ever have a wife, and concluding his reasons for this philosophic exhortation with these words: "Who among Christians would not be overwhelmed by such arguments as these advanced by Theophrastus?"

Now, she added, if laymen and gentiles, bound by no profession of religion, lived after this fashion, what ought you, a cleric and a canon, to do in order not to prefer base voluptuousness to your sacred duties, to prevent this Charybdis from sucking you down headlong, and to save yourself from being plunged shamelessly and irrevocably into such filth as this? If you care nothing for your privileges as a cleric, at least uphold your dignity as a philosopher. If you scorn the reverence due to God, let regard for your reputation temper your shamelessness. Remember that Socrates was chained to a wife, and by what a filthy accident he himself paid for this blot on philosophy, in order that others thereafter might be made more cautious by his example. Jerome thus mentions this affair, writing about Socrates in his first book against Jovinianus: "Once when he was withstanding a storm of reproaches which Xantippe was hurling at him from an upper story, he was suddenly drenched with foul slops; wiping his head, he said only, æI knew there would be a shower after all that thunder.'" Her final argument was that it would be dangerous for me to take her back to Paris, and that it would be far sweeter for her to be called my mistress than to be known as my wife; nay, too, that this would be more honourable for me as well. In such case, she said, love alone would hold me to her, and the strength of the marriage chain would not constrain us. Even if we should by chance be parted from time to time, the joy of our meetings would be all the sweeter by reason of its rarity.

But when she found that she could not convince me or dissuade me from my folly by these and like arguments, and because she could not bear to offend me, with grievous sighs and tears she made an end of her resistance, saying: "Then there is no more left but this, that in our doom the sorrow yet to come shall be no less than the love we two have already known." Nor in this, as now the whole world knows, did she lack the spirit of prophecy. So, after our little son was born, we left him in my sister's care, and secretly returned to Paris. A few days later, in the early morning, having kept our nocturnal vigil of prayer unknown to all in a certain church, we were united there in the benediction of wedlock her uncle and a few friends of his and mine being present. We departed forthwith stealthily and by separate ways, nor thereafter did we see each other save rarely and in private, thus striving our utmost to conceal what we had done.

But her uncle and those of his household, seeking solace for their disgrace, began to divulge the story of our marriage, and thereby to violate the pledge they had given me on this point. Heloise, on the contrary, denounced her own kin and swore that they were speaking the most absolute lies. Her uncle, aroused to fury thereby, visited her repeatedly with punishments. No sooner had I learned this than I sent her to a convent of nuns at Argenteuil, not far from Paris, where she herself had been brought up and educated as a young girl. I had them make ready for her all the garments of a nun, suitable for the life of a convent, excepting only the veil, and these I bade her put on.

When her uncle and his kinsmen heard of this, they were convinced that now I had completely played them false and had rid myself forever of Heloise by forcing her to become a nun. Violently incensed, they laid a plot against me, and one night while I all unsuspecting was asleep in a secret room in my lodgings, they broke in with the help of one of my servants whom they had bribed. There they had vengeance on me with a most cruel and most shameful punishment, such as astounded the whole world; for they cut off those parts of my body with which I had done that which was the cause of their sorrow. This done, straightway they fled, but two of them were captured and suffered the loss of their eyes and their genital organs. One of these two was the aforesaid servant, who even while he was still in my service, had been led by his avarice to betray me.

V

Renaissance & Reformation

Introduction

By 1400 Western Europe was poised to embark upon one of the most culturally creative periods of history: the Renaissance, meaning "rebirth." It was characterized by the rediscovery and new appreciation of the civic traditions, literature, and art of the ancient Greeks and Romans. During the fifteenth century there flourished numerous, highly talented artists who revolutionized painting and sculpture through their realistic style. The intellectual vigor of this period also eventually resulted in the questioning of the authority of the Roman Catholic Church and its traditional beliefs and practices, thus producing the Protestant Reformation that shattered the religious unity of Western Europe. The wars of religious intolerance that arose from this religious diversity ultimately led to the notion of religious toleration in the Western tradition. In addition, European technological innovation, especially in the area of ship construction and navigation, enabled Europeans to sail across the Atlantic and to circumnavigate Africa, thereby resulting in the discovery of North and South America, the establishment of trade routes all around the globe, and the European expansion into all these regions. ✢

Pico on the Dignity of Man

One of the most characteristic features of the Italian Renaissance was its glorification of the individual human being for all that he could achieve. The following passage is perhaps the most eloquent and forceful statements of this idea. It was expressed by Giovanni Pico, Count of Mirandola in northern Italy. In addition, this text with its numerous references to a wide range of writers and writings reflect the great learning and scholarship that also characterized the renaissance. Pico composed this text in 1486 when he was twenty-three years old, and it was intended to be part of an oration delivered at the beginning of a debate in Rome in which Pico was prepared to defend the validity of 900 propositions derived from Pico's own study. Thus, Pico himself represents a fine example of the individualism intellectual endeavors of the renaissance.

 (Taken from the translation of Mary Martin McLaughlin in The Portable Renaissance Reader, by James Bruce Ross and Mary Martin McLaughlin, [Viking Press 1953] pp.476-9)

Oration on the Dignity of Man

I HAVE READ, reverend Fathers, in the works of the Arabs, that when Abdala the Saracen was asked what he regarded as most to be wondered at on the world's stage, so to speak, he answered that there was nothing to be seen more wonderful than man. To this opinion may be added the saying of Hermes [Trismegistus]: "A great miracle, Asclepius, is man." But when thought about the reason for these statements, I was not satisfied by the many remarkable qualities which were advanced as arguments by many menthat man is the intermediary between creatures, the intimate of higher beings and the king of lower beings, the interpreter of nature by the sharpness of his senses, by the questing curiosity of his reason, and by the light of his intelligence, the interval between enduring eternity and the flow of time, and, as the Persians say, the nuptial bond of the world, and by David's testimony, a little lower than the angels. Great indeed as these attributes are, they are not the principal ones, those, that is, which may rightfully claim the privilege of the highest admiration. For why should we not admire the angels themselves and the most blessed choirs of heaven more?

At last I seem to have understood why man is the most fortunate creature and thus worthy of all admiration, and what precisely is the place allotted to him in the universal chain, a place to be envied not only by the beasts, but also by the stars, and the Intelligences beyond this world. It is an incredible and wonderful thing. And why not? For this is the very reason why man is rightly called and considered a great miracle and a truly marvellous creature. But hear what this place is, Fathers, and courteously grant me the favour of listening with friendly ears.

Now the Highest Father, God the Architect, according to the laws of His secret wisdom, built this house of the world, this world which we see, the most sacred temple of His divinity. He adorned the region beyond the heavens with Intelligences, He animated the celestial spheres with eternal souls, and He filled the excrementary and filthy parts of the lower world with a multitude of animals of all kinds. But when His work Was finished, the Artisan longed for someone to reflect in the plan of so great a creation, to love its beauty, and to admire its magnitude. When, therefore, everything was completed, as Moses and the Timaeus [of Plato] testify, He began at last to consider the creation of man. But among His archetypes there was none from which He could form a new offspring, nor in His treasure houses Was there any inheritance which He might bestow upon His new son, nor in the tribunal seats of the whole World was there a place where this contemplator of the universe might sit. All was now filled out; everything had been apportioned to the highest, the middle, and the lowest orders. But it was not in keeping with the Paternal power to fail, as though exhausted, in the last act of creation; it was not in keeping with His wisdom to waver in a matter of necessity through lack of a design; it was not in keeping with His beneficent love that the creature who was to praise the divine liberality with regard to others should be forced to condemn it with respect to himself.

Finally the Great Artisan ordained that man, to whom He could give nothing belonging only to himself, should share in Common whatever properties had been peculiar to each,of the other creatures. He received man, therefore, as a creature of undetermined nature, and placing him in the middle of the universe, said this to him: "Neither an established place, nor a form belonging to you alone, nor any special function have We given to you, O Adam, and for this reason, that you may have and possess according to your desire and judgment, whatever place, whatever form, and whatever functions you shall desire. The nature of other creatures, which has been determined, is confined within the bounds prescribed by Us. You, who are confined by no limits, shall determine for yourself your own nature, in accordance with your own free will, in whose hand I have placed you. I have set you at the centre of the world, so that from there you ulay more easily survey whatever is in the world. We have made you neither heavenly nor earthly, neither mortal nor immortal, so that, more freely and more honourably' the moulder and maker of yourself, you may fashion yourself in whatever form you shall prefer. You shall be able to descend among the lower forms of being' which are brute beasts; you shall be able to be reborn out of the judgment of your own soul into the higher beings, which are divine."

O sublime generosity of God the Father! O highest and most wonderful felicity of man! To him it Was granted to have what he chooses. At the moment when they are born, beasts bring with them from their mother's womb, as Lucilius says, whatever they shall possess. From the beginning or soon afterwards, the highest spiritual beings have been what they are to be for all eternity. When man came into life, the Father endowed him with all kinds of seeds and with the germs of every way of life. Whatever seeds each man cultivates will grow and bear fruit in him. If these seeds are vegetative, he will be like a plant; if they are sensitive, he will become like the beasts; if they are rational, he will become like a heavenly creature; if intellectual, he will be an angel and a son of God. And if, content with the lot of no created being, he withdraws into the centre of his own oneness, his spirit, made one with God in the solitary darkness of the Father, which is above all things, will surpass all things. Who then will not wonder at this chameleon of ours, or who could wonder more greatly at anything else? For it was man who, on the ground of his mutability and of his ability to transform his own nature, was said by Asclepius of Athens to be symbolized by Prometheus in the mysteries.

Reading 39

Vasari's Lives of the Famous Artists

V asari's *Lives of the Famous Artists* is a vast storehouse of valuable information on the art and intellectual achievements of the Italian Renaissance. Below are excerpts from his biographies of Filippo Brunelleschi and Leonardo da Vinci. These passages present fascinating illustrations of how these two men used their extraordinary powers of observation, reasoning, and mechanical skill to advance architecture and painting.

(Taken from the translation of E. L. Seeley)

A. EXCERPTS FROM FILIPPO BRUNELLESCHI

they [Brunelleschi and Donatello] determined to set out together from Florence and to spend some years in Rome, that Filippo might study architecture and Donatello sculpture. And when he came to Rome, and saw the grandeur of the buildings and the perfection of the form of the temples, he remained lost in thought and like one out of his mind; and he and Donatello set themselves to measure them and to draw out the plan of them, sparing neither time nor expense. And Filippo gave himself up to the study of them, so that he cared neither to eat or to sleep, having two great ideas in his mind, the one to restore the knowledge of good architecture, hoping thus to leave behind no less a memory of himself than Cimabue and Giotto had done, and the other to find a way, if it were possible, of raising the cupola of S. Maria del Fiore in Florence, the difficulty of which was so great that since the death of Arnolfo Lapi none had had courage enough to attempt it. He confided his intention neither to Donatello or any soul living, but gave himself no rest until he had considered all the difficulties of the Pantheon and had noted and drawn all the ancient vaulted roofs, continually studying this matter, and if by chance they found any pieces of capitals or columns they set to work and had them dug out. And the story ran through Rome that they were " treasure seekers," the people thinking that they studied divination to find treasures, it having befallen them once to find an ancient pitcher filled with medals.

Then money becoming scarce with Filippo, he set himself to work for the goldsmiths, and remained thus alone in Rome when Donatello returned to Florence. Neither did he cease from his studies, until he had drawn every kind of building, temples round and square and eight-sided, basilicas, aqueducts, baths, arches, and others, and the different orders, Doric, Ionic, and Corinthian, until he was able to see in imagination Rome as she was before she fell into ruins.

In the year 1407 he returned to Florence, and the same year there was held a meeting of architects and engineers to consider how to raise the cupola of S. Maria del Fiore. Among them came Filippo, and gave it as his opinion that it should not be done according to the design of Arnolfo, but in another fashion, of which he made a model. Some months after, Filippo being one morning in the Piazza of S. Maria del Fiore with Donatello and other artists, talking about ancient sculpture, Donatello began telling them how when he was returning from Rome he had journeyed by Orvieto to see the famous marble facade of the cathedral, and afterwards passing through Cortona went into the church there and found a most beautiful piece of ancient sculpture, which was then a rare thing, for they had not then disinterred such an abundance as they have in our times. So Donatello, going on to describe the manner of the work and its perfection and excellence, kindled such an ardent desire in Filippo to see it that, without saying where he was going, he set out on foot in his mantle and hood and sandals, and was carried to Cortona by the love he bore to art. The sculpture pleasing him much, he made a drawing of it with the pen, and returned to Florence before Donatello or any one else had discovered that he was gone. And when he showed him the careful drawing he had made, Donatello marvelled greatly at his love for art.

The other architects meanwhile being dismayed at the difficulties in raising the cupola, the masters of the works in S. Maria and the consuls of the Guild of the Woollen Merchants assembled together, and sent to pray Filippo to come to them. And he being come, they laid before him the difficulties small and great which the architects felt who were also present. And Filippo answered them, "Sirs, there is no doubt that in great undertakings you have always to encounter great difficulties, and in this one of yours there are greater than you perhaps imagine, for I do not think that even the ancients ever raised such a vaulted roof as this will be. And I, having considered it much, have never been able to come to any conclusion, the width as well as the height of the building dismaying me. But remembering that it is a temple consecrated to God and the Virgin, I believe that the wisdom and skill of any one who undertook it would not be allowed to fail, and if it were my affair I would resolutely set myself to find out a way. But if you resolve upon doing it you must take counsel not alone of me, who am not sufficient to give counsel in so great a matter, but summon to Florence upon a fixed day within a year's time architects, not only Tuscan and Italian but German and French, and those of every nation, and lay before them this matter, that having been discussed and decided by so many masters, it may be entrusted to him who has the best judgment and knows the best way."

And this counsel pleased them well, and they desired that he also would consider the matter and make a model for it. But he made believe not to care about the matter, and took his leave of them to return to Rome. And they, seeing that their prayers availed not to stop him, made many of his friends implore him also; and when he would not be moved, the members of the council voted him an offering of money. But he, keeping firm to his resolution, left Florence and returned to Rome, where he applied himself to continual study of the matter, thinking, as was true, that none but he could accomplish it.

So the Florentine merchants who dwell in France and England and Spain were commanded to obtain from the princes of those lands, without sparing expense, the most skilled and gifted men in those regions. And when the year 1420 was come, there were assembled in Florence all these masters from other lands and those of Tuscany, and the skilled artificers of Florence itself, and Filippo returned from Rome. And they came together in S. Maria del Fiore, with the consuls and members of the guild, and some ingenious men chosen from among the citizens, that the minds of all might be known, and the manner of raising the dome decided upon.

So one by one each architect was called upon to give his opinion and describe the way in which it should be done. And it was a fine thing to hear the strange and diverse opinions in the matter. For 'some proposed that it should be built of sponge-stone that the weight might be less, and many agreed that it would be best to put a pillar in the middle, while there were not wanting those who suggested that they should fill the space with earth, mixing money with it, and when the dome was built give leave to every one to take the money, by which means the earth would be cleared away without expense. Filippo alone declared that he could make a vaulted roof without much wood, without pillars or supports, and with little expense of arches. It seemed to all who heard him that what he had said was foolish, and they mocked him and laughed at him, saying he was speaking like a madman. Then Filippo, being offended, said, "Though you laugh at me, you will find out that it can be done in no other manner." And as he grew warm in explaining his ideas, they doubted him the more, and held him to be a mere chattering fool. And when they had bidden him depart several times and he would not go, he was carried out by force, all supposing him to be mad. And this was how it came about that Filippo used to say afterwards that he dared not at that time pass along any part of the city lest it should be said, "There goes that madman." So the consuls in the assembly were left altogether confused with the difficult methods proposed by the other masters, and Filippo's plan, which seemed to them foolish.

And on his part Filippo was many times tempted to leave Florence ; but desiring to conquer, he had to arm himself with patience. He might have shown a little model that he had made, but he would not, knowing how little the consuls understood the matter, and aware of the jealousy of the artists, and the unstable character of the citizens, who favoured now one, now another. And I do not marvel at this, for in that city every one professes to know as much as skilled masters themselves, although there are few who really understand such things. So Filippo, not having succeeded at the assembly, began to treat with them separately, talking now to this consul, now to that member of the guild, and to some of the citizens, showing them part of his design. And so, having been moved by his arguments, they met again and disputed of the matter. The other architects desired that Filippo would tell all his mind and show his model. This he would not do, but made a proposal that the building of the cupola should be given to him who could make an egg stand firmly on the smooth marble, for by doing this he would show his skill. And an egg being brought, all the masters tried to make it stand upright, but none found the way. And when they bade Filippo set it up, he took it, and striking it on the marble made it stand. And the architects murmured, saying that they could have done that ; but Filippo replied laughing that they could have built the cupola, too, if they had seen his model and designs. So it was resolved that the charge of the work should be entrusted to him.

But while he was making ready to begin to build, some began to say that such a work as this ought not to be entrusted to one only, as too great a burden for one to bear alone. And Lorenzo Ghiberti, having obtained great credit by his gates of S. Giovanni, and being beloved by certain who had power with the Government, he was joined with Filippo in this work. What was Filippo's bitter despair when he heard of this may be imagined from his desiring to leave Florence; and had it not been for Donatello and Luca della Robbia, who comforted him, he would have gone out of his mind. He set to work with little will, knowing that he should have all the trouble and yet be obliged to share the honour and fame with Lorenzo.

In this state of torment they went on working together until the end of 1426, when they had raised the walls twelve braccia [24 feet], and it was time to begin works of wood and stone to strengthen it, which, being a difficult thing, he consulted Lorenzo to see whether he had considered this difficulty, and he was so barren of suggestions that he only replied that he would leave it to him. The answer pleased Filippo, for he thought he had found a way of driving him from the work. One morning, therefore, he did not come to the place, but took to his bed, and lay groaning and causing hot cloths to be brought him constantly, pretending to be ill. So the masons, having waited for his orders in vain, went to Lorenzo, and asked what they were to do. But he replied that it was for Filippo to order, and they must wait for him. And one asked him, "Do you not know his mind?" and Lorenzo answered, "Yes, but I will do nothing without him." And this he said to excuse himself, for he had never seen Filippo's model.

But when this had lasted two days, the chief masons went to Filippo to ask what they were to do. And he answered, "You have Lorenzo, let him do a little." So there arose great murmuring among the men, some saying that Lorenzo was good at taking his salary, but not at giving orders. Then the wardens of S. Maria went to see Filippo, and after having condoled with him on his sickness, told him how it had brought all the building into confusion. But he answered with passionate words, "Is not he there Lorenzo?" And they answered, "He will do nothing without you." "I could do very well without him," said Filippo.

But seeing that Lorenzo was willing to take his salary without any work for it, he thought of another way of bringing him to scorn; so, returning to his work, he made proposition to the wardens, Lorenzo being present, that as they had divided the salary so they should divide the work. "There are now two difficulties to be overcome, the one the matter of the scaffolding to bear the men, and the other the chain-work to bind the building together. Let Lorenzo take which he will, and I will do the other, that no time may be lost." Lorenzo, being forced in honour not to refuse, chose the chain-work, trusting to the advice of the masons, and remembering that there was something like it in S. Giovanni. So they set to work, and Filippo's scaffolds were made so that the men could work as if they were on firm ground. Lorenzo with great difficulty made the chain-work on one of the eight faces, and when it was finished the wardens took Filippo to see it, but he said nothing. But to his friends he said that it ought to be secured in another way to that, and that it was not sufficient for the weight to be put upon it. And his words being heard, they called upon him to show how the thing ought to be done. So he brought out his models and designs, and they saw into what an error they had fallen in favouring Lorenzo. Then they made Filippo sole head and manager of the building, and commanded that none should work thereon but with his consent. Lorenzo, although vanquished and shamed, was so favoured by his friends that he was allowed to go on drawing his salary, having proved that they could not legally withdraw it for three years.

So the works went forward, but the masons, being urged on by Filippo more than they were used to, began to grow weary, and joining together in a body, they said it was hard work and perilous, and they would not go on without great pay, although they had more than was usual. Thereupon Filippo and those who had the management of the works, being displeased, took counsel together, and resolved on the Saturday evening to dismiss them all. And on the Monday following Filippo set ten Lombards to the work, and being constantly with them, saying, "Do this here, and do that there," he taught them in a day so much that for many weeks they were able to carry on the works. The masons, on the other hand, seeing themselves dismissed and their work taken from them, and finding no other work so profitable, sent men to intercede for them with Filippo. But for many days he kept them in suspense, and then received them at lower wages than they had received before.

The building had now proceeded so far that it was a long way for any one to climb, and much time was lost in going down to dinner and to drink, for they suffered much from thirst in the heat of the day. So Filippo ordered that eating-houses should be opened in the cupola, where wine should be sold, and that no one should leave his work till the evening, which was a great convenience to them and profit to the work. Although he had now overcome envy and was everywhere praised, he could not prevent all the architects in Florence, after they had seen his model, from producing others; even a lady of the Gaddi family venturing to compete with him. He, however, laughed at them all, and some of them having introduced in their models parts of Filippo's work, he remarked one day when looking at them, "The next model will be all mine." His own was infinitely praised, but because people could not see the staircase leading up to the ball, they said it was defective. So some of those presiding over the work came to him concerning the matter, and Filippo, raising a little piece of wood in his model, showed them the staircase in one of the piers, formed like a pipe, with bars of bronze on one side by which one could climb up. He did not live to see the lantern finished, but he left orders in his will that it should be done as it was in his model, otherwise he protested the building would fall....

Filippo at his death was greatly lamented by other artists, especially by those who were poor, whom he often assisted. So having lived as a Christian should, he left behind him a fragrant memory of his goodness and his great talents.

B. EXCERPTS FROM LEONARDO DA VINCI

There is a story that Ser Piero [Leonardo's father], being at his country house, was asked by one of the country people to get a round piece of wood, which he had cut from a fig-tree, painted for him in Florence, which he very willingly undertook to do, as the man was skilled in catching birds and fishing, and was very serviceable to Ser Piero in these sports. So having it brought to Florence without telling Leonardo where it came from, he asked him to paint something upon it. Leonardo, finding it crooked and rough, straightened it by means of fire, and gave it to a turner that it might be made smooth and even. Then having prepared it for painting, he began to think what he could paint upon it that would frighten every one that saw it, having the effect of the head of Medusa. So he brought for this purpose to his room, which no one entered but himself, lizards, grasshoppers, serpents, butterflies, locusts, bats, and other strange animals of the kind, and from them all he produced a great animal so horrible and fearful that it seemed to poison the air with its fiery breath. This he represented coming out of some dark broken rocks, with venom issuing from its open jaws, fire from its eyes, and smoke from its nostrils, a monstrous and horrible thing indeed. And he suffered much in doing it, for the smell in the room of these dead animals was very bad, though Leonardo did not feel it from the love he bore to art. When the work was finished, Leonardo told his father that he could send for it when he liked. And Ser Piero going one morning to the room for it, when he knocked at the door, Leonardo opened it, and telling him to wait a little, turned back into the room, placed the picture in the light, and arranged the window so as to darken the room a little, and then brought him in to see it. Ser Piero at the first sight started back, not perceiving that the creature that he saw was painted, and was turning to go, when Leonardo stopped him saying, "The work answers the purpose for which it was made. Take it then, for that was the effect I wanted to produce." The thing seemed marvellous to Ser Piero, and he praised greatly Leonardo's whimsical idea. And secretly buying from a merchant another circular piece of wood, painted with a heart pierced with a dart, he gave it to the countryman, who remained grateful to him as long as he lived. But Leonardo's Ser Piero sold to some merchants in Florence for a hundred ducats, and it soon came into the hands of the Duke of Milan, who bought it of them for three hundred ducats.

When Giovan Galeazzo, Duke of Milan, was dead, and Lodovico Sforza became duke in the year 1494, Leonardo was brought to Milan to play the lute before him, in which he greatly delighted. Leonardo brought an instrument which he had made himself, a new and strange thing made mostly of silver, in the form of a horse's head, that the tube might be larger and the sound more sonorous, by which he surpassed all the other musicians who were assembled there. Besides, he was the best improvisatore of his time. The duke, hearing his marvellous discourse, became enamoured of his talents to an incredible degree, and prayed him to paint an altar-piece of the Nativity, which he sent to the emperor.

He also painted in Milan for the friars of S. Domenic, at S. Maria delle Grazie, a Last Supper, a thing most beautiful and marvellous. He gave to the heads of the apostles great majesty and beauty, but left that of Christ imperfect, not thinking it possible to give that celestial divinity which is required for the representation of Christ. The work, finished after this sort, has always been held by the Milanese in the greatest veneration, and by strangers also, because Leonardo imagined, and has succeeded in expressing, the desire that has entered the minds of the apostles to know who is betraying their Master. So in the face of each one may be seen love, fear, indignation, or grief at not being able to understand the meaning of Christ; and this excites no less astonishment than the obstinate hatred and treachery to be seen in Judas. Besides this, every lesser part of the work shows an incredible diligence; even in the table-cloth the weaver's work is imitated in a way that could not be better in the thing itself.

It is said that the prior of the place was very importunate in urging Leonardo to finish the work, it seeming strange to him to see Leonardo standing half a day lost in thought; and he would have liked him never to have put down his pencil, as if it were a work like digging the garden. And this not being enough, he complained to the duke, and was so hot about it that he was constrained to send for Leonardo and urge him to the work. Leonardo, knowing the prince to be acute and intelligent, was ready to discuss the matter with him, which he would not do with the prior. He reasoned about art, and showed him that men of genius may be working when they seem to be doing the least, working out inventions in their minds, and forming those perfect ideas which afterwards they express with their hands. He added that he still had two heads to do ; that of Christ, which he would not seek for in the world, and which he could not hope that his imagination would be able to conceive of such beauty and celestial grace as was fit for the incarnate divinity. Besides this, that of Judas was wanting, which he was considering, not thinking himself capable of imagining a form to express the face of him who after receiving so many benefits had a soul so evil that he was resolved to betray his Lord and the creator of the world; but this second he was looking for, and if he could find no better there was always the head of this importunate and foolish prior. This moved the duke marvellously to laughter, and he said he was a thousand times right. So the poor prior, quite confused, left off urging him and left him alone, and Leonardo finished Judas's head, which is a true portrait of treachery and cruelty. But that of Christ, as we have said, he left imperfect.

The excellence of this picture, both in composition and incomparable finish of execution, made the King of France desire to carry it into his kingdom, and he tried every way to find architects who could bring it safely, not considering the expense, so much he desired to have it. But as it was painted on the wall his Majesty could not have his will, and it remained with the Milanese.

In the refectory, and while he was working at the Last Supper, he painted Lodovico with his eldest son, Massimiliano, and on the other side the Duchess Beatrice with Francesco her other son, both afterwards Dukes of Milan. While he was employed upon this work he proposed to the duke that he should make a bronze equestrian statue of marvellous size to perpetuate the memory of the Duke (Francesco Sforza). He began it, but made the model of such a size that it could never be completed. There are some who say that Leonardo began it so large because he did not mean to finish it, as with many of his other things. But in truth his mind, being so surpassingly great, was often brought to a stand because it was too venturesome, and the cause of his leaving so many things imperfect was his search for excellence after excellence, and perfection after perfection. And those who saw the clay model that Leonardo made, said they had never seen anything more beautiful or more superb, and this was in existence until the French came to Milan with Louis, King of France, when they broke it to pieces. There was also a small model in wax, which is lost, which was considered perfect, and a book of the anatomy of the horse which he made in his studies.

Afterwards with greater care he gave himself to the study of human anatomy, aided by, and in his turn aiding, that Messer Marc Antonio della Torre who was one of the first to shed light upon anatomy, which up to that time had been lost in the shades of ignorance. In this he was much helped by Leonardo, who made a book with drawings in red chalk, outlined with a pen, of the bones and muscles which he had dissected with his own hand. There are also some writings of Leonardo written backward with the left hand, treating of painting and methods of drawing and colouring.

In his time the King of France came to Milan, and Leonardo was entreated to make something strange for his reception, upon which he constructed a lion, which advanced some steps and then opened his breast and showed it full of lilies. Having returned to Florence, he found that the Servite monks had entrusted Filippino with the work of painting an altar-piece; but when Filippino heard that Leonardo had said he should have liked such a piece of work, like the courteous man he was he left off working at it, and the friars brought Leonardo to their convent that he might paint it, providing both for himself and his household. For a long time, however, he did nothing, but at last he made a cartoon of our Lady with S. Anne and the infant Christ, which not only astonished all artists, but when it was finished, for two days his room was filled with men and women, young and old, going as to a solemn festival to see Leonardo's marvels. This cartoon afterwards went to France. But he gave up the work for the friars, who recalled Filippino, but he was surprised by death before he could finish it.

Leonardo undertook to paint for Francesco del Giocondo a portrait of Mona Lisa his wife, but having spent four years upon it, left it unfinished. This work now belongs to King Francis of France, and whoever wishes to see how art can imitate nature may learn from this head. Mona Lisa being most beautiful, he used, while he was painting her, to have men to sing and play to her and buffoons to amuse her, to take away that look of melancholy which is so often seen in portraits ; and in this of Leonardo's there is a peaceful smile more divine than human.

BENVENUTO CELLINI

Nothing expresses the robust and rough-and-tumble spirit of the Italian Renaissance and its artists than does the autobiography of Benvenuto Cellini. He was born in 1500 in Florence and became a highly talented goldsmith. Toward the end of his life he composed an autobiography that has rightly attracted attention ever since its publication. By tracing Cellini's travels from place to place (Florence, Pisa, Rome, Siena, Mantua, and Paris), the narrative illustrates the itinerant nature of the great artists of the day, as they pursued their fame and fortune and created magnificent works of art for their numerous patrons. Meanwhile, their lives were often filled with chaos, conflict, and violence.

(Taken from the translation of John Addington Symonds)

1. ALL men of whatsoever quality they be, who have done anything of excellence, or which may properly resemble excellence, ought, if they are persons of truth and honesty, to describe their life with their own hand; but they ought not to attempt so fine an enterprise till they have passed the age of forty. This duty occurs to my own mind now that I am travelling beyond the term of fifty-eight years, and am in Florence, the city of my birth. Many untoward things can I remember, such as happen to all who live upon our earth; and from those adversities I am now more free than at any previous period of my career-nay, it seems to me that I enjoy greater content of soul and health of body than ever I did in bygone years. I can also bring to mind some pleasant goods and some inestimable evils, which, when I turn my thoughts backward, strike terror in me, and astonishment that I should have reached this age of fifty-eight, wherein, thanks be to God, I am still travelling prosperously forward....

    19. AT Siena I waited for the mail to Rome, which I afterwards joined; and when we passed the Paglia, we met a courier carrying news of the new Pope, Clement VII. Upon my arrival in Rome, I went to work in the shop of the master-goldsmith Santi. He was dead; but a son of his carried on the business. He did not work himself, but entrusted all his commissions to a young man named Lucagnolo from Iesi, a country fellow, who while yet a child had come into Santi's service. This man was short but well proportioned, and was a more skilful craftsman than any one whom I had met with up to that time; remarkable for facility and excellent in design. He executed large plate only: that is to say, vases of the utmost beauty, basons, and such pieces. Having put myself to work there, I began to make some candelabra for the Bishop of Salamanca, a Spaniard. They were richly chased, so far as that sort of work admits. A pupil of Raffaello da Urbino called Gian Francesco, and commonly known as Il Fattore, was a painter of great ability; and being on terms of friendship with the Bishop, he introduced me to his favour, so that I obtained many commissions from that prelate, and earned considerable sums of money.

During that time I went to draw, sometimes in Michel Agnolo's chapel, and sometimes in the house of Agostino Chigi of Siena, which contained many incomparable paintings by the hand of that great master Raffaello. This I did on feast-days, because the house was then inhabited by Messer Gismondo, Agostino's brother. They plumed themselves exceedingly when they saw young men of my sort coming to study in their palaces. Gismondo's wife, noticing my frequent presence in that house-she was a lady as courteous as could be, and of surpassing beauty-came up to me one day, looked at my drawings, and asked me if I was a sculptor or a painter; to whom I said I was a goldsmith. She remarked that I drew too well for a goldsmith; and having made one of her waiting-maids bring a lily of the finest diamonds set in gold, she showed it to me, and bade me value it. I valued it at 800 crowns. Then she said that I had very nearly hit the mark, and asked me whether I felt capable of setting the stones really well. I said that I should much like to do so, and began before her eyes to make a little sketch for it, working all the better because of the pleasure I took in conversing with so lovely and agreeable a gentlewoman. When the sketch was finished, another Roman lady of great beauty joined us; she had been above, and now descending to the ground-floor, asked Madonna Porzia what she was doing there. She answered with a smile: "I am amusing myself by watching this worthy young man at his drawing; he is as good as he is handsome." I had by this time acquired a trifle of assurance, mixed, however, with some honest bashfulness; so I blushed and said: 'such as I am, lady, I shall ever be most ready to serve you." The gentlewoman, also slightly blushing, said: "You know well that I want you to serve me;" and reaching me the lily, told me to take it away; and gave me besides twenty golden crowns which she had in her bag, and added: 'set me the jewel after the fashion you have sketched, and keep for me the old gold in which it is now set." On this the Roman lady observed: "If I were in that young man's body, I should go off without asking leave." Madonna Porzia replied that virtues rarely are at home with vices, and that if I did such a thing, I should strongly belie my good looks of an honest man. Then turning round, she took the Roman lady's hand, and with a pleasant smile said: "Farewell, Benvenuto." I stayed on a short while at the drawing I was making, which was a copy of a Jove by Raffaello. When I had finished it and left the house, I set myself to making a little model of wax, in order to show how the jewel would look when it was completed. This I took to Madonna Porzia, whom I found with the same Roman lady. Both of them were highly satisfied with my work, and treated me so kindly that, being somewhat emboldened, I promised the jewel should be twice as good as the model. Accordingly I set hand to it, and in twelve days I finished it in the form of a fleur-de-lys, as I have said above, ornamenting it with little masks, children, and animals, exquisitely enamelled, whereby the diamonds which formed the lily were more than doubled in effect.

20. WHILE I was working at this piece, Lucagnolo, of whose ability I have before spoken, showed considerable discontent, telling me over and over again that I might acquire far more profit and honour by helping him to execute large plate, as I had done at first. I made him answer that, whenever I chose, I should always be capable of working at great silver pieces; but that things like that on which I was now engaged were not commissioned every day; and beside their bringing no less honour than large silver plate, there was also more profit to be made by them. He laughed me in the face, and said: "Wait and see, Benvenuto; for by the time that you have finished that work of yours, I will make haste to have finished this vase, which I took in hand when you did the jewel; and then experience shall teach you what profit I shall get from my vase, and what you will get from your ornament." I answered that I was very glad indeed to enter into such a competition with so good a craftsman as he was, because the end would show which of us was mistaken. Accordingly both the one and the other of us, with a scornful smile

upon our lips, bent our heads in grim earnest to the work, which both were now desirous of accomplishing; so that after about ten days, each had finished his undertaking with great delicacy and artistic skill.

Lucagnolo's was a huge silver piece, used at the table of Pope Clement, into which he flung away bits of bone and the rind of divers fruits, while eating; an object of ostentation rather than necessity. The vase was adorned with two fine handles, together with many masks, both small and great, and masses of lovely foliage, in as exquisite a style of elegance as could be imagined; on seeing which I said it was the most beautiful vase that ever I set eyes on. Thinking he had convinced me, Lucagnolo replied: "Your work seems to me no less beautiful, but we shall soon perceive the difference between the two." So he took his vase and carried it to the Pope, who was very well pleased with it, and ordered at once that he should be paid at the ordinary rate of such large plate. Meanwhile I carried mine to Madonna Porzia, who looked at it with astonishment, and told me I had far surpassed my promise. Then she bade me ask for my reward whatever I liked; for it seemed to her my desert was so great that if I craved a castle she could hardly recompense me; but since that was not in her hands to bestow, she added laughing that I must beg what lay within her power. I answered that the greatest reward I could desire for my labour was to have satisfied her ladyship. Then, smiling in my turn, and bowing to her, I took my leave, saying I wanted no reward but that. She turned to the Roman lady and said: "You see that the qualities we discerned in him are companied by virtues, and not vices." They both expressed their admiration, and then Madonna Porzia continued: "Friend Benvenuto, have you never heard it said that when the poor give to the rich, the devil laughs?" I replied: "Quite true! and yet, in the midst of all his troubles, I should like this time to see him laugh;" and as I took my leave, she said that this time she had no will to bestow on him that favour.

When I came back to the shop, Lucagnolo had the money for his vase in a paper packet; and on my arrival he cried out: "Come and compare the price of your jewel with the price of my plate." I said that he must leave things as they were till the next day, because I hoped that even as my work in its kind was not less excellent than his, so I should be able to show him quite an equal price for it.

21. ON the day following, Madonna Porzia sent a major-domo of hers to my shop, who called me out, and putting into my hands a paper packet full of money from his lady, told me that she did not choose the devil should have his whole laugh out: by which she hinted that the money sent me was not the entire payment merited by my industry, and other messages were added worthy of so courteous a lady. Lucagnolo, who was burning to compare his packet with mine, burst into the shop; then in the presence of twelve journeymen and some neighbours, eager to behold the result of this competition, he seized his packet, scornfully exclaiming "Ou! ou!" three or four times, while he poured his money on the counter with a great noise. They were twenty-five crowns in giulios; and he fancied that mine would be four or five crowns 'di moneta.' I for my part, stunned and stifled by his cries, and by the looks and smiles of the bystanders, first peeped into my packet; then, after seeing that it contained nothing but gold, I retired to one end of the counter, and, keeping my eyes lowered and making no noise at all, I lifted it with both hands suddenly above my head, and emptied it like a mill hopper. My coin was twice as much as his; which caused the onlookers, who had fixed their eyes on me with some derision, to turn round suddenly to him and say: "Lucagnolo, Benvenuto's pieces, being all of gold and twice as many as yours, make a far finer effect." I thought for certain that, what with jealousy and what with shame, Lucagnolo would have fallen dead upon the spot; and though he took the third part of my gain, since I was a journeyman (for such is the custom of the trade, two-thirds fall to the workman and one-third to the masters of the shop), yet inconsiderate envy had more power in him than avarice: it ought indeed to have worked quite the other way, he being a peasant's son from Iesi. He cursed his art and those who taught

it him, vowing that thenceforth he would never work at large plate, but give his whole attention to those brothel gewgaws, since they were so well paid. Equally enraged on my side, I answered, that every bird sang its own note; that he talked after the fashion of the hovels he came from; but that I dared swear that I should succeed with ease in making his lubberly lumber, while he would never be successful in my brothel gewgaws. Thus I flung off in a passion, telling him that I would soon show him that I spoke truth. The bystanders openly declared against him, holding him for a lout, as indeed he was, and me for a man, as I had proved myself....

24. WHILE I was pushing forward Salamanca's vase, I had only one little boy as help, whom I had taken at the entreaty of friends, and half against my own will, to be my workman. He was about fourteen years of age, bore the name of Paulino, and was son to a Roman burgess, who lived upon the income of his property. Paulino was the best-mannered, the most honest, and the most beautiful boy I ever saw in my whole life. His modest ways and actions, together with his superlative beauty and his devotion to myself, bred in me as great an affection for him as a man's breast can hold. This passionate love led me oftentimes to delight the lad with music; for I observed that his marvellous features, which by complexion wore a tone of modest melancholy, brightened up, and when I took my cornet, broke into a smile so lovely and so sweet, that I do not marvel at the silly stories which the Greeks have written about the deities of heaven. Indeed, if my boy had lived in those times, he would probably have turned their heads still more. He had a sister, named Faustina, more beautiful, I verily believe, than that Faustina about whom the old books gossip so. Sometimes he took me to their vineyard, and, so far as I could judge, it struck me that Paulino's good father would have welcomed me as a son-in-law. This affair led me to play more than I was used to do.

It happened at that time that one Giangiacomo of Cesena, a musician in the Pope's band, and a very excellent performer, sent word through Lorenzo, the trumpeter of Lucca, who is now in our Duke's service, to inquire whether I was inclined to help them at the Pope's Ferragosto, playing soprano with my cornet in some motets of great beauty selected by them for that occasion. Although I had the greatest desire to finish the vase I had begun, yet, since music has a wondrous charm of its own, and also because I wished to please my old father, I consented to join them. During eight days before the festival we practised two hours a day together; then on the first of August we went to the Belvedere, and while Pope Clement was at table, we played those carefully studied motets so well that his Holiness protested he had never heard music more sweetly executed or with better harmony of parts. He sent for Giangiacomo, and asked him where and how he had procured so excellent a cornet for soprano, and inquired particularly who I was. Giangiacomo told him my name in full. Whereupon the Pope said: "So, then, he is the son of Maestro Giovanni?" On being assured I was, the Pope expressed his wish to have me in his service with the other bandsmen. Giangiacomo replied: "Most blessed Father, I cannot pretend for certain that you will get him, for his profession, to which he devotes himself assiduously, is that of a goldsmith, and he works in it miraculously well, and earns by it far more than he could do by playing." To this the Pope added: "I am the better inclined to him now that I find him possessor of a talent more than I expected. See that he obtains the same salary as the rest of you; and tell him from me to join my service, and that I will find work enough by the day for him to do in his other trade." Then stretching out his hand, he gave him a hundred golden crowns of the Camera in a handkerchief, and said: "Divide these so that he may take his share."

When Giangiacomo left the Pope, he came to us, and related in detail all that the Pope had said; and after dividing the money between the eight of us, and giving me my share, he said to me: "Now I am going to have you inscribed among our company." I replied: "Let the day pass; to-morrow I will give my answer." When I left them, I went meditating whether

I ought to accept the invitation, inasmuch as I could not but suffer if I abandoned the noble studies of my art. The following night my father appeared to me in a dream, and begged me with tears of tenderest affection, for God's love and his, to enter upon this engagement. Methought I answered that nothing would induce me to do so. In an instant he assumed so horrible an aspect as to frighten me out of my wits, and cried: "If you do not, you will have a father's curse; but if you do, may you be ever blessed by me!" When I woke, I ran, for very fright, to have myself inscribed. Then I wrote to my old father, telling him the news, which so affected him with extreme joy that a sudden fit of illness took him, and well-nigh brought him to death's door. In his answer to my letter, he told me that he too had dreamed nearly the same as I had.

24. KNOWING now that I had gratified my father's honest wish, I began to think that everything would prosper with me to a glorious and honourable end. Accordingly, I set myself with indefatigable industry to the completion of the vase I had begun for Salamanca. That prelate was a very extraordinary man, extremely rich, but difficult to please. He sent daily to learn what I was doing; and when his messenger did not find me at home, he broke into fury, saying that he would take the work out of my hands and give it to others to finish. This came of my slavery to that accursed music. Still I laboured diligently night and day, until, when I had brought my work to a point when it could be exhibited, I submitted it to the inspection of the Bishop. This so increased his desire to see it finished that I was sorry I had shown it. At the end of three months I had it ready, with little animals and foliage and masks, as beautiful as one could hope to see. No sooner was it done than I sent it by the hand of my workman, Paulino, to show that able artist Lucagnolo, of whom I have spoken above. Paulino, with the grace and beauty which belonged to him, spoke as follows: "Messer Lucagnolo, Benvenuto bids me say that he has sent to show you his promises and your lumber, expecting in return to see from you his gewgaws." This message given, Lucagnolo took up the vase, and carefully examined it; then he said to Paulino: "Fair boy, tell your master that he is a great and able artist, and that I beg him to be willing to have me for a friend, and not to engage in aught else." The mission of that virtuous and marvellous lad caused me the greatest joy; and then the vase was carried to Salamanca, who ordered it to be valued. Lucagnolo took part in the valuation, estimating and praising it far above my own opinion. Salamanca, lifting up the vase, cried like a true Spaniard: "I swear by God that I will take as long in paying him as he has lagged in making it." When I heard this, I was exceedingly put out, and fell to cursing all Spain and every one who wished well to it.

Amongst other beautiful ornaments, this vase had a handle, made all of one piece, with most delicate mechanism, which, when a spring was touched, stood upright above the mouth of it. While the prelate was one day ostentatiously exhibiting my vase to certain Spanish gentlemen of his suite, it chanced that one of them, upon Monsignor's quitting the room, began roughly to work the handle, and as the gentle spring which moved it could not bear his loutish violence, it broke in his hand. Aware what mischief he had done, he begged the butler who had charge of the Bishop's plate to take it to the master who had made it, for him to mend, and promised to pay what price he asked, provided it was set to rights at once. So the vase came once more into my hands, and I promised to put it forthwith in order, which indeed I did. It was brought to me before dinner; and two hours before sunset the man who brought it returned, all in a sweat, for he had run the whole way, Monsignor having again asked for it to show to certain other gentlemen. The butler, then, without giving me time to utter a word, cried: "Quick, quick, bring the vase." I, who wanted to act at leisure and not to give up to him, said that I did not mean to be so quick. The serving-man got into such a rage that he made as though he would put one hand to his sword, while with the other he threatened to break the shop open. To this I put a stop at once with my own weapon, using therewith spirited language, and saying: "I am not going to give it to you! Go and tell Monsignor, your master, that I want the money for my work before I let it leave this shop." When the fellow saw he could not obtain it by swaggering, he fell to praying me, as one prays to the Cross, declaring that if I would only give it up, he would take care I should be paid. These words did not make me swerve from my purpose; but I kept on saying the same thing. At last, despairing of success, he swore to come with Spaniards enough to cut me in pieces. Then he took to his heels; while I, who inclined to believe partly in their murderous attack, resolved that I would defend myself with courage. So I got an admirable little gun ready, which I used for shooting game, and muttered to myself: "He who robs me of my property and labour may take my life too, and welcome." While I was carrying on this debate in my own mind, a crowd of Spaniards arrived, led by their major-domo, who, with the headstrong rashness of his race, bade them go in and take the vase and give me a good beating. Hearing these words, I showed them the muzzle of my gun, and prepared to fire, and cried in a loud voice: "Renegade Jews, traitors, is it thus that one breaks into houses and shops in our city of Rome? Come as many of you thieves as like, an inch nearer to this wicket, and I'll blow all their brains out with my gun." Then I turned the muzzle toward their major-domo, and making as though I would discharge it, called out: "And you big thief, who are egging them on, I mean to kill you first." He clapped spurs to the jennet he was riding, and took flight headlong. The commotion we were making stirred up all the neighbours, who came crowding round, together with some Roman gentlemen who chanced to pass, and cried: "Do but kill the renegades, and we will stand by you." These words had the effect of frightening the Spaniards in good earnest. They withdrew, and were compelled by the circumstances to relate the whole affair to Monsignor. Being a man of inordinate haughtiness, he rated the members of his household, both because they had engaged in such an act of violence, and also because, having begun, they had not gone through with it. At this juncture the painter, who had been concerned in the whole matter, came in, and the Bishop bade him go and tell me that if I did not bring the vase at once, he would make mincemeat of me; but if I brought it, he would pay its price down. These threats were so far from terrifying me, that I sent him word I was going immediately to lay my case before the Pope.

In the meantime, his anger and my fear subsided; whereupon, being guaranteed by some Roman noblemen of high degree that the prelate would not harm me, and having assurance that I should be paid, I armed myself with a large poniard and my good coat of mail, and betook myself to his palace, where he had drawn up all his household. I entered, and Paulino followed with the silver vase. It was just like passing through the Zodiac, neither more nor less; for one of them had the face of the lion, another of the scorpion, a third of the crab. However, we passed onward to the presence of the rascally priest, who spouted out a torrent of such language as only priests and Spaniards have at their command. In return I never raised my eyes to look at him, nor answered word for word. That seemed to augment the fury of his anger; and causing paper to be put before me, he commanded me to write an acknowledgment to the effect that I had been amply satisfied and paid in full. Then I raised my head, and said I should be very glad to do so when I had received the money. The Bishop's rage continued to rise; threats and recriminations were flung about; but at last the money was paid, and I wrote the receipt. Then I departed, glad at heart and in high spirits.

READING 41

ERASMUS OF ROTTERDAM

Desiderius Erasmus (1466-1536) was regarded as the most learned man of his day. Although born in Rotterdam in what was then Flanders (now the Netherlands), he spent much of his adult life traveling about Western Europe, visiting the major cities in order to interact with other scholars. In addition to being well versed in both Greek and Latin and their literature from classical antiquity, he was a devout Christian and was a scholar of *The Bible*, especially of *The New Testament*. He therefore combined in himself both the ancient Greco-Roman and Christian traditions, which are quite evident in his numerous writings. Although he was devoted to Christianity, he found much to criticize in contemporary Catholic practices, and he often expressed these criticisms in the form of humorous dialogues, of which the following text is an excellent example. Erasmus' writing and scholarship therefore represent the culmination of the humanist learning of the Renaissance and also anticipate the Protestant Reformation that shattered the religious unity of Western Europe as embodied in the Roman Catholic Church.

THE RELIGIOUS PILGRIMAGE

(Taken *from The Familiar Colloquies of Desiderius Erasmus of Rotterdam, translated by Nathan Bailey, London 1877 pp.238-257*)

Me. = Menedemus

    Og. = Ogygius

    Me.   What novelty is this? Don't I see my old neighbour Ogygius, that nobody has set their eyes on. this six months. There was a report he was dead. It is he, or I am mightily mistaken. I will go up to him and give him his welcome. Welcome, Ogygius.

    Og.   And well met, Menedemus.

    Me.   From what part of the world came you? for here was a melancholy report that you had taken a voyage to the Stygian shades.

    Og.   Nay, I thank God, I never was better in all my life than I have been ever since I saw you last.

    Me.   And may you live always to confute such vain reports. But what strange dress is this? It is all over set off with shells scolloped, full of images of lead and tin, and chains of straw-work, and the cuffs are adorned with snakes' eggs, instead of bracelets.

    Og.   I have been to pay a visit to St. James at Compostella [in northern Spain], and after that to the famous virgin on the other side the water in England; and this was rather a re-visit, for I had been to see her three years before.

    Me.   What? out of curiosity, I suppose?

Og.   Nay, upon the score of religion.

Me.   That religion, I suppose, the Greek tongue taught you.

Og.   My wife's mother had bound herself by a vow, that if her daughter should be delivered of a live male child, I should go to present my respects to St. James in person, and thank him for it.

Me.   And did you salute the saint only in your own and your motherin-law's name?

Og.   Nay, in the name of the whole family.

Me.   Truly I am persuaded your family would have been every whit as well if you had never complimented him at all. But, pray thee, what answer did he make you when you thanked him?

Og.   None at all, but upon tendering my present he seemed to smile, and gave me a gentle nod, with this same scollop shell.

Me.   But why does he rather give those than anything else?

Og.   Because he has plenty of them, the neighbouring sea furnishing him with them.

Me.   O gracious saint, that is both a midwife to women in labour and hospitable to travellers too! But what new fashion of making vows is this, that one who does nothing himself shall make a vow that another man shall work? Put the case that you should tie yourself up by a vow that I should fast twice a week if you should succeed in such and such an affair, do you think I would perform what you had vowed?

Og.   I believe you would not, although you had made the vow yourself, for you make a joke of fobbing the saints off. But it was my mother-in-law that made the vow, and it was my duty to be obedient. You know the temper of women, and also my own interest lay at stake.

Me.   If you had not performed the vow what risk had you run?

Og.   I do not believe the saint could have laid an action at law against me, but he might for the future have stopped his ears at my petitions, or slily have brought some mischief or other upon my family; you know the humour of great persons.

Me.   Pray thee, tell me how does the good man St. James do, and what was he doing?

Og.   Why, truly, not so well as by far he used to be.

Me.   What is the matter; is he grown old?

Og.   Trifler, you know saints never grow old. No, but it is this new opinion that has been spread abroad through the world is the occasion that he has not so many visits paid to him as he vised to have, and those that do come give him a bare salute, and either nothing at all, or little or nothing else; they say they can bestow their money to better purpose upon those that want it.

Me.   An impious opinion.

Og.   And this is the cause that this great apostle, that used to glitter with gold and jewels, now is brought to the very block that he is made of, and has scarce a tallow candle.

Me.   If this be true, the rest of the saints are in danger of coming to the same pass.

Og.   Nay, I can assure you that there is a letter handed about which the Virgin Mary herself has written about this matter.

Me.   What Mary?

Og.   She that is called Maria a Lapide.

Me.   That is up towards Basil, if I am not mistaken.

Og.   The very same.

Me.   You talk of a very stony saint. But who did she write it to?

Og.   The letter tells you the name.

Me.   Who did she send it by?

Og.   An angel, no doubt, who laid it down in the pulpit, where the preacher to whom it was sent took it up; and to put the matter out of all doubt, you shall see the original letter.

Me.   Do you know the angel's hand that is secretary to the Virgin Mary?

Og.   Well enough.

Me.   By what token?

Og.   I have read St. Bede's epitaph that was engraven by the same angel, and the shape of the letters are exactly the same; and I have read the discharge sent to St. Egidius, and they agree exactly. Do not these prove the matter plain enough?

Me.   May a person see it?

Og.   You may, if you will damn your soul to the pit of hell if ever you speak about it.

Me.   It is as safe as if you spoke it to a stone.

Og.   But there are some stones that are infamous for this, that they cannot keep a secret.

Me.   If you cannot trust to a stone, speak to a mute then.

Og.   Upon that condition I will recite it to you; but prick up both your ears.

Me.   I have done so.

Og.   Mary, the mother of Jesus, to Glaucoplutus sendeth greeting. This is to let you know that I take it in good part, and you have much obliged me in that you have so strenuously followed Luther, and con inced the world that it is a thing altogether needless to invoke saints. For before this time I was even wearied out of my life with the wicked importunities of mortals. Everything -was asked of me, as if my gon was always a child, because He is painted so, and at my breast, and therefore they take it for granted I have Him. still at my beck, and that He dares not deny me anything I ask of Him, for fear I should deny Him the bubby when He is thirsty. Nay, and they ask such things from me, a virgin, that a modest young man would scarce dare to ask of a bawd, and which I am ashained to commit to writing. A merchant that is going a voyage to Spain to get pelf recommends to me the chastity of his kept mistress; and a professed nun, having thrown away her veil in order to make her escape, recommends to me the care of her reputation, which she at the same time intends to prostitute. The wicked soldier, who butchers men for money, bawls out to me with these words, O blessed Virgin, send me rich plunder. The gamester calls out to me to give him good luck, and promises I shall go snips with him in what he shall win; and if the dice do not favour, I am railed at and cursed because I would not be a confederate in his wickedness. The usurer prays, Help me to large interest for my money, and if I deny them anything they cry out I am no mother of mercy. And there is another sort of people whose prayers are not properly so wicked as they are foolish. The maid prays, Mary, give me a handsome, rich husband; the wife cries, Give me fine children; and the woman with child, Give me a good delivery. The old woman prays to live long without a cough and thirst; and the doting old man, Send that I may grow young again. The philosopher says, Give me the faculty of starting difficulties never to be resolved; the priest says, Give me a fat benefice; the bishop cries out for the saving of his diocese, and the mariner for a prosperous voyage; the magistrate cries out, Shew me thy Son before I die; the courtier, that he may make an effectual confession when at the point of death; the husbandman calls on me for seasonable rain, and a farmer's wife to preserve her sheep and cattle. If I refuse them anything, then presently I am hardhearted. If I refer them to my Son they cry, If you will but say the word, I am sure He will do it. How is it possible for me a lone body, a woman, and a virgin, to assist sailors, soldiers, merchants, gamesters, brides and bridegrooms, women in travail, princes, kings, and peasants? And what I have mentioned is the least part of what I suffer. But I am much less troubled with these concerns now than I have been, for which I would give you my hearty thanks, if this conveniency did not bring a greater inconveniency along with it. I have indeed more leisure, but less honour and less money. Before I was saluted queen of the heavens and lady of the world, but now there are very few from whom I hear an Ave Mary. Formerly I was adorned with jewels and gold, and had abundance of changes of apparel: I had presents made me of gold and jewels; but now I have scarce half a vest to cover me, and that is mouse-eaten too. And my yearly revenue is scarce enough to keep alive my poor sexton, who lights me up a little wax or tallow candle. But all these things might be borne with, if you did not tell us that there were greater things going forward. They say you aim at this, to strip the altars and temples of the saints every-where. I advise you again and again to have a care what you do, for other saints do not want power to avenge themselves for the wrong done to them, peter, being turned out of his church, can shut the gate of the kingdom of heaven against you; Paul has a sword, and St. Bartholomew a knife. The monk William has a coat of mail under his habit, and a heavy lance too. And how will you encounter St. George on horseback, in his cuirassier's arms, his sword, and his whinyard? Nor is Anthony without his weapon; he has his sacred fire. And the rest of them have either their arms or their mischiefs, that they can send out against whom they please. And as for myself, although I wear no weapons, you shall not turn me out unless you turn out my Son too, whom I hold in my arms. I will not be pulled away from Him; you shall either throw us both out or leave us both, unless you have a mind to have a church without a Christ. These things I would have you know, and consider what answer to give me, for I have the matter much at heart. From our Stone House, the Calends of August, the Year of my Son's Passion, 1524. I, the Stony Virgin, have subscribed this with my own hand.

Me.   In truth, this is a very terrible threatening letter, and I believe Glaucoplutus will take care what he does.

Og.   He will, if he is wise.

Me.   But why did not honest James write to him about this matter?

Og.   Truly I cannot tell, except it is because he is a great way off, and now-a-days all letters are intercepted.

Me.   But what wind carried you to England?

Og.   A very favourable wind, and I had made half a promise to the beyond-sea she-saint to pay her another visit within two or three years.

Me.   What did you go to ask for of her?

Og.   Nothing new but those common matters, the health of my family, the increase of my fortune, a long and a happy life in this world, and eternal happiness in the next.

Me.   But could not our Virgin Mary have done as much for you here? She has at Antwerp a temple much more magnificent than that beyond sea.

Og.   I will not deny that she is able, but one thing is bestowed in one place and another thing in another; whether this be her pleasure merely, or whether she being of a kind disposition, accommodates herself in this to our affections.

Me.   I have often heard of James, but, pray thee, give me some account of that beyond-sea lady.

Og.   I will do it as briefly as I can. Her name is very famous all over England, and you shall scarce find anybody in that island who thinks his affairs can be prosperous unless he every year makes some present to that lady, greater or smaller, according as his circum-stances are in the world.

Me.   Whereabouts does she dwell?

Og.   Near the coast, upon the furthest part between the west and the north, about three miles from the sea; it is a town that depends chiefly upon the resort of strangers. There is a college of canons there, to which the Latins have added the name of Regulars, which are of a middle sort between monks and those canons that are called Seculars.

Me.   You tell me of amphibious creatures, such as the beavers are.

Og.   Nay, so are crocodiles too. But trifling apart, I wrill tell you in three words: in odious cases they are canons, in favourable cases they are monks.

Me.   You have hitherto been telling me riddles.

Og.   Why, then, I will give you a mathematical demonstratum. If the pope of Rome should throw a thunderbolt at all monks, then they will be all canons; and if he will allow all monks to marry, then they will be all monks.

Me.   These are new favours I wish they would take mine for one.

Og.   But to return to the matter in hand. This college has little else to maintain it but the liberality of the Virgin, for all presents of value are laid up; but as for anything of money or lesser value, that goes to the support of the flock and the head of it, which they call the prior.

Me.   Are they men of good lives?

Og.   Not much amiss. They are richer in piety than in revenue. There is a clever neat church, but the Virgin does not dwell in it herself, but upon point of honour has given it to her Son. Her church is on the right hand of her Son's.

Me.   Upon His right hand! which way then does her Son look?

Og.   That is well taken notice of. When He looks toward the west He has His mother on the right, and when He looks toward the east she is on His left hand. And she does not dwell there neither, for the building is not finished; the doors and windows are all open, and the wind blows through it; and not far off is a place where Oceanus the father of the winds resides.

Me.   That is a hard case; where does she dwell then?

Og.   In that unfinished church that I spoke of, there is a little boarded chapel with a little door on each side to receive visitors. There is but little light to it but what comes from the tapers; but the scent is very grateful.

Me.   All these things conduce to religion.

Og.   Nay, Menedemus, if you saw the inside of it you would say it was the seat of the saints, it is all so glittering with jewels, gold, and silver.

Me.   You set me agog to go thither too.

Og.   If you do you will never repent of your journey.

Me.   Is there any holy oil there?

Og.   Simpleton, that oil is only the sweat of saints in their sepulchres, as of Andrew, Catherine, fec. Mary was never buried.

Me.   I confess I was under a mistake; but make an end of your story.

Og.   That religion may spread itself the more widely, some things are shewn at one place and some at another.

Me.   And it may be that the donations may be larger, according to the old saying, Many hands will carry off much plunder.

Og.   And there are always some at hand to shew you what you have a mind to see.

Me.   What, of the canons?

Og.   No, no, they are not permitted, lest under the colour of religion they should prove irreligious, and while they are serving the Virgin lose their own virginity. Only in the inner chapel, which I call the chamber of the holy Virgin, a certain canon stands at the altar.

Me.   What does he stand there for?

Og.   To receive and keep that which is given.

Me.   Must people give whether they will or no?

Og.   No; but a certain religious modesty makes some give, when anybody stands by, who would not give a farthing if there were no witness of it, or give more than otherwise they would give.

Me.   You set forth human nature as I have experienced in myself.

Og.   There are some so devoted to the human nature, that while they pretend to lay one gift on the altar, by a wonderful sleight of hand they steal what another has laid down.

Me.   But put the case, if nobody were by, would the Virgin thunder at them?

Og.   Why should the Virgin do that any more than God himself does, whom they are not afraid to strip of His ornaments, and to break through the walls of the church to come at them?

Me.   I cannot well tell which I admire at most, the impious confidence of those wretches or God's patience.

Og.   At the north side there is a certain gate, not of a church, don't mistake me, but of the wall that encloses the churchyard, that has a very little wicket, as in the great gates of noblemen, that he that has a mind to get in must first venture the breaking of his shins and afterwards stoop his head too. Me, In truth, it would not be safe for a man to enter in at such a little door.

Og.   You are in the right of it. But yet the verger told me that some time since a knight on horseback, having escaped out of the hands of his enemy, who followed him at the heels, got in through this wicket. The poor man at the last pinch, by a sudden turn of thought, recommended himself to the holy Virgin that was the nearest to him, for he resolved to take sanctuary at her altar, if the gate had been open. When, behold, which is such a thing as was never heard of, both man and horse were on a sudden taken into the churchyard and his enemy left on the outside of it stark mad at his disappointment.

Me.   And did he give you reason to believe so wonderful a relation?

Og.   Without doubt.

Me.   That was no easy matter to a man of your philosophy.

Og.   He shewed me a plate of copper nailed oil the door, that had the very image of this knight that was thus saved, and in the very habit which was then in fashion among the English, which is the same we see in old pictures, which, if they are drawn truly, the barbers and dyers and weavers in those days had but a bad time of it.

Me.   Why so?

Og.   Why, he had a beard like a goat, and there was not a wrinkle in any of his clothes-they were made so strait to his body that the very straitness of them made his body the more slender. There was also another plate that was an exact description of the chapel and the size of it.

Me.   Then there was no doubt to be made of it.

Og.   Under the little wicket there was an iron grate, no bigger than what a man on foot could just get in at; for it was not fit that any horse afterwards should tread upon that place which the former knight had consecrated to the Virgin.

Me.   And very good reason.

Og.   From hence towards the east, there is another chapel full of wonders; thither I went. Another verger received me. There we prayed a little; and there was shewn us the middle joint of a man's finger. I kissed it, and asked whose relic it was? He told me it was St. Peter's. What, said I, the Apostle? He said it was. I then took notice of the bigness of the joint, which was large enough to be taken for that of a giant. Upon which, said I, Peter must needs have been a very lusty man. At this, one of the company fell a laughing. I was very much vexed at it; for if he had held his tongue the verger would have shewn us all the relics. However, we pacified him pretty well, by giving him a few groats. Before this little chapel stood a house, which he told us, in the winter time, when all things were buried in snow, was brought there on a sudden from some place a great way off. Under this house there were two pits brimful, that were fed by a fountain consecrated to the holy Virgin. The water was wonderful cold, and of great virtue in curing pains in the head and stomach.

Me.   If cold water will cure pains in the head and stomach, in time oil will quench fire.

Og.   But, my good friend, you are hearing that which is miraculous; for what miracle is there in cold water quenching thirst?

Me.   Thab shift goes a great way in this story.

Og.   It was positively affirmed that this spring burst out of the ground on a sudden at the command of the holy Virgin. I, observing everything very diligently, asked him how many years it was since that little house was brought thither? He said it had been there for some ages. But, said I, methinks the walls don't, seem to carry any marks of antiquity in them. He did not much deny it. Nor these pillars, said I. He did not deny but those had been set up lately; and the thing shewed itself plainly. Then, said I, that straw and reeds, the whole thatch of it seems not to have been so long laid. He allowed it. Nor do these cross beams and rafters that bear up the roof seem to have been laid many years ago. He confessed they were not. And there being no part of that cottage remaining, said I to him, How then does it appear that this is the very cottage that was brought so far through the air?

Me.   Pray thee, how did the sexton extricate himself out of this difficulty?

Og.   He presently shewed us an old bear's skin tacked there to a piece of timber, and almost laughed at us to our very faces for not having eyes to perceive a thing that was so plain. Therefore, seeming to be satisfied, and excusing our dulness of apprehension, we turned ourselves to the heavenly milk of the blessed Virgin.

Me.   O mother like her Son! for as He has left us so much of His blood upon earth, so she has left us so much of her milk, that it is scarce credible that a woman who never had but one child should have so much, although her child had never sucked a drop.

Og.   And they tell us the same stories about our Lord's cross, that is shewn up and down both publicly and privately in so many places, that if all the fragments were gathered together, they would seem to be sufficient loading for a good large ship; and yet our Lord himself carried the whole cross upon his shoulders.

Me.   And don't you think this is wonderful?

Og.   It may be said to be an extraordinary thing, but not a wonderful one, since the Lord, who increases these things according to His own pleasure, is omnipotent.

Me.   You put a very pious construction upon it, but I am afraid that a great many such things are forged for the sake of getting money.

Og.   I cannot think God would suffer any one to put these mockeries upon Him.

Me.   Nay, when both the mother and Son, Father and Spirit are robbed by sacrilegious persons, they don't seem to be moved the least in the world, so as to deter wicked persons, so much as by a nod or a stamp, so great is the lenity of the divine being.

Og.   This is true, but hear me out. That milk is kept upon the high altar in which Christ is in the middle, and his mother, for respect sake, at his right hand; for the milk represents the mother.

Me.   Why, is it plain to be seen then?

Og.   It is preserved in a crystal glass.

Me.   Is it liquid then?

Og.   What do you talk of being liquid, when it has been put in above 1500 years ago. It is so concreted, you would take it for beaten chalk tempered with the white of an egg.

Me.   But why don't they shew it open?

Og.   Lest the milk of the Virgin should be defiled by the kisses of men.

Me.   You say very well, for I believe there are some who put lips to it, that are neither pure nor virgin ones.

Og.   As soon as the officer sees us, he runs presently and puts on a surplice and a stole about his neck, and falls down very devoutly and worships, and by and by gives us the holy milk to kiss. Then we prostrated ourselves at the lowest step of the altar, and having first paid our adoration to Christ, we applied ourselves to the Virgin in the following prayer, which we had. framed beforehand for this very purpose: "Virgin Mother, who hast merited to give suck to the Lord of heaven and earth, thy Son Jesus, from thy virgin breasts, we desire that, being purified by His blood, we may arrive at that happy infant state of dove-like innocence which, being void of malice, fraud, and deceit, we may continually desire the milk of the evangelical doctrine, until it grows up to a perfect man, and to the measure of the fulness of Christ, whose blessed society thou wilt enjoy for evermore, with the Father and the Holy Spirit. Amen."

Me.   Truly, a devout prayer. But what answer did she make?

Og.   If my eyes did not deceive me, they were both pleased, for the holy milk seemed to give a leap, and the eucharist seemed to look somewhat bigger than usual. In the meantime the shower of the relics came to us, without speaking a word, holding out such a kind of table as they in Germany that take toll on the bridges hold out to you.

Me.   In truth, I have oftentimes cursed those craving tables when I travelled in Germany.

Og.   We laid down some pieces of money, which he presented to the Virgin. After this, by our interpreter (if I remember right), one Robert Aldridge, a well-spoken young man, and a great master of the English tongue, I inquired as civilly as I could, what assurance he had that this was really the Virgin's milk. And truly I desired to be satisfied of this with a pious intention, that I might stop the mouths of some impious persons who are used to scoff at all these things. The officer first contracted his brow without speaking a word; thereupon I pressed the interpreter to put the same question to him again, but in, the fairest manner that could be, and he did it in so obliging a manner that if he had addressed himself to the mother herself in these terms, when she had but newly lain in, she would not have taken it amiss. But the officer, as if he had been inspired with some enthusiasm, looking upon us with astonished eyes, and with a sort of horror, cursing our blasphemous expression, said, What need is there for your putting this question, when you have an authentic record? and had turned us out of doors for heretics, had not a few pence pacified his rage.

Me.   But how did you behave yourselves in the interim?

Og.   Just as if we had been stunned with a cudgel, or struck with thunder; we sneaked away, humbly begging his pardon for our boldness; for so a man ought to do in holy matters. Thence we went to the little chapel, the dwelling of the Virgin Saint. In our way thither an expounder of sacred things, one of the minors, offers himself; he stares upon us as if he had a mind to draw our pictures; and having gone a little farther, another meets us, staring upon us after the same manner; and after him a third.

Me.   It may be they had a mind to have drawn your picture.

Og.   But I suspected far otherwise.

Me.   What you imagine then?

Og.   That some sacrilegious person had stolen of the Virgin's vestments, and that I was suspected as the thief. Therefore, having entered the chapel, I addressed myself to the Virgin mother with this short prayer: "O thou who only of all women art a mother and a virgin, the most happy of mothers and the purest of virgins, we that are impure do now come to visit and address ourselves to thee that art pure, and reverence thee with our poor offerings, such as they are. Oh that thy son would enable us to imitate thy most holy life, that we may deserve, by the grace of the Holy Spirit, to conceive the Lord Jesus in the most inward bowels of our minds, and having once conceived him, never to lose him. Amen." So I kissed the altar, laid down some money, and withdrew.

Me.   What, did the Virgin hear? Did she give you no nod as a token that she had heard your prayer?

Og.   As I told you before, it was but an uncertain light, and she stood in the dark at the right side of the altar. And the check of the former officer had made me so dejected that I did not dare to lift up my eyes again.

Me.   Then this adventure had not a very happy conclusion?

Og.   Nay, the happiest of all.

Me.   Nay, now you put me in courage again; for, as your Homer says, my heart was even sunk into my breeches.

Og.   After dinner we go to church again.

Me.   How did you dare to do that, being suspected of sacrilege?

Og.   It may be I was; but I did not suspect myself. A clear conscience fears nothing. I had a great mind to see the record that the shower of the relics had referred us to. Having hunted a great while for it, we found it at last; but it was hung up so high that he must have good eyes that could read it; and mine are none of the best, nor none of the worst. Therefore, not being willing wholly to trust to him in a matter of such moment, I went along with Aldrisius as he read it.

Me.   Well! and were all your doubts removed?

Og.   I was ashamed of myself that I should doubt of a matter that there was made so plain before one's eyes, the name, the place, the order of the proceeding—in one word, there was nothing omitted. There was one William of Paris, a man of general piety, but more especially religious in getting together the relics of saints all over the earth, he having travelled over a great many countries, and having everywhere diligently searched monasteries and churches, at last arrived at Constantinople (for this William's brother was a bishop there). When he was preparing to return home, the bishop acquainted him that there was a certain nun that had the Virgin's milk, and that he would be the happiest man in the world if he could possibly get any of it, either for love or money, or by any other means, for that all the relics he had hitherto collected were nothing compared to that sacred milk. Upon this William never was at rest till he had obtained one-half of this milk, and having gotten this treasure, thought himself richer than Croesus.

Me.   And very well he might. It was a thing so unexpected too.

Og.   He goes straight homeward, but falls sick by the way.

Me.   Oh, how little trust is to be put in human felicity that it shall be either perfect or long-lived!

Og.   Finding himself in danger he sends for a Frenchman, a faithful fellow-traveller, and makes him swear secrecy, and then delivers the milk to him upon this condition, " That if he got tome safe he should deposit that treasure on the altar of the holy Virgin that is worshipped at Paris in that noble church that has the river Seine on each side of it, as if itself gave place in reverence to the divinity of the Virgin. To sum up the matter in few words, William was buried; the other rides post, but he falls sick by the way, and thinking himself past recovery, he delivers the milk to an Englishman that was his fellow-traveller, making him take a solemn oath that he would perform that which he himself was to have done. The one dies, the other takes it and puts it upon the altar in the presence of all the canons of the place, those that at that time were called regulars, as they are yet at St. Genoveve. He obtained half this milk of them and carried it into England, and made a present of it to this beyond-sea place, his mind being moved thereunto by a divine impulse.

Me.   Truly this story hangs very handsomely together.

Og.   Nay, further, that there might not be left the least room to doubt, the very names of the bishops were set down that were authorised to grant releases and indulgences to such as should come to see the milk according to the power to them given, but not without some donation or another.

Me.   And how far did that power extend?

Og.   To forty days.

Me.   But are there days in purgatory?

Og.   For certain there is time there.

Me.   But when they have disposed of this stock of forty days have they no more to bestow?

Og.   No; for there ever and anon arises something for them to bestow, and it is in this quite otherwise than it is with the tub of the Danaides; for though that is continually filling, it is always empty; but in this, though you are continually drawing out, there is never the less in the vessel.

Me.   But if the remission of forty days were given to a hundred thousand men would every one have so much?

Og.   Yes, so much.

Me.   And suppose that they that have received forty days in the morning should ask for forty days more at night, would they have wherewithal to give them?

Og.   Yes, ten times over in an hour.

Me.   I wish I had such a cabinet at home. I would not wish for above three groats if they might be doubled and tripled after that manner.

Og.   You might as well have wished to be all turned into gold yourself, and as soon, have had what you wished for. But to return to my story, there was one argument added by a mail of great piety and candour, which is, that though the Virgin's milk, which is shewn in many other places, is indeed venerable enough in that it was scraped off from stones, yet this was more venerable than all the rest, because this was saved as it flowed from the Virgin's breast without touching the ground.

Me.   But how does that appear?

Og.   Oh, the nun at Constantinople that gave it said so.

Me.   It may be she had it of St. Bernard.

Og.   I believe she had.

Me.   He, when he was very old, had the happiness to taste milk from the same nipple which the child Jesus sucked, whence I wonder that he was not rather called lactifluous than Mellifluous. But how is that called the Virgin's milk that did not flow from her breasts?

Og.   That did flow from her breasts, but dropping upon the stone she sat upon while she was giving suck it concreted, and was afterwards by Providence so multiplied.

Me.   Right. Go on.

Og.   These things being over, we were just upon the point of going away, but walking about and looking round us to see if there was anything worth taking notice of, the chapel officers come to us again, leering at us. Pointing at us with their fingers, they advance to us retreat, run backward and forward, nod as if they would fain have said something to us, if they had had courage enough to have done it.

Me.   And were you not afraid then?

Og.   No, not at all; but I looked them full in the face very cheerfully, as who should say speak and welcome At length one of them comes up to me and asked my name. I told it him. He asked me if I was the person that a matter of two years ago set up a votive table in Hebrew letters? I told him I was.

Me.   Can you write Hebrew then?

Og.   No; but they call everything Hebrew that they cannot understand. But by and by, upon calling, as I suppose, came the Trpwroe uo-tpoe of the college.

Me.   What title of dignity is that? Have they not an abbot?

Og.   No.

Me.   Why so?

Og.   Because they do not understand Hebrew.

Me.   Have they no bishop?

Og.   None at all.

Me.   Why so?

Og.   Because the Virgin is so poor that she has not wherewith to buy a staff and mitre.

Me.   Have they not so much as a president?

Og.   No, nor that neither.

Me.   What hinders?

Og.   Because a president is a name of dignity and not of holiness, and therefore the colleges of canons reject the name of an abbot, but they willingly allow the name of a president.

Me.   But this Trpwroe i/iTEpoe is what I never heard of before.

Og.   In truth you are but an indifferent grammarian then.

Me.   I know what iKrepoVpwrov is in rhetoric.

Og.   Why, that is it. He that is next the prior is posterior-prior. You mean a sub-prior.

Og.   Ho saluted me very courteously. He told me what great pains had been taken to read those verses; what wiping of spectacles there had been to no purpose; how often one grave doctor of divinity, and another of law, had been brought thither to expound the table. One said the letters were Arabic, another said they were fictitious ones; but at last they found one that made a shift to read the title. It was written in Latin words and Latin capitals. The verses were Greek in Greek capitals, which at first sight looked like Roman capitals. Being requested, I turned the verses into Latin, word for word. They would have given me a reward for this small service, but I positively refused it, affirming that there was nothing so difficult that I would not, with all the readiness in the world, undertake for the sake of the holy Virgin, even if she should command me to carry a letter for her from thence to Jerusalem.

Me.   What occasion can she have for you to be her letter-carrier that has so many angels for her secretaries and pages?

Og.   He pulled out of his pouch a little piece of wood, cut off from the beam on which the Virgin mother stood. The admirable fragrancy of it shewed it to be a thing that was highly sacred. I having received this present in the lowest posture of humility and bare headed, and having kissed it over and over, put it in my pocket.

Me.   May a person see it?

Og.   I will let you see it if you will. But if you have eaten or drank to-day, or have had to do with your wife last night, I would not advise you to look upon it.

Me.   Let me see it; there is no danger.

Og.   Here it is for you.

Me.   O happy man art thou that hast such a present!

Og.   Whether you know it or no, I would not exchange this little fragment for all the gold in the Tagus [a gold-bearing river in Spain]. I will set it in gold, and put it in a crystal case so that it may be seen through it. When this hysteroprotos saw me so religiously transported with that small present, thinking I deserved to have things of greater moment imparted to me, he asked me if I had seen the Virgin's secrets. That word startled me a little, but I durst not ask him what he meant by the Virgin's secrets, for in matters so sacred there is danger in a slip of the tongue. I told him I had not seen them, but I had a very great desire to see them. Then I am conducted in as one in an ecstacy. A wax taper or two was lighted, and a little image was shewn me that made no extraordinary figure, neither for magnitude, matter, nor workmanship, but of extraordinary virtue.

Me.   Bulk has no great matter in it as to the doing of miracles. I have seen St. Christopher at Paris, not him of a cartload or of the size of a colossus, but rather of a large mountain; but I never heard he was famous for doing miracles.

Og.   At the feet of the Virgin there is a jewel that neither the Latins nor Greeks have yet given a name to. The French have given it a name from a toad, because it has the resemblance of a toad in it so lively that no art can match it. And that which is the more miraculous is that it is a very small stone, and the image does not stand out of it, but is included in the very body of the stone, and may be seen through it.

Me.   Perhaps they may fancy they see the likeness of a toad cut in it, as some fancy they see that of an eagle in the stalk of a brake or fern; and as boys, who see everything in the clouds, as dragons breathing out fire, burning mountains, and armed men fighting.

Og.   Nay, that you may be thoroughly satisfied in the matter, no living toad ever shewed itself more plainly than that is expressed there.

Me.   I have been hearing your stories all this while, but I would have you find out somebody else to give credit to your story of the toad.

Og.   I do not at all wonder, Menedemus, that you are so incredulous; I should not have believed it myself if the whole tribe of divines had asserted it, unless I- had seen it with these eyes-I say beheld it with these very eyes, and had experienced the truth of it. But methinks you seem not to be curious enough upon these natural rarities.

Me.   Why so? what, because I will not believe that asses fly.

Og.   But do you not observe how nature sports herself in imitating the shapes and colours of everything in other things, but especially in precious stones? And also what admirable virtues it has planted in them, which are altogether incredible if common experience did not force us to a belief of them? Pray thee, tell me, would you ever have believed without seeing it with your eyes that steel could have been drawn by the loadstone without touching it, or be driven away from it without being touched by it?

Me.   No, indeed, I never should, although ten Aristotles had taken their oaths of the truth of it.

Og.   Well, then, do not say everything is a fable that has not fallen within the compass of your experience. We find the figure of a bolt in a thunder-stone, fire in the carbuncle, the figure of hail and the coldness of it in the hail-stone, nay, even though you throw it into the midst of the fire; the deep and transparent waves of the sea in the emerald; the carciuias imitates the figure of a sea-crab, the echites of a- viper, the scarites of a gilt head, the theracites of a hawk, the geranites shews you the figured neck of a, crane, the segophthalmus shews the eye of a goat, and some shew that of a hog, and another three human eyes together; the lycophthalmus paints you. out the eye of a wolf in four colours, fiery and bloody, and in the middle black encompassed with white. If you open the black cyamea you will find a bean in the middle; the dryites represents the trunk of a tree, and burns like wood; the cissites and narcissites represent ivy, the astrapias darts forth rays, of lightning out of the midst of white or blue, the phlegontites shews a flame within that does not come out; in the anthracitis you may see certain sparks running to and fro; the crocias represents the colour of saffron, the ihodites that of a rose, the chaleites of brass, the aietites the figure of an eagle with a white tail, the taos represents a peacock, the chelidonia an asp, the merrnecites has the image of a creeping pismire growing within it; the cantharias shews a perfect beetle, and the scorpites admirably deciphers a scorpion. But whyshould I proceed to recount that which is innumerable, when there is no part of nature, either in elements, animals, or plants, which nature, as it were to sport herself, does not give us some resemblance of in stones' And do you then admire that the form of a toad is represented in the bufonites?

Me.   I wonder that nature has so much spare time as to divert herself in drawing the pictures of everything.

Og.   It has a mind to exercise the curiosity of mankind, and by that means to keep us from being idle. And yet, as though we were at a loss to know how to pass away our time, we run a madding after buffoons, dice, and jugglers.

Me.   You say true.

Og.   And some persons of credit add, that if you put this toadstone into vinegar it will move its legs and swim.

Me.   But why is this dedicated to the Virgin?

Og.   Because she has overcome, trampled upon, and extinguished all uncleanness, malice, pride, avarice, and all manner of earthly desires. Me,. Woe to us, then, who carry so much of the toad still in our hearts!

Og.   But We shall be pure if we worship the Virgin as we ought.

Me.   How would she have us worship her?

Og.   You will perform most acceptable service to her if you imitate her.

Me.   That is soon said, but not so easily performed.

Og.   It is hard indeed, but then it is very well worth the pains.

Me.   Come on, go forwards in what you have begun.

Og.   Afterwards he shewed me statues of gold and silver. This, says he, is solid gold, and this is only silver gilt. He told me the weight of every one, the price, and the name of the donor. I being full of admiration at everything, and congratulating the Virgin being mistress of so much wealth, says the officer to me, Inasmuch as I perceive you are so pious a spectator, I think I should not do fairly by you if I should conceal anything from you, therefore you shall see the greatest privacies the Virgin has. And presently he takes out of a drawer from under the altar a world of admirable things, the particulars of which, if I should proceed to mention, the day would not be long enough; so that thus far the journey succeeded to my wish. I satisfied my curiosity abundantly with fine sights, and brought home with me this inestimable present, a pledge of the Virgin's love, given, me by herself.

Me.   Did you ever make trial of the virtues of this piece of wood?

Og.   I have. Three or four days ago I, being in an house of entertainment, found a man stark mad, whom they ere just going to put into chains; I put this piece of wood privately under his bolster, and he fell into a sound sleep and slept a long time, and when he rose in the morning he was as sober as ever.

Me.   Perhaps he was not dis tracted but drunk, and sleep commonly cures that distemper. Og Menedemus, since you love to use raillery, take another subject. It is neither pious nor safe to make sport with saints; nay, the man himself told me that there was a woman appeared to him in his sleep of an incomparable beauty, that held forth a cup to him to drink.

Me.   Hellebore, I believe.

Og.   That is uncertain; but this ia certain, that the man recovered his reason.

Me.   Did you pass by Thomas, Archbishop of Canterbury?

Og   No, I think I did not. It is one of the most religious pilgrimages in the world.

Me.   I long to hear it, if it will not be too much trouble to you.

Og.   It is so far from that, that you will oblige me in hearing of it. That part of England that looks towards Flanders and France is called Kent; the metropolis of it is Canterbury. There are two monasteries in it that are almost contiguous, and they are both of Benedictines. That which bears the name of Augustine is the ancienter of the two; that which is now called by the name of St. Thomas seems to have been the seat of St. Thomas the archbishop, where he had led his life with a few monks whom he chose for his companions, as now-a-days deans have their palaces near the church, though separate from the houses of other canons. For, in old time, both bishops and canons were monks, as appears by the manifest vestigia of things. But the church that is dedicated to St. Thomas raises itself up towards heaven with that majesty that it strikes those that behold it at a great distance with an awe of religion, and now with its splendour makes the light of the neighbouring palaces look dim, and as it were obscures the place that was anciently the most celebrated for religion. There are two lofty turrets which stand as it were bidding visitants welcome from afar off, and a ring of bells that make the adjacent country echo far and wide with their rolling sound. In the south porch of the church stand three stone statues of men in armour, who with wicked hands murdered the holy man, with the names of their countries-Tusci, Fusci, and Betri.

Me.   Why have such wicked men so much honour done them?

Og.   They have the same honour done to them that is done to Judas, Pilate, Caiaphas, and the band of wicked soldiers whose images you may see carved upon stately altars; and their names are added that none after them might arrogate to themselves the glory of the fact. They are set there in open sight to be a warning to wicked courtiers, that no one may hereafter presume to lay his hand on either bishops or the possessions of the church. For these three ruffians ran mad with horror of the fact that they had committed; nor had they come to themselves again, had not holy Thomas been implored in favour of them.

Me.   Oh, the perpetual clemency of martyrs!

Og.   When you are entered in, a certain spacious majesty of place opens itself to you, which is free to every one. Me, Is there nothing to be seen there?

Og.   Nothing but the bulk of the structure, and some books chained to the pillars, containing the gospel of Nicodemus and the sepulchre of I cannot tell who. He. And what else?

Og.   Iron grates enclose the place called the choir, so that there is no entrance, but so that the view is still open from one end of the church to the other. You ascend to this by a great many steps, under which there is a certain vault that opens a passage to the north side. There they shew a wooden altar consecrated to the holy Virgin; it is a very small one, and remarkable for nothing except as a monument of antiquity, reproaching the luxury of the present times. In that place the good man is reported to have taken his last leave of the Virgin, when he was at the point of death. Upon the altar is the point of the sword with which the top of the head of that good prelate was wounded, and some of his brains that were beaten out, to make sure work of it. We most religiously kissed the sacred rust of this weapon out of love to the martyr. Leaving this place, we went down into a vault underground; to that there belong two showers of relics. The first thing they shew you is the skull of the martyr, as it was bored through; the upper" part is left open to be kissed, all the rest is covered over with silver. There also is shewn you a leaden plate with this inscription, Thomas Acrensis. And there hang up in a great place the shirts of hair-cloth, the girdles, and breeches with which this prelate used to mortify his flesh, the very sight of which is enough to strike one with horror, and to reproach the effeminacy and delicacy of our age.

Me.   Nay, perhaps of the monks themselves.

Og.   That I can neither affirm nor deny, nor does it signify much to me.

Me.   You say right.

Og.   Hence we return to the choir. On the north side they open a private place. It is incredible what a world of bones they brought out of it, skulls, chins, teeth, hands, fingers, whole arms, all which we having first adored, kissed; nor had there been any end of it had it not been for one of my fellow-travellers, who indiscreetly interrupted the officer that was shewing them.

Me.   Who was he?

Og.   He was an Englishman, his name was Gratian Pullus, a man of learning and piety, but not so well affected to this part of religion as I could wish he were.

Me.   I fancy he was a Wickliffite.

Og.   No, I believe he was not, though he had read his books; but I do not know where he had them.

Me.   Did he make the officer angry?

Og.   He took out an arm having yet some bloody flesh upon it; he shewed a reluctance to the kissing it, and a sort of uneasiness in his countenance: and presently the officer shut up all his relics again. After this we viewed the table of the altar, and the ornaments; and after that those things that were laid up under the altar: all was very rich; you would have said Midas and Croesus were beggars compared to them, if you beheld the great quantities of gold and silver.

Me. And was there no kissing here?

Og. No, but my mind was touched with other sorts of wishes.

Me. What were they?

Og. I made me sigh to think I had no such relics in my own house.

Me. A sacrilegious wish!

Og. I confess it, and I humbly begged pardon of the saint before I set my foot out of the church. After this we were carried into the vestry. Good God! what a pomp of silk vestments was there, of golden candlesticks! There we saw also St. Thomas's foot. It looked like a reed painted over with silver; it hath but little of weight, and nothing of workmanship, and was longer than up to one's girdle.

Me. Was there never a cross?

Og. I saw none. There was a gown shewn; it was silk, indeed, but coarse and without embroidery or jewels, and a handkerchief, still having plain marks of sweat and blood from the saint's neck. We readily kissed these monuments of ancient frugality.

Me. Are these to everybody?

Og. No, certainly, my good friend.

Me. How then did you come to have such credit with them, that none of their secrets were concealed from you?

Og. I had some acquaintance with the reverend prelate, William Wai'ham, the archbishop, and he recommended me.

Me. I have heard he was a man of great humanity.

Og. Nay, if you knew the man, you would take him for humanity itself. He was a man of that learning, that candour of manners, and that piety of life, that there was nothing wanting in him to make him a most accomplished prelate. From hence we were conducted up higher; for behind the high altar there is another ascent as into another church. In a certain new chapel there was shewn to us the whole face of the good man set in gold, and adorned with jewels; and here a certain unexpected chance had near interrupted all our felicity.

Me. I want sadly to hear what mischievous matter this was.

Og. My friend Gratian lost himself here extremely. After a short prayer, he says to the assistant of him that shewed us the relics, Good father, is it true, as I have heard, that Thomas, while he lived, was very charitable to the poor? Very true, replies he, and began to relate a great many instances of his charity. Then, answers Gratian, I do not believe that good inclination in him is changed, unless it be for the better. The othEr assented. Then, says he again, if this holy man was so liberal to the poor when he was a poor man himself, and stood in need of charity for the support of his own body, do you not think he would take it well now, when he is grown so rich and wants nothing, if some poor woman having a family of children at home ready to starve, or daughters in danger of being under a necessity to prostitute themselves for want of portions, or a husband sick in bed, and destitute of all comforts; if such a woman should ask him leave to make bold with some small portion of these vast riches for the relief of her family, taking it either as by consent, or by gift, or by way of borrowing? The assistant making no answer to this, Gratian being a warm man, I am fully persuaded, says he, that the good man would be glad at his heart, that when he is dead he could be able to relieve the necessities of the poor with his wealth. Upon this the shower of the relics began to frown, and to pout out his lips, and to look upon us as if he would have eaten us up; and I do not doubt but he would have spit in our faces, and have turned us out of the church by the neck and shoulders, but that we had the archbishop's recommendation. Indeed I did in some measure pacify him with good words, telling him that Gratian did not speak this from his heart, but had a droll way with him, and also laid down a little money.

Me.   Indeed, I exceedingly approve of your piety. But I sometimes seriously think of it, how they can possibly excuse themselves from being guilty of a fault who consume such vast sums in building, Beautifying, and enriching churches, setting no bound to their expenses. I allow that there ought to be a dignity in the sacred vestments, the vessels of a church, agreeable to the solemn service, and would have the structure of it to have a certain air of majesty; but to what purpose 'are so many golden fonts, so many candlesticks, and so many images? To what purpose is such a profusion of expense upon organs, as they call them? Nor are we, indeed, content with one pair. What signify those concerts of music, hired at So great an expense; when in the meantime our brothers and sisters, Christ's living temples, are ready to perish for hunger and thirst!

Og.   There is no man, either of piety or wisdom, but would wish for a moderation in these matters; but since this error proceeds from a certain extreme of piety, it deserves some favour, especially when we reflect, on the other hand, on the contrary errors of others, who rob churches rather than build them up. They are commonly endowed by great men and monarchs, who would employ the money worse in gaming or war. And, moreover, if you take anything away from the church, in the first place it is accounted sacrilege; and in the second place, it shuts up the hands of those who had an inclination to give; and besides, it is a temptation to rapine. The churchmen are rather guardians of these tkings than masters of them. And lastly, I had rather see a church luxuriant with sacred furniture, than as some of them are, naked and sordid, more like stables than churches.

Me.   But we read that the bishops of old were commended for selling the sacred vessels and relieving the poor with the money.

Og.   And so they are commended at this day; but they are only commended; for I am of the mind, they neither have the power nor the will to follow the example.

Me.   But I hinder your narration; I now expect to hear the conclusion of your story.

Og.   Well, you shall have it, and I will be very brief. Upon this, out comes the head of the college.

Me.   Who was he, the abbot of the place?

Og.   He wears a mitre, and has the revenue of an abbot-he wants nothing but the name; he is called the prior, because the archbishop is in the place of an abbot; for in old time every one that was an archbishop of that diocese was a monk.

Me.   I did not matter if I was called a camel, if I had but the revenue of an abbot.

Og.   He seemed to me to be a godly and prudent man, and not unacquainted with the Scotch divinity. He opened us the box in which the remainder of the holy man's body is said to rest.

Me.   Did you see the bones?

Og.   That is not permitted, nor can it be done without a ladder. But a wooden box covers a golden one, and that being craned up with ropes, discovers an inestimable treasure.

Me.   What say you?

Og.   Gold was the basest part. Everything sparkled and sinned with very large and scarce jewels, some of them bigger than a goose's egg. There some monks stood about with the greatest veneration. The cover being taken off, we all worshipped. The prior, with a white wand, touched every stone one by one, telling us the name in French, the value of it, and who was the donor of it. The principal of them were the presents of kings.

Me.   He had need to have a good memory.

Og.   You guess right, and yet practice goes a great way, for he does this frequently. Hence he carried us back into a vault. There the Virgin Mary has her residence; it is something dark; it is doubly railed in and encompassed about with iron bars.

Me.   What is she afraid of?

Og.   Nothing, I suppose, but thieves. And I never in my life saw anything more laden with riches.

Me.   You tell me of riches in the dark.

Og.   Candles being brought in we saw more than a royal sight.

Me.   What, does it go beyond the Parathalassian virgin in wealth?

Og.   It goes far beyond in appearance. What is concealed she knows best. These things are shewn to none but great persons or peculiar friends. In the end we were carried back into the vestry. There was pulled out a chest covered with black leather; it was set upon the table and opened. They all fell down on their knees and worshipped.

Me.   What was in it?

Og.   Pieces of linen rags, a great many of them retaining still the marks of the snot. These were those, they say, that the holy man used to wipe the sweat off from his face and neck with, the snot out of his nose, or any other such sort of filth which human bodies are not free from. Here again my Gratian behaved himself in none of the most obliging manners; for the gentle prior offered to him, being an Englishman, an acquaintance, and a man of considerable authority, one of the rags for a present, thinking he had presented him with a very acceptable gift; but Gratian unthankfully took it squeamishly in his fingers, and laid it down with an air of contempt, making up his mouth at it as if he would have smacked it. For this was his custom, if anything came in his way that he would express his contempt to. I was both ashamed and afraid. Nevertheless the good prior, though not insensible of the affront, seemed to take no notice of it; and after he had civilly entertained us with a glass of wine, dismissed us, and we went back to London....

Martin Luther

The following text is excerpted from a very lengthy treatise that Martin Luther wrote in 1520, which well encapsulates the reasons that compelled Luther to break with the Roman Catholic Church and to found his own Lutheran Church. This text also illustrates Luther's tremendous power and passionate nature as a writer, thinker, and leader.

🕊️ *(Taken from the translation of C. A. Buchheim in the Harvard Classics) Address to the Christian Nobility of the German Nation Respecting the Reform of the Christian Estate*

To his most Serene and Mighty Imperial Majesty [Emperor Charles V] and to the Christian Nobility of the German Nation. Dr. Martinus Luther.

The grace and might of God be with you, Most Serene Majesty, most gracious, well-beloved gentlemen!

It is not out of mere arrogance and perversity that I, an individual poor man, have taken upon me to address your lordships. The distress and misery that oppress all the Christian estates, more especially in Germany, have led not only myself, but every one else, to cry aloud and to ask for help, and have now forced me too to cry out and to ask if God would give His Spirit to any one to reach a hand to His wretched people. Councils have often put forward some remedy, but it has adroitly been frustrated, and the evils have become worse, through the cunning of certain men. Their malice and wickedness I will now, by the help of God, expose, so that, being known, they may henceforth cease to be so obstructive and injurious. God has given us a young and noble sovereign [Emperor Charles V], 1 and by this has roused great hopes in many hearts; now it is right that we too should do what we can, and make good use of time and grace....

THE THREE WALLS OF THE ROMANISTS

The Romanists have, with great adroitness, drawn three walls round themselves, with which they have hitherto protected themselves, so that no one could reform them, whereby all Christendom has fallen terribly. Firstly, if pressed by the temporal power, they have affirmed and maintained that the temporal power has no jurisdiction over them, but, on the contrary, that the spiritual power is above the temporal. Secondly, if it were proposed to admonish them with the Scriptures, they objected that no one may interpret the Scriptures but the Pope. Thirdly, if they are threatened with a council, they pretend that no one may call a council but the Pope.

Thus they have secretly stolen our three rods, so that they may be unpunished, and intrenched themselves behind these three walls, to act with all the wickedness and malice, which we now witness. And whenever they have been compelled to call a council, they have made it of no avail by binding the princes beforehand with an oath to leave them as they were, and to give moreover to the Pope full power over the procedure of the council, so that it is all one whether we have many councils or no councils, in addition to which they deceive us with false pretences and tricks. So grievously do they tremble for their skin before a true, free council; and thus they have overawed kings and princes, that these believe they would be offending God, if they were not to obey them in all such knavish, deceitful artifices. Now may God help us, and give us one of those trumpets that overthrew the walls of Jericho, so that we may blow down these walls of straw and paper, and that we may set free our Christian rods for the chastisement of sin, and expose the craft and deceit of the devil, so that we may amend ourselves by punishment and again obtain God's favour.

(A) THE FIRST WALL

⊹ That the Temporal Power has no Jurisdiction over the Spirituality

Let us, in the first place, attack the first wall. It has been devised that the Pope, bishops, priests, and monks are called the spiritual estate, princes, lords, artificers, and peasants are the temporal estate. This is an artful lie and hypocritical device, but let no one be made afraid by it, and that for this reason: that all Christians are truly of the spiritual estate, and there is no difference among them, save of office alone. As St. Paul says (1 Cor. xii.), we are all one body, though each member does its own work, to serve the others. This is because we have one baptism, one Gospel, one faith, and are all Christians alike; for baptism, Gospel, and faith, these alone make spiritual and Christian people.

As for the unction by a pope or a bishop, tonsure, ordination, consecration, and clothes differing from those of laymen-all this may make a hypocrite or an anointed puppet, but never a Christian or a spiritual man. Thus we are all consecrated as priests by baptism, as St. Peter says: "Ye are a royal priesthood, a holy nation" (1 Peter ii. 9); and in the book of Revelations: "and hast made us unto our God (by Thy blood) kings and priests" (Rev. v. 10). For, if we had not a higher consecration in us than pope or bishop can give, no priest could ever be made by the consecration of pope or bishop, nor could he say the mass, or preach, or absolve. Therefore the bishop's consecration is just as if in the name of the whole congregation he took one person out of the community, each member of which has equal power, and commanded him to exercise this power for the rest; in the same way as if ten brothers, co-heirs as king's sons, were to choose one from among them to rule over their inheritance, they would all of them still remain kings and have equal power, although one is ordered to govern.

And to put the matter even more plainly, if a little company of pious Christian laymen were taken prisoners and carried away to a desert, and had not among them a priest consecrated by a bishop, and were there to agree to elect one of them, born in wedlock or not, and were to order him to baptise, to celebrate the mass, to absolve, and to preach, this man would as truly be a priest, as if all the bishops and all the Popes had consecrated him. That is why in cases of necessity every man can baptise and absolve, which would not be possible if we were not all priests. This great grace and virtue of baptism and of the Christian estate they have quite destroyed and made us forget by their ecclesiastical law. In this way the Christians used to choose their bishops and priests out of the community; these being afterwards confirmed by other bishops, without the pomp that now prevails. So was it that St. Augustine, Ambrose, Cyprian, were bishops.

Since, then, the temporal power is baptised as we are, and has the same faith and Gospel, we must allow it to be priest and bishop, and account its office an office that is proper and useful to the Christian community. For whatever issues from baptism may boast that it has been consecrated priest, bishop, and pope, although it does not beseem every one to exercise these offices. For, since we are all priests alike, no man may put himself forward or take upon himself, without our consent and election, to do that which we have all alike power to do. For, if a thing is common to all, no man may take it to himself without the wish and command of the community. And if it should happen that a man were appointed to one of these offices and deposed for abuses, he would be just what he was before. Therefore a priest should be nothing in Christendom but a functionary; as long as he holds his office, he has precedence of others; if he is deprived of it, he is a peasant or a citizen like the rest. Therefore a priest is verily no longer a priest after deposition. But now they have invented characteres indelebiles, 2 and pretend that a priest after deprivation still differs from a simple layman. They even imagine that a priest can never be anything but a priest-that is, that he can never become a layman. All this is nothing but mere talk and ordinance of human invention. It follows, then, that between laymen and priests, princes and bishops, or, as they call it, between spiritual and temporal persons, the only real difference is one of office and function, and not of estate; for they are all of the same spiritual estate, true priests, bishops, and popes, though their functions are not the same-just as among priests and monks every man has not the same functions. And this, as I said above, St. Paul says (Rom. xii.; 1 Cor. xii.), and St. Peter (1 Peter ii.): "We, being many, are one body in Christ, and severally members one of another." Christ's body is not double or twofold, one temporal, the other spiritual. He is one Head, and He has one body....

... what do the Romanist scribes mean by their laws? They mean that they withdraw themselves from the operation of temporal Christian power, simply in order that they may be free to do evil, and thus fulfil what St. Peter said: "There shall be false teachers among you, . . . and in covetousness shall they with feigned words make merchandise of you" (2 Peter ii. 1, etc.). Therefore the temporal Christian power must exercise its office without let or hindrance, without considering whom it may strike, whether pope, or bishop, or priest: whoever is guilty, let him suffer for it. Whatever the ecclesiastical law has said in opposition to this is merely the invention of Romanist arrogance. For this is what St. Paul says to all Christians: "Let every soul" (I presume including the popes) "be subject unto the higher powers; for they bear not the sword in vain: they serve the Lord therewith, for vengeance on evildoers and for praise to them that do well" (Rom. xiii. 1-4). Also St. Peter: "Submit yourselves to every ordinance of man for the Lord's sake, . . . for so is the will of God" (1 Peter ii. 13, 15). He has also foretold that men would come who should despise government (2 Peter ii.), as has come to pass through ecclesiastical law....

It is, indeed, past bearing that the spiritual law should esteem so highly the liberty, life, and property of the clergy, as if laymen were not as good spiritual Christians, or not equally members of the Church. Why should your body, life, goods, and honour be free, and not mine, seeing that we are equal as Christians, and have received alike baptism, faith, spirit, and all things? If a priest is killed, the country is laid under an interdict. why not also if a peasant is killed? Whence comes this great difference among equal Christians? Simply from human laws and inventions. It can have been no good spirit, either, that devised these evasions and made sin to go unpunished. For if, as Christ and the Apostles bid us, it is our duty to oppose the evil one and all his works and words, and to drive him away as well as may be, how then should we remain quiet and be silent when the Pope and his followers are guilty of devilish works and words? Are we for the sake of men to allow the commandments and the truth of God to be defeated, which at our baptism we vowed to support with body and soul? Truly we should have to answer for all souls that would thus be abandoned and led astray....

(B) THE SECOND WALL

✣   That no one may interpret the Scriptures but the Pope

The second wall is even more tottering and weak: that they alone pretend to be considered masters of the Scriptures; although they learn nothing of them all their life. They assume authority, and juggle before us with impudent words, saying that the Pope cannot err in matters of faith, whether he be evil or good, albeit they cannot prove it by a single letter. That is why the canon law contains so many heretical and unchristian, nay unnatural, laws; but of these we need not speak now. For whereas they imagine the Holy Ghost never leaves them, however unlearned and wicked they may be, they grow bold enough to decree whatever they like. But were this true, where were the need and use of the Holy Scriptures? Let us burn them, and content ourselves with the unlearned gentlemen at Rome, in whom the Holy Ghost dwells, who, however, can dwell in pious souls only. If I had not read it, I could never have believed that the devil should have put forth such follies at Rome and find a following.

But not to fight them with our own words, we will quote the Scriptures. St. Paul says, "If anything be revealed to another that sitteth by, let the first hold his peace" (1 Cor. xiv. 30). What would be the use of this commandment, if we were to believe him alone that teaches or has the highest seat? Christ Himself says, "And they shall be all taught of God." (St. John vi. 45). Thus it may come to pass that the Pope and his followers are wicked and not true Christians, and not being taught by God, have no true understanding, whereas a common man may have true understanding. Why should we then not follow him? Has not the Pope often erred? Who could help Christianity, in case the Pope errs, if we do not rather believe another who has the Scriptures for him?

Therefore it is a wickedly devised fable-and they cannot quote a single letter to confirm it-that it is for the Pope alone to interpret the Scriptures or to confirm the interpretation of them. They have assumed the authority of their own selves. And though they say that this authority was given to St. Peter when the keys were given to him, it is plain enough that the keys were not given to St. Peter alone, but to the whole community. Besides, the keys were not ordained for doctrine or authority, but for sin, to bind or loose, and what they claim besides this from the keys is mere invention. But what Christ said to St. Peter: "I have prayed for thee that thy faith fail not" (St. Luke xxii. 32), cannot relate to the Pope, inasmuch as the greater part of the Popes have been without faith, as they are themselves forced to acknowledge; nor did Christ pray for Peter alone, but for all the Apostles and all Christians, as He says, "Neither pray I for these alone, but for them also which shall believe on Me through their word" (St. John xvii.). Is not this plain enough?

Only consider the matter. They must needs acknowledge that there are pious Christians among us that have the true faith, spirit, understanding, word, and mind of Christ: why then should we reject their word and understanding, and follow a pope who has neither understanding nor spirit? Surely this were to deny our whole faith and the Christian Church. Moreover, if the article of our faith is right, "I believe in the holy Christian Church," the Pope cannot alone be right; else we must say, "I believe in the Pope of Rome," and reduce the Christian Church to one man, which is a devilish and damnable heresy. Besides that, we are all priests, as I have said, and have all one faith, one Gospel, one Sacrament; how then should we not have the power of discerning and judging what is right or wrong in matters of faith? What becomes of St. Paul's words, "But he that is spiritual judgeth all things, yet he himself is judged of no man" (1 Cor. ii. 15), and also, "we having the same spirit of faith"? (2 Cor. iv. 13). Why then should we not perceive as well as an unbelieving pope what agrees or disagrees with our faith?

By these and many other texts we should gain courage and freedom, and should not let the spirit of liberty (as St. Paul has it) be frightened away by the inventions of the popes; we should boldly judge what they do and what they leave undone by our own believing understanding of the Scriptures, and force them to follow the better understanding, and not their own. Did not Abraham in old days have to obey his Sarah, who was in stricter bondage to him than we are to any one on earth? Thus, too, Balaam's ass was wiser than the prophet. If God spoke by an ass against a prophet, why should He not speak by a pious man against the Pope? Besides, St. Paul withstood St. Peter as being in error (Gal. ii.). Therefore it behoves every Christian to aid the faith by understanding and defending it and by condemning all errors.

(C) THE THİRD WALL

✣ That no one may call a council but the Pope

The third wall falls of itself, as soon as the first two have fallen; for if the Pope acts contrary to the Scriptures, we are bound to stand by the Scriptures, to punish and to constrain him, according to Christ's commandment, "Moreover, if thy brother shall trespass against thee, go and tell him his fault between thee and him alone; if he shall hear thee, thou hast gained thy brother. But if he will not hear thee, then take with thee one or two more, that in the mouth of two or three witnesses every word may be established. And if he shall neglect to hear them, tell it unto the Church; but if he neglect to hear the Church, let him be unto thee as a heathen man and a publican" (St. Matt. xviii. 15-17). Here each member is commanded to take care for the other; much more then should we do this, if it is a ruling member of the community that does evil, which by its evil-doing causes great harm and offence to the others. If then I am to accuse him before the Church, I must collect the Church together. Moreover, they can show nothing in the Scriptures giving the Pope sole power to call and confirm councils; they have nothing but their own laws; but these hold good only so long as they are not injurious to Christianity and the laws of God. Therefore, if the Pope deserves punishment, these laws cease to bind us, since Christendom would suffer, if he were not punished by a council. Thus we read (Acts xv.) that the council of the Apostles was not called by St. Peter, but by all the Apostles and the elders. But if the right to call it had lain with St. Peter alone, it would not have been a Christian council, but a heretical conciliabulum. Moreover, the most celebrated council of all-that of Nicaea-was neither called nor confirmed by the Bishop of Rome, but by the Emperor Constantine; and after him many other emperors have done the same, and yet the councils called by them were accounted most Christian. But if the Pope alone had the power, they must all have been heretical. Moreover, if I consider the councils that the Pope has called, I do not find that they produced any notable results.

Therefore when need requires, and the Pope is a cause of offence to Christendom, in these cases whoever can best do so, as a faithful member of the whole body, must do what he can to procure a true free council. This no one can do so well as the temporal authorities, especially since they are fellow-Christians, fellow-priests, sharing one spirit and one power in all things, and since they should exercise the office that they have received from God without hindrance, whenever it is necessary and useful that it should be exercised. Would it not be most unnatural, if a fire were to break out in a city, and every one were to keep still and let it burn on and on, whatever might be burnt, simply because they had not the mayor's authority, or because the fire perchance broke out at the mayor's house? Is not every citizen bound in this case to rouse and call in the rest? How much more should this be done in the spiritual city of Christ, if a fire of offence breaks out, either at the Pope's government or wherever it may! The like happens if an enemy attacks a town. The first to rouse up the rest earns glory and thanks. Why then should not he earn glory that descries the coming of our enemies from hell and rouses and summons all Christians?

But as for their boasts of their authority, that no one must oppose it, this is idle talk. No one in Christendom has any authority to do harm, or to forbid others to prevent harm being done. There is no authority in the Church but for reformation. Therefore if the Pope wished to use his power to prevent the calling of a free council, so as to prevent the reformation of the Church, we must not respect him or his power; and if he should begin to excommunicate and fulminate, we must despise this as the doings of a madman, and, trusting in God, excommunicate and repel him as best we may. For this his usurped power is nothing; he does not possess it, and he is at once overthrown by a text from the Scriptures. For St. Paul says to the Corinthians "that God has given us authority for edification, and not for destruction (2 Cor. x. 8). Who will set this text at nought? It is the power of the devil and of antichrist that prevents what would serve for the reformation of Christendom. Therefore we must not follow it, but oppose it with our body, our goods, and all that we have. And even if a miracle were to happen in favour of the Pope against the temporal power, or if some were to be stricken by a plague, as they sometimes boast has happened, all this is to be held as having been done by the devil in order to injure our faith in God, as was foretold by Christ: "There shall arise false Christs and false prophets, and shall show great sings and wonders, insomuch that, if it were possible, they shall deceive the very elect" (Matt. xxiv. 23); and St. Paul tells the Thessalonians that the coming of antichrist shall be "after the working of Satan with all power and signs and lying wonders" (2 Thess. ii. 9)....

OF THE MATTERS TO BE CONSIDERED IN THE COUNCILS

1. It is a distressing and terrible thing to see that the head of Christendom, who boasts of being the vicar of Christ and the successor of St. Peter, lives in a worldly pomp that no king or emperor can equal, so that in him that calls himself most holy and most spiritual there is more worldliness than in the world itself. He wears a triple crown, whereas the mightiest kings only wear one crown. If this resembles the poverty of Christ and St. Peter, it is a new sort of resemblance. They prate of its being heretical to object to this; nay, they will not even hear how unchristian and ungodly it is. But I think that if he should have to pray to God with tears, he would have to lay down his crowns; for God will not endure any arrogance. His office should be nothing else than to weep and pray constantly for Christendom and to be an example of all humility.

However this may be, this pomp is a stumbling-block, and the Pope, for the very salvation of his soul, ought to put if off, for St. Paul says, "Abstain from all appearance of evil" (1 Thess. v. 21), and again, "Provide things honest in the sight of all men" (2 Cor. viii. 21). A simple mitre would be enough for the pope: wisdom and sanctity should raise him above the rest; the crown of pride he should leave to antichrist, as his predecessors did some hundreds of years ago. They say, He is the ruler of the world. This is false; for Christ, whose vicegerent and vicar he claims to be, said to Pilate, "My kingdom is not of this world" (John xviii. 36). But no vicegerent can have a wider dominion than this Lord, nor is he a vicegerent of Christ in His glory, but of Christ crucified, as St. Paul says, "For I determined not to know anything among you save Jesus Christ, and Him crucified" (2 Cor. ii. 2), and "Let this mind be in you, which was also in Christ Jesus, who made Himself of no reputation, and took upon Himself the form of a servant" (Phil. ii. 5, 7). Again, "We preach Christ crucified" (1 Cor. i.). Now they make the Pope a vicegerent of Christ exalted in heaven, and some have let the devil rule them so thoroughly that they have maintained that the Pope is above the angels in heaven and has power over them, which is precisely the true work of the true antichrist.

2. What is the use in Christendom of the people called "cardinals"? I will tell you. In Italy and Germany there are many rich convents, endowments, fiefs, and benefices, and as the best way of getting these into the hands of rRome, they created cardinals, and gave them the sees, convents, and prelacies, and thus destroyed the service of God. That is why Italy is almost a desert now: the convents are destroyed, the sees consumed, the revenues of the prelacies and of all the churches drawn to Rome; towns are decayed, the country and the people ruined, because there is no more any worship of God or preaching; why? Because the cardinals must have all the wealth. No Turk could have thus desolated Italy and overthrown the worship of God.

Now that Italy is sucked dry, they come to Germany and begin very quietly; but if we look on quietly Germany will soon be brought into the same state as Italy. We have a few cardinals already. What the Romanists mean thereby the drunken Germans are not to see until they have lost everything - bishoprics, convents, benefices, fiefs, even to their last farthing. Antichrist must take the riches of the earth, as it is written (Dan. xi. 8, 39, 43). They begin by taking off the cream of the bishoprics, convents and fiefs; and as they do not dare to destroy everything as they have done in Italy, they employ such holy cunning to join together ten or twenty prelacies, and take such a portion of each annually that the total amounts to a considerable sum. The priory of Wurzburg gives one thousand guilders; those of Bamberg, Mainz, Treves, and others also contribute. In this way they collect one thousand or ten thousand guilders, in order that a cardinal may live at Rome in a state like that of a wealthy monarch. After we have gained this, we will create thirty or forty cardinals on one day, and give one St. Michael's Mount, near Bamberg, and likewise the see of Wurzburg, to which belong some rich benefices, until the churches and the cities are desolated; and then we shall say, We are the vicars of Christ, the shepherds of Christ's flocks; those mad, drunken Germans must submit to it. I advise, however, that there be made fewer cardinals, or that the Pope should have to support them out of his own purse. It would be amply sufficient if there were twelve, and if each of them had an annual income of one thousand guilders. What has brought us Germans to such a pass that we have to suffer this robbery and this destruction of our property by the Pope? If the kingdom of France has resisted it, why do we Germans suffer ourselves to be fooled and deceived? It would be more endurable if they did nothing but rob us of our property; but they destroy the Church and deprive Christ's flock of their good shepherds, and overthrow the service and word of God. Even if there were no cardinals at all, the Church would not perish, for they do nothing for the good of Christendom; all they do is to traffic in and quarrel about prelacies and bishoprics, which any robber could do as well.

3. If we took away ninety-nine parts of the Pope's Court and only left one hundredth, it would still be large enough to answer questions on matters of belief. Now there is such a swarm of vermin at Rome, all called papal, that Babylon itself never saw the like. There are more than three thousand papal secretaries alone; but who shall count the other office-bearers, since there are so many offices that we can scarcely count them, and all waiting for German benefices, as wolves wait for a flock of sheep? I think Germany now pays more to the Pope than it formerly paid the emperors; nay, some think more than three hundred thousand guilders are sent from Germany to Rome every year, for nothing whatever; and in return we are scoffed at and put to shame. Do we still wonder why princes, noblemen, cities, foundations, convents, and people grow poor? We should rather wonder that we have anything left to eat.

Now that we have got well into our game, let us pause a while and show that the Germans are not such fools as not to perceive or understand this Romish trickery. I do not here complain that God's commandments and Christian justice are despised at Rome; for the state of things in Christendom, especially at Rome, is too bad for us to complain of such high matters. Nor do I even complain that no account is taken of natural or secular justice and reason. The mischief lies still deeper. I complain that they do not observe their own fabricated canon law, though this is in itself rather mere tyranny, avarice, and worldly pomp, than a law. This we shall now show.

Long ago the emperors and princes of Germany allowed the Pope to claim the annates 6 from all German benefices; that is, half of the first year's income from every benefice. The object of this concession was that the Pope should collect a fund with all this money to fight against the Turks and infidels, and to protect Christendom, so that the nobility should not have to bear the burden of the struggle alone, and that the priests should also contribute. The popes have made such use of this good simple piety of the Germans that they have taken this money for more than one hundred years, and have now made of it a regular tax and duty; and not only have they accumulated nothing, but they have founded out of it many posts and offices at Rome, which are paid by it yearly, as out of a ground-rent. Whenever there is any pretence of fighting the Turks, they send out some commission for collecting money, and often send out indulgences under the same pretext of fighting the Turks. They think we Germans will always remain such great and inveterate fools that we will go on giving money to satisfy their unspeakable greed, though we see plainly that neither annates, nor absolution money, nor any other-not one farthing-goes against the Turks, but all goes into the bottomless sack. They lie and deceive, form and make covenants with us, of which they do not mean to keep one jot. And all this is done in the holy name of Christ and St. Peter.

This being so, the German nation, the bishops and princes, should remember that they are Christians, and should defend the people, who are committed to their government and protection in temporal and spiritual affairs, from these ravenous wolves in sheep's clothing that profess to be shepherds and rulers; and since the annates are so shamefully abused, and the covenants concerning them not carried out, they should not suffer their lands and people to be so piteously and unrighteously flayed and ruined; but by an imperial or a national law they should either retain the annates in the country, or abolish them altogether. For since they do not keep to the covenants, they have no right to the annates; therefore bishops and princes are bound to punish this thievery and robbery, or prevent it, as justice demands. And herein should they assist and strengthen the Pope, who is perchance too weak to prevent this scandal by himself, or, if he wishes to protect or support it, restrain and oppose him as a wolf and tyrant; for he has no authority to do evil or to protect evil-doers. Even if it were proposed to collect any such treasure for use against the Turks, we should be wise in future, and remember that the German nation is more fitted to take charge of it than the Pope, seeing that the German nation by itself is able to provide men enough, if the money is forthcoming. This matter of the annates is like many other Romish pretexts....

But this may suffice for the present. For of what concerns the temporal authority and the nobles I have, I think, said enough in my tract on Good Works. For their lives and governments leave room enough for improvement; but there is no comparison between spiritual and temporal abuses, as I have there shown. I daresay I have sung a lofty strain, that I have proposed many things that will be thought impossible, and attacked many points too sharply. But what was I to do? I was bound to say this: if I had the power, this is what I would do. I had rather incur the world's anger than God's; they cannot take from me more than my life. I have hitherto made many offers of peace to my adversaries; but, as I see, God has forced me through them to open my mouth wider and wider, and, because they do not keep quiet, to give them enough cause for speaking, barking, shouting, and writing. Well, then, I have another song still to sing concerning them and Rome; if they wish to hear it, I will sing it to them, and sing with all my might. Do you understand, my friend Rome, what I mean?

I have frequently offered to submit my writings for inquiry and examination, but in vain, though I know, if I am in the right, I must be condemned upon earth and justified by Christ alone in heaven. For all the Scriptures teach us that the affairs of Christians and Christendom must be judged by God alone; they have never yet been justified by men in this world, but the opposition has always been too strong. My greatest care and fear is lest my cause be not condemned by men, by which I should know for certain that it does not please God. Therefore let them go freely to work, pope, bishop, priest, monk, or doctor; they are the true people to persecute the truth, as they have always done. May God grant us all a Christian understanding, and especially to the Christian nobility of the German nation true spiritual courage, to do what is best for our unhappy Church. Amen!

At Wittenberg, in the year 1520.

John Calvin

Through his massive work, *Institutes of the Christian Religion*, John Calvin (1509-1564) proved to be the most influential theologian of the Protestant Reformation. He elaborated the long-standing Christian doctrine of original sin and developed his own peculiar theological perspective by combining it with the idea of predestination: namely, that from the very beginning of creation God in His infinite power and knowledge has determined everything that is to happen, including all our own actions. From these ideas Calvin asserted that from the very beginning God has either chosen us for eternal salvation through His grace or has condemned us to everlasting hell. This is Calvin's famous doctrine of the elect vs. the damned. This theological scheme was adopted by the Huguenots of France, the Puritans of England, and the Presbyterians of Scotland, as well as other Protestant groups.

INSTITUTES OF THE CHRISTIAN RELIGION

(Taken from the translation of Henry Beveridge)

We have now to speak of the creation of man, not only because of all the works of God it is the noblest, and most admirable specimen of his justice, wisdom, and goodness, but, as we observed at the outset, we cannot clearly and properly know God unless the knowledge of ourselves be added. This knowledge is twofold,—relating, first, to the condition in which we were at first created; and, secondly to our condition such as it began to be immediately after Adam's fall. For it would little avail us to know how we were created if we remained ignorant of the corruption and degradation of our nature in consequence of the fall. At present, however, we confine ourselves to a consideration of our nature in its original integrity. And, certainly, before we descend to the miserable condition into which man has fallen, it is of importance to consider what he was at first. For there is need of caution, lest we attend only to the natural ills of man, and thereby seem to ascribe them to the Author of nature; impiety deeming it a sufficient defence if it can pretend that everything vicious in it proceeded in some sense from God, and not hesitating, when accused, to plead against God, and throw the blame of its guilt upon Him. Those who would be thought to speak more reverently of the Deity catch at an excuse for their depravity from nature, not considering that they also, though more obscurely, bring a charge against God, on whom the dishonour would fall if anything vicious were proved to exist in nature. Seeing, therefore, that the flesh is continually on the alert for subterfuges, by which it imagines it can remove the blame of its own wickedness from itself to some other quarter, we must diligently guard against this depraved procedure, and accordingly treat of the calamity of the human race in such a way as may cut off every evasion, and vindicate the justice of God against all who would impugn it. We shall afterwards see, in its own place how far mankind now are from the purity originally conferred on Adam....

Man excelled in these noble endowments in his primitive condition, when reason, intelligence, prudence, and Judgment, not only sufficed for the government of his earthly life, but also enabled him to rise up to God and eternal happiness. Thereafter choice was added to direct the appetites, and temper all the organic motions; the will being thus perfectly submissive to the authority of reason. In this upright state, man possessed freedom of will, by which, if he chose, he was able to obtain eternal life. It were here unseasonable to introduce the question concerning the secret predestination of God, because we are not considering what might or might not happen, but what the nature of man truly was. Adam, therefore, might have stood if he chose, since it was only by his own will that he fell; but it was because his will was pliable in either directions and he had not received constancy to persevere, that he so easily fell. Still he had a free choice of good and evil; and not only so, but in the mind and will there was the highest rectitude, and all the organic parts were duly framed to obedience, until man corrupted its good properties, and destroyed himself. Hence the great darkness of philosophers who have looked for a complete building in a ruin, and fit arrangement in disorder. The principle they set out with was, that man could not be a rational animal unless he had a free choice of good and evil. They also imagined that the distinction between virtue and vice was destroyed, if man did not of his own counsel arrange his life. So far well, had there been no change in man. This being unknown to them, it is not surprising that they throw every thing into confusion. But those who, while they profess to be the disciples of Christ, still seek for free-will in man, notwithstanding of his being lost and drowned in spiritual destruction, labour under manifold delusion, making a heterogeneous mixture of inspired doctrine and philosophical opinions, and so erring as to both. But it will be better to leave these things to their own place At present it is necessary only to remember, that man, at his first creation, was very different from all his posterity; who, deriving their origin from him after he was corrupted, received a hereditary taint. At first every part of the soul was formed to rectitude. There was soundness of mind and freedom of will to choose the good. If any one objects that it was placed, as it were, in a slippery position, because its power was weak, I answer, that the degree conferred was sufficient to take away every excuse. For surely the Deity could not be tied down to this condition,—to make man such, that he either could not or would not sin. Such a nature might have been more excellent; but to expostulate with God as if he had been bound to confer this nature on man, is more than unjust, seeing he had full right to determine how much or how little He would give. Why He did not sustain him by the virtue of perseverance is hidden in his counsel; it is ours to keep within the bounds of soberness. Man had received the power, if he had the will, but he had not the will which would have given the power; for this will would have been followed by perseverance. Still, after he had received so much, there is no excuse for his having spontaneously brought death upon himself. No necessity was laid upon God to give him more than that intermediate and even transient will, that out of man's fall he might extract materials for his own glory....

Without reason that the ancient proverb so strongly recommended to man the knowledge of himself. For if it is deemed disgraceful to be ignorant of things pertaining to the business of life, much more disgraceful is self-ignorance, in consequence of which we miserably deceive ourselves in matters of the highest moment, and so walk blindfold. But the more useful the precept is, the more careful we must be not to use it preposterously, as we see certain philosophers have done. For they, when exhorting man to know himself, state the motive to be, that he may not be ignorant of his own excellence and dignity. They wish him to see nothing in himself but what will fill him with vain confidence, and inflate him with pride. But self-knowledge consists in this, first, When reflecting on what God gave us at our creation, and still continues graciously to give, we perceive how great the excellence of our nature would have been had its integrity remained, and, at the same time, remember that we have nothing of our own, but depend entirely on God, from whom we hold at pleasure whatever he has seen it meet to bestow; secondly, When viewing our miserable condition since Adam's fall, all confidence and boasting are overthrown, we blush for shame, and feel truly humble. For as God at first formed us in his own image, that he might elevate our minds to the pursuit of virtue, and the contemplation of eternal life, so to prevent us from heartlessly burying those noble qualities which distinguish us from the lower animals, it is of importance to know that we were endued with reason and intelligence, in order that we might cultivate a holy and honourable life, and regard a blessed immortality as our destined aim. At the same time, it is impossible to think of our primeval dignity without being immediately reminded of the sad spectacle of our ignominy and corruption, ever since we fell from our original in the person of our first parent. In this way, we feel dissatisfied with ourselves, and become truly humble, while we are inflamed with new desires to seek after God, in whom each may regain those good qualities of which all are found to be utterly destitute....

As the act which God punished so severely must have been not a trivial fault, but a heinous crime, it will be necessary to attend to the peculiar nature of the sin which produced Adam's fall, and provoked God to inflict such fearful vengeance on the whole human race. The common idea of sensual intemperance is childish. The sum and substance of all virtues could not consist in abstinence from a single fruit amid a general abundance of every delicacy that could be desired, the earth, with happy fertility, yielding not only abundance, but also endless variety. We must, therefore, look deeper than sensual intemperance. The prohibition to touch the tree of the knowledge of good and evil was a trial of obedience, that Adam, by observing it, might prove his willing submission to the command of God. For the very term shows the end of the precept to have been to keep him contented with his lot, and not allow him arrogantly to aspire beyond it. The promise, which gave him hope of eternal life as long as he should eat of the tree of life, and, on the other hand, the fearful denunciation of death the moment he should taste of the tree of the knowledge of good and evil, were meant to prove and exercise his faith. Hence it is not difficult to infer in what way Adam provoked the wrath of God. Augustine, indeed, is not far from the mark, when he says, that pride was the beginning of all evil, because, had not man's ambition carried him higher than he was permitted, he might have continued in his first estate. A further definition, however, must be derived from the kind of temptation which Moses describes. When, by the subtlety of the devil, the woman faithlessly abandoned the command of God, her fall obviously had its origin in disobedience. This Paul confirms, when he says, that, by the disobedience of one man, all were destroyed. At the same time, it is to be observed, that the first man revolted against the authority of God, not only in allowing himself to be ensnared by the wiles of the devil, but also by despising the truth, and turning aside to lies. Assuredly, when the word of God is despised, all reverence for Him is gone. His majesty cannot be duly honoured among us, nor his worship maintained in its integrity, unless we hang as it were upon his lips. Hence infidelity was at the root of the revolt. From infidelity, again, sprang ambition and pride, together with ingratitude; because Adam, by longing for more than was allotted him, manifested contempt for the great liberality with which God had enriched him. It was surely monstrous impiety that a son of earth should deem it little to have been made in the likeness, unless he were also made the equal of God. If the apostasy by which man withdraws from the authority of his Maker, nay, petulantly shakes off his allegiance to him, is a foul and execrable crime, it is in vain to extenuate the sin of Adam. Nor was it simple apostasy. It was accompanied with foul insult to God, the guilty pair assenting to Satan's calumnies when he charged God with malice, envy, and falsehood. In fine, infidelity opened the door to ambition, and ambition was the parent of rebellion, man casting off the fear of God, and giving free vent to his lust. Hence, Bernard truly says, that, in the present day, a door of salvation is opened to us when we receive the gospel with our ears, just as by the same entrance, when thrown open to Satan, death was admitted. Never would Adam have dared to show any repugnance to the command of God if he had not been incredulous as to his word. The strongest curb to keep all his affections under due restraint, would have been the belief that nothing was better than to cultivate righteousness by obeying the commands of God, and that the highest possible felicity was to be loved by him. Man, therefore, when carried away by the blasphemies of Satan, did his very utmost to annihilate the whole glory of God.

As Adam's spiritual life would have consisted in remaining united and bound to his Maker, so estrangement from him was the death of his soul. Nor is it strange that he who perverted the whole order of nature in heaven and earth deteriorated his race by his revolt. "The whole creation groaneth," saith St Paul, "being made subject to vanity, not willingly." If the reason is asked, there cannot be a doubt that creation bears part of the punishment deserved by man, for whose use all other creatures were made. Therefore, since through man's fault a curse has extended above and below, over all the regions of the world, there is nothing unreasonable in its extending to all his offspring. After the heavenly image in man was effaced, he not only was himself punished by a withdrawal of the ornaments in which he had been arrayed—viz. wisdom, virtue, justice, truth, and holiness, and by the substitution in their place of those dire pests, blindness, impotence, vanity, impurity, and unrighteousness, but he involved his posterity also, and plunged them in the same wretchedness. This is the hereditary corruption to which early Christian writers gave the name of Original Sin, meaning by the term the depravation of a nature formerly good and pure. The subject gave rise to much discussion, there being nothing more remote from common apprehension, than that the fault of one should render all guilty, and so become a common sin. This seems to be the reason why the oldest doctors of the church only glance obscurely at the point, or, at least, do not explain it so clearly as it required. This timidity, however, could not prevent the rise of a Pelagius with his profane fiction—that Adam sinned only to his own hurt, but did no hurt to his posterity. Satan, by thus craftily hiding the disease, tried to render it incurable. But when it was clearly proved from Scripture that the sin of the first man passed to all his posterity, recourse was had to the cavil, that it passed by imitation, and not by propagation. The orthodoxy, therefore, and more especially Augustine, laboured to show, that we are not corrupted by acquired wickedness, but bring an innate corruption from the very womb....

But lest the thing itself of which we speak be unknown or doubtful, it will be proper to define original sin. I have no intention, however, to discuss all the definitions which different writers have adopted, but only to adduce the one which seems to me most accordant with truth. Original sin, then, may be defined a hereditary corruption and depravity of our nature, extending to all the parts of the soul, which first makes us obnoxious to the wrath of God, and then produces in us works which in Scripture are termed works of the flesh. This corruption is repeatedly designated by Paul by the term sin; while the works which proceed from it, such as adultery, fornication, theft, hatred, murder, revellings, he terms, in the same way, the fruits of sin, though in various passages of Scripture, and even by Paul himself, they are also termed sins. The two things, therefore, are to be distinctly observed—viz. that being thus perverted and corrupted in all the parts of our nature, we are, merely on account of such corruption, deservedly condemned by God, to whom nothing is acceptable but righteousness, innocence, and purity. This is not liability for another's fault. For when it is said, that the sin of Adam has made us obnoxious to the justice of God, the meaning is not, that we, who are in ourselves innocent and blameless, are bearing his guilt, but that since by his transgression we are all placed under the curse, he is said to have brought us under obligation. Through him, however, not only has punishment been derived, but pollution instilled, for which punishment is justly due. Hence Augustine, though he often terms it another's sin (that he may more clearly show how it comes to us by descent), at the same time asserts that it is each individual's own sin. And the Apostle most distinctly testifies, that "death passed upon all men, for that all have sinned;" that is, are involved in original sin, and polluted by its stain. Hence, even infants bringing their condemnation with them from their mother's womb, suffer not for another's, but for their own defect. For although they have not yet produced the fruits of their own unrighteousness, they have the seed implanted in them. Nay, their whole nature is, as it were, a seed-bed of sin, and therefore cannot but be odious and abominable to God. Hence it follows, that it is properly deemed sinful in the sight of God; for there could be no condemnation without guilt. Next comes the other point—viz. that this perversity in us never ceases, but constantly produces new fruits, in other words, those works of the flesh which we formerly described; just as a lighted furnace sends forth sparks and flames, or a fountain without ceasing pours out water. Hence, those who have defined original sin as the want of the original righteousness which we ought to have had, though they substantially comprehend the whole case, do not significantly enough express its power and energy. For our nature is not only utterly devoid of goodness, but so prolific in all kinds of evil, that it can never be idle....

Having seen that the dominion of sin, ever since the first man was brought under it, not only extends to the whole race, but has complete possession of every soul, it now remains to consider more closely, whether from the period of being thus enslaved, we have been deprived of all liberty; and if any portion still remains, how far its power extends. In order to facilitate the answer to this question it may be proper in passing to point out the course which our inquiry ought to take. The best method of avoiding error is to consider the dangers which beset us on either side. Man being devoid of all uprightness, immediately takes occasion from the fact to indulge in sloth, and having no ability in himself for the study of righteousness, treats the whole subject as if he had no concern in it. On the other hand, man cannot arrogate any thing, however minute, to himself, without robbing God of his honour, and through rash confidence subjecting himself to a fall. To keep free of both these rocks, our proper course will be, first, to show that man has no remaining good in himself, and is beset on every side by the most miserable destitution; and then teach him to aspire to the goodness of which he is devoid, and the liberty of which he has been deprived: thus giving him a stronger stimulus to exertion than he could have if he imagined himself possessed of the highest virtue. How necessary the latter point is, everybody sees. As to the former, several seem to entertain more doubt than they ought. For it being admitted as incontrovertible that man is not to be denied any thing that is truly his own, it ought also to be admitted, that he is to be deprived of every thing like false boasting. If man had no title to glory in himself, when, by the kindness of his Maker, he was distinguished by the noblest ornaments, how much ought he to be humbled now, when his ingratitude has thrust him down from the highest glory to extreme ignominy? At the time when he was raised to the highest pinnacle of honour, all which Scripture attributes to him is, that he was created in the image of God, thereby intimating that the blessings in which his happiness consisted were not his own, but derived by divine communication. What remains, therefore, now that man is stript of all his glory, than to acknowledge the God for whose kindness he failed to be grateful, when he was loaded with the riches of his grace? Not having glorified him by the acknowledgment of his blessings, now, at least, he ought to glorify him by the confession of his poverty. In truth, it is no less useful for us to renounce all the praise of wisdom and virtue, than to aim at the glory of God. Those who invest us with more than we possess only add sacrilege to our ruin. For when we are taught to contend in our own strength, what more is done than to lift us up, and then leave us to lean on a reed which immediately gives way? Indeed, our strength is exaggerated when it is compared to a reed. All that foolish men invent and prattle on this subject is mere smoke....

All this being admitted, it will be beyond dispute, that free will does not enable any man to perform good works, unless he is assisted by grace; indeed, the special grace which the elect alone receive through regeneration. For I stay not to consider the extravagance of those who say that grace is offered equally and promiscuously to all. But it has not yet been shown whether man is entirely deprived of the power of well-doing, or whether he still possesses it in some, though in a very feeble and limited degree—a degree so feeble and limited, that it can do nothing of itself, but when assisted by grace, is able also to perform its part. The Master of the Sentences [Peter Lombard], wishing to explain this, teaches that a twofold grace is necessary to fit for any good work. The one he calls Operating. To it, it is owing that we effectually will what is good. The other, which succeeds this good will, and aids it, he calls Co-operating. My objection to this division is, that while it attributes the effectual desire of good to divine grace, it insinuates that man, by his own nature, desires good in some degree, though ineffectually. Thus Bernard, while maintaining that a good will is the work of God, concedes this much to man—viz. that of his own nature he longs for such a good will. This differs widely from the view of Augustine, though Lombard pretends to have taken the division from him. Besides, there is an ambiguity in the second division, which has led to an erroneous interpretation. For it has been thought that we co-operate with subsequent grace, inasmuch as it pertains to us either to nullify the first grace, by rejecting its or to confirm it, by obediently yielding to it. The author of the work De Vocatione Gentium expresses it thus: It is free to those who enjoy the faculty of reason to depart from grace, so that the not departing is a reward, and that which cannot be done without the co-operation of the Spirit is imputed as merit to those whose will might have made it otherwise. It seemed proper to make these two observations in passing, that the reader may see how far I differ from the sounder of the Schoolmen. Still further do I differ from more modern sophists, who have departed even more widely than the Schoolmen from the ancient doctrine. The division, however, shows in what respect free will is attributed to man. For Lombard ultimately declares, that our freedom is not to the extent of leaving us equally inclined to good and evil in act or in thought, but only to the extent of freeing us from compulsion. This liberty is compatible with our being depraved, the servants of sin, able to do nothing but sin....

OF THE ETERNAL ELECTION, BY WHICH GOD HAS PREDESTINATED SOME TO SALVATION, AND OTHERS TO DESTRUCTION.

The covenant of life is not preached equally to all, and among those to whom it is preached, does not always meet with the same reception. This diversity displays the unsearchable depth of the divine judgment, and is without doubt subordinate to God's purpose of eternal election. But if it is plainly owing to the mere pleasure of God that salvation is spontaneously offered to some, while others have no access to it, great and difficult questions immediately arise, questions which are inexplicable, when just views are not entertained concerning election and predestination. To many this seems a perplexing subject, because they deem it most incongruous that of the great body of mankind some should be predestinated to salvation, and others to destruction. How ceaselessly they entangle themselves will appear as we proceed. We may add, that in the very obscurity which deters them, we may see not only the utility of this doctrine, but also its most pleasant fruits. We shall never feel persuaded as we ought that our salvation flows from the free mercy of God as its fountain, until we are made acquainted with his eternal election, the grace of God being illustrated by the contrast—viz. that he does not adopt all promiscuously to the hope of salvation, but gives to some what he denies to others. It is plain how greatly ignorance of this principle detracts from the glory of God, and impairs true humility. But though thus necessary to be known, Paul declares that it cannot be known unless God, throwing works entirely out of view, elect those whom he has predestined. His words are, "Even so then at this present time also, there is a remnant according to the election of grace. And if by grace, then it is no more of works: otherwise grace is no more grace. But if it be of works, then it is no more grace: otherwise work is no more work." If to make it appear that our salvation flows entirely from the good mercy of God, we must be carried back to the origin of election, then those who would extinguish it, wickedly do as much as in them lies to obscure what they ought most loudly to extol, and pluck up humility by the very roots. Paul clearly declares that it is only when the salvation of a remnant is ascribed to gratuitous election, we arrive at the knowledge that God saves whom he wills of his mere good pleasure, and does not pay a debt, a debt which never can be due. Those who preclude access, and would not have any one to obtain a taste of this doctrine, are equally unjust to God and men, there being no other means of humbling us as we ought, or making us feel how much we are bound to him. Nor, indeed, have we elsewhere any sure ground of confidence. This we say on the authority of Christ, who, to deliver us from all fear, and render us invincible amid our many dangers, snares and mortal conflicts, promises safety to all that the Father has taken under his protection. From this we infer, that all who know not that they are the peculiar people of God, must be wretched from perpetual trepidation, and that those therefore, who, by overlooking the three advantages which we have noted, would destroy the very foundation of our safety, consult ill for themselves and for all the faithful. What? Do we not here find the very origin of the Church, which, as Bernard rightly teaches., could not be found or recognized among the creatures, because it lies hid (in both cases wondrously) within the lap of blessed predestination, and the mass of wretched condemnation?

But before I enter on the subject, I have some remarks to address to two classes of men. The subject of predestination, which in itself is attended with considerable difficulty is rendered very perplexed and hence perilous by human curiosity, which cannot be restrained from wandering into forbidden paths and climbing to the clouds determined if it can that none of the secret things of God shall remain unexplored. When we see many, some of them in other respects not bad men, every where rushing into this audacity and wickedness, it is necessary to remind them of the course of duty in this matter. First, then, when they inquire into predestination, let then remember that they are penetrating into the recesses of the divine wisdom, where he who rushes forward securely and confidently, instead of satisfying his curiosity will enter in inextricable labyrinth. For it is not right that man should with impunity pry into things which the Lord has been pleased to conceal within himself, and scan that sublime eternal wisdom which it is his pleasure that we should not apprehend but adore, that therein also his perfections may appear. Those secrets of his will, which he has seen it meet to manifest, are revealed in his word—revealed in so far as he knew to be conducive to our interest and welfare....

I admit that profane men lay hold of the subject of predestination to carp, or cavil, or snarl, or scoff. But if their petulance frightens us, it will be necessary to conceal all the principal articles of faith, because they and their fellows leave scarcely one of them unassailed with blasphemy. A rebellious spirit will display itself no less insolently when it hears that there are three persons in the divine essence, than when it hears that God when he created man foresaw every thing that was to happen to him. Nor will they abstain from their jeers when told that little more than five thousand years have elapsed since the creation of the world. For they will ask, Why did the power of God slumber so long in idleness? In short, nothing can be stated that they will not assail with derision. To quell their blasphemies, must we say nothing concerning the divinity of the Son and Spirit? Must the creation of the world be passed over in silence? No! The truth of God is too powerful, both here and everywhere, to dread the slanders of the ungodly, as Augustine powerfully maintains in his treatise, *De Bono Perseverantiae*. For we see that the false apostles were unable, by defaming and accusing the true doctrine of Paul, to make him ashamed of it. There is nothing in the allegation that the whole subject is fraught with danger to pious minds, as tending to destroy exhortation, shake faith, disturb and dispirit the heart. Augustine disguises not that on these grounds he was often charged with preaching the doctrine of predestination too freely, but, as it was easy for him to do, he abundantly refutes the charge. As a great variety of absurd objections are here stated, we have thought it best to dispose of each of them in its proper place. Only I wish it to be received as a general rule, that the secret things of God are not to be scrutinized, and that those which he has revealed are not to be overlooked, lest we may, on the one hand, be chargeable with curiosity, and, on the other, with ingratitude. For it has been shrewdly observed by Augustine, that we can safely follow Scripture, which walks softly, as with a mother's step, in accommodation to our weakness. Those, however, who are so cautious and timid, that they would bury all mention of predestination in order that it may not trouble weak minds, with what color, pray, will they cloak their arrogance, when they indirectly charge God with a want of due consideration, in not having foreseen a danger for which they imagine that they prudently provide? Whoever, therefore, throws obloquy on the doctrine of predestination, openly brings a charge against God, as having inconsiderately allowed something to escape from him which is injurious to the Church.

The predestination by which God adopts some to the hope of life, and adjudges others to eternal death, no man who would be thought pious ventures simply to deny; but it is greatly caviled at, especially by those who make prescience its cause. We, indeed, ascribe both prescience and predestination to God; but we say, that it is absurd to make the latter subordinate to the former. When we attribute prescience to God, we mean that all things always were, and ever continue, under his eye; that to his knowledge there is no past or future, but all things are present, and indeed so present, that it is not merely the idea of them that is before him (as those objects are which we retain in our memory), but that he truly sees and contemplates them as actually under his immediate inspection. This prescience extends to the whole circuit of the world, and to all creatures. By predestination we mean the eternal decree of God, by which he determined with himself whatever he wished to happen with regard to every man. All are not created on equal terms, but some are preordained to eternal life, others to eternal damnation; and, accordingly, as each has been created for one or other of these ends, we say that he has been predestinated to life or to death....

We say, then, that Scripture clearly proves this much, that God by his eternal and immutable counsel determined once for all those whom it was his pleasure one day to admit to salvation, and those whom, on the other hand, it was his pleasure to doom to destruction. We maintain that this counsel, as regards the elect, is founded on his free mercy, without any respect to human worth, while those whom he dooms to destruction are excluded from access to life by a just and blameless, but at the same time incomprehensible judgment. In regard to the elect, we regard calling as the evidence of election, and justification as another symbol of its manifestation, until it is fully accomplished by the attainment of glory. But as the Lord seals his elect by calling and justification, so by excluding the reprobate either from the knowledge of his name or the sanctification of his Spirit, he by these marks in a manner discloses the judgment which awaits them.

THE COUNCIL OF TRENT

During the Middle Ages the Roman Catholic Church had enjoyed a virtual monopoly of religious authority throughout western Europe, and this situation had been one of the principal reasons for the various abuses and shortcomings that characterized the Medieval Church. The Protestant Reformation forever ended Catholicism's monopoly and prompted the latter to undergo a thorough reexamination of itself: for henceforth there existed in western Europe several different competing views of Christianity. Catholicism's response to the Protestant challenge took several forms, which are collectively termed the Counter Reformation or Catholic Reformation by modern scholars. One important feature of this Counter Reformation was the council of Trent, a series of meetings of Catholic bishops and priests held in the northern Italian city of Trent and extending over an eighteen-year period (1545-1563). During these meetings Catholic clergy discussed all beliefs and practices of the Catholic Church and issued decrees defining what constituted orthodox Catholic doctrine. As can be seen from the following excerpts from these decrees, the council of Trent changed very little of existing Catholic doctrines and practices; but the clergy's reaffirmation thereof was often formulated in such a way as to condemn Protestant deviations from Catholicism. The one important innovation was the establishment of the seminary system, which was designed to recruit, educate, and train young men to become Catholic priests, so that they would be properly suited for lifetime service to their fellow Catholics.

(Taken from The Canons and Decrees of the Sacred and Oecumenical Council of Trent, by J. Waterworth, London 1848)

DECREE CONCERNING THE EDITION AND THE USE OF THE SACRED BOOKS.

Moreover, the same sacred and holy Synod,—considering that no small utility may accrue to the Church of God, if it be made known which out of all the Latin editions, now in circulation, of the sacred books, is to be held as authentic,—ordains and declares, that the said old and vulgate edition, which, by the lengthened usage of so many years, has been approved of in the Church, be, in public lectures, disputations, sermons and expositions, held as authentic; and that no one is to dare, or presume to reject it under any pretext whatever.

Furthermore, in order to restrain petulant spirits, It decrees, that no one, relying on his own skill, shall,—in matters of faith, and of morals pertaining to the edification of Christian doctrine, —wresting the sacred Scripture to his own senses, presume to interpret the said sacred Scripture contrary to that sense which holy mother Church,—whose it is to judge of the true sense and interpretation of the holy Scriptures,—hath held and doth hold; or even contrary to the unanimous consent of the Fathers; even though such interpretations were never (intended) to be at any time published. Contraveners shall be made known by their Ordinaries, and be punished with the penalties by law established.

DECREE CONCERNING ORIGINAL SIN.

That our Catholic faith, without which it is impossible to please God, may, errors being purged away, continue in its own perfect and spotless integrity, and that the Christian people may not be carried about with every wind of doctrine; whereas that old serpent, the perpetual enemy of mankind, amongst the very many evils with which the Church of God is in these our times troubled, has also stirred up not only new, but even old, dissensions touching original sin, and the remedy thereof; the sacred and holy, ecumenical and general Synod of Trent,—lawfully assembled in the Holy Ghost, the three same legates of the Apostolic See presiding therein,—wishing now to come to the reclaiming of the erring, and the confirming of the wavering,—following the testimonies of the sacred Scriptures, of the holy Fathers, of the most approved councils, and the judgment and consent of the Church itself, ordains, confesses, and declares these things touching the said original sin:

1. If any one does not confess that the first man, Adam, when he had transgressed the commandment of God in Paradise, immediately lost the holiness and justice wherein he had been constituted; and that he incurred, through the offence of that prevarication, the wrath and indignation of God, and consequently death, with which God had previously threatened him, and, together with death, captivity under his power who thenceforth had the empire of death, that is to say, the devil, and that the entire Adam, through that offence of prevarication, was changed, in body and soul, for the worse; let him be anathema.

2. If any one asserts, that the prevarication of Adam injured himself alone, and not his posterity; and that the holiness and justice, received of God, which he lost, he lost for himself alone, and not for us also; or that he, being defiled by the sin of disobedience, has only transfused death, and pains of the body, into the whole human race, but not sin also, which is the death of the soul; let him be anathema:—whereas he contradicts the apostle who says; By one man sin entered into the world, and by sin death, and so death passed upon all men, in whom all have sinned.

3. If any one asserts, that this sin of Adam,—which in its origin is one, and being transfused into all by propogation, not by imitation, is in each one as his own,—is taken away either by the powers of human nature, or by any other remedy than the merit of the one mediator, our Lord Jesus Christ, who hath reconciled us to God in his own blood, made unto us justice, santification, and redemption; or if he denies that the said merit of Jesus Christ is applied, both to adults and to infants, by the sacrament of baptism rightly administered in the form of the church; let him be anathema: For there is no other name under heaven given to men, whereby we must be saved. Whence that voice; Behold the lamb of God behold him who taketh away the sins of the world; and that other; As many as have been baptized, have put on Christ.

4. If any one denies, that infants, newly born from their mothers' wombs, even though they be sprung from baptized parents, are to be baptized; or says that they are baptized indeed for the remission of sins, but that they derive nothing of original sin from Adam, which has need of being expiated by the laver of regeneration for the obtaining life everlasting,—whence it follows as a consequence, that in them the form

of baptism, for the remission of sins, is understood to be not true, but false, —let him be anathema. For that which the apostle has said, By one man sin entered into the world, and by sin death, and so death passed upon all men in whom all have sinned, is not to be understood otherwise than as the Catholic Church spread everywhere hath always understood it. For, by reason of this rule of faith, from a tradition of the apostles, even infants, who could not as yet commit any sin of themselves, are for this cause truly baptized for the remission of sins, that in them that may be cleansed away by regeneration, which they have contracted by generation. For, unless a man be born again of water and the Holy Ghost, he cannot enter into the kingdom of God.

That a rash presumptuousness in the matter of Predestination is to be avoided.

No one, moreover, so long as he is in this mortal life, ought so far to presume as regards the secret mystery of divine predestination, as to determine for certain that he is assuredly in the number of the predestinate; as if it were true, that he that is justified, either cannot sin any more, or, if he do sin, that he ought to promise himself an assured repentance; for except by special revelation, it cannot be known whom God hath chosen unto Himself.

ON THE SACRAMENTS IN GENERAL.

CANON I.   If any one saith, that the sacraments of the New Law were not all instituted by Jesus Christ, our Lord; or, that they are more, or less, than seven, to wit, Baptism, Confirmation, the Eucharist, Penance, Extreme Unction, Order, and Matrimony; or even that any one of these seven is not truly and properly a sacrament; let him be anathema.

CANON II.   If any one saith, that these said sacraments of the New Law do not differ from the sacraments of the Old Law, save that the ceremonies are different, and different the outward rites; let him be anathema.

CANON III.   If any one saith, that these seven sacraments are in such wise equal to each other, as that one is not in any way more worthy than another; let him be anathema.

CANON IV.   If any one saith, that the sacraments of the New Law are not necessary unto salvation, but superfluous; and that, without them, or without the desire thereof, men obtain of God, through faith alone, the grace of justification;-though all (the sacraments) are not ineed necessary for every individual; let him be anathema.

CANON V.   If any one saith, that these sacraments were instituted for the sake of nourishing faith alone; let him be anathema.

CANON VI.   If any one saith, that the sacraments of the New Law do not contain the grace which they signify; or, that they do not confer that grace on those who do not place an obstacle thereunto; as though they were merely outward signs of grace or justice received through faith, and certain marks of the Christian profession, whereby believers are distinguished amongst men from unbelievers; let him be anathema.

CANON VII.   If any one saith, that grace, as far as God's part is concerned, is not given through the said sacraments, always, and to all men, even though they receive them rightly, but (only) sometimes, and to some persons; let him be anathema.

CANON VIII.   If any one saith, that by the said sacraments of the New Law grace is not conferred through the act performed, but that faith alone in the divine promise suffices for the obtaining of grace; let him be anathema.

CANON IX.   If any one saith, that, in the three sacrments, Baptism, to wit, Confirmation, and Order, there is not imprinted in the soul a character, that is, a certain spiritual and indelible Sign, on account of which they cannot be repeated; let him be anathema.

CANON X.   If any one saith, that all Christians have power to administer the word, and all the sacraments; let him be anathema.

CANON XI.   If any one saith, that, in ministers, when they effect, and confer the sacraments, there is not required the intention at least of doing what the Church does; let him be anathema.

CANON XII.   If any one saith, that a minister, being in mortal sin,-if so be that he observe all the essentials which belong to the effecting, or conferring of, the sacrament,- neither effects, nor confers the sacrament; let him be anathema.

CANON XIII.   If any one saith, that the received and approved rites of the Catholic Church, wont to be used in the solemn administration of the sacraments, may be contemned, or without sin be omitted at pleasure by the ministers, or be changed, by every pastor of the churches, into other new ones; let him be anathema.

On the real presence of our Lord Jesus Christ in the most holy sacrament of the Eucharist.

In the first place, the holy Synod teaches, and openly and simply professes, that, in the august sacrament of the holy Eucharist, after the consecration of the bread and wine, our Lord Jesus Christ, true God and man, is truly, really, and substantially contained under the species of those sensible things. For neither are these things mutually repugnant,- that our Saviour Himself always sitteth at the right hand of the Father in heaven, according to the natural mode of existing, and that, nevertheless, He be, in many other places, sacramentally present to us in his own substance, by a manner of existing, which, though we can scarcely express it in words, yet can we, by the understanding illuminated by faith, conceive, and we ought most firmly to believe, to be possible unto God: for thus all our forefathers, as many as were in the true Church of Christ, who have treated of this most holy Sacrament, have most openly professed, that our Redeemer instituted this so admirable a sacrament at the last supper, when, after the blessing of the bread and wine, He testified, in express and clear words, that He gave them His own very Body, and His own Blood; words which,-recorded by the holy Evangelists, and afterwards repeated by Saint Paul, whereas they carry with them that proper and most manifest meaning in which they were understood by the Fathers,-it is indeed a crime the most unworthy that they should be wrested, by certain contentions and wicked men, to fictitious and imaginary tropes, whereby the verity of the flesh and blood of Christ is denied, contrary to the universal sense of the Church, which, as the pillar and ground of truth, has detested, as satanical, these inventions devised by impious men; she recognising, with a mind ever grateful and unforgetting, this most excellent benefit of Christ.

On Transubstantiation.

And because that Christ, our Redeemer, declared that which He offered under the species of bread to be truly His own body, therefore has it ever been a firm belief in the Church of God, and this holy Synod doth now declare it anew, that, by the consecration of the bread and of the wine, a conversion is made of the whole substance of the bread into the substance of the body of Christ our Lord, and of the whole substance of the wine into the substance of His blood; which conversion is, by the holy Catholic Church, suitably and properly called Transubstantiation.

ON THE MOST HOLY SACRAMENT OF THE EUCHARIST.

CANON I.   If any one denieth, that, in the sacrament of the most holy Eucharist, are contained truly, really, and substantially, the body and blood together with the soul and divinity of our Lord Jesus Christ, and consequently the whole Christ; but saith that He is only therein as in a sign, or in figure, or virtue; let him be anathema.

CANON II.   If any one saith, that, in the sacred and holy sacrament of the Eucharist, the substance of the bread and wine remains conjointly with the body and blood of our

Lord Jesus Christ, and denieth that wonderful and singular conversion of the whole substance of the bread into the Body, and of the whole substance of the wine into the Blood-the species Only of the bread and wine remaining-which conversion indeed the Catholic Church most aptly calls Transubstantiation; let him be anathema.

CANON VIII.   If any one saith, that Christ, given in the Eucharist, is eaten spiritually only, and not also sacramentally and really; let him be anathema.

On the Ecclesiastical hierarchy, and on Ordination.

But, forasmuch as in the sacrament of Order, as also in Baptism and Confirmation, a character is imprinted, which can neither be effaced nor taken away; the holy Synod with reason condemns the opinion of those, who assert that the priests of the New Testament have only a temporary power; and that those who have once been rightly ordained, can again become laymen, if they do not exercise the ministry of the word of God. And if any one affirm, that all Christians indiscrimately are priests of the New Testament, or that they are all mutually endowed with an equal spiritual power, he clearly does nothing but confound the ecclesiastical hierarchy, which is as an army set in array; as if, contrary to the doctrine of blessed Paul, all were apostles, all prophets, all evangelists, all pastors, all doctors. Wherefore, the holy Synod declares that, besides the other ecclesiastical degrees, bishops, who have succeeded to the place of the apostles, principally belong to this hierarchial order; that they are placed, as the same apostle says, by the Holy Ghost, to rule the Church of God; that they are superior to priests; administer the sacrament of Confirmation; ordain the ministers of the Church; and that they can perform very many other things; over which functions others of an inferior order have no power. Furthermore, the sacred and holy Synod teaches, that, in the ordination of bishops, priests, and of the other orders, neither the consent, nor vocation, nor authority, whether of the people, or of any civil power or magistrate whatsoever, is required in such wise as that, without this, the ordination is invalid: yea rather doth It decree, that all those who, being only called and instituted by the people, or by the civil power and magistrate, ascend to the exercise of these ministrations, and those who of their own rashness assume them to themselves, are not ministers of the church, but are to be looked upon as thieves and robbers, who have not entered by the door. These are the things which it hath seemed good to the sacred Synod to teach the faithful in Christ, in general terms, touching the sacrament of Order.

Method of establishing Seminaries for Clerics, and of educating the same therein.

Wereas the age of youth, unless it be rightly trained, is prone to follow after the pleasures of the world; and unless it be formed, from its tender years, unto piety and religion, before habits of vice have taken possession of the whole man, it never will perfectly, and without the greatest, and well-nigh special, help of Almighty God, persevere in ecclesiastical discipline; the holy Synod ordains, that all cathedral, metropolitan, and other churches greater than these, shall be bound, each according to its means and the extent of the diocese, to maintain, to educate religiously, and to train in ecclesiastical discipline, a certain number of youths of their city and diocese, or, if that number cannot be met with there, of that province, in a college to be chosen by the bishop for this purpose near the said churches, or in some other suitable place. Into this college shall be received such as are at least twelve years old, born in lawful wedlock, and who know how to read and write competently, and whose character and inclination afford a hope that they will always serve in the ecclesiastical ministry. And It wishes that the children of the poor be principally selected; though It does not however exclude those of the more wealthy, provided they be maintained at their own expense, and manifest a desire of serving God and the Church. The bishop, having divided these youths into as many classes as he shall think fit, according to their number, age, and progress in ecclesiastical discipline, shall, when it seems to him expedient, assign some of them to the ministry of the churches, the others he shall keep in the college to be instructed; and shall supply the place of those who have been withdrawn, by others; that so this college may be a perpetual seminary of ministers of God. And that the youths may be the more advantageously trained in the aforesaid ecclesiastical discipline, they shall always at once wear the tonsure and the clerical dress; they shall learn grammar, singing, ecclesiastical computation, and the other liberal arts; they shall be instructed in sacred Scripture; ecclesiastical works; the homilies of the saints; the manner of administering the sacraments, especially those things which shall seem adapted to enable them to hear confessions; and the forms of the rites and ceremonies. The bishop shall take care that they be present every day at the sacrifice of the mass, and that they confess their sins at least once a month; and receive the body of our Lord Jesus Christ as the judgment of their confessor shall direct; and on festivals serve in the cathedral and other churches of the place.

All which, and other things advantageous and needful for this object, all bishops shall ordain-with the advice of two of the senior and most experienced canons chosen by himself-as the Holy Spirit shall suggest; and shall make it their care, by frequent visitations, that the same be always observed. The froward, and incorrigible, and the disseminators of evil morals, they shall punish sharply, even by expulsion if necessary; and, removing all hindrances, they shall carefully foster whatsoever appears to tend to preserve and advance so pious and holy an institution.

ON THE SACRAMENT OF MATRIMONY.

CANON I.   If any one saith, that matrimony is not truly and properly one of the seven sacraments of the evangelic law, (a sacrament) instituted by Christ the Lord; but that it has been invented by men in the Church; and that it does not confer grace; let him be anathema.

CANON II.   If any one saith, that it is lawful for Christians to have several wives at the same time, and that this is not prohibited by any divine law; let him be anathema.

CANON IX.   If any one saith, that clerics constituted in sacred orders, or Regulars, who have solemnly professed chastity, are able to contract marriage, and that being contracted it is valid, notwithstanding the ecclesiastical law, or vow; and that the contrary is no thing else than to condemn marriage; and, that all who do not feel that they have the gift of chastity, even though they have made a vow thereof, may contract marriage; let him be anathema: seeing that God refuses not that gift to those who ask for it rightly, neither does He suffer us to be tempted above that which we are able.

CANON X.   If any one saith, that the marriage state is to be placed above the state of virginity, or of celibacy, and that it is not better and more blessed to remain in virginity, or in celibacy, than to be united in matrimony; let him be anathema.

ON THE INVOCATION, VENERATION, AND RELICS OF SAINTS, AND ON SACRED IMAGES.

The holy Synod enjoins on all bishops, and others who sustain the office and charge of teaching, that, agreeably to the usage of the Catholic and Apostolic Church, received from the primitive times of the Christian religion, and agreeably to the consent of the holy Fathers, and to the decrees of sacred Councils, they especially instruct the faithful diligently concerning the intercession and invocation of saints; the honour (paid) to relics; and the legitimate use of images: teaching them, that the saints, who reign together with Christ, offer up their own prayers to God for men; that it is good and useful suppliantly to invoke them, and to have recourse to their prayers, aid, (and) help for obtaining benefits from God, through His Son, Jesus Christ our Lord, who is our alone Redeemer and Saviour; but that they think impiously, who deny that the saints, who enjoy eternal happiness in heaven, are to be invocated; or who assert either that they do not pray for men; or, that the invocation of them to pray for each of us even in particular, is idolatry; or, that it is repugnant to the word of God; and is opposed to the honour of the one mediator of God and men, Christ Jesus; or, that it is foolish to supplicate, vocally, or mentally, those who reign in heaven. Also, that the holy bodies of holy martyrs, and of others now living with Christ,-which bodies were the living members of Christ, and the temple of the Holy Ghost, and which are by Him to be raised unto eternal life, and to be glorified,—are to be venerated by the faithful; through which (bodies) many benefits are bestowed by God on men; so that they who affirm that veneration and honour are not due to the relics of saints; or, that these, and other sacred monuments, are uselessly honoured by the faithful; and that the places dedicated to the memories of the saints are in vain visited with the view of obtaining their aid; are wholly to be condemned, as the Church has already long since condemned, and now also condemns them.

Moreover, that the images of Christ, of the Virgin Mother of God, and of the other saints, are to be had and retained particularly in temples, and that due honour and veneration are to be given them; not that any divinity, or virtue, is believed to be in them, on account of which they are to be worshipped; or that anything is to be asked of them; or, that trust is to be reposed in images, as was of old done by the Gentiles who placed their hope in idols; but because the honour which is shown them is referred to the prototypes which those images represent; in such wise that by the images which we kiss, and before which we uncover the head, and prostrate ourselves, we adore Christ; and we venerate the saints, whose similitude they bear: as, by the decrees of Councils, and especially of the second Synod of Nicaea, has been defined against the opponents of images.

Cardinals and all Prelates of the churches shall be content with modest furniture and a frugal table: they shall not enrich their relatives or domestics out of the property of the Church.

It is to be wished, that those who undertake the office of a bishop should understand what their portion is; and comprehend that they are called, not to their own convenience, not to riches or luxury, but to labours and cares for the glory of God. For it is not to be doubted, that the rest of the faithful also will be more easily excited to religion and innocence, if they shall see those who are set over them, not fixing their thoughts on the things of this world, but on the salvation of souls, and on their heavenly country. Wherefore the holy Synod, being minded that these things are of the greatest importance towards restoring ecclesiastical discipline, admonishes all bishops, that, often meditating thereon, they show themselves conformable to their office, by their actual deeds, and the actions of their lives; which is a kind of perpetual sermon; but above all that they so order their whole conversation, as that others may thence be able to derive examples of frugality, modesty, continency, and of that holy humility which so much recom mends us to God.

Wherefore, after the example of our fathers in the Council of Carthage, It not only orders that bishops be content with modest furniture, and a frugal table and diet, but that they also give heed that in the rest of their manner of living, and in their whole house, there be nothing seen that is alien from this holy institution, and which does not manifest simplicity, zeal towards God, and a contempt of vanities. Also, It wholly forbids them to strive to enrich their own kindred or domestics out of the revenues of the church: seeing that even the canons of the Apostles forbid them to give to their kindred the property of the church, which belongs to God; but if their kindred be poor, let them distribute to them thereof as poor, but not misapply, or waste, it for their sakes : yea, the holy Synod, with the utmost earnestness, admonishes them completely to lay aside all this human and carnal affection towards brothers, nephews and kindred, which is the seed-plot of many evils in the church. And what has been said of bishops, the same is not only to be observed by all who hold ecclesiastical benefices, whether Secular or Regular, each according to the nature of his rank, but the Synod decrees that it also regards the cardinals of the holy Roman Church ; for whereas, upon their advice to the most holy Roman Pontiff, the administration of the universal Church depends, it would seem to be a shame, if they did not at the same time shine so pre-eminent in virtue and in the discipline of their lives, as deservedly to draw upon themselves the eyes of all men.

DECREE CONCERNING INDULGENCES.

Whereas the power of conferring Indulgences was granted by Christ to the Church; and she has, even in the most ancient times, used the said power, delivered unto her of God; the sacred holy Synod teaches, and enjoins, that the use of Indulgences, for the Christian people most salutary, and approved of by the authority of sacred Councils, is to be retained in the Church; and It condemns with anathema those who either assert, that they are useless; or who deny that there is in the Church the power of granting them. In granting them, however, It desires that, in accordance with the ancient and approved custom in the Church, moderation be observed; lest, by excessive facility, ecclesiastical discipline be enervated. And being desirous that the abuses which have crept therein, and by occasion of which this honourable name of Indulgences is blasphemed by heretics, be amended and corrected, It ordains generally by this decree, that all evil gains for the obtaining thereof,—whence a most prolific cause of abuses amongst the Christian people has been derived,—be wholly abolished. But as regards the other abuses which have proceeded from superstition, ignorance, irreverence, or from what soever other source, since, by reason of the manifold corruptions in the places and provinces where the said abuses are committed, they cannot conveniently be specially prohibited; It commands all bishops, diligently to collect, each in his own church, all abuses of this nature, and to report them in the first provincial Synod; that, after having been reviewed by the opinions of the other bishops also, they may forthwith be referred to the Sovereign Roman Pontiff, by whose authority and prudence that which may be expedient for the universal Church will be ordained; that this the gift of holy Indulgences may be dispensed to all the faithful, piously, holily, and incorruptly.

READING 45

CHRISTOPHER COLUMBUS

The year 1492 was a momentous one in the history of Western Europe. It marked the end of the centuries-long reconquest of the Iberian Peninsula by Queen Isabella of Castile and King Ferdinand of Aragon. In that same year these monarchs also furthered their Christianization of their realms by ordering all Jews either to convert to Christianity or to emigrate elsewhere. In that same year Christopher Columbus, a highly skilled navigator from northern Italy, set out on the first of his four voyages that took him across the Atlantic Ocean and into the Carribean. Columbus' goal was not to discover the continents of North and South America, but to find a westward route to the eastern coast of Asia in order to reestablish Western Europe's spice trade with Asia, which had been interrupted during the fifteenth century by the Ottoman Turks and their conquest of the Byzantine Empire.

The following two passages were written by Columbus himself. The first is a preface that he composed for the journal that he kept throughout the course of his first voyage; and it is addressed to Queen Isabella and King Ferdinand, who sponsored the enterprise. The second text is a letter addressed to Luis De Sant Angel, the treasurer of Aragon, written by Columbus as he was sailing back across the Atlantic. In it Columbus set forth his first impressions of what he had encountered. He was convinced that he had come upon the offshore islands of eastern Asia, and that the inhabitants were living in a state of primitive innocence akin to Adam and Eve in the Garden of Eden. On the other hand, the inhabitants seem to have regarded as god-like beings these peculiar humans, sailing in enormous ships, wearing clothes and shoes, and equipped with strange objects made of glass and iron.

(Taken from American Historical Documents, Vol. XLIII [1904])

PREFACE TO THE JOURNAL

IN THE NAME OF OUR LORD JESUS CHRIST: Whereas, Most Christian, High, Excellent, and Powerful Princes, King and Queen of Spain and of the Islands of the Sea, our Sovereigns, this present year 1492, after your Highnesses had terminated the war with the Moors reigning in Europe, the same having been brought to an end in the great city of Granada, where on the second day of January, this present year, I saw the royal banners of your Highnesses planted by force of arms upon the towers of the Alhambra, which is the fortress of that city, and saw the Moorish king come out at the gate of the city and kiss the hands of your Highnesses, and of the Prince my Sovereign; and in the present month, in consequence of the information which I had given your Highnesses respecting the countries of India and of a Prince, called Great Can, which in our language signifies King of Kings, how, at many times he, and his predecessors had sent to Rome soliciting instructors who might teach him our holy faith, and the holy Father had never granted his request, whereby great numbers of people were lost, believing in idolatry and doctrines of perdition. Your Highnesses, as Catholic Christians, and princes who love and promote the holy Christian faith, and are enemies of the doctrine of Mahomet, and of all idolatry and heresy, determined to send me, Christopher Columbus, to the above-mentioned countries of India, to see the said princes, people, and territories, and to learn their disposition and the proper method of converting them to our holy faith; and furthermore directed that I should not proceed by land to the East, as is customary, but by a Westerly route, in which direction we have hitherto no certain evidence that any one has gone. So after having expelled the Jews from your dominions, your Highnesses, in the same month of January, ordered me to proceed with a sufficient armament to the said regions of India, and for that purpose granted me great favors, and ennobled me that thenceforth I might call myself Don, and be High Admiral of the Sea, and perpetual Viceroy and Governor in all the islands and continents which I might discover and acquire, or which may hereafter he discovered and acquired in the ocean; and that this dignity should be inherited by my eldest son, and thus descend from degree to degree forever. Hereupon I left the city of Granada, on Saturday, the twelfth day of May, 1492, and proceeded to Palos, a seaport, where I armed three vessels, very fit for such an enterprise, and having provided myself with abundance of stores and seamen, I set sail from the port, on Friday, the third of August, half an hour before sunrise, and steered for the Canary Islands of your Highnesses which are in the said ocean, thence to take my departure and proceed till I arrived at the Indies, and perform the embassy of your Highnesses to the Princes there, and discharge the orders given me. For this purpose I determined to keep an account of the voyage, and to write down punctually every thing we performed or saw from day to day, as will hereafter appear. Moreover, Sovereign Princes, besides describing every night the occurrences of the day, and every day those of the preceding night, I intend to draw up a nautical chart, which shall contain the several parts of the ocean and land in their proper situations; and also to compose a book to represent the whole by picture with latitudes and longitudes, on all which accounts it behooves me to abstain from my sleep, and make many trials in navigation, which things will demand much labor.

Letter

SIR:

AS I know you will be rejoiced at the glorious success that our Lord has given me in my voyage, I write this to tell you how in thirty-three days I sailed to the Indies with the fleet that the illustrious King and Queen, our Sovereigns, gave me, where I discovered a great many islands, inhabited by numberless people; and of all I have taken possession for their Highnesses by proclamation and display of the Royal Standard without opposition. To the first island I discovered I gave the name of San Salvador, in commemoration of His Divine Majesty, who has wonderfully granted all this. The Indians call it Guanaham. The second I named the Island of Santa Maria de Concepcion; the third, Fernandina; the fourth, Isabella; the fifth, Juana; and thus to each one I gave a new name. When I came to Juana, I followed the coast of that isle toward the west, and found it so extensive that I thought it might be the mainland, the province of Cathay; and as I found no towns nor villages on the sea-coast, except a few small settlements, where it was impossible to speak to the people, because they fled at once, I continued the said route, thinking I could not fail to see some great cities or towns; and finding at the end of many leagues that nothing new appeared, and that the coast led northward, contrary to my wish, because the winter had already set in, I decided to make for the south, and as the wind also was against my proceeding, I determined not to wait there longer, and turned back to a certain harbor whence I sent two men to find out whether there was any king or large city. They explored for three days, and found countless small communities and people, without number, but with no kind of government, so they returned.

I heard from other Indians I had already taken that this land was an island, and thus followed the eastern coast for one hundred and seven leagues, until I came to the end of it. From that point I saw another isle to the eastward, at eighteen leaguesÆ distance, to which I gave the name of Hispaniola. I went thither and followed its northern coast to the east, as I had done in Juana, one hundred and seventy-eight leagues eastward, as in Juana. This island, like all the others, is most extensive. It has many ports along the sea-coast excelling any in Christendomùand many fine, large, flowing rivers. The land there is elevated, with many mountains and peaks incomparably higher than in the centre isle. They are most beautiful, of a thousand varied forms, accessible, and full of trees of endless varieties, so high that they seem to touch the sky, and I have been told that they never lose their foliage. I saw them as green and lovely as trees are in Spain in the month of May. Some of them were covered with blossoms, some with fruit, and some in other conditions, according to their kind. The nightingale and other small birds of a thousand kinds were singing in the month of November when I was there. There were palm trees of six or eight varieties, the graceful peculiarities of each one of them being worthy of admiration as are the other trees, fruits and grasses. There are wonderful pine woods, and very extensive ranges of meadow land. There is honey, and there are many kinds of birds, and a great variety of fruits. Inland there are numerous mines of metals and innumerable people. Hispaniola is a marvel. Its hills and mountains, fine plains and open country, are rich and fertile for planting and for pasturage, and for building towns and villages. The seaports there are incredibly fine, as also the magnificent rivers, most of which bear gold. The trees, fruits and grasses differ widely from those in Juana. There are many spices and vast mines of gold and other metals in this island. They have no iron, nor steel, nor weapons, nor are they fit for them, because although they are well-made men of commanding stature, they appear extraordinarily timid. The only arms they have are sticks of cane, cut when in seed, with a sharpened stick at the end, and they are afraid to use these. Often I have sent two or three men ashore to some town to converse with them, and the natives came out in great numbers, and as soon as they saw our men arrive, fled without a momentÆs delay although I protected them from all injury.

At every point where I landed, and succeeded in talking to them, I gave them some of everything I hadùcloth and many other thingsùwithout receiving anything in return, but they are a hopelessly timid people. It is true that since they have gained more confidence and are losing this fear, they are so unsuspicious and so generous with what they possess, that no one who had not seen it would believe it. They never refuse anything that is asked for. They even offer it themselves, and show so much love that they would give their very hearts. Whether it be anything of great or small value, with any trifle of whatever kind, they are satisfied. I forbade worthless things being given to them, such as bits of broken bowls, pieces of glass, and old straps, although they were as much pleased to get them as if they were the finest jewels in the world. One sailor was found to have got for a leathern strap, gold of the weight of two and a half castellanos, and others for even more worthless things much more; while for a new blancas they would give all they had, were it two or three castellanos of pure gold or an arroba or two of spun cotton. Even bits of the broken hoops of wine casks they accepted, and gave in return what they had, like fools, and it seemed wrong to me. I forbade it, and gave a thousand good and pretty things that I had to win their love, and to induce them to become Christians, and to love and serve their Highness and the whole Castilian nation, and help to got for us things they have in abundance, which are necessary to us. They have no religion, nor idolatry, except that they all believe power and goodness to be in heaven. They firmly believed that I, with my ships and men, came from heaven, and with this idea I have been received everywhere, since they lost fear of me. They are, however, far from being ignorant. They are most ingenious men, and navigate these seas in a wonderful way, and describe everything well, but they never before saw people wearing clothes, nor vessels like ours. Directly I reached the Indies in the first isle I discovered, I took by force some of the natives, that from them we might gain some information of what there was in these parts; and so it was that we immediately understood each other, either by words or signs. They are still with me and still believe that I come from heaven. They were the first to declare this wherever I went, and the others ran from house to house, and to the towns around, crying out, ôCome! come! and see the men from heaven!ö Then all, both men and women, as soon as they were reassured about us, came, both small and great, all bringing something to eat and to drink, which they presented with marvellous kindness. In these isles there are a great many canoes, something like rowing boats, of all sizes, and most of them are larger than an eighteen-oared galley. They are not so broad, as they are made of a single plank, but a galley could not keep up with them in rowing, because they go with incredible speed, and with these they row about among all these islands, which are innumerable, and carry on their commerce. I have seen some of these canoes with seventy and eighty men in them, and each had an oar. In all the islands I observed little difference in the appearance of the people, or in their habits and language, except that they understand each other, which is remarkable. Therefore I hope that their Highnesses will decide upon the conversion of these people to our holy faith, to which they seem much inclined. I have already stated how I sailed one hundred and seven leagues along the sea coast of Juana, in a straight line from west to east. I can therefore assert that this island is larger than England and Scotland together, since beyond these one hundred and seven leagues there remained at the west point two provinces where I did not go, one of which they call Avan, the home of men with tails. These provinces are computed to be fifty or sixty leagues in length, as far as can be gathered from the Indians with me who are acquainted with all these islands. This there, Hispaniola, is larger in circumference than all Spain from Catalonia to Fuentarabia in Biscay, since upon one of its four sides I sailed one hundred and eighty-eight leagues from west to east. This is worth having, and must on no account be given up. I have taken possession of all these islands, for their Highnesses, and all may be more extensive than I know, or can say, and I hold them for their Highnesses, who can command them as absolutely as the kingdoms of Castile. In Hispaniola, in the most convenient place, most accessible for the gold mines and all commerce with the mainland on this side or with that of the great Khan, on the bother, with which there would be great trade and profit, I have taken possession of a large town, which I have named the City of Navidad. I began fortifications there which should be completed by this time, and I have left in it men enough to hold it, with arms, artillery, and previsions for more than a year; and a boat with a master seaman skilled in the arts necessary to make others; I am so friendly with the king of that country that he was proud to call me his brother and hold me as such. Even should he change his mind and wish to quarrel with my men, neither he nor his subjects know what arms are, nor wear clothes, as I have said. They are the most timid people in the world, so that only the men remaining there could destroy the whole region, and run no risk if they know how to behave themselves properly. In all these islands the men seem to be satisfied with one wife, except they allow as many as twenty to their chief or king. The women appear to me to work harder than the men, and so far I can hear they have nothing of their own, for I think I perceived that what one had others shared, especially food. In the islands so far, I have found no monsters, as some expected, but, on the contrary, they are people of very handsome appearance. They are not black as in Guinea, though their hair is straight and coarse, as it does not grow where the sunÆs rays are too ardent. And in truth the sun has extreme power here, since it is within twenty-six degrees of the equinoctial line. In these islands there are mountains where the cold this winter was very severe, but the people endure it from habit, and with the aid of the meat they eat with very hot spices.

As for monsters, I have found no trace of them except at the point in the second isle as one enters the Indies, which is inhabited by a people considered in all the isles as most ferocious, who eat human flesh. They possess many canoes, with which they overrun all the isles of India, stealing and seizing all they can. They are not worse looking than the others, except that they wear their hair long like women, and use bows and arrows of the same cane, with sharp stick at the end for want of iron, of which they have none. They are ferocious compared to these other races, who are extremely cowardly; but I only hear this from the others. They are said to make treaties of marriage with the women in the first isle to be met with coming from Spain to the Indies, where there are no men. These women have no feminine occupation, but use bows and arrows of cane like those before mentioned, and cover and arm themselves with plates of copper, of which they have a great quantity. Another island, I am told, is larger than Hispaniola, where the natives have no hair, and where there is countless gold; and from them all I bring Indians to testify to this. To speak, in conclusion, only of what has been done during this hurried voyage, their Highnesses will see that I can give them as much gold as they desire, if they will give me a little assistance, spices, cotton, as much as their Highnesses may command to be shipped, and mastic as much as their Highnesses choose to send for, which until now has only been found in Greece, in the isle of Chios, and the Signoria can get its own price for it; as much lign-aloe as they command to be shipped, and as many slaves as they choose to send for, all heathens. I think I have found rhubarb and cinnamon. Many other things of value will be discovered by the men I left behind me, as I stayed nowhere when the wind allowed me to pursue my voyage, except in the City of Navidad, which I left fortified and safe. Indeed, I might have accomplished much more, had the crews served me as they ought to have done. The eternal and almighty God, our Lord, it is Who gives to all who walk in His way, victory over things apparently impossible, and in this case signally so, because although these lands had been imagined and talked of before they were seen, most men listened incredulously to what was thought to be but an idle tale. But our Redeemer has given victory to our most illustrious King and Queen, and to their Kingdoms rendered famous by this glorious event, at which all Christendom should rejoice, celebrating it with great festivities and solemn Thanksgivings to the Holy Trinity, with fervent prayers for the high distinction that will accrue to them from turning so many peoples to our holy faith; and also from the temporal benefits that not only Spain but all Christian nations will obtain. Thus I record. What has happened in a brief note written on board the Caravel, off the Canary Isles, on the 15th of February, 1493.

Yours to command,
THE ADMIRAL

Postscript:

within the letter

Since writing the above, being in the Sea of Castile, so much wind arose south southeast, that I was forced to lighten the vessels, to run into this port of Lisbon to-day which was the most extraordinary thing in the world, from whence I resolved to write to their Highnesses. In all the Indies I always found the temperature like that of May. Where I went in thirty-three days I returned in twenty-eight, except that these gales have detained me fourteen days, knocking about in this sea. Here all seamen say that there has never been so rough a winter, nor so many vessels lost.

Done the 14th day of March [1493].

THOMAS MORE'S UTOPIA

Perhaps nothing better encapsulates the intellectual climate of early sixteenth-century Western Europe than Sir Thomas More's little book, *Utopia*. Published in 1516, when western Europeans were excited about the recent discovery of North and South America, and coming one year before Western Europe was convulsed by the beginning of the Protestant Reformation, *Utopia* combines contemporary interest in the New World with the scholarship of renaissance humanism. The work's author, Thomas More, was an Englishman, born in 1478. After being trained as a lawyer, More entered government service and was highly respected and trusted by King henry Viii until the latter orchestrated his break with Roman Catholicism and the creation of the Church of England. When More refused to take an oath to acknowledge King Henry as head of the new Anglican Church, he was arrested, imprisoned in the Tower of London, and beheaded (1535), thereby earning himself a place among Catholic saints.

Besides his training as a lawyer, More was a leading figure in fostering renaissance humanism in England. As a result of their shared Christian piety and love of classical antiquity, Erasmus and More became close life-long friends. Like Erasmus, More was well educated in ancient Greek and Latin, possessed a thorough knowledge of ancient Greek and Roman literature, and was equally at home in Biblical scripture. Yet, as a man experienced in the high politics of government, he was no ivy-tower intellectual grounded in book learning alone; and *Utopia* reflects all these facets of More's education and life experience.

This small work, comprising approximately 65 pages in a modern edition, is divided into two parts: Book I and Book II. The former serves as a lengthy introduction to the latter, and the latter treats Utopia proper. It is all cast into the form of a Platonic philosophical dialogue, in which an actual event brings together several men of learning, who proceed to while away their time in a serious discussion of the political, social, and economic problems confronting the nations and monarchs of Western Europe. When Thomas More travels to Flanders to represent King Henry VIII in negotiations with Charles V of Castile, he happens to come into the company of a cardinal and other learned men, including a Portuguese explorer named Rafael, recently arrived from having lived for several years in the New World. During their first discussion these men commiserate over the sad state of affairs throughout Europe, in which monarchs are not interested in ruling their subjects well and justly, but instead, devote most of their time and attention to waging wars to try to enlarge their kingdoms, thereby inflicting upon their subjects the oppression of taxation and upon people generally the violence of war. Eventually the discussants agree with the famous maxim of Plato, found in his own utopian work *The Republic*, that the kingdoms of Europe will never be ruled justly until a philosopher becomes king, or a king becomes a philosopher. More hereby connects his own early modern utopian work with the most famous one from classical antiquity.

❧ *(Taken from the translation of Henry Morley)*

A. THE MISERIES OF ENGLAND

✢ Book I

Every day's experience shows that the mechanics in the towns [of England], or the clowns in the country, are not afraid of fighting with those idle gentlemen, if they are not disabled by some misfortune in their body, or dispirited by extreme want, so that you need not fear that those well-shaped and strong men (for it is only such that noblemen love to keep about them, till they spoil them) who now grow feeble with ease, and are softened with their effeminate manner of life, would be less fit for action if they were well bred and well employed. And it seems very unreasonable that for the prospect of a war, which you need never have but when you please, you should maintain so many idle men, as will always disturb you in time of peace, which is ever to be more considered than war.

But I do not think that this necessity of stealing arises only from hence; there is another cause of it more peculiar to England.' "'What is that?' said the cardinal. "'The increase of pasture,' said I, 'by which your sheep, which are naturally mild, and easily kept in order, may be said now to devour men, and unpeople, not only villages, but towns; for wherever it is found that the sheep of any soil yield a softer and richer wool than ordinary, there the nobility and gentry, and even those holy men the abbots, not contented with the old rents which their farms yielded, nor thinking it enough that they, living at their ease, do no good to the public, resolve to do it hurt instead of good. They stop the course of agriculture, destroying houses and towns, reserving only the churches, and enclose grounds that they may lodge their sheep in them. As if forests and parks had swallowed up too little of the land, those worthy countrymen turn the best inhabited places in solitudes, for when an insatiable wretch, who is a plague to his country, resolves to enclose many thousand acres of ground, the owners as well as tenants are turned out of their possessions, by tricks, or by main force, or being wearied out with ill-usage, they are forced to sell them.

By which means those miserable people, both men and women, married and unmarried, old and young, with their poor but numerous families (since country business requires many hands), are all forced to change their seats, not knowing whither to go; and they must sell almost for nothing their household stuff, which could not bring them much money, even though they might stay for a buyer. When that little money is at an end, for it will be soon spent, what is left for them to do, but either to steal and so to be hanged (God knows how justly), or to go about and beg? And if they do this, they are put in prison as idle vagabonds; while they would willingly work, but can find none that will hire them; for there is no more occasion for country labor, to which they have been bred, when there is no arable ground left. One shepherd can look after a flock which will stock an extent of ground that would require many hands if it were to be ploughed and reaped.

This likewise in many places raises the price of grain. "'The price of wool is also so risen that the poor people who were wont to make cloth are no more able to buy it; and this likewise makes many of them idle. For since the increase of pasture, God has punished the avarice of the owners by a rot among the sheep, which has destroyed vast numbers of them; to us it might have seemed more just had it fell on the owners themselves. But suppose the sheep should increase ever so much, their price is not like to fall; since though they cannot be called a monopoly, because they are not engrossed by one person, yet they are in so few hands, and these are so rich, that as they are not pressed to sell them sooner than they have a mind to it, so they never do it till they have raised the price as high as possible. And on the same account it is, that the other kinds of cattle are so dear, because many villages being pulled down, and all country labor being much neglected, there are none who make it their business to breed them. The rich do not breed cattle as they do sheep, but buy them lean, and at low prices; and after they have fattened them on their grounds sell them again at high rates. And I do not think that all the inconveniences this will produce are yet observed, for as they sell the cattle dear, so if they are consumed faster than the breeding countries from which they are brought can afford them, then the stock must decrease, and this must needs end in great scarcity; and by these means this your island, which seemed as to this particular the happiest in the world, will suffer much by the cursed avarice of a few persons.

Besides this, the rising of grain makes all people lessen their families as much as they can; and what can those who are dismissed by them do, but either beg or rob? And to this last, a man of a great mind is much sooner drawn than to the former. "'Luxury likewise breaks in apace upon you, to set forward your poverty and misery; there is an excessive vanity in apparel, and great cost in diet; and that not only in noblemen's families, but even among tradesmen, among the farmers themselves, and among all ranks of persons. You have also many infamous houses, and, besides those that are known, the taverns and ale-houses are no better; add to these, dice, cards, tables, foot-ball, tennis, and quoits, in which money runs fast away; and those that are initiated into them, must in the conclusion betake themselves to robbing for a supply. Banish these plagues, and give orders that those who have dispeopled so much soil, may either rebuild the villages they have pulled down, or let out their grounds to such as will do it: restrain those engrossings of the rich, that are as bad almost as monopolies; leave fewer occasions to idleness; let agriculture be set up again, and the manufacture of the wool be regulated, that so there may be work found for those companies of idle people whom want forces to be thieves, or who, now being idle vagabonds or useless servants, will certainly grow thieves at last.

If you do not find a remedy to these evils, it is a vain thing to boast of your severity in punishing theft, which though it may have the appearance of justice, yet in itself is neither just nor convenient. For if you suffer your people to be ill-educated, and their manners to be corrupted from their infancy, and then punish them for those crimes to which their first education disposed them, what else is to be concluded from this, but that you first make thieves and then punish them?' ...

'It seems to me a very unjust thing to take away a man's life for a little money; for nothing in the world can be of equal value with a man's life: and if it is said that it is not for the money that one suffers, but for his breaking the law, I must say extreme justice is an extreme injury; for we ought not to approve of these terrible laws that make the smallest offences capital, nor of that opinion of the Stoics that makes all crimes equal, as if there were no difference to be made between the killing a man and the taking his purse, between which, if we examine things impartially, there is no likeness nor proportion. God has commanded us not to kill, and shall we kill so easily for a little money? But if one shall say, that by that law we are only forbid to kill any, except when the laws of the land allow of it; upon the same grounds, laws may be made in some cases to allow of adultery and perjury: for God having taken from us the right of disposing, either of our own or of other people's lives, if it is pretended that the mutual consent of man in making laws can authorize man-slaughter in cases in which God has given us no example, that it frees people from the obligation of the divine law, and so makes murder a lawful action; what is this, but to give a preference to human laws before the divine? "'And if this is once admitted, by the same rule men may in all other things put what restrictions they please upon the laws of God. If by the Mosaical law, though it was rough and severe, as being a yoke laid on an obstinate and servile nation, men were only fined and not put to death for theft, we cannot imagine that in this new law of mercy, in which God treats us with the tenderness of a father, he has given us a greater license to cruelty than he did to the Jews. Upon these reasons it is that I think putting thieves to death is not lawful; and it is plain and obvious that it is absurd, and of ill-consequence to the commonwealth, that a thief and a murderer should be equally punished; for if a robber sees that his danger is the same, if he is convicted of theft as if he were guilty of murder, this will naturally incite him to kill the person whom otherwise he would only have robbed, since if the punishment is the same, there is more security, and less danger of discovery, when he that can best make it is put out of the way; so that terrifying thieves too much, provokes them to cruelty.

B. THE PERFECT CONDITIONS IN UTOPIA

When the discussants meet to renew their conversation on a second day, they allow Rafael to describe for them the perfect conditions prevailing in utopia in the New World. As is the case with so many utopian creations of the human mind, they often are little more than the author's critique of what he finds wrong in his own society. Thomas More was himself well aware of this phenomenon and plays with it throughout the entire work, often alerting his readers to this by his clever word play: for Utopia in Greek simply means "nowhere," so that despite More's careful placement of this region in the New World, he is telling his readers that it really does not exist. Similarly, the river that flows through the principal city of Utopia is named the Anhydor, meaning in Greek "the unwater." Consequently, although More's *Utopia* is the earliest modern work of its type, it is probably best read as a learned and scholarly satire upon the woeful state of affairs in western European society during More's day.

✤ Book II

THE island of Utopia is in the middle 200 miles broad, and holds almost at the same breadth over a great part of it; but it grows narrower toward both ends. Its figure is not unlike a crescent: between its horns, the sea comes in eleven miles broad, and spreads itself into a great bay, which is environed with land to the compass of about 500 miles, and is well secured from winds. In this bay there is no great current; the whole coast is, as it were, one continued harbor, which gives all that live in the island great convenience for mutual commerce; but the entry into the bay, occasioned by rocks on the one hand, and shallows on the other, is very dangerous. In the middle of it there is one single rock which appears above water, and may therefore be easily avoided, and on the top of it there is a tower in which a garrison is kept; the other rocks lie under water, and are very dangerous. The channel is known only to the natives, so that if any stranger should enter into the bay, without one of their pilots, he would run great danger of shipwreck; for even they themselves could not pass it safe, if some marks that are on the coast did not direct their way; and if these should be but a little shifted, any fleet that might come against them, how great soever it were, would be certainly lost....

AGRICULTURE is that which is so universally understood among them that no person, either man or woman, is ignorant of it; they are instructed in it from their childhood, partly by what they learn at school and partly by practice; they being led out often into the fields, about the town, where they not only see others at work, but are likewise exercised in it themselves. Besides agriculture, which is so common to them all, every man has some peculiar trade to which he applies himself, such as the manufacture of wool, or flax, masonry, smith's work, or carpenter's work; for there is no sort of trade that is not in great esteem among them.

Throughout the island they wear the same sort of clothes without any other distinction, except what is necessary to distinguish the two sexes, and the married and unmarried.

The fashion never alters; and as it is neither disagreeable nor uneasy, so it is suited to the climate, and calculated both for their summers and winters. Every family makes their own clothes.

But all among them, women as well as men, learn one or other of the trades formerly mentioned. Women, for the most part, deal in wool and flax, which suit best with their weakness, leaving the ruder trades to the men. The same trade generally passes down from father to son, inclinations often following descent; but if any man's genius lies another way, he is by adoption translated into a family that deals in the trade to which he is inclined: and when that is to be done, care is taken not only by his father, but by the magistrate, that he may be put to a discreet and good man. And if after a person has learned one trade, he desires to acquire another, that is also allowed, and is managed in the same manner as the former. When he has learned both, he follows that which he likes best, unless the public has more occasion for the other. The chief, and almost the only business of the syphogrants, is to take care that no man may live idle, but that every one may follow his trade diligently: yet they do not wear themselves out with perpetual toil, from morning to night, as if they were beasts of burden, which, as it is indeed a heavy slavery, so it is everywhere the common course of life among all mechanics except the Utopians; but they dividing the day and night into twenty-four hours, appoint six of these for work; three of which are before dinner, and three after. They then sup, and at eight o'clock, counting from noon, go to bed and sleep eight hours. The rest of their time besides that taken up in work, eating and sleeping, is left to every man's discretion; yet they are not to abuse that interval to luxury and idleness, but must employ it in some proper exercise according to their various inclinations, which is for the most part reading. It is ordinary to have public lectures every morning before daybreak; at which none are obliged to appear but those who are marked out for literature; yet a great many, both men and women of all ranks, go to hear lectures of one sort of other, according to their inclinations. But if others, that are not made for contemplation, choose rather to employ themselves at that time in their trades, as many of them do, they are not hindered, but are rather commended, as men that take care to serve their country. After supper, they spend an hour in some diversion, in summer in their gardens, and in winter in the halls where they eat; where they entertain each other, either with music or discourse.

They do not so much as know dice, or any such foolish and mischievous games: they have, however, two sorts of games not unlike our chess; the one is between several numbers, in which one number, as it were, consumes another: the other resembles a battle between the virtues and the vices, in which the enmity in the vices among themselves, and their agreement against virtue, is not unpleasantly represented; together with the special oppositions between the particular virtues and vices; as also the methods by which vice either openly assaults or secretly undermines virtue, and virtue on the other hand resists it.

But the time appointed for labor is to be narrowly examined, otherwise you may imagine, that since there are only six hours appointed for work, they may fall under a scarcity of necessary provisions. But it is so far from being true, that this time is not sufficient for supplying them with plenty of all things, either necessary or convenient, that it is rather too much; and this you will easily apprehend, if you consider how great a part of all other nations is quite idle. First, women generally do little, who are the half of mankind; and if some few women are diligent, their husbands are idle: then consider the great company of idle priests, and of those that are called religious men; add to these all rich men, chiefly those that have estates in land, who are called noblemen and gentlemen, together with their families, made up of idle persons, that are kept more for show than use; add to these, all those strong and lusty beggars, that go about pretending some disease, in excuse for their begging; and upon the whole account you will find that the number of those by whose labors mankind is supplied, is much less than you perhaps imagined. Then consider how few of those that work are employed in labors that are of real service; for we who measure all things by money, give rise to many trades that are both vain and superfluous, and serve only to support riot and luxury. For if those who work were employed only in such things as the conveniences of life require, there would be such an abundance of them that the prices of them would so sink that tradesmen could not be maintained by their gains; if all those who labor about useless things were set to more profitable employments, and if all they that languish out their lives in sloth and idleness, every one of whom consumes as much as any two of the men that are at work, were forced to labor, you may easily imagine that a small proportion of time would serve for doing all that is either necessary, profitable, or pleasant to mankind, especially while pleasure is kept within its due bounds. This appears very plainly in Utopia, for there, in a great city, and in all the territory that lies round it, you can scarce find 500, either men or women, by their age and strength, are capable of labor, that are not engaged in it....

indeed the only commonwealth that truly deserves that name. In all other places it is visible, that while people talk of a commonwealth, every man only seeks his own wealth; but there, where no man has any property, all men zealously pursue the good of the public: and, indeed, it is no wonder to see men act so differently; for in other commonwealths, every man knows that unless he provides for himself, how flourishing soever the commonwealth may be, he must die of hunger; so that he sees the necessity of preferring his own concerns to the public; but in Utopia, where every man has a right to everything, they all know that if care is taken to keep the public stores full, no private man can want anything; for among them there is no unequal distribution, so that no man is poor, none in necessity; and though no man has anything, yet they are all rich; for what can make a man so rich as to lead a serene and cheerful life, free from anxieties; neither apprehending want himself, nor vexed with the endless complaints of his wife? He is not afraid of the misery of his children, nor is he contriving how to raise a portion for his daughters, but is secure in this, that both he and his wife, his children and grandchildren, to as many generations as he can fancy, will all live both plentifully and happily; since among them there is no less care taken of those who were once engaged in labor, but grow afterward unable to follow it, than there is elsewhere of these that continue still employed.

I would gladly hear any man compare the justice that is among them with that of all other nations; among whom, may I perish, if I see anything that looks either like justice or equity: for what justice is there in this, that a nobleman, a goldsmith, a banker, or any other man, that either does nothing at all, or at best is employed in things that are of no use to the public, should live in great luxury and splendor, upon what is so ill acquired; and a mean man, a carter, a smith, or a ploughman, that works harder even than the beasts themselves, and is employed in labors so necessary, that no commonwealth could hold out a year without them, can only earn so poor a livelihood, and must lead so miserable a life, that the condition of the beasts is much better than theirs? For as the beasts do not work so constantly, so they feed almost as well, and with more pleasure; and have no anxiety about what is to come, whilst these men are depressed by a barren and fruitless employment, and tormented with the apprehensions of want in their old age; since that which they get by their daily labor does but maintain them at present, and is consumed as fast as it comes in, there is no overplus left to lay up for old age. Is not that government both unjust and ungrateful, that is so prodigal of its favors to those that are called gentlemen, or goldsmiths, or such others who are idle, or live either by flattery, or by contriving the arts of vain pleasure; and on the other hand, takes no care of those of a meaner sort, such as ploughmen, colliers, and smiths, without whom it could not subsist? But after the public has reaped all the advantage of their service, and they come to be oppressed with age, sickness, and want, all their labors and the good they have done is forgotten; and all the recompense given them is that they are left to die in great misery. The richer sort are often endeavoring to bring the hire of laborers lower, not only by their fraudulent practices, but by the laws which they procure to be made to that effect; so that though it is a thing most unjust in itself, to give such small rewards to those who deserve so well of the public, yet they have given those hardships the name and color of justice, by procuring laws to be made for regulating them. Therefore I must say that, as I hope for mercy, I can have no other notion of all the other governments that I see or know, than that they are a conspiracy of the rich, who on pretence of managing the public only pursue their private ends, and devise all the ways and arts they can find out; first, that they may, without danger, preserve all that they have so ill acquired, and then that they may engage the poor to toil and labor for them at as low rates as possible, and oppress them as much as they please....

Thus you see that there are no idle persons among them, nor pretences of excusing any from labor. There are no taverns, no alehouses nor stews among them; nor any other occasions of corrupting each other, of getting into corners, or forming themselves into parties: all men live in full view, so that all are obliged, both to perform their ordinary tasks, and to employ themselves well in their spare hours. And it is certain that a people thus ordered must live in great abundance of all things; and these being equally distributed among them, no man can want, or be obliged to beg....

It is certain that all things appear incredible to us, in proportion as they differ from our own customs. But one who can judge aright will not wonder to find that, since their constitution differs so much from ours, their value of gold and silver should be measured by a very different standard; for since they have no use for money among themselves, but keep it as a provision against events which seldom happen, and between which there are generally long intervening intervals, they value it no farther than it deserves, that is, in proportion to its use. So that it is plain they must prefer iron either to gold or silver; for men can no more live without iron than without fire or water, but nature has marked out no use for the other metals, so essential as not easily to be dispensed with. The folly of men has enhanced the value of gold and silver, because of their scarcity. Whereas, on the contrary, it is their opinion that nature, as an indulgent parent, has freely given us all the best things in great abundance, such as water and earth, but has laid up and hid from us the things that are vain and useless. If these metals were laid up in any tower in the kingdom, it would raise a jealousy of the Prince and Senate, and give birth to that foolish mistrust into which the people are apt to fall, a jealousy of their intending to sacrifice the interest of the public to their own private advantage. If they should work it into vessels or any sort of plate, they fear that the people might grow too fond of it, and so be unwilling to let the plate be run down if a war made it necessary to employ it in paying their soldiers. To prevent all these inconveniences, they have fallen upon an expedient, which, as it agrees with their other policy, so is it very different from ours, and will scarce gain belief among us, who value gold so much and lay it up so carefully. They eat and drink out of vessels of earth, or glass, which make an agreeable appearance though formed of brittle materials: while they make their chamber-pots and close-stools of gold and silver; and that not only in their public halls, but in their private houses: of the same metals they likewise make chains and fetters for their slaves; to some of which, as a badge of infamy, they hang an ear-ring of gold, and make others wear a chain or coronet of the same metal; and thus they take care, by all possible means, to render gold and silver of no esteem. And from hence it is that while other nations part with their gold and silver as unwillingly as if one tore out their bowels, those of Utopia would look on their giving in all they possess of those (metals, when there was any use for them) but as the parting with a trifle, or as we would esteem the loss of a penny. They find pearls on their coast, and diamonds and carbuncles on their rocks; they do not look after them, but, if they find them by chance, they polish them, and with them they adorn their children, who are delighted with them, and glory in them during their childhood; but when they grow to years, and see that none but children use such baubles, they of their own accord, without being bid by their parents, lay them aside; and would be as much ashamed to use them afterward as children among us, when they come to years, are of their puppets and other toys....

They have but few laws, and such is their constitution that they need not many. They very much condemn other nations, whose laws, together with the commentaries on them, swell up to so many volumes; for they think it an unreasonable thing to oblige men to obey a body of laws that are both of such a bulk and so dark as not to be read and understood by every one of the subjects. They have no lawyers among them, for they consider them as a sort of people whose profession it is to disguise matters and to wrest the laws; and therefore they think it is much better that every man should plead his own cause, and trust it to the judge, as in other places the client trusts it to a counsellor. By this means they both cut off many delays, and find out truth more certainly: for after the parties have laid open the merits of the cause, without those artifices which lawyers are apt to suggest, the judge examines the whole matter, and supports the simplicity of such well-meaning persons, whom otherwise crafty men would be sure to run down: and thus they avoid those evils which appear very remarkably among all those nations that labor under a vast load of laws. Every one of them is skilled in their law, for as it is a very short study, so the plainest meaning of which words are capable is always the sense of their laws. And they argue thus: all laws are promulgated for this end, that every man may know his duty; and therefore the plainest and most obvious sense of the words is that which ought to be put upon them; since a more refined exposition cannot be easily comprehended, and would only serve to make the laws become useless to the greater part of mankind, and especially to those who need most the direction of them: for it is all one, not to make a law at all, or to couch it in such terms that without a quick apprehension, and much study, a man cannot find out the true meaning of it; since the generality of mankind are both so dull and so much employed in their several trades that they have neither the leisure nor the capacity requisite for such an inquiry.